KT-148-423

DOC HOLLIDAY'S GONE

A Western Duo

DOC HOLLIDAY'S GONE

A Western Duo

Jane Candia Coleman

Thorndike Press • Chivers Press
Thorndike, Maine USA   Bath, England

This Large Print edition is published by Thorndike Press, USA and by Chivers Press, England.

Published in 2000 in the U.S. by arrangement with Golden West Literary Agency.

Published in 2000 in the U.K. by arrangement with Golden West Literary Agency.

U.S. Hardcover 0-7862-1855-X (Western Series Edition)
U.K. Hardcover 0-7540-4368-1 (Chivers Large Print)
U.K. Softcover 0-7540-4369-X (Camden Large Print)

The text of this Large Print edition is unabridged.
Other aspects of the book may vary from the original edition.

Set in 16 pt. Plantin by Minnie B. Raven.

Printed in the United States on permanent paper.

British Library Cataloguing-in-Publication Data available

Library of Congress Cataloging-in-Publication Data

Coleman, Jane Candia.
    Doc Holliday's gone : a western duo / Jane Candia Coleman.
        p. cm.
    Contents: Doc Holliday's gone — Mrs. Slaughter.
    ISBN 0-7862-1855-X (lg. print : hc : alk. paper)
    1. Western stories. 2. Large type books. I. Coleman, Jane Candia. Mrs. Slaughter. II. Title.
PS3553.O47427 A6   2000
    813'.54—dc21   00-042622

My thanks to Michael Horony and the entire Horony family for sharing with me new information about their famous relative and for inviting me to a spectacular Horony family reunion in June, 1997. Also to Wilbur and Charles White who walked me over the old town of Dos Cabezas and who provided their personal memories of Kate and Jack Howard. And to Karen Holliday Tanner, author of DOC HOLLIDAY, A FAMILY PORTRAIT, for her invaluable insights into Doc and his early life.

Jane Candia Coleman
February 1999

Table of Contents

DOC HOLLIDAY'S GONE

Part One

Prologue

Dos Cabezas, March, 1930

Doc Holliday's gone. And Wyatt Earp. George Cummings, my second husband is dead, and now Jack Howard, who gave me thirty years and a different kind of love, different from all the rest.

The lantern flickers. It's early April and windy, and the night is cold. I put more wood in the stove, pour myself coffee from the big enamel pot. I suppose if I stay here I'll have to cut down on luxuries like firewood and coffee, but that is to think about later. Tonight I'll be warm, comforted, if comfort there is, by the heat of the stove, the quilt around my shoulders, memories.

Tonight I'll sit with Jack as we have sat every night for so long — the happiest years

9

of my life. I won't pull the sheet over his face just yet. I want to watch him a while, to say good bye and thanks.

In the morning I'll walk the three miles to town and ask the Whites for help with the burying. But tonight is mine, and I'll use it to remember, because memories, at least to me, are prayers.

I

Glenwood Springs, 1887

Doc Holliday fought a long and futile battle, and I was with him at the last, unable to help or to give him breath. After the funeral I packed his things. Such a few things he had to show for his thirty-six years! Some clothes, his razor, the diamond stickpin he'd brought with him from Georgia, minus the diamond that he'd pawned in Leadville when his luck at the tables ran out. I wanted to put a letter in the trunk. A note saying that he hadn't died alone or unloved. That I'd been with him whenever he needed me for over ten years and had done my best that, in the long run, wasn't good enough.

But I knew his family, and the nun to whom I was sending the trunk wouldn't appreciate any words from me — mistress, fallen woman. No matter that I couldn't help my past, relive it, change it, make of myself anything other than who I was — Mary Katherine Horony, Kate Fisher, Mary May, Big Nose Kate, Kate Elder, a different name for every place I'd been and left, sometimes with the law on my heels.

So I wrote nothing, and, standing in the bitter cold that gray November day, I closed the door to my heart and made a vow never to look back, a futile promise as it turned out, for my past has shaped my present. What I was is what I am.

"We'll go on home." My brother, Alex, helped me into the wagon and handed me a robe to wrap around myself.

"Yes," I said, though his words sounded out of place. What did it mean to have a home? I'd never stayed anywhere long enough to put down roots and find out.

"Eva and I want you to stay with us," he added, picking up the reins.

"Yes," I said again. "For a while anyhow."

"As long as you like. The children love you. *We* love you."

Frankly, all love scared me. What had it

gotten me but loneliness?

As if he'd read my thoughts, he said: "Doc had his own way to make, Mary. You did the best you could."

Anger replaced grief. "If I could have gotten him out of Tombstone. If I could have gotten him away from those Earps so we could've stopped running and fighting. But they always came first with him. I hardly counted."

"That's not true."

I shrugged and looked out at the Roaring Fork. It reminded me of myself, running madly to nowhere. "We really didn't suit except we were both two black sheep on the lam."

"You weren't the first woman to do what you had to."

"But the fact is . . . I did. I'm not the kind a man like Doc takes to meet his family."

He clucked to the team and turned up the trail by the Crystal River. "Like I said, you aren't the first. And you're a Horony. That counts for something, even if we're the only ones who care or know what that means."

He was right. The West was filled with whores who'd married and turned respectable, their pasts swept under the carpet. I supposed he was hinting that I could do the same.

"Mama wouldn't know me," I said.

His smile was wry. "She wouldn't know me, either. Chopping wood, digging holes in mountains. Her life wasn't ours. It was another world, face it."

I didn't want to face any of it. In a few short years, I'd gone from being the pampered daughter of Hungarian aristocrats, to the wife of a St. Louis businessman, to prostitution, simply to stay alive. That was my excuse, and it was, to me, a good one. Faced with the prospect of starving, I'd sold myself as had a good many others.

And then I met Doc, and that made all the difference. For a long time we were happy — alone and carefree — before the Tombstone years and disaster.

I said: "There's probably still a warrant out for me in Texas. For arson." — and Alex looked at me with an expression that was part amazement, part devil-may-care Horony.

"Best tell me what else you've been up to," he said with a grin.

I closed my eyes against the stark winter mountains, the naked trees, and was back in Griffin in the spring of 1876.

"It was one of those crazy things you do without thinking too much. Doc was in jail, and they were going to hang him, and I

13

wasn't about to sit there and let it happen."

Alex's grin widened. "Even when you were little you were always in trouble."

"I wasn't!" What I remembered was tiptoeing around the house, taking care of Mama and the little ones.

"I remember, if you don't," he said. "You should've been a boy."

"Well, that's what I did in Texas. Dressed up in pants and started a fire in a stable to distract everybody so I could get Doc out. It worked, too." I stopped, seeing it, hearing Doc's voice as plain as if he sat beside me. *"By Christ, Kate! You set the whole damn' town on fire!"*

Looking back, the whole plan had been crazy, but it had worked. Doc was free, and I'd saved him. All we had had to do was get out of Texas.

We had good horses and the rest of our lives ahead of us. We were young, and the West was a different place from what it is now. There weren't any roads or fences. We had only the stars and the sun to go by — and the cattle trails that gouged out the prairie, stripped the grass, left a map anyone could follow.

If ever Doc loved me, it was then, unencumbered by past or future, two fugitives with a single purpose and a passion for life that tinged our love-making with a kind of glory.

Each time we kissed, touched, it seemed it might be the last time for us. We threw ourselves at one another with a sense of desperation, the knowledge that the law was on our heels, that time was running out. Death lurked everywhere — on the plains, in the sky, in our own poor bodies. Especially Doc's.

Sometimes, with his arms around me, my head against his chest, I could hear the faint rattle of the disease that had ruined his life, his hopes — hear it and taste my own fury because I was helpless, a pawn in a game we were both bound to lose.

Funny that, for all our intimacy, I never caught it from him, that I should be the strong one. But why? Here I was, thirty six years old, the past buried in a grave in Glenwood, and a future that held no promise.

Behind my closed eyes I saw the plains spreading out like a painting by an artist gone wild — bluebonnets, white poppies with petals like tissue, the brilliant, color-streaked faces of galliardias, and the grass rippling like a scarf of green silk in the never-ending wind. Far away, where the heat waves made illusions against the horizon, Doc and I were riding north, the wind making music in our ears.

Tears I'd held in started then, slipping down my cheeks and turning to ice. Alex leaned over and took my hand.

"I thought you were never going to let it out," he said.

I reached for my handkerchief. "I thought I didn't have any tears left."

Crying doesn't do anybody any good. Tears can't raise the dead, and, if they go on long enough, people avoid you. So I stopped crying and tried to think of something to say so Alex wouldn't blame himself for what he hadn't done.

"It was a good life for a while."

He looked straight ahead. "You're still young. You'll marry again."

"No." I shook my head, determined, then thought better of it. "Maybe. But not soon."

Still, who wanted to be the unmarried sister or aunt? I'd seen enough of those — living off their relatives, always in the way, humbling themselves in thanks for their keep. I wasn't one to be humble, even on my worst days.

"I'll stay the winter," I said. "Then I'll figure something."

I still had some money from the sale of my hotel in Globe and more energy than two people. Cooking was what I did best; everyone said so, even Doc who was hard to please. Perhaps I could open a restaurant — a small one, with a room for myself in the back.

"Just so you know you're welcome." Alex pulled up at the door of the cabin, and Eva came out, her arms open wide.

"Ah, Mary, poor child," she said.

I took offense, though her motive was kind. I wasn't anybody's child but a woman who'd seen enough death for ten, who'd slept with more men than Eva had ever met.

"Don't!" I said, avoiding her embrace, fearful that tears would start again, and I'd be unable to stop them.

She looked behind me at Alex, her eyes questioning him. I went inside, taking off my bonnet and going to the fire to warm my hands. The house was comforting, cheerful, but I didn't belong. A person gets used to making decisions, being on her own. Here, I was a cipher. Aunt Mary or poor child fallen on hard times. At that thought I laughed to myself. Since leaving home, it seemed I'd had nothing but hard times, but I'd survived, and would again. I'd make do or die.

II

The dream is always the same. It's Tombstone in October, 1881, and the trouble that's been festering between the Earps and Doc and the cowboy gang is about to boil over. It's serious trouble, good against evil, and I'm in the middle of it though I never wanted to be.

Ike Clanton comes into Fly's boarding house looking like a gargoyle, and I want to run away, but my feet are stuck to the floor so all I can do is wrap my arms around myself for protection. Not that Ike is going to rape me. Ike doesn't much care for women. I'm simply trying to keep my distance.

"Where's Holliday?" He has a high, squeaky voice like a young girl's. It's at odds with his face, his pale, cruel eyes.

I shake my head. No words come. I run then, back to Doc who straps on his pistol and goes quickly out the door. A few minutes later the shooting starts. They are all there — Wyatt, Morg, Virge, and Doc; the McLaurys, Billy Clanton, Ike, Johnny Behan in that big, white hat you can see a mile off.

The shots come in two bursts and sound like

cannon fire. A bullet comes through the window over my head, covering me with splinters of glass. I see Morg spin around and go down, see Doc fall, and my own face and hands blood-covered so it seems I've been shot, too. But I can run. I'm running out onto the street toward Doc who's alive and cussing. There's dirt on his face, but his eyes shine, blue and hard, like jewels.

"That's three less of the murdering bastards."

The women are there — Allie, Lou, and Josie Marcus, hatless, her face carved out of ivory, her hands stretched out toward Wyatt who's standing grim as death, who's done what he meant to do all along.

Except he hasn't finished. The killing will go on, and Doc will go with him, ignoring my pleas, shaking me off like I'm an annoyance, a clinging vine of a woman who only wants peace and her man home with her instead of out some-where, a target for the rustlers and con-men who run Cochise County.

There's the taste of blood in my mouth. My lip is cut. I lick it, spit out blood like I'd like to spit out my anger. I'm a victim, too — caught like we're all caught in this nasty little town that has no reason to exist but greed.

I wake up whimpering. It's dark, and the house is cold. Outside, the moon reflects off fresh snow. The mountains hold up the sky on massive white shoulders. I miss the desert. Cloud shadows riding purple over those endless valleys, the fragrance of secret bloomings. I miss Doc with an ache in my heart, my loins. For all our anger, bitter words, foolish betrayals, I miss him.

Maybe someday I'll get over this; stop dreaming, stop wanting. Maybe.

Spring came slowly that year, as it always does in the high Rockies, and I was impatient to be gone. "Cabin fever," they call what I had, the feeling of being locked in, locked out, every crack in the walls, every bump in the floor memorized until I could find my way blindfolded.

In spite of the deep snow, I went down to the river and watched the magpies arguing in the trees. In Hungary, magpies were considered pests, and there was a bounty on them. Here they were simply winged jewels flashing against snow and sky.

Somewhere I'd heard that, if you could catch a young one, it would learn to talk, like a parrot, and I wondered what it would be like to have a magpie as a companion, one that, unlike humans, said only what it had been taught and sat on your shoulder, preening its iridescent blue and white feathers.

Only a few months before, Doc had sat here and watched them with me. Now, in his place, was a space I couldn't fill. Even the splendor of the day — the brilliant snow, the sweeping flight of birds — had no meaning. It wasn't only cabin fever that had me by the throat. Sorrow had turned me numb, stitched me into myself as if I, too, was wrapped in a shroud and buried.

I said — "Doc!" — and the hills caught the word, sent it back in echoes, and the magpies, startled, flew toward the mountains and left me lonelier than before.

Slowly I trudged toward the cabin, leaning into my own shadow, blue on the snow in front of me. Eva was outside doing a wash, and she waved.

"I decided to hang the clothes out since the sun's shining," she said.

"What can I do?"

She pointed at a tub of freshly rinsed sheets. "Hang those, if you would."

I set to work pinning them to the line, smelling the sweetness of soap, the mountain air. Unconsciously I must have sighed, because Eva turned and watched me a minute.

"I wish I could make you happy," she said.

How could she erase the past, bring Doc back? Everything seemed hopeless, but I couldn't tell her so. "Nobody's happy all the time," I said.

She stirred the clothes in the wash tub with a wooden paddle. "What I mean is . . . you're not happy with us."

She didn't understand. How could she, with her home, her husband, her children to keep her warm?

"It's not you," I said. "I love you all. But Doc's here. His ghost, his memory. I've been thinking about everything, and I decided I'll go into Aspen when the snow melts. Maybe open another restaurant."

She came closer and patted me on the arm. "I think that's a good idea. Maybe you'll meet somebody."

When I started to protest, she silenced me. "Let me say it. You're the kind of woman who gets along better with men than with women. Men like you. Alex and I both think you'd be happier if you had someone."

She was right. Whether I'd been born that way or experience had molded me, I wasn't made to be a hen in a hen house. My stay in the convent, even my months at Bessie Earp's, had been proof of that.

"Nobody can take Doc's place," I said, though I agreed with her premise.

"Of course not! But life goes on, and you're still young."

In my heart I was old. The heart can only break so much, and then it atrophies, turns into a mockery of itself.

"I'm thinking about Aspen," I said.

Colorado was booming. The treasure trove of gold and silver that lay buried in the mountains was luring miners from all over the world. In the big camps — Aspen, Leadville, Silverton — you could hear a dozen languages spoken at once, and many prospectors paid their way with a bag of gold dust, a handful of nuggets. There was money to be made, and, though I was grieving, I knew I had to earn my own way.

Eva pulled me into her arms and hugged me. "Don't think I'm trying to get rid of you. I just hate seeing the shadows in your eyes."

I submitted to her embrace. She was a warm, motherly soul, and I'd been motherless for longer than I cared to remember. "I'll come back and visit. And you can bring the children for a day or two. Aspen isn't far."

Aspen had another point in its favor, one I didn't mention. Aspen wasn't Glenwood Springs or Leadville, those places haunted by ghosts. I'd never figured why Doc stayed in Leadville even though he knew it was hurrying his death. Sometimes I thought he'd simply decided to die.

III

Leadville, 1885

"You start out with a dream. Then it all goes to hell," Doc said, and coughed until I thought he'd die right then.

He had pneumonia. Leadville wasn't the place for a man with his lungs as he had to have known.

I wanted to shake him but didn't dare. "Listen to me. Let's get out of here. You beat this before, you can do it again. I know you can. We'll go to California, change our names, and you can sit in the sun and breathe real air and get well. We'll be happy there like we used to be."

He didn't answer, just turned away and looked out the window. It was snowing. It seemed it was always snowing in Leadville.

"Go ahead and die then," I said. "Go ahead and leave me."

He hunched his shoulders and coughed again. "You'll find somebody else to boss around soon enough."

"You're a quitter!" I stomped across the room.

His smile shivered across the bones of his face that were so prominent they seemed ready to break through the skin. "Go away, Kate. I'm a realist, and you're the kind of female I hate."

"So hate me!"

A sigh shook him. "Go next door and get me a drink."

"No."

"That's you. Always telling me what's good for me. Who in hell do you think you are?"

I straightened up and looked down my nose at him, a look I'd learned in my cradle from my mother and that never failed to intimidate. "I'm a Horony. My family's been in Hungary since Arpad, and don't you forget it."

He snorted, then laughed, and I felt better. Putting him in a good mood had become an almost impossible challenge. "Kate, Kate," he said, "I'll bet you can't even tell me who Arpad was, but that's all right. I don't feel up to a history lesson. And anyway, I agree. There's not a one like you. Not a whore in five states."

It hurt. He had the power to hurt because I loved him and wished I didn't. We were bound together by our upbringing and by a passion to conquer one another. Except now I had the upper hand. I was young and healthy. Still, the nasty words spilled out.

"I hope you die tonight. I hope you go straight to hell where you belong."

He looked at me with those incredible blue eyes, and I saw what he would have been without trouble and disease. "You believe everything I say. Won't you ever learn I love to tease you?"

"You love torturing me."

He reached out a hand that trembled. "No, sweetheart. It's just you take it all so seriously."

What other way was there? I said: "I'm going back to Globe."

"Good. Then I can die drunk and in peace."

I kicked a chair and wished it was him. "If you hadn't followed Wyatt, if you hadn't gone off with him and killed those cowboys, there wouldn't be a warrant out on you. You could come with me. But you wouldn't listen. You never do."

He shut his eyes. "It was a matter of honor. Something you obviously can't understand."

I snickered, misrepresenting what had happened to suit my own purpose. "A bunch of big city gunmen with pistols killing a bunch of no-good cowboy rustlers who couldn't shoot their way out of a barn. That's not honor."

He didn't answer, and I saw that he'd fallen asleep. I covered him, lowered the lamp, and went out and down the stairs. Outside it was still snowing, and the thin air had a bite to it that made my eyes water. How had we come to such a brutal parting?

26

"Fool, fool," I said, and didn't know if I meant Doc or myself.

Prescott, Arizona, 1880

"What is it now?" Doc was pacing the floor of the room we'd rented. It was the spring of 1880, and we were bound for Tombstone at the urging of Wyatt Earp, except I didn't want to go.

That morning I'd gotten a letter from my brother, Alexander, who was homesteading in Colorado. He was urging me to come for a visit to Leadville, where he and my younger brother, Louis, had staked a mining claim and were hoping to strike it rich.

"You always want what you can't have," Doc said, when I showed him the invitation. "Nobody can satisfy you. I give you a week before you come running back."

He was right. I wanted him, but on my terms, and I wanted my family that I hadn't seen since I'd run away at age sixteen. I felt like one of those tumbleweeds that were beginning to become a nuisance on the plains, blowing here, touching down there, sailing on at the whimsy of the wind. And I was sick of the Earps, all of them, but Wyatt in particular. It seemed that all he had to do was snap his fingers and Doc

27

jumped, while I had to beg, plead, argue even to be listened to.

For Doc, the Earps took the place of his family. I came second — or last — and the fact rankled. At least Doc and I shared similar backgrounds, while the Earps were a tough, noisy bunch, always on the move, always looking for the main chance, dragging their women along like so much baggage.

Again, though I loved those women, I hated being classed as one of them, and I hated Wyatt's Mattie on principle. After all, in my mind, I'd had him first, and I never could understand what he saw in her with her violent temper, her country ways, and how, when that temper flared, she'd get drunk and smart-mouthed, ripping into Wyatt and the rest of us without a care. She and I avoided each other, though sometimes that was hard to do, traveling together as we were.

"Go if you want," Doc said. "Just don't expect to find me when you come back."

"I'm not going to this Tombstone place with you and them. That's final."

"Suit yourself. Do you have enough money?"

I didn't, and it riled me. I hated taking money from him, being dependent for every little necessity.

"I'll pay you back," I said.

He came closer and cupped my face in his

hands. "No need. Just take care of yourself. Those mining camps can get pretty rough."

When he was gentle like that, I was willing to do anything. "I don't have to go," I said.

"Yes, you do. You miss your family. God knows I can understand that." His eyes took on that look of longing they always did when he thought of his own family and the life he'd been forced to leave. "I'll miss you," he said.

I stared at him. "You will?"

He smiled. "You're like a toothache. Pull the tooth and it leaves a hole."

It wasn't flattering, but I didn't get mad as I usually did. "I'll miss you, too." I kissed him, and he returned it with passion, holding me a long time.

Then he said: "What a strange business life is."

"At least, we found each other. At least, there's that."

As usual, he reversed himself. "Yes. And now you're off some place. Talk's cheap, Kate. And don't expect me to come after you."

I pushed him away. "I don't expect anything. You taught me not to."

He went out, and I packed and left for Colorado.

The Denver and South Park Railroad at that time only went as far as Buena Vista. I got out of the train, retied my bonnet, shook the soot out of my skirt, and looked around for directions to the stage dépôt. Another woman stood on the platform with me, obviously as confused and as tired as I was. When our eyes met, she gave a dazzling smile and walked over to me.

"I hope you're going to Leadville, too," she said without preamble.

"I am." I decided she had to be the wife of a mining magnate, or, at least, the mistress of one, dressed as she was in a blue suit that matched her eyes, and wearing a Tuscan straw bonnet I'd have killed for.

"Good!" A blonde curl slipped out from under one of the bonnet's ribbons and blew across her cheek. "I wasn't looking forward to going on alone with all those strange men. They stare so. My name's Elizabeth Doe, but everybody calls me Baby."

I blinked. It was a ridiculous name, one more suited to a prostitute, but then, in view of my past, I couldn't be particular. "Mary Holliday."

"Well, Mary, where do you suppose we catch the stage?"

"Just what I was wondering. But two women ought to be able to find out anything."

She laughed at that. Not one of your muffled, lady-like sounds, but a genuine laugh like a good bell. "You're so right."

With a gesture she summoned a porter who was so taken with her beauty he could only stammer a few directions, but she seemed to understand him. "See that our trunks get there, will you please?" She opened her purse and searched for a tip, then took my arm. "We'll walk. Won't it feel good to walk after that awful train?"

And so together we boarded the stage for Leadville and settled ourselves in the most comfortable seats, if so they could be called.

"Is someone meeting you?" she asked.

"My brothers. One I haven't seen in fifteen years." As I spoke, I was shocked at how old I felt, at the things I'd seen — and done.

"A reunion!" She clapped her hands. "That's wonderful. I'm going to meet the man I love." She spoke as if there was no one else present but me, as if the other passengers, all male, weren't watching her, hanging on every word.

With some amusement, I saw their faces fall, their hopes destroyed by her obvious excitement. She, however, paid them no mind, continuing on with her story. How she'd been married to one Harvey Doe, a shiftless drunk; how she'd fallen in love with

Jake Sandelowsky, lost his child, lost everything in her subsequent divorce from Doe. "So you see, I'm a fallen woman," she said, eyes sparkling. "And it doesn't matter any more, if it ever did. I'm going to meet Jake and be married, and that's an end to it."

At the mention of her dead child, I thought of little Michael, named for my father and buried in St. Louis, taken away by the yellow fever.

"What is it?" She reached out a hand in a pale blue glove and took mine.

When I told her, her eyes filled with tears. "I'm sorry. For us both. Life is so unfair sometimes."

"Especially to children. He was so little. So dear. After that, I didn't care about anything. Not for a long time." No, I hadn't cared. I'd gone from respectable married woman to Bessie Earp's brothel in Wichita in a descent so rapid I even now couldn't recall all of it.

Baby nodded. "They say that sorrow makes you tough. I think it only cuts away little pieces until there's not much left."

Neither of us could know what the rest of life had in store for us. Baby would become the mistress, then the wife of millionaire H. A. W. Tabor, a fairy tale with a bad ending. When I last heard from her, she was living alone and broke in a shed near the Matchless Mine that had made Tabor — and for a brief time Baby — rich.

And I? Well, that's my story, and I'll tell it as it comes — in fragments, scenes, like the unfolding of a flower, petal by petal, until I reach the heart.

IV

Leadville, 1880

They were Horonys. There was no way I'd have missed finding my brothers, even in the milling crowds at the dépôt. There were the blue eyes in the bony faces, the prominent ears, the long, thin noses so much like my own that had given me the name I detested. Big Nose Kate! I hated it the minute it was given me — and have spent the rest of my life trying to live it down.

Hugging my brothers, my heart beating so hard I thought I'd faint — from altitude as well as emotion — I suddenly understood Doc's attachment to the Earps. They were fellow adventurers, a warm-hearted bunch of Gypsies, and as much of a family as he could hope to have. One woman, and that one as rootless as he, couldn't supply the security he needed. I sighed and looked at Louis, now a head taller than I was.

"You grew up!"

His eyes twinkled. "And so did you, big sister. His hands were large and rough, miner's hands, hardened by shovel and pick axe. "Come on. Let's get you something to eat and catch up on things."

At that moment, over his shoulder, I saw what looked like an army marching down the street — a platoon of armed men, determined and in step.

"Is there a war?" Dim pictures of soldiers and cavalry came back and frightened me. Maximillian in Mexico on his prancing stallion; my father and Kossuth, planning freedom for the Hungary they loved.

"There's a strike," Alex said. "The mine owners cut wages. There's so many workers in town, the bosses can hire who they want at the price they want, which doesn't sit too well with the old-timers. That's one of the local militias, hoping to scare the strikers into accepting the pay cut and going back to work."

Looking around, I saw a bunch of rough men carrying clubs and in some cases pistols, their eyes following the progress of the gaily dressed militia with hatred.

"Is that them? The miners?"

"Some of them. The rest are up at the mines, hoping to organize and get more followers. Things will get violent, Mary. In fact, we've been thinking of getting out before the whole town goes up."

"But I just got here!" I was stiff, sore, hungry. The idea of getting on another stage to nowhere held less appeal than a war.

He took my arm. "They might settle quickly. Particularly if the governor gets involved. But these men are mad. And they're right, even if no one wants to admit it. Let's get off the street, and then we'll talk."

Baby waved at me from across the street, where she stood with, I supposed, her beloved Jake. "Come see me, when you're settled!" she called.

My brothers stared at her with fascination. "Who's that?" they asked simultaneously.

I told them. Alex shook his head. "Jake's a lucky man. If he can hold her."

"Why shouldn't he?"

"She looks like a fortune-hunter, and who's to blame her with a face like that?"

I thought about other women I'd known — Blanche in St. Louis, Bessie and the girls

35

in Wichita, Lottie Deno in Griffin. "She's not a bad woman," I said, knowing that in reality there weren't any bad women, just frightened ones down on their luck. Alex didn't know about that part of my life, what I'd done to keep body and soul together, and I wasn't about to tell him.

"Let's go eat," I said, changing the subject.

We hadn't gone a block when the madness erupted.

Someone hurled a stone that was followed by a hailstorm of them, crashing into the window of a newspaper office and into the shop windows on either side. There were shouts, more stones flying without direction, gunshots, and bodies milling and pushing like a herd of maddened longhorns. Alex lost his grip on my arm, and I was swept into the midst of the mob, fighting to stay on my feet, to get to the relative safety of the sidewalk. I felt as if I were drowning, struggling to catch my breath, flailing my arms, and trying to keep hold of my purse at the same time.

Around me were angry men fighting for their livelihood in a rebellion that had been repeated in one way or another since the beginning of history. The strong against the weak, the rich against the poor. I could smell their anger. It was tainted with the smell of fear — my own and theirs, those men who had been pushed too far.

One of them, with hard boots, stepped on my feet, and I cried out, but the sound was lost in the shouting. Like a leaf I was shunted back and forth until, by a miracle, I got shoved into a post and, panting, wrapped my arms around it.

"Mary!" Louis came toward me, dodging fists and bodies. "Hold on!"

I held on so well he had to pry my hands away. Then he dragged me into an alley between a wall of buildings. "Are you hurt?"

I flexed my toes inside my shoes and tried to find enough breath to answer. "No," I said finally.

"Come on, then." He put an arm around my waist, and in spite of myself I laughed. My little brother had, indeed, grown up. We'd all survived life in a new country, without parents or guidance or any help at all but our wits. Or maybe because of dumb luck. If it was that, I wasn't pushing it any further.

Straightening my hat I said: "Alex was right. Let's get out of here. I've seen enough. Leadville's a disaster."

How much of a disaster I'd learn a few years later.

V

Ruby, Colorado, 1880

Ruby was never a big mining camp, but there was enough gold being taken out to keep a thousand or so hopefuls burrowing into the mountains, my brothers, who had claims there, included. Louis worked the prospects, and Alexander came and went, dividing his time between his homestead and prospecting. To me it seemed paradise after the smoke and furor of Leadville, and I hadn't been there a week before I rolled up my sleeves and went into business.

Men had to eat, and there was money to be made feeding them. Besides, I've never been one to sit still and do nothing. When I broached the subject to Louis, he was baffled.

"You're supposed to be on vacation."

"I can't just sit here and look at the scenery all day," I said. "But I'll need some dishes and a few cooking pots to start. And a little extra cash."

"If you mean it, I've got credit in Leadville," he said. "You can pay me later. You'll be able to. These guys'll jump at decent cooking."

So I retraced my steps and went back to Leadville, and spent a day buying the essentials, contracting with a freighter to bring everything over the mountain, including sacks of flour, beans, potatoes, and rice.

I also mailed a letter to Doc, telling him about my plan and hoping against all hope that he'd give up his notion about Tombstone and come and find me.

When I'd finished, I stepped outside and looked up and down the street. As usual, it was bustling, but the strike had been settled and no angry mob greeted me. Instead, I came face to face with Baby Doe.

"Mary!" she exclaimed. "Where have you been? I looked all over town for you, but you disappeared."

I explained, and she listened, then said: "Come have lunch with me. The most wonderful thing has happened, and I need to tell somebody, but none of the women here will talk to me." She laughed. "Like I said, I'm a fallen woman. A second time. So I'm doubly in disgrace."

She was wearing a diamond ring as big as an egg, and her eyes were sparkling. Disgraced or not, she was making the best of it, but Jake Sands, as he now called himself, had never bought her a jewel like that one.

We settled ourselves at a table in the dining room of the Clarendon, where, she informed me, she was now living in a suite.

"Who is it?" I asked.

"It's the strangest, most romantic thing, and I have no defense. I met Horace at a ball. He asked me to dance, and, of course, I said yes. The minute he took my hand, we both felt it. Like we were meant to be. I can't explain it any other way, Mary. Who ever could explain how love happens?"

That she meant what she said, I had no doubt. Her face was radiant. She looked like a young girl in the throes of first love. Had I looked like that, I wondered, when I first met Doc, when we were making our way over the cattle trail to the safety of Dodge?

"Horace who?" I couldn't restrain my curiosity.

"Horace Tabor." She waved her hand to stop my words. "I know what you're thinking. That he's rich and I'm in love with his wallet, but it's not so, Mary. He's kind and good and. . . ."

"Married," I put in.

"To a dreadful woman who won't give him a divorce."

And she wondered why the town society women shunned her! I chose my next words carefully, knowing exactly the dilemma she'd let herself in for.

"You'll always be unacceptable to the old cats. Even if he does get a divorce and marry you. You'll never fit in, and, if that's going to eat at you, you'd better decide now. You can't have it both ways. The world isn't made like that."

"I already made up my mind." Her voice was soft, but her look was determined. "For better or worse," she added. Then, with a lift of her chin, she said: "Are you going to scorn me, too? I thought you were cut from a different bolt of cloth."

I chuckled. "I'm not in a position to criticize, believe me."

"Then you understand."

"Of course."

"And you'll be my friend?"

Millionaire's mistress or not, she seemed like a child, helpless, vulnerable, and I understood her situation only too well. And there was also a great deal to be said about having access to H. A. W. Tabor and the power of his influence. I reached across the table and took her hand. "If you'll be mine."

Dimples framed her mouth. "We make a fine pair, Mary, and I thank you."

When I went back to Prescott at the end of the short mountain summer, I had five hundred dollars squirreled away. Some I'd earned cooking at Ruby. The rest came from H. A. W. Tabor's largesse via his much-adored mistress and soon to be wife, Baby Doe, who turned out to be a very good friend, indeed.

VI

Prescott, Arizona 1880

"So you're back. Like the proverbial bad penny." Doc softened his words with a kiss. *"Have you changed your mind?"*

"About what?"

"Tombstone." He gave me a wicked look.

I felt my purse, heavy with the gold of freedom. "No."

"Too bad." He folded a shirt and put it in his bag. "For you," he added.

"I'll go with you," I said, needing him more than I wanted to admit. "But I won't stay."

"Then why bother?" He turned to face me. "What's in it for you? Or for me? What's this

crazy game you play all the time? Go or stay, Kate, but don't do both. Make up your mind and stick with it."

"I can't."

"Why not?"

A good question, and one I couldn't answer because I couldn't make him understand my hopes.

I said: "We always end up in a fight, but it doesn't have to be like that."

"You want a lap dog. I'm not it."

"I want you."

"As much as there is to have, you have me." He smiled, but it was a cautious smile.

"What's in Tombstone for you anyhow?" I asked, changing the subject. "You can set up a dentist's office any place."

"No, Kate, I can't. People are afraid of me. Of it. I'm a leper."

"You're a good dentist."

"And you're biased. Of course, I'm good. Or was." He shrugged. "But I can't just lie down and wait for the bugs to get me. I'm not built right for that. Wyatt's got some layouts going, and I'll be earning my way, such as it is, so don't try and take that from me. Let me have some pride, and there's an end to it."

It hurt me to see him fighting for some male notion of manhood, so I shut up, repacked my trunk, and went with him to that damned town that grew like an evil weed in the valley of the

San Pedro River. I went, looked, and felt the wickedness with an intuition I hadn't known I possessed. I lasted a week.

"Stay if you have to. I'm going to Globe."

"With what?" He faced me across the table where we'd just finished our dinner.

"I saved my money. Don't worry, I won't ask for a loan."

His eyes burned until I thought my face would be scorched. "Don't look at me like that," I said. "I can't help it. This place . . . those people. They'll destroy you, and I won't hang around to watch."

"I didn't ask you to."

He hadn't, but just once I wished he would, wished he'd say what I wanted to hear whether it was true or not. Certainly I had other options. Colorado was full of men who were looking for a wife and not choosy about her background. I could have stayed there, dignified by a proper marriage and my connection to my family, and given up on Doc and our explosive relationship. But I didn't, and for all the trouble and sorrow that happened, I still can't say I have any regrets.

In Ruby the men had flocked to my tent restaurant where I dished out good meals. They came, they ate, they returned again, and they proposed marriage, regardless of the fact that I told them I was already taken.

Only one actually caught my eye — a tall, lean, determined prospector, George Cummings. George had come to Colorado early, had fought off Utes, claim-jumpers, the unpredictable mountain weather, and he had fallen in love with my cooking first, then with me.

"Stay with me, Mary," he said, when I was packing up to leave before the first snow. "You'll bring me luck, and I'll buy you the biggest mansion in Aspen. You'll never be sorry."

He was handsome, I had to admit — dark-haired, muscular, with a wry twist to his mouth that appealed. But there was Doc somewhere in Arizona, and we were tied together by our strange hungers — for each other, for the need of a rough respectability. God knows I wanted to live down what I'd been. And Doc — well, he wanted what he'd been born to. The Southern aristocracy. If it hadn't been for what I'd done, I'd have filled the bill. Except I'd been a whore, and he knew it, couldn't trust me to assume the demeanor he demanded. And no matter what I said or did, he couldn't believe me.

There's the tragedy. To know one's self and to have one's lover scoff at the truth. And tragedy it was. I've spent the rest of my life attempting to figure it, wondering what I could have said or done to prove my worth.

I still don't know, and now it doesn't matter. He's gone. I'm old. For better or worse, I've lived my life, and what matters now is that I can open my eyes in the morning, look out and see the mountains, the desert, the stubborn trees whose roots go hundreds of feet into the earth. What matters is the singing of birds, the lifting of thunder clouds in late summer, the music of the senses that clutch the heart. What matters is life itself, and the fleeting moments of unadulterated joy.

VII

Globe, 1880

From Globe I watched the drama in Tombstone unfold like a play, the ending of which I knew in my bones would be disaster, and I was involved in spite of myself.

I couldn't stay away from Doc. Like an opium smoker, I was addicted, and he was the same, always writing me to come for a visit, to stay a while with him. And I went, though I feared for his life and my own, though I'd proved I could survive without him.

So I went back and forth between the towns, the outcome of my journeys always predictable. Trouble. Pain. Anguish. And at the last, the street fight in Tombstone where three badmen got what they deserved, and Doc and the Earps were branded murderers by snotty, little Sheriff Behan.

I'd had my own run-in with Behan before then. Doc and I had had a bitter fight, and I had been alone and miserable until Johnny Behan came along, all smooth-talking and oily. He had calmed me down, flattered me in that way he had, then bought me dinner and enough wine so I couldn't think straight. Back in his office, he had twisted my arm, had pulled it back, and had twisted till the pain got so bad I had cried out.

"Just sign the paper, Kate." His voice had been low in my ear. "Sign it and you'll never have to have anything to do with Doc again."

"You're hurting. . . ."

He had given another twist, and I had thought I'd pass out. "Sign it, Kate. He's no good. You know it. I know it."

There had been the pain, the haze of liquor, Behan's breath warm on my face, the blurred light of the lamp on his desk where the paper lay ready for me, and nothing had mattered but an end to the torture. Doc would understand what I was doing. He'd make it right, come morning.

Except in the morning I had found out I'd signed a paper implicating Doc in a stagecoach hold-up and the murder of Bud Philpot. Doc and Wyatt had fixed it all right, and I had had to go to court and swear I'd been drunk and forced, and that I didn't know anything at all about the hold-up or Doc's whereabouts on that night. And then I had gone back to Globe, stung by Doc's fury and Wyatt Earp's contempt.

Some years ago, I read about Johnny's funeral in the Tucson paper and said to myself: "Good riddance! A pity it didn't happen sooner." If it had, maybe things would have turned out differently. But who knows?

Certainly nobody could have stopped Wyatt from doing what he did after the cowboy gang murdered his brother Morgan. Wyatt went out for revenge, and he got it — Frank Stilwell in Tucson, Curly Bill at Iron Springs, Indian Charley in the Dragoons, and nobody ever counted or found the others. Wyatt rode through Cochise County like the devil on horseback, visiting every ranch, camp, rustler hide-out, and Doc was with him, as set on revenge as Wyatt.

Morgan had been Doc's friend, and Wyatt

was the brother he never had. Call it a blood feud, call it honor, call it what you will. They rode out, and they didn't stop until they'd cleaned up the den of thieves that had been running roughshod for years. And then, with murder warrants hanging over them, they headed for Colorado.

I'd written to Baby Doe as soon as Doc told me his bad news. Baby and I had kept in touch, and I was one of the few who knew about Tabor's secret divorce and his even more secret marriage to Baby.

Governor Evans was out of the state, and Tabor was lieutenant governor of Colorado when the extradition papers got there. It was like an act of God, especially when Tabor turned down the Arizona warrant, refusing to send Doc back to Arizona. They didn't even try for Wyatt after that. So I had still another reason to bless my friendship with Baby.

Doc wrote from Colorado and told me the whole story, and urged me to come for a visit. But I was stuck in Globe with a hotel I'd bought mainly to prove my independence. Now it was a millstone around my neck, profitable though it was. I put it up for sale, but no one wanted to pay my price, and I wasn't about to cheat myself after all the work I'd put into it. So I stayed, and was there when Doc and Wyatt came back in that hot summer of 1882 — came back in secret, by train and on horseback, and caught the last of the outlaw gang, John Ringo, while he was camped in a cañon near West Turkey Creek.

His body was found propped in a tree, his gun belt upside down, no boots on his feet, and a hole in his head. The coroner's verdict was suicide, but I knew better. Doc made a quick stop in Globe on his way back to Colorado.

"You haven't seen me, sweetheart." He had his arms around me, and I was crying because I was so happy to see him. "If anybody asks, tell them that."

"I'm glad you got Ringo," I said, still sniffing. "He was no good for all he tried to pretend he was a gentleman. When he was sober," I added.

Doc snorted. "He was trash like the rest of them."

"Is there going to be more of it? More killing? Or are you through?"

"We've got most of them. Except that bastard Behan. I'll drill him dead center for what he did to you that night, if I ever catch him."

"Forget him," I whispered. "He's not worth killing."

"I'll forget him for now, but only because time's running out." He kissed me — softly at first, then harder. The fire was still there between us, the passion that was love, anger, hate, despair, all of those things. When he let me go, my legs were trembling.

"Take care, sweetheart," he said. "And remember, you haven't seen me."

Then he was gone into the first gray light of morning — gone into exile yet another time, the last.

VIII

Aspen, Colorado, 1888

Alexander went with me to Aspen. "Till I'm sure you're settled in," he said.

I smothered a smile. Settling in, as he called it, was what I'd been doing for years in one town after another, one country after another. Like the Gypsies of Hungary, I knew what to look for, how to make out, no matter what. Still, his concern touched me. It was sweet to have a brother again, someone who shared a past, however distant, someone who cared.

Aspen had grown since I'd seen it last. It had wide, well-planned streets lit by electricity, with running water and even a sewage system. And it had the mansions of the mine owners, private clubs, hotels, stores that stocked everything from bonnets and lace to musical instruments, baseball teams, and a race track. Above it all loomed the mountains, and the tunnels, shafts, mills that twenty four hours a day spit out silver — thousands of tons of it.

There was talk of telephone service, and the skeleton of what would become the opera house dwarfed the neighboring buildings. All in all, it was a splendid place to go into business, and go I did, buying out an already established restaurant named, of all things, Aunt Mary's.

"A good omen," I said to Alex, who was amazed at the determined way I'd conducted my transactions.

"You go after what you want just like a man," he said.

"What's wrong with that?"

He shook his head. "Nothing. I guess."

"I've learned the hard way," I said. "And I don't like wasting time."

"Then I'll leave you to get on with it. You'll be all right?" He was having trouble giving up his self-appointed rôle as protector.

I gave him a hug. "I'll be fine. And thank you for being there when I needed you."

The first thing I did was to clean up the place, starting with the kitchen that had been run by a man who had no interest in cleanliness, and ending in the dining room where I made sure the waitresses had fresh aprons and clean hands. Mining town or not, no one was going to serve tables in my restaurant with dirty fingernails!

One of the girls looked at me with surprise and what I thought was a hint of fear.

"You," I said. "What's your name?"

"Magda."

That caught my attention. "From where?"

"Hungary, missus." She was doing her best to be polite, at the same time sniffing back tears.

"Well, then, Magda," I said in rusty but grammatical Magyar, "would you want to disgrace your country by having people say we're all peasants?"

Her mouth opened. "You?" she said at last.

"Yes. And if you know anything about cooking, and if you do what I tell you, I'll take you into the kitchen as cook's helper. I just fired that dirty old man in there."

Already I was remembering the meals I'd made in past years — food with the flavors of my long-ago home.

She clasped her hands. "Missus . . . anything you tell me, I will do. My father died in an explosion in the mine, and there is my mama and four little ones."

She reminded me of myself, with her long yellow braid and that flash of determination. Here was one who wouldn't end up walking the street, selling herself, not if I could help it.

"Just close your eyes and think about something else." That was Bessie Earp's advice when she hired me in Wichita.

Except it wasn't as easy as that. My first customer was a kid in from a cattle drive, a kid hardly old enough to leave home. We went to my room, and he stood there, his Adam's apple moving up and down, his eyes looking everywhere but at me. Obviously, he'd been to the bath house and the barber. I could smell soap and shaving lotion, and it was all I could do to keep from smoothing the cowlick on his freshly cut hair.

"Come sit beside me," I said, patting the bed.

He did, gingerly. I asked him his name and where he was from and what it was like on the Texas trail, and after a couple minutes he relaxed and I kissed him like he was my child instead of a paying customer.

"Is this your first time?" I asked.

"Yes, ma'am." He was polite, well-raised, and blushing like a girl.

Some woman had done a good job with him, and now it was my turn to teach him a few more things. If my son had lived, I'd have prayed that

54

he learned the right ways with a woman, and that he found one capable of showing him.

"Take off those spurs and boots," I told him. "Then help me out of this dress. There's no hurry about anything."

The men who came to Bessie's weren't all like him, and thinking about something else wasn't always easy. As a result, I learned more than a woman needs to know about the peculiarities of humanity, men in particular.

I made up my mind that Magda wouldn't ever have to go through what I'd gone through, that she'd have what was denied me — the freedom to choose.

"Wash your hands and face," I said. "Then come back to the kitchen."

It turned out to be one of the smartest moves I ever made. Magda had learned cooking at her mother's knee, and she had an uncle who refused to work in the mines. "I won't be buried before I die," was how he put it.

Karoly was a hunter. He kept me supplied with venison and elk and anything else that walked or flew, usually for the price of a few meals and some rounds of ammunition. After a few months, he proposed, but by that time George Cummings had come back into my life, a disaster had I only known it.

IX

"There's a gentleman looking for you, missus." Magda was obviously impressed, either by the fact that I had a caller, or by the man himself.

"Who is it?"

"He say his name is Yurp. Something like that." Magda was still having trouble with English.

"And he's the last person I want to see."

She frowned. "He's very handsome."

"He's trouble." I took off my apron. "Never mind. I'll go find out what he wants."

By keeping busy, I'd managed to dull the edges of grief. Sometimes a day would go by without my thinking about Doc. Now here was Wyatt, bringing back what I'd tried so hard to forget.

He was sitting at a table, his back to the wall, sipping a cup of coffee, but, seeing me, he stood up. "Well Kate," he said, smiling a little.

"I'm not Kate any more. Kate's dead and gone. My family always called me Mary."

He pulled out a chair and held it for me. "Mary, then. I was in town and heard you were here."

"Where's Josie?" I asked, hoping he hadn't abandoned her the way he'd done Mattie.

"Out shopping. I had enough of it. Thought I'd just drop by and see how you were. If you needed anything."

"I'm fine."

My short answers made him uncomfortable, and I was glad of it. Once I thought I knew him well, but I'd never really understood him. Maybe no one did, not even Josie Marcus. Not even Doc.

As if he'd read my mind, he said: "He was a good man. None better."

And you killed him, I thought. *You dragged him along and never thought what it did to him. Or to me.*

It was uncanny how he seemed to know my feelings. He said: "I couldn't stop him, Mary. He lived on his own terms, the way he wanted. And I miss him. I never had a better friend."

"You never will, either." I felt tears beginning, and anger. Damn him! He'd brought it all back, the whole tangled mess. Once I thought I loved him, that he was the prince in the fairy tale who'd rescue me from the life I hated, that he'd ride up to Bessie's whore house and take me away. And then in walked Mattie, the wife he'd left back on the farm, and all my dreams vanished the way dreams usually do. And then I found Doc.

I pushed back my chair. "I have to get to work. Give my best to Josie."

He reached out and took my hand. "I'm glad you were with him, Mary. Glad he didn't have to go alone."

"He shouldn't have had to go at all. Not so soon. And whose fault is it?" I yanked my hand away and stood there trembling with pent-up rage.

Wyatt stood, too. "Not mine. Not yours, either. He made his choice. And for what it's worth, he told me he wanted to finish up and go back to you. Only it didn't work out that way, and I'm sorry."

It was like being shot, hearing him say that. Like having a slug tear through me, ripping apart all the walls I'd put up to keep the pain away.

"Please." I choked on tears. "Go away. You only make it worse."

He put on his hat and looked at me, and I saw a hint of my own sorrow in those ice-blue eyes. "Stay well," he said softly, and left, stopping at the counter to pay for his coffee before opening the glass door and going out onto the street.

I stood a minute, trying to compose myself. Damn him! Always so sure of himself, always in control. It was what made him so dangerous — both in a gunfight and with women. Whoever he was after never stood a chance.

I was wishing I'd never left home, never met a one of the men I'd loved and lost, when from behind me came a voice.

"Mary! Mary Holliday! What are you doing back here?"

X

George Cummings wasn't the kind of man I'd have picked for myself twenty years before, but I'd lived in the West long enough to learn that what was necessary for success wasn't always what was acceptable in drawing rooms.

He was a rough diamond, and he had a merry eye that promised a woman a good time. In spite of misgivings, I was drawn to him, or maybe it was that I'd simply had enough of feeling sorry for myself.

Working was fine and profitable, but I've

never been one to sit at home alone doing nothing when the work was done. And there was plenty of fun to be had in Aspen — ball games, horse races, touring theatrical troops, dances, none of which I felt comfortable about attending alone.

A decent woman needed a male escort, and George was the answer to my unspoken prayer. With his beard trimmed and in clean clothes, I thought he would solve my problem quite nicely, so I smiled and said: "Why, George Cummings! Have you struck it rich and come to town to spend it all?"

He had those wicked hazel eyes, and they shot sparks at me. "I've come to take you to the Independence Day celebration," he said. "And I won't take no for an answer."

"I'd be delighted." The words slipped out. I was thirty eight years old, but I wasn't dead. Not by a long shot. It was past time for some fun.

The face in the mirror was the one I'd been looking at all my life — long, with high cheekbones under eyes that slanted just a bit.

"Cat's eyes," Doc had called them. Gambler's eyes, giving nothing away.

And there was the thin Horony nose that I'd thought was elegant until the day that whore in Wichita gave me the name I couldn't get rid of. Big Nose Kate. It made me sound like a clown. An elephant. A creature in a freak show instead of a woman with an interesting face.

Fortunately, no one in my new life had ever heard the hated nickname, and I had no intention of revealing it. I was Mary Holliday, recent widow, respectable restaurateur. A woman who, as Shakespeare wrote, had played many parts. And played them well!

I smiled at myself and searched for gray hairs. Not finding any, I smiled harder. I was ready to live again. Fortunately Doc had always insisted on my being well-dressed, and paid generously for it. There were enough clothes in my trunk to see me into the next century with a little careful needlework. And very few of the dresses had bustles.

"Bear traps," Doc had called them with a wicked grin. "How can I pinch your bottom, if it's protected by that contraption?"

It seemed he was in the room with me, lying on the bed and watching me dress as he often had, and teasing me in that slow, Southern drawl I loved. Only this time, I refused to give in to sorrow.

"Quit haunting me," I told him. "You're dead, but I'm not, and it's not fair, you coming back all the time, making me feel bad. And guilty. I'm not guilty, and you know it."

I was talking to myself. The face in the mirror mocked me. "Damn' fool," it said. "You're the one lugging the baggage around. Put it to rest once and for all."

I snapped back into reality and pulled out a yellow linen suit with hand embroidery on the jacket and skirt — several years old but still flattering, and best of all there was a parasol to match. Only the ladies of the Aspen social set would have anything like it, and I could be proud, and George Cummings would be pleased to have me on his arm.

"So there!" I said to the empty room, and stepped out into the brilliant July sunlight where George stood waiting.

The whole town was on holiday. Buildings were draped with bunting; flags flew everywhere; and Main Street was lined with people waiting for the parade that was led by the fife and drum corps playing spritely marches. They were followed by the wagons of the local fire departments; each one decorated with crepe paper and painted signs, the firemen, shouting and spraying water at the screaming crowd.

Around us rose the mountains — Aspen, Smuggler, the tip of Snowmass, ice-covered even in the middle of summer. It was a far cry from Tombstone that always managed a certain drab, sinister appearance, or even Globe, buttoned into its jagged hills.

So I was happy. Happier still to see Alex and Eva and the children coming toward us.

"We decided to take a holiday," Eva said. And then in my ear whispered: "And here we find you already with a man."

"It's nothing," I protested, but she flashed a conspirator's smile.

"You could do worse."

"Or better." I was thinking of Baby Doe and Tabor and the millions of dollars he was taking out of his mines, the mansion he had built for his new family in Denver. Not that I envied her. It just seemed, somehow, that there had to be a middle ground between absolute wealth and utter poverty, that too much or too little money, either one, corrupted.

To my dismay, I saw Wyatt, with Josie clinging to his arm, walking toward us.

I made the introductions, praying neither of them would refer to my past, Josie in particular. Although I liked her and admired her beauty, she did have a way of going on about things.

"Kate." She reached out a slender hand. "How good to see you again. And looking so well. I was sorry about Doc. We both were. I guess Wyatt's told you."

"I'm Mary now," I said, cutting in on her. "It's what my family called me."

"Oh good!" She was all sparkle and the best of intentions. "Big Nose Kate was really an awful name when you think of it. Not flattering at all."

Under cover of our skirts, I stepped on her foot. Too late.

"What's this? What's this?" George had ears like a fox. "Who dared call this lovely lady such a horrible name?"

I took his hand. "It was a joke. Now let's go over and watch the horse races." How did I know he'd use it against me one day in the far future? How did I know that a slip of the tongue would contribute to my undoing?

Josie looked at me, stricken. "Shouldn't I. . . . ?"

"Hush!" I said. "Just never mind!"

Wyatt saved me. "Let's all go. There's a gray somebody brought up from Denver in the second race that looks promising." And he led Josie away, though she looked back at me bewildered, and, I thought, in some pain. I hadn't been exactly gentle, but it served her right.

George and I followed them, laughing.

"Some joke," he said. "Who'd insult you like that?"

I shrugged. "It was a long time ago. I forget. So should you."

The gray Wyatt picked came in first by six lengths, and since we'd all placed small bets, we were in fine spirits as we made our way to the picnic grounds.

Josie tugged at my sleeve. "Did I say something wrong?"

"I'm not her any more," I hissed. "She's gone . . . Doc's gone . . . they're all gone. Even Mattie. Understand?"

She nodded. "I do. We never talk about any of it. But it's hard. How do we live it down? How do we forget it all . . . and what we did?"

A good question, one I'd been asking myself. "We don't," I said. "We just hope to God nobody brings it up."

Her dark eyes flickered. "Somebody always does. Wyatt can't hide and neither can I. I'm sorry, if I embarrassed you. I should have known better. It wasn't meant."

"I know."

"Friends?" She cocked her head under a bonnet covered with plumes, reminding me of Baby again — another adventurous woman who had no qualms about what she wanted or how to get it.

"Sure," I said. "Just call me Mary from now on."

"If you'll call me Missus Wyatt Earp," she said, and winked.

XI

Every week-end for the rest of the summer George made the trip over the mountain and into town. He was determined and persistent, and he never left without proposing at least once.

For my part, I wasn't anxious to give up a thriving business and move to what was little more than a prospector's shack in the woods. My life was under control, and I was enjoying the freedom.

Every Friday afternoon I walked over to the Wheeler Bank and made a deposit. I'd also visited the Aspen stock exchange and bought shares in some of the local mines. In addition, having learned from experience, I was hoarding a stack of gold coins in the bottom of my trunk. Mary Katherine Horony wasn't ever going to be broke and down on her luck again!

I listened to the men talking over at the

exchange. Although the mines were producing millions of tons of ore, there was a limited market for silver. Even I could see that, and sometimes wondered how the boom would end. The country was run on the gold standard, leaving silver to find its own place — a risky one in my view and in the view of some big-time investors who were a lot shrewder than I.

The fate of Aspen — and every silver mining town — depended on the price of silver, and, for that matter, so did my restaurant and all the businesses that had grown up due to the mines.

George sometimes laughed at me — portioning out my profits, collecting my small interest on my stocks — but, when the end came, we were both glad I'd had the foresight to keep my eggs in different baskets.

One of the reasons I said yes, when George proposed for maybe the hundredth time, was his willingness to give up prospecting and take a job blacksmithing for the Smuggler Mine.

He announced his plan with a kind of glee, as if he'd outwitted me by removing the last obstacle between us. It was January, 1890, and we'd gone to the skating rink for the afternoon — one of those glorious Rocky Mountain afternoons, when the sun shines, the snow catches fire, and every tree and rock is etched in glass.

"I'll do it!" he exclaimed, his hat in his hand. "I'll do it and move into town, if you'll just say yes and stop putting me off. You drive a man crazy, Mary, and I'm tired of it."

His eyes were solemn, almost pleading, and I felt a surge of pity for him, so earnest, so determined. Pity isn't enough to build a good marriage, but I didn't know that, then. I thought I knew everything, but I didn't. Somewhere inside I was still that little motherless girl running away from her past, grabbing at any life line that was offered.

And what, after all, was my objection? He wasn't Doc. But neither was any one of the other men who'd come courting — miners who enjoyed my cooking; the clerk at the bank who was eyeing my savings account; the doctor I'd visited when I'd burned my hand on the stove whose false teeth came loose when he examined me; and Magda's Uncle Karoly who'd finally given up and married his brother's widow.

A woman without a husband was at a disadvantage in those times, whether or not she was a success in business, and George was a hard worker, often fun, and he was giving up a large part of his freedom for me. How could I object to that?

I took a deep breath and balanced carefully on my skates. "Yes," I said, and watched as his face broke into a grin.

"You will?"

"I will."

He pulled me into his arms, and we both staggered, clutching each other and laughing, and it seemed like the mountains caught the sound and threw it back — peals of laughter and the applause of the other skaters who joined in the excitement.

We were married in the St. Charles Hotel, in March in the middle of a blizzard. George, not wanting anything to go wrong, asked both Judge Wiley and Judge England to do the honors.

No sooner had Judge Wiley pronounced us man and wife, than Judge England appeared ready to do it again.

Amidst much laughter, George, dressed in a new suit and starched white shirt, raised his glass in a toast — and an explanation.

"For two years I've been courting Mary, and she finally said yes. But I wasn't about to take any chances, so I decided to marry her twice!"

"It's good you're settled." Eva was beaming. "You'll be happy now with a husband to look out for you."

Poor, innocent Eva! She believed that a woman was nothing without a man at her side — an attitude that suited my brother completely. Neither of them held with women's suffrage, or with the ability of a woman to think and live independently.

And none of us, on that blustery March afternoon, could foresee the future and my descent into poverty and humiliation, regardless that I had, indeed, married a man who had promised to take care of me, forsaking all others.

XII

I should have known that George and I were headed for trouble even before the wedding, when Horace and Baby Tabor sent us a silver tea service as a wedding present. George had stared at the ornate teapot, the creamer and sugar bowl, and the silver tray where they sat like it was a nest of snakes.

"What're we supposed to do with this?" His voice had been icy. "And what's that woman doing sending us presents?"

"She's an old friend." I was enjoying the weight, the dull sheen of the silver. It had seemed a century had passed since I'd seen anything as lovely as this.

"We don't hobnob with mine owners and their fancy women," he had said.

I had laughed. "Don't be silly! I've known Baby for years, and she and Horace really love each other. Besides, I owe both of them. A lot."

"Is that what you want? To be a society lady? Then you're marrying the wrong man."

I had wondered what he'd say if I had told him that my parents had hobnobbed with emperors; that we'd had not only a silver tea set but a service for twenty four and the Limoges china to go with it. I had pictured my mother sweeping down the stairs in a velvet gown, diamonds in her ears and around her neck, and my father in uniform, every bit as splendid. But that life was gone, and I was here, and, having accepted George's proposal, I had no intention of telling him about my past, the good or the bad.

"I knew Baby when she was poor," I had said. "I can't help it if she married the richest man in Colorado, or what people think about her. And no . . . ," I had held up a hand to stop his protest, "I don't want to

71

be a society lady. It's too damn' much trouble."

He had grinned at that and came around the table to take my face in his big, rough hands. "We're ordinary people, aren't we?" he had asked, his eyes searching mine for confirmation.

I wasn't sure what made anybody ordinary. As far as I knew, we were all different, but to please him I had nodded. "I guess."

He had kissed me then, hard and with a hint of possessiveness, like he had wanted to leave a mark that told the world I was his. For a day or two I had been troubled — by the kiss and the conversation — and then I had forgotten as I got busy getting ready for my wedding.

Baby Doe Tabor met us at the train station in Denver.

"You'd never find a hack in this weather, so I came to get you." She was bundled in fur, only her face visible as she smiled up at George who was stunned into silence, whether from anger or amazement I couldn't tell.

Baby didn't seem to notice, babbling on and leading the way to her carriage, an ostentatious affair done in blue enamel, driven by a liveried coachman, and pulled by a matched pair of bays.

George grabbed my elbow. "Did you know about this?"

"No. She's just being nice. It's the way she is."

"Look at her. Look at the damn' carriage. She makes me feel like a dirt farmer."

I lost my temper. "Well, for God's sake, you don't have to act like one!"

"Is that what you think?"

"Listen to yourself," I said. "Having a hissy because a friend was worried and nice enough to come to meet us. It's a little silly, if you ask me."

He pulled away. "I'm going back to Aspen." With those words he walked away toward the ticket office.

This was my honeymoon. This was my husband whom I'd married only the day before, and he was walking away, hands thrust in his pockets, while Baby watched, as shocked as I.

"Go after him." Her breath came out in a cloud. "Hurry!"

I knew about male pride. I'd seen enough of it, God knew. And I thought I knew George, but obviously didn't. We'd struck a fear or an anger in him, and I didn't understand its source or how to take anything back.

I planted myself in front of him and said the first thing that came into my head. "Don't go."

"Why not? You and your fancy friend can have all the fun you want without me along."

"You're my husband. This is our honeymoon!"

One corner of his mouth jerked up. "And you're my wife. You coming with me or not?"

"Let's find a hack and go to the hotel," I said, though at that moment I wasn't sure I wanted to go anywhere with him. "Please. Don't be like this. Just let me tell Baby to go on home."

His eyes bored into me. "Tell her, then. She's just a whore dressed up in fancy clothes. I don't want you to have anything to do with a woman like that."

A whore. I wanted to laugh. To cry. Instead, I put my head in my hands so he wouldn't see my face. A whore. So that was it. And what would he do if he learned the truth about his wife? Quickly I walked back to the carriage.

"It's me, isn't it?" Baby's cheeks were flushed from cold and mortification. "He's like all the rest. All those good people who cross the street when they see me." She laughed, a single, harsh note. "Well, the hell with them. I've got my life. What about you?"

"Please don't blame me," I got out, conscious of George, waiting and watching. "I don't understand, so I can't explain, but you're my friend. One of my only friends, and I'm ashamed. I brought presents for the girls, too. I wanted to see them. And Horace. And you. If I can get away, I'll come for a visit. Just don't be mad, and don't blame me. He's my husband, you see."

She stood there, looking like a little queen in her furs with the snow falling on her face. Then she reached out and hugged me. "We do what we have to, even at the cost of friendship. But it's all right, Mary. You go on and have fun. Just don't forget me." Then she slipped inside without looking back.

I watched the carriage drive away, watched until it disappeared in a flurry of snow. George had come up beside me.

"Happy now?" I asked, unable to keep the bitterness out of my voice.

He tugged at the brim of his hat. "Let's get out of here," he said, and pulled me into the storm.

Close your eyes and think about something else.

George got drunk that night, and what should have been joyous became an act I had to live through. The man I'd known for more than two years became a rutting bull, as clumsy and unfeeling as any buffalo hunter or cowboy off the trail.

I wanted Doc back, never mind his waspish tongue, his way of igniting anger. The proof of what we had was in our bed where all anger vanished, and what was between us was honest and true. I wanted Doc, but I had married a stranger.

XIII

In the morning George whistled as he shaved, admiring himself in the mirror. "Ah, Mary, Mary, what a pair we make!" he said, catching me watching him.

I managed a smile that set him off whistling again. It was as if the day and the night before had never happened, and we were the same happy couple who had set out so merrily from Aspen.

Who are you? I wanted to ask. *Who were you yesterday?* But I kept quiet, not wanting a repeat of his earlier performance. With

Doc I could shout and vent my grievances, and they bounced off him like stones. With George I resolved to be wary. And quiet. And to stay out of his way as much as I could.

He made it easy for me that day, asking me what I wanted to do. We were at breakfast, and, in spite of myself, I was enjoying being served good food in fine surroundings.

"I need to do some shopping, if that's all right with you."

He pushed back his chair. "Just as long as I don't have to go along."

"What will you do?"

He flashed his merry grin. "Try out the billiard table. It's been a long time since I had a good game."

We were staying at the Windsor that boasted a saloon, billiard tables, and three thousand silver dollars laid in the floor in front of the bar — a decoration which at first had shocked him, but which now he decided was clever.

"There's how you can save your money, Mary. Glue it to the floor and attract more customers."

In spite of myself, I laughed. "My customers wouldn't appreciate me throwing money away. Most of them would be on

77

their hands and knees, trying to pry it loose."

"You sure you don't mind shopping alone?"

On the contrary, I was delighted. The first thing I intended to do was call on Baby. I stood up. "It's fine this way. I won't feel like I'm boring you."

I'd never felt that with Doc. He'd gone with me much of the time, picking dresses and hats with the eye of a connoisseur, seeing to it that I was always dressed as well as he, and never quibbling over the cost.

"I'll just run upstairs and get my coat," I said, and then — so as not to appear too eager — "Have a good time. I'll be back for lunch."

"And I got us tickets for the show at the Opera House tonight. Some Eastern troupe doing Shakespeare. I figured you'd like that."

He looked so proud of himself, standing there on the morning after his wedding night — the typical bridegroom without the slightest notion or concern about what pleased the bride. From thinking of him as a monster, I suddenly saw him as a little boy, perhaps five years old. Not my own child, but belonging to some other woman who'd done a bad job. *Were all men like this?* I asked myself, then shook my head. I'd been fortunate enough to know men who were men, in bed and out. Just my luck I'd not married one.

"I knew you'd come!" Baby came toward me down the long, marble-floored front hall. "How'd you get away? Did he make a fuss? Here, take off your coat and come in and let's have a good talk. I'll ring for some coffee." She summoned a servant who took my coat and gloves and disappeared as silently as he'd come.

"Is it all right? With George?" she wanted to know when we were seated in a parlor the size of my restaurant, the walls hung with paintings, the floor covered by an immense Aubusson carpet.

"He doesn't know I'm here."

She leaned toward me, her silk skirts rustling. "Do you really love him? Tell the truth, Mary."

I met her eyes with a kind of shock at what I was going to say. "No."

"Then why?"

"I don't know. I thought I did, but I'm not sure any more. I guess he just wore me down."

Another servant appeared, carrying a silver tray and a steaming coffee pot. Baby gestured at the inlaid table in front of us. "Put it here, please," she said. "I'll do the rest." Then she began pouring the coffee into fragile china cups.

"What'll you do now?" she asked, handing me a napkin.

I shrugged. "Live with it. I've lived with worse mistakes. You don't know all of them, and you don't want to, either."

"Living down the past isn't easy." She sipped her coffee and looked at me over the gold rim of the cup. "Heaven knows, I haven't been able to. But you're tough. You made something of yourself, by yourself. And I have Horace. And the girls."

"I want to see them. I brought presents."

"You shouldn't have. We've tried not to spoil them, but it's hard." She rang for a maid, and, when the girl came, asked that Elizabeth and Rose Mary be brought down to us.

Didn't she see her own children? I wondered. And if not, what did she do with herself alone in this house that was more like a palace and as filled with servants?

"Are you happy?" I asked on impulse. "With all this . . . this . . . ?" I couldn't find the word for the opulence surrounding us and waved my hand. I'd seen Miramar and the Emperor's palaces in Mexico, but even in memory they weren't as grand as Baby's mansion.

"Horace and the girls are my life," she said with a hint of irritation. "This . . . as you call it . . . just makes everything easier."

"It's like a fairy tale." A chill ran down my back as I spoke, remembering that a lot of those old tales had bad endings.

"And if I had three wishes, I'd wish the same for you," she said.

"Too late for me."

She shook her head, and her blonde curls bounced. "It's never too late. You just have to believe." And then: "Here they are, the darlings!"

A nursemaid stood at the door, little Rose Mary Echo Silver Dollar in her arms, and Elizabeth Lillie by her side, dressed like a small angel in white taffeta.

"Mama!" She ran to Baby, who lifted her onto her lap.

"This is my best friend, Missus Holliday. No . . . ," she caught herself, "Missus Cummings. Can you say how do you do?"

Elizabeth looked at me from under her lashes, then smiled widely, Baby's smile in a tiny face. Hopping off her mother's lap, she came to me and curtsied, then asked: "Did you bring me a present?"

Baby and the nurse gasped in unison, but

I held out my arms to the little minx, and she came willingly. "Of course, I did. But first you must ask nicely."

It was good to hold a child again, especially one as sweet and as sweet-smelling as this one, her hair still damp from a bath, her skin as fresh as a peach — child of privilege but innocent of her heritage and secure in herself.

How I wished for one of my own! A daughter, a son like little Michael with his blue eyes and utter trust in me, dead now for more than twenty years. Time had passed in a heartbeat. Soon I'd be too old even to think of child bearing. I put my package in her hands and blinked back tears.

She looked around at her mother. "May I, Mama?"

"First say, thank you. Then go over to the window seat with nurse. And don't forget your manners again." She turned back to me. Seeing my face, she said: "There's always something to keep life from being perfect, isn't there?"

"You seem to have everything," I said. "Children, the man you love, security."

"But for how long? I worry about Horace. I worry about kidnappers taking the girls. And you know what the silver market's been like. Sometimes I wonder if this isn't all a dream, and I'll wake up some morning back in Central City poor as a church mouse and still married to Harvey Doe."

"You know that won't happen," I said.

"I don't know. Sometimes I'm scared." Her blue eyes were wide. "Why me? It came so easily. It can get taken away just as fast."

That was true, as I knew very well. "Keep a stash," I told her. "Don't trust anybody, especially all those Easterners who come out and take advantage of your hospitality, then try to sell you something."

I'd read of the parties she and Horace gave — the private railroad cars, the oysters, caviar, champagne, hunting trips, foolishness. "Put some money aside, just in case," I said. Advice that had been given to me and that I'd never forgotten.

She sat back and laughed. I'll never forget how she laughed, peal after peal like church bells ringing. Then she said: "Oh, Mary, Mary, it's not that bad. It'll never get that bad, believe me."

Except it did. In July, 1893, President Cleveland repealed the Sherman Silver Act, and all the silver mines in the West shut down, putting thousands out of work and bankrupting many of Colorado's millionaires, including Horace Tabor and Jerome B. Wheeler, whose Wheeler Bank was where most of my money had been deposited.

XIV

In simple terms, the Sherman Silver Act was a subsidy, with the government buying several million dollars' worth of silver each month in an effort to provide a market. President Cleveland's repeal doomed the mines, the towns that had grown up around them, and the miners and their families whose lives depended on the production of silver.

In a matter of days, Aspen changed from a lively, prosperous community into a place of hunger and despair. The men gathered at the street corners and in the saloons, talking useless solutions, while their women stretched out what food was left and tried not to think of the day when there would be nothing to eat and no money to buy more. Their children collected coal from the railroad tracks, trudging along with buckets swinging from filthy hands.

My business slowed to a trickle, then stopped altogether. No one had cash to spend on a meal, and I hadn't enough to replace supplies that wouldn't be used. Along with the rest, George had lost his job, and he spent his days with his friends in the saloon.

It was the silence that bothered me most. No more trains coming in and leaving loaded with ore, no mine whistles announcing the changing of shifts, no rumbling of machinery, or even the tramp of feet as the men made their way up the mountains to work.

It seemed as if Aspen had changed into Sodom; that death had come swiftly, overnight, and all that was left was what had been there before — sky, mountains, the rush of the Roaring Fork, the laughter of magpies like a mockery of us all.

On the First of September I closed the restaurant with apologies to those who'd worked so hard and whom I couldn't afford to pay any longer.

"I hate this as much as you," I told them. "But I can't figure a way to keep going."

Magda patted my arm. "We know, missus. And we thank you for trying. For being so good to us."

I saw them out, shut the door, and sat down at an empty table, tired to my bones. Everything that I'd worked so hard for was gone. My savings had vanished; my stocks in the mines were worthless. All I had were the gold coins in my trunk that I'd never told anyone about, not even George. Especially not George who'd have drunk it up.

What to do? I hadn't a clue and couldn't think. I looked up as the door opened and Alex came in and sat down across from me. He hadn't been to town for more than two months, and in those months he'd grown older, more like our father, with deep lines running from his nose to the corners of his mouth.

"I figured you'd be here," he said.

"Where else? There's no place to go, except out of Aspen." I spoke what I'd been trying to avoid — an uprooting, a move to still another place, another beginning.

To my surprise, he nodded. "That's what I've been thinking. The mines are dead. At least for a while. But I can't make a go of farming without a market, and I sure can't find a buyer for my claims. Eva and I have about decided to pull out and go to California."

"When?" I whispered.

"Soon as we can. We just wanted you to know, and to say you and George are welcome to throw in with us."

Once I'd wanted to go to California — with Doc — but no more. My heart was buried in the Rockies and in the desert of Arizona. My heart and the best years of my life.

"I'll miss you," I said. "But I think we'll stay on. Maybe not here. I don't know. It all happened so fast it's hard to believe."

He was drawing rings on the table top with a callused finger. "I guess we all hoped, but that wasn't enough. Seems like we're two countries, East and West, and neither understands the other or gives a damn."

What he said was true. I'd seen enough of folks from the East — investors, tourists, wide-eyed spectators — come to town to see the inhabitants, the scenery, as if we were foreign species in a zoo. How then could the President, or even Congress, recognize our problems, speak our language enough to understand? And as far as I was concerned, California was as bad — only on the other coast — a place where I didn't belong.

"George and I haven't talked about leaving," I said. In fact, we'd hardly talked at all since that morning in July when the news came over the wire, and he went out, cramming his hat on his head as if he were in pain. "He's been drinking." It was a difficult admission, but Alex was my brother.

He sighed. "So has everybody. What else is there?"

"You saw them. The men on the street. Just standing and waiting."

He slapped his palm on the table. "And

they'll be there until the snow flies, but I won't, and neither will you. Let me go find George and see if I can't snap him out of it."

"Go ahead. But I'm not going to California, so don't even suggest it."

"Stubborn," he said.

"A family trait."

"God help us all." He got up, then reached out and pulled me close. "I hate splitting up again."

For a minute I leaned against him, comforted by familiarity. "Me, too. But I can't keep hanging on your coat tails. At least this time I'll know where you are."

When he was gone, I put on the coffee pot and cut thin slices off a loaf of bread I'd made using the last of the flour. Then I went out and down the street to the house we'd been renting.

The locked trunk sat in a corner of the bedroom, its top serving as a bureau where I kept my hairbrush and comb, a silver-backed mirror Doc had bought me, a tray of hairpins, and a bottle of cologne. Removing those, I knelt and unlocked it, burrowed down to the bottom where my hoard was hidden, the very weight of it inside a stocking a comfort.

Two hundred dollars — a fortune to a great many, a ticket out of Aspen, and a new start. Without hesitation, I counted out fifty dollars, then replaced everything and turned the key, happy that I could at least give some security to Alex and Eva and the children, repay them for their kindness to me and to Doc that year that seemed so long ago, that summer when we had all tried to reverse the tide of his illness and failed.

He was so wasted I could almost lift him myself. On sunny days he sat outside the house, a quilt wrapped around him, sleeping fitfully, then waking to watch the children play. Sometimes he walked with me, a short way only, and we talked about the good times, avoiding argument because there was no longer a reason to argue, and because the passion that had fueled our fighting had gone, replaced by the painful acceptance that our luck had run out.

Sometimes he played the old card game, Skinning, with the children, the way Sophie Walton had played with him as a child, his fingers still quick enough to catch them unawares and leave them giggling.

"You cheated, Uncle Doc!"

"And how do you know?"

"I just know."

"Did you see me?"

A shake of the head.

"Then mind your tongue. Don't ever accuse a

man of cheating, if you can't prove it."

"That's no fair!"

"Nothing's fair, Hattie. Nothing at all. Next time watch closer. Your deal."

Later, little Mary, my namesake, watched as he stacked the pile of pennies.

"Did you win them all, Uncle Doc?"

"Yep."

"Are you going to buy something nice?"

The ghost of a smile flew across his face. "No. But you are. You're going to buy candy for you and Hattie."

He leaned back and closed his eyes. I think he was already dead, that he had chosen to die, perhaps because of what happened in Tombstone where he, indeed, became a killer.

I like to blame everything on that town and on Wyatt. I like to believe that, if he hadn't had to run to Colorado with a warrant hanging over him, he'd have gone home again, with or without me, and lived the life he'd been born for.

The desert air had cured him, yet he stayed on with the Earps until, in fact, he had become what everybody said he was. A murderer.

And then it was too late — for him and for us all.

"I couldn't find him." Alex stood in the doorway, his hands spread, his expression one of confusion.

"It's all right." God knew, of late I'd not been able to find George, either. The man I'd married had disappeared, and in his place was a stranger whose mind wandered, who stumbled over words, who drank and looked at me as if what had happened were my fault. Of course, he wasn't any different from the rest of the men whose jobs had dried up, who wandered like ghosts and stared at the mountains, the mine shafts, the skeletons of empty buildings as if they could bring Aspen to life again simply by wishing.

I poured coffee and put my bread on the table. "Eat," I urged Alex. "Eat. And take this for your trip."

He looked at the coins I held out in astonishment, then shook his head. "I can't take your savings."

"There's more. There's enough."

"Mary. . . ."

I pressed the money into his hand and closed his fingers over it. "Take it," I said. "I owe you, and you have a family to think about. George and I . . . we'll be fine."

"Big Sister," he said. "Always looking out for the rest of us."

"That's what sisters . . . and brothers . . . are for." I was close to tears, and so was he. "I'll be out to say good bye before you leave, and we'll keep in touch. Maybe even visit once in a while, who knows?"

"We started out so hopeful," he said, sounding the way Doc had sounded years before. "It's hard to understand why things happen like they do."

I stood and put my hands on his shoulders, not about to let him feel sorry for himself. "Think about our parents. And what they went through, coming here with nothing but a dream and a promise."

"And then they died."

"Stop it!" I shook him gently. "They came, and so did thousands like them. They didn't all die, and neither will we. We'll keep starting over."

He gave a grim smile. "You will, anyhow."

"It's the way I am. I can't just quit. That's the easy way. You're a Horony, same as me, and we're fighters, all of us, even when the dream turns nightmare. So what, if the mines closed? There's other ways of making a living. So what, if you have to move on? You're young, and I'm not so old I can't do a good day's work and get paid for it. As a matter of fact, I've been thinking of going back to Arizona."

The words slipped out, startling me. What had been a vague notion had become suddenly real.

"Why there?" He looked up at me, curious.

"Because of the mines. Copper. Gold. Silver. They can always use a cook and a blacksmith, and we sure won't freeze in the winter like here."

"Does George know?"

I laughed. "I didn't know myself till I said it. But now it sounds right, and besides. . . ." I hesitated, searching for the words to speak a vision. "Besides, I miss it. The desert. The mountains. They're part of me, and I can't explain, so don't ask."

They danced in my head as I stood there, those red rock mountains so different from Colorado's. And the purple shadows moving across as if they were being painted by a giant brush. And the green of the cottonwoods in the river bottoms, how they changed to gold in late fall, dancing, setting sail into the bright air.

Doc was there, too, at least in spirit; a man full of health and determination, a man who had loved me once, of that I was sure. Arizona was where I belonged. It was past and future. It was home.

XV

After all, it wasn't hard to convince George to leave Aspen. He listened to my argument and nodded.

"Might as well," he said. "There's nothing here for us, even if I went back to prospecting. The market's shot to hell, and I don't see anybody stepping in to save it." He fumbled for his pipe and tobacco, and I noticed that his hands were shaking.

Too much booze, I thought, and sighed. Well, we'd make a new start, he and I, and maybe we'd get back what we'd lost in our marriage and financially.

"When?" I asked, thrusting the rest of the decision onto him.

He lit a match, puffed a minute, then sat back in the chair. "As soon as you can get ready."

So it was all up to me — the packing, the figuring, even the purchase of our tickets to Denver, then to Albuquerque, Deming, and Bisbee, where, with luck, the copper mines would stay productive until we had some money put by.

Pack up and move. Pack up and move. The words played in my head like a Negro spiritual, with all the anguish of those who know only too well what despair is made of.

I said: "Give me a week."

"Don't take too long. We don't want to be the last rats leaving the ship."

"A nice way to put it."

He laughed, a hollow sound unlike his old boisterousness. "There's thousands out of work and starving, and no good way to say it, except damn the government, damn the President, damn us all for a bunch of fools."

Not wanting to hear a repetition of that constant refrain, I went into the bedroom and started sorting through our clothes, but his words wouldn't let me alone. *A bunch of fools.* That's what came when you looked to someone else for salvation; when you expected the government to bail you out, feed you, clothe you; when you abdicated responsibility for self and drifted. That's what could happen to me . . . if I relied on George.

I said my good byes to Alex, Eva, and the children whom I might never see again, to Magda, Karoly, all my friends in Aspen and in Denver, and, risking George's anger, I said good bye to Baby Doe.

The Tabor mansion on Sherman Street had been the first thing to go — that palace with its Turkish carpets, plush velvet draperies, the conservatory filled with palms, ferns, orchids, the garden and its marble statues brought from villas in Rome, Florence, who knew where?

"Did you save anything?" I asked her as we sat in the tiny parlor of her rented house. She still dressed in silk, shivering in the cold, and I was in my old woolen traveling costume.

"I have the Queen of Spain's pearls," she said with what I thought was foolish pride. Getting up, she left the room and came back with an ornate box. Inside lay the pearls, her wedding gift from Horace Tabor.

As I held them, I thought that he'd been duped, that he'd handed over a small fortune for pearls that had probably been strung by some clever jeweler in New York City or Philadelphia, and that he'd believed simply because he wanted to believe, just as his wife was doing. But I held my tongue. Enough dreams had been shattered.

"Lovely," I said instead, and they were lovely, regardless of their lack of age or provenance.

Baby gazed at them, her blue eyes filled with tears. "I'll sell all the rest, but not these.

I'll even go to work, if I have to."

She did sell the rest — the diamonds, the sapphires, the rubies and emeralds — and, in the end, the Queen of Spain's pearls. Now, she's up at the Matchless Mine with the girls, wearing rags and miner's boots and waiting for the price of silver to rise, for the mother lode to be discovered, for the return of the days of glory. The Matchless, H. A. W. Tabor's greatest purchase, root of his fortune, seed of his destruction and hers.

We've seen the heights and the bottom of the pit, she and I, and what has it gotten us? Are we wiser? More sophisticated? Better, for our hard-earned knowledge? This is a question I can't answer, except to say that life must be lived — and dealt with — to the best of our ability. Beyond that, who ever knows?

George was happy in Bisbee, having found a job immediately, and happier still to have a new bunch of cronies to drink with. We rented a tiny house perched precariously on the side of a mountain overlooking town, and I spent a week scrubbing, washing, arranging the few things we'd brought with us. That done, I went out to call on my neighbors.

Anna Pasquale was twenty two, a little

woman with her hair in a bun and a catch in her throat as she talked in a mix of languages about leaving home and making the long voyage to America.

How different the trip had been for me! No cramped quarters in steerage, no noise or disease, no waiting in line at Ellis Island, the taste of fear in my mouth. Although at the time I had longed for Hungary, I was still child enough to be enthralled by what I saw — ocean, clouds, sky, the occasional leap of fish, the sound of wind in the huge sails that drove the ship westward like the wings of a white bird.

And then there was Mexico, all color and light, scents and sounds. Was it then that I fell in love with mountains and deserts, I wonder, or was it later? — Doc and me in New Mexico, our backs to the Sangre de Cristos, our eyes on the roll of the high plains, and around us the music of the language of Spain like the notes of a guitar on a summer night, like the falling of rain?

"I'm going to beat this, Kate."
"If we don't freeze first."
It was Christmas Eve, and Las Vegas was deep in snow with the temperature at zero. In spite of the cold, the townspeople were reënacting the Posada, *the search of Mary and Joseph to*

find shelter for the birth of their son. Long shadows fell on the snow and on the walls of the houses that lined the narrow streets as the candle-lit procession moved from house to house, and the sound of ancient hymns resonated in the pure, dry air.

Doc stood with me, watching, as the singing died away, and his hands closed on my shoulders.

"I will beat it. I'm not ready to consign my soul to hell."

"And I'm not ready to let you." I leaned against him, still under the spell of the procession. "Maybe what we just saw was a kind of sign. Like we've been blessed."

"I'd like to believe you."

"Other people have gotten cured here," I said, and shivered as an icy wind blew around the window frame.

He leaned down and kissed my ear. "It's Christmas Eve. Let's forget about the cure for tonight. I have a present for you, and from the look of things, you need it."

"What is it?"

"Greedy as a child," he said. "I think that's why I love you."

My heart jumped. "Do you?"

"Most of the time." He grinned, wicked as a cat, and handed me a package wrapped in tissue and tied with silver ribbon.

It was so beautiful I hated to open it. "I have something for you, too," I said, "but you'll have to wait."

"My pleasure." He sat on the bed and crossed his legs.

I untied the ribbon carefully, then curiosity got the better of me. "Oh, hell!" I exclaimed, and ripped open the paper to the sound of his laughter.

Inside the box lay a shawl, a lovely thing of blue and black embroidery, with twining silver threads and silken fringe. I wrapped it around myself and found it warm in spite of what appeared to be its fragility, and I danced, there in that small room, whirling and stamping my feet, as wild and as happy as any Gypsy, while Doc watched and clapped his hands and, for a few moments, forgot that death hung over us both like a pall.

"Brava," he said, when I collapsed, breathless. "Sometimes I think you're somebody I've never seen before and can't catch. Like swamp fire. Who are you really? Do you know?"

I'd been so many selves, acted so many parts. "I'm me," I said finally, then got up and rummaged in my trunk for his gift that I'd managed to hide.

"Your turn."

I'd gotten him a vest, a fancy one embroidered with flowers and vines and our linked initials hidden in the design.

"Clever of you," he said, spotting our names right away. "Is it marriage you're after?"

I answered softly. Though I wanted marriage to him above all else, the time wasn't right to ask. "Just luck for us both. I thought it might do that."

"Ah, Kate, Kate." He held out his arms, and I went into them gladly. "I'm not sure I deserve anything. I've made such a mess of it. But we'll have better days. I promise."

And then I wept as if my heart had broken. Wept like a woman with nothing more to lose — not her man, not her self, not anything meaningful. It was as if I saw it all, that Christmas Eve in little Las Vegas, New Mexico — the future that held nothing but violence and the pain of loss.

XVI

"Please. Take." Anna offered a chipped plate that held a braided cake. It brought back memories that shoved against each other like children playing. Wedding cakes and merriment. Cakes rolled over logs and baked in huge ovens. Cakes in the shape of rings, decorating the arms of the newborn.

"*Kolacs!*" I exclaimed.

Her eyebrows rose at the unfamiliar word. "Is old recipe. From *Italia*. My mama, she make, and now me. Is good."

And it was. Light, yeasty, faintly flavored with fruit I couldn't identify, a treat from a woman who might have been a master baker had she been born in another place, a different time. I ate two pieces, then left her with the promise of a recipe of my own, and all that night and the next day I thought and planned.

Keeping house was simple. And George, who never minded what he ate as long as there was lots of it, made no demands on my time, often working double shifts or staying late to drink with his new friends.

We hadn't much of a marriage. It seemed as if once he got me he forgot about me except at meals or on those nights when he grabbed me and relieved himself without a thought as to how I felt.

So I was bored. And unhappy. Alone in a town of strangers except for Anna and the Ortega family who lived in the house below. Bisbee wasn't Aspen. It lacked the shops, the cosmopolitan atmosphere, running water, and anything beyond the basic supplies needed for a meal was hard to come by.

Certainly it hadn't a decent bakery. Oh, there were places to buy *tortillas* and plain loaves, but where were the pies, the cakes, the strudels for fancy occasions, desserts fit for the tables of the bosses and mine owners in their big houses?

I put on my hat, took my purse, and carefully descended the steep steps that led to the cañon below. From the bottom it was a short walk to Brewery Gulch with its saloons and gambling houses, its raucous mining town life complete with whores, dandies, Mexicans leading burros that moved slowly under burdens of firewood and canvas water bags, and around it all the mountains rose, cutting off the horizon, piercing the sky.

I found what I was looking for, then retraced my steps a little breathless. Anna came to the door when I knocked, a welcoming smile on her face. When we were seated at the round oak table in her kitchen, I told her my plan.

"We're going to start a bakery, you and me. I've already rented a store. It'll be extra money, and God knows we can use it."

To my surprise, her face turned solemn. "My Tony . . . he won't like," she muttered.

There it was — that old-country way of thinking. Annoyed, I wriggled in my chair.

"Look," I said, "I'm sure he won't mind the extra money, and, anyhow, I'll do the selling. You stay home and bake. I'll buy you the supplies and get a boy who'll make deliveries, if we need to. Let me handle the business part . . . I've done it before. What do you say?"

She looked at her hands that already showed signs of hard work, then up at me. "*Si.* I will. Is good idea, and I have so many recipes and nobody to eat them."

Within a year we had more business than we could handle. I hired two more women, miner's wives with a flair for pie crust and *empanadas*, and two little Mexican boys who made our deliveries with a great sense of pride.

Word got around. For a taste of paradise, people came to Mary's Bakery. There are still times when I wish they hadn't.

XVII

"I'll take six of those . . . and six of these." The young man pointed, then raised his eyes to mine. "Don't I know you from somewhere?"

"No!" I was firm. The last thing I wanted was to be recognized.

"But . . . ?" He seemed perplexed.

For my part, I couldn't place him, and said: "I'm new here. My husband works at the mine."

"Funny. You look familiar." He took the cookies and fished in his pocket. "I don't forget faces."

In the years I'd been away I'd changed, put on weight, and there was gray in my hair that I now wore differently. I smiled. "Everybody has a twin, or so they say."

He looked at me again, and I decided that I didn't like him, but smiled harder. "Enjoy the cookies."

"I will. And I'll remember. It'll come to me."

I hoped not. "Perhaps," I said. "Perhaps."

It came to him all right, just like it came to everybody he met, including George who came home drunk and shouting.

"Bitch! Whore! A joke! You said it was a joke, but it wasn't. You're a whore like that gal in Denver, putting on airs." He picked up a kitchen chair and smashed it against the wall. The whole house shook.

"Stop it!" I might as well have had no voice for all the attention he paid.

"You made me a laughingstock. My wife. Big Nose Kate."

"It's not what you think."

"Don't tell me what to think. Don't tell me anything. It'll be lies." He reached out and slapped me. Hard.

I fell against the stove and whimpered as the corner of it slammed my hip. No man had ever hit me except that snake Behan, when he got me drunk and forced me to sign the paper, saying Doc had held up the stage. But George was my husband, and, though he'd changed, I still couldn't believe what he'd done.

"You're drunk," I accused him. "When you're sober, I'll talk to you. Not before."

He staggered and leaned on the table. "I've got a right to get drunk. My dear wife, the Tombstone whore."

Anger was replacing pain. Inside me pure rage was building — at him, at life, at the young man who'd leaked my past to the town. I wrapped my fingers around the handle of an iron skillet. "Don't you hit me again, George. You hear?" Then I watched as my warning played through the haze of liquor.

"Big Nose Kate," he sneered, but backed off. "Why'd you lie to me?"

I took the offensive. "Get out and don't

come back till you can walk straight. Until you can listen to reason and keep your hands to yourself. You hear me?" I hefted the skillet.

He went, still snarling. I hoped he'd fall down the steps and break his neck, but he made it to the bottom and turned toward Brewery Gulch and consolation in a bottle.

I cleaned up the pieces of the chair and threw them in the woodbin, anger bubbling like boiling oil. This was what I'd come to — the wife of a drunk who hit me. At that moment, I'd have rather still been a whore.

George didn't come home for three days, and I can't say I missed him. Marriage wasn't all it was supposed to be. The way it seemed, the woman got the worst of it and put up with beatings along with everything else. I wasn't the only wife in town sporting a black eye, though it shamed me to be seen with one, as if I was to blame for whatever had happened. Well, in a way I was, but the facts of my past couldn't be helped.

As mad as Doc got sometimes, he never laid a hand on me, just lashed out with that tongue of his and let me have it in words. But then, Doc was a gentleman. George, obviously, was not.

When I heard him fumbling at the door

that evening, I took the offensive again and was waiting when he walked in. "Well?" I said, giving him a hard look.

"I figured you'd be gone." He wasn't drunk, but he'd had a few.

"Gone where?"

"Wherever whores go."

"I don't know what you've heard, or from whom, but I want you to listen to me, and listen good." I pointed to the chair. "Sit on it. Don't smash it like you did the other one. Just sit there and shut up."

His mouth dropped open in surprise, but he did as he was told.

I stayed standing, the better to avoid him if he lost his temper and came after me. Why it was so important for me to justify my life to him, I didn't understand. Still don't. Thinking about it, maybe I was explaining me to myself, and about time.

"You think you know it all, but you don't," I began, my eyes on his. "In the first place, you're a man. It's easy for you. You can always find work, a place to sleep, get along, somehow. But for a woman? A girl?" I laughed bitterly, remembering myself at sixteen, frightened, wanting, needing my mother's arms and kindness, except that she was buried in a Davenport, Iowa cemetery and I was alone, without advice or instruction.

Taking a deep breath to banish emotion, I went on. "When I was sixteen, I ran away. On account of a man, George. A man who tried to rape me. Did I ask for it? No, I didn't. I was scared witless. Does that make me a whore? Does it?"

He stared at me like he was hypnotized, and responded with a reluctant shake of his head.

Satisfied, I said: "I was all right for a while. I even married and had a son, but, when he died, everything stopped. You wouldn't know about how that is. You're not a mother. And you wouldn't know how it feels to be in a strange town alone, no money, no job, starvation staring you in the face, and no way out except. . . . No!" I stopped him from interrupting. "No, you stay still and learn how it is for a woman with nothing that's worth anything, except her body. Men pay for that. They *pay*, George! You know they do. The world's filled with prostitutes and the men who use them. The world's full of scared girls selling themselves to be able to eat. And maybe dream about the day they can be decent again, take their bodies back. And their souls, if there's anything left of them."

"Stop!" The word came out guttural.

"I won't. You think I'm filthy and degraded, but who made me that way? You and your kind, thinking women are nothing but animals. I was lucky to meet Doc Holliday, let me tell you. He wasn't happy about what I'd done, either, but he was a gentleman. He never raised a hand to me, George, unlike you. He never left me to explain a black eye to the neighbors. I should've known better than to let myself be talked into marrying you just because we were friends and both of us lonely. We don't suit, you and me. You think I'm a whore, and I think you're a damned disgusting drunk and a lousy lover. That's something I do know about, only I'm stuck with you, God help me."

He was on his feet in an instant, and I realized my mistake. I'd brought him down to what he saw was my level, and he had pride. Misplaced, maybe, but pride it was.

Before I could reach the skillet, he was on me, shaking me so hard I saw stars just before he cracked my cheek open with one of those big blacksmith's hands. Then he tossed me away, limp as a doll. I hit the edge of the stove again, and heard another crack when my arm snapped.

I think I screamed, in anger and pain, before I passed out.

When I came to, Anna was there holding a

cloth to my face and sobbing.

I said — "My arm." — and nearly fainted again, when the split in my cheek widened.

"Doctor." She forced herself to stop crying. "I get. You stay."

For sure I wasn't going anywhere. I closed my eyes and lay on the hard floor. "Go," I whispered, trying not to move the muscles in my face.

I heard her quick feet taking the stairs, and the mine whistle shrieking like a crazy person, for the change of shifts. Where was George? I wondered, turning my head slightly. Gone. He'd done his worst and gone, and good riddance.

I wasn't dying, though I wished I was — wished I could drift away past the pain, above the cañons, the red hills, the topsy-turvy shacks of miners and prospectors. Lying there I felt old, worn out, as lost as I'd been at sixteen, and no place to go. Forty five years had come and gone, and I had nothing to show for my life — not happiness or security or children to care for me. A wasted life is what it was, and the best part of it gone where I couldn't bring it back.

Anna, in spite of my protests, moved me into her house, helped by the doctor who set my arm and stitched my cheek together. I didn't know which were worse, the wounds or the fixing of them there on the kitchen table.

"You shouldn't be alone, Missus Cummings." The doctor, a man with spectacles and a ratty beard, patted my shoulder.

"I'll be fine," I said through the darting pain in my face.

He peered at me out of eyes like bright pebbles. "You will. You're healthy enough, not like some I see. But you won't be able to do much for a while or defend yourself, if you have to."

I tried to laugh and failed. "He won't be back."

"You can't be sure. The world's a sorry place. No explaining what people will do."

While I didn't think George would attack me again, I agreed with him on principle. "The bastard," I said.

He wasn't shocked. "Exactly my point, Missus Cummings. Now let's get you on your feet and into bed."

I slept on a pallet in Anna's kitchen for two days, and, when I woke up, I'd come to a decision.

"I'm getting a divorce."

Anna turned to me, shocked. No one, especially Catholics, even thought of such a thing. You married for better or worse and stuck to it.

"Talk to the priest," she said. "He will help."

"To hell with the priest. He's not the one who's married."

She crossed herself, probably to keep from getting tarred by my heresy. "Is not good," she insisted.

I raised up slowly. "Getting beat all the time isn't so good, either. Don't worry. God won't condemn you, just me. He gave up on me a long time ago."

Her eyes widened in horror, and she crossed herself again. Then, taking no chances, she made the old sign of the horns with her fingers before she dropped to her knees beside me.

"Please, Mary. Is ask for trouble. Think. I am friend, and I tell you, don't do this thing."

But I did, and it was easier than getting married. Living in Bisbee afterwards was not.

XVIII

Business fell off slowly but surely, and it was a while before I realized why. Divorce was a stigma, and a divorced, one-time lady of the night carried a double curse. Anna, for all her superstition, had been right. Women, who'd come in to buy and gossip, stayed away, pretended not to see me if we met on the street, as if my reputation, like some dreadful disease, was somehow communicable. And all because of that pudding-faced young man and his memory. Wouldn't I give him a piece of my mind when I saw him?

It was summer, and the rains were late. I was tired, discouraged, irritable on the day I went to have the splints taken off my arm.

"How is it?" Dr. Feldman sat me in a chair and checked out the scar on my face.

"It'll be good to have two hands again."

He nodded, then cut the tape and removed the heavy splints. "Good as new," he said after a minute. "Just don't use it too hard at first."

I sighed, thinking of my loss of business.

He was perceptive. "Is something wrong?"

"You might say so."

"The divorce?" Behind his spectacles, his eyes were bright and compassionate.

"Partly."

"We live in peculiar times, Missus Cummings," he said. "There are many who believe a woman should allow herself to be mutilated or even murdered instead of trying to save her own life. I'm not one of them, however."

I leaned back in the chair, comforted by his understanding. "Thank you," I murmured.

He nodded, as if to say thanks weren't needed, then poured water out of a pitcher and washed his hands while I watched, appreciating his attention to cleanliness.

Doc had been like that, always freshly shaved, always insisting on a bath and clean clothes for us both. I sighed again, and Feldman heard.

"Can you cook as well as you bake?" he asked.

I laughed and decided to boast. "I ran one of the best restaurants in Aspen, and I'd still be there, if the mines hadn't closed. And before that I had a hotel in Globe. I'm a cook and a darn' good one."

He came to stand beside me, and ran a finger over the scab on my face. "You heal fast. I doubt you'll have much of a scar in a few months." Then, as if he'd made a decision: "Would you be interested in moving out of town?"

For one minute I had the notion he was making me a proposition, and my heart sank. But when I opened my mouth to protest, he cut me off with a blush of apology.

"I'm sorry. It's not what it sounded like. I have a friend who's mining near Pearce. Has quite a few men working for him. He's looking for a cook. It sounds like a kind of rough operation, not like what you've been used to, but you'd not be bothered by anybody, and from what I understand the pay is good."

I was forty five years old, a little plump, with a mark on my cheek, and gray woven through my hair, but youth dies hard if it ever does. I chuckled to myself. Who would want me now? And worse, why had I misunderstood an act of kindness?

"Can I tell him you're interested?" He was watching me as if he could read my thoughts.

I didn't hesitate. "I am."

Within a week it was arranged. I'd met with Percy Clark, the mine owner, accepted the job, and given him a list of the supplies I needed. I'd turned the bakery over to Anna, Lupe Ortega, and Lena Sestric, and taken my share of the profits, storing the money, as always, in a stocking in the bottom of one of my trunks.

To hell with Bisbee, George, and the so-called ladies who'd ostracized me! And to that young man who said he'd been a child in Tombstone at the time of the troubles. I gave him a piece of my mind one afternoon in the middle of the street, called him every bad name I could think of, and marched away before he had a chance to answer. Naturally the ladies jabbered — at my language, at how I'd "forgotten myself," as, of course, was to be expected from someone like me. What did they know, those twittering creatures who gave themselves airs? And what did a kid know about how I'd lived, where I'd been, what I'd had to do?

Once more I was on the move, waving good bye to my true friends from the seat of a wagon loaded with supplies and the trunks that held all that was left of the me that I'd been.

Once upon a time. . . . That's how all the old tales began. Once upon a time there was a princess. Me. Only the happy ending hadn't happened, and I doubted that it would. I was an aging female drifting across the endless sea of America, across the high desert that's like a sea in itself — sand, mountains, blue sky and never an end to it, on and on with the horizon always moving away, until you feel like you're swimming in the air like the shadows that fall and sail on in whatever direction they please, and the vastness takes you like a current, and you go with it, not caring, swept away.

XIX

The Sulphur Springs Valley fans out like the delta of a yellow river as it runs into Mexico. To the east, the Chiricahua Mountains thrust up like the frozen waves of an ancient sea. The copper-colored Mules and the Dragoons form the western boundary of the great valley, hemming it in, keeping it in place.

The Apache leader, Cochise, is buried somewhere in the Dragoons. Over the years, several search parties have climbed over those rocks and passes, hoping to find him — or what's left — but I've always wished them bad luck. Let the dead lie. Let him be, that Apache who, like the rest of his people, loved the land where they were born, and fought for it. And lost.

I can understand him because this is my country. By adoption, it's true, but I love it in an almost sensual way, feel it in my bones, respond to it with something like passion — as if I want to take it inside me, all of it, grass, mountains, spirals of rock, cañons that twist into secret places that might or might not speak out like oracles to one who knows how to listen.

I was mostly silent on that trip to Pearce — silent and looking, and I saw some of the changes that had happened because of the white man and his cattle and greed. The range had been overstocked and overgrazed. In many places the grass was gone, and tumbleweed and catclaw had taken root. Other stretches were bare, and dust devils coiled up from the surface like transparent serpents.

In the fifteen years I'd been away, the face of these valleys had been wiped clean and repainted, not for the better. So I was silent, and stunned, but happy, nonetheless, for I was home again.

Dr. Feldman had been right about one thing. Pearce, compared to Bisbee, was downright primitive. Percy Clark came out to meet me and take me to the shack that would be my headquarters. It contained a stove, a large table, and rough shelves on which were stacked rusty pans and Dutch ovens and a mess of tin plates and cups. A cubbyhole off to one side had a cot and a rickety table with a pitcher filled with sulphurous water. A layer of grit and grease covered everything, and cobwebs hung from the rafters. Both rooms were stifling and would only get worse when I fired up the stove.

I glanced out the back door and saw a ramada. "I want the stove moved out there. And the table, too," I said to Percy. "There's no way I can cook in here and stay on my feet. Who had the job before me?"

Percy looked embarrassed. "Nobody. We've been kind of making do on our own . . . but my men don't like it much."

"I'll bet." I took off my hat and hung it on a hook beside the cot, then looked around for a broom and bucket, smothering a grin at the look on Percy's face.

"Don't worry. I'll have this place clean before it's time to start supper," I said, hoping to calm him. "It's a wonder you haven't poisoned yourselves in this mess."

He opened his mouth, then closed it, and turned away. In any operation — ranching, mining, running a hotel — the cook's word counts for something. Men live for their stomachs, and so do women for that matter. I had the upper hand and intended to use it, both for myself and the hungry miners.

All in all, once I'd established some order and a routine, it wasn't a bad place to be. The men were respectful and friendly, and appreciated the meals I put out. And then there was the country, the freedom of it, the beauty that was like life, both violent and peaceful, and accepting of me as no human ever was.

On my Sundays off I explored, either on foot or on horseback, borrowing one of Percy's old saddle mares and heading out, returning with my saddlebags full of rocks, weeds, desert flowers that fascinated me with their toughness. I couldn't name them, only marvel over shapes and colors — orange, yellow, the purple of storm clouds, the shell pink of sunrise.

"Miss Mary's back. Better get her a bucket of water," someone would call when I rode into camp with my treasures, and they'd help me arrange the grasses and flowers, though they probably figured I was crazy.

For me, it was like having a family again — a family of rough but well-meaning brothers who flattered, teased, begged for their favorite meals, and did their best to keep me happy. A hard life, but I didn't complain.

I stayed a year, and then on one of my Sunday rides I passed by the little Cochise Hotel and met Mrs. Rath, the owner. She was a fussy woman with a fringe of false curls and an air of helplessness that was equally false, as I found out.

Seeing me pass, she invited me in, and was horrified to hear that I was cooking for the miners.

"My dear Missus Cummings," she said in a whisper, "you can't. It's not decent . . . you and all those men."

Hypocrite! I thought but said nothing.

"People will talk, you know," she went on. "Why not come and work for me? I've been needing someone with experience to help out, and that's hard to find here."

I sipped the coffee she'd brought, then said: "It's really all right. The men are my friends. I've not had any problem."

Her eyebrows lifted to the false fringe. "Not yet. But you know how men are."

"I'm a little old to worry about such things, don't you think?" I asked, trying for humor.

She shook her head, dropped her voice to an even lower whisper. "Some of them lust after anything, especially in a place like this. Even women of our age. Think about it. If you work for me, you'll have your own room, your meals, a decent place to bathe, and forty dollars a month." She paused to let her generosity sink in. "And Sunday's off, of course. What do you say?"

"It sounds interesting." And it did. The idea of sleeping on a decent bed in a room where the wind didn't cut through the cracks in the walls was appealing. But the woman herself made me cautious — all that piety and doom-saying.

She changed her tactics, when I didn't answer. "Please," she said, folding her hands on the table. "I really need the help. I wouldn't offer, if I didn't. And we women have to stick together. Safety in numbers, don't you know."

"I'll think about it," I said, and got up to leave.

"Fifty dollars a month!" Her eyes were like steel darts. "You won't be sorry!"

Well, I was and I wasn't. The widow Rath had a tendency to fuss over small things and overlook necessities, and her daughters were lazy creatures who gave themselves airs and looked down on me — the hired help. If I'd told them I'd once known the Emperor of Mexico, they wouldn't have believed it. "Mary's making up stories again," they'd say, snickering. "Mary thinks she's better than us."

No doubt about that! The poor girls didn't even know how to set a table, where to put the knives and forks. Not that the travelers coming through knew better or even cared. Still, I showed them, much to their irritation and their mother's.

"Snooty," they called me behind my back, then relished the fact that I was the one who changed beds and did the laundry, who oversaw the kitchen while they were off flirting with guests or with some of the neighboring cattlemen.

That was just as well. Their absence allowed me to do things my way, to enjoy the hanging of clothes on the line, while the hawks soared overhead and the thrashers whistled at me from the brush; to pretend that the kitchen was my own, that I was back once again cooking as I chose for appreciative diners. At least the people who ate at the hotel were appreciative — travelers who'd had their fill of beef and beans, jerky and cornbread. They talked to me, and I to them, exchanging news and stories. And it was one of those exchanges that led to my downfall.

He was a book salesman, taking orders for editions of Shakespeare, Dickens, the Old and New Testaments, and he was frustrated to find so few on his route who could read or who even wanted to.

I pounced on his sample of the Shakespeare, leather-bound and illustrated with engravings. It had been a long time since I'd held a book like that one in my hands, or read anything besides the week-old newspapers that came in on the train.

"Can I borrow it?" I asked him. "Just overnight. I'll be careful with it, I promise."

His face crinkled like wet taffeta. "Of course, Missus Cummings. Enjoy it, and tell your friends. Perhaps you might even start a reading room here in the hotel."

I snickered at the thought of the girls indulging in anything that would improve their minds. "Doubtful," I told him. "But it's been an age since I've read a real book."

"You've been out here quite a while then?" He was interested, not so much in me as to what I could tell him that would improve his business.

"Since the early 'Eighties," I said.

"Wild times then, or so I hear. Robbings, killings, bandits behind every bush and tree. Am I right?"

I thought back to those days, to Tombstone when it was alive, throbbing with dissension, rude but vital. We'd been young, all of us — Doc, Wyatt, Josie, myself — young and as devil-may-care as the town.

"It was different," I said. "But it's gone now, and all the actors with it."

Something in my tone struck him. He said: "I've heard stories. About outlaws, the Earps, Doc Holliday. Are they true?"

"Depends on what you heard and who did the telling."

He nodded. "Yes. I can see that. People will twist things just to make a good tale. Even Shakespeare, there, did it." He cleared his throat. "In Bisbee last week someone told me about a woman named Big Nose Kate. Did you ever run across her?"

Now it was coming! Now I'd hear it all again — distorted, a fantasy told by someone who hadn't known me, didn't give a damn.

I said: "I knew her."

"Then you've heard she was murdered. By that Holliday fellow. Buried out here somewhere, so they say. Pity to do that to a woman. But dramatic, you have to agree."

Laughter got the best of me. When I was in control again, I said: "She's not dead. And Doc wouldn't have done that. He was a gentleman, and they loved each other. I know that much."

His face fell, then brightened. "You knew them both?"

"Oh yes. And the Earps and all the rest."

"Interesting."

"Maybe."

Out of the corner of my eye I saw the widow, her eyes fastened on me with something like horror. *Trouble,* I thought, and cursed myself for talking too much.

★ ★ ★

"You never mentioned that you were involved with those people."

It was the next morning, and the widow was grilling me like my life was on the line, which in a way it was.

"You never asked."

"Well, I'm asking now. How is it you know so much?"

"I was there for a while," I said, and went on chopping peppers for the stew pot.

"In what capacity?"

I wanted to shake her until her fake hair fell off, until her teeth rattled and fell out, but I controlled the urge.

"I was visiting. Other than that, my life isn't your business."

She grabbed the knife out of my hand and waved it like a saber. "It certainly is! I have my girls to think of! And my hotel. We're reputable people, and I can't have someone whose life's indecent working here."

I'd have bet her life wasn't lily-white, either, but that hardly mattered. What did matter was that she was painting me black without knowledge or charity. I picked up the vegetables and tossed them on the floor at her feet.

"Fine," I said. "I quit."

And that was that. By the end of that week

I had answered an ad in the paper and been hired as a housekeeper by one John Howard whom I'd never met. That didn't matter, either. All I wanted was out — away from hypocrites, prudes, and spoiled children.

When he arrived to pick me up, neither the widow Rath nor her daughters were there to say good bye, a fact that Howard noticed as he noticed most things.

"Where's the widow?" he asked, hefting my trunks into the wagon bed.

"Probably counting the spoons."

He made a noise that I thought was laughter. "Did you take them?"

"No."

"Too bad. She's an old biddy, if ever there was one."

With that, he helped me onto the seat, climbed up himself, and took the reins. "You'll be better off with me," he commented. "As long as you're not too particular."

About what? I wondered, and then forgot as we moved off at a trot through heat waves that shimmered above the valley floor.

Part Two

XX

Camp Supply, 1876

I'm holding the horse's big head between my hands. His breath is warm, his eyes have a glimmer of a twinkle in them. I'm saying good bye to Gidran who carried me safely out of Fort Griffin and across Indian Territory, and to the little mouse-colored mustang that was Doc's.

"Take care of him." It's a plea and an order to the buyer.

He seems to understand. "I will, that. He's a good horse."

"The best."

With the money from the sale I go back to Doc, trying not to cry.

He says: "Out here horses are a commodity. You know that. We're on our way to Dodge and Denver and need money not horses."

I wipe my nose on my ragged sleeve. "It's like I lost something. Some piece of me. Understand?"

"Sure. But vagabonds like us can't afford to be sentimental."

"I wasn't born to be like this!"

"Neither was I, sweetheart. Neither was I. It's the luck of the draw."

Jack Howard and I drove across the valley toward the mountain peak known as Dos Cabezas — Two Heads. The afternoon was brilliant, the sky a deep and cloudless blue. I was feeling young again, and adventurous. It was that kind of day. A little touch of autumn in the air, a hint of excitement that was infectious.

The team of sorrels trotted out boldly, and I admired the way Jack handled the reins. He wasn't anything to look at — sharp-featured and angular — but there was determination in him and a gleam in his eye, as if he made his own rules and stuck to them come hell or high water. I had the eerie sense of having known him before, and only hoped it hadn't been at Bessie's house which would have been hard to explain, especially if he should turn out to be like George.

"A nice team," I said over the sound of hoofs and wheels.

"They get me where I want to go." He glanced at me out of the corner of his eye. "Can you handle a gun, Missus Cummings?"

A strange question to ask one's housekeeper. "Yes," I said. "Will I have to?"

"You might. I've got claims, and I don't want anybody jumping them. Or me."

"Maybe you should have advertised for a bodyguard, instead," I said.

He chuckled, and it came out rusty, as if he'd forgotten how. "You'll do. You've got an honest face, and you aren't some flighty young 'un pining for city lights and compliments."

"Not any more."

"That's good, then." He clucked to the team, and we turned off onto a track that led into the mountains. "My daughter took off for the city. 'Not enough excitement,' she said. That's why I advertised. A man isn't made right for things that need doing in a house."

"And your wife?" I hesitated to ask, but, since I was working for him, I figured I should know something about him.

"Dead," he said shortly. "Died and left me with Jessie to raise, and I wasn't cut out for it."

"Not too many men are," I said to ease what was obviously a sore spot. "But don't worry. She'll probably make out fine."

"Huh!" He spat over the side of the wagon. " 'Twon't be my fault, if she gets herself in trouble!"

"No, indeed!" I agreed, deciding he was a man of character in spite of his cranky way of putting things. "Why do I have the feeling I met you before?" I asked then, because I couldn't escape the tug of memory.

He shrugged. "People get around. Like me. Born in England, made my way here, worked at jobs across the country. But here I'll stay. Mark me."

It came, then, in a flood. Me, holding Gidran's big head, fighting tears. Me saying: "Promise you'll treat him right." And the buyer stroking the horse's neck, not looking beyond my boy's clothes. "For sure, lad. I can see what he is, don't doubt it."

"You bought a big paint horse years ago at Camp Supply," I said to him. "Do you remember?"

He gave me an astonished look as if I were a Gypsy, reading palms. "How do you know that?"

"He was mine. I was that boy."

"I'll be damned. The best horse I ever owned. Had him till he died, like I promised." He spat again. "That was you? That lad?"

"It was."

"You fooled me. What the devil were you doing out there dressed like that?"

"A long story."

"And you'll tell me sometime."

"Why not?" Nights are long on the high desert, and a housekeeper earns her living in more ways that cleaning and cooking. I laughed. Maybe, just maybe, I'd lucked out at last.

Dos Cabezas never had the glitter and flash of the big mining camps, and the people who lived there liked it that way. There was a store, a livery, a church, a school, a post office, and the houses of the people who ran the businesses.

Jack pointed out everything as we drove through, and added a caution. "You can get what you need at the store, or wait till I go into Willcox, but I'm not made of money, so don't go running up a bill."

"Aren't your claims paying anything?" I asked, worried that I'd agreed to a life of poverty.

"I get by . . . but I'm no millionaire. Even if I was, I'd be out here where I'm free to do what I please when it pleases me. If you don't like it, say so, and I'll take you back."

But I did like it. All of it. The little town nestled in the hills, the quiet broken only by the thud of hoofs, the jingle of trace chains, and every now and again the squawking of startled jays in the oak trees.

"So far it suits me fine," I said.

Two dogs snarled at us, when we drove into the yard — the biggest dogs I'd ever seen. I stayed where I was, holding tight to my skirts and looking to Jack to tell me what to do.

He jumped down and ignored me. "Hey, boys," he said to the pair. "Did you think I'd gone off and left you?"

They quieted and stood, wagging their tails.

"Is it safe?" I called.

"Just come slow. They'll get used to you."

I certainly hoped so. Although I'd always wanted a dog, these hardly seemed like lap dogs. Their huge tongues hung out between curving, white teeth, and their eyes were unreadable as they stood, watching me.

"It's all right, Bear," Jack said as I put out a hand to the bigger of the two.

"That's his name? Bear?"

"He's damn' near as big as one."

The creature sniffed me, then investigated my skirt before wagging his tail. The other, slightly smaller, followed suit, and I got down on my knees and patted them both.

"I always wanted a dog," I told them, "but

you're a bit more than I figured on."

"Don't mollycoddle them," Jack ordered. "They're guard dogs, not pets."

His tone, his manner, irritated me. "You're trouble is you've lived alone too long." I scrambled to my feet, and he jumped like I'd shot him.

"Don't think you're going to come here and boss me, woman! You can go at any time."

"And don't think I'll stand quiet and let you shoot off your mouth at my expense," I said. "It's obvious you need looking after."

His jaw dropped, and then, surprisingly, he laughed. "You've got a sharp tongue on you," he said. "But so have I. We'll have some disagreements, we will."

"I've lived through worse."

"And you've promised to tell me."

"Only if you behave yourself, and give me a free hand in the house." I wasn't about to take chances with his changeable nature. The rules were going to be laid out from the start.

"Why do I get the feeling I just sealed my fate?" he asked.

I grinned. "Because you have. Now let's see the house."

It was a house like any other in that part of

the country. Put up fast with board and batten, quick shelter, added on to as needed. There was a front room, kitchen, and sitting room combined, complete with iron stove, plank table, a rocking chair, and two straight chairs. Behind that, two small bedrooms with narrow beds, primitive chests, and hooks on the walls for clothes.

Hardly a palace, I thought, remembering Baby Doe's mansion, the elegance of some of the hotels I'd stayed in — and some of the other places as well — the stone house in Fort Griffin, the adobe in New Mexico — places I'd turned into a home with my own hands and determination.

"Say it! It's not what you're used to!" Jack was beside me, belligerent as one of the dogs.

"You don't know what I'm used to," I snapped back. "Stop apologizing."

He took off his hat, and I saw that he was as bald as an egg with only a few grizzled hairs around his ears.

"Best keep your hat on when you're out in the sun." I spoke automatically, so used to taking care of someone.

"Looking out for me, are you?"

I guess I was. I nodded.

"That's nice." He put the hat back on and walked to the door. "I'll get you settled, then

I've got things to do. You want to hear how I lost my hair?"

"How?"

"I was in one of my prospects. Took off my hat and laid it down. When I put it back on, damn' if a vinegaroon wasn't in it. Scared me so bad my hair fell out!" He stood there grinning, waiting for me to catch on.

"Liar!" I said with a chuckle.

"Damn' right. Now, tell me where to put these trunks of yours. Heavy as lead they are. What's in 'em?"

"None of your business, Mister Howard," I said, and preceded him out the door.

XXI

"I need wash tubs, lye soap, a washboard, clothespins, and some calico for curtains. And a coffee pot, a good frying pan, moth balls, and flour that doesn't have bugs in it."

We were facing each other across the table like duelists. I wasn't spending any more nights under dirty quilts, or fighting a losing battle with infested flour. And Jack wasn't happy. In fact, he was roaring.

"You'll break me! We'll both be paupers! You with your wash pots! The spring up the cañon's good enough, always has been. You'll use your legs and your wits, woman, or I'll let you go!" He slammed his cup on the table.

By now I had him figured. A lot of bluster, a lot of noise, and then he saw sense. I only had to stand up to him and stay calm, which wasn't always easy given my own temper.

"You want bugs in your bread? Fine. You want fleas in your blankets from those beasts of yours? That's fine, too. Just don't complain about your stomach or your itches. There! I've told you. Now make up your mind."

I got up and went outside where the view always pacified me. Rolling hills dotted with oaks and mesquite, yellow chamiza flowers, and the peaks of the mountains like sculpted faces turned to the sky. Closer to home was the garden plot I'd started to dig, and the sapling trees — apples, peaches, apricots. In a few years — if I lasted that long — we'd have fruit and vegetables of our own, good, fresh produce to supplement Jack's beans, beef, and occasional venison.

Oh, he was tight-fisted, but I knew he was taking gold out of those prospects he was so proud of, and I'd found where he kept his money in a sack under a loose floor board. There was more than enough for the simple way he lived, and which I intended to stick to.

"Missus Cummings. . . ." He was at my elbow, coffee cup in hand.

I said: "It's time you just called me Mary."

He blinked, distracted as I'd intended. "I . . . it's not right," he said after the minute it took to follow me. "People might get the wrong idea."

"There's nobody here but us," I reminded him. "We can do and say what we want. And anyhow, I'm divorced. Missus Cummings is long gone."

"What happened? With you and him?"

I told him, leaving nothing out.

When I finished, he was quiet, frowning. "It's not right, raising your hand to a woman. A man who does that isn't a man, and you such a little thing."

I gave him a pleading look, not having forgotten how it was to flirt and get my way. "And now here I am, trying to earn a living and having to fight for every little thing I need to make you comfortable."

He sighed. "All right. All right. This time you can have your way, but don't think I can't recognize when a woman's trying to get 'round me. I'm soft in the head this morning is all."

I smiled sweetly. "Thank you, Jack."

He stalked across the yard to the horse pen. "Save your thanks," he called back. "I deserve whatever happens. God help me."

He rode off without another word, and I spent the morning sweeping and laughing to myself. Jack Howard was ornery, penny-pinching, argumentative, and, in spite of it all, charming. He was himself, and there's a lot to be said for that.

It's a funny thing, but I've never been lonely all these years, even though so much of my early life was spent in towns surrounded by people. Maybe a person gets so she has enough of noise, excitement, the tug and pull of other people's demands. I don't know. I haven't thought much about it until now. I've been too busy doing things — making this house comfortable, doing the garden and putting up the produce, writing letters and getting answers, making sure Jack didn't work too hard and come in bent over so I had to heat water and get him in a wash tub, then rub liniment on him and keep him inside while he groused about how, if he couldn't work, we'd end up in the poor house, both of us.

"Shoot me through the head, Mary," he'd say. "If it comes to that, shoot me and toss me in a hole."

"And leave me to look out for myself."

"My money's on you. You're the only woman I ever met who never complained. Can't stand whining females. Never could. You're all right, no matter what anybody says."

We came to understand each other, Jack and I, in spite of our shouting matches. All my years with Doc and that wicked tongue of his made it easy for me. I was used to a man who used words, instead of blows, to get his points across. In fact, I liked it. We kept our wits sharpened, our humor intact, and that was, I see now, our way of showing affection, as strange as that sounds.

Jack brought back the wash tubs and everything else on my list, and then watched as I stitched and hung the curtains.

"Damn' place looks like a brothel," he said, when I admired the bright calico.

"Is that where you were in town?"

He made a rude noise. "Waste of money."

"Why not?" I was baiting him.

"What kind of woman are you, talking like that?" His roar rattled the windows.

"Curious," I said.

"You're not supposed to be. You're not supposed to know about things like that."

I smothered a laugh. "Who said?"

He stalked across the room, and stood facing me. "Shut your mouth, woman. It's not decent."

"You're a prude, Jack Howard!"

"I'm not!"

"Seems like it. I mean, after all, we're here in the same house, we ought to be able to talk. And we both know what the world's like."

"There's better things to talk about!"

"Like what?"

"Like what's for supper?"

I burst out laughing, and after a minute so did he. "You made a fool of me, Mary Cummings," he said. "You and your wicked tongue."

"I wanted to see if I could make you laugh," I said. "You're always so ready to go up in smoke. Like one of those dynamite sticks you keep in the outhouse. And that's another thing. I want a door put on it. It's not right, me having to be out there for everybody to see."

He always took his shotgun with him and sat there in full view, which didn't bother him, but which I thought was awful.

His laughter ended as quickly as it had

begun. "Nobody's sneaking up on me. Especially not out there. They want my claims, Mary. A man has to protect what he's worked for."

"I know that. But a woman needs some privacy."

He gave me a piercing look. "Just like a man's life is his own."

We were, it seemed, back to the beginning. "All right," I said. "I won't ask where you've been, if you'll put a door on the outhouse for me. Agreed?"

With another spurt of laughter, he sat down and plunked his arms on the table. "You drive a hard bargain, but I'll do it. And I'll see what I can do about piping that spring down here to the house for the wash and our water. I been meaning to do it, but there's never enough time. And just so you know, I've got no use for fancy women. Never have. Anyhow, now I've got you."

"But you don't," I said softly. "Have me, I mean."

"There's always hope." His eyes glinted up at me.

It was as if I was young again, slender, still pretty, believing in dreams. It seemed I was being given another chance at what I'd come to believe would always be denied me. So I weighed my answer carefully.

Finally, I went to him and kissed the top of his bald head. "I'm not pretty any more," I said.

He kept his elbows planted on each side of his plate and wouldn't look at me when he spoke. "A man wants more than a pretty face, Mary. And I'm a bit long in the tooth, myself."

I put my hands on his shoulders. They were rigid, as if he'd scared himself. "You suit me just fine," I said.

XXII

"I suppose now you'll be wanting to get married."

We were having breakfast — eggs, beef, fried potatoes — a huge meal that Jack said he needed to get through the day.

He caught me by surprise, and I looked down into my cup as if I could find an answer there. Finally, I shook my head. "I've been married. It never brought me anything but trouble."

He took a forkful of eggs. "That's fine then."

But like a sinner, I had the sudden urge to

144

confess and be forgiven, to have the slate of my conscience wiped clean. "There's a lot about me you don't know," I said.

"Let the past rest. I know enough."

"But. . . ." I was insistent.

"Mary, whatever you did is done. Same with me. I'm no saint, and probably neither are you, but we don't have to start blabbing just because of last night."

Regardless of consequences, I blurted out what bothered me most. "They called me Big Nose Kate! You understand me? You want to kick me out, now's your chance."

His eyebrows shot up to where his hair should have been. "That was you? Back in Tombstone with that Holliday fella?"

"That's only part of it."

"Then spit out the rest, if it'll make you feel better."

Why was he being so calm about it all? By now he should be shouting about women and deception, and how he never trusted a one of them. Taking a deep breath, I went on and didn't stop till I reached the end.

"That's it. All of it. Now you know and can send me packing."

He cut another piece of meat. "You should see yourself," he said. "Nervous as a whore in church. No offense," he added with what looked like a smile.

"But . . . ?"

"Stop with your buts, and listen to me. It seems like you did what you had to do like everybody else. Like I did. Staying alive beats dying all to hell, at least in my book. And you stuck with him, didn't you?"

"I was there when he died."

"Well, then. As for the rest, everybody knew the Earps and Holliday were the law. You were on the right side." Then he went on eating as if my revelation was of no interest at all.

I leaned across the table. "You don't mind?"

"Like I said. What's done's done. I killed a man in Tombstone back then. He tried to jump my claim."

"Why doesn't that surprise me?" I said.

"It shouldn't." His eyes crinkled with silent humor. "We're quite a pair, you and me."

"Why aren't you in jail?" I wanted to know. "Why aren't you in Yuma?"

"Self-defense. The fella needed killing like a lot of them in that town. A bad place, Tombstone. It's better here."

I looked past him through the open door. The desert broom was covered with silver plumes, and the mountains seemed farther away, their fall appearance, as if they'd

146

drawn into themselves for protection against the coming winter.

"This is the best place I've ever been," I said softly. "I hope you don't ever decide you don't want me any more."

"Just don't start thinking for me," he said. "I can't stand a woman does that."

I figured with his quick temper somebody had to think for him at times, calm him down before he got apoplexy. But a clever woman knows how to make her influence felt without being caught at it. I sipped my coffee and didn't say another word until Jack, who was looking out the window, jumped up, scattering the dishes.

"Now what?"

"That damned Hurtado fellow's gathering cattle. Probably gathering mine along with his. They all try it. Every damn' year."

He grabbed his shotgun. I grabbed him. "You can't go shooting the neighbors," I said firmly. "Let me go."

He glared. "And what'll you do about it?"

"Bring our cows back."

He gave that cackle of his that passed for a laugh. "What do you know about it? Those cows are wild."

He could be infuriating, never believing I was capable of doing more than keep a house, set a table. I stamped my foot hard. It hurt, but I paid no attention. "I know as much as you. Now, go saddle me a horse and put that damn' gun away, because I won't need it."

He stopped short, belligerent as one of the dogs. "I won't have you riding out there with your skirt up to your waist."

"Oh, stop!" I said. "My skirt will be only above my ankles, and nobody's interested in an old woman's legs anyhow."

"I am!"

"And we're both long in the tooth, like you said." I sounded harsh, but inside my heart was pattering like a girl's, and I put out a hand and laid it on his arm. "Thank you for that. It was . . . it was nice."

"Huh!" he said. "You listen to flattery but not to common sense. Like every other woman," he added, refusing to look at me out of what was, I thought, embarrassment.

"And where would you men be without women? Out shooting at each other. Let me go, Jack. It scares me . . . you ready to kill somebody, and maybe get killed yourself. And then what?" What I said was the truth. I didn't want Jack dead, and I'd seen enough killing to last me.

"You mean it, don't you?" He raised his eyes to mine.

"Yes."

He cleared his throat. "All right. Just this once. You hear me? Either that, or you get yourself something decent to ride in."

"I will," I promised, with every intention of doing so as quickly as I could. I'd missed my rides — the freedom I felt on horseback, and the land rolling past, each scene different from the last, each curve of the trail beckoning.

I scrambled up on the old horse without any help and rode off down the cañon. "See you soon!" I called back, and Jack waved, a stiff motion of hand and arm as if he wasn't used to waving to anybody, had never done it before. Probably he hadn't, I decided, as I headed for the dust cloud that was the main body of the herd. Probably he hadn't had much love in his life or any close friendships at all. He'd grown up distrustful of everybody and never had reason to change.

Well, I thought, *I'm going to change that. You just wait and see, Jack Howard.* Then I put the horse into a fast trot, laughing at how good it felt to be on the move again.

Regardless of Jack's state of mind, Florencio Hurtado was a gentlemen, and so were the other ranchers, Charley Busenbark and Harvey Newell, who'd joined him in the roundup. Seeing me, they all pulled up their horses and tipped their hats.

"We thought you were Jack. That's his horse isn't it?" Busenbark said with a grimace of what seemed like relief.

"I came, instead," I said, and introduced myself.

Hurtado was riding a rangy bay that was dancing under him, and I admired the way he controlled it, with a light hand on the bit. "*Señora*," he said, "we'll find your cattle. You, please, stay here. Have coffee and rest until we come back."

Then he was gone and the others with him, leaving me to marvel at the courtesy that seemed born into every Mexican I'd ever known — so different from most of those who'd made their way West and had no knowledge or understanding of manners.

Jack had only four cows that ran loose on the range and were bred by whatever bull wandered by. All, this year, had calves at their sides, good, big youngsters as wild as their mothers.

"If you wish, *señora*, I can take them to market for you and get a good price." Hurtado stood beside me, hat in his hand.

Jack wouldn't like it, but it was one less chore to do, so I smiled and nodded. "*Gracias, señor.* I would be grateful."

"And *Señor* Howard?" His eyes were alight with humor.

"I'll manage."

"*Bueno.*" He turned to his horse. "My men will drive your cows back for you. They won't want to leave their calves, and I don't think you could manage four at once." He hesitated, then gave a small bow. "Even if you are brave enough to face Jack Howard by yourself."

Looking at them — bony mamas with wicked horns — I didn't think I could manage them, either. Facing Jack looked like a much easier proposition.

"His bark is worse than his bite," I said.

"A barking dog and a shotgun are always dangerous," came the response.

And Jack had admitted to killing a man. I wondered how many of his neighbors knew about that, and thus stayed as far away from the home place as they could.

"Perhaps you better leave the money for the calves at the post office," I said.

He bowed again. "As you wish."

That's how I got to know some of the neighbors — by interceding for Jack. And they are good neighbors, all of them, just wary of Jack's temper. There's the school-teacher, who lends me books to read; the local ranchers who to this day have kept an eye out for our few cows; the Whites, our closest neighbors and best friends, who in these last years have made sure we never wanted anything, made trips to town for us, and never paid the slightest bit of attention to Jack's frequent bad humor.

It was Mrs. White who found me standing in the road that day in 1929, when Josie Earp's letter reached me. Wyatt was dead. The man I'd loved and hated, the man who'd cleaned up Cochise County then left with a warrant hanging over his head — left, taking Doc Holliday to ruin — was dead.

Almost fifty years had passed since those nightmarish days at Tombstone. I was old. Everyone who'd been there was old and dying. Where had the years gone? Where was our youth, and what had we done with all that energy, all those hopes?

Tears blinded me, and I stopped walking and stood there feeling lost, crying — not for Wyatt, but for the passage of time, the foolishness of passion.

The men were gone — all of them. The women, Allie, Josie, myself, and the lovely Baby Doe, remained — links with the violence of history, the reasons underlying that violence.

What would have happened if Josie had never come to Tombstone, intending to marry Johnny Behan but falling in love with Wyatt, instead? What would my life have been if Doc had loved me enough to leave the Earps and settle down somewhere? It seemed we'd all been the instruments of our own destruction, our lives braided together in a long rope that held firm even all these years later.

We were all widows. As for me, I'd been widowed or abandoned so many times I'd lost count. Even George Cummings was dead — a suicide. They said he'd had a brain tumor, and maybe that was so. Maybe that accounted for the way he'd acted, but who could tell?

"Are you all right?" Mrs. White was standing beside me, looking worried.

I nodded. "Just some bad news."

"I'm sorry. I'll get somebody to drive you home."

Company was the last thing I wanted, so I managed a smile. "I'll be fine. It's just a kind of shock when somebody you know dies."

"Come in the house and rest a minute, then," she said. "I'm just through baking, and the coffee's still hot."

She was a good woman, and kind. And young. I wanted to tell her to hold on to life, to savor every minute, to treasure her two sons, active boys as nice as their parents, because too soon everything would change, and she'd be like me — an old woman with a life that had passed in the blink of an eye, and nothing to show for it but a trunkful of clothes, old photographs, and memories.

I said: "I'll just go on home. Jack isn't feeling too well. Thanks just the same."

And then I went on up the dusty road in the brilliant late-winter afternoon, the sky so blue, the mountains so clear, it seemed they'd just been made. They'd been here all along, though. They'd seen it all, silent witnesses. They'll be here when we're gone, all of us. And there was a comfort in that, like there's a comfort in believing in heaven.

It's first light now — that ghostly pale gray that forecasts morning — and the wind has died down. I'll get my shawl and walk down to the Whites'. And then?

Then, who knows? It's hard to think about the future when the present is so sad. But everything changes. In eighty years my life has changed more times than I can count, and the world around me with it. I've gone from horses and stagecoaches to trains and automobiles; from waiting months for news of my family to being able to hear their voices over the telephone. There has been a war in Europe, a prolonged, fierce thing, and the Hungary I knew, the land of my birth, is a different place from the land that lives in my heart.

But all the time these things were happening, I was here, in these mountains that belong to me because I've looked at them, loved them, more perhaps than I've ever loved a person, and with good reason. People get old and sick. They die, and nothing's left of them. But the land's different. It's always been here and always will, and there's a mercy in that, a strength I once took for granted.

The road to town has never been so long. Three miles seems like a hundred. My feet drag in the dust, and my breath comes hard. The sun is lifting, a great jug pouring light down the cañons, turning the leaves of the mesquites to jade.

A new day — and empty. So empty without Jack to make me laugh, fire my temper, touch my hand. I'll go on alone as I've done so many times before, my tears like salt in my mouth. So many tears — for all of those I've loved and buried, for all the miles traveled, running away, moving toward something.

Where am I going? Who am I now?

Epilogue

Dos Cabezas, Arizona
April 6, 1931

Secretary of Board of Directors
of State Institutions
Phoenix, Arizona

Dear Mr. Zander,

No doubt you have received documents in regard to my application for admittance to the pioneer home from Mr. C. O. Anderson, my Attorney.

When may I leave Dos Cabezas for that home? I have money to pay my fare to Prescott, but when I arrive in the city I won't know where to go or what to do with myself. I would like to leave here as soon as you have accommodation for me. I am very anxious to leave here as I have no income to pay my expenses here.

If you write me when I may come, please give me a few days to dispose of some furniture and a few other things. If I stay here much longer, I won't have money enough left to pay my fare or anything else.

Please let me hear from you at your earliest convenience.

> I remain most respectfully,
> Mrs. Mary K. Cummings

MRS. SLAUGHTER

I

Governor Lew Wallace was frustrated. In place of a diplomatic post in Italy, he'd been offered the governorship of New Mexico Territory, and he'd accepted only because he needed the money and because he'd hoped that, in the far reaches of the West, he'd have the peace and solitude necessary to finish the novel that had occupied his time for so many years. Instead, he'd inherited a war, and it was difficult, if not impossible, to ascertain just who was in the right, who were the killers, and who the preyed upon.

It was enough to keep him awake at night, pacing the cold floors of what was called the Governor's Mansion, a sprawling adobe compound in a city that had seen Spanish conquest, Indian uprisings, and now the machinations of white men bound and determined to become rich in a land far enough from Washington to escape justice.

In September, 1878, he had been sent to replace Governor Samuel Axtel. From then on his troubles had mounted. It was impossible to gain a hold on the warring factions

— Dolan, Murphy, McSween, Tunstall, Chisum, the Kid known as Billy Bonney and a few other aliases, the drunken Colonel Dudley at Fort Stanton, and the crew down at Seven Rivers that had earlier been known by the ignominious name of Dog Town.

In his whole life — that encompassed the Mexican and Civil Wars — he'd never seen such a labyrinthine mess. And all the time the manuscript, *Ben Hur*, lay untouched and unfinished in his desk drawer.

"All right," he snapped at the young lieutenant who stood at the door. "Come in and let's go over that list again."

At least, he could attempt a beginning, weed out the bad from the good, the outlaws from the citizens simply trying to make a living and survive in this magnificent country — a country of mountains, desert, sky — populated by descendants of the early Spaniards, homesteaders, and the dregs of Texas who'd been chased out of their stamping grounds into what was now his domain.

Adjusting his spectacles, he peered down at the paper where unfamiliar names were written along with those only too familiar, then he glanced up at Lieutenant Dawson.

He pointed to the first. "John Slaughter. Who's he?"

"A Texan, sir. He came in a few years ago with some cattle he sold to the fort, and Chisum claimed he rustled some of his. It turned out that time he was only cutting out his own, and since then he's come and gone. Now they say he's stolen Tunstall's cattle, or what was left of them. And he was under suspicion of murder a few years back."

Murder. Everyone was murdering someone, or so it seemed, and it had to be stopped. If it wasn't, New Mexico was lost, and he'd go the same way Axtel had — in disgrace, replaced by another poor fool without the faintest notion of the hell that awaited him.

"Who was the victim, and why wasn't this Slaughter tried?"

The lieutenant shrugged. "Bitter Creek Gallagher. A drifter. Slaughter claimed self-defense, and there weren't any witnesses. At least not any who wanted to testify. Slaughter's a hard man, and his riders are as bad or worse than he is."

"Where is he now?"

"Probably down near Seven Rivers with the rest of them. Some that's on the list."

"Who?"

"Joe Hill, for one. Jesse Evans. John Selman. Probably some other hardcases he brought in from Texas. Hill works for him,

163

when he's not off working for himself."

Wallace sighed. New Mexico was big enough for every hoodlum running out of Texas to hide in. "All right. Bring him in as soon as you can, and any of his cronies you can find."

"Yes, sir." Lieutenant Dawson turned sharply on his heel.

"Dawson!"

"Yes, sir?"

"Be careful. I want him alive and able to talk. Understand?"

Dawson nodded. "Slaughter's a cut above the usual saddle tramp, sir. I doubt he'll give me any trouble."

Wallace leaned back in his chair. "Even the best of families has a rogue or two, and there's no accounting for it. Shut the door on your way out."

Alone again, the governor opened a drawer and pulled out his manuscript. He'd been working on it so long the pages were wrinkled and torn, battered, the way he felt. There were times, and this was one, when, like Diogenes, he doubted the possibility of finding even ten honest men in the entire territory.

II

"Soldiers! There's soldiers coming!" No matter that the war had been over for almost fifteen years, the sight of blue-coated men still frightened Mary Anne Howell. That was one reason she'd been glad to leave Missouri with her husband, Amazon. The other was that the damn' Yankees hadn't left them with anything except feelings of fear and hatred. A way of life was gone and, with it, her confidence.

"Go see what they want, Vi, honey."

Eighteen-year-old Viola Howell wasn't afraid of much except maybe Indians and snakes. She put a calming hand on her mother's arm. "Sit down, Mama. I'll take care of them."

She stepped through the door and stood blinking in the brilliant, late-winter sunlight. "May I help you?" she inquired of Lieutenant Byron Dawson who had dismounted at first sight of her.

A pretty little thing, he thought, removing his broad brimmed hat. Pretty, and defiant, her brown eyes meeting his directly.

"Sorry to bother you, miss, but we're looking for a man named Slaughter. Somebody said we might find him here."

With an effort she controlled herself and forced a smile. "Is it important?"

"Yes, ma'am."

"Oh." She lifted a hand and covered the quick pulse at her throat. Never would she betray John to a bunch of damn' Yankees! Let them go search! "I'm afraid I can't help you," she said. "He's waiting for a herd to come in and might be anywhere."

Anywhere in that broad plain west of the Pecos covered a lot of country, Dawson thought. The girl was lying through her teeth like everybody else he'd questioned, but he couldn't blame her. The situation was such that a man couldn't trust his own neighbors, let alone the law.

"I'm sorry to have bothered you, miss."

She didn't answer, just nodded, and stood watching as he mounted his horse and trotted out of the yard, his men in formation behind him. When they had disappeared behind a rise, she turned and went inside.

"They're looking for John," she said to her mother, her face white. "I'd better go find him."

"You'll do no such thing. It's not our business, whatever it is. Let the men handle it. I think I'll lie down for a minute. I have a headache coming on."

"You do it, and I'll bring you a cloth for your head." Viola was thinking fast. With her mother out of the way, she could take her mare, cut across country to the post office where John had been headed. It was pitiful the way he waited for news of his children whom he'd left with friends after his wife died of smallpox. He was a good man. She knew it. And she loved him. She knew that, too, although she'd have died rather than admit it to anyone, especially her mother.

A half hour later, she slipped a bridle onto the mare and rode off slowly, hoping the dust muffled the sound of hoofs. Her mother, brought up in comfort, disapproved of the way she sometimes rode — bareback and astride — disapproved, in fact, of almost everything she did or wanted to do, regardless of the fact that the rules on the frontier were not the same as those that had governed her youth.

Viola frowned, thinking about how inept she was at things that mattered in a wife. She couldn't even cook, hadn't the vaguest notion about how to fry an egg, or what went into a stew. That was a cook's job, her mother maintained. A lady didn't go into the kitchen except to check that things were in order and see that she wasn't being stolen blind by her help.

Viola sighed. Being a lady was fine except when you butted up against reality and discovered that lady equated with useless. What man out here wanted a woman who couldn't do anything except play the piano and sing and look pretty while doing it?

John Slaughter didn't strike her as the type to admire a helpless female. He was a man who knew what he wanted and aimed to get it. One glance at his face had told her that much, and for her it had been love at first sight although she'd done her best to hide it. Ladies never showed what they felt. That was as bad as showing their legs.

She grinned, looking down at her own slim legs that gripped the mare's sides. Somehow she believed that John Slaughter wouldn't mind the sight. *If* she found him before the lieutenant did.

At that she pushed the mare into a lope, forgetting appearances. There was a time and a place for everything, and she, Cora Viola Howell, wasn't about to let the man she loved be taken away, perhaps put in jail, just because she was admiring her own legs.

Seven Rivers had grown from a few adobe huts into a town boasting stores, saloons, and its own post office where Slaughter's big black stood hitched. She slipped off the mare's sweated back and ran inside, found him standing beside the stove, a letter in his hand.

"Mister Slaughter!" She was formal still, in spite of her feelings.

He looked up quickly, a man cautious of sudden approaches. Then he smiled. "Why, Miss Viola. What's the matter?"

"The soldiers. They're looking for you. I thought . . . I thought you ought to know."

The change in his expression was swift, quick as a threatened snake's. "What?" he said. "What, what?" in that way he had of stuttering when taken by surprise.

Her eyes blazed, fierce in the dim room. "They asked where you were. A lieutenant and some men with him. I said I didn't know."

"So. So. They've come, have they?" He put a careless arm across her shoulders, noted how firm she stood, how full of fight, noted the loyalty in her eyes as if she'd take on the world. Except she was a girl, over her head in the turmoil of the place, the times. She didn't understand, had no knowledge of what he'd done, only that ferocity which he understood deep in his bones.

"I'll take care of it." He gave her a smile

that didn't reach his eyes.

"You mustn't let them take you."

"They won't. Not for long, anyhow." Wasn't he doing only what the rest were, even her father, if she'd known it? Making money with cattle that strayed among his own? And if his riders brought in others, it paid to look the other way because money was where you found it. New Mexico was a hot bed of thieves, and no one was free of sin, least of all John Chisum.

He tightened his arm around Viola's shoulders. "Go on back home, honey. It'll be all right, and that's a promise. And tell your daddy to get ready to move."

She reared back at that, her eyes frightened. "Move?" she said. "Move where? Not again."

He had a plan, he and Amazon. In Arizona nobody questioned your papers or your bill of sale. You sold your cattle in town, to the forts, the reservations, and got paid. Then you repeated the operation, only, if you were smart, you ran Mexican cattle across the line and sold them as your own. Nobody cared as long as they got beef to eat. Nobody gave a damn, and John Slaughter gave less than that.

He pulled her close. "Do you trust me?"

She felt bonded to him, her blood running

hot, screaming like the hawks screamed over the mesas. "Yes," she said. "Yes, I do."

And with that, her destiny was sealed.

III

Back at the house she found chaos — her mother hysterical, her father attempting to comfort.

"You!" Mary Anne turned on her daughter. "Where have you been? The minute my back's turned you go sneaking off and leave me to face trouble."

"What trouble, Mama? What's happened?" Viola put her arms around her mother and felt her trembling.

"They came back. The soldiers. For your father."

"Papa?" She looked across the room at Amazon. "Is this true?"

" 'Fraid so, honey." Amazon Howell was a big man with a weathered face and a thatch of graying hair.

"Why?"

He shrugged. "They say I don't have a proper bill of sale for the cattle I brought in from Nevada. It's true. I don't. And there's a bunch of unbranded calves they say I stole."

"They can't believe that."

"They do. And John's cows are in with mine . . . some they claim he rustled from what's left of Tunstall's herd. Looks like we both have to go up to Lincoln and try to talk sense into the governor."

"Another Yankee!" Mary Anne snapped, her tears gone. "It's not bad enough they took everything once, they have to try again."

"No sense going over that." He put a hand on her shoulder. "We're not the only ones, nor the only folks with unbranded cattle, either."

"But. . . ." Viola was puzzled. "But isn't that kind of like taking what's not yours?" She had to ask to keep things straight in her own mind, but she wasn't sure she wanted to hear the answer.

Her father smiled. "It's the way it is. There's Chisum up at South Spring, helping himself to our stock . . . there's Dolan and Murphy who rustle anything that moves . . . and there's us down here, the little folk, trying to even it up. Only big cowmen have the governor's ear. They can say we stole their cows, and now we've got to stand up and say we didn't. And hope we're believed."

She listened, and the knowledge sank in. If you were big enough, you could do as you wished. If you were John Chisum, you called the shots, while she and her family and men like John Slaughter got sent to prison. Rustling, it seemed, was only a crime if you got caught and couldn't defend yourself.

"Still, it doesn't sound right," she said.

"Everybody does it."

Mary Anne's mouth was a grim line in her once beautiful face as she turned to her daughter. "Leave it be. I told you before, this is men's business. And dinner's ready."

In a daze, Viola sat and pretended to eat, but she was turning over what she'd heard in her mind. The Commandment plainly stated — "Thou shalt not steal." — and she'd been brought up to believe that.

Now everything was changed, like a backward reflection in a mirror. Both her father, whom she worshipped, and the man she'd come to love, were thieves by their own admission. And how, she wondered, was she supposed to reconcile that?

IV

She was born just before the Civil War began, but she remembered very little of those years. For her life had begun on the trail, in a wagon train headed to Montana, the first time Amazon took her up on the saddle with him.

She had spent her babyhood surrounded by women — frightened ones — because Amazon had been off fighting, but her five-year-old mind recognized the warmth and security of his big arms, the pride in his voice as he praised her fearlessness, and how that voice rumbled in his chest as she leaned against him. It was a new experience, and she reveled in it, made excuses to leave her mother in the wagon and ride with the father she had missed without knowing she did so.

With them was her brother, Stonewall Jackson, still an infant, and Sally, her mother's black servant who had refused to be left behind. It was Sally who drove the wagon, cooked their meals, and soothed Mary Anne during fits of weeping for her lost home. Although she was delighted to have her husband back safe, she looked on the journey as the end, rather than the beginning of her life. Behind them lay the known and familiar. Ahead, who knew? They might be murdered by Indians or die of cholera. The trail was marked by the rough graves of those who hadn't made it. They shaped her nightmares, those rough crosses, those rude stones with their pitiful names and dates, solitary reminders of lost hopes.

What Viola remembered were her mother's tears, and how they put a pall on her own new-found happiness. Was it then, she wondered later, that her own survival instincts were honed? In the attempt to be something more than a lost and weeping woman? To be admired instead of pitied for female weakness?

Whatever the case, by the time the family reached Montana, her babyhood was ended and her character formed. For the rest of her life she would be independent, determined, and as unlike her mother as possible.

It was she who, along with Sally, supervised their constant moves as Amazon failed in one job after another from gold panning to restaurant owning, and as Mary Anne grew more timid and bitter-tongued.

But when her father announced they were moving to a farm in Nevada, even the indomitable Sally gave up.

"I think I'll be stayin' here," she said. "My seat bones are tired of that wagon." And she was tired to death of trying to keep Mary Anne's spirits high.

At her announcement, Mary Anne burst into tears, but Sally was adamant. "Miss Vi's old enough to help. As for me, I'm gettin' married and stayin' put."

So it was ten-year-old Viola who drove the wagon to Nevada, who set up the house, and then turned her efforts toward helping her father with his sheep and cattle, but who paid no attention to the rate at which the herds increased or how often they were bought and sold.

Perhaps she should have, she thought now, elbows on the table. Looking back, she realized that the herd they'd brought into New Mexico was larger than the original, but her mind had been elsewhere — seeing to Mary Anne and the new baby, James, and on the excitement of the journey — the desert spread out around them like a painted quilt framed by mountains, a country that went on and on, harsh, lonely, fascinating in its moods, in the odd shapes of the plants that grew, surviving year after year through sheer determination, nothing more.

Well, she hadn't come this far to quit, either. Somehow the governor had decided that Amazon and John threatened his vision of law and order, and so her own life and future hung in the balance.

She straightened her shoulders and looked across the table at Amazon. "I'm coming with you to Lincoln," she said, and her tone brooked no opposition.

Amazon nodded. Mary Anne wailed. "You can't!"

"Yes, Mother. I can. And I will." And if necessary she was going to break the two men she loved out of jail. Then she'd be on the governor's list, too. Lady outlaw. She didn't care, not as long as the men were safe.

The door opened, and John came in, weariness carved on his face. "Reckon we've got to go see the governor, Cap," he said, calling Amazon by the name he'd preferred since the early days when he'd been a riverboat captain.

"Looks like it. What do they have against you aside from cattle?"

"Murder. That saddle tramp Gallagher. And then there's the cows of Tunstall's." He smiled briefly at Viola who was staring at him.

"Tunstall is dead," she said.

"Yes. And some of his cattle are in with

mine. Better me than Murphy and Dolan. They took the rest."

Everybody knew how, after the murder of the Englishman, Tunstall, Murphy and Dolan's riders had looted his place, cleared off his range. No matter whose side you were on — and sometimes it was hard to tell — their greed hadn't gone unnoticed by the smaller cattlemen.

"How do they know you have his cows?" she asked after a minute.

He shrugged. "Somebody must've been watching me pretty close. But those cattle have Missus Casey's brand on 'em, and I aim to tell Wallace I bought them from her. It'll be hard to prove, seeing as she's gone back to Texas." He walked over to the hearth and stood warming his hands before he spoke again.

"While Wallace is trying to prove I'm guilty, I'm heading for Arizona, and I'd advise you to do the same, Cap." He turned to Amazon, and the two looked at each other in silence.

"I won't go!" Mary Anne's face crumpled.

"Now, Mother, don't get upset before time." Amazon reached across the table and patted her hand.

She shook it off. "Don't treat me like a baby. I'm just sick and tired of always being on the move, never settling, never having anything. I want a home. A place that's ours for once and for all."

Each of them heard the misery in her voice and understood it, Amazon most of all. For nearly fifteen years he'd dragged her across the West, always hoping to better their circumstances, to give her what she desired. And now here he was, threatened with jail, simply for doing what everybody did. Suddenly he felt old — too old to keep on moving.

"I'll think on it," was all he said.

Viola studied their faces in the lamplight — her mother's, tearful and defeated, her father's, perplexed. And at the last, Slaughter's, whose eyes blazed at the thought of confrontation. He was a fighter, she thought, just as she was, and never mind that he was twenty years older and under suspicion of murder.

She had pieced together the facts from listening to others. How Gallagher had been rustling John's cattle and come at him with a shotgun. Self-defense is what it had been, and no one had ever said otherwise until now.

She stood up. "I don't know much about Arizona," she said, "but any place seems better than here."

If she wasn't so damn' young, John thought. She was a woman in a thousand, standing there ready to take on whatever enemy threatened. He wanted her — so badly it was all he could do to stay where he was, hands held out to the warmth of the fire. He was a thirty-eight-year-old widower with two children, a weak set of lungs, and no prospects except jail. Hardly an ideal candidate as a husband.

She turned then and met his eyes, and he was stunned to read the stirring of passion in her, a need that seemed as great as his own.

V

To the east and south the high plains rolled and tumbled as if they were alive, as if there was a giant heart beating under the buffalo-grass-covered hide of the beast that was earth. From the back of her mare, Viola could see a hundred miles or more. Distance here wasn't measured by human invention but by the sweep of wind, the motion of clouds, the lure of El Capitán, snow-covered, rearing at the edge of sight.

Here the Río Hondo spilled out of its narrow valley, and the valley itself beckoned, offering shelter to those who had come across the plains and grown weary of unbounded space.

"It's grand!" she exclaimed. "Isn't it?"

John, riding beside her, agreed. "And free for the taking."

"Is it like this in Arizona?"

"It's different."

"My mother's against it. She wants to go on to Texas." And for herself, she'd go where Slaughter went, if it was ten thousand miles.

"We aren't likely to change Wallace's mind," he said. "You know that. Staying here could get dangerous."

"You're saying my father's a thief. And yourself, too."

He heard pain in her voice, and a tinge of anger. She was young. And innocent. A jewel in a den of opportunists, and he'd fallen for her. He sighed. "An unbranded cow has no owner," he said at last. "It belongs to whoever finds it. And a man who doesn't mark his cattle is plain foolish."

What he said made sense, but would the governor understand? Somehow, she doubted it, and when Byron Dawson rode up, she was glad of the distraction.

"We'll be stopping here a while, Miss Howell. I thought you might want to know." He pointed toward the narrow river, a silver thread under the noon sun.

"Race you there, Lieutenant!" For a moment her face shone with mischief, and then she was gone, feather-light on her mare, laughter spilling out in her wake.

Watching them, John felt too old to make a fool out of himself over a slip of a girl, no matter how much he wanted her. He sighed again.

Amazon, who had come up beside him, read the longing on his face. "Best not wait too long, man," he said with a grin.

"You don't mind?"

"I'd like to see her settled. Mind you, she's a handful, but her heart's pure gold."

For a moment he was happy. Then the knowledge of what lay ahead of him blotted it out. "I can't ask her to marry a jailbird, Cap."

Amazon spat. "There's not enough evidence to convict either of us. Nor enough jails to hold every man who ever took a few unbranded cows. Wallace knows that. This whole thing's just to put a scare into people, but it won't work."

"Maybe not. But I'm planning to leave as soon as I can. *If* I can. Then we'll see."

Up ahead, Lieutenant Dawson was helping Viola off her mare. She was still laughing. The sound was sweet as music, as painful as a shard of glass.

"By God, he'll not have you," John said under his breath. "And that's a promise."

VI

Lincoln was smaller than Viola had expected, simply a main street framed by a few wood and adobe buildings, with Bonita Creek murmuring between its banks, and behind it, a mountain covered with oak and juniper.

"Is this all?" she asked her father as they rode past the Ellis House and the Torreón, a tower of yellow stone that had been built to protect the town from raiding Apaches.

"Reckon so, honey. But don't go by size. There's places that attract trouble, and this is one."

She felt it then, the violence, the ghosts that seemed to linger in the burned ruins of the McSween house. "How long do we have to stay?" she asked.

"Long as it takes Wallace to make up his mind."

In that moment she made up her mind a second time. They were leaving Lincoln and New Mexico, and be damned to anyone who tried to stop them! She wasn't about to spend her life waiting for her father's and John's release from jail and catering to her mother's whims. She might as well be imprisoned, too, sentenced to spend her youth reaching through the bars of a cell toward a dream that was leaving her behind.

The Wortley Hotel sat at the western end of the street, an adobe building much like all the others. In the late afternoon, lamps were already lit, and fragrant piñon smoke wreathed its chimneys, welcoming travelers.

Obviously, she thought, the governor was also staying in the little hotel, and, therefore, she could arrange to meet him before her father and John went to testify. She, after all, was a woman, and he, well, he was merely another man, and a Yankee at that. If not for him and his blue-coated kind, they'd be back in the big house in Missouri, instead of here in a wilderness accused of everything from murder on down.

She waited until her father and John were shown to a room before questioning the clerk at the desk.

"The governor is staying here, isn't he?"

"*Sí, señorita.* And it is an honor to have

such a man in our town." The young New Mexican, hardly older than she, smiled widely, impressed by her beauty as much as by the visit of the territorial leader.

Viola smiled back. "Is he here alone?"

"Oh, no. He brings with him many men . . . a *mayordomo,* a *segretario,* even soldiers."

"And does he eat with the rest?"

"He eats in his room, when he is finished his work. It is said that he sits all night writing, but I don't know this for certain."

When he turned to reach for the key to her room, she quickly scanned the register, noting the location of the room she wanted. It wouldn't be seemly to knock on his door, but she could be waiting outside and would be, even if she had to get up in the dark.

A rooster crowed outside, and others joined in, announcing sunrise although the town in the valley lay in darkness. It was cold — the water in the pitcher only a few degrees warmer than the room — and Viola shivered as she washed, brushed out her hair, and recoiled it at the back of her head.

Day came slowly, a subtle change from black to gray, and, when she looked out, she saw that the town and the red hills surrounding it were deep in snow. The scene

185

was one of brooding desolation, and she wrapped her arms around herself in an attempt to stifle the chill that came from within as much as from without. For the first time she doubted the success of her plan, the future she'd imagined with such surety. Here, in this valley of cold shadows, optimism had no place. Here were only greed and the wickedness of men.

Voices and the rattle of china in the hall brought her out of her dark mood. Obviously, in spite of the weather and his night-time occupation, the governor was an early riser. And she intended to be waiting when he opened his door.

The glow of a lamp brightened the passage. Against it, he stood in silhouette — a tall man, and slender, even in the greatcoat and hat he'd put on for his walk to the courthouse.

"Your Excellency." Viola hadn't the faintest notion how to address him, but chose the most respectful way she could think of and cursed that her voice wavered like a child's and not the woman she wanted to appear.

At her words, Wallace turned toward her, and she saw his face — *a scholar's face,* she thought, noting the spectacles, the high forehead, dark hair, graying in places.

He took off his hat, bowed slightly. *Who on earth was this girl, and what did she want, hovering like an apparition in the shadows?* "What is it, child?" He bit off his words as she came close. *No child certainly, but a young woman, and beautiful with her large eyes and carefully arranged dark hair.* "Speak up. Don't be afraid."

"I'm not."

If she was, she hid it well, he thought, noting the tilt of her chin. "Good. Who are you and what is it you want?"

She took a breath. *Where to start?* "My name is Cora Viola Howell. My father is Amazon Howell who you've accused of being a cattle thief."

Ah. Now it was clear. He nodded and held out his arm. "Walk with me, Miss Howell. Did your father send you to plead his case?"

How dare he say such a thing? On top of it all, he now accused her father of cowardice! She drew away, eyes flashing. "He did not! It's my idea. My father has always been an honorable man, sir. A riverboat captain, an officer in the Confederate Army. He has always tried his best for his family. If it hadn't been for the war. . . ." She stopped, not wanting to hurl accusations at this Yankee.

The war. Always one came back to that —

a war that had accomplished its purpose but that had left so many — black and white — homeless and destitute. And here was another war with equally dark results. Worse, he had no way of ascertaining who was innocent, except, perhaps, for this woman who stood filled with the courage to fight for those she loved.

"What do you want me to do?" he asked quietly. "Your father is in possession of cattle without a bill of sale."

"It doesn't mean he stole them! Or that John Slaughter stole his! You have to believe me. And them."

"Slaughter's is a different case. As I recall, he's also a murderer."

"It was self-defense!"

Behind the spectacles Wallace's eyes were keen. "You know this for a fact, Miss Howell?"

"I know John. He's not a Regulator or involved with any of the others. He's a businessman. A cattleman."

Wallace stroked his beard. "And what is Slaughter to you?"

Everything! But that was a secret that belonged only to her. "He's a friend. A family friend. And a good man. Oh. . . ." Her hand tightened on his arm. "I'm not asking for much. Only that you understand that without my father, my mother and I won't have anyone. And my mother isn't. . . ." She searched for the word. "Isn't strong, sir. She depends on him, and so do my brothers."

"No other family?"

"No, sir. Just us." She looked at the stern but kindly face lit now by the lamps in the small lobby. "I beg you . . . don't send him to jail. Or Mister Slaughter. All I'm asking is that you give them a chance."

The tears in her eyes were real, and the desperation, he had no doubt. And she was several cuts above most of the women he'd seen — those who lived with the wanted men on his list. She was educated, too, judging by her speech. He couldn't afford to ignore her, even if he wanted to. Educated citizens were a valuable asset — more so than the riffraff that poured into the territory, the law on their heels.

He patted her hand. "Miss Howell, don't cry. I'll give your father and John Slaughter a fair hearing and the chance to prove themselves. And. . . ." A smile flickered across his face. "I won't mention our meeting. Agreed?"

The smile she gave in return was worth any promise, and he doubted she had any idea of its effect. He wished he had a child like her, willing to face the enemy with nothing but her beliefs.

"Yes, sir. Thank you, sir." She choked over the words. "I owe you my life!"

"You owe me nothing. Only your honesty."

And who was honest in this land? The weight of her errand lay on her like a stone. "God bless you," was all she said.

"And you, Miss Howell." He bowed again — she deserved the courtesy — and, replacing his hat, set out for the courthouse to listen to the excuses of her father and those of John Slaughter, family friend.

From the door to the room he shared with Amazon, John Slaughter heard the entire interview. He'd gotten up early and was on his way out when Viola had stepped into the hall and intercepted Wallace.

So that was why she'd insisted on coming along! Why she'd faced down Mary Anne's objections with a cold determination he hadn't understood! He'd thought she only wanted an outing, or perhaps a flirtation with the handsome lieutenant. But he'd thought wrong. Viola Howell was a most unusual woman, one any man would be proud to have at his side.

Well, if she would have him, he'd keep her beside him as long as he lived. And God willing, that would be many years.

"He let me off, but John's been sent to jail at Fort Stanton." Amazon stood in the door to his daughter's room, distress creasing his broad face.

Viola felt her legs give way. She'd been so certain. So sure of herself. "Why?" she asked. "What reason could he have?"

"Those Tunstall cattle, pure and simple. We both told Wallace how it was, but he wasn't listening. Seems like he's deaf where the real trouble lies."

"But. . . ." She was clutching the bed post that, at least, seemed solid. "What can we do?"

Amazon shook his head. "Nothing. We'd just best head home before your mother worries herself sick."

And leave John? She let go of the bed and took a step toward him. "We can't just go off and leave him in jail. He's our friend. And he's got nothing to do with this . . . this *war* that's going on. All he wants is to go to Arizona. We have to help, Papa."

He was watching her closely and hid a smile. So he hadn't been wrong, after all. The girl was smitten with the Texan who had a dream of a cattle empire. No matter that the man was hardly bigger than a banty rooster. As far as Amazon was concerned, Slaughter still stood head and shoulders above the scum that was causing all the trouble.

He stepped into the room and closed the door behind him. "How do you figure we can help?" he asked his daughter quietly. "We're only a little bit better off than he is."

"We'll go back to the governor."

Her chin was set firmly. She reminded him of himself in the days when he'd been young. Cock-sure and determined.

"I've been," he said.

"Then I'll go myself." She came closer and put a hand on his arm. "Let me try. And we won't tell John or Mother."

At the thought of Mary Anne, he snorted. "Honey, we can't tell her the half of it."

She took it as approval, although that hardly mattered to her. "I'll talk to him in the morning before he leaves."

Her certainty alerted him. "What've you been up to?"

"Nothing," she said. "Yet." But she didn't meet his eyes.

She had the spirit of a man, and all the charm of a Southern woman. Her mother's charm that had swept him off his feet years before and that, in spite of her disappointments and sharp tongue, still captivated him. In his experience there was nothing like a woman who'd made up her mind about what she wanted. He almost pitied Wallace — and Slaughter, too.

"Mind you remember who you are and act like a lady," was all he said, and he was rewarded by a smile of pure mischief.

"A lady is as a lady does." She linked her arm through his. "Is it dinner time? I'm hungry."

She was waiting for the governor in the morning, hands clasped together to stop their trembling.

"Miss Howell," he said. "Are you always up so early?"

"Yes, sir. When I have to be."

"And what is it today?" he asked, although he thought he knew.

"John Slaughter. I . . . I hoped you'd let him go."

"And you want to question my reasons, is that it?"

For a moment he thought she was going to cry, that female trick that had undone so many men, himself included. He hoped she wouldn't. It would spoil everything, including his opinion of her.

Instead she squared her shoulders and

drew herself up. "Yes, sir. And to tell you my own reasons."

"Heaven help me," he said with a chuckle, and was rewarded by a sharp glance.

Was he making fun of her? She struggled with sudden anger. He hadn't the right to laugh simply because she was a girl who had come to plead for the man she loved.

"Perhaps I made a mistake." Her voice was cold. "I thought you, more than all the rest, were a fair and honest person."

"I thought so, too, my dear. But fairness isn't always simple. Not when I'm surrounded by deceit and must discover the truth by myself. Perhaps you can help me. I'd be glad of it."

That earned a swift smile. "I don't know how much help I can be," she said. "But I do know that Mister Slaughter doesn't deserve jail. He isn't a part of what's happened here except as someone passing through who got caught up in the troubles. If I may say so . . . there are others who need punishment more than he does."

"Who?" His eyebrows rose above his spectacles.

She shook her head. "I only know what I've heard. That hardly gives me the right to say. But there have been murders right here in this town, and the killers are still free.

And out there" — she waved her hand — "are little people who're afraid to sleep at night for fear they'll be murdered in their beds or all their stock rustled. Murder is a worse crime than owning unbranded cattle, I think."

If it were only that simple. But, of course, it was. "I ask you again, Miss Howell, what is Slaughter to you?"

This time she gave him a direct answer. "The man I hope to marry."

It was as he'd suspected. Well, there wasn't anything wrong in a woman fighting for the man she loved. "I see," he said. Stalling for time to think, he reached for his handkerchief and wiped his spectacles. "And neither your father nor Slaughter plan to settle here?"

"Mister Slaughter has only been waiting for the rest of his cattle. We've all been caught in something we had no knowledge or warning of. Please believe that."

Strangely enough, he did. There were always minor players in every great drama, always the small folk who got dragged along by the turbulence. Some survived, while others were crushed and lost, but he would hate to see this girl become one of the latter, hate to see her spirit crushed, the fire gone from her magnificent dark eyes.

He made up his mind quickly. "Give me your word, my dear, that you and your family and John Slaughter will leave New Mexico."

The responsibility overwhelmed her. How could she speak for the rest? If she gave her word, her family might never forgive her. Well, she'd gotten herself into it and now, somehow, had to get herself out. She put out her hand, and Wallace took it. "You have it, sir," she said.

Wallace walked the short distance to the courthouse, head bowed against the cold wind that funneled down the street.

Love strikes where it will, he thought, although it was odd that so young a girl should have fallen for a man old enough to be her father. Still, there was steel in Slaughter, a toughness that belied his size. By no means an ordinary man, in another time he might have sought him out, learned something of this land about which he knew so little. And in another time he'd have delighted in the girl, the determination behind her lovely face.

Perhaps he'd put her in his book. She belonged there. Well, if he ever had time to get back to writing, he'd think about it. He would, indeed.

At his desk, he picked up his pen, dipped it in the ink pot, and scrawled a brief message. Then he called his secretary.

"Have this taken to the fort," he ordered. "Tell them John Slaughter is to be released on his own parole, but that someone will be checking his cattle and his papers shortly. Then bring me all the information you have on this boy they call Billy the Kid. I keep wondering if he isn't being falsely accused."

Viola found the note slipped under her door. **John Slaughter released**, it said. **Pending his departure and that of your family for Arizona, and may God go with you.** It was signed simply with the initials: **L.W.**

For the first time, she understood her own power. For the first time, she realized that a woman was not simply baggage carried along on a man's quest. And she had done it all with dignity, unlike her mother's nagging complaints. She had done it with her mind, her wit, and, she conceded, her smiles. It was a lesson that was never to be forgotten.

She permitted herself a dance around the little room, arms wide, feet skipping under her skirts. Nothing was impossible. Any obstacle could be overcome. She was nineteen years old, filled with hope and with the knowledge of her own indomitable will.

With the note tucked into her pocket, she went down the narrow hall to find her father.

VII

God, the weather was miserable! Cold and wet, and it had been even colder in the jail cell at Fort Stanton. John came into the hotel, shaking water off his coat and stamping his feet. What he wanted most was a hot meal and a good wash, and with luck he'd find Amazon and Viola still here, waiting for decent weather before heading home. He wondered what she was thinking — her father released, himself sent off to prison in spite of her pleas. Damn Wallace! Damn them all! He was free and intended to stay that way!

Viola half rose from her chair at the sight of him, haggard, wet, but with eyes shining. "You're here!"

"It seems Wallace can't make up his mind," he said. "First I'm sent to jail, and the next thing I'm out and given three months to come up with a bill of sale."

"How?" Relief and concern were written on her lovely face.

"It doesn't matter. As soon as the cattle come, I'm out. I doubt he'll follow me."

"And we'll be with you," Amazon said.

She squirmed in her chair. With any luck she wouldn't have to tell them about her promise to Wallace. "What about Mother?"

Amazon sighed. "She'll come along or be left."

"She won't like it."

"Child, she's been unhappy for years. Nothing to do with you or me. She wants what isn't there any more, and there's nothing we can do about it. I'm hoping to settle in Arizona, once and for all. Maybe then she'll come alive again." Or maybe not. He wasn't sure of much these days, least of all his wife's frame of mind.

A surge of affection swept her for this man who had done his best for all of them. "It'll be all right, Papa. You'll see. And neither you nor John will ever have to worry about being tried as criminals."

She sounded almost smug. John, who had been watching her, wondered what she knew, what else she'd done. He wouldn't have put it past her to threaten old Wallace and keep it all to herself. Maybe on the long trek he'd find out.

He pushed back his chair. "If you'll excuse me, I'm going to wash the jail off me and get ready to start back. Is that all right with you, Cap?"

"The sooner the better."

The ride home was for the most part silent, each of them isolated by their own thoughts.

John left them on the second day to round up riders for the drive to Arizona, and Viola and Amazon continued on alone. Mary Anne met them at the door, her face creased with worry.

"I worried every minute," she said by way of greeting. "Anything could have happened. To any of us."

Amazon gave the reins to Stonewall. "Put the horses up, Son, and rub 'em well. Thanks for looking after your mother for me."

"It wasn't anything." Stonewall couldn't wait to be old enough to ride with the men. He'd been humiliated when his sister had gone off and he'd been left behind like a child.

Amazon remembered what it felt like to be on the verge of manhood. "I left you in charge because I knew you'd handle it," he said. Then he put an arm around his wife's waist and led her into the house.

For the rest of her life Viola remembered the scene that took place — the bitter accusations, the anger, her mother's tears that, once started, never stopped until Amazon, tried to the limit of patience, laid down the law in a voice that, although stern, was filled with anguish.

"I've done my best for you, Mother. Done what I figured was right with what we had, and Lord knows we didn't have much. Now I'm asking you to go with me one last time. If you don't, I'll send you on to your San Antonio cousins. But I'm going to take one last chance, and the children are coming with me. You think on it. Don't answer now. Morning's soon enough." Then he crossed the room and went out, leaving a stricken Mary Anne and a stunned daughter alone.

"He means it," Viola said to break the silence that seemed to have dragged on forever.

When her mother answered, it was in a monotone, without hope or her earlier hysteria. "He's all I have."

What of her and her brothers? Obviously, they didn't count. "Then you'd best keep him," she said bitterly. Then she, too, went out and left Mary Anne to her decision.

VIII

They pulled out at the end of March, 1879, the Howells, John Slaughter, and one thousand head of cattle driven by Slaughter's men — Joe Hill, Billy Grounds, Jesse Evans, and a surly Texan known only as Curly Bill. John's servant, Bat, drove the combination supply and chuck wagon, and young Stonewall Howell was on the seat of the wagon that held all of the Howell's possessions. Beside him, a sun-bonneted Mary Anne, who had decided that life with Amazon was preferable to that with her unmarried cousins, sat silently, although at times her lips moved as if she was praying.

Perhaps she was, Viola thought, and perhaps they needed praying for. They were a rag-tag bunch, thrown together out of necessity, even the cowboys, most of whom she knew were in trouble with the law and as eager to leave New Mexico as her father and John.

The way some of them looked at her made her feel vulnerable, aware of herself as female and defenseless, even though she was carrying the pistol Amazon had given her as they left.

"Keep it on you," he said, his face betraying nothing.

"Why?"

"In case you need it, why else? We're going through some hard country, and the Apaches aren't going to like it, either."

"In hard company," she said, slipping the pistol into her belt.

He looked at her sharply. "Anybody been bothering you? Speak up!"

She decided not to mention the men, their eyes hungry as wolves. "No. Nobody."

"That's good, then. Just don't go riding off out of sight. Anything happens to you, your mother'll have my scalp, and never mind about the Apaches."

She reached out and patted his hand. "She'll be all right when we're settled once and for all."

"It's been hard on her. All this. And you've been a good daughter." He cleared his throat and looked after the slow-moving herd. "Best catch up now, and remember what I said about keeping in sight."

She had no intention of disappearing. Her intention was to stay as close to John as she could manage. The thought of being on the trail with him excited her. Surely she would have chances to find him alone, away from Mary Anne's supervision. Surely she hadn't been mistaken about the longing in his eyes. Except, what she knew about courtship was nothing at all. She'd never had a beau, never spoken about such things with anyone, especially not with her mother. Oh, she and Josefina Beckwith had giggled about boys often enough, but she'd been a child then, unaware of the lightning strike of passion.

With a sigh, she lifted her reins and set the mare into a long trot, keeping well upwind of the herd and the dust it raised, a cloud that rose high in the air and announced their passage to anyone watching. Pray God there were no Apaches. Her fear of Indians stemmed from their trek to Montana, the threat of Indian attack and snatches of conversations she'd overhead but hadn't understood, not until they came upon the remains of a wagon train that hadn't made it through. Until the end of her days she would see the carnage — bodies sprawled like rag dolls, and overhead the buzzards attracted by the sight of death, the bloodied faces and scalps.

They followed the Río Peñasco, then turned north through a country of grass and brush, cut by rocky washes and miniature cañons, swept by the wind that came out of the southwest, steady and cold. Overhead, the sky was a hard and perfect blue, ragged only at its edges where the mountains rose, Sierra Blanca the highest of all, a white beacon marking the way.

Although the Howells had come to New Mexico on this same route, everything seemed new to Viola, as if she was seeing it for the first time, and the beauty of the land pierced her, grabbed her throat, clutched at her heart.

Time after time she drew up and stared around, putting out a hand as if to touch the mountains, opening her mouth to capture the wind that tasted of snow and pine trees, sage and rock and trail dust, and to her it was sweet, as everything she sensed was sweet because John was nearby, sharing these moments with her.

It seemed to her that they came upon the mountains suddenly. One day they were driving over the plains, the next they were camped at the base of the trail that led over the pass. The pines were thick here, and patches of snow still lay in their shade. To the north, Sierra Blanca gleamed red in the sunset, as if the snow was burning with a cold fire.

They camped for the night between the

hills, the sighing of the pines, the rush of water, a song in counterpoint to the sound of cattle bedding down. One of the night riders was playing a harmonica, and the tune drifted back to camp like a lullaby.

Viola walked away from the light of the fire and stood listening, looking up at the sky. Had she ever seen it before? she wondered. Had she ever bothered to notice the stars? It seemed she'd been so caught up in herself and her narrow world she hadn't seen much of anything, or even cared.

Now she tilted her head and let the pale light sweep across her, and she thought the sky seemed covered with ice crystals, billions of tiny flakes that glinted like snow that had fallen upward.

"Magnificent, isn't it?" John had been watching for the chance to find her alone.

"I don't think I ever saw so many stars." She turned to him slowly. "I don't think I ever saw anything at all. I've been asleep all my life like the princess in the story."

It was an old tale. Even he had heard it somewhere, sometime, but had paid no attention until now, standing next to her whose eyes reflected the immensity of the night.

"It took a kiss to wake her," he said. "If I remember the story right." Then he won-

206

dered if he'd misunderstood and made a fool of himself.

He meant it! Suddenly she was frightened. She'd never been kissed, had only lately tried to imagine such a thing. "I don't know how!" she blurted, and hated herself for her ignorance in front of this man far more worldly than she.

He chuckled, from relief and happiness. "It's the easiest thing in the world to learn," he said. "And a pleasure to teach."

From somewhere, she never knew how or why, came courage, and with it the mischief that, with her, was never far from the surface. "I'll be a good pupil, sir," she said.

He didn't wait. Life had taught him to take the advantage and that there were few second chances. In his arms she was light-boned, but with a hint of steel, and after the first kiss she laughed up at him with a recklessness he recognized.

"Well?" She was teasing, barely containing what he thought was joy.

"I say, Viola . . . I say . . . marry me." The words were out before he could stop them, even if he'd wanted to.

She leaned against him, almost as tall as he was, her lips next to his ear. "Yes," she whispered. "Yes, gladly."

Oh, more than gladly! They were bound,

had been from the first, and blessed, she thought, when she could think at all. Life was a gamble, as was love, and she was ready to throw her heart out and follow where it led, regardless of what troubles lay ahead.

She pulled away slowly. "Let's not wait. I'm tired of waiting."

So was he, by God. "There'll be a judge in Tularosa. Or maybe a priest, if you want."

"I don't care." And she didn't. "Let's go tell my parents."

He took her hand. "Amazon knows."

She looked at him, amazed. "You mean . . . you mean you asked him?"

"No. But he told me to hurry up about it. I tried."

That was her father, all right. No nonsense there. Mary Anne was a different cup of tea. "My mother will have lots to say," she said, "but I won't listen, and neither should you."

"I won't." As a rule, he didn't listen to anybody, particularly not dissatisfied women.

They were both rebels, both risk-takers, she thought. Odd that until now she hadn't realized that about herself. But then, as she'd said, she'd been asleep, undisturbed by want or turmoil. This was what butterflies felt like emerging from their cocoons, spreading their wings, tasting freedom. And freedom, she decided, was precious, almost, but not quite, as precious as love.

IX

"I won't have it! He'll ruin your life! Gamble it away. And he's too old. He's got children, and you're just a child yourself. What'll you do with them? They'll walk all over you, and so will he. All he wants is a place to leave them so he can run around the country with a herd of cattle, getting into trouble."

Mary Anne had been carrying on for ten minutes, and all Viola wanted to do was scream. Worse, she was certain that her mother's objections carried well beyond the thin walls of their tent, and that not only John but the cowboys were listening to it all.

"Please!" she hissed at her mother. "Hush! You don't understand."

Mary Anne came so close that she could see the wrinkles on her face. "Don't hush me! I'm your mother, and I can see it all. He's been after you for months in that sly way of his."

"And I've been after him."

Her mother reeled back, one hand to her heart. "Are you in trouble? Speak up."

Bewildered, Viola shook her head. "No. Why should I be? And where's the disgrace in wanting to get married?"

"You'll rue this day . . . wait and see."

"Now, Missus Howell, calm down." Amazon had come through the tent flap. "I've already given John my permission."

"Men!" Her mouth tightened in scorn. "He's a rustler. A murderer. And you're handing your daughter over to him."

He put his arms around her. "There's plenty worse than John Slaughter around. I'll sleep easy, knowing Viola's with him, and so will you, once you think about it. He'll give her a good life."

"He's too old!"

"He's not!" Viola jumped into the fray, hands clenched. "And I think I have sense enough to pick out a decent husband."

"I brought you up for better things." Mary Anne's lip quivered. "I wanted something better for you than a life with a man who's not settled and not likely to be, that's all. Those are my feelings, but, since you're both set on it, I wash my hands of the whole thing."

As her mother had intended, Viola felt

guilty and ungrateful, the wayward daughter she'd never, in truth, been. "Don't be angry, Mother," she said. "Please just try and be happy for me."

"I'm not angry. Just disappointed."

Because of her. Because she'd made a choice and stood up for herself. Because she loved. She looked at Amazon, her eyes filled with tears, and saw understanding on his face.

"Go on out and find him, honey," he said. "I've got a few things to talk over with your mother."

John was standing by the chuck wagon, lighting a cigar with a twig he'd pulled out of the fire. For a moment she stood studying his face — a pugnacious one but with kindness in the lines around his mouth and in the dark eyes that met hers across the flames.

"I guess you heard," she whispered, ashamed. "I'm so sorry."

"Not your fault. Not anybody's fault, and she'll come 'round. Don't worry. Day after tomorrow, you and I'll ride on down to Tularosa. We'll stay there till they catch up. It's a pretty place. You'll like it."

But for the next two nights she would have to put up with her mother's aggrieved complaints and accusations. Well, it would be the last time. With her head against his shoulder, she nodded agreement.

"Nothin' like a young bitch to wake up an old dog." From where he hunkered by the campfire, Curly had been watching the two lovers.

"Wish it was me, instead of the boss," Jesse Evans muttered. "She's a fancy piece, all right."

"And neither of you's fit to wipe their shoes!" Bat, whose loyalty belonged only to John, stepped out of the shadows. "Best you both mind your own business and keep your mouths tight shut."

"Just wishful thinkin'," Curly said. "No harm meant."

Bat gave him a hard look. "Make sure you keep it that way."

They were trash, both of them. He couldn't figure why the boss had hired such men, but he sure could keep them in line, come to it. The camp cook held the reins in more ways than one.

Before their nasty tongues had started wagging, he'd been thinking of a special wedding dinner — a cake, maybe, if he had the right fixings. And he'd make damned sure those two hands and their pals got the crumbs. He would, indeed, or his name wasn't Bat Hennings.

★ ★ ★

The trail was steep, the pines thick, the sky a narrow opening framed by branches. Up and up — and over her shoulder Sierra Blanca, immovable, serene. At her side, her husband-to-be on his big, black gelding, telling her his life and his plans.

She hardly heard, didn't care what the future brought as long as he was in it, as long as she was with him. Mrs. John Slaughter. She repeated the words to herself and laughed low so he wouldn't hear and think she was crazy.

Missus Slaughter, she said to herself. *That's me.* Only it was someone else, a different Viola from the one she was now, a woman she didn't know, couldn't foresee.

"I don't want you to be worrying about my children," John was saying. "When we're settled, I'll bring them to stay for a week or two and then send them back to Texas."

So much for Mary Anne's prediction. Viola flashed him a smile. "I don't mind a ready-made family."

"Those are my plans. I'm not going to burden you with children." Sometimes it was hard to believe he'd ever been married, ever fathered Addie and Willie, his life had changed so drastically. And now it was about to change again, for the better.

213

By tomorrow evening this lovely woman would be his. Too old was he? Not with his blood running hot as a young stud's at the thought of her he wasn't.

X

They came down into a country of red earth and deep arroyos, yellow grass and juniper trees that clung to the gullies with thick, twisted roots. Against the foot of the mountain, apple trees were blooming, and the perfume rode the air as lightly as the bees that flashed and sipped and buzzed among the flowers. The town, itself, was prosperous, built of adobe, shaded by cottonwoods, watered by the *acequia* with its source in the river that rushed down the cañon.

A perfect place for a honeymoon, Viola thought, then blushed.

John, who had been watching her, asked: "Second thoughts?"

She shook her head. "No. It's only. . . ." She stopped, confused. How could she tell him her fears, her eagerness? Such things weren't talked about, not in her family, not in anyone's. A woman kept her feelings to herself. "It's nothing," she said finally. "Do you think I'll be able to wash and change my dress before?"

"We'll stop at the hotel. While you're getting ready, I'll find the judge."

When, as a child, she had pictured her wedding, it had always been in a church, with attendants and her parents looking on. She would have a new dress, in the latest fashion. The dress, of course, had changed with the times, but always she would be carrying flowers and smiling, the way all brides smiled out of sheer bliss at having been chosen.

How different was her reality — alone, with her husband to be, in a town where she knew no one, had come as a stranger, her best dress strapped behind her saddle, and only her father's blessing to give her courage.

Not only had she been chosen, she, too, had made her choice, and that she saw was more important than waiting, breathlessly, for a man's declaration. By choosing she had defined herself as a person, as John's equal, and she intended to have an equal voice in their combined future.

For now, however, she wanted a bath, the luxury of warm water after having been in the saddle for days, and the scented soap carried in her saddlebags. When she went to John as a bride, it would be at her most desirable, in her pale blue silk dress with kid boots on her small feet, smelling of lavender water instead of horse sweat and trail dust.

What in God's name had he done? John paced the hall outside the room where Viola, now his bride, was getting ready for bed. He'd married a child! He'd allowed himself to be carried away by his own hungers and now had to prove himself equal to the task of educating her without shocking her sensibilities.

He tried to remember his first wedding night, but Viola kept intruding — her laughter and how she'd taken his arm and leaned against him, offering her lips as soon as they'd been pronounced man and wife.

"Mister Slaughter," she'd whispered, looking up at him with adoration and a hint of something more, as if she expected him to take her there and then. But damn, how could she know her affect on a man? She couldn't, and he'd go slowly. She was too precious to hurt.

With a curse he put out his cigar and knocked on the door.

"Come in."

She was already in bed, her dark hair

spread out on the pillow, her eyes shining. With a smile, she held out her arms. "Why, Mister Slaughter," she said, "what took you so long?"

And with that, he forgot his fears and good intentions and went inside and locked the door.

So *that* was what marriage was about! Viola grinned and gave a healthy yawn. That was what the wives and old ladies whispered about when they got the chance; what her mother had never mentioned at all. Well, her body hadn't lied any more than her heart had misled her.

Life was a wonderful adventure, and the world and John Slaughter were hers. She threw back the covers, got out of bed, and stretched, admiring herself and the body she'd given over so joyously. A glance in the tiny mirror showed her no different except for, perhaps, a glimmer of knowledge in her eyes, lips that seemed bruised from too many kisses. What fun it was! She dressed quickly. The morning air was cold; John was waiting to take her to breakfast, and, after the night's activities, she was starving.

"Well, are you happy now?" Mary Anne made her question sound like a curse.

"Yes," Viola said. "Yes, I am."

She and John had ridden out to the herd, racing each other and laughing, and even her mother's dour countenance couldn't darken her spirits. She was no longer the dutiful daughter. She was a faithful wife. Her allegiance was to John, and she gave it gladly.

Old Bat helped her dismount. "This is one happy day, Miz Slaughter," he said. "Mister Slaughter, he was needing a wife somethin' awful. Now he can have a family again. Seems he ain't himself without a family. A place where he can be his own self, 'stead of what folks make him out to be."

Did he mean children? she wondered. And what was expected of her that she didn't understand? "I'll do the best I can," she said with a smile. "And I hope you'll help me."

"Yes'm. I'll sure do that."

"I don't know how to cook, Bat."

"Nothin' to it. I can show you easy. But cookin' don't make a home."

His words went straight to her heart. She'd been worried about all the wrong things, when what was most important — love, kindness, respect — had been furthest from her mind.

"You're a wise man," she said.

218

He shook his head. "No'm. I just know what's needed."

"Like in a recipe."

He chuckled deep in his throat. "If you want to put it that way. I made us a honey cake for the wedding, and after, I can play my fiddle. Seems like we ought to celebrate, even way out here."

John had told her about Bat's music-making. "None like him," he'd said. "He can make the thing talk."

"I'd be proud to have you play for us," she said, realizing the worth of the black man's loyalty. "We'll have us a dance!"

She was something, this new wife. Pretty as a little bird, and with sweetness written all over her. Mr. John had outdone himself this time. Yes, he had!

Bat checked on the cake he'd hidden in one of the wagon's cupboards. Just as well to keep it out of the sight of those no-good trail hands. Then he pulled his fiddle out from under the seat where he kept it wrapped in a piece of quilt.

That night they danced to the enchantment of Bat's fiddle, even Amazon and Mary Anne who finally, breathless and laughing, sat down on a log beside the fire.

"Goodness! I haven't had so much fun in I can't remember when!" She patted her curls and looked at John and Viola who were waltzing in a circle.

Amazon sighed with relief. Maybe his daughter's marriage would mean happiness for them all. Over his wife's head, his eyes met Viola's. She was smiling, her cheeks flushed, the filigree earrings John had given her brilliant in the firelight. *Good or bad, life went on,* Amazon thought. He'd had enough of the bad, but the future looked promising.

"Are you ready for bed, Missus Howell?" He bent close to his wife's ear.

"Wedding fever! It's best left to the young," she said, but she put her hand in his and let him lead her to the tent.

XI

They headed out the next day, Viola on horseback and John at her side, down into the valley where the white sands edged the trail — a mysterious stretch of what appeared to be empty dunes — empty except for a few fragile trees that cast dark shadows on the whiteness out of which, somehow, they grew.

"I think this is the strangest place I ever saw," Viola said. "It's just here . . . for no reason. And lonely." She looked north across the pure white expanse of gypsum and shivered. What was the purpose of such a place? What could live there, and how?

"There's supposed to be mustangs running in there." John answered her unspoken question. "That means water and grass. But it's not my idea of cattle country."

"And where we're going is?" She was eager to be settled in her own home.

"It's fine country. You'll see soon enough."

"How soon?"

He glanced at her. "A few weeks. If you're tired. . . ." She worried him, small as she was, riding like a man day in and day out with enough energy left at the end of each day to welcome him with passion.

"I'm never tired. I'm just curious. Who can get tired, when there's so much to see? And do." She gave him a wicked, sideways look.

She was a flirt. A temptress. And he loved her the better for it. Still, he spoke what was on his mind. "I say, I say, Viola, I don't want you exhausting yourself. There'll be a lot to do when we get to Arizona, and we don't even have a place to live. We'll have to camp out like we're doing, and it won't be easy."

"I'm not afraid of hard work. Not when

we're building a life together." She was serious, hoping to impress him with her sense of purpose.

Odd that he hadn't looked at it that way himself. Until this minute he'd simply been doing a job, trying to get ahead, gain an advantage, and stay there. But his life had taken a new path. He had a past, and now, with this bright-faced girl at his side, the future seemed a pleasant prospect.

He said: "I hope I don't disappoint you."

She gave an unlady-like snort. "You won't. And even if you did, it wouldn't last."

"You're sure of that?"

"Mister Slaughter," she said, turning to look squarely at him, "life is full of little problems, and we can't escape them. But I do love you with all my heart."

With that, she pressed a heel against the mare's side. "Now let's take a closer look at this sand just in case we're never back this way. I want to be able to remember it all. It *is* our honeymoon trip. Something to tell our children about."

They crossed the Río Grande at Las Cruces, then strung out across a wide and desolate plain bordered by mountains — the Hatchets, the Floridas, Cooke's Range, and on the floor of the valley the white cascades of blooming yucca rose in stalks as high as her head, like candles marking the way.

On and on, and every day the wind in their faces, strong gusts out of the southwest, stirring up sand devils, spiraling, dancing whirlwinds that made the cattle restless and the horses unmanageable. At night they shook the dust out of their clothes, splashed precious water on their faces, ignored the grit in old Bat's beans, and fastened their eyes on Arizona.

"You'll look sixty, time you're thirty at this rate," Mary Anne told her daughter whose face was tanned in spite of her wide-brimmed hat.

"I'll still be me," came the stubborn reply.

Mary Anne rummaged in the back of the wagon. "Here," she said, handing Viola a small bottle. "Use it every night, and try not to lose it. And just for once take my advice like it's meant."

From the unmarked bottle came a faint scent of roses, a scent Viola had associated with her mother since childhood. And her face was as smooth as a child's in spite of the hard life she'd led. Now the secret was being passed, mother to daughter. The realization, that her mother cared for her more than she'd ever shown, came swiftly. Love showed itself in so many ways, some so small as to go unrecognized.

Viola put out her arms and hugged her in a rare display of affection. "So that's how you stayed so pretty," she whispered.

"I've done the best I could. I'm telling you to do the same." Mary Anne submitted to the embrace for a brief moment, then stepped away. "Men are fools for a pretty face."

If she put her hand on paper and outlined it — fingers and the spaces in between — the result would look like a map of southeastern Arizona, Viola decided. Here were mountain ranges that separated broad valleys, each range different from the next, each valley more lush than the last. But the common denominator of them all was grass that grew as high as her mare's shoulders, that leaned in the wind and rippled as if it were fluid, an endless, inland sea. Grama, galleta, red clover, love grass, brome — the names sounded like a song, one of the liquid tunes Bat coaxed out of his fiddle. Cattle, grass, an end to striving.

She dreamed of a home, an island in the ocean of grass, an end to the trail and constant motion. She dreamed of featherbeds and meals on a table set with fine linen, a roof overhead instead of the endless sky, and children. Always there were children, laughing, playing, tugging at her skirt, at John's coat tails.

Someday, she vowed, *someday I will have these things.* For now they struggled, as all newcomers to a new country struggled, to have money in their pockets, to make a life regardless of hardship. For now, life was the trail with its dust and sounds of hoofs and horns, the sameness of days, wind, sun, and wind again, motion of grass, dancing of new leaves on mesquites and cottonwoods.

XII

When they reached the San Pedro River, Amazon and Mary Anne left them and headed south toward Tombstone. John had a beef contract with J. L. Hart, the agent at the San Carlos Reservation, and, although he and Mary Anne did their best to discourage Viola from going with him, their best wasn't good enough.

"You should come with us and get settled," Mary Anne said, "instead of trailing along with the men."

"A woman's place is with her husband,"

Viola insisted. "I belong with John." Besides, she had no intention of staying with her parents and becoming a daughter again.

"I didn't know you were a stubborn woman," John said.

"Now you do. How soon do we start?"

He knew when he was bested. "As soon as we put a little weight on these steers."

They were a sorry lot, she thought. Texas longhorns, gaunt from the long drive, their ribs like washboards, their heads almost too heavy for their bodies. "They hardly seem worth selling," she said, looking them over.

"Beggars aren't picky. Neither's the Indian Agency. The Indians are starving. They're not cut out to farm, and that's the truth. When they get hungry enough, they jump the reservation and go back on the war path. And Hart isn't the most honest fellow I ever met."

"Will we . . . will we see any? Apaches, I mean?" As usual, at the thought of Indians, she was terrified.

"I said you didn't have to come. You'll see more than you bargained for."

With a visible effort, she controlled her fear. "But I am coming. Indians or not. If the agent is dishonest, why are you selling to him?"

He gave her a blank stare. "Understand

this. In this business everybody shades the law, no matter what you think. He's got the money. I've got the cattle. What he does after . . . that's not my problem."

"But. . . ."

"This is business, my dear," he said. "Best leave it to me."

What Indian Agent Hart did was a common practice. He paid for cattle, then turned half the herd back to the supplier, supposedly to be put on grass until they were needed, but which were actually resold elsewhere. The agreement benefited both parties who profited twice, splitting the money from the second sale. The only losers in the game were the Apaches who existed on weevily flour and handfuls of beans.

The Apaches that crowded around Bat's wagon were, therefore, far from the way Viola had imagined. Half-starved, with barely enough clothes for decency, they begged for tobacco, sugar, coffee without any appearance of shame.

Still, she held to Bat's arm for fear they would drag her off the seat. "Go faster," she urged him.

"They're just hungry," he said. "They ain't gonna hurt us. Tell the truth, they don't look like they got strength enough."

She knew she'd see them in her sleep —

the broad, dark faces, the impenetrable eyes, the hands held out in supplication. And she knew she would feel an unexamined guilt in the face of such misery.

"In a war," John had told her, "there's winners and losers. The Indians are the losers, though they're putting up a good fight. But you're better off with them on the reservation than losing your scalp when you're asleep."

Oh, yes, better! But . . . there were women in the group, and scrawny infants, and she, who had never known real hunger, drew back in fear and revulsion and chided herself for being helpless.

Her confusion changed to indignation the next morning as she sat watching a young lieutenant cut out the cattle he wanted. He turned back what seemed like half the herd.

She squirmed in the saddle. "He doesn't know a cow from a donkey," she muttered to John. "At this rate, we'll go back with all our cattle. What on earth is he doing?"

"Throwing his weight around." John's eyes twinkled, as if he knew a joke that she didn't. "And don't worry. If we can't sell here, we'll sell in Tombstone. The town's booming."

"But there's nothing wrong with those steers," she protested. "Even I can see that."

"Keep watching." He was still smiling.

To her amazement, she saw their riders run the rejects back again, and this time the lieutenant made no objection. "He can't tell!"

"Greenhorn," John said with hidden satisfaction. The young man, whether knowingly or not, was only adding to the general confusion. By the time John settled up with Hart, half the herd would be back in his possession, and he would, indeed, sell it in Tombstone.

He turned his attention to the horse the lieutenant was riding — a well-muscled gray that was too good for him or for the Army. He had in mind a good poker game after dinner — when his money was safely in his pocket. In his mind, letting a well-trained horse go to waste was more sinful than gambling.

John and Viola had been given a room in the officers' quarters, and she was delighted at the fact that they would be sleeping in a real bed for a night.

When John told her he was going out and not to wait up, she was disappointed enough to show it. "Where?" she asked. "Can't I come, too?"

"Business."

"And wives aren't allowed?"

He tugged at his beard. "I say, Viola, you aren't going to turn into a nag, are you?"

She was horrified. Become like her mother? "No, Mister Slaughter, I'm not," she said, her tone cold. "You just go on about your business."

He kissed her cheek. "Don't sulk, my dear. It doesn't suit you."

By midnight, the young lieutenant, Cowper, an Army scout, Clay Beauford, and Hart were well on their way to being drunk, and most of their money was on John's side of the table. As usual, he'd followed his rule of never mixing liquor and cards, and he was pleased with his night's work. Not for the first time, either. He'd gambled with old Chisum back in New Mexico for cows that had actually belonged to Chisum, and had won that time, too.

"Guess I'm out." Cowper threw down his cards.

"Me, too." Beauford tilted away from the table.

"One more hand." John shuffled with a gambler's ease.

"I'm broke till payday," Cowper said.

John smiled. "What about that horse you were riding?"

The lieutenant's chair crashed down on

the dirt floor. "That horse has been with me three years."

"And can be replaced. My wife took a fancy to it."

"Replaced how?" He squinted across the table.

"Out of my remuda. Agreed?"

"I. . . ." Cowper hesitated, looked at his pay on the table beside John. "He's a good horse."

"And the Army uses up good horses faster than a good man can blink. Shall we play?"

"Count me out," Hart said. "I don't need a horse. Damn' redskins'd likely try to eat it when my back's turned."

John flicked him a quick glance. "Better watch how you renege on the beef rations, then."

"Better watch your mouth." Hart lit a cigar and stared at John through the smoke.

John nodded. "Of course. Like you'll watch yours." The threat was there just below the surface. "Gentlemen," he said, "are we ready?"

Viola eyed the big gray with suspicion. "That's the lieutenant's horse," she said.

"He's mine now." John refused to meet her eyes.

Realization came swiftly. "That's where

you were last night! Gambling with our beef money!" God, what if he'd lost?

"Now, Viola . . . ," he began.

She threw up her head. "Don't now me, Mister Slaughter. We could've been paupers, thanks to you."

"I don't lose."

Her mother had been right. The man was a risk-taker, a gambling fool, and she was married to him. "That's what they all say!"

He lifted his reins and moved off, and she followed, hurt, angry, suddenly unsure of everything. "Promise me. . . ."

He kept on riding. The big gray had a fast jog that was almost a dance, and her mare had to trot to keep up. Now she'd done it. Precipitated an argument, when all she had wanted was to be reassured. "I'm not nagging," she pleaded. "Honest I'm not."

"Making a big thing out of nothing, then," he said.

"It scares me. All that money at risk."

"I didn't stake it all, and I have a good market for the rest of the herd. I'm not the fool you think I am."

His stern response made her feel childish, as if she were the fool. "I'm sorry," she said. "Am I forgiven?"

He glanced at her then, saw her flushed face, her eyes filled with tears. Still, he had no intention of giving up his happy habit of winning at poker, not for her, not for anyone.

"You said you'd get over little disappointments," he reminded her gently. "And you may be disappointed, but last night I doubled our money and got me the horse I wanted. So . . . so what do you have to say to that?"

She swallowed hard. Admiration struggled with her mother's warnings and her old beliefs — and after a long moment won out.

Mimicking him, she said: "I say, I say, Mister Slaughter, what'll we do with the money?"

"We'll go to Tucson. Send the boys down the valley with the cattle, and you and I will have a decent honeymoon and pick up my children. Not for long, just long enough for me to make sure they don't want for anything. Do you mind?"

"Not at all." How could she mind? At this rate, they'd be rich in no time. And above all else, she wanted to be rich.

XIII

Willie Slaughter, almost three years old, had forgotten his father and had never really known his mother. He looked at John and Viola out of round eyes while he chewed on a moldy bacon rind.

Viola took in his filthy clothes, matted hair, dirty bare feet, and lost her temper. No matter that Amazon had provided a poor living, even as children, she and her brothers had been fed and kept clean. This child, John's child, looked like a ragamuffin and was starving to boot.

She knelt down in the dusty yard and held out her arms. "Poor baby. Come here to Aunty Viola."

Willie did so eagerly. Although unaware of his own miserable state, the pretty lady seemed to promise what, unconsciously, he yearned for — warmth, sweetness, a soft breast for comfort. Once in her arms, he gave a delighted squeal and held fast.

She kept her voice level so as not to alarm him, but over his head her eyes blazed with fury. "What's been done to this child is unconscionable, Mister Slaughter. He needs a bath, clean clothes, and decent food. And possibly a doctor. Why, I can feel his poor bones, and I don't like the way he was coughing. Give me your handkerchief."

John had been stunned into silence by the sight of his son. He'd left money with Mabel and Harvey Ryan for his and Addie's care, but they'd turned the boy out and used the money for themselves. Sick at heart, he gave her the handkerchief and watched as she wiped the child's streaming nose.

"Poor little mite. We'll have you better in no time. Can you smile for Aunty? Can you?"

Willie regarded her solemnly, as if he'd forgotten — or had never learned — how to smile.

"This child has been neglected," she said after a minute. "But no more. And I'll hear no more about sending him and Addie back to Texas, either. Their place is with us, with their father, no matter what. And I'm going to give those awful people . . . that dreadful woman . . . a piece of my mind! It's shameful is what it is!"

She turned on her heel and started walking, indignation in every line of her body. Over her shoulder she said: "While Willie has his bath, you're going to buy him some decent clothes and a pair of shoes, no matter what they cost. And something for Addie, too. We can't forget her, the dear thing."

At that moment, John knew he would forgive Viola anything — her tantrums about his gambling, her tight-fisted ways. She had opened her heart to his motherless waifs and taken them in, and that was what counted. They were a family, and she was at the center, dispensing love and down-to-earth pragmatism. By some stroke of good fortune, she was his. No. He shook his head. He was hers. And heaven help them all, he thought, when he returned and heard his wife's voice raised in wrath.

"You'll get me a tub of hot water this minute or I'll have the law on you for mistreating a child and stealing my husband's money that he gave you in good faith! God knows what you've done to Addie, though she's clean enough. But I'll find out. You can bet on it!"

Frightened, Willie began to cry, a high, thin wail, and Viola's voice lowered. "There, little one. No one's hurting you. We'll have you all clean in a trice, as soon as the water comes. *Won't we, Missus Ryan?*"

John couldn't hear the other woman's response, probably because she, too, was frightened out of her wits. His guess was proved correct when Mabel Ryan came scuttling toward him looking like a small, round spider.

"I didn't mean no harm, Mister Slaughter. Honest I didn't. I just couldn't take care of the both of them and run this hotel. Not with my Harvey laid up like he's been." She clasped her hands as if she were praying.

"Do what my wife w-wants," he stammered. "I'll settle with you later. And I *will* settle, Mabel."

She turned white and fled.

In the room he found Viola wielding scissors, locks of Willie's baby hair on the floor around both of them.

"Pray he doesn't have lice," she said in greeting.

"What's lice?" Addie, who was sitting on the bed enthralled, asked.

"Bugs," Viola answered.

Addie laughed. "Willie has bugs, Papa."

Viola turned, scissors in hand. "I haven't found any by some miracle. So be good and don't scare your brother. I'll be checking you next."

"No!" Addie ran to John and clasped his leg. "Don't let her find bugs, Papa!"

As if on cue, Willie shrieked and wriggled off the chair. "No-o-o bugs! No-o-o!"

Family life. John hadn't envisioned it as a mad house. He disengaged Addie's hands from his trouser leg and lifted her back onto the bed, then turned to Willie. "Be good and do what Aunty says." Then he beat a hasty retreat.

Viola seethed but tried not to show it. The little boy was skin stretched over bone, and he had bruises on his knees and shins. But for all that, he seemed a perfectly bright three year old, splashing in his bath and giggling when the water caught her in the face.

"Aunty's wet," he crowed in pleasure.

"Aunty Vi will take her bath later." She tried to sound stern but failed, and giggled instead.

Addie joined in, then asked: "Are you really our Aunty?"

"I guess I'm your step-mama. Your daddy and I are married."

"Are we going to stay with you? We don't like it here." Addie came to stand beside Viola, her eyes serious.

"Yes, indeed, because your daddy's been missing you, and because I always wanted a girl and boy of my own." And be damned to Mary Anne and her hateful predictions! These two needed her. And God knew how many other orphans there were in the world. If she had her way, she'd adopt them all.

"Bring me a towel," she said to Addie. "I'm putting you in charge as my helper."

"Because Willie's still a baby." Addie skipped over to the dresser where Mabel had left two skimpy towels. Handing one to Viola, she said: "Is Missus Ryan a bad lady?"

Viola sighed. How to explain? "Let's just say she should have kept you two together."

"I told her, but she wouldn't listen."

"Did you?" Viola pictured the scene and smothered a laugh.

"I told her my daddy would come back and be awful mad. That was before I knew he was bringing you. You yelled really loud."

At that, Viola's laughter bubbled over. "I guess I did."

Addie's eyes gleamed in admiration. "Yes," she said. "It was fine."

XIV

Home! They were headed home to a place near Charleston in the San Pedro Valley. Viola let her imagination run wild as she pictured a snug adobe house shaded by cottonwood trees. The children would have their own room, and a swing hung from one of the large tree branches. And she and John would have rest and privacy in a real bed behind a door that closed. Best of all, Bat would be around to supervise her cooking lessons. She was going to learn to cook so many things, to be a good wife to John and mother to the children, who were bouncing like excited puppies in the wagon.

She did her best to keep them occupied, teaching the names of the mountains, having them count the hawks and buzzards that spiraled overhead, riding the wind as easily as kites. But they were overjoyed at being with their father and new aunty, and their happiness spilled out, uncontrolled.

Viola could smell the river long before they reached it — the sweetness of water in dry, desert air, the darkness of old leaves rotting on the banks.

"Almost there!" she said to Addie and Willie. "Now how do you think I can tell?"

In unison they shook their heads. Viola sniffed the wind like a hound. "Use your noses. What do you smell?"

They imitated her so perfectly, John chuckled. "A real bunch of little Injuns."

"They need to learn about the country," Viola said. "It's their home now."

"So it is."

Addie interrupted. "Flowers. I smell flowers."

"What else?"

"Something soft."

Viola was delighted. "Very good! That's water. You can tell when it's close by, just like you can tell when it's raining, by using your nose."

Willie sneezed, and she took him on her lap. "You must cover your mouth when you do that," she instructed. "Will you remember next time?"

He sneezed again.

"His manners have been neglected along with everything else," she said.

John cleared his throat. "I have no doubt you'll take care of all that."

"Count on it!"

"Look there!" He pointed ahead, and she saw the river, its curving course marked by trees whose tops appeared to explode in the midday sun. On the far bank, cattle were grazing, taking advantage of the shade.

She squinted to read the brand, and was startled to see John's Z, a duplicate of Amazon's but on the right shoulder.

"Why," she said, "why those are ours! Where on earth did they come from?"

John smiled into his beard. Obviously the boys had been busy. There were enough unbranded cattle in Mexico to stock a hundred ranches, and everyone knew it and took advantage of the fact.

"Mexico." He pointed again, this time to the south. "There it is. Those mountains you see are almost at the border."

"So close. Yet so different from here."

"It is at that. A hot bed of renegade Apaches in addition to the rest." He slapped the reins once. "Now let's get across the river and see what they've done about a place for us to live."

She leaned forward, hands clasped. "Hurry!" she urged. "Hurry. I've waited long enough!"

Ten minutes later she was doing her best not to cry.

Called by the Spanish word, *jacal,* the house she had imagined was built out of ocotillo stalks held together with mud and frayed lengths of rope. The floor was hard-packed earth, the roof assorted branches laced together and covered with sacaton. Some of the ocotillo had begun to put out leaves that did little to disguise dangerous thorns. The door was a cowhide hung from a rod jammed between roof and walls.

On the hearth of the clay fireplace, Viola saw one of Mary Anne's treasured Dutch ovens, a pot that she remembered from childhood. Though Mary Anne had left her fine mahogany chest of drawers, her dining table and chairs on the trail to Montana, Sally had insisted on keeping the cooking pots.

"We don't need no chests. We got nothin' to put in 'em. But we all got to eat."

Funny how clear Sally was in memory, standing there beside the wagon, one arm around a tearful Mary Anne, determined to see her people through their troubles.

What was needed, and what Sally had in plenty, was courage. The frontier wasn't the place for weeping women, timid men. Somehow, her mother had made it through those difficult years, although they had shaped her, marked her, embittered her.

And if Mary Anne could do it, swallow one disappointment after another, so could she — Cora Viola Howell Slaughter — who had cast her lot with the man she loved, and who, because of that love, would do whatever was required of her.

She put her carpetbag down on the table — three rough planks on crude sawhorses — and squared her shoulders.

"Looks like my work's cut out for me," she said. "I'd best get to it."

XV

The summer rains were heavy and constant that year. Every afternoon, thunderclouds rose over the mountains, changing shape, feeding on their own energy, until at last they covered sun and sky and burst open in crashes of thunder.

The river swelled to the top of its banks, and the roof of the *jacal* leaked steadily, rivulets of muddy water that soaked the beds and turned the dirt floor to pudding.

Viola gave up trying to keep the house clean, the sheets and clothes washed. Mud was everywhere, and in the mud were toads, released by the rain and surging like a wave out of earth and into the fields and through the rawhide door. She stationed Willie and Addie at the opening with brooms Bat had made out of sacaton, with orders to sweep the creatures away. They worked diligently, accompanied by much shrieking, and Viola didn't know what irritated her more — the constant noise or the sight of the creatures skulking in corners and hopping underfoot.

At least she hadn't had any snakes inside,

she thought. Only toads, tarantulas, and vinegaroons that released their vile odor as soon as they were threatened.

She was trying to cook dinner, but it was impossible to concentrate. The air was sultry, made even hotter by the fire that, somehow, she'd managed to start with wet kindling. Her head ached; her hair had come out of its bun and hung in her eyes, glued to her skin by perspiration. Lord, she was dripping wet, and her hands were filthy. If, as Mary Anne was so fond of saying — "A man liked a pretty face." — then John would soon ride off and leave her with the screaming children, a pot of boiling potatoes, and an army of critters intent on storming the door.

She picked up a long-handled wooden fork and leaned over the kettle, so absorbed in her own misery that she never saw the toad sitting by the hearth. It picked that minute to jump against her leg and entangle itself in her petticoat. She screamed, tipped the potatoes and hot water onto the floor, just missing her feet. Everything ruined! Everything! Her dinner, her life, her sanity. Still screaming, she ran out the door toward the river, where John found her, trembling, her tears mixing with rain on a face smudged with mud and ashes.

"Ruined, ruined. Everything's spoiled!" She sobbed against his shoulder, unable to control herself, too weary to try. It seemed she'd been working like a field hand for months, learning to cook, keeping the dirt and dust at bay, lugging water for the family wash and hanging it up to dry, only to have to do it all over again a few days later. And what had she to show but potatoes on the floor?

"What's ruined?"

"Everything!"

"Come back to the house and get dry, my dear, then we'll see what's the matter."

She snorted through her tears. "House? It's not a house. It's a mud hole full of varmints."

"That bad?" He could feel her shaking, more from emotion than cold.

"Worse. Next thing, we'll have them in our bed."

He sighed. Sometimes he forgot how young she was. Perhaps he'd asked too much of her, first with the children, then with what even he had to admit were miserable quarters. He patted her shoulder, then took her hand. "Let's go see what I can do to help."

Reluctantly, she let him lead her back. Her headache was worse, and she'd had a nagging pain in her stomach all afternoon.

All she wanted was to lie down on dry sheets and sleep — and let supper take care of itself.

He saw Addie and Willie at their stations and the overturned kettle, potatoes lying in the muck. "Wash them off," he directed. "Get some clean water out of the barrel. Aunty Viola's going to lie down a while."

She held tightly to his arm. "Yes, please," she said, and then felt a rush of blood between her legs — warm, the blood of her womb. Oh, God! She had been so busy, she'd overlooked the fact that she'd missed her monthlies. And now she was losing a child. John's child. Hers. At the realization, she wept harder.

How she'd wanted a child of her own. And now, for a reason she couldn't understand, it was leaving her body as if fleeing from a foreign place. She was not wanted. Her body was unsuitable. She lay down and tasted tears, bitterness, the emptiness of a leaking and useless vessel.

"I want my mother," she whispered, and was stunned that, truly, she longed for Mary Anne, the touch of one who had loved and lost several children.

Her blood was on his clothes. He knew enough to understand what was happening, but not why, and he called to Addie who was dutifully washing each potato and dropping it back into the pot.

"Call Tad," he said. "He's out in the south pasture. Tell him to go get Missus Howell and quick. Can you do that?"

Addie read his pain, denied it in herself. Aunty Vi was ailing, and the burden rested on her own narrow shoulders, the swiftness of her feet. "Yes," she said. "Yes, I can." Then she was gone, a tiny figure parting the tall grasses, a black speck in the hugeness of afternoon.

Viola drifted in and out of consciousness. It seemed that she and Stonewall were back in Nevada, huddled together by the fire — for comfort more than for warmth.

"Stay here," Amazon had told them. "Don't bother your mother unless she calls for you."

From behind the closed door they could hear their mother's moans. Once she screamed, and the sound cracked through the stillness like breaking glass.

"Is Mama going to die?" Stonewall whispered, clutching his sister's shoulders.

If she said what she thought, she'd say yes, and then it would happen, and she and her brother would be alone here, keeping watch over the dead.

"I don't know, Stoney," she whispered back.

"What's the matter with her?"

"A baby's coming."

He shut his eyes. "Don't want a baby. I want Mama."

"So do I," she said. "So do I."

By the time Amazon returned with the doctor, the baby had been born and had died. It was buried quickly. They never saw its face.

"Don't cry any more. It won't help." Mary Anne wiped her daughter's forehead where the dark curls were matted with sweat. "You aren't the first to lose a child, though it hurts every time, God knows."

"John," Viola whispered.

"He's outside. Soon as you're cleaned up, I'll call him. Hush, now. You're messing your face."

She didn't give a fig about her face. It was her body that had betrayed her. The body she'd never thought about, worried about, had betrayed her — and John.

"She'll be all right." In spite of herself, Mary Anne took pity on her son-in-law. He was haggard, his expression anguished. "I . . . I didn't know," he said. "She never told me."

"I doubt she knew herself. It was too early. But there's time enough for a family, John."

"I lost one wife. I couldn't stand to lose Viola."

He meant it, bless him. Possibly he was a better man than she'd given him credit for. She reached out and patted his arm. "Go on in. But she needs to sleep."

"I guess I ruined everything." Viola's voice was weak.

John knelt beside the bed. "You're all right. That's all that counts."

She saw his worried eyes, and how his mouth drooped at the corners, read devotion in every gesture. "Next time. . . ."

"Next time I'll take care this doesn't happen. I'll take care of *you*."

"I'm so sorry," she said.

He leaned and kissed her cheek. "Be well, my dear."

"Ummm." She was almost asleep.

The rain had stopped. In its place, without warning, they heard the singing that rose from the riverbanks, a music that wound around them, the *jacal,* the darkness of night like a silver wire or the vibration of Bat's fiddle strings.

Viola opened her eyes. "Listen!" she said. "What on earth?"

"Toads. Calling each other."

She lay back on the pillow, exhausted but with a growing excitement. Out of the mouths of those repulsive creatures came magic — a chorus of exultation, a celebration of life — and it was joyful, insistent, too demanding to be ignored. Instinctively, she understood.

You sang to your mate, crooned in your throat, threw up your head to the sky and embraced the world and the one you loved. And you put fear, pain, loss out of mind and went on making music, moving in rhythm with the ancient dance and giving thanks.

"Next time," she murmured, reaching for his hand. "Next time I promise." And fell asleep.

When he came into the front room, he found Mary Anne braiding Addie's hair. She looked up briefly. "Asleep?"

"Yes." He sat down on a bench and drummed his fingers on the table. "When . . . when she's up to it, I wonder if you'd take her to your place. I have to leave for Hermosillo to pick up some cattle, and I'd rather not leave her alone."

Mary Anne gave a dry chuckle and pushed Addie off her lap. "She won't like it."

"Can't be helped."

"You'll have to be firm. She'll say she's going, no matter what."

"Not this time."

"Who's going to tell her?"

John stood up. "I'll do it in the morning."

XVI

As they expected, Viola was furious. Sick or well, she would go with her husband, and that was that.

"I say, I say . . . I didn't think you were a fool, Viola. But you're beginning to convince me." John paced the floor beside the bed, startled at his wife's vehemence.

She pushed herself up, anger giving her strength. "How dare you, Mister Slaughter!"

"I dare, my dear, because I don't want to lose you. You and the children are going to your parents. I've made up my mind, and that's that."

She punched the pillow with impotent wrath. "I hate it! Hate having my mind made up by somebody else! Even you. I hate being in bed. I've never been sick in my life, and I'm not now. I want to go."

He thought she might fly at him if he attempted to touch and comfort her, but Christ she was lovely in her anger. Hair tumbling down, dark eyes made larger, brighter by hot tears. He jammed his hands in his pockets.

"The answer is still no," he said and, turning, left the room. Behind him he heard the thud of her pillow as it hit the wall.

Of course, he was right. And so was her mother, much as she hated to admit it. She wasn't up to the long trip to Hermosillo. Even the buggy ride to her parents' milk ranch was tiring.

Amazon had, for once, been lucky. When he and Mary Anne arrived in the valley, he'd sold off his herd and bought the ranch and the dairy cows from a widow who wanted to return to Tennessee. The sale included a stone-floored adobe house and the Mexican couple who had worked on the place.

It was the house Viola had imagined for herself — shaded by cottonwoods, thick-walled, with a massive wooden door and shutters that could be closed and barred against any trouble, including marauding Apaches.

"By the time I'm home, you'll be well again," John said, kissing her good bye.

"Hurry back." She held to him for a minute, fighting down fear. If anything happened to him. . . .

He read her mind. "Nothing's going to happen. Don't worry."

Other women were brave. Left behind,

they went about their lives, taking on duties and doing a man's work, and if they had fears, they kept them hidden lest the children, too, be frightened.

She clenched her teeth to keep her chin steady and stepped back. "Go with God," she said, and watched him mount the gray and ride off down the valley, watched until the distance swallowed him and he was one with grass and plain.

Amazon came up behind her. "Don't fret, child. The man has work to do, and you can't be around every minute."

"I just have a feeling," she said. "I can't explain it."

He chalked that up to her miscarriage. In his experience, women were prone to fancy at such times. "Put it out of your head. It can't help and might hurt. And your mother and Inez have supper nearly ready."

Obediently, Viola spent the next few weeks doing as she was told. She ate, she slept, she began teaching Addie her letters, but a part of her was cut off, shut away. A part of her brooded and mourned, not only for herself but for the lost child, for the emptiness she carried within, as if at any moment she or John could disappear, be taken by the wind and dispersed in the vastness of the valley. Life hung by a thread as illusory as a spider's web, and no one, least of all herself, knew the precise time when the thread would be broken.

She was at the corral watching Stonewall break a horse. He had a way with them and, in addition to helping Amazon, had begun to work on the rough strings belonging to several local ranchers.

"I call this one Traveler," he said over his shoulder. "He's one of those Nez Percé horses that found his way down here." The horse, white with leopard spots, stood in the middle of the corral, eyes showing white, muscles bunched.

"He looks like a handful," she said. "And how do you know where he came from?"

"We saw enough of them up north. Don't you remember?"

She didn't. Anything to do with Indians had been blotted out, and, besides, it was Stoney who went chasing after horses as if he wanted to own every one he saw.

"Are you going to ride him now?" She had a vision of her brother, bones shattered, face down in the dust.

"Not today. I've got a hunch about this one. He's smart, and he's thinking, but right now he doesn't much like or trust me. I could take the buck out of him, but he wouldn't be broke. Today I'm just getting him used to the sight and sound of me."

She relaxed. One less life to worry about. At least for the day.

The sound of a horse coming fast caused them both to turn and squint down the lane that led to the house. She recognized the horse before she identified the rider, and stood for a second, one hand to her throat as if to still the scream.

"It's Tad!" And then she was running, lifting her skirt high above her boots, her white stockings flashing in the sunlight.

"John!" The word hung in the air between them like a dust mote.

"Miz Slaughter . . . ma'am." Tad dismounted, came toward her, hands stretched out to catch her if she fell.

"It's John. Isn't it?"

He bobbed his head, couldn't meet her eyes, couldn't bear to see her expression. "Miz Slaughter . . . we were ambushed on our way back. Mexican bandits. I was . . . I was riding point . . . out ahead when they jumped the others. Mister Slaughter, he yelled at me to keep going, to get to you. I wanted to fight but he . . . he cussed me out good. Last I saw, they were surrounded. It looked mighty bad."

No husband. No child. No solid ground anywhere. She'd been right to fear, wrong to stay behind. Better to have gone and died fighting alongside him, to let the buzzards pick their flesh, their bones sink into common ground.

She fought the pain, the blackness behind her eyes. Had he suffered? Gone quickly? No one knew, not Tad standing beside her, not herself. And his body lay in some un-named, unmarked place in an alien country far from home. It wasn't right.

She wiped her eyes on her sleeve, then stood straight, disregarding Tad's hand on her shoulder. When she spoke, it was slowly, each word enunciated as if she had just learned the language. "I am going to bring him back."

"Ma'am! You can't!"

"You'll kill yourself, Sis." That was Stoney who'd followed her.

"Yes . . . I . . . can." Again the painful spacing between words. "And I will. With or without you."

"Ma'll have a hissy."

Color flooded back into her face. "Ma be damned! Hissy or no hissy, can't or won't, I'm going to bring my husband's body home for a decent burial. And there's an end to ar-gument."

Without waiting to hear further, she spun on her heel and walked quickly toward the house, the men following her, looking at each other helplessly.

"Don't argue with her," Stoney advised. "It'll only make it worse. She don't know what she's in for, and, believe me, she don't care. We'll just have to go along and try to keep her out of trouble."

They left the next morning, Viola driving the wagon with Stoney and Tad as outriders, leaving an outraged Mary Anne and a stoic Amazon behind.

The children hadn't been told. Time enough when their father's body was put in the ground, when the mourners gathered, when the dream had come to its end.

"Aunty Vi's going to meet your daddy," she told them, holding back tears with an iron will. "You stay right here and be good, and I'll be back before you can blink. You hear?"

Addie put her arms around Viola's neck. "I want to come, too. I want my daddy."

She buried her face in the child's hair and prayed for strength, for the ability to be a mother to Addie and her brother, now orphans for real. "No, honey," she whispered after a minute. "It's a long, hard trip. Maybe some other time." Except there would be no other time. Never again. She stood up quickly, turned away, hiding the tears that couldn't be hidden, and without looking back climbed unassisted onto the seat of the wagon.

Two riders pulled up and watched the slow procession.

"Who d'you think that is?"

"Nesters. Just what we don't need any of."

The bigger man squinted. "Looks to me like part of the Slaughter outfit. There's a woman in the wagon."

"What's a woman doing out here?"

"Let's go see!" He slapped his reins on his horse's rump and took off at a lope, pulling up alongside Viola and staring at her with barely disguised lust.

"It's Missus Slaughter, ain't it? Billy Clanton. This's my brother Ike. We're neighbors." He grinned, and the expression in his eyes reminded Viola of a wolf.

What on earth did he want from her? Whatever it was, she wasn't about to give anything away, not to one such as he. "I'm Missus Slaughter," she said, her voice cold.

"I was looking for your husband. He at home?"

She bit her lip before answering. "No. He isn't. But . . . but I expect he will be shortly. Is there a message?"

He shook his head. "Naw. Just wondered

if he was around anywheres."

"I'll be sure and tell him we met." She picked up the reins in dismissal, aware that his eyes lingered on her body for what seemed too long a time. Trash! That was it. Both these men were trash, neighbors or not. "Good afternoon, Mister Clanton."

She drove off without looking back, and after a minute said to Tad: "I lied. Don't say it. But I didn't like those men. And what's happened isn't their business."

She seemed so small, sitting there on the wagon seat, small but tough for all a good wind could have blown her away. "You did right, ma'am," he said. "The boss has run them off once or twice for takin' what's not theirs to take, if you get my meaning."

She clucked to the horse. "Sometimes I wonder if anybody out here is civilized," she said. "And sometimes it isn't worth thinking about." But in spite of herself she kept picturing the two brothers, their pale eyes and how they sat their horses, as if they were looking for trouble and knew just where to find it.

It seemed to her that they moved in slow motion down the valley, along the river, heat waves dancing, San José Peak and Cananea dancing in the distance, and the little slant-sided mesa that she kept watching, neither mountain nor hill, simply a small, distorted cone rising out of the hot and rippling ocean that was grass — and herself lost in it, lost in a continent of loneliness, a widow on a quest, a lone female on a wagon seat headed into Mexico to bring back the remains of what had been, what in her mind would always be, a great and enduring love.

XVII

Tad rode ahead, watching for any sign of Indians or Mexican bandits. You went into Mexico, you took your chances. John Slaughter had understood that, and look where it got him. He was dead, but Tad had no intentions of endangering the lady boss any more than she'd already done by insisting on this journey.

It was a sorry business, and her not well. She was a tough little thing, but he'd seen how she nearly fell over from exhaustion when they'd camped the night before — how white she was, and how her eyes seemed too big for her face.

With any luck, he'd find the bodies first.

Or what was left of them. He was going to spare her that much, at least — the sight of death and what happened after. Out here, it didn't take long for a body to disappear, not with a thousand hungry critters in search of a meal, and the sun burning down like a brand.

At the thought, he spurred his horse into a lope and rode up a small rise. From the top he'd be able to see ahead and behind, spot danger, if it was possible to spot those damned Indians in their disguises, the *bandidos* who knew every hidey hole in the country.

The wagon was coming slowly along a bed of rock, Stoney riding beside, his young face set. A good kid, one who didn't panic easily. Any sign of Indian trouble, he knew what he had to do. If necessary, he'd shoot his sister. Better dead than a prisoner of the Apaches.

Damn it all! He'd left life on the farm to find adventure. Only what he'd found was harsh reality — not that much different from home, except that out here death lurked in a thousand places and didn't wait patiently to take you in old age.

He spat out dust, reached for his canteen. They'd made a dry camp the night before, and it was imperative that he find water for the horses before they camped again. Regretfully, he limited himself to one swallow.

In the distance something was moving. He squinted hard, saw dust and what looked like a team of horses pulling an unwieldy wagon. But the country played tricks. He'd seen mirages — on the plains, in the middle of the desert — seen the enormous reflections of men on horseback, lakes of water where nothing existed but sand.

Motionless, he sat watching, shaking his head at what he thought he saw. If that wasn't Bat and the chuck wagon, he'd eat his hat. Cautiously he rode down the rise toward what he hoped was more than a ghostly vision.

"No, suh! We ain't dead! Mister Slaughter, he's comin' behind with the herd." Bat's grin split his face into two parts.

"How?" Tad slumped in his saddle, too stunned to talk.

"They made it to the pile of rocks where I was and holed up. Then we shot it out. There's six dead men back there, but they ain't us."

"You're sure?"

Bat's grin disappeared. "Now why would I make a joke over that?"

"You wouldn't. But just the same, I've got the lady boss comin' behind with a wagon to get the body."

"Then you better go tell her there ain't no body. Leastways, no dead one. And don't go scarin' her. You break it to her easy. That's a fine lady."

"He's alive! John's alive?" All the determination that had held her body upright vanished, and she huddled on the seat, her face in her hands, tears coming unchecked. So many tears! How could one person produce such a flowing, and where did they come from? She wept and didn't stop until Bat pulled up and came to her side.

"You goin' to mess your pretty face," he said in a parody of her mother. "And Mister John, he sets a store by that face. Now you come on down here and set in the shade and let Bat get you something to eat. I bet you ain't ate right in a week."

It seemed longer. It seemed a year since food had any appeal, since life itself was anything but forced labor. She had lost a child and a husband, except that John was alive. She couldn't quite take that in, couldn't quite believe what they were telling her. Hope was such a precarious emotion, prey to dangers she couldn't name, couldn't begin to imagine. Fear hovered, held her by the throat, refused her permission to believe what the men were saying.

And then he came riding on his big gray — out of the haze of dust and distance — and if he was surprised to see her, she couldn't tell, couldn't find words to ask. He was real, and she was in his arms, and they were strong and solid. That was what she knew the moment before she fainted.

When she came to, she was lying on her bedroll in the shade of the wagon, and John was kneeling beside her.

"It's true. You're really here!" She pushed herself up on one elbow. With her other hand she reached out and touched his cheek.

"I'm here," he said. "But you shouldn't be."

"I wasn't about to leave you in this place. I wanted you home . . . where you belong."

Her obvious adoration touched him. "Wh . . . when it's my time, I'll die in bed," he said. "Out here's for the living. For you, and me, and the children. You don't ever have to worry about me."

"Men!" she said scornfully. "You think you're invincible!"

He looked at her a long time before answering. "But I am, Viola," he said. "Believe it. I am."

XVIII

She sat as close to John on the wagon seat as propriety allowed, and once in a while reached out to touch his sleeve, as if to reassure herself. He was alive, and she felt her own life singing in her veins. How different everything looked now! The cottonwoods lush with summer, their leaves in constant, glittering motion, the craggy Huachuca Mountains buttressing sky, the Mule Mountains, softer, the soil under oak and juniper a dark red, indicative of the mineral wealth that lay hidden below the surface.

"Probably not silver like over at Tombstone," John said in answer to her question. "But it won't be long before someone comes along and finds whatever it is. This country's going to bust wide open, mark my words, and I aim to supply all the beef I can."

He frowned, and sensitive to his moods she asked: "What's the matter with that?"

"When they start coming, it'll mean the end of the range. We'll need our own place ... plenty of grass and water. I've even been thinking about Oregon."

"Oregon!" The very idea of it horrified her. "What's wrong with where we are?" she demanded, then laughed. "Apart from the house."

"The range is already crowded, and new folks are coming every month. Now I've got this herd and the one coming in from Texas this winter. About Oregon . . . it's just a thought."

She hoped he kept it that way, even if she did have to live in what she called to herself "a picket house."

As if he'd read her mind, he said: "About the house . . . before I left I gave orders to have one built. It should be ready before Christmas."

She clasped his arm. "A house? A real one?"

He chuckled. "I say, Vi . . . do you have to repeat everything?"

"Yes," she said. "Just to make sure." Then she threw her arms around him. Be damned to propriety! He was alive, and she loved him down to her toes in her sturdy boots. She'd have a house with solid walls and a roof that didn't threaten to collapse. And, if the gods were good, a cookstove instead of that hated fireplace that threatened her every move.

"A door," she said breathlessly. "Will it have a door we can close?"

He glanced at her out of the corner of his eye and saw her hope imposed on the trials she'd endured for his sake, and he patted her knee. "The door," he said with great satisfaction, "is in Bat's wagon. I bought it myself in Hermosillo. A present for you, my dear, I hope one of many."

True to his word, the house was ready in early December — four rooms with plank floors and the carved door from Mexico to shut out weather and what Viola labeled, in no uncertain terms, "varmints."

This was happiness, she thought, as she went from room to room exclaiming. A home of her own and a ready-made family. The memory of her recent miscarriage brought a moment's pain, but she pushed it away. What was done was done, and the future was bright.

"We'll have a tree," she told the children. "And a real Christmas."

"What's Christmas?" Willie looked doubtful.

Startled, she knelt down beside him. Why, the poor child had no idea of anything, no memories to hold to, pleasurable or otherwise.

"It's a celebration," she said, her arms around him. "It's Christ's birthday, only we all get the presents."

"What's presents?"

How to explain? She sat back on her heels and thought, then said: "A present is something you've wished for with all your heart. And sometimes, on Christmas, your wish comes true."

"I want a pony," he said.

Addie came to stand beside them. "Me, too."

"Ponies," Viola repeated, revising her vision of caps and scarves, sticks of candy, a new dress for Addie. "I see. Well. . . ."

"Why not?" John asked, when she reported the conversation. "We can't be carrying them on our saddles forever. They're old enough. And besides, your brother's got two ponies nearly ready."

Once again, he'd surprised her. "How do you always know what's in people's minds?"

"Better that way," he said. "No surprises for anybody."

And that, she decided, was how he managed to stay alive — with a kind of intuition, an animal sense that read the unspoken, deciphered scents and sounds that rode the air. It was a gift that benefited them all, particularly herself.

With John she had a sense of security she'd found in no one else, certainly not her own family, much as she loved them. With John she was able to relax, to be herself, and the discovery of just who that self was brought her a happiness she'd never known.

"Can I . . . can we afford a shopping trip?" she asked. "To Tombstone? It is almost Christmas."

He couldn't refuse her. "As long as you go easy."

She threw her arms around his neck. "I'll go tomorrow. Just for little things, I promise. But won't it be fun to have Christmas in our first real home?"

"It will. Shall we invite your family? Don't worry. Bat can take over the cooking."

Smiling, she agreed. Now she could entertain and be able to hold up her head.

"And maybe some of the neighbors?" he asked.

Viola's smile was replaced by a frown. "Not if you mean those Clanton boys. I've never seen such a disgusting pair. There's something wrong with both of them, Mister Slaughter. And I won't have them in the house."

He raised his eyebrows. "I say, Vi, isn't that a little harsh?"

"No!" She stamped her foot. "That big

brute Billy came by when I was setting out with Tad for Mexico. He was looking for you, and I swear, if I'd given him any encouragement, he'd have come along. And as for his brother. . . ." Her nose twitched. "He *smells*."

John stifled a laugh. What she said was true enough, but he'd come to an agreement with all his disreputable neighbors, some of whom he'd brought into the valley along with his cattle. They left him alone, and he turned his back on their forays outside the law.

"Better let Tad drive you to Tombstone," he said, changing the subject. "God forbid you should run into Billy."

She peered into his eyes. "Are you laughing at me?"

"No, my dear. But I don't think you should travel alone, and, right now, I can't go with you. Besides, Tombstone's not the place for a lady by herself."

"You think I can't take care of myself."

He shook his head. "I don't think you should have to. Do you?"

Put that way, she had to admit he was right. Billy Clanton had frightened her more than she wanted to admit, and who knew who she would find in town or on the way there?

She hugged him again. "I'll take Tad. And I'll find you a wonderful present. I've been saving my house money."

"You are the best present I've ever had," he said. "I don't need much else."

XIX

Tad dropped her off at the San José House and repeated John's warnings. "When you're ready, send somebody for me. This place is full of riffraff."

As she stood looking around, she realized that the town had more than doubled in size in only a few months. It was like an ant hill, teeming with activity. Ore wagons, freight wagons, strings of mules and burros passed in a steady flowing down the dusty streets, and the wooden sidewalks were crowded with men and women going about their varied chores. It was noisy, colorful, and alive, and she responded to it with that part of her that loved gaiety of any kind, be it parties, dances, or merely good conversation.

"Don't worry about me," she said to Tad with a grin. "I'll be fine."

"Mister Slaughter's orders." He tipped

his hat and drove off to the livery, hoping it was all right to leave her.

Viola stepped into the small lobby, blinking at the sudden contrast with the brilliant light from the street, and didn't notice the sharp glance of the woman behind the desk.

"I'll need a room for two nights," she said.

"We're full up." The words were ungracious and unexpectedly harsh, and for a moment Viola was startled.

"Oh, dear. Now where will I go? We always stay here, you know." She gave a tentative smile, and the proprietress leaned across the counter.

"My gracious, Missus Slaughter, is it you?"

"It certainly is."

The woman waved her hands in a placating gesture. "Lordy! I didn't recognize you. Thought you were somebody else. I can't have single women, you know. It leads to trouble, 'specially in this town where we've got all the trouble we can handle and some left over. Sure I have a room. The one at the end of the hall, same as always. But if you don't mind, I'll have your supper sent in. There's a political meeting in the dining room tonight, not the place for you, if you don't mind my saying so."

It appeared that she wasn't safe anywhere

in town, Viola thought. The place was worse than the whole of Lincoln County, probably because most of those who had deserved their place on Governor Wallace's list had headed here where they were free to make as much trouble as they wished. And she and John were responsible for bringing some of them. With determination, she forced that idea out of her mind. People did what they had to do as best as they could, and neither she nor John had looked any further into the future than leaving New Mexico. At least she hadn't.

With an effort, she resumed the conversation. "A political meeting? What about?"

The proprietress let indignation spill out. "Town lots, is what. Folks came here early on and set up businesses, then along comes the mayor and what they call 'The Town Lot Company,' who say we don't own the property we're setting on. Says we got to pay or get out, and there's those of us who don't aim to do either one, seeing as we already paid once."

"It doesn't sound right."

"It doesn't, and it isn't, and there's plenty of hot tempers set to go off. Maybe right in my own dining room. That's why I say, take your supper in your room, and stay out of it."

Viola picked up her bag and took the key. "I'll just have a bath and supper and go to bed early, then. I have shopping to do in the morning."

Regardless of her intentions, she lay awake until long after midnight. Sleep was impossible in the racket that drifted in from the street, the shouting that echoed from the dining room, occasional gunshots that frightened her so that she pulled her pillow over her head and lay waiting for a stray bullet to fly through the window.

John had been right, and Tad, when they called Tombstone no town for a lady.

She was awakened by the shouts of a mob and the screeching of what sounded like metal being dragged over rock. A glance out the window told her nothing. She dressed quickly and went down the hall.

"What on earth?" she said to the proprietress who looked, if possible, even more distraught than she had the night before.

"It's those men I told you about. With the town lots. They're moving poor Mister Reilly's house into the street."

"Whatever for?"

"Eviction. They're kickin' him off his own property." The woman's mouth snapped shut.

Viola had a vivid picture of a house in

ruins. "Is anyone hurt?"

"Nobody's home. Reilly's out of town. If he was here, he'd shoot the cowards." She waved a hand toward the empty dining room. "Best eat some breakfast while you can."

"I will, and thank you," Viola said. "But can't the law do anything about all this?"

The woman laughed. "The law around here is . . . if you can get away with it, it's legal. We're going from bad straight to the devil, and the country with us, and nobody man enough to take charge except maybe one of those Earps."

Viola buttered a piece of toast. "Who are they?"

"Brothers. Come here, like most, hoping to strike it rich, but they're honest at least. Wyatt's deputy sheriff. It was him who put Curly Bill in jail after Marshal White was killed, and over this same problem. Curly said it was an accident, but there's a lot of us that has doubts."

Viola stopped chewing and stared. "Curly!" she exclaimed. "Goodness, I know him."

The woman gave her a hard look. "I wouldn't admit it, if I was you. He runs with a bad crowd. Those Clantons and that Ringo fella. Your neighbors, come to think of it."

"I see," Viola murmured, although she wasn't sure she did. But she did remember her unease when they had left New Mexico, and how some of the men, and Curly in particular, had aroused her dislike. At the mention of the Clantons she remembered only the circumstances of that painful day and the two men staring at her, one with obvious lust, the other as if she was no more to him than an annoyance, an obstacle in his path.

Her little kingdom, that had seemed so secure, had revealed cracks in its structure. Suddenly, irrationally, she longed for home and John, who would put all her worries to rest.

In bed, in the crook of his arm two nights later, Viola brought up the subject of her fears.

"Curly was one of ours," she said. "And Joe Hill. And that . . . that Ringo creature. And now they're outlaws."

His arm tightened beneath her, but all he said was: "Do you expect me to be responsible for men's characters?"

She pushed herself up. "Yes," she said, "if that means we've brought outlaws into the territory. Maybe we'd better be more careful."

"They'd have come with or without us," he said. "Leave well enough alone, my dear, and don't trouble your pretty head." He bent and kissed her, but to his surprise she pulled away.

"But, Mister Slaughter, these men are terrorizing everybody."

"And because they are who they are, you won't kiss me good night?"

"I'm trying to understand. Trying to make sure we don't make the same mistake again."

He sighed and pulled her closer, seeing no way to explain the close-knit network of rustling that went on, and that would continue to go on in the territory, with or without him.

"Will you stop worrying about it?" he whispered against her hair. "Just leave it to me and trust my judgment." And he was relieved when she relaxed against him and opened her mouth for a kiss that, for him, blotted out any necessity to explain the tangled affairs of the soon to be formed county of Cochise.

XX

Willie left the house and went out to the corral where his pony was cropping grass. *His* pony! Excitement and happiness bubbled up in his throat until he felt he was going to burst. Now he could ride out with his father and Aunty Vi like a real man, mounted on his own horse — the gray pony that was a miniature of his father's and that now came over and stood looking at him.

"Hello," Willie whispered, his voice catching in wonder. "Hello, Christmas."

The name slipped out before he thought; a good name, he decided. Every time he said it, he'd remember this astonishing day — the scent of the wild turkeys Bat was roasting in the new iron stove, and how he and Addie and Aunty Vi had made popcorn and threaded it on strings for decoration. And how he'd felt when his father had brought him and Addie outside and helped them get on the two ponies — his gray, Addie's a brown and white pinto.

He wriggled through the fence and put his arms around the sturdy neck and felt the warmth of the animal even through his new jacket — warmth and something like how it was when Aunty Vi hugged him — an explosion of goodness, as if everything that was wrong had come right, and he was safe in a place where hunger and loneliness never came.

"Christmas," he said again, and the horse turned its head and nuzzled his ear, blowing warm, sweet-scented breath.

From the door of the house Viola watched. "Come see," she called to John. "Come see your son."

He stood beside her, one arm around her waist. "He'll make a horseman," he said. "Thanks to you."

"To us, Mister Slaughter," she said. "We've done it together, and that's how it should be."

From overhead came a sudden, wild music, and they looked up to see a formation of cranes flying into the sunset, their motion like a dance to an ancient song.

In the corral, Willie stood, his face turned up to the sky, his mouth open in wonder.

Viola leaned her head against John's shoulder. "I think we've just been blessed," she said.

Three weeks later, huddled next to a campfire made of twigs and cow chips, she remembered her words and wondered if, instead, they had been cursed.

She, John, and Addie had taken the train as far as the Río Grande where they met their third Texas herd — two thousand five hundred longhorns possessed of one thought — to stay on the east bank of the river.

From the opposite side, Viola and Addie had watched as the boys pushed the cattle toward the crossing, only to have them turn off and stampede away in all directions.

"Cattle," she said crossly. "They're dumber than sheep. Why does anybody bother?"

"Because they're gold on the hoof," John answered. "You know it as well as I do." He spurred his horse and rode down to the river edge to confer with John Swain, his black foreman who'd brought the herd from Texas.

When he came back, he was grim-faced. "Swain's got an idea. It's tricky, but it might work."

Her hands tensed on the reins. "What is he going to do?"

John studied the river, a steel-blue ribbon between sandy banks. "Water's low right now. Those cows don't even have to swim, if they only knew it. But they haven't seen a river since the Pecos, so they're spooked. Swain's fixing to drag a couple while the boys try to drive the rest behind. It might work, or it might not. But I want you and Addie back with Bat, out of the way."

"And you?" she asked. "What are you going to do?"

"I'll be right here, pushing them to high ground."

"Be careful."

He studied her face. "Don't worry. It's not my time."

There he went again. So sure of himself. She wished she could be as certain, but she never shared his faith and optimism. Life was too full of danger. She knew it and hated the fact. Obediently, she clucked to the horse and drove the buggy toward the chuck wagon set up in the lee of a brush-covered sandhill.

Bat offered her a cup of coffee from the big enamel pot he kept hot on the fire. "Can't have you freezin' yourself," he said. "Or you, missy." Addie was a favorite. For her he'd brought along a package of the Mexican chocolate she loved.

Viola warmed her hands on the steaming cup and watched the scene across the river. Behind the massed and restless herd, the

Organ Mountains, a barrier of crags, turrets, twisted rock, blocked the way to the east and the desert of white sand, while to the north and south the Río Grande wound itself between bare cottonwoods and pink sandhills. In all the wide stretch that she could see, only cattle and riders were moving, a living flood of mottled bodies and flashing horns. Suddenly she closed her eyes. "I can't watch."

Bat patted her shoulder. "Don't you fret. John Swain's nobody's fool. If he says he's gonna do something, it's as good as done, and Mister Slaughter, he's got an angel sits on his shoulder."

Addie giggled. "Where?"

"Why, right there." Bat pointed down to where John sat his big gelding. "I can see him plain as day."

What Addie saw was a spiral of dust rising, caught by the afternoon sun, whirling overhead and shining like flakes of gold.

"I see him, too!" her child's voice rang out. "Aunty Vi, look!"

Bat winked at Viola. "What'd I tell you? You just listen to old Bat who's been with your daddy since before you was born."

Oh, to be a child again, Viola thought. To have such belief. But with love came danger, the insidious fears that at times rendered her helpless. What would become of them all in this empty land with only their wits, their puny strength standing between them and destruction?

"I see," she forced herself to say, then turned and faced away.

With an expertise born of years handling ornery range steers, John Swain roped one of the leaders and urged his horse, a muscled sorrel, toward the river. Simultaneously Tad and Stoney did the same.

"Come on you bone-headed sons-of-bitches!" Swain's voice rose above the din as, reluctantly, the steer began to follow.

It was risky as they all knew. A maddened steer could as easily charge a rider as come along tamely, and with the rope tied fast, Texas-style, rider and horse had few choices — run or cut loose and hope you did it before a horn gored your horse and you got thrown and trampled.

Swain went down the low bank and into the water with the steer that, discovering its footing, crossed calmly, reached the opposite shore, and then bawled for company.

Stoney crossed next, and then Tad. Behind them, riders pushed the herd, forcing them into a narrow opening where their only choice was to follow their leaders and cross the river.

In mid-stream, Tad's steer, pushed from behind, lowered its head and charged horse and rider, but, hampered by the muck of the river bottom, lost its footing, fell, and lay still, a dead weight at the end of Tad's rope. Just like a cow to quit and leave you in a tight spot, Tad thought as his horse struggled for its own footing, while a thousand longhorns hit the water behind them. He reached for the knife he carried in a scabbard, his fingers hampered by the gloves he wore. He'd been in tight spots and lived to tell about them, but a glance over his shoulder told him this was one of the worst.

Fumbling, he sawed at the taut rope, watched it fray too slowly for comfort. "Come on," he muttered, and heard his teeth grinding, heard the cattle sloshing the water close behind. He spurred his horse, and it leaped forward, snapping what was left of the rope and scrambling up the bank a stride ahead of the oncoming herd.

"That was close!" John pulled up alongside.

"Too damn' close." Tad's face was white under his perpetual tan. "Why I ever wanted to be a cowman beats me."

John smiled. "It's a sickness. Can't be cured."

"Except by accident." Tad wiped his face

on his sleeve. "Here they come. You want to point them upriver?"

John spun his horse around. "There's good grass up there."

"And the weather's due to change."

"Change or not. They're waiting for us at Fort Bayard. We'll push on tomorrow." Once there, they would have shelter, and he had the women to worry about. Still, it was a comfort to have Viola with him. At that, he squinted up the hill where she and Addie stood watching, probably aghast at Tad's close escape.

"Be back in a minute," he said, and put his big horse into a lope.

XXI

Tad had been right. The morning dawned cold and overcast, and the wind had a bite to it, a taste like cold iron. Above the Organs, the sky was streaked with red, a distant fire that gave no warmth and promised none.

Bat sniffed the air. "Snow comin'," he said. "You can smell it plain. Best keep under that buffalo robe today."

Viola was shivering. Even hot coffee and

biscuits weren't enough to warm her. "How soon?" she asked.

He sniffed again. "Weather makes its own rules. If it gets too bad, you and young miss ride in the chuck wagon out of the wind."

Addie was already shivering, but kept quiet. She had pleaded to be able to come along, had sworn she'd not be in the way or ask for special treatment. Now she sipped her chocolate and pretended imperviousness to storm and cold, when all she wanted was to burrow back into her blankets like a little animal safe in its den.

Viola had a sixth sense where Addie was concerned. "I'll drive the buggy," she said to Bat. "But Addie can go with you."

He looked from woman to child and nodded. "Missy, go get your blankets and pile 'em up back of my seat. That way we can talk and maybe even sing, if we feels like it. No storm's gonna bother us." He turned back to Viola. "You be all right?"

"If not, I'll holler."

"Make sure you do." He gave orders with the confidence of familiarity.

"Yes, sir," Viola said, grinning, used to his over-protective ways and enjoying them. With John and Bat she was safe, and the knowledge was comforting.

And she needed that comfort as the day

went on and the cold deepened like a chasm, surrounded her, threatened to steal her breath, a white cloud that hung in the air and frosted her eyelashes, numbed the tip of her nose. Behind her, the herd moved slowly, hoofs hitting the hardened ground like the beating of a thousand drums.

"All right?" John rode alongside.

"How much longer?"

"A week. Maybe more if it snows."

She gritted her teeth. "I'm fine."

Except she wasn't. She'd never been so cold with no chance of getting warm, no way to avoid the rising wind that cut like a knife. This was what it must be like to freeze to death. She'd heard the symptoms. How you simply closed your eyes and slept, and your blood changed into ice, and your heart with it. Only pride, the fear that she'd be a nuisance, kept her going throughout the long afternoon.

That night the snow came, burying the hands in their blankets, threatening the coals of Bat's fire that he struggled to keep burning with a pitiable amount of fuel. She and John slept with Addie between them under the buffalo robe, sharing the heat of their bodies while the cold crept up from the ground and through the frail bulwark of their tent, an invisible intruder, harbinger of death.

In the morning, they pushed on through the slush churned up by the hoofs of slow-moving cattle, through the dampness that penetrated their clothes, and, around them, the black mountains, the white plain, all color stripped from earth and sky as if, overnight, the world had lost its vitality and lay wretched and still, marked only by the trudging herd, a chuck wagon, a light buggy, and the steam rising above the cavalcade in a bank of gray fog.

Viola's horse was stumbling. Every mile or two she had to stop and let one of the boys chop the balled ice out of its hoofs, and the other horses were no better. Horses and cattle all had icicles dripping from mouths and chins, yet they moved on, sluggish but recognizing the need to keep moving, to head away from the bitter wind.

How many days and nights passed in the bitter whiteness, Viola never could remember. What she recalled was the cold that tasted like metal in her mouth, that crept into her body and almost succeeded in taking not only her life but the lives of her husband and daughter, and of the men who struggled to keep themselves and the exhausted cattle moving.

They built fires of yucca stalks and cow chips, of brush and of the few branches of mesquite that dotted the desert, and, when they reached what they hoped would be the shelter of the mountains, the storm increased, the snow grew deeper, stunning them all. The men went out then and stripped branches from the pine and oak trees and built fires around the herd, around the wagon and the remuda, and prayed their efforts would see them through to safety. And they worked and prayed in silence, too beaten, too fearful to speak what they were thinking aloud.

Old Bat squinted through the driving snow, wiped his eyes on a frozen sleeve and squinted again, then slapped the reins over the backs of the stumbling mules. "Look there!" he shouted to Addie, huddled behind him. "Look like we made it, missy."

Addie stuck her head out beside him and stared, and fought back tears. Safe! She was safe, and John, and Viola, and old Bat who'd done the best he could to keep her warm and out of the way of the storm.

"I didn't think we would," she said in a small voice that wobbled, although she tried her best to stop it.

Bat hadn't, either, but refused to admit such a thing to her. "I told you about that angel," he said. "It's watchin' over us all, and don't you never forget it."

But she had. Somewhere on the harrowing, frigid trail, she had forgotten not only about the angel, but about everything except trying to keep warm and not complain. "I won't," she said, still in the same falsetto. "I won't ever again."

Viola had to be carried inside where she sat, wracked by chills and then by pain as feeling returned to her frostbitten feet. Of them all, only Addie, wrapped in her blankets, had escaped frostbite. Bat's right hand had been frozen, and John's ears, but they were alive, all of them.

John knelt beside Viola, rubbing her feet. "Never again," he mumbled. "Never again, you hear? If I lose my ears, will you still love me?" It was a feeble attempt at light-heartedness.

"And if I lose my feet?" she asked, voicing her fright.

"You won't."

"Optimist."

"I forbid it."

In spite of everything, her eyes kept closing. Sleep was what she wanted, what it was now safe to have. "That's good, then."

She was so small! He studied her slender foot and perfect toes, saw the faint flush of pink returning, and sat back on his heels. Lucky. They'd been damned lucky. But he'd be damned if he'd go on like this, risking lives, taking chances, putting his determined wife through hell because of a dream. Enough was enough.

He'd had his eye on Oregon and the land along the Snake River for a while. With the sale of his cattle they'd have enough to start over, to ranch and farm and be sufficient unto themselves, and be damned to high desert weather that burned one day and froze the next. Be damned to Apaches and *bandidos,* and his renegade neighbors who were running hellbent into trouble and liable to drag him along.

He put another log on the fire, then carefully lay down beside Viola, and pulled up the blanket. They'd survived. This time. For himself he had no fears, but all his instincts urged protection for his wife and children, and logic said that the responsibility was his.

In her sleep, Viola relived the ordeal — Tad struggling in the muddy river; John hunched over a plodding horse, his hat pulled down, icicles in his beard, only his eyes blazing out through falling snow; and herself, on the point of succumbing to cold.

She came awake with a start and lay listening to her heart beating wildly, and to the wind battering the roof. Cautiously she moved a foot, wriggled her toes, and gave a sigh of relief. She was safe. And whole. And John slept soundly beside her, the sleep of exhaustion.

She turned and watched his face in the last of the firelight, memorizing its shape, imprinting each line, the planes of his cheekbones, the faintly arrogant nose, so that, if, by hideous chance, he was taken from her, she would have this, the imprint of his face to carry with her always.

XXII

It would be good to be home again, Viola thought as they drove up the valley of the San Pedro. Home and in one piece, and with the cash from the sale of their cattle in a belt around old Bat's waist.

"They look for me to be carrying it," John had explained. "Who'd believe the cook had it?"

It was a clever ruse, but then he was clever, always planning ahead, never making a move he hadn't thought out.

She smiled up at him. "Won't it be good to get home? Pretty soon I can start my garden."

Now he was in for it. Now he had to shatter her plans. He cleared his throat once, then again. "I say . . . I say," he began, then stroked his beard and was silent.

Under raised brows her eyes were huge and curious. "Is something wrong?"

"We're going to Oregon." He blurted it out, looking straight ahead between his horse's ears.

She gave a gasp of surprise. "You mean walk away from all this? Turn our backs on everything we've done?"

"What have we done except nearly get ourselves killed?"

"Why . . . why. . . ." Her hands went slack on the reins for an instant before she pulled back and brought horse and buggy to a stop.

In the late January sun the valley glittered. Small birds, stirred by their presence, flew up and out of the brush and swept overhead with a flutter of wings, and somewhere a lark was singing its mating song.

It was happening again, she thought miserably. No sooner settled than she was taken away, forced to move and begin again. The pattern of her life and her mother's before her.

"I . . . we . . . we have a home," she said in a low voice. "We have a life here. And the children. It's not fair to them."

"They'll make do. But we almost lost Addie. Almost died ourselves. I want. . . . I want to make sure that doesn't happen again, Vi. And I intend to make sure it doesn't. The climate's better . . . we can breed our own cattle. Blood stock, not these blasted longhorns. And we won't have to worry about Apaches or the law coming down on us for what our neighbors are doing."

"Neighbors!" She snorted. "We brought them in here."

"A lack of foresight on my part."

"And who will our neighbors be in Oregon?"

Her voice was bitter, and it irritated him. "You sound like it's my fault."

She stared at her hands clenched in her lap. "I'm not blind or foolish, Mister Slaughter. I've seen how our herds increase. I figured out how my father made enough to buy his place. I also know that it's common practice. Everybody does it. But I've heard about how those cowboys are terrorizing the county, and I won't have that affecting us or be in league with them, here or any place else. Do you understand?"

He sighed, then dismounted, and led his horse to the rear of the buggy and tied it before climbing onto the seat beside her. "So you think I'm a cow thief?" he asked. "You think I'm like the others, even after it's been explained to you?"

She sat mute and stubborn, refusing to look at him, and he resisted the urge to shake her.

"Don't you?" His voice was harsh.

She responded wearily, by rote. "An unbranded cow belongs to whoever finds it. I know. But we have thousands of them. Where have they come from? Tell me."

"I can't."

"Why not?"

"Because I don't know. It's as simple as that. Our boys find them and bring them in. *Our boys.* Tad. Even your brother. Are you trying to incriminate him along with me?"

"Stoney? You asked Stoney to steal for us?"

"Stoney's his own man. He's built a herd for himself, too, in case you didn't notice. Also, in case you haven't noticed, I don't change brands like the Clantons and their daddy over in the Animas Valley do. Or like Curly . . . or anybody else I could name. Once and for all, Vi, I do not steal branded cattle. Am I making that clear?"

He was asking for her belief, and she wasn't sure what she believed. In her mind she visualized the herds that grazed in the pastures by the river — several thousand head that had appeared, so it seemed, out of nowhere, but all bearing a single brand, that distinctive Z that had been Amazon's and was now theirs.

She knew how a man clever with a running iron could change a brand, then keep the animals out of sight until the wound healed over. That, too, was common practice — among rustlers. But she'd seen no sign of tampering on their cattle, nor had she seen a running iron anywhere on the place. It was a puzzle, and she solved it the only way she could.

John was her husband whom she had vowed to love, honor, and obey. And he was not a liar. If he swore he was honest, she had to believe him.

She let out a breath. "I understand," she said slowly. Then, because she knew that she belonged with him regardless of circumstances, she said: "And I'll go to Oregon when you do. But I want to settle some place. I want to put down roots and stay. I've been moving all my life, and it's past time to stop. Can *you* understand *that?*"

He supposed it had been hard on her, the constant upheaval, leaving behind the things she loved and was used to. For himself, he carried with him what was important — cattle, horses, opportunity. But he did have a family, and his duty was to them first and foremost — to his children and to this woman who so unaccountably had fallen in love with him, this woman who had nearly died rather than be separated from him.

He reached over and took one of her hands in his — a small, square hand with strong fingers, a hand that had known hard work, much of it on his behalf. Gently he kissed the palm. "I understand more than you think," he said. "I'll make you a home to be proud of, and that's a promise."

XXIII

"Men are all the same. They have to cross the plains, have to climb the mountains, and then, when they get to the sea, they have to build boats and sail away and leave the women behind to do all the work."

In spite of herself, Viola had to laugh at her mother's dour view. They were at the dépôt in Benson, waiting for the train that would take them to the connection to Colorado and the north, and, as always, Mary

Anne was having her say.

"John isn't leaving me, Mama. And he's certainly not going to sail to China. As soon as we're settled, we want you to come and visit."

The June wind was blowing in gusts. Mary Anne held her hat with one hand, her skirts with the other. "I'm done with traveling, even if this blasted wind does want to blow me to some place else. If you want to see your father and me, you'll have to come back here. But mind you take good care of those dear children. And of your own, when they come."

Her mother, Viola thought, had mellowed, taking Willie and Addie in as if they were her own, and without complaint. "You know I will," she said.

But Mary Anne was determined to have the last word. "I don't know anything for sure. The world's a tricky place, and who's to say what will happen, or if we'll meet again in this life?"

Viola struggled against tears as Mary Anne's doomsaying exaggerated what she herself was feeling. "Don't," she said. "Please, Mama. Let me leave here happy."

"You chose your man," came the harsh response. "Do as best you can, but never say you weren't warned."

There it was. The lack of support, the constant disapproval. Viola straightened her shoulders. "I did choose," she said clearly. "And I'm happy in my choice. It would be nice if you would be happy with me for a change."

She bent then and kissed Mary Anne's cheek, missing contact on purpose, making a gesture for the sake of good manners. Then she turned and threw her arms around Amazon. "Good bye," she whispered. "Good bye, Papa."

"God go with all of you." She was his only daughter — brave, beautiful, adventurous — and he loved her, the girl who should have been a boy, who marched to her own drummer without regret or apologies. Damn but he loved her! And damn if he didn't want to go along — to Oregon, to whatever challenge awaited in a new place, on a different frontier.

"Mind you write," he ordered. "You tell us everything."

"I will," she murmured into his shoulder. "You know I will, always."

In spite of herself, Viola found the trip interesting, pointing out various sights to Addie and Willie who gawked out the window and who, in a matter of hours, captivated the hearts of every passenger in the car.

Yet there was a part of her, kept hidden for fear of dampening John's enthusiasm, that ached at being taken away from the high desert country. All the important events of her life belonged to that empty piece of land labeled Arizona Territory — to its plains, mountains, and long valleys, in one of which what would have been their child was buried.

Who would know in fifty years or a hundred, that beneath the red earth, under the waist-high grama grass, was the end of a scarcely formed life? Who would know of her sorrow, or how so often she stood watching morning lift above the mountains in an exuberant bursting of light?

They left New Mexico behind, stopped for several days in Denver, then headed west for Salt Lake City where they were to board a stage for the long run into Boise.

Her depression deepened as they crossed the heavily forested Rockies, teetered above river gorges, passed mountains whose peaks were white with perpetual snow. She longed for the familiar — the crying of cranes, the rocky face of the Dragoons, the rattle of old Bat's chuck wagon, and the plaintive music of his fiddle winding through the night.

Nothing would ever be quite the same. She'd been marked as clearly as if she carried a brand, except the mark was stamped on her senses and on her heart.

Beside her, John was coughing but trying to make light of the cold he'd caught during the storm, and that had never entirely left him.

"Are you sure you're all right?" she asked, more worried than she wanted to admit.

"Positive." He spat into his handkerchief. "I've had worse colds, my dear."

"How much longer?"

"A few days yet to Salt Lake. Rest easy."

She couldn't. Not with the children to entertain and care for, and not with the heaviness of spirit that grew worse with every mile.

"When we get there, I'll make you a mullein tea. That should help." Her herbs and medicines were in the baggage car, and she wished she'd had the foresight to keep them with her.

He leaned back in the seat and closed his eyes. "That will be good. For now, I'll take a nap."

He could sleep anywhere simply by closing his eyes. She envied him that ability. With her own eyes closed, she could still see the country moving past, smell the acrid smoke from the engine, feel the ash and cinders that, even with the windows closed, blew into the car and covered them with grime.

"Where's Christmas?" Willie whined suddenly. "I want Christmas."

Neither Viola nor John had been able to convince the little boy that his beloved pony had been shipped ahead in the care of Tad and John Swain.

She reached across and took him onto her lap. He was still small enough that he fit comfortably. "Christmas will be waiting for you in Boise," she told him. "And just as happy to see you as you will be to see him. He's been on a train, too, you know."

"Tell me." He laid his head on her bosom. "Tell me again, Aunty."

This was what you did as a wife, a mother. You gave comfort when you yourself were in need; you spun tales to soothe anxious children; and you bit down on your own anxieties, covered them up, plastered a smile on a grimy face, put courage into a body that ached from sitting still and from pouring out balm on wounds not your own.

She closed her eyes, began to rock slowly with the motion of the train. "Once upon a time . . . ," she began. "Once upon a time in Arizona Territory. . . ."

XXIV

Viola was wearing John's money belt under her skirt. It was heavy and awkward, and, when she sat, it lay in her lap like a stone, a constant reminder that outside the coach, in the brush, in the folds of barren mountains were men whose only purpose in life was the theft of the hard-earned money of innocent travelers. They had stayed two nights in Salt Lake City, and on the morning of their departure John had insisted that she carry their cash.

"I didn't like the way that fellow was asking questions," he told her, his eyes bright as they always were when he was forming a plan. "We've got a week's travel through hard country, and I'd guess our host out there is the point man for an outlaw gang."

Outlaws! Viola put a hand to her throat. "What if they search me?"

"They won't. They're not about to maul a woman, and, besides, I told him our money was safe in the bank." He coughed, a dry, hacking cough. "But just to make sure, you wear the belt, and, if there's trouble, keep Willie on your lap. Leave the rest to me."

They were four days into their journey, and with the passing of every mile she grew more frightened. Civilization, all that was familiar, lay behind them. They were deep into a country of mountains and gorges, cañons and sagebrush desert, and they had no one to turn to but each other, no family or hired hands to come to their aid.

Her eyes stung from the dust that blew, and her head ached from being constantly alert, watching, waiting for the appearance of masked riders. And all the while she was aware of John's coughing which he did his best to hide. If he died here, in this wilderness? She set her chin. He would not. She wouldn't allow it, and that was final. Perhaps there was a doctor in Boise who could prescribe something other than her own remedies. Before they set out again, she was going to find him, if only to set her mind at ease.

Above the clatter of hoofs, the creak of wheels, and jingle of harness, she said: "When we get to Boise, I want you to consult a doctor."

His mouth twisted in annoyance. "Don't fuss."

"I will, too. I'm your wife."

"More like a setting hen."

"And you're stubborn as a mule. Humor me in this, Mister Slaughter. Please."

"Blast it, Vi. . . ." Coughing shut off the rest of his words. Damnation! Weak lungs were a curse. He could ignore the problem in hopes it would go away, but it was always there, and he knew it better even than his wife.

"All right," he said after a moment. "If it'll make you feel better, I'll go see a sawbones, but he won't tell me anything I haven't heard before."

"He can tell me, then," she said.

He chuckled. "I trust you'll pick his brains for everything he knows, my dear. I've seen you in action."

It had been raining all day when they reached Boise, and Viola shivered as she stood ankle-deep in mud while John gave directions for their luggage to be carried to the hotel.

Willie clung to her neck like a sodden kitten, and Addie clapped her hands to her ears and whimpered when thunder boomed directly overhead.

What was worse, Viola wondered, freezing to death or drowning? Her mouth tilted in a bitter smile. She couldn't recommend either. Life was precious, and she hadn't come this far to give it up.

With her free hand she pulled Addie close. The little girl had been an heroic traveler, amusing Willie and never once uttering a complaint about late hours, indigestible meals, or physical discomfort. Now, however, she had reached the end of her patience — like the rest of them.

"Don't cry, sweetheart," Viola said. "We'll be inside in a minute and get dry and have something to eat."

"I want to go home," Addie wailed. "Please, Aunty Vi."

She knew. Oh, she knew! Standing there in the mud, her hat brim sagging and dripping rain, she summoned her last bit of strength. "Come along, Addie. We'll go to the hotel and wait for your papa where it's warm."

With a look of despair, Addie followed, sloshing through the mud, her eyes fastened on her feet and her new boots, now ruined. She was remembering Amazon and how he'd held her on his knee, and how he'd taken her into the cow barn and taught her how to milk one of the gentle cows. How it had been warm there, and peaceful, the cows munching hay and giving milk, while up in the loft swallows swooped and twittered, their bodies like tiny kites blown by the wind.

Mary Anne had given her a doll made out of a corncob and dressed in a scrap of red calico. She had it with her still in the bottom of her trunk. She wished she'd thought to carry it with her — a thing familiar, a souvenir of the place she'd grown to love and that, for the rest of her life, she'd call home.

Blood spattered the front of John's nightshirt, and, even as Viola watched, stricken into paralysis, he coughed up more. How could there be so much blood? How could she stand frozen while he bled to death? She jerked into frenzied motion.

"You must lie down!"

"And you must get hold of yourself." His words came out in a ragged whisper.

Get hold of herself! And him half dead. But this wasn't the time to vent her anger. As always, practicality took over.

"Lie down and stay still. I'm going to find a doctor." Surely a town like this one had a doctor.

A check into the next room showed Addie and Willie asleep, clutching each other for warmth and security. "Poor babies," Viola said in a low voice. "Poor, sweet children." She shut the door and clattered down the stairs to the small lobby where Tad and John Swain stood up at her approach.

"Miz Slaughter." They held their hats in their hands, and she wanted to tell them that courtesy at this point didn't matter, that who she was, who they thought she was, was irrelevant. But a look at their caring faces brought relief, and she went to them, her hands outstretched.

"We need a doctor," she said. "It's urgent. Mister Slaughter is upstairs in bed and he's hemorrhaging. If one of you will go, I'll stay with him. I think . . . ," her voice broke, "I think I should be there."

"I'll go." Tad slammed his hat on his head. "John" — he turned to the foreman — "you stay and make yourself useful. Do whatever has to get done. All right?"

Swain nodded curtly. "I'm here, and here's where I stay. Miz Slaughter . . . ?" He looked at Viola. "You need anything at all, you just ask. I'll be right outside that door till you tell me otherwise."

"Bless you both." She took their rough hands for an instant, felt the warmth in each. She wasn't alone, after all.

She was pacing up and down the narrow hall outside the room where the doctor had been for what seemed like ten years.

"She gonna wear a hole in the floor," Swain muttered to Tad who had taken up the vigil with him.

"And she'll keep walkin' till she falls through, so forget it," Tad answered.

"Poor little thing's plumb wore out."

Tad knew better. "She's never wore out. Believe it. You 'n' me'll be ready for the bone yard, and she'll still be on her feet givin' orders. That's the goin'est woman I ever saw."

John Swain flashed a wide grin. "Then Mister John picked himself a Thoroughbred."

It was as good a description as any Tad could think of. "Damn' right." He sat up as the door opened and the doctor stepped into the hall.

"Is he all right? Will he be all right?" Viola couldn't control the tremor in her voice.

Doctor Timothy J. MacFarland hadn't been out of medical college long enough to acquire a decent bedside manner. He looked down at the tiny woman clinging to his arm and spoke his mind. "Not if he insists upon continuing this journey, madam. I advise you to go back to the Southwest where his lungs might have a chance. This isn't the climate for a man with your husband's disease."

Viola continued to peer up at him, and, to

his astonishment, he thought he saw something like triumph flickering in her dark eyes. "You're certain of this?"

Was she questioning his diagnostic ability? He pulled away from her. "I am, madam. His condition should be apparent, even to you."

She, too, stepped away, annoyed. "It is, sir. But I wanted a learned opinion, and I thank you for your honesty. Now, if I can settle your bill?"

When he had gone, she turned to Tad and John Swain. "You heard what he said?"

They nodded in unison.

"Very well. We're going home as soon as Mister Slaughter can travel. I'll make arrangements for you to start back as soon as possible. I'm sorry you had to come on a fool's errand, but . . . but, oh. . . ." She clasped her hands, and they both saw the happiness on her face. "Oh, boys, we're going home!"

By the next morning John was sitting up in bed, irritated at his own weakness.

"Don't scold, Vi," he said, when she came in. "I've been scolding myself."

She sat down beside him and took his hand. "I won't," she said. "I'm just glad you're alive."

"I'll be up in a few days. Tell the children that, and don't scare them."

A woman could hold in, deny her emotions for only so long. Viola drew a deep breath. "I told them that we're going home, Mister Slaughter. That we're going back where we belong."

He pushed himself higher against the pillows. "Wh . . . what?" he stammered. "What did you just say?"

"You heard me. And I heard what the doctor said last night. I didn't marry you to become a widow quite so soon, and your children need their father. *I* need you. So we're going back to where we have a chance and forget the dream about Oregon. We had our dream, only we left it, but we can have it again. Except it won't be here. And if you persist, you'll have to do it alone, because I won't be a party to suicide . . . yours, mine, anybody's, and that's final!"

Actually he was quite proud of her, filled with admiration for her ability to take charge and make what she said stick, but all he said was: "And that's your decision?"

"It is for a fact." She was on her feet and moving, her heels striking the floor like castanets. "We don't belong here. We're desert rats. That's obvious. At least to me."

"Why didn't you say so before?" he

wanted to know. "Why wait till we burned our bridges?"

She folded her arms under her breasts and faced him, love and anger warring in her dark eyes. "Because you're my husband, and I'm supposed to follow where you go. But I'm not foolish. Or blind. And I know disaster when I see it. We've got a second chance, Mister Slaughter, and I for one intend to take it. And take you back with me, if I have to hog-tie you and throw you on that stage. So, there!"

She had never lost her temper with him, never spoken a harsh word in more than two years. For that, he thought, he should be grateful. Viola in a temper was magnificent. Unfortunately, she also made perfect sense.

He sighed. And coughed. And hated the perfidy of his body. Without opening his eyes he said: "Go down to the stage office and buy our tickets back. I'll sleep for a while, but I'll be ready to leave day after tomorrow."

XXV

Suddenly there it was! The San Pedro Valley with its pink sandhills, the river winding through, and the rock shoulders of the Dragoon Mountains rising out of the brush in the east.

Viola stood on the station platform breathing the high desert air with a relief felt down to her toes. The trip back had seemed interminable. She felt she hadn't slept more than a few hours, always waking to check on John, fearful that she'd see that frightening gush of blood she had no way to prevent or stop.

"Happy?" he asked, coming to stand beside her.

She felt the heat of the sun, the stirring of wind against her face. "Yes," she said. "Here is where we belong."

"You're sure you won't mind living in Tombstone a while?"

She shook her head. Even the idea of town life couldn't shake her optimism, and Addie would be able to go to school, make friends with children her own age. "It won't be forever. Just till we find our own place."

He watched a troop of buffalo soldiers ride down the main street. They were well-armed and well-mounted, and gave credence to the rumors they'd been hearing about trouble on the San Carlos Reservation. If he had his way, his family would stay in town until Geronimo and every one of his warriors was either dead or permanently confined.

"It's true, isn't it?" Viola clutched his arm, her face white. "Geronimo's out and the Apaches are raiding again."

"Now, Vi, don't go getting jumpy before time." He patted her hand. "Let's go over to the stage office and find out what's happening."

He sounded jovial, but she knew. Even the short run from Benson to Tombstone could be perilous. Always, it seemed, there had to be a flaw in paradise, a scimitar hanging over them threatening happiness.

She swept Addie and Willie to her. "We'll make it, won't we?" Her voice trembled.

"Or die trying." He bit off the words that only made the situation worse and tried again. "No need to fear. We're all armed."

Yes, she thought. And much good a few men would be against a horde of murderous Indians. For the sake of the children, she called on her self-control. "Let's just go, then," she said, and headed toward the dépôt, head high.

"No sign of the devils around here, yet." The ticket seller pushed his spectacles high on his nose. "Heard they're south of Globe, but can't say for sure. What's worse is the roads. The summer rains washed out near everything from here to the border. Good for the grass, but hard on travel."

In Silver City, John had contracted to sell beeves to the railroad crews and, cattleman that he was, had already taken into account the lushness of the valley, a sea of moving grass, fodder for the cows he intended to fatten, Apaches or no Apaches, bad lungs or good. Already he felt better. Viola had been right as usual. Here was where they'd make a life, and be damned to anyone, red or white, who attempted to stop him!

The ticket agent had been right about the condition of the road. They hadn't gone ten miles when the heavy coach bogged down.

"Everybody out!" The driver and guard swung down. Seeing Viola's face, the driver added: "Sorry, ma'am. We'll have to dig her out, but it shouldn't take long."

Long enough, she thought as she and the children stood to one side in the shade of a white-barked sycamore tree. At least the walls of the stage offered some protection. In the open they were defenseless, targets to Apaches or the outlaw gangs who regularly held up the coaches. And she'd been the one who wanted to return!

"Don't go out of sight," she warned Addie and Willie who were picking up stones and tossing them into the brush where, suddenly, a thrasher whistled and was answered by another.

She strained her ears. Was that a bird or could it be an Apache, coming closer? They could all die here, their bones picked over by buzzards, their dreams scattered in the dust. She heard the grunts of the men, the clang of shovels, and one of the horses blew and stamped. She heard the children's voices, a sweet music, and beyond that, nothing. In the whole valley, beneath the dome of blue sky, nothing broke the silence — the hush of the first day of creation before man and his greed came to pass.

She put out her hands clutching at air and space as if they were tangible, and she could hold them, examine them as she might a jewel or a piece of glass. How strange it was to be a part of everything yet separate, with only her own thoughts circling in her head. Fear had no place here — or violence. Only the moment mattered, a moment that stretched out, as the valley stretched out, and the silence, and the small kernel of her intense awareness.

"Aunty Vi!" The peace shattered, her heart jumped.

"What on earth?"

Everything was as it had been — the men struggling to dig the coach out of the mud, the children scampering toward her, faces alight. Where had she been? She didn't know, only that she would cling to her vision, return to it when problems and despair threatened as they inevitably would.

"Gold!" Addie shrieked. "We found gold!" — and held out a piece of quartz that glittered with delicate flakes of mica.

Viola sank to her knees in the sand and examined the rock. Fool's gold, of course, but she hadn't the heart to disappoint. "Goodness," she said. "What will you do with it?"

Addie beamed. "I'll buy us a big house like you and Papa talk about. And we'll have a cook. A real one so you won't have to bother."

"And horses," Willie put in. "Lots of horses."

"That many?"

He nodded solemnly. "Maybe more."

"Well," she said, getting to her feet, "we'll have this assayed in town. But don't be disappointed if it isn't gold."

"It is!" Addie stamped her foot.

"We'll show your papa." A glance toward the road showed the coach out of the mire and the horses impatient.

Once back inside, John took Addie on his lap. "I say, I say, it's a rock that wanted to be gold so badly it painted itself."

She frowned, thinking. "Rocks can't do that," she said finally. "They don't know things like we do."

"You're sure?"

"Yes."

"But the Indians believe that everything has a spirit. Even rocks."

Indians again. Viola peered anxiously out the window but saw nothing except the glittering mesquite leaves and the dust, heavy in the air.

"That's them," Addie said. "We know better."

John chuckled. "Maybe," he said. "Maybe."

Addie's eyes were closing in spite of her excitement. "And we'll buy a house and lots of horses," she mumbled before she fell asleep.

"That we will, eh, Vi?" He looked across at his wife who seemed as if she, too, needed a nap.

He'd dragged her across half the West to satisfy his own notions, but no more. She'd have her house and her servants as soon as he could manage it. She deserved the best, his Cora Viola.

"I'll just be grateful, if we get to Tombstone without Indian trouble," she said. "Time enough then to think about the future."

"We'll make it all right. We haven't come this far to lose. From here on, things are going our way."

As usual, being John Slaughter, he was planning ahead. And as usual he failed to take into account the world in which he lived.

XXVI

They rented a house at Third and Fremont Streets. John left the furnishing of it to Viola and went off with Tad, John Swain, and old Bat to gather cattle.

"This won't take long, my dear." He kissed her hard. "When I can, I'll be home, but you'll be safe in town, and you're not to worry, you hear?"

He might as well tell her not to breathe. Her fears, however, weren't for herself but for him, out riding the valleys and mountain passes, gathering cattle to be fattened and sold.

Every day came new stories about the Apaches. They were raiding ranches, setting fire to buildings, stealing stock, murdering helpless homesteaders and ranchers. They were in Dragoon Pass, and then in the Sulphur Springs Valley where they swooped down and ran off Frink's horses. They were in the Swisshelms and the Chiricahuas, but no one, not the volunteers from Tombstone or the buffalo soldiers from the fort, found more than beaten trails leading south into Mexico.

In spite of her constant worry, Viola found life in Tombstone pleasant. She was no sooner settled than the ladies called to invite her to church suppers, to join the literary society, to afternoon lunches and teas, and she went to everything with a pleasure that startled her until she recognized that she had been lonely for the company of women.

She had never had a close woman friend, and since her marriage she had spent all her time with John and the children, not realizing the comfort to be had in exchanging ideas, problems, even gossip with others of her sex. From the ladies of Tombstone she learned which dressmaker to patronize, which butcher gave the best value, which tailor took advantage of his customers, and, most important of all, she learned the political complications that slowly but surely were pulling the town apart.

"If you ask me, it's all the fault of that Marcus woman." Mrs. Berry sipped her coffee elegantly, eyeing her audience over the rim of her cup.

"Who?" Viola leaned across the table, curious about the town and its undercurrents, the small truths that men usually overlooked when talking to their wives.

"Josephine Marcus. An actress. She came here to marry our sheriff" — Mrs. Berry allowed herself a sniff of disdain — "but the marriage never took place. And now she's been seeing Wyatt Earp. Oh, he's handsome enough, and worth ten of Sheriff Behan, but . . . ," she lowered her voice to a whisper, "but you know, he's a married man. The whole affair is quite scandalous, and the two men have been at odds ever since she changed her mind. To the detriment of the good of this town, I might add."

Jessica Pridham gave a tinkling laugh. "We don't know for sure that he's married. Only that he lives with that bedraggled

Mattie creature. There's no comparing her with Miss Marcus."

"Chasing skirts!" Elizabeth Goodfellow's mouth clamped shut. "He'd do better to pay attention to what's going on."

Mrs. Berry gave her a severe look. "He and his brothers have been chasing those cowboys as well, don't forget."

"So our sheriff can let them out of jail as soon as they're brought in. Isn't that so?" Elizabeth's look challenged them all, even Viola, who was attempting to understand the tangled web.

"Are you saying he's dishonest?" she asked. "The sheriff, I mean."

They laughed in unison, but Elizabeth answered. "The truth is obvious. The sheriff has the cowboys in his pocket. And maybe it's the other way around. All of them . . . Curly Bill, the Clanton boys, that drunken Ringo. It's all about money, of course. Bad men lining their pockets at the expense of decent, hard-working folk. Sometimes I wish we'd never come here."

There were the names again, the names of men she knew, however slightly. Viola shuddered. "The Clantons were our neighbors down on the San Pedro. I thought . . . I thought they were dreadful. They frightened me."

"So they should. They're men without conscience. Of course, the one called Ike isn't interested in the ladies. You needn't be afraid of him." Elizabeth giggled and sat back to wait for the sure-to-follow interrogation.

"What on earth do you mean?"

"How?"

"I eavesdrop in the doctor's surgery," she said with a smug grin. "And sometimes I hear the most interesting things. You should all be careful what you say, my dears."

Startled, her friends straightened in their chairs, forgetting her comments about the Clantons and wondering instead what secrets they might have divulged in the supposed privacy of Dr. Goodfellow's surgery.

"Why Elizabeth Goodfellow," Jessica said. "You should be ashamed!"

"Well, I'm not. It's been very instructive," came the answer. "How else can I expect to learn what's going on? Our husbands never tell us anything and say they're protecting us, and even the newspapers can't agree. We all know that much at least."

Viola listened with private amusement, vowing never to confide anything to the good doctor whom she intended to visit soon. Not that she had any confessions to make. Far from it. But she was almost certain she was with child. The thought brought a smile to her face. John would be so happy. As for herself, she wanted a child of her own more than anything else.

"Are the Clantons part of what you call the cowboys?" she asked, breaking the silence. "I'm sorry to appear ignorant, but the fact is" — she spread her hands — "I am."

With reluctance, Mrs. Berry put her curiosity aside. She had a long neck, like that of a turtle, and she thrust her head forward as she answered. "In this town it doesn't pay to remain ignorant. What's happening is a simple question of morality. Of right versus wrong. And which side you choose . . . the cowboys, and that includes the Clantons, and what is called the County Ring, and our sheriff, or the other, the decent citizens and the Earps. All of those Earps were raised Methodist, by the way," she added, as if that, in itself, constituted righteousness.

"Methodists or not," Elizabeth snapped, "the Earps aren't saints. They gamble, you know."

"They represent order, and you know that, too. Or you should. But it will come to a showdown one of these days. I feel it in my bones. The situation has gone from bad to worse, and we're sitting on a powder keg about to go off. Mark my words."

Even as she uttered her prophecy, the sound of gunfire reverberated through the room.

XXVII

Viola's first thought in the silence that followed was for Addie who walked home from school every day. She pushed away from the table and stood, and a second burst of gunfire rattled the windows.

The four women looked at each other, cocked their heads toward the street, and listened to the shouting, the thud of running feet.

"I've got to see that Addie's all right." Viola reached for her cloak that was hanging on the coat rack near the door.

"We'll all go," Mrs. Berry said. "Safety in numbers, don't you know."

Outside they found confusion, a crowd surging toward Fremont Street. Mrs. Berry collared a delivery boy. "What is it? What's happened?"

"Big fight. Up by Fly's," he said, and wriggled free.

"Who?"

But he was gone.

"It was the Earps and some of the cow-boys." A man with a red beard had stopped beside them. "Maybe you ladies should go back home. Might be dangerous out here."

"Nonsense!" Elizabeth gave him a withering look. "Is anyone hurt?"

"Dunno."

They hurried — as fast as their corsets and narrow skirts would permit — toward the scene. A group of men passed them pulling a cart, and a wagon stopped to let a young woman out on Fremont Street.

"There!" Mrs. Berry nudged Viola. "There's the Marcus chit come to see if she's a widow before the marriage vows."

Viola stared at the young woman and was struck by her beauty and by the yearning of her body as she ran toward the tall figure of Wyatt Earp, who was engaged in what seemed like a bitter argument with John Behan.

"Why, she loves him!" she said to her friends. "The poor thing was probably frightened out of her wits."

"My foot!" Mrs. Berry snapped. "I just got through telling you. . . ." Her words were cut off as the crowd parted and they saw a body lying on the corner of the street.

Elizabeth stood on tiptoe. "Why," she

said, "it's Tom McLaury. Dead as a door-nail."

Viola's stomach turned. She'd never seen a man shot, never imagined that in death a face froze in agony, or that sightless eyes could carry the remnants of fear and shock. She turned away, wanting the security of her own house, but Mrs. Berry took her elbow.

"There's more than one." She pushed her way through the crowd, dragging Viola with her.

"Billy Clanton. Doesn't look like he's going to make it." The man next to them shook his head. "Bad times," he said. "Bad times and worse ones coming. And you ladies shouldn't be here seeing this."

"Where's Ike?" Mrs. Berry surveyed the onlookers.

The man snorted. "They said he run off. Left his brother in the lurch."

The four women huddled together and watched as Billy was carried into a house. He was clutching his chest with bloody hands and whimpering.

Viola shut her eyes, but Elizabeth stared with obvious interest. "A goner," she announced with satisfaction. "And I guess this means George will be late again for supper tonight. If he gets home at all."

"Who can eat after seeing this?" Viola asked.

Mrs. Berry gave a short laugh. "You'll get used to it. This is Tombstone. After a while you won't pay much attention."

A cold wind blew down Fremont Street, carrying the feel of snow, and a cloud blotted out the sun so that the scene suddenly darkened. The scurrying figures, the wagons bearing the dead and wounded looked, to Viola, like a photograph in a newspaper, black and white and slightly blurry as she stood fighting nausea and dizziness. She would go home and lock her doors, and pull the curtains tight, gather Willie and Addie together for safety, and pray that John would come back soon and put everything in perspective. She swallowed hard. "I'm going to look for Addie."

"We'll go with you," Elizabeth said. "And then we should all go home and stay there. This town won't be safe, day or night, until this is all settled."

"Vengeance is mine saith the Lord," Mrs. Berry quoted. "But it seems the Lord's gone someplace else."

"And left us in hell." Viola forced herself to cross the street.

Mrs. Berry, however, was determined to have the last word. "Stuff! Hell's much

329

worse. We're just a stop on the way, but this is as close as I want to get."

The town seethed, its tension almost visible in the cold October air, and she wished John would come home and dispel her anxiety.

The three dead men had been buried, their funeral attended by a huge crowd, not of mourners, but of the curious who used any excuse to alleviate small town boredom.

None of the ladies had come visiting, all opting to stay at home in safety, and Viola had kept Addie out of school for fear she might become the innocent victim of yet another street fight.

She missed John, she was frustrated at being locked up with only the children for company, and the pain in her side she'd been trying to ignore was growing worse with each passing hour. She couldn't think for the throbbing, and, when at last she fainted, it was on the kitchen floor beside the stove, leaving the two children frightened into immobility.

Tears ran down Willie's face. "Aunty Vi," he sobbed. "Aunty Vi."

With an effort, Addie conquered her fear, although her heart was thumping so hard it threatened to choke her, and her stomach felt like she'd been punched. She crouched down beside her little brother and then, cautiously, reached out and touched Viola's cheek.

"Willie," she whispered, "can you be good and stay right here till I bring the doctor?"

"Stay with Aunty?"

"Yes. Will you do it?"

He nodded. "Is she sick?"

"I think so. But we'll make her better."

Willie moved closer and patted Viola's shoulder. "I love Aunty," he said.

Addie kissed the top of his head. "Me, too. I'll be back quick as I can."

She slipped out into the street and looked carefully up and down. Then she started toward Dr. Goodfellow's at a trot, careful to stay close to the store fronts for fear she might be shot by a stray bullet, leaving two of the three people she loved best alone and helpless.

John had been edgy for several days for no reason he could put his finger on.

When news of the gunfight reached Tubac, where he'd just finished a purchase of two hundred and fifty head of cattle, he made up his mind without hesitation.

To Tad and John Swain he said: "I'm riding on back. Tonight. You boys bring the cattle, and, if you need extra hands, ask Elias to lend us a couple. I'm worried about Missus Slaughter with what's been going on."

He took off on Old Gray without waiting for their answer, rode under a sliver of moon and tattered clouds, rode until morning when he stopped and rested himself and the horse for an hour before continuing east in a gray light and a wind that carried the scent of snow.

In Tombstone, he left the horse at the livery, giving orders to rub him down, cool him off, and give him a good feed, and learning the particulars of the gunfight in a few words. Then he took off at a run through streets that were quieter than usual, as if the town was waiting for another eruption of violence, sure it would come.

Amazon and Mary Anne met him at his door. Mary Anne was weeping. A haggard Amazon put out his hand and clasped John's.

"Wh . . . what is it? Viola? The ch . . . children? Tell me, man," he stammered.

"It's Viola. She's lost another child, and the doctor . . . he's afraid we're going to lose her, too." Amazon's voice broke. "He's in with her now, doing what he can."

"He's operating," Mary Anne spoke

around her handkerchief. "He said it was the only way."

John felt he himself was bleeding, shot in the gut, and everything that was good and familiar, everything he cherished was being taken away. "Let me by!" He pushed past them and threw open the door to the bedroom.

"For God's sake, shut the damn' door and let me do what I have to!" George Goodfellow didn't look around, simply shouted his orders without raising his head.

The room stank of sweat, blood, and chloroform. Viola was hidden under a stained sheet.

"Is she all right?" John whispered.

"I don't know, and I won't until she wakes up. *If* she does." Goodfellow dropped something into a bowl on the floor. "I went in. Only thing to do. If she makes it, she won't have any more children."

"George . . . damn it! If you've killed her . . . !"

Goodfellow wiped his hands on a towel and spat into the bloody basin. "Damn it, yourself! She was dying and might anyhow. At least this way she's got a chance, so don't fault me for trying. I did what I had to, and there's an end to discussion." He stood up, a tall man, a surgeon with a reputation for brilliance and daring and pulling lives, like a magician, out of his hat.

"It's been one hell of a week around here," he said. "You probably heard."

John sat wearily on the chair beside the bed. "When . . . when did this happen?"

"Probably she was in pain for a few days, but Addie only came for me this morning. I wasn't home. I came as quick as I got word. Elizabeth sent for the Howells and watched the children." He sighed. "I'm sorry, John. We all love her. But there's just so damned much we don't know about these things. I took a chance, but it was better than quitting."

"There's so damned much we'd planned on doing." John turned and looked at Viola who lay still, hardly breathing, her face colorless, her hair a dark, disordered mass.

Goodfellow put a hand on his friend's shoulder. "I'll be outside. I'll stay the night. . . . just in case."

When he had gone, closing the door carefully behind him, John put his head on the pillow beside his wife's and wept.

XXVIII

She had gone far away, into a place without pain or the necessity for speech, and she was floating there, emotionless, wrapped in a gentle light that soothed without sound, that was warm and sweet, and she welcomed it, submitted to it out of a deep weariness. But somewhere, at the periphery of her understanding, a person was crying hopelessly, bitterly, and, with the little energy she had, she responded.

Grief, she knew, was for the living. The dead felt only release, a great freedom, but she was touched with concern that anyone should weep so — and for her who didn't need it. With a great effort, she summoned the extremities of her body, pulled them together, and forced them into motion, forced open the lids of her eyes that were heavy as stone.

The familiar room spun around her — bureau, mirror, her lamp, the light burning low. *Why,* she thought, *I must have been dreaming! But what a strange dream it was!*

And there was John, his face next to hers,

the pillow wet with his tears. He wept for her!

She said: "Mister Slaughter," forming the syllables with care for she had almost forgotten how to speak. "Mister Slaughter."

At the faint sound, he raised his head, saw her dark eyes watching him with compassion and what seemed to him to be a kind of curiosity, as if the fact of his emotion was a wonder to her.

"Vi." He took her hand and warmed it in his callused ones.

"I . . . wanted you," she said slowly.

"I know. And I'm here. And I'm not letting you go."

Wherever she had been was receding, vanishing in the shadows where the lamp light couldn't reach.

"Light," she whispered. "Please."

He obeyed, turning the flame up until it dazzled him. Then he came back and knelt again beside the bed.

"I mean it, Vi. We need you. We love you, and that's the truth of it."

"The children?" She raised her eyebrows in question. "Are they all right?"

"Your parents are here. Not to worry. About anything."

"You," she said. "I worry about you." With a rush of longing, she came completely back into the moment, and her face crumpled. "I lost our child. Again. I'm s . . . sorry."

But she was here, and she was alive, and that was what mattered to him.

"The world's full of children, Vi. But there's only one you. Understand?"

She remembered the day she had first met him, at her parents' house — how she had recognized him immediately and had struggled to keep that recognition secret. Looking at him had been like looking into a mirror and finding her own person reflected, even the morass of unvoiced thought, unexamined emotions. Together they made one whole. To be apart, to leave him alone, was unthinkable.

He was, she saw, exhausted, travel-stained, his coat spattered with mud, his eyes red-rimmed. "Now that you're here, I can rest," she said. "And so should you. Everything's going to be all right."

Viola recovered slowly. To all appearances she was happy and healthy, but only she knew that each day she dressed and carefully painted on a mask that disguised her devastation. She had received a life sentence from which there was no reprive, and with the knowledge of her barrenness she felt increasingly useless, a woman without plan or purpose, save as an ornament.

She did not speak her feelings, even to John, especially not to him who assumed, in his masculine, good-hearted way, that all was well with her, and who strove to please by buying her jewelry and hats and a new riding horse, and who, when he was in town, squired her to parties, dances, the theater, and teased her unmercifully about what he called her "flirtations."

As if, she thought bitterly, anyone would want her if they knew. A man had a right to children, to wholeness in a wife. She could cover herself with feathers and baubles, but all the trimmings in the would could not disguise what she knew to be true — that inside she was empty, and that she ached with that emptiness and mourned a hope that was gone forever.

And around her the town seethed with venom and the accompanying plots and violence.

In December, Virgil Earp was brought down by shadow assassins who shattered his arm rather than killing him, and left him a partial cripple for life. In March, Morgan Earp was shot in the back in Hatch's Billiard Parlor, and the next day the entire Earp clan left Tombstone with the coffin, a line of mounted riders protecting the living family and the remains of the happiest and most insouciant of the brothers.

Viola and Mrs. Berry watched the silent procession as it moved slowly out of town, saw the grim faces of the riders, the even grimmer faces of the women who rode in the wagons.

"Where do you suppose Miss Marcus is?" Viola asked. "It's a wonder she isn't here to say good bye."

Mrs. Berry sniffed, and her mouth pursed as if she'd been handed a sour pickle. "She wouldn't dare show her face. Not now. She's not family, and she's the cause of all this killing. Probably she's home crying. She should be asking forgiveness, but that kind never does. And if you think we've heard the last of the Earps, you have another think coming." With that, she lifted her skirts and stepped into the street. "Come along," she ordered. "Miss Borland has some new dress material. Just the thing for summer."

Within days the proof of her statement drifted back. Frank Stilwell dead at Tucson, Curly Bill at Iron Springs, Indian Charley at South Pass, anyone who had ever given loyalty to the cowboy gang was not going to live to speak of it.

And Viola brooded over responsibility for

the deaths, foolish though she tried to tell herself she was.

"We brought some of them here," she said to John at the dinner table.

"We did, and I don't deny it." He looked at her over the rim of his glass, then set it down firmly. "But there's a difference. I hired men who knew one end of a cow from another because I needed them, just like your father did. We never asked about their breeding. If they kept bad company, we're not to blame, and, if I worried about it, why . . . why I'd give up cattle and become a minister like this Peabody fellow you ladies are so fond of." He put his elbows on the table and his chin in his hands.

"We do what we have to Vi, like we had to get out of New Mexico or be put in jail, and we brought our cash with us on the hoof. Thanks to those boys. What they were or made of themselves has nothing to do with us. We can't punish ourselves for the crimes of others. Understand?"

When she met his eyes without a response, he lost his temper. "D . . . damn it, Vi! You think I'm holier than holy? You want to blame me for what's happened here, but you can't. The seeds were sown long before we came. And I won't be any man's confessor any more than your father will. In this country, it's every man for himself, and that's the way it's always been. Now, you either agree or you don't, but I don't want to hear about it again. And I don't want to have you trying to make me feel guilty every time you hear the name of a dead man. It's over. It's done. Or will be when Earp's finished here. And more power to him. He bit off a chunk few men want to handle, but he's handling it. Maybe now we can all go about our business, and maybe you and I can get on with our plans."

She sat silent under what, for him, was a tirade. Silent and taking all the guilt upon herself. She'd been, she thought, a bad wife, questioning, accusing, failing to support him because she'd been preoccupied with herself. In short, she'd failed him in all the ways she knew, and her sorrow struck deep inside.

She toyed with her food, staring at the congealed fat, the soggy potatoes that made her nauseous. Was this where it ended, the love they had, the glorious expectations? In mutual disappointment? Her words stuck in her throat, but she got them out somehow.

"What must I do?"

He burst into laughter. "Do? Do?" Then he reached across the table and took her hand. "Be yourself. Be my own, sweet Vi, that's all."

And who was that? How did he see her? As a shadow that said what he wanted and nothing more? She shook her head. Never! She'd never be a ghost to him or to herself. She snatched back her hand and made it into a small fist.

"I'm not all sweet, and you know it, Mister Slaughter. I'll speak my mind when I feel it's time. When somebody has to tell you what's what because you aren't God, and that's the way of it. We chose each other, and we'll go on, and you'll not close your ears to what I have to say. I'm as worthy and as smart as anybody to be heard and listened to. You hear me?"

Her eyes flashed for the first time in months, and her cheeks grew pink with indignation. Inwardly, John applauded her — and himself.

"Pack a bag," he said suddenly.

She stared. "Why?"

"We're going to buy a ranch."

Her eyes narrowed. "What ranch? Where? You didn't say anything."

"I didn't know until an hour ago. It's an old Spanish grant in the San Bernardino Valley. Runs both sides of the border. Good grass, water, all we've ever wanted. Are you coming, or do I have to do it alone?" He held his breath and watched her.

It was the dream, wrenched out of night-mare, the offering of the old hope that hadn't, perhaps couldn't, be extinguished.

She said: "You've seen it and didn't tell me?"

"I haven't. But Tad has, and that's good enough for me. Will you come?"

He was pleading as much as he could bring himself to plead, and she felt her anger dissipate. What else, after all, was there? She loved. She had chosen.

She stood up, walked around the table, put her hands on his shoulders. "Of course, I'm coming, Mister Slaughter," she said, bending to kiss the top of his head. "Wild horses wouldn't keep me away."

XXIX

He drove the buggy down Silver Creek where it spilled into the San Bernardino Valley. To the east, the Peloncillo Mountains rose out of a broad plain, and behind them, like an illusion, the peaks of the Animas Range seemed to float against a sky the color of an iris petal.

Looking up the valley, she thought she could see nearly to the end of the world, across infinite space, endless grass interspersed with small hills, relics of fledgling volcanoes from a time so far past no one could remember it. There was distance distorted by dancing waves of heat, and beyond that more distance, and more still, and only a spiraling hawk, the flight of a herd of white-rumped antelope gave perspective to a landscape so large it seemed to have no boundaries at all.

The land called, and she responded with a joyousness she thought she'd lost with her lost children.

They would have a house here, and it would be a happy place, filled with ringing voices and the sound of the wind that blew constantly from the southwest. They would have a house and a life that spun out around them like the moving light, the shadows of rising thunderheads, the mountains whose names she spoke to herself, names that boomed like thunder, whispered with a softness like spring rain — Peloncillo, Pedregosa, Chiricahua, Guadalupe — the Old World and the New come together, the dream and the reality made one.

She blinked away tears. "There it is," she whispered. "There's our future. All that beauty waiting for us."

"We'll have it, Vi," he said, and reached

for her hand. "We'll have it here . . . what we planned."

She curled her fingers around his and let her imagination soar. The house would be large, with high windows and a porch to sit on after chores and supper were over. And there would be laughter, lots of it, visitors, neighbors, cattle buyers, and children.

She took a breath, let it out. "Mister Slaughter . . . ," she said slowly, thinking through her vision. "Mister Slaughter . . . there must be children who need a home, who haven't got anybody to care for them. Do you think we could . . . ?" Her voice trailed off, but she looked at him with hope in her eyes.

He understood what she hadn't spoken, caught a glimpse of the desolation she'd tried so hard to disguise, and pity welled up in him, but when he spoke it was jokingly, as if he didn't trust himself. "I say. . . . I say, Vi, I'll bring you all the babies I find and give you the raising of them. How's that, eh?"

After all, she thought, she had chosen wisely, followed her heart and her intuition. Her smile, when she looked at him, was radiant, and her eyes caught and held a reflection of sky.

"I love you, Mister Slaughter," she said. "And I thank you. For my life and for bringing us home."

Author's Note

I have taken a few liberties with dates in this novel, but not with the facts. It is fact that John Slaughter headed New Mexico Governor Lew Wallace's wanted list and that Amazon Howell also appeared on that list. However, it must be taken into consideration that the appropriation of unbranded cattle was a common practice, was, in fact, the foundation of the Texas cattle industry after the Civil War, so that neither John Slaughter, nor his father-in-law, nor any of the other cattle "barons" were any more guilty of "sweeping in" than anyone else.

It is also true that John Slaughter brought into Arizona many of those who became what was known as "The Cowboy Gang" — Curly Bill Brocius, Joe Hill, Billy Grounds, Billy Claiborn, and, possibly, even John Ringo. Again, however, in those days and in those circumstances, one hired men who were capable of sitting a horse and punching cows, regardless of their past records.

I have taken some liberties with Slaughter dates for the purposes of the novel. In 1881, the year of the famous gunfight in Tombstone, the Slaughters were still living on their ranch in the San Pedro Valley. There is, however, no reason to believe that Viola was not in Tombstone at this time as she frequented the town for visits and shopping trips. In addition, the Slaughters went on their ill-fated trip to Idaho in 1882 and were forced to return because of John's health. It was after this trip that they rented their house on Third and Fremont Streets in Tombstone.

Viola had several miscarriages and a life-threatening tubal pregnancy. Whether or not she was operated on by George Goodfellow is unknown, but, certainly, if that pregnancy occurred in Tombstone, Goodfellow, known for his brilliant surgical procedures, would have been called and would not have hesitated to operate.

John Slaughter was elected sheriff of Cochise County and served two terms, after which he and Viola moved to the San Bernardino Ranch and lived there until a few months before his death in 1922. Viola Slaughter died in Douglas, Arizona in 1941.

Acknowledgments

Without the assistance of Ben T. Traywick, Tombstone town historian, I could not have written "Mrs. Slaughter." Ben provided me with two boot boxes filled with Slaughter material and with much encouragement.

Thanks also to John Tanner, whose overview of the cattle kings clarified their actions and way of life for me.

And to Glenn Boyer, who first took me to the Slaughter Ranch and introduced me to its magic. The ranch is now a National Historic Landmark and a testimony to the lives of two extraordinary Arizona pioneers.

About the Author

Born and raised near Pittsburgh, Pennsylvania, Jane Candia Coleman majored in creative writing at the University of Pittsburgh but stopped writing after graduation in 1960 because she knew she "hadn't lived enough, thought enough, to write anything of interest." Her life changed dramatically when she abandoned the East for the West in 1986, and her creativity came truly into its own. *The Voices of Doves* (1988) was written soon after she moved to Tucson. It was followed by a book of poetry, *No Roof but Sky* (1990), and by a truly remarkable short story collection that amply repays reading and re-reading, *Stories from Mesa Country* (1991). Her short story, "Lou" in *Louis L'Amour Western Magazine* (3/94), won the Spur Award from the Western Writers of America as did her later short story, "Are You Coming Back, Phin Montana?" in *Louis L'Amour Magazine* (1/96). She has also won three Western Heritage Awards from the National Cowboy Hall of Fame. *Doc Holliday's Woman* (1995) was her first novel and one of vivid and extraordinary power. The highly acclaimed *Moving On: Stories of the West* contains her two Spur award-winning stories. It was followed in 1998 with the novel, *I, Pearl Hart*. It can be said that a story by Jane Candia Coleman embodies the essence of what is finest in the Western story, intimations of hope, vulnerability, and courage, while she plummets to the depths of her characters, conjuring moods and imagery with the consummate artistry of an accomplished poet.

The employees of Thorndike Press hope you have enjoyed this Large Print book. All our Large Print titles are designed for easy reading, and all our books are made to last. Other Thorndike Press books are available at your library, through selected bookstores, or directly from us.

For information about titles, please call:

(800) 223-1244
(800) 223-6121

To share your comments, please write:

Publisher
Thorndike Press
P.O. Box 159
Thorndike, ME 04986

Cambridge History of Medicine

EDITORS: CHARLES WEBSTER and CHARLES ROSENBERG

AIDS and contemporary history

The advent of AIDS has led to a revival of interest in the historical relationship of disease to society. Now, after ten years, there is a new consciousness of AIDS and history, and of AIDS itself as an historic event. This is the starting-point of this new collection of essays.

Its twin themes are the 'pre-history' of the impact of AIDS, and its subsequent history. The section on the 'pre-history' of AIDS includes articles which analyse the contexts against which AIDS should be measured. The second section – on AIDS as history – presents chapters by historians and policy scientists on such topics as British and US drugs policy, the later years of AIDS policies in the UK, and the development of AIDS as a political issue in France. A final chapter looks at the archival potential in the AIDS area. As a whole the volume demonstrates the contribution which historians can make in the analysis of near-contemporary events.

Cambridge History of Medicine

EDITED BY
CHARLES WEBSTER
Reader in the History of Medicine, University of Oxford,
and Fellow of All Souls College

CHARLES ROSENBERG
Professor of History and Sociology of Science,
University of Pennsylvania

For a list of titles in the series, see end of book

AIDS and contemporary history

EDITED BY

VIRGINIA BERRIDGE

AND

PHILIP STRONG

AIDS Social History Programme, London School of Hygiene and Tropical Medicine

CAMBRIDGE
UNIVERSITY PRESS

Published by the Press Syndicate of the University of Cambridge
The Pitt Building, Trumpington Street, Cambridge CB2 1RP
40 West 20th Street, New York, NY 10011–4211, USA
10 Stamford Road, Oakleigh, Victoria 3166, Australia

First published 1993

Printed in Great Britain at the University Press, Cambridge

A catalogue record for this book is available from the British Library

Library of Congress cataloguing in publication data
AIDS and contemporary history / edited by Virginia Berridge
and Philip Strong.
p.   cm. – (Cambridge history of medicine)
Includes index.
ISBN 0 521 41477 6 (hardback)
1. AIDS (Disease) – History. I. Berridge, Virginia, 1946– .
II. Strong, Philip, 1945– . III. Series.
RC607.A26A3455517 1993
362.1'969792'009–dc 20   92–14276 CIP

ISBN 0 521 41477 6 hardback

Contents

Notes on contributors

WARWICK ANDERSON is a medical doctor and Assistant Professor in the History of Science Department at Harvard. His research interest is in the historical development of health policy and medical care. In addition to this, he is the principal investigator for an epidemiological and ethnographic study of the recourse to complementary therapies by patients with HIV infection.

VIRGINIA BERRIDGE is Senior Lecturer in History at the London School of Hygiene and Tropical Medicine and Co-Director of the AIDS Social History Programme there. She is currently researching the policy history of AIDS in the UK. Her publications include *Opium and the People: Opiate Use in Nineteenth-Century England* (1987) (main author); 'Health and disease 1750–1950', in the *Cambridge Social History of Britain* (ed. F. M. L. Thompson) (1990) and *Drugs Research and Policy in Britain: A Review of the 1980s* (1990).

EWAN FERLIE is currently Associate Director of the Centre for Corporate Strategy and Change, University of Warwick. He was previously Research Fellow at the Personal Social Services Research Unit, University of Kent. His wide range of research interests in NHS management includes: innovation processes, the management of change and strategic management in the context of managed competition.

JANET FOSTER is a professional archivist now working as a consultant. She has considerable experience with medically related archives, working for St Bartholomew's Hospital and the Wellcome Institute for the History of Medicine before joining the AIDS Social History Programme at the London School of Hygiene and Tropical Medicine. Her publications include *British Archives: A Guide to Archive Resources in the UK* (1989) and *AIDS Archives in the UK* (1990).

VICTORIA A. HARDEN is the Director of the National Institutes of Health Historical Office and the DeWitt Stetten, Jr Museum of Medical Research. In 1989 she co-chaired a conference 'AIDS and the Historian', whose proceedings were published in 1991. The author of two books and a number of articles, Dr Harden has written about federal biomedical research policy in the US, the history of infectious diseases and twentieth-century biomedical research instrumentation. Her current interests include the history of AIDS at NIH and twentieth-century biomedical research instrumentation.

JANE LEWIS is a Professor of Social Policy at the London School of Economics. She is the author of: *Women and Social Action in Victorian and Edwardian England* (1991); with D. Clark and D. Morgan, *Whom God Hath Joined: The Work of Marriage Guidance, 1920–1990* (1992); with Barbara Meredith, *Daughters Who Care. Daughters Looking after Mothers at Home* (1988); and *What Price Community Medicine?* (1986).

ILANA LÖWY is at the Institute National de la Santé et de la Recherche Médicale (INSERM). Her interest in the relationships between biological knowledge and medical practice has led her to studies in the history of bacteriology, immunology and cancer research and to investigation of the epistemological thought of Ludwik Fleck. She has recently published *The Polish School of Philosophy of Medicine: From Tytus Chalubinski (1820–1889) to Ludwik Fleck (1896–1961)* (1990).

WILLIAM MURASKIN, PhD, is Associate Professor of Urban Studies, Queens College, City University of New York. His recent publications include 'Individual rights versus the public health: the controversy over the integration of retarded hepatitis B carriers into the New York public school system', *Journal of the History of Medicine and Allied Sciences* (1990) and 'The silent epidemic: the social, ethical, and medical problems surrounding the fight against hepatitis B', *Journal of Social History* (1988). He is currently working on a book entitled *Scientists in Service to Humanity: A History of the International Task Force for Hepatitis B Immunization and the Fight to Eradicate Liver Cancer.*

DENNIS RODRIGUES is Executive Assistant to the Director of the National Institutes of Health Historical Office and the DeWitt Stetten, Jr Museum of Medical Research. Before joining this office, he was a laboratory research technician and, later, a policy analyst who helped to establish the NIH Office of AIDS Research. Mr Rodrigues has written numerous internal NIH policy studies and is a co-author of seventeen scientific papers. His current research interests include the history of AIDS at NIH and twentieth-century biomedical research instrumentation.

MONIKA STEFFEN is a researcher in political sciences at the National Centre of Scientific Research (CNRS). She is author of publications on public health policies in France, including international comparisons. At present, she is researching a comparison of AIDS policies in four European countries.

JOHN STREET is a Lecturer in Politics and Director of the Centre for Public Choice Studies at the University of East Anglia. He has written extensively on British AIDS policy and is the co-author (with John Greenaway and Steve Smith) of *Deciding Factors in British Politics* (1992).

PHILIP STRONG is Co-director of the AIDS Social History Programme and Senior Lecturer in Sociology in the Department of Public Health and Policy, London School of Hygiene and Tropical Medicine. He is the author of *The Ceremonial Order of the Clinic* (1979), editor and co-author of the eight-volume series *Health and Disease* (1985) and co-author of *The NHS: Under New Management* (1990).

BRIDGET TOWERS is a Senior Lecturer at Kingston Polytechnic in the Faculty of Human Sciences where she teaches social policy and is a member of the Gender Studies Group. Her research and publications are in the field of the history of medicine, with a particular focus on the politics of international health organ-isations. Her current work is a mixture of empirical research on the impact of policy changes on the occupational identity and morale of district nurses, and historical research on the disappearance of the concept of convalescence in British health care provision.

JEFFREY WEEKS is Professor of Social Relations at Bristol Polytechnic. He is the author of numerous articles and books on various aspects of the social regulation of sexuality. These include *Sex, Politics and Society* (1981), and *Against Nature: Essays on History, Sexuality and Identity* (1991).

PAUL WEINDLING is Senior Research Officer at the Wellcome Unit for the History of Medicine, University of Oxford. He is the author of *Health, Race and German Politics between National Unification and Nazism, 1820–1945* (1989). He is currently researching into aspects of international health between the First and Second World Wars.

Acknowledgements

The editors would like to acknowledge the Nuffield Provincial Hospitals Trust for funding the AIDS Social History Programme at the London School of Hygiene and Tropical Medicine and the conference 'AIDS and Contemporary History' in April 1990 from which the proposal for this book stemmed. Virginia Berridge wishes to thank Philip Bean and David Whynes for their permission to reprint a substantially revised version of 'AIDS and British drug policy' which appeared in their edited collection *Policing and Prescribing: the British System of Drug Control* (London 1991). Warwick Anderson is grateful to the editors of the *American Journal of Public Health* for their permission to republish his paper 'The New York needle trial: the politics of public health in the age of AIDS'. Both editors wish to thank Ingrid James for unfailing secretarial support, and Diana LeCore for compiling the index.

Introduction   AIDS and contemporary history

VIRGINIA BERRIDGE

There is a different historical consciousness around AIDS at the end of ten years. AIDS now has its own history, rather than borrowing from the more distant past. Surveys of the recent past, looking back over a decade, are common. There is a realisation, too, that understanding AIDS requires an assessment of the 'larger agenda' of health, social and science policy development in the post-war period. The impact of the disease cannot be assessed without knowing something of this 'pre-history'. This book is therefore framed around the twin areas of AIDS as history and the pre-history of the disease. Its concern is very much with AIDS as an issue in contemporary history and with the perspectives on the history of post-war health policy which it has revealed.

The purpose of this introductory chapter is not just to survey AIDS as a problem in contemporary history, but to reflect on the changing relationship of AIDS and history over the past ten years. For even in its early stages, the disease brought history in its train. The function of the discipline was different at that time. Much historical commentary aimed to point a 'lesson of history'. Its concern was to draw parallels with the distant past rather than to locate AIDS in its immediate pre-history. The form of history has therefore changed over time. It has shifted from far distant events to those of only a few years ago. The function of history, too, has shifted. Three functions of historical policy writing can broadly be identified: 'policy relevant' history feeding in to current policies or used in forecasting future developments; 'recreating the past' for its own sake, academic 'voyeurism' or journalism; and policy analysis, the understanding of past events according to particular theoretical models and empirical under-standing, analysing the past without specific current policy intent (although the insights provided may feed into perceptions of the present). The relationship between AIDS and history has developed away from the first function, the 'lesson of history', through journalism and towards historical policy analysis. In doing so, it has brought a realisation of the strengths of the historical approach, what makes it unique and appropriate for the analysis of recent, as well as more distant, events.

1

AIDS, epidemic disease and the 'lesson of history'

Let us begin by tracing the 'history of AIDS and history'. The initial role of history was very much that of the first function of 'policy relevant' history. The 'lesson of history' was to the fore. The novelty and shock of a life-threatening infectious disease of potentially epidemic proportions in the late twentieth century led to a search for explanatory models from the past with some degree of predictive power. How had society reacted to and dealt with past epidemics? Could the past give a clue to the end of this particular disease story? What forms of reaction were appropriate? The initial historical input focused on three broad areas: the role of epidemic disease in past societies, in particular the association between disease and 'moral panic' or disease and stigmatised minorities; the historical record in the area of sexually transmitted disease, in particular the traditions of voluntarism and confidentiality in this area in Britain; and more general questions of ends and means in public health policy, focusing on practices such as quarantine and notification, and contributing to the classic public health debate between the rights of the individual and the good of society. Papers and collected editions on these themes proliferated.[1]

Nor was historical consciousness confined to historians. The annual international AIDS conference, an enormous gathering, early on developed a history strand amid a primarily clinical, scientific and epidemiological focus. Historians of 'relevant' areas such as cholera and plague suddenly found their work and thoughts of interest to participants in AIDS conferences, actively seeking the 'lesson of history'. This lesson was mediated by different national cultures. In France, for example, the earlier history of regulation in the area of sexually transmitted diseases was one which included central state regulation in particular of prostitution. It was this national history which entered the French debates around AIDS in the 1980s. The United States, perhaps in line with its own pluralist and federal structures, saw a plurality of competing 'lessons' around the issues of compulsion and confidentiality.[2] But in Britain the 'lesson of history' almost without exception stressed a voluntaristic, non-punitive and confidential response. The historian Roy Porter's editorial in the *British Medical Journal* in 1986 headlined 'History says no to the policeman's response to AIDS' was a high point in historical judgement on the present, drawing on analogies from the history of public health in relation to civil liberties and on the British example in the area of sexually transmitted diseases (STDs).[3]

These historical arguments were of some policy significance. Two key protagonists in early AIDS policy making in Britain, Professor Michael Adler at the Middlesex Hospital and Sir Donald Acheson, Chief Medical Officer at the Department of Health, had a keen interest in historical precedent.[4] The reports of the Chief Medical Officer in the early AIDS years were consciously historical, citing parallels between AIDS and the great nineteenth-century battles against disease.[5] History was used both to construct and defend a liberal consensus around AIDS. The 'lesson of history' came into the debates in 1985 about whether AIDS should be made a compulsorily notifiable disease (it was not); and in the general defence of a liberal line. Acheson in his evidence to the Commons Social Services Committee hearing on AIDS in 1987 cited the historical record as a prime reason for avoiding a punitive response to AIDS.[6]

AIDS as a 'chronic disease' and history

The historical arguments and analogies were of importance in early British policy formation. AIDS was an 'open' policy area and it was possible for policy to be directly influenced in ways which would be more unusual in an established policy arena. But the early period of AIDS as an 'epidemic disease' passed and with it passed the role of epidemic history. AIDS policy development in Britain over the past decade has passed through three stages: an initial period from 1981 to 1986 of surprise and shock, with relatively little official action, succeeded in 1986–7 by a brief period of 'war-time emergency' when politicians publicly intervened and AIDS was officially established as a high level national emergency.[7] 'Epidemic history' fitted well into these initial stages and was itself an active policy force in the British context. But from 1987 onward, these two initial 'heroic' phases have been followed by a calmer period, by what has been termed the 'normalisation' of the disease and of the public reaction to it. The model of chronic rather than epidemic disease has come to the fore.[8] History has been less of an active policy force; and the historical analogies used to understand the disease have themselves changed to accommodate this change in perception. Take, for example, a piece by Charles Rosenberg in a 1989 issue of *Daedalus*. Distinctly post-heroic and post-epidemic in tone, it notes the range and stages of policy choices in an epidemic. Rosenberg cites the 'chronic disease' model of tuberculosis, which, although far more widespread in the nineteenth century, did not elicit the moral and political pressure for immediate action as did yellow fever or cholera.[9] How and why the chronic disease model came so swiftly to establish hegemony is a valid area of investigation. In policy terms AIDS was assimilated to the pre-existing dominant twentieth-century models of disease, those of chronic degenerative, not epidemic infectious disease. The work of historians played little part in challenging the hegemony of that perspective. For 'the lesson of history' in both the later and the early stages of AIDS policy development mirrored the preconceptions of the present.

'Relevant history' of this type has its dangers. In an open policy situation, the case with AIDS in the first half of the 1980s, history could play a practical rather than a symbolic role. How far that role was justified was a different matter. For what lay behind this form of historical intervention was a Whiggish assumption that there was indeed a 'lesson of history' which could be learnt, that the past could provide a blueprint for a present-day policy reaction. Historical reaction was predicated on the assumptions of the present. The implication was that history was incontrovertible 'fact' rather than a welter of differing interpretations, themselves in turn historically specific. The belief that historical evidence was some higher form of truth, although useful in establishing particular policy positions, down-played some of its subtler strengths of analysis.

This was an approach which accorded well with the ethos of the time. In the United States, as Elizabeth Fee and Daniel Fox have commented, the study of history had seemed less relevant prior to AIDS; the revival of history as a policy science came with the disease.[10] In the UK, the situation was somewhat different. The status of history as what one commentator had called a 'profoundly ideological subject' had revived even prior to AIDS.[11] In the 1980s, the initiative had come from the right rather than the left. While history on the left, a dynamic force in the 1960s and early 70s, had often seemed on the defensive, or preoccupied with its own historiography and with internal debate, history on the right increasingly made the running in relation to practical policy issues.[12] The demand for a return to nineteenth-century 'self-help' and to 'Victorian values' and the debates round the place of history in the British schools national curriculum may be cited as particular examples. Discussion round this latter issue had also centred on the role of fact in history and the 'lesson of history' approach. In Britain, therefore, the early relationship between AIDS and history continued and extended the existing interface between policy and history. And in Europe in general, especially eastern Europe, the 'lesson of history' seemed particularly appropriate in the late 1980s as a series of revolutions overturned communist governments. In Czechoslovakia for example, radicalism was built around historical example; and parallels with the revolutions of 1848 were commonly made. In general, then, there was a heightened European sense of the historical relationships of policy change in the 1980s. Such consciousness can have its dangers. As Pat Thane has commented, it looks at events through the 'wrong end of the telescope', taking little account of the necessity of understanding past events in the very different context of their time.[13] Other historians too have commented on the dangers of 'presentism'. Hugh Trevor Roper put it baldly; historians were in danger of being 'great toadies of power', simply justifying, and not analysing, or challenging dominant perspectives.[14]

The focus of this volume is not the 'lesson of history', but a different form of historical analysis. At the end of the first decade of epidemic, different types of history have come to the fore. The notion of AIDS itself as history is more prominent and with it the potential role of the 'contemporary history' of health policy in general. Nonetheless historical analogy should not be discounted. Such historical intervention is valuable in challenging dominant preconceptions and in locating contemporary reactions in their context. As Shirley Lindenbaum has argued, 'history as background' has a useful role to play. She has pointed, for example, to the historic specificity of stigma in relation to diseases such as leprosy; and to the 'cultural construction' of the individual liberty/public good dichotomy which is now presented as at the heart of the public health debate.[15] The particular focus of this volume is on two areas of historical analysis – the 'contemporary history' of AIDS and what we call the 'pre-history' of the disease. AIDS itself is a study in history; and the significance of almost contemporary events cannot be understood without locating them in context. We cannot assess the impact of AIDS across a whole range of policy arenas – from research policy to drug policy, from the church to the gay response – without analysing developments in post-war policy in those areas and, in particular, the issues which have been of importance since the 1960s and 70s. AIDS has under-lined the lack of historical study of many areas of health and social policy in recent decades.

A growing body of work is focusing on the concept of 'AIDS as history', from a variety of different perspectives. One early example was Dennis Altman's *AIDS and the New Puritanism* (1986), which documented and analysed the early gay response to the crisis.[16] This has been joined by other histories. Gerald Oppenheimer, for example, has seen AIDS as a case study in the construction of disciplinary ownership of an issue and has analysed the role played by epidemiologists and virologists in the scientific construction of AIDS.[17] Daniel Fox, Patricia Day and Rudolf Klein have compared the development of AIDS policies in Sweden, the UK and USA.[18] The form and functions of such histories has varied – from a brief reconstruction of the early history of the Terrence Higgins Trust, to an analysis of the pre- and contemporary history (and possible future) of the Federal Drugs Agency (FDA) and drug regulation in the United States under the impact of AIDS.[19] At the end of the first decade of the disease, even ostensibly non-historical analysis routinely includes a survey of particular histories of the past decade and before. Papers on volunteering and AIDS; on doctors and AIDS patients; and on the issues for reproductive freedom raised by AIDS published in a recent volume located their analysis in the histories both of contemporary events and of preceding decades.[20] The journal *AIDS Care* had a historical survey of the past ten years as part of its tenth anniversary issue.[21] Professor Tony Coxon, a sociologist and leading AIDS researcher, introduced his remarks at an AIDS conference aimed at bringing social scientists and policy makers together with a history of the Economic and Social Research Council's involvement in the area.[22] The examples are legion.

Such reflectiveness is a natural process. The new historical face of AIDS has continued to have a number of functions; and its practitioners have also been varied. Policy relevance as well as policy analysis has continued to be the order of the day; and some surveys have adopted what Roy Porter has called a 'heroes and villains' approach, which tends to ignore the social and structural underpinning of events. The American journalist Randy Shilts's history of the early years of the AIDS epidemic in the United States, *And the Band Played On* has been criticised for the emphasis it places on personal culpability rather than the slowness and ineptitude of the American Federal state.[23] Journalists have in fact played a particular role in writing the 'contemporary history' of AIDS. Several, both in the United States and in Britain, used their vantage point on events to produce speedy accounts of the initial crisis.[24] Other accounts have derived from a different mix of perspectives. Science and history proved a powerful combination in M. D. Grmek's *History of AIDS*.[25] Contributions have also come from sociology, from anthropology (where the interest in cultural formation and change over time has meshed with the historical approach) and from political science.[26] In Britain, the annual meeting and proceedings of the Social Aspects of AIDS conference have provided not just a vantage point for British sociology, but also a wealth of source material for contemporary history.[27] There are thus a variety of disciplinary approaches mingling in the recent history fold. Added to them is what can be termed 'activist contemporary history'. There is concern that the early dimensions of the voluntary and largely gay response, subsequently overlain by one which attracted statutory funding, which was professionalised, normalised and non-gay, may be 'hidden from history'. There has been a concern to document this early response before memories and participants are lost.[28] Such historical consciousness can also have its dangers. 'History from below' for AIDS, as more generally, runs the risk of presenting an alternative 'official history' also cast in the heroes and villains mould.[29] The 'invention of tradition' can also be a feature of the reconstruction of the recent past.

Given the incipient vitality of the field, what can historians contribute? It might indeed be asked what the particular strengths of the discipline are. Some policy scientists have stoutly maintained that the historian has no business in dabbling with contemporary events.[30] So why is AIDS a problem in contemporary history? Three broad strengths can be presented for consideration: the historian's sense of chronology; the historical sense of continuity as well as change; and, within an overall chronology, a synthetic and critical ability to interweave and assess different forms of source material and different levels of interpretation. Chronology may not be everything and much fundamental work in history cannot be done within a purely chronological framework. Nonetheless, academic history, more than any other social science, has made a disciplinary specialty of the passage of time. Another potential strength lies in the historian's implicit cynicism about the routine proclamations of a new departure in policy. Historians, more than most other social scientists, have the capacity to locate policy change in past practice, to seek out antecedents and tendencies which feed into present policy development. At its worst, this ability can prove an obsessive desire to show that nothing ever changes, to deny the relevance of individual or collective effort. At its best, it provides a powerful means of setting policy development in its proper context. For AIDS, for example, supposedly new policies such as those in research or illegal drugs, turn out to possess deep roots in the past. The final strength of the historical approach lies in its generalising ability both in terms of methodology and of theoretical approach. The relative atheoreticity of the subject has been a matter of comment from other disciplinary standpoints. Historians certainly engage in theoretical development; but it is rare that theory overtly dominates. Herein lies a strength. For sociologists, political scientists and others can, on occasion, drown in a welter of theory grounded on a slim empirical base. The historical approach is unique in its potential ability both to deal with and assess a range of primary source material bearing on the subject, to interweave that complex story with levels of theoretical explanation – and all within a framework which takes account of the passage of time. Historical cynicism as well as sensitivity to the assessment of competing sources and accounts must be accounted strengths. No historian would accept a single account or source at face value – a besetting sin in 'policy history' accounts emanating from non-historical sources. Historians as ideologically distant as Michael Howard and Christopher Hill are agreed that it is structure and process which are important in history.[31] We need, writes Hill, 'an understanding of history as a process, not just a bran-tub full of anecdotes'.[32] The generalising nature of history is central, as is its conceptual appreciation of change.

In researching contemporary history – of AIDS or any other area – that process is not without its difficulties. There is of necessity a reliance on oral sources. Contemporary history is particularly difficult for British historians for the lack of a Freedom of Information Act inhibits access to government departments under the thirty year rule. A journalistic 'contemporary history' such as Crewdson's analysis of Robert Gallo's laboratory notebooks would be impossible in the UK; the US legislation made access possible to National Institute of Health (NIH) data.[33] In fact, few of the historical accounts beginning to emerge have used conventional historical source material. Keith Alcorn's study of the genesis of the British government's mass media response to AIDS in 1987 is one of the few British accounts to use the minutes of the relevant committees.[34] Leaving aside these problems of sources, the writing and publishing of contemporary history has its own problems – not least where living 'historical actors' disagree with historians' interpretation of events. Nonetheless, AIDS has demonstrated important and in some senses unrealised potential in the historical approach to policy issues. The papers in this volume, mostly by historians, but with a sprinkling of policy scientists and an archivist, demonstrate some of the vitality of the contemporary history of AIDS and of its historical location in the social and health policy issues of the twentieth century and especially of the post-war period. The first part of the book concentrates on the 'larger agendas' into which AIDS fitted. Jeffrey Weeks in 'AIDS and the regulation of sexuality' locates reactions to AIDS in the history of sexuality and in particular the changing responses to sexual diversity in the post-war period. He draws attention to a complex matrix of reactions – liberalisation, but also moral confusion and a new conservatism emerging in the late 1970s and 1980s. AIDS emerged at a time when the political impetus of the UK gay movement had exhausted itself, but other strengths – a commercial subculture, self-help agencies – had emerged. This male community bound by ties of sex and of friendship was inevitably a vector for the rapid spread of the disease. But those friendship ties were also the bonds which made possible the spread of safer sex and community self-organisation. The nature of the policy response has also been complex in its relationship to the gay community. The government relied on that community to promote safe sex education while at the same time limiting sex education in schools and the promotion of homosexuality by local authorities. The same duality is apparent in the impact on the gay community, at one and the same time doubly stigmatised, yet also achieving new legitimacy and public acceptability.

AIDS fitted into that pre-history of gay politics and self-organisation; but it also fitted into other agendas. Jane Lewis in 'Public health doctors and AIDS as a public health issue' shows how AIDS' own initial definition as an 'epidemic disease' and subsequent redefinition as a chronic disease has mirrored the shift which public health doctors have been struggling to make since the late nineteenth century. They have attempted to redefine their role in a society no longer dominated by infectious disease. Public health, since the 'bacteriological revolution' of the late nineteenth century, has defined itself in terms of individual prevention, but has also seen its role very much in terms of the particular functions it has undertaken, for example hospital administration in the inter-war years. Public health, via the 1988 Acheson Report, has redefined its role again in the 1980s, this time in response to AIDS. But as Lewis argues, this 'new public health', although rooted in public health's past in theoretical terms at least, has not adopted that nineteenth-century determination to consider the social and environmental determinants of health, or to take issue with those in authority. What has continued is instead a focus on individual prevention; an intersectoral approach has failed to develop. The discipline continues to define itself around epidemiology as a means of scientific legitimacy.

AIDS has brought not just a revival of public health and the focus on epidemiology, but also revival of interest in 'testing' and surveillance. Bridget Towers in 'Politics and policy: historical perspectives on screening' shows in her analysis of past debates round 'sifting' and 'sorting', in case studies of radiography and TB; of testing for venereal diseases; of paternity testing; and the medical inspection of aliens, how the debates of the 1980s were mirrored in earlier discussions of screening. The epidemiological data thus produced tell us more about the social operation of the service provided rather than any model of scientific and technical progress or of objective 'knowing'. Towers also raises the continuing theme of confidentiality. This arose, she demonstrates from her case studies, not just out of the individually focused doctor–patient relationship but had wider bureaucratic ramifications in terms of the empowering of groups with access to information deemed to be confidential. Confidentiality can have managerial implications, and has historically been dependent on the status of the person concerned. In discussing the question of screening for commercial purposes (most notably by insurance companies), Towers comments how the practice has been legitimated by its definition as a medical activity. Yet insurance companies as much as state bureaucracies face real potential costs.

Ilana Löwy looks in 'Testing for a sexually transmissible disease 1907–1970: the history of the Wassermann reaction' at the 'pre-history' of testing from another perspective. Integrating perspectives derived from science, history and sociology, she demonstrates the emergence and establishment of the Wassermann test for syphilis between 1906 and 1940, a test which, unbeknown to its users at the time, brought with it a high rate of false positives and consequently artificially high diagnoses of syphilis. The development of specific 'treponemal tests' and the analysis of results of mass screening for syphilis brought a reassessment of its use and specificity. For AIDS, too, the problem of the high ratio of false positives in low risk populations and the social costs of such false positives have been important arguments in debates on mandatory or large-scale AIDS testing. Other uncertainties also surround the test; and, as Löwy comments, the history of the Wassermann reaction reminds us of the fragility of apparently uncontestable 'medical facts'.

Paul Weindling in 'The politics of international co-ordination to combat sexually transmitted diseases, 1900–1980s' traces the battleground of inter-national health as illustrated by the particular example of sexually transmitted disease. In the inter-war years the League of Nations, the International Labour Office, Red Cross and the International Office of Public Health provided the organisational bases for the complex interaction of pro-natalism and social purity movements; of feminists and pacifists. Medical science was an important legitimating source of expertise; and the League of Nations concentrated on a restricted range of scientific issues – the Wassermann test, salvarsan – and on technical input in terms of medical education. The World Health Organisation model as it developed post-1948 was a medical one and the introduction of antibiotics strengthened this tendency. Weindling points to how scientism, militarism and state controls have dominated international initiatives. The powers and responsibilities of international organisations remain unresolved, between a minimalist role as agencies of epidemiological intelligence and a universalist drive to formulate optimum standards transcending the interests of ruling elites in nation states.

Weindling's call for a blending of medical priorities with humanitarian values is echoed by William Muraskin in 'Hepatitis B as a model (and anti-model) for AIDS'. Muraskin sees a very clear historical lesson in the case of hepatitis B, a disease with some clear similarities – and differences – with AIDS. The scientific lessons were learnt from hepatitis B, argues Muraskin, but the social lessons were not. Hepatitis B remained a low profile disease and the problem of carriers of the disease was not dealt with, largely, in this interpret-ation, because carrier status affected health care workers. Concern about Asian immigrants and hepatitis B and about schoolchildren carriers were perceived as problems of discrimination. Muraskin castigates the policy decision to put the protection of the rights of carriers above the rights of the uninfected population. The result was a failure to generate solutions, such as safe sex, needed subsequently during the AIDS epidemic.

Although it deals with the 'pre-history' of AIDS, Muraskin's is a paper which draws a direct policy lesson. The second part of the book moves to the theme of AIDS itself as history – the 'contemporary history' of the past decade. Virginia Berridge in 'AIDS and British drug policy: continuity or change?' surveys the apparent changes which AIDS has brought in British drug policy. Many commentators have focused on the change to a health-based rather than a penal approach via the concept of harm-minimisation and the incorporation of drug policy within a public health paradigm. Berridge, while acknowledging the immediate reality of change, locates the shifts which have taken place within the context of tensions and concepts legitimised in drug policy since the late 1970s. Harm-minimisation was already the objective of a revisionist drug 'policy community'; AIDS gave the concept political acceptability. Berridge analyses current policy in the light of some continuing themes in drug policy; of medical legitimacy; the relationship between technological and policy change; and the long-term history of harm-minimisation as a guiding theme in British policy.

Warwick Anderson in 'The New York needle trial: the politics of public health in the age of AIDS' tells the very different story of US drug policy and in particular of the history of the attempt to establish controversial policy change in New York City. The attempt to secure the acceptability of needle exchange in New York was to be legitimised by a technical scientific procedure, that of the clinical trial. In Britain the apparent scientific neutrality of research – via the epidemiological assessment conducted by the Monitoring Research Group – did help secure controversial policy change. But the local limitations in New York on the role of expert groups meant that science did not have this autonomous authority. Anderson's aim is not to draw a 'lesson of history' from this; his paper does not discuss what might or should have been.

Victoria A. Harden and Dennis Rodrigues in 'Context for a new disease: aspects of biomedical policy in the United States before AIDS' also focus on US politics round AIDS, in this case the response of the federal research organisations to AIDS. The authors use two case studies against which to contextualise that response. These are the establishment of the structure of the NIH system for distributing grants, and the emergence of targeted disease programmes and planning. The new concept of planning for research (a process which had its parallel in the UK with the Rothschild 'customer–contractor' changes) and of targeting specific diseases is illustrated via the politics of the response to DNA and to Legionnaires' disease. As Harden and Rodrigues note, the quick NIH response in that latter case may have heightened optimism around AIDS. But the research planning process proved useless in response to this new disease. Using internal documents, the authors survey the initial NIH reaction to AIDS and compare the changes required to those needed laboriously to re-direct a large ship already set on a particular course. They stress the importance of the mid-1982 move from an 'environmental agent' model to an infectious pathogen, and relate the stages of reaction to Charles Rosenberg's three-stage model of an epidemic.

Ewan Ferlie in 'The NHS responds to HIV/AIDS' has also had access to internal policy documentation. But his paper deals with the local dimension of policy making in British District Health Authorities. Ferlie, trained as an historian, writes from within a business school and from an organisation theory perspective. Many of the concepts are shared with historical ones, in particular the problem of organisational change over time, and the particular role of crisis in stimulating innovation. Here there is an organisation theory literature as well as an historical one. Ferlie delineates a cycle from innovation to institutionalis-ation which is also underlined by 'historical' work on AIDS. Managers, seen as key figures in National Health Service (NHS) policy at the local level in the 1980s, he finds 'dull' in relation to AIDS. Far more important were the clinical 'product champions', and the politics of the particular District were crucial where funding was concerned.

Ferlie's analysis of the District Health Authorities' response found new agendas being defined and a second generation of 'product champions' emerging as part of the move towards institutionalisation. John Street, in 'A fall in interest? British AIDS policy, 1986–1990' also deals with this later stage of AIDS, this time from a policy science perspective. Using the theme of 'crisis to complacency' as the normal pattern of response to pressing social policy issues, he uses AIDS as a case study to see if this model is indeed appropriate. Street scrutinises the issues raised by the 1987 Report of the Social Services Committee Enquiry into AIDS to see what has happened in the intervening years. He also examines the particular role of politicians and in particular of Mrs Thatcher as Prime Minister. The role of the All Party Parliamentary Group on AIDS is seen as important in maintaining consensus. The arrival of reform of the NHS on the political agenda also served to deflect attention from AIDS. Street concludes that the crisis–complacency model is too simplistic. Quite significant changes and developments in policy can take place without the overt intervention of political or media interest. This has been the case for AIDS policy development since 1987. Nonetheless, the role of politicians cannot simply be discounted.

Politics has played a key role in French policy making, according to Monika Steffen's analysis in 'AIDS policies in France'. Steffen, like Street, a policy scientist, views AIDS in France within a perspective of change over time. Steffen locates the liberal reaction to AIDS in France in pre-existing traditions of politics of health service organisation and public policy formation. The reaction to AIDS fitted into the pre-existing norms of social policy over the preceding three decades. But a large-scale policy 'push' was delayed in France until the late 1980s, despite the existence of larger relative numbers of AIDS cases in France than in other western European countries. Steffen locates this delay in the initial absence of scientific consensus around AIDS and, crucially, in the delayed emergence of political consensus. Split political control between a liberal Prime Minister and a socialist President and the emergence of a strong National Front movement made AIDS more of a potentially politically contentious issue than in Britain. The response, when it came, was ultimately one which protected individual liberty; and, as in Britain and the US, gave legitimacy to gay and other non-medical groups.

Finally, Janet Foster presents in 'AIDS: the archive potential' the work of the pilot survey of AIDS archives carried out through the AIDS Social History Programme. This unique study set out not to collect archival material, but to indicate how much material there was and the problems involved in its preservation. This was an exercise in raising archival consciousness, but also in defining key problem areas. The archives of voluntary sector organisations with a national role appear she concludes to be especially at risk.

No volume on contemporary history, let alone on AIDS, can claim to be comprehensive. There are areas of pre-history and of AIDS as history where, as yet, little has been researched or written. Nevertheless, the papers in this collection demonstrate both the vitality of the more recent historical approaches to AIDS and the cross-fertilisation with the perspectives of other disciplines which is possible. They will, it is hoped, encourage further analysis of the social and health policy issues of the post-war period.

NOTES

1 Among the earlier examples were the 1986 issue of the Millbank Quarterly, subsequently republished as E. Fee and D. M. Fox (eds.), *AIDS: The Burdens of History* (Berkeley, 1988); 'In time of plague', *Social Research*, 55, 3 (1988); A. M. Brandt, *No Magic Bullet. A Social History of V.D. in the U.S. since 1880* (Oxford, 1985), was republished in 1987 with a new chapter on AIDS. British examples

include F. Mort, *Dangerous Sexualities: Medico-Moral Politics in England since 1830* (London, 1988); R. Davenport-Hines, *Sex, Death and Punishment* (London, 1990).

2 A. Brandt, 'AIDS in historical perspective: four lessons from the history of sexually transmitted diseases', *American Journal of Public Health*, 78 (1988), 367–71.

3 R. Porter, 'History says no to the policeman's response to AIDS', *British Medical Journal*, 293 (1986), 1589–90. See also R. Porter, 'Plague and Panic', *New Society*, 12 December 1986, 11–13.

4 M. W. Adler, 'History of the development of a service for the venereal diseases', *Journal of the Royal Society of Medicine*, 75 (1982), 124–8. M. W. Adler, 'The terrible peril: a historical perspective on the venereal diseases', *British Medical Journal*, 281 (1980), 206–11. See also J. Austoker, 'AIDS and homosexuality in Britain: an historical perspective', in M. W. Adler (ed.), *Diseases in the Homosexual Male* (London, 1987).

5 Chief Medical Officer, *On the State of the Public Health. The Annual Report of the Chief Medical Officer of the DHSS for the Year 1986* (London, 1987).

6 House of Commons, Social Services Committee, *Third Report. Problems Associated with AIDS Volume 1*, Session 1986–8 (London, 1987), vii.

7 See V. Berridge and P. Strong, 'AIDS policies in the UK: a study in contemporary history', *Twentieth Century British History*, 2, 2 (1991), 150–74.

8 For some discussion of the concept, see D. M. Fox, 'Chronic disease and disadvantage: the new politics of HIV infection', *Journal of Health Politics, Policy and the Law*, 15 (1990), 341–55.

9 C. Rosenberg, 'What is an epidemic? AIDS in historical perspective', in S. R. Graubard (ed.), *Living with AIDS* (Cambridge, Mass., and London, 1990), republishing spring and summer 1989 issues of *Daedalus*, 118, 2 and 3.

10 Fee and Fox, 'Introduction: AIDS, public policy and historical inquiry', in Fee and Fox (eds.), *AIDS: The Burdens of History*.

11 D. Parker, 'History as bunk', *Times Higher Education Supplement*, 1 June 1990, 14.

12 As one example of the historiography of radical history, see R. Samuel (ed.), *History Workshop 1967–1991. A Souvenir and Collectanea* (Oxford, 1991). A survey of the vitality of the right and some possibilities for a response is given in P. Curry, 'Thompson, Clark and beyond: the future of English Marxist social history' (unpublished paper). See also Juliet Gardiner (ed.), *The History Debate* (London, 1990).

13 P. Thane, 'Introduction', in P. Thane (ed.), *The Origins of British Social Policy* (London, 1978).

14 E. Fee and D. M. Fox, 'The contemporary historiography of AIDS', *Journal of Social History*, 23 (1989), 303–14.

15 G. Herdt and S. Lindenbaum (eds.), *The Time of AIDS. Social Analysis Theory and Method* (Newbury Park, Ca., 1992).

16 D. Altman, *AIDS and the New Puritanism* (London, 1988).

17 G. Oppenheimer, 'In the eye of the storm: the epidemiological construction of AIDS', in Fee and Fox (eds.), *AIDS: The Burdens of History*.

18 D. M. Fox, P. Day and R. Klein, 'The power of professionalism: AIDS in Britain, Sweden and the United States', *Daedalus*, 118 (1989), 92–112.

19 Z. Schramm-Evans, 'Responses to AIDS, 1986–1987', in P. Aggleton, P. Davies and G. Hart (eds.), *AIDS: Individual, Cultural and Policy Dimensions* (London, 1990); H. Edgar and D. J. Rothman, 'New rules for new drugs: the challenge of AIDS to the regulatory process', in D. Nelkin, D. P. Willis and S. V. Parris (eds.), *A Disease of Society: Cultural and Institutional Responses to AIDS* (Cambridge, 1991).

20 Nelkin, Willis and Parris (eds.), *A Disease of Society*.

21 J. Elford, R. Bor, L. Sherr and G. Hart, 'AIDS – ten years on', *AIDS Care*, 3 (1991), 235–8.

22 Prof. Tony Coxon, introducing a conference on HIV/AIDS: Research and Policy at the King's Fund, 3 May 1991.

23 R. Porter, 'Epidemic of Fear', *New Society*, 4 March 1988, 24–5, reviewing R. Shilts, *And the Band Played On: Politics, People and the AIDS Epidemic* (London, 1988).

24 For example in Britain, R. McKie, *Panic: The Story of AIDS* (Wellingborough, 1986).

25 M. D. Grmek, *History of AIDS. Emergence and Origin of a Modern Pandemic*, trans. R. C. Maulitz and J. Duffin (Princeton, 1990).

26 For the entwining of anthropological and historical perspectives, see Herdt and Lindenbaum (eds.), *The Time of AIDS*.

27 P. Aggleton and H. Homans (eds.), *Social Aspects of AIDS* (London, 1988); P. Aggleton, G. Hart and P. Davies (eds.), *AIDS: Social Representations, Social Practices* (London, 1989); Aggleton, Davies and Hart (eds.), *AIDS: Individual, Cultural and Policy Dimensions*; P. Aggleton, G. Hart and P. Davies (eds.), *AIDS: Responses, Interventions and Care* (London, 1991).

28 See, for example, the entries for the Aled Richards Trust and for Simon Watney in J. Foster, *AIDS Archives in the UK* (London, 1990).

29 See, for example, the outcry in the *Guardian* in 1991 in response to an article by R. Haselden, 'Gay abandon', *Weekend Guardian*, 7–8 September 1991, 20–1, which had suggested that not all gay men had adopted safe sex practices.

30 The author presenting an earlier version of this work to a seminar of policy scientists at the King's Fund was confronted by complete disbelief. Brendan Dunleavy in 'The study of public policy: do historians have a role?' (paper presented at the Institute of Historical Research May 1990) has also argued against the role of history. By contrast, P. N. Stearns, 'History and public policy', in G. J. McCall and G. H. Weber, *The Roles of Academic Disciplines in Policy Analysis* (London, 1984), demonstrates some strengths of the 'policy relevant' historical approach.

31 M. Howard, *The Lessons of History* (Oxford, 1991).

32 C. Hill, 'History and the Present', 65th Conway Memorial Lecture 1989.

33 J. Crewdson, 'Science under the microscope', *Chicago Tribune*, 19 November 1989.

34 K. Alcorn, 'AIDS in the public sphere', in E. Carter and S. Watney (eds.), *Taking Liberties: AIDS and Cultural Politics* (London, 1989).

I

The pre-history of AIDS

1

AIDS and the regulation of sexuality

JEFFREY WEEKS

Introduction

The HIV/AIDS epidemic is framed, if not burdened, by many histories. There are histories of past epidemics and diseases, including sexually transmitted diseases; histories of scientific investigation, and of medicine and social hygiene; histories of the various groups affected by HIV and AIDS: of homosexuals, of drug users, of the poor and racially disadvantaged in the urban centres of western nations, and of the poor and exploited in the developing world; and there are histories of social policy and of welfare policies, or of their absence, which can help us to understand the various phases of the political and governmental response to HIV and AIDS. AIDS is already a deeply historicised phenomenon.[1]

But at the centre of any attempt to understand the response to the epidemic in the west must be the history (or rather histories) of sexuality. At the most basic level this is because sexual intercourse is one of the most efficient means of transmission of the virus, and changing patterns of sexual interaction help explain its rapid spread from the late 1970s. There is, however, a more profound reason why we need to situate HIV and AIDS in a history of sexuality. AIDS was identified at a particular moment in that history, when values and behaviour were in a period of unprecedented flux, and when sex-related issues came close to the top of the political agenda.

The syndrome was first identified in a highly sexualised community, the gay community, which was the focus of heated controversy as well as (or perhaps because of) an unparalleled growth and public presence. It was also a period when to an extraordinary degree sexuality had become a major element in political debate and mobilisation. Not surprisingly, therefore, AIDS became for many a potent symbol for all that had changed, or threatened to change. Change was not, of course, confined to sexuality, but changes in sexual behaviour seemed to condense all the other changes (in personal behaviour, in the changing demographic make-up of western populations, in forms of social

17

regulation and in the changing relationship between First and Third Worlds) that were transforming western, and world, culture by the early 1980s. The AIDS crisis emerged at a crucial moment of cultural uncertainty, particularly with regard to sexuality, and the initial reaction to the epidemic, as well as the subsequent response at all levels, from popular fear and panic to national and international intervention, has been indelibly shaped by that fact.[2]

This paper, therefore, explores the responses to HIV and AIDS through an exploration of our current sexual preoccupations. I begin with an account of key tendencies in what I shall call the 'new history of sexuality', which can contribute to our understanding of the impact of the epidemic. Then I trace in more detail the changing patterns of the social organisation and regulation of sexuality in Britain which helped shape the initial, and continuing, reaction to the crisis. Attitudes towards homosexuality were central to the debates over the appropriate forms of regulation. The gay community in turn bore the brunt of the early 'moral panic' (a contested but to my mind still valuable concept, to which I shall return) and which at the end of the first decade of the crisis still faced the main burden of the epidemic. Responses to homosexuality, then, are necessarily central to the discussion. Finally, I attempt an assessment of the complexity of social responses to HIV and AIDS (both as a syndrome of diseases, and as a symbolic presence) in our deeply historicised present.

AIDS and the new history of sexuality

Since the 1960s there has been a revolution in the historical understanding of sexuality. From being (like gender) scarcely a spectral presence in social history, sexuality has increasingly been seen as a key element for understanding the social dynamics of modern society. At the centre of the new history is a recognition that sexuality is far from being the purely 'natural' phenomenon which earlier historians took for granted, and which largely shaped their avoidance of the subject. If sexuality is a constant, why bother to study it?

We now see, on the contrary, that far from being outside of history, 'sexuality', as the social organisation of sexual relations, is a product of many histories, from the *longue durée* of population changes and shifts in the economic and social structure of modern society, to the shorter term interventions of religious leaders, 'moral entrepreneurs', legislators and sexual activists and minorities. 'Sexuality' in an inadequate but now familiar, if controversial, term is 'socially constructed'.[3]

We can draw from this now substantial body of work three major themes which are central to any attempt to understand the impact of AIDS: the symbolic centrality of sexuality in modern society; the historical nature of sexual, like other social, identities; and the complexity of regimes of sexual regulation. Before deploying these themes for a more detailed analysis, I want to indicate briefly the general ways in which they can illuminate the crisis around HIV and AIDS.

First of all, let us take the symbolic centrality of sexuality. Sexuality has been at the heart of social discourse for a very long time. The regulation of sexual behaviour was central to the institutionalisation of Christianity, and hence to the formation of what we know as European civilisation. Within the period we now think of as 'modernity', since roughly the eighteenth century, sexual behaviour has been a besetting preoccupation in all the crises and initiatives of industrialisation and 'modernisation'. This is because sexuality, far from being the most natural thing about us, is in many ways the most socialised, the most susceptible to social organisation. To put it another way, the terrain of sexuality is like a conductor of currents, whose origins lie elsewhere, but whose battleground is sexual belief and behaviour. Sexuality, as Michel Foucault put it, has been assigned so great a significance in our culture because it has become the point of entry both to the lives of individuals and the life, well-being and welfare of the population as a whole. But it is also, of course, the focus of fantasy, individual and social, and of judgements about what is right or wrong, moral or immoral.[4]

It is not surprising, then, that the emergence of a sex-related disease, or set of diseases, in the early 1980s became the focus of social anxieties, fears and panics, just as the syphilis epidemic produced significant social, and symbolic, effects in the nineteenth century.[5] The origins of the sense of uncertainty, amounting in many people's minds to a generalised crisis of western culture, may have been complex and diverse, but the emergence of AIDS provided a convenient focus, a symbolic site, for articulating the new social imagery.

The question of identity was central to what for the sake of convenience I am calling a crisis around sexuality. Here the work of the new history has been perhaps most original and innovatory. What it has sought to demonstrate is that the socio-sexual identities (such as 'heterosexual' or 'homosexual') that we now take for granted as so natural and inevitable are in fact historical constructs, and fairly recent constructs at that.[6] To be more specific, since at least the nineteenth century, and possibly earlier – the debate is still open – western culture has become increasingly concerned with identifying what you do with what you are, with establishing object choice as the key to our sexual natures. In a phrase, heterosexuality and homosexuality may always have existed (if we take those terms to apply to general sexual activity), but 'homosexuals' and 'heterosexuals' have not.

The historicisation of sexual identities helps us to understand some of the most important features of the initial reaction to the AIDS epidemic. The existence of the 'homosexual' as a generally execrated category, the description of a particular type of person, the 'other' whose very presence served to define what is normal in the rest of the population, was central to the early definition of AIDS as a homosexual disease, the 'gay plague'. If homosexuality is the exclusive characteristic of the 'deviant', then necessarily the disease must have something to do with the lifestyle of homosexuals. From this stemmed the disastrous reluctance of many early scientists to come to terms with heterosexual transmission, and the dimensions of the heterosexual epidemic, especially in Africa.

This brings us to the third lesson we can draw from the new history, concerning the complex patterns of regulating sexuality. Two key elements stand out: the formal regulation of sexual behaviour through church and state; and the less formal, but frequently closely connected, forms of regulation of sexuality through the discourses of medicine, sexology, 'public health' and social hygiene. The important point here is that these are rarely articulated together in a neat fit; more often than not they are in contradiction with one another, and often are torn by self-contradictions. Different agents of the state (the bureaucracy and the political leadership, central and local bodies) take different views, have different priorities and strategies. Churches have their own moral agenda, and intervene with variable force and effect. The medical establishment might promote a health policy which is sharply at odds with political priorities. All these tensions were manifest in the response to the new health crisis.

At the same time, a deep historical awareness of the shaping roles of the state, religion, science and medicine in sustaining a model of homosexuality as deviant and 'other' helped to determine the early reaction of people with AIDS, and gay activists, to the epidemic. There was a deep-rooted fear that having only recently escaped from the opprobrious definitions of homosexuality (male homosexuals had only recently been partially decriminalised, the 'medical model' of homosexuality was still prevalent) AIDS could easily lead to the re-medicalisation, and possibly re-criminalisation, of homosexuality.[7]

All these factors suggest the complex ways in which sexuality is socially organised. Our sense of ourselves, and our place in the world, is shaped at the intersection of a series of often conflicting discourses: religious, legal, medical, educational, psychological, sexological, communal, and so on. Our subjectivities and identities are negotiated through the network of meanings and potentialities these offer. They entangle us, shaping our sense of what we are, and can become. But the very complexity of meanings that exist in the contemporary world suggests that we are not trapped within them; on the contrary, they provide the space for constant re-negotiations and re-definitions.

The period since the 1960s has seen rapid changes in social and cultural life,[8] and a closely related proliferation of new discourses around sexuality, re-shaping and re-ordering the possibilities for living our sexual lives. AIDS appeared in the midst of a cacophony of debate, experimentation and consequent reaction concerning sexuality. Responses to it were, not surprisingly, complex. In turn, the epidemic has initiated new discourses (for example, concerning 'safer sex', health, and social regulation) which are likely to shape powerfully the ways in which we think and live sexuality for the foreseeable future. The response to AIDS casts a strong searchlight on the sexual preoccupations of our time. It also throws a long shadow on what is to come.

The regulation of sexuality

The key to understanding the impact of the AIDS crisis lies in recognising that it emerged in the midst of what can best be described as an 'unfinished revolution' in attitudes towards, and in the regulation of, sexuality, and especially homosexuality. On the one hand there has been a striking double-shift in attitudes over the past generation. This has involved both a liberalisation of attitudes towards issues such as marriage and divorce, pre-marital sex, birth control and abortion, and towards homosexuality; and an apparent secularisation of belief systems, with the decline of traditional, usually Christian-based, absolutist standards, and the emergence of more pragmatic belief systems. The development from the early 1970s of a vigorously open and diverse lesbian and gay community is one index of the change, though far from being the only one.[9]

But these shifts have been accompanied by a high degree of moral confusion (where attitudes and beliefs have frequently lagged behind behavioural changes). Uncertainty and confusion, in turn, provided the elements for a moral mobilisation around sexual issues, which has given sexuality a new political salience. This is most dramatically illustrated by the emergence since the 1970s of a new conservatism, often allied – though less so in Britain than elsewhere – to fundamentalist religion, which has focused a great deal of energy on key moral issues: abortion, above all, especially in the USA, but also such themes as sex education and, most obviously in relation to AIDS, the claims of lesbian and gay politics. AIDS emerged as a focus of social concern at precisely the moment in the early 1980s when these new political forces were attempting to achieve a new cultural hegemony in North America and Britain especially.[10]

One way into the understanding of the complex forces at work is through the shifting patterns in the regulation of sexuality during this period. The late 1960s had witnessed the most striking changes in the legal framework of sexuality for almost a hundred years. Between 1967 and 1970 there was significant new legislation on abortion, homosexuality, stage censorship and divorce. Together with earlier changes (such as changes to the laws on obscene publications) these constituted what became known as 'permissiveness'.[11]

Behind the legal changes was a collapse of a whole pattern of regulating sexuality, enshrined in the assumption that the law had a right and a duty to state what was right and wrong in both public and private life. In place of a legal absolutism that was widely perceived as being incapable of responding appropriately to a more open and pluralistic culture, a new strategy of regulation emerged, most clearly articulated in one of the key statements of the period, the 'Wolfenden Report' of 1957.[12]

The report, and the raft of legislation that attempted to enact its implications, based its proposals on a clear distinction: between private morality and public decency. The role of the state, it declared, was not to impose a particular pattern of private morals; that was the role of the churches and of individual conscience. The law's role was to uphold acceptable standards of public order and decency.

The legislation of the 1960s was cautious and modest in the actual changes it sought to make. So, for example, the Abortion Act of 1967 did not allow abortion on demand; there was no divorce by consent; and, most significantly, homosexuality was not fully legalised, nor was it in any real sense legitimised. There was no attempt to create new rights, or positively to assert the values of different sexual lifestyles. The declared aim, rather, was to find a more effective way of regulating sexual behaviour than the draconian (and largely ineffective) methods of the old laws had allowed.[13]

So the Wolfenden strategy did not herald any espousal of 'sexual liberation'; its philosophy was well in the tradition of English liberalism, and its policy implications were modest and pragmatic. That was not, however, how it was seen by many, either at the time, or subsequently. For the upholders of legal absolutism and for the morally conservative the approach represented an abandonment of moral standards in favour of moral relativism. During the subsequent decades the legislative revolution of the 1960s became for many the symbol of all that had gone wrong in 'the sixties', the decade of supposed sexual liberation and moral collapse. As the conservative commentator, Ronald Butt, put it, 'In some matters, a charter of individual rights was granted which unleashed an unprecedented attack on old commonly held standards of personal behaviour and responsibility.'[14]

But for some of the radical forces that emerged from the late 1960s, around feminism and gay liberation, the reforms were a symbol also, but this time of a failed liberalism, too little, too late. The British gay movement that emerged in 1970 grew in the space that law reform had helped shape. The new generation of lesbian and gay activists acted *as if* they had been given new rights by law reform. But the spirit of the new radicalism was distinctly different from that of the Wolfenden strategy. By advocating 'coming out', that is declaring one's gayness, it sought to dissolve the privacy of sexual taste, to make sexuality a public issue. Through its militancy and the carnivalesque way in which it demonstrated its new sense of collective consciousness it attempted to break the taboos about public displays of homosexual love and affection.[15]

In other words, the Wolfenden approach, with its rationalistic assumptions about an acceptable distinction between public and private spheres, satisfied neither of the polarised sexual political forces that emerged vocally in the 1970s. For the radicals, it had not gone far enough; for the right, which was becoming politically dominant, especially after the election of the Thatcher government in 1979, it had gone too far. By the end of the 1970s and the beginning of the 1980s, there were clear signs that the Wolfenden strategy itself was losing its purchase on debate, as the political climate shifted.[16]

Behind this was a wider political and cultural crisis, for which the emergence of what Stuart Hall has called the 'authoritarian populism' of the Thatcher governments offered an apparent solution (at least, perhaps, to that section of the British electorate which voted for the Thatcher-led Conservative Party in 1979, 1983 and 1987).[17] Crucially, alongside its commitments to 'a strong state and a free economy' was a moral project, summed up polemically in Mrs Thatcher's potent espousal of a return to 'Victorian values'.[18]

It is important to recognise that this moral project was never during the 1980s pursued with the same enthusiasm as the economic revolution close to Mrs Thatcher's heart, and the impact of Thatcherism on moral attitudes, and even sexual regulation, was in the end limited.[19] Nevertheless, it is relevant to the understanding of the initial impact of, and response to, AIDS that such a forceful exponent of opposition to 'the sexual revolution' was in power in Britain during the early years of the AIDS epidemic. This was a decade when political issues were persistently moralised, and moral issues were ever in danger of becoming political issues, and that profoundly defined the parameters of the response to AIDS. Not least, AIDS raised difficult questions about the relationship between private behaviour and public policy in the most sensitive and controversial area of all, that of sexual behaviour.

The stress on family values, though somewhat erratically pursued, as some of Mrs Thatcher's ideological friends frequently complained, was perhaps the major moral response to 'permissiveness' during the period. Its inevitable accompaniment was a challenge to those who had most fervently sought to undermine the hegemony of the family, and of these homosexuality represented the most potent symbol.

Homosexuality, particularly as represented by the militancy of lesbian and gay politics, represented, in Anna Marie Smith's powerful term, an overflowing of 'radical difference', a challenge to the normality and inevitability of orthodox family life.[20] This not only threatened (at least in New Right discourse, if not elsewhere) the hierarchy of difference between men and women, adults and children represented by the traditional model of the family, but also made public what was best confined to the decency of the private sphere.

It was an historic accident that HIV disease first manifested itself in the gay populations of the east and west coasts of the United States, and subsequently in similar populations throughout the west. But that chance shaped, and has continued to form, the social and cultural response to AIDS. Originally officially designated by its association with the gay community ('gay cancer', GRID or Gay Related Immune Deficiency), and easily encapsulated in tabloid headlines as the 'gay plague', HIV and AIDS were immediately classified as the diseases of the diseased, caused by, and revealing, the problems inherent in a particular way of life: 'promiscuity', 'fast-lane' lifestyles, irresponsibility, and all the other terms deployed against what by the early 1980s was being identified as a clamant, but unpopular, minority.[21]

The lesbian and gay community in Britain never achieved the public presence or sophistication of the American, nor therefore the notoriety. It had grown significantly during the 1970s, largely through the stimulus of the radical gay liberation movement which was launched in 1970, in large part under American influence. During the subsequent decade the movement had developed rapidly, absorbing and transforming the older, more reformist, homophile groupings, and in turn stimulating an unprecedented growth of homosexual organisations, social facilities, publications, and a new self-confidence and sense of identity amongst lesbians and gay men.[22]

But by the early 1980s the initial political impetus had exhausted itself. The gay liberation movement itself had fragmented in the early 1970s, and the various militant groupings it had given rise to were themselves in crisis by the early 1980s. Even *Gay News*, which had been central to the identification and articulation of a sense of common experience in the 1970s, entered a terminal crisis in the early 1980s, and had effectively disappeared by 1983.[23] There was a felt mood of vulnerability in the British gay community as policies swung dramatically to the right under Margaret Thatcher. The close ties with the American gay scene, stimulated by a greater ease of transatlantic travel, fed the sense of apprehension. The various anti-gay campaigns of the late 1970s in the USA, most famously the crusade of Anita Bryant to save America from sodomy,[24] had been carefully watched in the UK, and there was a strong belief amongst many activists that the same would follow in Britain.

Yet this sense of vulnerability, and fear of a backlash against the gains of the 1970s, must not lead us to ignore the real strengths of the lesbian and gay communities by the early 1980s. There was a burgeoning commercial subculture, for men at least, which constantly expanded the possibilities for social and sexual interaction. The demise of broad-based campaigning organisations did not mean that a lesbian and gay politics had disappeared. On the contrary, the subsequent decade, in part despite, in part because of, AIDS, saw a new political energy: of lesbians active in the women's movement; of openly lesbian and gay activists in the major political parties, especially the Labour Party; the emergence of distinctive campaigns for lesbian and gay rights in various local government areas, especially in London, Manchester and other major cities; and a continued development of gay-related information and support services, such as London Gay Switchboard (subsequently Lesbian and Gay Switchboard), with similar organisations throughout the country. Moreover, the example of the gay movement stimulated a proliferation of alternative radical sexual identities, around paedophilia, sado-masochism, transvestism and the like, giving rise to what became known as a radical 'sexual fringe'.[25]

Of course, there was a paradox inherent in this expansion. The ties of community, at least amongst gay men, facilitated the rapid spread of HIV in the gay community. Sex, and a greater freedom in the pursuit of sexual freedom and choice, was a bond that bound the male community together, but that inevitably provided a vector for the rapid spread of disease. On the other hand, the bonds constructed and reaffirmed through a new ease with sexuality also made possible the emergence of a new discourse of 'safer sex', and provided the nexus of friendships and personal ties that was to be a vital factor in the community response to the developing health crisis.[26]

Inevitably, it was the sexuality of the male gay community, and the radical alternative it implied to the traditional values, 'the old virtues of discipline and self-restraint' endorsed by Mrs Thatcher,[27] which became the focus of the early fears aroused by AIDS. But beyond this, as I have already tried to indicate, were a wider set of fears about cultural change that the links between the gay revolution and HIV disease came to symbolise. At the heart of these fears, I would argue, was the challenge posed by diversity.

AIDS, as a syndrome of diseases that preeminently during the 1980s affected marginal and marginalised people – male homosexuals, drug users, the poor and black people of American cities, men and women of the Third World – became a symbol of diversity, of the problems posed by cultural and sexual change. AIDS was both global in its impact and implications, and local in its manifestations and effects. It could be represented as the harbinger of that 'sense of an ending' which was at the centre of the new cultural conservatism. It unsettled the enlightenment faith in the triumph of science, and reason. But it also demanded new resources at a time when conservative governments throughout the west were intent on reducing the role of public provision. And it required an empathetic understanding of the implications of cultural pluralism in a climate which was rife with the quest for new absolutes.[28] AIDS, as Nelkin et al. have argued, 'demonstrates how much we as a "culture" struggle and negotiate about appropriate processes to deal with social change, especially in its radical forms'.[29]

The unprecedented nature of the problems posed by the disease as it spread in Britain in the 1980s, combined with the peculiarly uncertain response evoked by the needs of the gay community, helped determine the contours of the immediate response to the crisis. This has been widely characterised as one of 'moral panic', though this description has also been sharply criticised.[30]

The setting of limits, the drawing of boundaries, is precisely one of the functions of the classic elements of 'moral panics', and we can, I believe, still use this concept, with caution, as a helpful heuristic device to explore the deeper currents which shaped the developing HIV/AIDS crisis. The concept was developed to describe the response to the problem of youth in the 1960s, and has been used in a variety of contexts since. Classically, moral panics focus on a condition, person or group of persons who become defined as a threat to accepted social values and assumptions. They tend to develop in situations of confusion and ambiguity, in periods when the boundaries between what are seen as acceptable and unacceptable behaviour become blurred, and need redefinition. Over the past generation there have been an apparently endless series of such panics, many of them around moral and sexual issues: areas, clearly, where boundaries are uncertain, where anxieties about the parameters of legitimate behaviour are most acute. They reveal above all an uncertainty about sexual beliefs, which made it possible to mobilise anxieties and promote symbolic solutions.

In the case of AIDS we can detect several key features. There was, first of all, the characteristic stereotyping of the main actors as peculiar types of monster, leading in turn to an escalating level of fear and perceived threat. The response to the perceived threat from the tabloid press was particularly important here between 1983 and 1986, in shaping the image of the 'gay plague'.[31] This in turn led to the 'manning of the barricades' by the moral entrepreneurs, and the seeking out of largely symbolic solutions: quarantine, compulsory blood testing, immigration controls.[32] More widely there were manifestations of what Susan Sontag has called 'practices of decontamination',[33] against lesbians who at this stage did not seem vulnerable to HIV, as well as gay men who were: restaurants refused to serve gay customers, gay waiters were sacked, dentists refused to examine the teeth of homosexuals, technicians refused to test blood of people suspected of having AIDS, paramedics fumigated their ambulances, hospitals adopted barrier nursing, rubbish collectors wore masks while collecting garbage, prison officers refused to move prisoners, backstage staff in theatres refused to work with gay actors, distinguished pathologists refused to examine bodies, and undertakers refused to bury them.[34]

These were not universal experiences; there was altruism, self-sacrifice and empathy as well. But all these things happened, to people vulnerable to a devastating and life-threatening disease; and the vast majority of these people were homosexual. It is difficult to avoid seeing such manifestations as anything but panic-driven. The real plague as the *Guardian* famously put it, was panic.[35]

Of course, AIDS-related illnesses in the early 1980s were mysterious; fear was legitimate. It was not simply dreamt up by the press. There was a general sense of uncertainty, which shaped the early responses of the medical profession as well as politicians. Moreover, to describe these happenings as simply manifestations of a moral panic does not do justice to the complexity of what was happening, nor to the prolonged nature of some of the responses. It is perhaps better to see what happened as a series of panics, occasioned by particular events or new information or rumours, unified through a continuing discourse of hostility towards homosexuality (and the pursuit of circulation). Moral panic theory, moreover, does not explain why these social flurries of anxiety occur: they simply draw our attention to certain recurring phenomena, providing a template for description rather than a full analysis. Explanations of the AIDS panic must be found in all the other factors we have discussed.

Nevertheless, with all these qualifications, there is still some merit in using the term 'moral panic' as a way of describing the first major public stage of the response to AIDS, between roughly 1983 and 1986, not least because a perception of how the public was reacting determined the responses both of the community most affected, and of the government.

The complexity of social responses

My argument is that initial reactions to AIDS were structured by a complex history, which in turn produced a complex set of responses. To illustrate this I want, first of all, to look again at the experiences of the gay community. Identities in the contemporary world, it may be argued, are the means by which we negotiate the hazards of everyday life, and assert our sense of belonging.[36] They are rooted in history, or at least 'History' is evoked, but their effectiveness depends on their strategic placing in a complex play of power relations. The response to the new health crisis from the gay community provides a classic example of this. In particular, the early voluntary response to AIDS was able to draw on the sense of a common identity that had developed in the 1970s in order to operate in a situation where national government responses were absent, and where hostility towards the community was increasing. The Terrence Higgins Trust, which emerged in 1983 as the first British voluntary grouping, drew on a wealth of gay organising and campaigning experience, and this was crucially important. But the emergence of the dozens of other voluntary bodies that followed owed as much to the sense of identity provided by the ties and networks of the community as a whole than to any previous activist experience. Individuals were confirming their sense of common identity through involvement in the fight against HIV and AIDS. At the same time, many who were HIV positive or had been diagnosed with AIDS were affirming new identities, as 'Body Positive' or 'People with AIDS'.[37]

This sense of identity and belonging was crucial to the other major development within the gay community in the early 1980s, the adoption of a regime of what became known as 'safer sex'. It has been suggested that it was precisely the development of a resilient sense of self-esteem that was the 'sine qua non of safer sex education', and this has been confirmed by detailed studies.[38] The idea of safer sex had emerged in the early years of the American epidemic, and became central to the initial work of voluntary bodies and to the coverage of the issue in the gay press. There were clear signs of the success of safer sex campaigns by the mid-1980s, with a substantial drop in the incidence of sexually transmitted diseases amongst gay men. The detailed reasons for this are unclear, and there were clear variations in the sexual behaviour of gay men. It seemed likely that it was the urban gay man who was most likely to adopt explicit safer sex guidelines, with self-identification as part of the gay community as a crucial factor, and a sense of equality between partners as perhaps a vital element.[39]

The response of the gay community, and the major voluntary effort it sustained, was an expression of concern and involvement. It was also necessary in the absence of an appropriate official response until 1986. There is now well-documented evidence for the gradual creation of a 'policy community' around the health crisis in the years running up to the adoption of an official government strategy in late 1986, which drew on the expertise of leading figures in genito-urinary medicine, public health officials and activists largely drawn from the gay community. The outlines of what was to become the government response – an emphasis, in the absence of a likely 'cure', on prevention and health education – emerged, building on a much older tradition of public health policy which had its origins in the responses to diseases such as typhoid and cholera in the early days of industrialisation and urbanisation.[40]

On the other hand, it is difficult not to conclude that the association of AIDS with homosexuality, and to a lesser extent with other forms of social marginality, with all the historical baggage which these factors brought, determined governmental responses throughout the 1980s, particularly in the light of the moral panic in the early years. There was virtually no government response until 1984, when it intervened to secure the blood supply from contamination. It was 1986 before the first major initiative was taken directly by the government, which included the powers to detain people who were highly infectious (though these powers were rarely if ever used). Half of the fifty-nine parliamentary questions on AIDS in 1984–5 dealt with the blood supply, followed by drugs.[41] It is not to minimise the threat of HIV transmission from these sources to note the extraordinary disparity between the actual problem, amongst homosexual men, and the political priorities this suggests. It was to be November 1986 before there was a major House of Commons debate on the subject, four years after the first British deaths.

Two points need to be made. The first is that the government was operating in a situation that was widely perceived to be a gay crisis, at a time when as a result homosexuality was becoming deeply unpopular. The surveys of sexual attitudes during the 1980s are clear on this. The British Social Attitudes Survey for 1987 found that public opinion had become marginally less discriminatory towards homosexuality since 1983, with a greater acceptance also that lesbians and gay men should not be banned from certain professions. But when asked if they approved of 'homosexual relationships', there was evidence of a significant increase in hostility. In 1983, 62% had censured such relations; in 1985, 69%;

and in 1987, 74%. There was countervailing evidence also. A 1988 Gallup Poll for the *Sunday Telegraph*, whilst reporting that 60% of those sampled believed that homosexuality was not an acceptable lifestyle, observed that 50% of those under twenty-five were accepting.[42] It is also worth noting that all these surveys of opinion reported increased disapproval of extra-marital sexual relations, suggesting that what was happening was not only a reaction against homosexuality, but a reassertion of more conventional family values amongst significant sections of the population. Nevertheless, it is clear that AIDS was affecting the acceptability of homosexuality, and there was no great public support for more liberal policies towards lesbians and gays.

The second point that needs underlining is that the Thatcher government was highly sensitive to morally conservative currents of opinion. Even as the government was formulating a more considered policy towards the AIDS crisis in late 1986, the Secretary of State for Education was engaged in a complex campaign to prevent schools from providing positive images of homosexuality in response to conservative fears that left-wing local authorities were promoting homosexuality 'on the rates'. And this policy orientation was central to the government's strongest intervention on the subject during the 1980s: the banning by the Thatcher government of 'the promotion of homosexuality' by local authorities through what became known as 'Section 28' of the Local Government Act of 1988.

Behind the specific political context (in particular a government willingness to embarrass the Labour opposition over its ambiguous support for gay rights) was a deeper issue, a concern precisely with the challenge posed to 'traditional family values' by the claim to legitimacy by homosexuals. The famous neologism embodied in Section 28 – rejecting homosexuality as a 'pretended family relationship' – signalled that the claims of the lesbian and gay community in their fullness could not be accepted, because they were outside, antithetical to, the family. Despite the fervent advocacy of the more right-wing supporters of Section 28, this did not represent a challenge to the 1967 settlement, narrowly interpreted. There was no attempt to make homosexuality illegal. It did, however, challenge the claims of the vastly expanded lesbian and gay community as it had developed since 1970. 'Privacy', as far as homosexuality was concerned, was to be narrowly defined according to the interpretation of 1967. Anything beyond that was seen as a threat to the publicly sanctioned private sphere of the family endorsed by the conservative moral discourse of the 1980s.[43]

But even as the government supported what was widely seen as a repressive measure, it had specifically to exclude information about AIDS from its provisions. This highlights the difficulty of policy formation concerning sexuality in a complex society. For the new AIDS policy adopted in 1986 had assumed the need to promote sex education as the only way of halting the threatened epidemic. Implicitly, that meant the co-operation and involvement of the community most at risk, the gay community, a policy that was anathema to the ideologues behind the Thatcherite project.

The new government policy when it came did largely follow the developing policy consensus. The government in practice adopted traditional public health policies aimed at prevention rather than the more punitive policies of detention and segregation advocated by some of its supporters. The simple reason for this was that there appeared to be no practical alternative that would achieve widespread acceptability.[44] The advice that the Health Secretary offered to the nation – to use condoms, and avoid needle sharing – was not only sensible, it was essential. Only a public education campaign to increase awareness of HIV and AIDS, it was believed, would change people's behaviour. This new policy was undoubtedly inspired by the threat of a heterosexual epidemic, which had been dramatised by the publication of the US Surgeon-General's report on AIDS in October 1986. This, combined with mounting evidence that HIV was spreading in the 'heterosexual community' in Britain, propelled the new policy. It made it possible for the proponents of the developing policy and medical consensus to seize the ears of ministers; and it provided ministers, wary of a volatile public opinion and a raucous press, with the opportunity to make a radical departure. Five years into the crisis, AIDS had achieved the 'critical mass' to put it at the top of the policy agenda.

But there were multiple ironies in the policy departure. The policy adopted was basically one of sex education, at a time when the government was elsewhere pursuing a policy of redefining and restricting sex education, by taking it out of the hands of the despised local education authorities and giving responsibility largely to parents, who were thought likely to be more con- servative. In part, too, the government was building on the achievements of the voluntary sector, largely led by the gay community which its policies otherwise sought to undermine.

The policy shift in 1986 signalled a new determination on the part of the government to manage the crisis, using by and large the traditional methods of what has been called the 'biomedical elite'. Yet once the period of 'emergency' passed, and crisis management became routinised, there were signs that the government's moral preoccupations had not changed. Hard on the heels of speculation that the heterosexual threat had been exaggerated in 1989, the special AIDS education unit of the Health Education Authority was disbanded, the Cabinet sub-committee overseeing the policy was wound up and Mrs Thatcher personally vetoed government support for a major academic study of sexual behaviour, designed to explore patterns of behaviour likely to facilitate spread of HIV. The media, not only the tabloids, seized the opportunity to state as a fact that AIDS was still a gay disease, and not a real heterosexual threat. It was hard to avoid the conclusion that for many people AIDS only mattered if it was a heterosexual problem.[45]

This certainly was the perception in the community still most at risk. There was a deep sense of frustration amongst lesbian and gay activists, confirmed by the passing into law of Section 28, that gave rise in the late 1980s to a new militancy in the HIV/AIDS and gay communities. A direct action grouping, ACT-UP (AIDS Coalition to Unleash Power), was established in 1989, echoing the American organisation set up in New York in 1987, and deliberately re-calling the militant gay activism of the early 1970s. A number of individuals who had been heavily involved in the earlier voluntary effort gave their support to the new venture, out of a sense that moderation and discreet behind the scenes lobbying had not fundamentally changed government attitudes.[46]

This seemed to be confirmed by an apparent increase in anti-gay prejudice and random violence following the passing of Section 28. By the end of the decade, there was also evidence that prosecutions for consensual homosexual offences had reached a new high (comparable with the previous high total in 1954, before the establishment of the Wolfenden Committee). New government initiatives in 1990/1, threatening to increase penalties for homosexual offences through the Criminal Justice Bill, and attempting to prevent lesbians and gay men from adopting children, sparked widespread opposition and the emergence of new militant lesbian and gay groupings, such as Outrage.[47]

Yet the paradoxical result of the first decade of AIDS was that homosexuality had achieved a voice as never before. Following extensive gay lobbying and activism, the penalties in the Criminal Justice Bill were modified, and new liaison procedures with the police were established. The new Prime Minister, John Major, had a much publicised meeting with a leading member of the gay community. In part such successes were the result of that 'legitimisation through disaster' which Altman has seen as a characteristic of the AIDS crisis.[48] As open lesbians and gays were drawn into policy formation and service delivery, as knowledge about gay lifestyles, and sexual practices, spread as a result of discussions of HIV and AIDS, so the homosexual community achieved a new openness and public presence. There was even some evidence that the 'blip' in public acceptability of homosexuality in the mid-1980s caused by the fear of AIDS had been overcome, with a small but important growth of support. Margaret Thatcher, despite AIDS and her conservative moral agenda, had in fact presided over a considerable growth in the self-confidence and social weight of the lesbian and gay community.

Yet the boundaries between acceptable and unacceptable sexual behaviour remained fluid and indeterminate and homosexuality remained ambiguously on the margins of social life, its acceptability still in doubt. Ambiguity was the hallmark also of government policy. During the 1980s there can be no doubt that government was constrained by its moral agenda. That did not stop the development of coherent policies by the policy and medical establishment, nor their implementation at national and local level when the crisis seemed acute. But the national policy was implemented in a climate of anxiety which the government's own moral agenda did little to alleviate, and that inevitably had a major impact on how the policy developed.

Meanwhile the health crisis ground on. Though the majority of deaths from AIDS by the beginning of the 1990s were still amongst gay men, the evidence of the underlying HIV epidemic suggested the pattern was beginning to change, with the rate of reported infection rising most rapidly amongst women. It was estimated that by the year 2001, 4,800 men and 1,200 women would die from AIDS annually; by 2011 the annual total would rise to 7,000. HIV, it seemed, would be increasingly a problem for heterosexuals, for women and for black people.[49] By the early 1990s there was evidence that the heterosexual spread was in large part amongst drug users and people from Africa, ominously echoing the development of the epidemic in the USA. But whatever the roots of transmission, the virus was slowly entering the heterosexual population. Once again, the government established a ministerial AIDS action group. Clearly the crisis was not over; in some ways it was still to come, with unpredictable implications for the future regulation of sexuality.

The histories I have outlined demonstrate the unpredictability and complexity of responses when a society is confronted by an unexpected and in many ways unprecedented crisis. In confronting the unpredictability of events 'History' is called upon to offer remedies. These could be drawn from a self-conscious history of resistance (the response of the gay community); from a history of public health (the response of the medical elite); or from a moral history which evoked a value system that probably by this time did not command widespread support, and which underlined a sensitivity to the dangers of rushing too far ahead of public opinion (by and large, the response of the Thatcher government during the 1980s). This suggests the key conclusion: the regulation of sexuality cannot be understood through a monocausal account. On the contrary, it reveals the interplay of diverse forces, burdened (like AIDS) by a multiplicity of often incompatible histories.

NOTES

1 For discussions of the multiple histories of AIDS, see Elizabeth Fee and Daniel M. Fox (eds.), *AIDS: The Burdens of History* (Berkeley, 1988), and Elizabeth Fee and Daniel M. Fox (eds.), *AIDS: The Making of a Chronic Disease* (Berkeley, 1992).

2 For a fuller development contextualisation of the points made here, see Jeffrey Weeks, *Sexuality and its Discontents: Meanings, Myths and Modern Sexualities* (London, 1985); and *idem, Sexuality* (Chichester and London, 1986).

3 The *locus classicus* of constructionist arguments is Michel Foucault, *The History of Sexuality*, vol. I: *An Introduction* (London, 1979). This little book made a major

impact, however, because it fed into theoretical debates already stimulated by the development of what was originally a 'grass-roots history', by feminist and lesbian and gay historians. For a general discussion of these developments, see Jeffrey Weeks, 'Sexuality and history revisited', in Lynn Jamieson and Helen Corr (eds.), *State, Private Life and Political Change* (Basingstoke and London, 1990), 31–49. For a sympathetic but appropriately critical overview of the various arguments, see Carole S. Vance, 'Social construction theory: problems in the history of sexuality', in Anja von Kooten Niekerk and Theo van der Meer (eds.), *Which Homosexuality?: Essays from the International Scientific Conference on Lesbian and Gay Studies* (Amsterdam and London, 1989).

4 Foucault, *The History*; Jeffrey Weeks, *Sex, Politics and Society: The Regulation of Sexuality since 1800* (Harlow, 1st edn, 1981, 2nd edn, 1989).

5 On the impact of the syphilis epidemic, see Judith R. Walkowitz, *Prostitution and Victorian Society: Women, Class and the State* (Cambridge, 1980).

6 For major contributions on this debate, see the essays in Edward Stein (ed.), *Forms of Desire: Sexual Orientation and the Social Constructionist Controversy* (New York and London, 1990).

7 See, for example, the discussion of this in Weeks, *Sexuality and its Discontents*, chapter 3.

8 On the ever-accelerating rapidity of social change, as the 'juggernaut of modernity' gathers speed, see Anthony Giddens, *The Consequences of Modernity* (Cambridge, 1990).

9 See Weeks, *Sex, Politics and Society* (1989 edn), chapter 15.

10 See the essays in Stuart Hall and Martin Jacques (eds.), *The Politics of Thatcherism* (London, 1983) and Ruth Levitas (ed.), *The Ideology of the New Right* (Oxford, 1986).

11 For a conservative view of the period, see Christie Davies, *Permissive Britain* (London, 1975). For a more radical analysis of the period see National Deviancy Conference (ed.), *Permissiveness and Control. The Fate of Sixties Legislation* (London, 1980).

12 Home Office and Scottish Home Department, *Report of the Committee on Homosexual Offences and Prostitution*, Cmnd 247 (London, 1957).

13 Weeks, *Sex, Politics and Society* (1989 edn), chapter 13. On the debates leading to the passing of the Sexual Offences Act 1967, which partially decriminalised male homosexuality, see Stephen Jeffery-Poulter, *Peers, Queers and Commons. The Struggle for Gay Law Reform from 1950 to the Present* (London, 1991). For a comparison with the rights-based developments in the USA during the same period see, Thomas B. Stoddard and Walter Rieman, 'AIDS and the rights of the individual: towards a more sophisticated understanding of discrimination', in Dorothy Nelkin, David P. Willis and Scott V. Parris (eds.), *A Disease of Society: Cultural and Institutional Responses to AIDS* (Cambridge, 1991), 241–71.

14 Ronald Butt, 'Lloyd George knew his followers', *Times*, 19 September 1985.

15 Jeffrey Weeks, *Coming Out: Homosexual Politics in Britain from the Nineteenth Century to the Present* (2nd edn, London, 1990), Part 5: 'The Gay Liberation Movement'.

16 The relation of these polarised *political* positions to actual public attitudes and behaviour is a complex one. Broadly, I would argue, there was a long term

'liberalisation' and 'secularisation' of attitudes, that continued despite AIDS and the dominance of a morally conservative government in the 1980s. See my *Sexuality*, and *Sex, Politics and Society* (1989 edn), chapter 15.

17 Stuart Hall, *The Hard Road to Renewal. Thatcherism and the Crisis of the Left* (London, 1989).

18 For a perceptive account of Mrs Thatcher's moral politics, based on her address to the General Assembly of the Church of Scotland in 1988, see Jonathan Raban, *God, Man and Mrs Thatcher* (London, 1988).

19 Martin Durham, *Sex and Politics: The Family and Morality in the Thatcher Years* (Basingstoke, 1991).

20 Anna Marie Smith, 'A symptomology of an authoritarian discourse. The parliamentary debates on the prohibition of the promotion of homosexuality', in *New Formations. A Journal of Culture/Theory/Politics*, 10 (Spring 1990), 41–65.

21 On the early American reaction to the burgeoning epidemic see Dennis Altman, *AIDS and the New Puritanism* (London, 1986), published in the USA as *AIDS in the Mind of America* (New York, 1986).

22 Weeks, *Coming Out*, chapter 17. For international comparisons, see Barry D. Adam, *The Rise of a Gay and Lesbian Movement* (Boston, Mass., 1987).

23 Gillian E. Hanscombe and Andrew Lumsden, *Title Fight: The Battle for Gay News* (London, 1983).

24 On the situation in the USA in the late 1970s and early 1980s, see Dennis Altman, *The Homosexualization of America, the Americanization of the Homosexual* (New York, 1972).

25 Weeks, *Coming Out*, chapter 15.

26 On the importance of relationships in the gay community, see my essay 'Male homosexuality in the age of AIDS', in Jeffrey Weeks, *Against Nature: Essays on History, Sexuality and Identity* (London, 1991), 100–13.

27 Speech of 27 March 1982.

28 On these themes, see, for example, the essays in Tessa Boffin and Sunil Gupta (eds.), *Ecstatic Antibodies: Resisting the AIDS Mythology* (London, 1990). On the 'sense of an ending', particularly in relation to AIDS, see Susan Sontag, *AIDS and its Metaphors* (London, 1989); and Elaine Showalter, *Sexual Anarchy: Gender and Culture at the Fin de Siècle* (London, 1991). On difference and identity, see the essays in Jonathan Rutherford (ed.), *Identity: Community, Culture, Difference* (London, 1990).

29 Nelkin, Willis and Parris (eds.), *A Disease of Society*, p. 3.

30 I first used the concept in relation to AIDS in 1985 in *Sexuality and its Discontents*, p. 45. The concept has been criticised by Simon Watney, 'AIDS, "moral panic" theory and homophobia', in Peter Aggleton and Hilary Homans (eds.), *Social Aspects of AIDS* (London, 1988), 52–64; and by Philip Strong and Virginia Berridge, 'No one knew anything: some issues in British AIDS policy', in Peter Aggleton, Peter Davies and Graham Hart (eds.), *AIDS: Individual, Cultural and Policy Dimensions* (London, 1990), 245–7.

31 On media response, see Simon Watney, *Policing Desire: Pornography, AIDS and the Media* (London, 1987); and Kaye Wellings, 'Perceptions of risk – media treatments of AIDS', in Aggleton and Homans (eds.), *Social Aspects of AIDS*, 83–105.

32 See the discussion in Jeffrey Weeks, 'Love in a cold climate', in Aggleton and Homans (eds.), *Social Aspects of AIDS*, 10–19.

33 Susan Sontag, *Illness as Metaphor* (New York, 1978).

34 All these incidents can be documented in the press between 1983 and 1986.

35 'The real plague is panic', leader column, *Guardian*, 19 February 1985.

36 See Albero Melucci, *Nomads of the Present: Social Movements and Individual Needs in Contemporary Society* (London, 1989) and Anthony P. Cohen, *The Symbolic Construction of Community* (Chichester, London and New York, 1985).

37 For some discussion of the voluntary response, see Strong and Berridge, 'No one knew anything: some issues in British AIDS policy', and Zoe Schramm-Evans, 'Responses to AIDS, 1986–1987', in Aggleton, Davies and Hart (eds.), *AIDS: Individual, Cultural and Policy Dimensions*, and Virginia Berridge, 'The early years of AIDS in the United Kingdom 1981–6: historical perspectives', in T. Ranger and P. Slack (eds.), *Epidemics and Ideas* (Cambridge, 1992).

38 Simon Watney, 'Safer sex as community practice', in Aggleton, Davies and Hart (eds.), *AIDS: Individual, Cultural and Policy Dimensions*; and Simon Watney, 'AIDS: the second decade: risk, research and modernity', and Mitchell Cohen, 'Changing to safer sex: personality, logic and habit', in Peter Aggleton, Graham Hart and Peter Davies (eds.), *AIDS: Responses, Interventions and Care* (London, 1991).

39 Ray Fitzpatrick, Mary Boulton and Graham Hart, 'Gay men's sexual behaviour in response to AIDS', in Peter Aggleton, Graham Hart and Peter Davies (eds.), *AIDS: Social Representations, Social Practices* (London, 1989); Ray Fitzpatrick, John McLean, Mary Boulton, Graham Hart and Jill Dawson, 'Variations in sexual behaviour in gay men', in Aggleton, Davies and Hart (eds.), *AIDS: Individual, Cultural and Policy Dimensions*; and Cohen, 'Changing to safer sex'. It is worth noting here that by the end of the 1980s there were ominous signs that younger gay men, identifying HIV as a disease of older men, were abandoning safer sex; and the rates of sexually transmitted disease (STD) infection showed signs of increasing once again. One London hospital noted twice the rates of gonorrhea infection in the first six months of 1990 as in the whole of 1989 (*Independent on Sunday*, 14 October 1990). Clearly the adoption of safer sex, though uneven, was much greater in the gay community than elsewhere, with heterosexual men proving particularly resistant to its messages (see Tamsin Wilton and Peter Aggleton, 'Condoms, coercion and control: heterosexuality and the limits to HIV/AIDS education', in Aggleton, Hart and Davies (eds.), *AIDS: Responses, Interventions and Care*). But another history, that making important generational differences within the gay community, was apparently reasserting itself.

40 V. Berridge and P. Strong, 'AIDS policies in the UK: a study in contemporary behaviour', *Twentieth Century British History*, 2, 2 (1991), 150–74; Berridge, 'The early years of AIDS in the United Kingdom'.

41 Berridge, 'The early years of AIDS in the United Kingdom'.

42 Roger Jowell, Sharon Witherspoon and Lindsay Brook, *British Social Attitudes: The 1986 Report* (Aldershot, 1988); *Sunday Telegraph*, 5 June 1988.

43 On the background to Section 28 see Smith, 'A symptomology of an authoritarian discourse'; also my essay 'Pretended family relationships', in Jeffrey Weeks, *Against Nature* (London, 1991).

44 See Berridge and Strong, 'AIDS policies in the UK', and Strong and Berridge, 'No one knew anything: some issues in British AIDS policy'.

45 See 'PM angers doctors by axing AIDS study', *Guardian*, 11 September 1989; 'Thatcher disbands Cabinet AIDS team', *Sunday Correspondent*, 17 September 1989.

46 Tony Whitehead, 'The voluntary sector: five years on', in Erica Carter and Simon Watney (eds.), *Taking Liberties: AIDS and Cultural Politics* (London, 1989).

47 See, for example, Labour Campaign for Lesbian and Gay Rights, *Emergency Briefing on Paragraph 16 and Clause 25* (London, 1990); 'Not fit to foster', *Pink Paper*, 5 January 1991; Jayne Egerton, 'Gay parents: nothing natural', *New Statesman and Society*, 16 November 1990; Sean O'Neill, 'Are the police looking the other way', *The Independent*, 18 December 1990; Nick Cohen, 'MPs oppose tough court penalties for homosexuals', *The Independent*, 10 January 1991; GALOP (Gay London Policing Project), *Annual Report* (London, 1990); 'Gay protest sealed with a kiss', *The Independent*, 6 September 1990; and '"Outing group" to name MPs as homosexual', *The Independent*, 29 July 1991.

48 Dennis Altman, 'AIDS and the reconceptualization of homosexuality', in van Kooten Niekerk and van der Meer (eds.), *Which Homosexuality?*

49 *OPCS Monitor*, PP2 91/1; Chris Mihill, 'AIDS figures prompt race backlash fears', *Guardian*, 9 August 1991.

2

Public health doctors and AIDS as a public health issue

JANE LEWIS

Most of the literature on HIV infection makes at least passing reference to 'public health'. However, the meaning of the term varies enormously. The public health implications of AIDS may be identified as the ways of protecting the population from infection, or, especially in the USA, may raise the issue of how to provide health care services for persons with AIDS within a badly fragmented system that offers only limited access. The public health issues arising from HIV are usually agreed to cover its epidemiology, to which disease control centres in both Britain and the USA have made the major contribution, and also the controversial debates arising from the interpretation of epidemiological data, which have focused on the protection of civil rights in face of measures to test for and control the spread of the infection. The behavioural changes believed to be necessary to prevent the infection may also be referred to under the heading of public health education. The lack of clarity that marks the discussion of public health in the literature merely reflects the wide-ranging – some would say, less flatteringly, 'rag-bag'[1] – nature of public health ideology and practice in the mid- and late twentieth century. Since the heroic battles of the nineteenth century for clean water and sanitation, and against infectious disease, the identity of public health as a specialty and in its relations to medicine has been far from clear. The extent to which its practice has been effective in promoting the health of the population has also been called into question by both contemporaries and historians.[2]

   Public health doctors have experienced major difficulties in taking up a collective as opposed to an individualist approach to the health needs of the population vis à vis both the rest of the medical profession and government. Within the medical profession, British public health doctors have occupied a low status throughout the twentieth century and, since the 1974 and more especially the 1984 reorganisations of the National Health Service (NHS) have become increasingly hard to identify as a professional body. In the USA, the public health establishment is more readily identifiable and specialists in infectious disease have continued to have good career prospects, even though public health

37

has become a much more interdisciplinary endeavour than in Britain. As an infectious disease, AIDS was, initially at least, perceived to call on the old tradition of public health expertise and the advice of public health practitioners was actively sought. Towards the end of the 1980s, the modelling of HIV infection underwent a significant change. The problem of managing persons with AIDS was increasingly viewed in relation to the management of chronic disease more generally. At the same time, the basis of prevention moved from an overwhelming emphasis on lifestyle prevention, in the sense of encouraging change in individual sexual behaviour, to a recognition of the problems in devising effective preventive measures among populations who could already be classified as materially disadvantaged in a number of respects.[3]

This chapter seeks, first, to chart the way in which the shift in the modelling of AIDS over a single decade has in fact mirrored the shift public health doctors have been struggling to make since the late nineteenth century in defining a role for themselves in a society no longer dominated by infectious disease. The changing meaning of health promotion and the prevention of disease, and the relationship of public health practice to health care delivery, have long been issues for public health. In Britain, AIDS posed a challenge to a public health profession that was severely demoralised. In making a response, public health also sought yet again to redefine its role. The last part of this chapter examines the extent to which public health in its revised form may be able to address the issues raised by AIDS as they are currently being defined. In many respects AIDS highlights the weaknesses of both public health and the NHS.

Modelling AIDS

Daniel M. Fox has recently described the way in which the diagrams that experts used to describe AIDS to audiences of health and policy professionals changed dramatically during the 1980s. For most of the decade they drew an iceberg, with only the top susceptible to treatment, but by 1989 they were drawing a time-line 'intersected by numerous and increasing opportunities for intervention'.[4] The perception of AIDS as a chronic disease requiring management was superseding the model that depicted it as a new plague.

Following the naming of AIDS and the perception of it as a novel, fatal and potentially widespread disease, responses were in large measure shaped by what Philip Strong has described as 'epidemic psychology'. He describes this as involving three components: an epidemic of fear, an epidemic of explanation and moralisation and an epidemic of action or proposed action.[5] Epidemiologists named the disease and epidemiologists continued to make the running during the first half of the 1980s (until the isolation of the HIV virus in 1984), as befitted the widespread fear of a new and apparently uncontrollable disease. The preoccupations revolved around establishing where the disease came from, how to protect endangered communities and how to put in motion research to develop vaccines and experimental cures.

The epidemiological data enabled researchers to describe the high incidence of the disease among the gay population. After that, it was open to a variety of interpretations. Epidemiology has historically been characterised (and some would argue restricted)[6] by its lack of theoretical context. There have been periods, for example in Britain during the late 1940s, when practitioners have attempted more firmly to tie the practice of epidemiology to social science methods. Thus J. N. Morris and Richard Titmuss stressed the importance of a multifactorial approach and of social variables in the study of factors inimical and favourable to health. But in both Britain and the USA the medical establishment proved suspicious of the social. Thus Morris and Titmuss's work on the epidemiology of rheumatic heart disease was criticised for emphasising the poverty factor too much and in the USA some epidemiologists set out explicitly to 'rescue' their discipline from such concerns and bring it back firmly into the 'laps of practising physicians'.[7]

While consideration of social factors could, in particular circumstances, lead to 'progressive' conclusions, especially when pitted against clinical or genetic factors, this was not necessarily the result. In the case of AIDS, the danger that social and moral judgements would be applied once the gay community was identified as a 'high risk group' was readily apparent. Thus the early years of AIDS saw suggestions that the disease resulted from 'immune overload' which was linked to recurrent bouts of sexually transmitted disease, which in turn could be attributed to promiscuity.[8] Such a chain of causality did little to illuminate the case of the middle-aged monogamous woman with AIDS that was to emerge in the mid-1980s. The search for cause proceeded from the identification of the group most at risk rather than from risk-bearing acts. This was arguably inevitable in the early stages of research, but it did not change as it logically should have done when the HIV virus was isolated, serving to redefine AIDS as a set of biomedical problems. Only when the heterosexual population was perceived as a population at risk did such a shift begin to take place.[9] As Ken Plummer has noted, the rhetoric of medicine and morality has been hard to distinguish;[10] the person with AIDS was constructed as the source of the disease rather than the sufferer.[11]

The second preoccupation of the plague model – the protection of endangered communities – thus immediately raised issues to do with the control of those infected with HIV, which both threatened to stigmatise the perceived risk group and to curtail their civil liberties. In the USA, the Institute of Medicine and the National Academy of Sciences summarised these issues as comprising: specific education for high risk groups, voluntary versus mandatory testing and reporting of test results, contact tracing, screening, regulations to close public places (as in the decision to close the gay bathhouses in San Francisco in 1984) and quarantine.

The impetus to compulsory public health measures was differently mediated in the USA and in Britain. In the latter, the voice of public health, embodied most influentially in the views of the Chief Medical Officer, Sir Donald Acheson, came out firmly against compulsion and appealed to the historical evidence in so doing. Dorothy and Roy Porter have reminded us of the historically weak alliance between public health and government in matters of compulsion. In the nineteenth century, success in imposing compulsory vaccination against smallpox and the Contagious Diseases Acts (which forced prostitutes to undergo medical examination for VD) was overthrown by repeal movements.[12] But as the Porters note, the most active component of medical opposition consisted of the GPs, who acted more out of a professional interest in preserving patient/doctor confidentiality than out of a regard for civil liberties. The position of public health has been historically ambivalent, population medicine offered a broad territory for population control. But on the whole the public health doctors' traditional concern with environmental factors has propelled them towards the educational end of the interventionist spectrum when it has been a matter of promoting change in the behaviour of individuals. Thus at the beginning of the twentieth century, when infant mortality was identified as one of the most significant public health issues, public health doctors eschewed the more Draconian features of extreme eugenic analysis in favour of 'educating mothers' in clinics, or, more intrusively, via health visitors.

In the context of AIDS, Simon Watney has identified two approaches, that of the 'terrorist' who, identifying an external invader, recommends testing, compulsion and even quarantine; and that of the 'missionary', who sees instead an evil spirit which thrives on immorality and possesses its victims, and recommends in response a return to traditional values.[13] It may be that it was the technical difficulty in securing exclusion that was most important in determining the approach to AIDS. The long incubation period, the very large numbers already infected before the epidemic was discovered, the initial absence of a quick and certain test and the huge numbers involved in international travel certainly all made the operation of quarantine regulations very difficult. Nevertheless, Watney's argument has the merit of signalling the elision between the moral and the social which has been historically present in public health policy and continues to be particularly prominent in the treatment of AIDS. In Britain, while public health doctors considered the issues of notifying, testing, screening and the like at length, a firm stand was taken against compulsion, notably by Acheson in, for example, both his evidence to the House of Commons Social Services Committee in 1987,[14] and his stand against the British Medical Association's (BMA) decision in 1987 to allow doctors to perform tests without consent, which was reversed the following year. While in 1984 regulations were changed to allow the compulsory removal of a person with AIDS to hospital, these were invoked only once. The position in the USA has been somewhat different, where, in Ronald Bayer's analysis, the public health voice found itself outflanked and where testing has been made mandatory for a range of employees of public institutions.[15]

The plague model of AIDS involved battles over what had been the public health territory of the nineteenth century – the control of epidemic, infectious disease. While the nature of the epidemiologists' multifactorial analysis of infection provided a space for a reactionary social politics, equally the public health profession's long consideration of environmental and social as well as biomedical factors served to moderate the policy response. It was not on the whole public health physicians who advocated that the legendary 1860s response to the cholera epidemic (consisting of the removal of the handle to the pump supplying infected water) be applied to the perceived source of AIDS, that is, the gay community.

As Fee and Fox have noted, the historical analogies to AIDS that were invoked were always epidemics such as smallpox and cholera, rather than, for instance, TB, which would have raised to mind rather different policy issues, involving problems of housing, poverty and community care.[16] The epidemic psychology of AIDS has, of course, been closely related to sexual politics and many commentators have made the connection between the fear of AIDS as a 'gay plague' and the great importance attached by New Right governments during the 1980s both to traditional sexual morality, and to the heterosexual two parent family as the motor of national stability and the chief provider of welfare.[17] However, towards the end of the 1980s expert models of HIV infection began to focus more on the problems of living with AIDS as opposed to the issues arising from the overwhelming fear of dying from the infection.

A number of factors account for the new construction of AIDS as a chronic disease. The isolation of the HIV virus meant that AIDS became redefined as a set of biomedical problems open to chemical resolution. Expensive treatments followed (principally involving the use of the drug AZT), which did not cure, but which made it possible to prolong life. The 'management' of the person with AIDS therefore became of increasing concern to the doctors and health service managers. At the same time, Virginia Berridge and Philip Strong have argued that in Britain the years after 1987 marked the assertion of the biomedical establishment's control over AIDS,[18] which contributed materially to the 'normalisation' of policy. During the first half of the 1980s, AIDS was increasingly perceived as a new kind of disease with a huge potential to kill. The British government became involved in a massive health education campaign in 1986 when the potential for infection among the heterosexual community was finally recognised. During these early years, Berridge and Strong have pointed to the existence of a relatively open 'policy community' around the Chief

Medical Officers at the then Department of Health and Social Security (DHSS). These were the years when 'no one knew anything'.[19] But between 1987 and 1989, expert opinion appeared to 'stabilise'. The 1989 House of Commons Social Services Committee commented on the scaling down of the figures for HIV infection during 1988;[20] in contrast to the Committee's report in 1987, AIDS was beginning to be perceived more as a long haul than an all-out battle. It was in 1987 too that the first estimate of the costs of caring for AIDS patients was published in the form of a letter to the *British Medical Journal*.[21] From 1987 the pattern of care for persons with HIV-related infection became more and more the focus of concern.

Just as it interlocked with the 1980s concern about 'the family', so AIDS also entered the debate over community care. The 1987 Social Services Committee Report stressed the achievements of gay voluntary organisations in San Francisco in providing continuous care whereby the hospitalisation of persons with AIDS was reduced to an average of two weeks a year. The movement towards community care, begun in the 1960s as a humanitarian policy by those desiring to promote 'normalisation' for both the elderly and mentally ill, had by the 1980s become part and parcel of the government's desire to reduce public expenditure, notwithstanding constant warnings from Titmuss as early as the 1960s that good community care could not be provided cheaply. In 1981, in a White Paper on the elderly, government warned that increasingly care 'in' the community would have to mean care 'by' the community, meaning that the sources of care would increasingly be 'informal', whether in the form of family members or voluntary organisations.[22]

Within this framework, the San Francisco model, which relied primarily on voluntary effort, looked very attractive. Health authorities feared the conflicting pressures of, for example, the hospital needs of persons with AIDS versus those of the elderly[23] at a time of cash crisis, NHS reform and the uncertainty surrounding the future of special funding for AIDS.[24] After 1987, authorities began to produce plans which allowed for only two weeks in-patient care a year with an appeal to a 'multiagency strategy' to facilitate the provision of housing, nursing and domestic help.[25] The response by the gay community to the shifting perceptions of AIDS and AIDS policies has been ambivalent, the fear being that while the perception of AIDS as a chronic disease may help those living with AIDS, it might also make it more difficult to exact money for basic research. The pride in caring, perhaps made more explicit by the American gay community than the British,[26] was strong, but was moderated by the desire for help, which the focus on the needs of those living with AIDS might be expected to bring. However, such a hope has been tempered by a political climate unsympathetic to further public expenditure and the increasing realisation that care in the community raises needs that are broader than health and personal social services, including crucially income and housing.[27] In this sense, the work of tertiary prevention in relation to persons with AIDS demands attention to structural as much as to lifestyle change. In addition, the population of those with HIV infection had become by the end of the 1980s considerably broader than the gay community. Drug addicts in particular could not fall back on voluntary aid.[28]

The new model of HIV infection therefore raises crucial issues as to the level of provision and co-ordination of different types of care for very different groups of people with AIDS. The plague model, with its focus on the cause of infection and the prevention of disease among the well, ignored what the medical profession has long referred to as tertiary prevention, meaning the promotion of health among the chronically or terminally ill. Such a shift in the modelling of AIDS has therefore brought new issues regarding health care and education on to the agenda. There is, of course, as Fox has cautioned, no guarantee that the AIDS model will not change dramatically again.[29] As recently as 1988, Fox himself, together with Fee, argued that health services were experiencing difficulty in dealing with AIDS because it was an infectious disease rather than the kind of chronic condition late twentieth-century medicine was used to dealing with (an argument which seemed to carry the controversial implication that the delivery of health care had indeed become successfully geared to the care of chronic conditions).[30] There is no guarantee that the issues of compulsion associated with the plague model will go away. Indeed, if the AIDS population becomes increasingly poor and, compared to the gay community, less powerful in terms of its lobbying capacity, these matters may regain importance. But the issues surrounding those living with HIV infection are not likely to go away. The shifting model of AIDS has meant that public health expertise has no longer been the frontline source of advice in the way in which it was when the infection was perceived to have much in common with nineteenth-century battles against epidemics. Indeed, the more recent model throws into sharp relief the difficulties public health has experienced in redefining its role in relation to the more general patterning of disease as overwhelmingly chronic, and in relation to the meaning of prevention and promotion. Some thirty years ago the public health profession was roundly criticised for not doing enough to co-ordinate community care; it remains to be seen whether recent efforts to define its role will make it more flexible in its future response.

Models for public health

Throughout the twentieth century, British public health doctors have been engaged in a redefinition of their role. During the 1980s this process has been closely bound up with the response to AIDS, but it is useful to understand the ways in which it is but the latest episode in a long renegotiation of public health's position. Nineteenth-century public health practitioners tackled water companies and other vested interests, as well as governments, in order to secure social reform that would prevent infectious disease. But in the twentieth century it has not been easy to address the full range of social, economic and environmental variables, including income and housing as well as personal lifestyle and health education, that may be considered to play a part in determining health status. The political battles involved in promoting the people's health have proved much larger than those required to attack specific environmental causes of disease. As a medical specialty, public health could be surer of its ground in fighting disease than in the murkier waters of promoting health; the latter all too easily became bound up with improving welfare, something both government and the medical profession itself considered to be outside the doctor's mandate. Nor has it proved straightforward to redefine prevention in relation to chronic disease; while efforts were made to minimise the division between prevention and cure, effective strategies for promoting tertiary prevention were developed but slowly.

From the early twentieth century, public health was reined in to focus on prevention and promotion in relation to the individual. As a result, the extent to which such a focus necessitated a consideration of health service administration and/or planning, and how it differed from the work of other, much more powerful, medical specialties became pressing problems. I have argued elsewhere that in this climate the practice of public health became effectively determined by the tasks it managed to accrue rather than by a strong sense of purpose and direction.[31] Arguably, the three major efforts to rethink the position of public health, embodied in the focus on personal preventive medicine in the early part of the century, and the further efforts to introduce social medicine in the 1940s and community medicine in the 1970s, were not very successful. Broad agreement greeted the mapping of the late twentieth-century health field by landmark documents such as the Lalonde Report of 1974,[32] which identified the areas of environment, lifestyle, health services and biomedical concerns as crucial. However, public health has not been able to assert a leadership role over environmental as well as lifestyle issues, or indeed over the balance of the health services needed for communities.

At the end of the nineteenth century, scientific advances in bacteriology helped to redefine the kind of intervention appropriate for public health. Once it was realised that dirt *per se* did not cause infectious disease, the broad mandate of public health to deal with all aspects of environmental sanitation and housing as the means of promoting cleanliness disappeared. Germ theory deflected attention from the primary cause of disease in the environment and from the individual's relationship to that environment and made a direct appeal from mortality figures to social reform much more difficult.[33] Increasingly public health authorities focused on what the individual should do to ensure personal hygiene. Paul Starr has characterised the shift in the changing nature of public health work in the twentieth century as a move towards a 'new concept of dirt'.[34]

As a result of germ theory, the twentieth-century concept of dirt 'narrowed' and also proved considerably cheaper to clean up. Thus in addition to developments in medical science, there was a political imperative to a more limited, less costly, mandate for public health.

Sir George Newman, the Chief Medical Officer at the newly formed Ministry of Health in 1919 offered a new model for public health, insisting that it 'must give up the idea that health is comprised in sewerage, disinfection, the suppression of nuisances, the burial of the dead, notification and registration of disease, fever hospitals, and endless restrictive by-laws and regulations. Health springs from the domestic, social and personal life of the people'.[35] Newman argued for preventive medicine based on the individual, which would involve a closer integration between preventive and curative medicine. However, the importance that Newman attached to public health as clinical medicine of a special kind – 'applied physiology' focused on the individual – brought the practice of public health confusingly close to that of general practice. During the late 1920s, GPs began to protest that they were the proper people to be dealing with all matters of health maintenance and disease prevention in respect of individuals.

Even though this claim substantially undercut the new rationale that public health was using to justify its existence, public health doctors were not unduly daunted during the inter-war years. For, notwithstanding the low status of the public health doctor as a salaried employee of local government, the public health departments became the administrators of the various piecemeal health service initiatives of the inter-war period. This work, rather than the model of individual prevention offered by Newman, became the mainstay of their practice, although many of the services they administered involved some elements of personal preventive medicine. By 1939, local authorities were permitted to provide maternal and child health services; a school medical service, including clinics treating minor ailments; dentistry; TB schemes, involving sanatorium treatment, clinics and aftercare services; infectious disease, ear, nose and throat and VD services; and health centres, the most elaborate being that built by the Finsbury Borough Council in 1938. In addition, the Local Government Act of 1929 allowed local authorities to take over the poor law hospitals and, by 1938, the number of acute beds provided by them equalled that provided by the voluntary sector. Finally, the Cancer Act of 1939 placed responsibility for the development of local regional cancer schemes on the local authorities rather than on the voluntary hospitals.

Public health doctors threw themselves into the work of medical administration, especially in regard to hospitals, the hub of the medical world, with gusto. There was a limited amount of contemporary criticism to the effect that public health was neglecting the work of prevention in favour of 'pathology'. The editor of one of the specialty's journals commented crossly that 'much recent public health work seems to aim at converting it into a gigantic hospital'.[36] In the case of both diphtheria and TB, the two major infectious diseases of the period, there was the tendency for public health doctors to associate themselves with institutionally based treatment, rather than with either effective immunisation procedures for diphtheria, or the spectrum of care services needed for TB sufferers.[37] Historians have also pointed out the extent to which the lead in raising questions concerning the health status of the population during the 1930s was taken by political lobby groups, such as the Children's Minimum Council and the Committee against Malnutrition; social scientists, for example, Richard Titmuss's investigation of infant mortality in relation to socio-economic class; a small number of medical specialists, particularly obstetricians and gynaecologists concerned about the incidence of maternal mortality; and by voluntary groups and organisations outside the medical establishment, such as the Women's Health Inquiry and the founders of the Peckham Health Centre, who were concerned to develop a philosophy of health.[38] The annual reports of public health doctors tended to take an optimistic view of the health of the people, even in areas of high mass unemployment. In so doing there is little doubt but that doctors were telling the Ministry what it wanted to hear.

Public health doctors remained confident during these years that they would gain a central place in any national organisation of health services as a result of the increased number of tasks they had collected. The preoccupation of public health had become inward looking, with an eye firmly on the medical politics of who would control the delivery of health care services. The meaning of the prevention of disease and the promotion of health in the context of the mid-twentieth century did not figure largely as matters for debate. But with the National Health Service Act of 1946, public health lost control of many of the tasks it had acquired during the 1920s and 1930s. Not surprisingly, the NHS was not unified under the control of local authorities and salaried public health doctors. This left the specialty bemoaning the remnants that remained.

The attempt to introduce 'social medicine' into the universities during the 1940s offered a second model for public health practice and held out a promising looking life-line to the specialty, but ended in deepening the division between academics and practitioners. John Ryle, appointed the first professor of social medicine at Oxford in 1942, argued that social medicine extended the interests of public health and altered its emphasis. Whereas public health was concerned primarily with environmental and personal health services, social medicine tried to study man in relation to all aspects of his nature and nurture. Second, while public health was preoccupied with infectious disease, social medicine was concerned with the epidemiology of all diseases. And finally, social medicine took within its province the whole work of medical sociology, defined by Ryle as the work of social diagnosis and aftercare services.[39] In this model, public health was invited to make epidemiological work its main concern, with a view to elucidating the determinants of health and disease.

Most professors of social medicine were convinced that the public health service was old-fashioned in its approach. W. Hobson, professor of social and industrial medicine at the University of Sheffield, commented on the public health departments' 'woeful lack of data on which to base a scientific approach'.[40] But social medicine failed to have the kind of impact on the medical schools that the new professors of the subject hoped for. While the 1944 Inter-Departmental Committee on the Medical Schools talked enthusiastically of a radical reorientation of the medical curriculum and of the need for social medicine to permeate all medical school teaching, most schools reacted only by slightly modifying their departments of public health. Furthermore, the concept of social medicine was progressively narrowed down in order to stake a claim to academic respectability. Ryle's own work increasingly emphasised the links between clinical medicine and epidemiology at the expense of social science and health policy, and the importance of the study of 'social pathology' – the quantity and cause of disease – at the expense of the more radical and difficult aim of promoting health.[41] Public health practitioners reacted against both what they regarded as 'ivory tower' academic criticism of their work and the increasingly clinical focus of social medicine. After the NHS was set up, they veered once more towards looking for new services to administer, finding them in the form of ambulances, social work and nursing homes.

Since the First World War public health doctors had concentrated increasingly on the performance of tasks associated with the delivery of health services. Even in their reduced circumstances after 1948, they controlled large numbers of staff, including health visitors, sanitary inspectors and social workers. During the 1950s and 1960s all these groups exerted claims to professional independence, culminating most notably in the secession of social workers with the setting up of the social service departments according to the recommendations of the 1968 Seebohm Committee.[42] In particular, public health doctors proved once again vulnerable to the argument that their clinical preventive work could be done by GPs, and were hard-pressed to answer the charge that they had proved ineffectual in organising good community care.[43] Not for the last time, public health doctors found themselves at the mercy of institutional reform, which at the end of the 1960s sought to rationalise community care and social services around the social worker and the GP.

It was in this context that a third major effort to provide public health with a new rationale and direction – as community medicine – took place. The main initiator was Professor J. N. Morris, who had played a central role with Richard Titmuss in promoting the co-operation between medicine and social science that had been the hallmark of early social medicine. Morris believed strongly that public health practice should be grounded more firmly in the principles of modern epidemiology and lifestyle prevention. His textbook on epidemiology identified the major uses of the subject as historical study, community diagnosis, analysis of the workings of health services, analysis of individual risks and changes, the identification of syndromes and the completion of the clinical picture.[44] From this he evolved the concept of a community physician responsible for community diagnosis and thus providing the 'intelligence' necessary for the efficient and effective administration of the health service. The community physician would carry out the studies that would provide the basis for a discussion of rationing and other issues involving the 'morality of medical care'. With the entry of community physicians into the NHS at a constant level (something always denied to them as employees of local government), Morris also envisaged them overseeing the integration of the three parts of the service: general practice, hospitals and community medicine. Believing that a multi-causal, epidemiological approach would ensure consideration of socio-economic and environmental variables and eliminate the danger of 'blaming the victim' for his or her illness, Morris built up examples around specific non-infectious diseases to emphasise the importance of co-operation between clinicians and community physicians, something that had also been important to Ryle. In regard to coronary heart disease, for example, he argued that the barriers between prevention and cure were crumbling and 'public health needs clinical medicine – clinical medicine needs a community'.[45]

From the beginning, government put more emphasis on the work of the new community physician in management of the health services than on his or her role as a specialist adviser using epidemiological skills; nor did government planning documents make any mention of prevention other than as it related to personal health services.[46] Most community physicians experienced considerable difficulty in adjusting to the positions that many were given on consensus management teams and to working with little support to provide specialist advice. Some found that they were expected to concern themselves only with health services in the community beyond the hospital and many others experienced a tension as to their accountability to the health authority on the one hand and to their populations on the other. Closely allied to the question of the community physician's accountability to the community as opposed to the NHS bureaucracy has been the responsibility some community physicians have felt to take up a broader mandate as spokespersons on the state of the people's health. While Morris had envisaged the community physician pursuing the 'applied physiology' first outlined by Newman early in the century and updated in the form of the 'lifestyle' approach, the Black Report on health inequalities drew attention to the need for a 'total and not merely a service-oriented approach to the problems of health'.[47]

The fortunes of community medicine were to a large extent bound up with the success or failure of the new NHS structure. While community physicians struggled to forge a role within it, both clinicians and government policy-makers tended to regard them as part and parcel of the new management structure of the service. When, in the 1980s, the concern of government became less the integration of the NHS and more the promotion of effective line management as a means to controlling spiralling costs, the role of the community physician faded from view. After general management was introduced in 1984, the community medicine establishment was reduced and the work allotted to community physicians varied widely from district to district. It was possible for energetic practitioners to prosper; the new emphasis on monitoring, for example, offered a new space for public health practice. But at the other (admittedly less common) extreme, community medicine virtually disappeared. Certainly, community medicine was not central in the way in which either the 1944 Inter-Departmental Committee on the Medical Schools or Morris had dreamed. It was sidelined with a much narrower remit. The role set out for the community physician was crucial for securing the public health, but by the mid-1980s, neither the community physician nor anyone else was performing it.

Public health and AIDS in the 1980s

At a time when community medicine faced declining credibility as a medical specialty the appeal engendered by AIDS to an earlier golden age of public health was attractive.

In 1986, the government set up a committee of inquiry into the future development of the 'public health function'. This followed two major outbreaks of infectious disease: salmonella at Stanley Royd Hospital in 1984 and Legionnaires' disease at Stafford in 1985. Reports on both episodes pointed to a decline of available expertise in environmental health and in the investigation and control of communicable disease. These had been the traditional concerns of public health, but the emphasis within the specialty had long been placed elsewhere. After 1974, the training of community physicians, one of whom remained the named medical officer for environmental health in each health district, gave little time to infectious disease.

The committee of inquiry was chaired by Sir Donald Acheson, who had already made explicit the connection he perceived between AIDS and earlier epidemics in his *Annual Report* for 1984: 'While the scourge of smallpox has gone and diphtheria and poliomyelitis are at present under control, other conditions such as legionellosis and AIDS have emerged. The control of the virus infection (HTLV III) which is the causative agent underlying AIDS is undoubtedly the greatest challenge in the field of communicable disease for many decades.'[48] The committee of inquiry referred at length to the demoralised position of community medicine. After the introduction of general management in 1984, thirteen authorities had no community physician on the district management boards and community physicians were often to be found in posts with titles such as director of planning, director of service evaluation or director of service quality, jobs that did not necessarily require a medically qualified incumbent. Public health at district level had achieved little by way of a coherent response to AIDS. In one London district, for example, the introduction of general management had resulted in an erosion of the power of community medicine in favour of the district general manager.[49] Where community physicians played a central role, as in Bradford, it happened more by accident than anything else.[50]

The Acheson Report included a section on the challenge posed by AIDS and this was used as a major prop for an enlarged model for public health practice, which included the provision of epidemiological advice, lifestyle and environmental prevention policies, health promotion and the co-ordination of the control of communicable disease.[51] Of these, the importance of epidemiology in giving public health scientific legitimacy was stressed as much as by Ryle in the 1940s, or Morris in the 1960s and 1970s.[52] It provided, the report suggested, the basis for the causal analysis of health problems, the health needs of populations and the provision, organisation and evaluation of services. Again it was suggested that the challenge of AIDS required such 'scientifically based analysis';[53] the battle over the interpretation and use of the data remained unacknowledged.

In many respects the report had a strong 'back to the future' flavour. It recommended that the name community medicine be abandoned and that the specialty call itself 'public health medicine'. There was also a sense in which public health was seen to be reclaiming a well-known niche for itself in relation to infectious disease. It was recommended that health authorities assign executive responsibility for communicable disease control to a District Control Infection Officer, who in regard to AIDS would take responsibility for liaison with GPs, hospitals and local authorities, and who would chair the District Control of Infection Committee.[54]

It is not clear how helpful such retrenchment will prove in regard to meeting the challenge of AIDS. First, the redefinition of community medicine's task was designed in large measure to provide the weakened specialty of community medicine with a more secure position in medicine, hence the addition of 'medicine' to 'public health'. But as John Ashton pointed out in the *British Medical Journal*, this reduced the likelihood of an effective intersectoral approach.[55] For while the report recognised the necessity of such an approach, the suggested membership of the District Control of Infection Committee was confined to the health district and to the medical profession, the only exception being the environmental health officer employed by the local authority. As Ashton remarked, in the case of AIDS this could do little to promote much needed liaison with voluntary organisations and the media.

Second, the addition of provisions designed to beef up the role of public health in preventing infectious disease has in part been overtaken by the changes in the modelling of AIDS. These have brought to the fore the problem of co-ordinating the continuous care that persons with AIDS need and the extent to which tertiary prevention raises issues of social and economic well-being as much as the need for lifestyle changes. On the former, several studies published in the late 1980s have commented as to the inadequacy of co-operation between health and social services and voluntary organisations in securing the full spectrum of care needed by persons with AIDS.[56] Beardshaw, Hunter and Taylor have noted that despite the emphasis on community care and prevention, most of the earmarked AIDS' money continues to go to the health authority in which most acute treatment is given.[57] In their research on six different sites, only one had succeeded in implementing joint planning to the point where a strategy had been accepted by all the principal local agencies. These findings point to the need for planning across the different parts of the health service and between community health and other services provided by local government and the voluntary sector. The 1974 job description for the community physician envisaged that they would undertake the planning across the full range of health services, but this (admittedly grandiose) vision faded swiftly. However, the lack of such planning for continuous care remains a major weakness, something that the failure to develop a fully fledged intersectoral approach in the Acheson Report will not help public health to remedy. It is possible that the 1990 NHS and Community Care Act may do more to promote change on this score and in so doing to bolster the position of public health. Arguably one of the most important parts of the legislation has been its stress on the importance of assessment for both health and social care, and in some, but by no means all, health districts, public health medicine has been asked to take the leading role in the work of assessing needs.

In his criticism of the Acheson Report, Ashton saw no reason to hope that public health doctors would be willing to address the wider social issues raised by tertiary prevention: 'Community physicians are keeping their heads down and avoiding contentious issues that affect public health . . . The public health voice on behalf of the homeless, the unemployed, and the poor and in defence of the National Health Service has been muted.'[58] In the case of AIDS, the issues of income and of providing safe housing of good design and with secure tenure have been raised with increasing frequency during the late 1980s, but there is little sign of public health deserting the focus on the individual that has characterised its preventive work since the early twentieth century. As Homans and Aggleton have argued, different understandings of health give rise to different preventive strategies: a predominantly biomedical understanding will tend to result in stress on the importance of changing individual behaviour, whereas a more social or holistic understanding will emphasise strategies based on community development and self-empowerment.[59] In this way, the failure to consider broader social and economic determinants of health may be linked to the failure to develop an intersectoral approach.

In the special edition of the *British Medical Journal* published to celebrate the journal's 150th anniversary, Roy and Dorothy Porter appealed to public health's heroic past and urged the specialty to resuscitate prevention and collective action, and to find the will to tackle governments in the manner of its nineteenth-century forebears.[60] Broadly speaking, this captures the spirit necessary to address the issues raised by AIDS, which have exposed the weakest points in health care provision. While it is not sufficient to advocate a return to the nineteenth-century model of public practice, a determination to consider social and environmental determinants of health and illness and to take issue with those in authority is necessary. However, it is not these aspects of public health's past that have inspired the model of practice offered by the Acheson Report.

NOTES

1 L. Jordanova, 'Review essay', *Social History*, 6 (1981), 371.

2 E.g., C. Webster, 'Healthy or hungry thirties?', *History Workshop Journal*, no. 13 (1982), 110–29.

3 This has been especially true of the USA, see Daniel M. Fox, 'Chronic disease and disadvantage: the new politics of HIV infection', *Journal of Health Politics, Policy and the Law*, 15 (1990), 341–55, but the tendency is the same in Britain with the increase in infection among drug users.

4 *Ibid.*, 344.

5 Philip Strong, 'Epidemic psychology: a model', *Sociology of Health and Illness*, 12 (1990), 249–59.

6 D. Roth, 'The scientific basis of epidemiology: an historical and philosophical enquiry', PhD thesis, University of California at Berkeley, 1976.

7 J. N. Morris and R. M. Titmuss, 'Health and social change I: the recent history of rheumatic heart disease', *Medical Officer*, 72 (1944); and J. N. Paul, *Clinical Epidemiology* (Chicago, 1958), 40.

8 Dennis Altman, *AIDS and the New Puritanism* (London, 1986), 35; and Hilary Homans and Peter Aggleton, 'Health education HIV infection and AIDS', in P. Aggleton and H. Homans (eds.), *Social Aspects of AIDS* (London, 1988), 155.

9 Gerald M. Oppenheimer, 'In the eye of the storm: the epidemiological construction of AIDS', in Elizabeth Fee and Daniel M. Fox (eds.), *AIDS: The Burdens of History* (Berkeley, 1988), 286.

10 Ken Plummer, 'Organising AIDS', in Aggleton and Homans (eds.), *Social Aspects of AIDS*, 28.

11 Erica Carter, 'AIDS and critical practice', in Erica Carter and Simon Watney (eds.), *Taking Liberties: AIDS and Cultural Politics* (London, 1989), 61.

12 Dorothy Porter and Roy Porter, 'The enforcement of health: the British debate', in Fee and Fox (eds.), *AIDS: The Burdens of History*, 107 and 114.

13 Simon Watney, 'Taking liberties: an introduction', in Carter and Watney (eds.), *Taking Liberties*, 20.

14 House of Commons, Social Services Committee, *Problems Associated with AIDS*, Minutes of Evidence, 182 – (i) (London, 1987).

15 Ronald Bayer, *Private Acts, Social Consequences. AIDS and the Politics of Public Health* (New York, 1989).

16 Elizabeth Fee and Daniel M. Fox, 'The contemporary historiography of AIDS', *Journal of Social History*, 23 (1989), 305.

17 See J. Weeks, 'Love in a cold climate', in Aggleton and Homans (eds.), *Social Aspects of AIDS*, 12; and Miriam David, 'Moral and maternal; the family in the right', in Ruth Levitas (ed.), *The Ideology of the New Right* (Oxford, 1986), 136–66.

18 Virginia Berridge and Philip Strong, 'AIDS policies in the UK: a preliminary analysis', in Elizabeth Fee and Daniel M. Fox (eds.), *AIDS: The Making of a Chronic Disease* (Berkeley, 1992).

19 Philip Strong and Virginia Berridge, 'No one knew anything: some issues in British AIDS policy', in Peter Aggleton, Peter Davies and Graham Hart (eds.), *AIDS: Individual, cultural and Policy Dimensions* (London, 1990).

20 Department of Health/Welsh Office, *Short Term Predictions of HIV Infection and AIDS in England and Wales*, Report of a Working Group (London, 1988).

21 Deirdre Cunningham and S. F. Griffiths to the editor, *British Medical Journal*, 295 (1985), 921.

22 J. Lewis, '"It all begins in the family": community care in the 1980s', *Journal of Law and Society*, 16 (1989), 83–96.

23 King's Fund Project Paper no. 68, *AIDS: Planning Local Services* (London, 1987).

24 Virginia Beardshaw, David J. Hunter and Rosemary C. R. Taylor, *Local AIDS Policies: Planning and Policy Development for Health Promotion*, Health Education Authority AIDS Programme papers no. 6 (London, 1990), 10.

25 E.g., Oxford Regional Health Authority, *Towards the Control of an Epidemic: Regional Policy and Strategy for HIV Infection, 1989–93*, consultation draft (Oxford, 1989).

26 See Cindy Patton's account of the USA in, 'The AIDS industry', and J. Weeks's comments on the differences in the British context in 'AIDS altruism and the New Right', both in Carter and Watney (eds.), *Taking Liberties*, 115 and 129.

27 Resource Information Service, *AIDS: The Issues for Housing* (London, 1987), and Alan Walker, 'Community care policy and AIDS', in Virginia Beardshaw (ed.), *AIDS: Can We Care Enough?*, report of a conference for World AIDS Day, 1988, organised by the National AIDS Trust in association with the King's Fund Centre (London, 1989), 49–52.

28 Nick Partridge, 'The role of AIDS-specific voluntary organisations', in Beardshaw (ed.), *AIDS: Can We Care Enough?*, 58–60.

29 Fox, 'Chronic disease and disadvantage'.

30 Elizabeth Fee and Daniel M. Fox, 'Introduction. AIDS, public policy and historical inquiry', in Fee and Fox (eds.), *AIDS: The Burdens of History*, 10.

31 Jane Lewis, *What Price Community Medicine? The Philosophy and Politics of Public Health since 1919* (Brighton, 1986).

32 Health and Welfare Canada, *New Perspectives on the Health of Canadians: A Working Document* (Ottawa, 1974).

33 N. Hart, *The Sociology of Health and Medicine* (Ormskirk, Lancs. 1985), 14–17.

34 Paul Starr, *The Social Transformation of American Medicine* (New York, 1982).

35 George Newman, *The Foundation of National Health*, the Charles Hastings Lecture (London, 1928).
36 'Preventive medicine in 1930', editorial, *Medical Officer*, 45 (1931), 1.
37 L. Bryder, *Below the Magic Mountain. A Social History of Tuberculosis in Twentieth-Century Britain* (Oxford, 1988).
38 Jane Lewis, *The Politics of Motherhood: Child and Maternal Welfare in England, 1900–1939* (London, 1980).
39 J. A. Ryle, *Changing Disciplines* (Oxford, 1949), 11–12.
40 W. Hobson, 'What is social medicine?', *British Medical Journal*, 2 (1949), 125.
41 Ryle, *Changing Disciplines*, 7.
42 PP, 'Report of the Committee on Local Authority and Allied Personal Social Services', Cmnd. 3703, 1967–8, p. 157.
43 'Medical Care', editorial, *Medical Officer*, 97 (1057), 104.
44 J. N. Morris, *The Uses of Epidemiology* (Edinburgh, 1969; 1st edn, 1957).
45 J. N. Morris, 'Tomorrow's community physician', *Lancet*, 2 (1969), 814.
46 Department of Health and Social Security, *Report of the Working Party on Medical Administrators* (London, 1972), para. 136.
47 P. Townsend and N. Davidson (eds.), *Inequalities in Health* (Harmondsworth, 1982), 41.
48 *Annual Report of the Chief Medical Officer of the DHSS for the Year 1984* (London, 1986), 35–7.
49 Ewan Ferlie and Andrew Pettigrew, 'Coping with change in the NHS: a frontline district's response to AIDS', *Journal of Social Policy*, 19 (1989), 191–220.
50 Dr Kathie Marfell and Jane C. Whitham, 'A public health response: the experience of Bradford', in Maryan Pye, Murkesh Kapila, Graham Buckley and Deirdre Cunningham (eds.), *Responding to the AIDS Challenge* (London, 1989), 131–42.
51 PP, *Public Health in England*. The Report of the Committee of Inquiry into the Future Development of the Public Health Function, Cm. 289 (London, 1988), para. 5.3.
52 *Ibid.*, para. 8.10.
53 *Ibid.*, 3.6.
54 *Ibid.*, paras. 7.16–17 and 7.25.
55 John Ashton, 'Acheson: a missed opportunity for the new public health', Leader, *BMJ*, 296 (1988), 231.
56 King's Fund Project paper no. 68, *AIDS: Planning and Local Services*, 26, and Andrew Bebbington and Pat Warren, *AIDS: The Local Authority Response* (Canterbury, 1988).
57 Beardshaw, Hunter and Taylor, *Local AIDS Policies*, 10.
58 Ashton, 'Acheson: a missed opportunity', 231.
59 Homans and Aggleton, 'Health education', 157.
60 Roy and Dorothy Porter, 'The ghost of Edwin Chadwick', *British Medical Journal*, 301 (1990), 252.

3

Politics and policy: historical perspectives on screening

BRIDGET TOWERS

Introduction

This paper grew out of the realisation that the governing context of my appraisal of contemporary AIDS policies was the historical material that I was dealing with in my research on tuberculosis policy and health education. The debates surrounding HIV serotesting had a deep resonance in the correspondence in the Public Record Office (PRO) files of the Ministry of Health dealing with policy formation on mass testing and health surveillance. Here too there was long, careful and critical consideration of the mandate and responsibility for the extension of routine health services into new territories. There was also concern at the Cabinet level about international co-operation in epidemiological data collection and the consequences of exclusionary immigration controls. I was struck too by the problems, both epistemological and practical, which the notion of 'presymptomatic illness' had posed for policy makers.

In saying this, I must, however, be cautious of the methodological trap of 'presentism'; i.e. attempting to interpret past actions and actors in terms of the cognitive structures, analytical paradigms and critical agendas of the present.[1] This is a particular danger for sociologists such as myself who look for the broader dynamics involved in policy changes over and above those which are situation specific. However, it would be overcautious in the extreme to fail to bring to the table of contemporary discussions the longer history of experience of creating preventive health programmes. I am of the belief that the historian's contribution can stand in its own right to furnish accounts and contexts and witness to the dimension of temporarity.

It was with this perspective that I looked in greater detail at four specific examples of screening programmes, in England, that were the subject of policy debate in the Ministry of Health during the last fifty years. These are: mass radiography for tuberculosis; ante-natal VD testing; paternity testing; and the medical inspection of aliens. In the second section of this paper I will briefly present these screening stories and in the final section I will attempt to draw

55

one or two connections between them and the questions that non-historians have raised about the expansion of screening as a health measure, not just for HIV but for chronic disease and more recently for genetically transmitted conditions.

Mass radiography for tuberculosis was the first attempt to use the new technology of miniature mobile radiography for the early detection of tuberculosis by chest X Ray. Ante-natal VD screening was a proposal to expand the routine rhesus factor serotesting of pregnant women to include an 'added-on' Kahn test for VD. Paternity testing was the attempt to develop a new serotest as a routine procedure in affiliation proceedings; it was an example of the use of laboratory knowledge in the field of serotesting for forensic purposes. The medical inspection of aliens had a long history in early international public health but in the 1940s the increase in immigration led to a requestioning of the relationship between exclusionary screening for infectious diseases and screening for projective health care demand, this led to a shift in the function of the medical inspection as a regulatory element in immigration control.

All of these programmes were the subject of issue at a time of the radical restructuring of the Health and Welfare Services in the 1940s and early 1950s. They have to be seen in the light of major changes in the financing, administration and control of public services both at the Treasury level of departmental budget allocations and also lower down the various intradepartmental sectors.

Mass radiography for tuberculosis has to be situated in the context of the disappearance of a separate tuberculosis section of public health and its integration into the work of the Regional Hospital Boards. The development of serotesting has to be understood with reference to the reorganisation of the separate Laboratory Services and their complex relationship to the new hospital and primary health care services. It was also a time in which the political economy of a war-time state generated and facilitated new administrative systems which entailed the logistical capacity to innovate and deploy on a mass scale, as can be seen in the introduction of mass radiography to screen military manpower.

At such times of major change there are always occupational groups who take the opportunity to advance their interests and position, and during this period the development of new technologies and procedures was an integral element in conflicts over the defence of new and maintenance of old occupational monopolies. For instance in the case of the new mass radiography the strict regulation of the operation of the machinery was designed to maintain the old distinction between radiologists as medical professionals and radiographers as technicians. Here also the distinction between the traditional 'diagnostic' X Ray and the 'indicative reading' of the miniature film was made with an eye to demarcating the provinces of 'clinical diagnostic activity' and 'public health case-finding'.[2]

What is 'screening'? Foltz and Kelsey in their critical case study of the Pap Test for cervical cancer screening present an 'anchor' definition: 'the presumptive identification of unrecognized disease or defect by the application of tests, examinations, or other procedures which can be applied rapidly to sort out apparently well persons who probably have a disease from those who probably do not' (Foltz and Kelsey, 1978, p. 427).

This is the same basic definition from which the World Health Organisation (WHO) Global Health Strategy for the Year 2000 identifies criteria that all screening procedures should fulfil before they are applied to populations. However, it is not clear that working with a fixed definition like this is the most satisfactory procedure when dealing with historical material.

Stanley Reisler (1978a) in his review of its history treats screening as an emergent concept and does not himself offer an authoritative definition. He documents a development throughout this century of preventive medical services, which began with individual routine health 'check ups', developed into case finding through mass testing for infectious disease, expanded to cover periodic individual testing for chronic conditions and has ended up as full multiphasic screening operated as part of the regular menu of modern health care provided by employers and medical practitioners.

This question of definitions brings us directly to the theoretical issue of what is the 'object' of study in historical interpretations of policy. How far can we assume even a fixed composite of activities, actors and material objects which we can identify as constituting 'screening'? I come from a radical sceptical background which sees 'policy objects' as differentially constituted by different groups and would argue that the historian's task in the telling of policy stories is essentially about describing who is sitting around which tables talking to whom, using what language when the particular topic was on the agenda. I should not want to be held to some a priori definition of what screening 'actually is' and by that criterion adjudicate whether these were really examples of it. It seems to me that it is precisely the ambiguity and conflict in the giving of interpretive accounts by participant actors that is the policy discourse.

In 1940 Lord Dawson described mass radiography as 'sorting',[3] the Medical Research Council (MRC) in 1942 referred to it as 'sifting'[4] and by 1954 the Ministry of Health was tentatively using the term 'screening'.[5] The Welsh Hospital Board saw it as an integral part of modern routine health maintenance[6] whereas the Ministry of Labour saw it as an exclusionary measure for service pension entitlement.[7] The statisticians in the Ministry of Health saw ante-natal VD testing as prevalence monitoring;[8] and the Home Office saw paternity testing as forensic evidence gathering.[9]

In this paper I retain a flexibility of definition and see my task as charting the various ways in which these programmes and procedures were both legitimised and differentiated from traditional medical diagnostic practice.

The stories

Mass radiography for tuberculosis

The technology of miniature radiography appears to have been invented in 1936 and developed and implemented for medical use in North America. As a procedure for use in health examinations, the chest X Ray was first introduced in Britain as a military measure in 1940. It was later taken up for use on selected civilian populations; in the beginning by the Welsh Board of Health and later, on an experimental basis, by the Ministry of Health in England. It was then more widely deployed by the Ministry of Labour to cover all military recruits and by 1948 it had become a standard part of the Tuberculosis Service's repertoire of the new Regional Hospital Boards. Between 1936 and 1948 government's attitudes towards mass X Ray passed from low key acceptance to high enthusiasm.

The foundation of the British TB scheme based on a public health service organised around dispensaries, sanatoria and chest hospitals had been laid by the Astor Committee Reports of 1912 and 1913 but it was not until the issue of tuberculosis in the post-war period and the particular problem of ex-servicemen was raised by the Barlowe Report of 1919 that large-scale development funding was provided by Exchequer grants and a network of services was fully established.

Although there had been a long history during the inter-war years to expand community-based tuberculosis work, both in alliance with other public health and child welfare services, the Tuberculosis Service remained a separate and directly funded branch of public health. It had its own section and statistical bureau within the Ministry of Health and enjoyed the patronage of senior civil servants who found that their participation in the Tuberculosis section of the Health Committee of the League of Nations and the League of Red Cross Societies in Geneva provided a useful political base for British health policy initiatives to be legitimated and advanced both domestically and internationally (Howard-Jones, 1978). It was therefore not unusual to find that a foreign initiative in tuberculosis policy was enthusiastically considered; although it should be noted that another anti-TB measure popular in Europe, BCG vaccination, had been critically rejected.[10]

The initiative for mass radiography in a military capacity came from Lord Dawson in February 1940. In a private memo to the Chief Medical Officer of Health he expressed concern about the level of wastefulness caused by tuberculosis amongst enlisted men and pointed to the standard procedure of mass radiographic chest examination of all enlisted men that had been adopted in Germany.[11] On the basis of a crude cost-benefit calculation he advised that the savings to the military authorities of the costs of returning men, paying for their hospital treatment and subsequent pensions would be substantially greater than the costs of implementing mass radiography.

This conclusion was based on an assumption of an initial outlay of £2,500 for the scheme and a modest 1% of positive identifications amongst those examined.

He described the objective of mass radiography as a 'preliminary sorting', 'a selection of suspects who would need subsequent detailed investigation'. The method of 'sorting' could equally have been clinical examination or skin testing, but he favoured radiography because of its efficiency and cheapness in specialist time, its practicability and the availability of apparatus.

However, although it initially appeared that the 'economic savings' argument was conclusive, the question soon arose as to who precisely was to bear the costs or make the savings. Most economic costing of health care during this period was usually made without reference to transactional costs or externalities and costs were calculated on the narrow basis of departmental budgets. The organisation and funding of tuberculosis care was similar in complexity to mental health services during the inter-war years, and by 1940 was made even more labyrinthian by the general mobilisation and the involvement of the Ministry of Labour and the War Office. There were a number of departments involved that had very different interests: the Ministry of Health was responsible for civilian health; the Ministry of Labour was responsible for recruits; the services were responsible for enlisted personnel; and the Ministry of Pensions was responsible for invalided ex-service personnel.

The future costs of health care fell to different ministries depending upon the status of the person at the time of diagnosis of TB: a recruit not being enlisted was *de facto* a civilian and therefore the responsibility of the Ministry of Health; an enlisted person although invalided out was the responsibility of the Ministry of Pensions; an enlisted person prior to invaliding out was the responsibility of the Services.

Dawson in his crude calculation had fundamentally misunderstood the complexity of the issue of economic costs of screening. For if screening is about the identification of cases that will require some treatment costs, then unless there is a congruence between those departments which provide the screening service and those which provide the treatment and those which will benefit from the prevented future costs of the disease, then there is no way that an aggregation of pooled costs and benefits will be accepted in the real political world of departmental budgeting unless elaborate transfer payments are worked out.

The branches of the military had their own clinical examination schemes for enlisted persons. However, the military had an incentive to under-diagnose, since although they stood to lose manpower, the long-term costs of treatment fell not to them but to the Ministry of Pensions; so they could afford to gamble on men's future health risks. There was a natural reluctance on their part to admit that their procedures were inadequate and that they failed to pick up a substantial number of cases.

In its turn, the Ministry of Labour had an incentive to 'weed out' future costs of pensionable cases before they came on to the books of Service Entitlements. However, it was resistant to any extension of mass radiography beyond its own narrow remit of existing and called-up service personnel. It was not prepared to meet the costs for what could be seen as 'future manpower'; this being a liability it saw as falling strictly to the Ministry of Health as part of its general responsibility for the health of the country.

The primary concern of the military was to make conscription practices efficient, equitable and not subject to local variation. What was critical for them was that any testing procedure for tuberculosis should be standardised and not subject to local interpretation. They therefore had an interest in it being fully under the control of the Ministry of Labour, tied to the Recruitment Centres and operated under strictly standardised procedures.[12] From the beginning of the discussions between the War Office, the Ministry of Labour and the Ministry of Health the main focus was upon the need to have a comprehensive and standardised system that could be introduced quickly and with minimum disturbance to existing administrative procedures. Issues of logistics, standardisation of equipment and centralisation of recording systems took prominence in decision making.[13] In order for the scheme to be truly comprehensive it was deemed to be best implemented through the Recruitment Centres, but centred at specifically designated radiographic recruitment centres, the equipment was to be provided, operated and tested by the Ministry of Health. However, the Medical Advisory Committee was unclear whether the existing legal powers requiring all recruits to submit to a medical examination could be deemed also to cover a compulsory X Ray.[14] This query was never properly answered but it was decided to exclude volunteers from any compulsory requirement.

The decision that the Ministry of Health was to provide facilities, training and the whole package of mass radiography was applauded by Lord Horder as a welcome opportunity for expanding access and provision of health services and a possible entering wedge for other future development of public health.[15] The Welsh Board of Health had already established a small mobile mass radiography service for civilians and was enthusiastic about the potential for expanding it and linking it to the military scheme in Wales.[16] However, the Ministry of Labour and other voices from the Medical Advisory Committee strongly resisted any expansion of mass radiography to cover civilians, workers or students on the grounds of its expense, fears that it might interfere with war effort in the factories and concern about its effect on morale; 'people should not be troubled today by having their attention concentrated on potential ills'.[17]

This was an echo of the sceptical attitude towards presymptomatic tuberculosis that had been common in Britain in the 1930s. Journals and newspapers of the time contained long and often ironic discussions about the notion of 'pre-tuberculosis' and a dismissive attitude towards the French policy of establishing 'preventoriums' was common. There was a suspicion that the concepts of the 'delicate child' and the 'pre-tubercular child' were inventions of tuberculosis officers faced with a declining client group.[18]

By contrast the Lindsay Committee in its MRC Report on mass radiography wholeheartedly endorsed an expansion of mass radiography (M/R) to the whole population, under a rigorous and centrally controlled system operated by the Ministry of Health and linked to the local authority tuberculosis services.[19] Although local authorities might administer a future scheme, it was envisaged that the central Ministry would retain overall control over target groups, systems of record keeping and all data analysis, the design and deployment of apparatus and the precise terms and conditions of staffing of the facility. The difficult question of defining the status of M/R within traditional medical practice was handled by emphasising that it was 'not diagnosis but the *sifting* out from a number of apparently normal persons those whose condition requires further diagnosis by established methods'.[20]

By 1948 the issue of M/R became dominated by consideration of the Sickness Benefit system introduced to replace Sanatorium Benefit and to be administered by local tuberculosis officers for all new cases. The financial consequences of an increase in positive diagnosis of tuberculosis shifted to the Central Exchequer for benefit payments and to the county councils in their responsibility for providing treatment. In 1948 the Regional Hospital Boards took over responsibility for the planning and financing of tuberculosis services and thereby the Ministry of Health picked up the bulk of all treatment costs as well as responsibility for control and planning. It was clear that early diagnosis of tuberculosis through M/R might lead to benefit claims and thereby incur opposition from the Treasury; however, if cases could be diagnosed early enough, it would not involve the Ministry of Health in any greater costs in actual treatment provision. Mass radiography was enthusiastically defended and promoted by the Ministry as a common service for the country as a whole under the central control of the Ministry and by 1949 the Chief Medical Officer was arguing for an expansion of its tuberculosis focus to cover other cardiovascular and respiratory diseases, and characterising its function as 'screening'.[21]

There are a number of seams which may have contributed to the expansion of medical screening in the post-war years throughout western Europe. There was the obvious link between the war-time medical inspection of recruits and the continuity of military medicine as conscription remained and demobilisation was only slowly implemented. Here the experience of the 1914–18 war and the problems of demobilisation, displaced populations, impoverishment and chronic malnutrition of civilians created a realistic attitude towards the need for co-ordinated public health programmes to prevent epidemics and long-term destabilisation. Anti-tuberculosis work was a priority with most European Red Cross Societies and although the Health Committee of the League of Nations had been dissolved, it was quickly reconstituted as the new organisational shell of the WHO and its co-ordinated work on tuberculosis control in Europe was revived in the late 1940s.

American influence on international public health during the inter-war years, through the sponsorship of the Rockefeller Foundation and the American Red Cross, reinforced a medical model of community health (Kniebler, 1979, Lert, 1982, Towers, 1987). The Rockefeller mission to France in 1919 had pioneered an anti-tuberculosis campaign based upon mobile health education teams with their motorised caravans and film shows that bore a striking resemblance to the promotional fanfares organised for mobile mass radiographic screening units.

At the level of ideas, the 1920s had witnessed a steady coupling of the 'scientific' claims of medical procedures to legitimate state regulatory activities in the fields of family policy, deviance and criminal justice (Donzelot, 1979, Foucault, 1977, Pfohl, 1985). One can see the legitimation of medical inter- vention through the increasing involvement of medical professionals in a broader range of social policy making and also in the expansion of the domain of medical work, both by the creation of new fields and the adoption and transformation of others (Conrad and Schneider, 1980). Screening would seem to be one such area where there was a consolidation of existing monitoring and surveillance work in the specific field of tuberculosis coupled to a more general mandate to expand into new areas to be deemed 'health work'.

Ante-natal VD screening

The emergence of preventive VD policies in Britain is a long and turbulent story involving conflicts between the Ministry, the Army Medical Corps, the British Medical Association (BMA) and a number of pressure groups (Towers, 1980). The most prominent and vocal group was the National Committee for Combating Venereal Disease (NCCVD), later renamed the British Council of Social Hygiene, under the leadership of Mrs Neville Rolfe who has become characterised as an 'ogre' figure of lampoon in the received history of the Ministry of Health and similarly stereotyped by modern historians.

In 1951 the question was put to the Ministry of Health whether VD testing should be made routine in all pregnancy tests.[22] A policy ruling was sought in the context of the emerging reorganisation of the Laboratory Services. The working practice had been that Kahn tests were done as a matter of course by the Blood Transfusion Centre on specimens of blood from women attending local authority ante-natal clinics who were being routinely tested for Rh-factor. If a woman was found Rh-negative she would be tested at all subsequent pregnancies, but if positive she would not be tested again. The VD test was simply an added-on test, and the Blood Transfusion Laboratory, not being a Public Health Laboratory, was not prepared to take blood specifically to be tested for VD and produce separate VD data.

A lobby from the British Council of Social Hygiene, supported by one from the National Society for the Prevention of Cruelty to Children (NSPCC) led by the head of the Great Ormond Street laboratory, urged the Ministry to deal with what they claimed was an alarming increase in the incidence of congenital syphilis. They argued for a campaign based upon two measures; routine ante-natal VD testing and compulsory treatment of children with congenital syphilis.[23]

In a departmental position paper, Ministry officials saw the key issues as whether VD testing should be routine, discretionary or compulsory, and where it should be done. They needed evidence to make an assessment of whether there was even a need for it, but found themselves caught in the dilemma of how to get the information without breaching the confidentiality of the Blood Transfusion Service (BTS) and linking data sets. The British Council of Social Hygiene argued that routine ante-natal tests would provide just such an information source on venereal disease and its control; they made a strong case for its epidemiological and service monitoring potential. The compulsory treatment initiative was made on the economic grounds that congenital syphilis was not being treated and was generating future health care costs. The change proposed was for an administrative order covering the removal of secrecy and confidentiality in the VD regulations in cases of children. Venereal Disease Officers could then be empowered to give evidence to magistrates and parents could be prosecuted for failure to ensure treatment of their children. There was strong resistance to any compulsory treatment legislation, or even threat of it, from the School Medical Service and the new clinics who saw it as threatening to undermine the whole basis of their work with parents and children.[24]

On both issues Ministry of Health documents reveal a solid line of resistance to any form of compulsion and a commitment to the encouragement of service use. The question of confidentiality was positioned as a central factor to be safeguarded throughout their deliberations and although it finally overruled considerations of the needs for epidemiological data, a disquieting dodge was mooted. The possibility was explored of getting the Blood Transfusion Laboratories to pass details of cases testing positive on to the local Medical Officer of Health; this was rejected because of the likely complaints it would provoke from GPs concerned about their patients' confidentiality.[25] The laboratories continued to produce figures for the Ministry based on the old pattern of testing and the Ministry settled for the limited data on the incidence of VD in the general population of pregnant women.

VD testing as a specific part of the diagnosis/treatment VD Service was becoming repositioned as part of the newer practice of monitoring the level of VD infection in the general population. There was a convergence of interests between the British Council of Social Hygiene (BCSH) which was concerned to preserve the invincibility of the threat of VD and its own jurisdiction over the defending crusade and the straightforward interest that the epidemiologists had in securing a regular and convenient sample base. It is a nice example of the different language of legitimation which different occupational groups might use in defending a particular test as 'compulsory' or 'added-on'. It is also note-worthy that this was by definition a gender specific group and it cannot have been completely forgotten that there was a long history of viewing women as the 'reservoirs of infection' in venereal disease.

Paternity testing

This area reflects a link with the role of paediatricians in lobbying for an occu-pational monopoly of medical inspections in adoptive cases and the function of the Blood Transfusion Laboratories. The question of whose domain they fell within was first raised in 1948 by the Welsh Hospital Board.[26] The National Blood Transfusion Service (NBTS) did not want to handle blood testing for the purpose of affiliation proceedings. The Ministry of Health was similarly concerned about NBTS Officers giving evidence in court and thereby raising suspicions about the confidentiality and professionalism of the whole blood donation scheme.

Affiliation proceedings fell under the auspices of the Home Office but since blood testing was not specifically required under legislation on Bastardy, it disclaimed any responsibility for making arrangements for its availability. The Ministry of Health estimated that although there was a demand of 2,000 tests per year in England alone, they were not prepared to simply extend laboratory facilities to cover this new area of work which smacked of forensic pathology. This was a good example of the Ministry of Health refusing to yield to the Home Office strategy of 'hand washing', and to the potential to expand 'health work' in directions they saw as undesirable for their ethos. It was the university laboratories which eventually picked up this work on a private fee for service basis.

This particular issue raised a lot of opposition from pathologists who saw it as further evidence of the declining status of laboratory work and the undermining of their occupational monopoly and professional credibility by the commercial laboratories. The Ministry of Health files record a deep loathing of what they referred to as the 'shop model' of laboratory work; one such example can be found in a position paper on the private laboratories written in 1949:

no-one who knows the facts doubts the evil influence they have exerted on medicine as a whole. They are in no sense an important or useful industry and the sooner they are put out of business the better. The universities case is not much stronger – in many perhaps most universities, the earnings of fees for routine diagnostic work has reacted very badly on the pathology and bacteriology departments concerned.[27]

The distinction between medical work and technical laboratory work raises issues about the nature of expert knowledge that become more complex when such work is positioned in a forensic context as can be seen in the recent use and development of DNA fingerprinting which have been confined to the commercial sector in Britain. The new work being done on the social construction of forensic knowledge needs contributions from historians of such antecedents (Smith and Wynne, 1989).

The medical inspection of aliens

Since the 1920s the medical inspection of aliens had been the responsibility of Port Medical Officers. The Home Office was responsible for immigration but the Ministry of Health had a key role in the granting or withholding of medical certificates. The significance of this role was raised in 1947 during the period of increased immigration through post-war resettlement and manpower schemes. This issue of medical involvement with immigration policy came at the same time as other cases were being considered in which health services were being reformulated and a number of different Ministries were negotiating their jurisdiction over health work.

The issue was first publicly raised by the xenophobic concern that foreigners were coming into the country with Home Office approval but became sick and were a 'drain' upon local authority health services. Concerned rate payers wanted to know whose responsibility it was to make sure it did not happen.

The Ministry of Health saw it as a matter of medical inspection at ports of entry being grossly inadequate. However, if it was made adequate then delays and complex arrangements for 'holding' immigrants would have had to be made and it was feared that this would attract political attention and result in a possible retaliatory action by other countries against Britain.[28]

The problem for the Ministry of Health was that even if the Medical Inspectors of Aliens (MIAs) could effect satisfactory examinations the immigration officers had the power to overrule them. Here was a clear confusion about the primary function of immigration control.

There was great variation in what a medical examination entailed, despite the confidential and specific guidelines issued by the Ministry of Health and its characterisation as an 'examination'. There were two elements:

1. A visual examination. (In practice this meant giving the queue on the disembarkation plank a once over.)
2. A thirty-second examination of selected passengers in a set-aside corner of the exit hall.

What the MIAs were having to decide in this inspection was primarily whether the immigrant was suffering from a current infectious disease or was likely to become a dependent on state health services. There was a gross confusion between social and medical issues on which the MIA was called to adjudicate and yet was not provided with such critical information as age, marital status or occupational category.[29]

Reviewing the whole policy objectives of the medical inspection of aliens in light of the new National Health Service structure, the Ministry concluded that its function was to prevent any increase in the burden of demand on health care resources. This it was assumed was likely to be heaviest in cases of chronic disease and yet it was virtually impossible to identify these cases in the sort of medical inspection possible in thirty seconds in a busy landing concourse.[30]

The Home Office had no specific interest in preventing long-term health care demand, but was concerned to prevent confusion in issuing entry permits and to minimise deportations. It made a primary distinction regardless of health status between those who stated they were prepared to seek private health care and those who were not. The MIAs refused to accept the responsibility of having to ascertain the motives and reliability of such statements.

Conflict between the Home Office and the Ministry of Health continued and the vexed question of the purpose of inspection was raised regularly throughout the 1950s. The service continued to be subject to low morale, sudden flare-ups, panics and chronic delays.

Connections and issues

Out of these brief sketches I should like to draw out one or two simple connections. There is not the space to give detailed systematic attention to a full range and I have traded off the benefits of depth and detail against the wish to raise discussion points that come out of not just this research but hopefully pertain to the broader range of material covered in the book. The background thematic considerations are the related issues of what is meant by 'knowing' and what are the associated costs and benefits of knowing.

In the field of TB work there was a long inter-war history, both nationally and internationally, of trying to discover what was the 'real' epidemiological picture of this disease. Attempts to establish an international clearing house at the League of Nations of a whole range of epidemiological data collected by nation states was fiercely contested. The British government feared that although it was a desirable plan, those countries with the most developed and bureaucratised health care systems would produce artefactually high rates of TB mortality and morbidity. When the International Classification of Diseases (ICD) standard was introduced in a patient record system for panel doctors in 1921 it was vehemently attacked by the *Times* newspaper as part of the Ministry of Health's craving for useless but sonorous statistics and it was claimed that overworked doctors would simply compound their clinical ignorance with the production of unreliable data. It was argued that the record system, by forcing doctors to name diseases such as TB, rather than simply record general observations, would generate political problems: 'the new record cards . . . tell us nothing but untruths, untruths will go to Whitehall and be bound in blue covers. We shall learn anew that we are the least healthy nation in Europe or the world and great and costly schemes of regeneration will be submitted to Parliament.'[31]

I am sympathetic to a constructionist view of the production of epidemiological knowledge and would start from a position that sees the production of any statistical knowledge as a labour process in which a number of occupational groups are involved, whose interests and claims are often in conflict (Whiston, 1979). Existence of this in Britain is found in the number of detailed complaints made to the Ministry of Health from the Joint TB Council, panel doctors, medical officers of health and tuberculosis officers. General practitioners objected to compulsory notification of a disease, which they saw as an attempt to trespass upon their relationship with their patients and further placed them in a subservient position to the public health departments. Tuberculosis officers complained that the amount of administrative and statistical work they had to do encroached upon their time to do clinical work and reinforced their low status within the medical profession. In a context of much distrust, low levels of co-operation, lack of administrative support and a general climate of resistance to the authority of central government departments, which were seen as remote, coercive and regulating centres of power, it is not surprising that the quality of data was variable. There is a fundamental difference between record keeping as an administrative function and using the records for research purposes; the data may give a good picture of organisational reality but they should not be mistaken for a picture of the social distribution of tuberculosis. This is a familiar difficulty facing any researcher using government health statistics in any field; namely that the state is in the business of collecting data not on social conditions but rather data on the operation of its agencies responsible for dealing with them and that inevitably the categories and units of analysis are grounded on particular theoretical assumptions and are not objective technical instruments.

Before mass radiographic screening, data on tuberculosis were generated primarily through the clinical diagnosis of the individual presenting patient. The major problem was that one of the characteristics of pulmonary TB is that as a disease it usually is presented with symptoms, however, that is not always the case and many people, even with extensive disease had symptoms which they ignored or interpreted within a social rather than a medical diagnostic typology and some patients were truly asymptomatic. However tight the diagnostic categories and descriptions might have been drawn, diagnosis was a practical activity undertaken with an individual patient and was not only a matter of judgement but often a highly subjective judgement. Mildred Blaxter (1978) has suggested when diagnosis as a category gets out of step with diagnosis as a process then the result may be arbitrary choice of label and perhaps inappropriate action. In the case of TB, positive diagnosis had implications of compulsory notification and a therapeutic action based on institutional treatment, both of which had severe consequences for the patient in terms of stigma and loss of earning capacity which could not be compensated for by any confident prognosis of future recovery.

How far was this element of subjectivity removed by the development of laboratory tests and X Rays? Shyrock (1961) has demonstrated in the case of Wassermann tests for VD that subjective elements lurk behind a facade of statistical and quantitative exactitude; and Reisler (1978b) has analysed the reality of laboratory work where contaminants, random variations, human errors, the profitability ethic and the speed of the work process structure the production of 'knowledge'. Radiologists since the 1920s have cautioned against an unquestioning acceptance of their readings, pointing out that sensory acuity is related to the context and amount of film reading that is done (Lynham, 1925).

My own tentative conclusion is that the knowledge produced by these screening procedures was of the same order as before. It tells us about the social operation of the service provided but it must not be confused with the rhetoric of legitimation of 'scientific truth' that it was given. This knowledge was evaluated by different interested parties according to partial, selective and instrumental criteria. In the case of the medical inspection of aliens, the visual examination and interviews failed to pick up on the most basic exclusionary categories of VD, TB, mental infirmity, pregnancy and epilepsy, all of which were likely to result in future health care demand. But without health economists to provide calculations based on pro-rata treatment costs, or even 'future productive life years', the Home Office settled for the cursory inspection and subjective interviewing as a system which generated the least political and administrative disbenefits. At the same time the medical practitioners were able to retain a territorial domain within the field of immigration control, despite the erosion of its clinical legitimacy. This example would suggest that the ability to retain a contested knowledge field in the face of its declining internal validity is related to occupational and class power and is in line with an externalist view of the history of medicine.

An internalist history of testing and screening would look to developments within the medical technology as a record of increasing scientific accuracy. This raises the question of what could be characterised as an 'engineering' versus a 'managerial' view of accuracy. The first is based upon principles of scientific validation, the second upon the notion of optimisation. In these stories of screening this is reflected in the overt recognition by policy makers that the reliability of the procedures was to be appraised on the bases of the economic consequences or outcomes of the results. A false clear medical certification was a problem for the Home Office if subsequent health care costs were generated by a landed immigrant if deportation on health grounds was not permitted. False positives in VD testing had significance for doctors and patients if the network of follow-up services was involved, but if it was a general surveillance exercise then this could be allowed for within margin errors. The issue of false negatives was of limited importance in paternity testing since the test result could only be used to exclude paternity – i.e. as negative evidence in affiliation procedures. It was generally recognised that the consequences of this meant that the forensic nature of the test was only part of the legal case and a false negative bias fitted more easily within the legal presumption of innocence and an adversarial approach to use of forensic evidence (Fortess and Kapp, 1985).

Calculations of economic costs during this period were crude and it is probably not surprising that patients' costs were generally not considered. The costs of stigma and anxiety to patients from false positive results in both mass radiography and VD testing were only considered in terms of the impact upon future service utilisation. The devastating personal costs borne by aliens deported on the basis of the cursory medical examination were never considered unless they reached the open forum of Parliament and became a subject of special political interest.

Here we can see the thread of the issue of confidentiality. It was generally believed that whilst in the case of TB, the consequences of treatment coupled with insurance entitlement would not be detrimental in the case of false positive diagnosis, nevertheless the stigma caused by the loss of confidentiality, which hospitalisation and notification would entail, was significant. Employers' costs in lost production were given due weight and reimbursed. It was even seriously considered in the Ministry of Health that employers who provided site facilities and time off to attend M/R might be entitled to know the results of any of their own participating employees.[32]

The question being touched upon is how far confidentiality of medical information is to be seen in strict terms of the doctor/patient dyad or whether there is an inevitable interconnectedness of wider medical practices which necessitate shared information. Debates about the confidentiality of information in modern bureaucratic states are usually centred around the control of access to that information and the licensing or empowering of groups to gain access. Administrative efficiency in the case of ante-natal VD testing was found to override the confidentiality of the clinic but it was regarded as defensible provided the circulation of information was only within professional groups. Here it was the medical statisticians, the Blood Transfusion Laboratories and the Ante-Natal Clinic who were designated as 'fit persons' to share data which could still be regarded as confidential.

The matter of where the boundaries of information sharing are drawn must in part be connected with the further implications of managerial action that interested parties have. If employers are to be given information on their employees in a voluntary, state-funded scheme to which they also make additional contributory expenditure, do they have greater claims and how does this situation differ from employer-organised schemes in which a condition of employment is mandatory screening? The new developments of occupational screening for conditions which might give rise to sickness claims or have an impact on the health and safety of production raise just such questions, particularly in the USA where employer-financed health insurance is extensive. Occupational genetic testing for conditions with a prognosis of long-term disability and dependency will compound the debate further.[33] In an indirect way this whole matter was considered in the discussions between the Home Office and the BMA in 1958 over the development of medical screening of adoptive parents, with a view to weeding out those putative parents whose life expectancy and health status would prevent them from being financially responsible for the adopted child before the age of maturity.[34] The Home Office regarded such medical information as clearly their own property to be shared with appointed probation officers, and sometimes had a reluctance even to allow it to be shared with the adoptive parents themselves.

It is apparent that even the decisions to ascribe confidential status to information on people is contingent upon the status of the person in question. Despite enthusiastic weeding of PRO files, detailed medical records of named aliens are openly available. As a researcher I am caught between a desire to gain access to material and a disquiet about the selective availability of it and the privilege of access which is differentially allocated.

Although the screening procedures discussed in this paper have been situated in a medical domain and legitimised as aspects of a preventive health policy, they can also be seen as a set of activities that are open to critical review when they are operated outside of the medical domain and legitimised by commercial criteria. When insurance companies are found to be using HIV tests for actuarial purposes, they may be indicted but in the light of historical practice by what criteria could this be called an immoral form of medical screening? Insurance companies now, just like the Ministries of Defence and Labour then, face real potential costs. In the past they have screened for opiate addiction and TB and in the future, with genetic screening and the much greater emphasis on health checks, they may well screen for a whole variety of conditions. Looking back in fifty years' time it may well be that it is the last few decades in which they have made very few exclusions that seem historically odd.

Acknowledgements

I should like to thank Rudolf Klein for his encouragement of my interest in screening, and Marilyn Lawrence and David Painting for their sustaining help in the production of this paper.

NOTES

1 A point made by Daniel Fox, discussant at Aids and Contemporary History Conference, 1990, London School of Hygiene and Tropical Medicine.
2 PRO MH55/1256, 8 Oct. 1942, Report of Advisory Committee on Tuberculosis, Mass Radiography Subcommittee (chairman: Lindsay).
3 PRO MH55/1264, Feb. 1940, memo from Dawson to McNalty.
4 PRO MH55/1262, 1942, Report of Mass Radiography Subcommittee of MRC.
5 PRO MH55/1269, 1954, memo from Ainsworth to Chief Medical Office.
6 PRO MH55/1067, 1941, Report of Medical Committee of Welsh Board of Health.
7 PRO MH55/1269, Nov. 1947, memo Alex Hoad.
8 PRO MH55/1525, 1953, memo McElligott.
9 PRO MH55/1658, 1949, memo Dr Maurant.
10 The British position, put by Major Greenwood, the Chief Statistician at the MRC was extensively discussed in the *Bulletin of the Health Organisation of the League of Nations* (1932). Greenwood wanted a rigorous analysis of Calmette's work since the MRC had some vaccine and would not proceed until a strong *prima facie* case could be established for its reliability or otherwise, it was claimed, it might be seen as an experiment on human beings. But others have argued that Greenwood delivered a devastating statistical attack on Calmette's work and, whilst his conclusions were justified, it had the effect of throwing the baby out with the bath water and no constructive contribution to the BCG programme came from Britain for the next twenty-five years. (P. D'Arcy Hart, 'Efficacy and applicability of mass TB vaccination in TB control', *British Medical Journal*, 1 (1967), 587.)
11 PRO MH55/1264, Feb. 1940, memo from Dawson to McNalty.
12 PRO MH55/1264, May 1940, memo from Medical Advisory Committee to McNalty on Administrative, Financial and Legal Aspects of Mass Radiography.
13 PRO MH55/1264, note on reactions of Admiralty, War Office and Ministry of Labour to Dawson memo.
14 PRO MH55/1264, May 1940, memo from Medical Advisory Committee on Administrative, Financial and Legal Aspects.
15 PRO MH55/1264, 5 Feb. 1941, memo from National Conference of Friendly Societies.
16 PRO MH55/1067, 1941, Report of Medical Committee of Welsh Board of Health.
17 PRO MH55/1067, 19 Sept. 1941, letter from Robinson to Glynn Jones of Welsh Hospital Board (WHB).

18 It was acknowledged that there was no firm medical basis for this diagnostic
    category; it was, however, widely used by those in the TB Service to select children
    for particular educational and welfare attention. A. S. MacGregor, Medical Officer
    of Health (MOH) for Glasgow admitted in 1931 that 'administrative provision has
    followed the view of clinicians very closely, often up dubious paths and blind alleys.
    We can remember the days when in search of the early case upon whom to exercise
    preventive measures, the pre tuberculosis child received extremely prominent
    treatment . . . it now appears that the pre tuberculosis child is something of an
    abstraction' (Transactions of the TB Society of Scotland, 1930–1). In Britain these
    children were usually those who were on the books of the dispensary in the 'under
    observation' category; however, public health administrators were loathe to let them
    remain there for any length of time since the category would become unwieldy. By
    recategorising them as 'delicate' the children became eligible for help by the School
    Medical Service with access to open air schools and food supplements. Whilst the
    category of 'delicate child' was recognised by the Educational Service it was derided
    by Tuberculosis Officers (TOs) as 'vague'. This group of 'delicate' children was a
    strange category of illnesses and behaviours, including 'weak lung', 'stammerers',
    'asthmatics', 'chronic eye infections', 'anaemia'. They were the forerunners of the
    'maladjusted' child who sat at the borderline of the medical diagnostic categories
    and ones being developed by the new occupational groups (social workers and child
    psychologists) involved in child care.

19 PRO MH55/1256, 8 Oct. 1942, Report of Advisory Committee on Tuberculosis,
    Mass Radiography Subcommittee (chairman: Lindsay).

20 PRO MH55/1262, 1942, Report of Mass Radiography Subcommittee of MRC.

21 PRO MH55/1269, 1949, memo from Ainsworth to Chief Medical Office.

22 PRO MH55/1525, 28 Nov. 1951, Position Paper on Syphilis Testing in Pregnancy.

23 PRO MH55/1329, 13 Aug. 1941, memo from British Social Hygiene Council
    (BSHC) on Routine Ante Natal Test for Syphilis.

24 First raised in PRO MH55/274, Congenital Syphilis in Children, memo from
    McNalty, 10 Nov. 1932.

25 PRO MH55/1525, 28 Nov. 1951, Position Paper on Syphilis Testing in Pregnancy.

26 PRO MH55/1658, 16 March 1948, letter from National Blood Transfusion Service
    to Welsh Board of Health.

27 PRO MH55/2146, 1949, memo on possible schemes of Hospital and Public Health
    Laboratory Service.

28 PRO MH55/1885, June 1949, correspondence of Ministry of Health with Home
    Office.

29 PRO MH55/1885, 1951, Account of Medical Inspection of Aliens, Harwich:
    'I cannot help feeling a thirty second medical examination is really of little
    value'.

30 PRO MH55/1885, June 1949, letter from Ministry of Health to Home Office.

31 Times, 5 Jan. 1921.

32 PRO MH55/1256, 1943, memo on Records.

33 This was extensively discussed at the conference on 'Biological Monitoring and
    Genetic Screening in the Industrial Workplace', Washington, May 1983, Report in
    Field 1983.

34 PRO BN 29/39, 1958, Discussion Papers on Childrens Act, Medical Certificate.

REFERENCES

Barlowe Report, 1919   HMSO Cmnd 31.

Blaxter, M., 1978   'Diagnosis as category and process: the case of alcoholism', *Social Science and Medicine*, 12: 9–17.

Conrad, P., and Schneider, J., 1980   *Deviance and Medicalization*, St Louis.

Donzelot, J., 1979   *The Policing of Families*, London.

Field, R. I., 1983   'Biological monitoring and genetic screening in the industrial workplace: a synopsis and analysis', *Law, Medicine and Health Care*, June: 125–9.

Foltz, A. M., and Kelsey, J. L., 1978   'The annual pap test: a dubious policy success', *Millbank Memorial Quarterly*, 56, 4: 426–62.

Fortess, E., and Kapp, M., 1985   'Medical uncertainty, diagnostic testing and legal liability', *Law, Medicine and Health Care*: 213–17.

Foucault, M., 1977   *Discipline and Punish: The Birth of the Prison*, London.

Howard-Jones, N., 1978   *International Public Health between the Two World Wars*, WHO, Geneva.

Kniebler, Y., 1979   ' "La lutte anti tuberculose". Instrument de la medicalisation des classes populaires 1870–1930', *Annales Bretagne et des Payes de l'Ouest*, 86.

Lert, F., 1982   'Emergence et devenir du systeme de prise en charge de la tuberculose en France entre 1900 et 1940', *Social Science and Medicine*, 16: 2073–82.

Lynham, J. E., 1925   'The use of X Rays in the diagnosis of pulmonary TB', *Tubercle*, June.

MacGregor, A. S., 1931   'The TB schemes, administrators and clinicians', *Transactions of the TB Society of Scotland* (1930–1).

Pfohl, S., 1985   *Images of Deviance and Social Control: A Sociological History*, New York.

Reisler, S. J., 1978a   'The emergence of the concept of screening', *Millbank Memorial Quarterly*, 56, 4: 403–25.

1978b   *Medicine and the Reign of Technology*, Cambridge.

Shyrock, R. H., 1961   'A history of quantification in medical science', *ISIS*, 5, 2.

Smith, R., and Wynne, B., 1989   *Expert Evidence: Interpreting Science in the Law*, London.

Towers, B., 1980   'Health education policy 1916–26: venereal disease and the prophylaxis dilemma', *Medical History*, 24: 70–87.

1987   'The politics of tuberculosis in western Europe 1914–40', unpublished dissertation, University of London.

Whiston, T., 1979   *The Uses and Abuses of Forecasting*, London.

4

Testing for a sexually transmissible disease, 1907–1970: the history of the Wassermann reaction

ILANA LÖWY

Introduction: *Genesis and Development of a Scientific Fact* revisited

'If one wants to study scientific facts', explained the bacteriologist and philosopher of science Ludwik Fleck in 1935 in the introduction of his book *Genesis and Development of a Scientific Fact* – today viewed as a pioneering study in the sociology of scientific knowledge – 'a medical fact, the importance and applicability of which cannot be denied, is particularly suitable, because it also appears to be very rewarding historically and phenomenologically. I have therefore selected one of the best established medical facts: the fact that the so-called Wassermann reaction is related to syphilis.'[1]

Fleck's choice of the Wassermann reaction was motivated by two reasons. One was the central role of this test in the development and the present structure of his own scientific specialty – serology. The other was the observation that the most famous serological reaction was based on the use of a non-specific antigen and was thus squarely in contradiction with fundamental principles of immunology and serology.[2] These principles had been summed up in 1910 by Wassermann's collaborator Julius Citron. The fundamental law of immunology, Citron explained, is that 'every true antibody is specific and that all nonspecific substances are not antibodies. The law of specificity is the precondition of immunodiagnostic.'[3] This particularity of the Wassermann reaction was central to Fleck's argument that additional, sociologically based explanations are needed to account for the genesis and rapid diffusion of this test.

The discovery that the Wassermann test is in contradiction with the theoretical principles of serodiagnostic did not diminish the practical impact of this test. Just the opposite was true: in the years following the publication of Wassermann's original paper, the test attracted considerable interest on the part of scientists and physicians. It was perfected through a sustained effort of numerous individual investigators, then standardised in a series of international conferences and meetings. The relation of the Wassermann reaction to syphilis, Fleck claimed, could become a generally accepted 'scientific fact' only through the collective activity of the appropriate scientific community. But how was this activity possible in the first place? Why did scientists obstinately look for a blood test for syphilis, all technical and conceptual obstacles notwithstanding? Fleck's answer is that the Wassermann reaction was made possible on the one hand by the persistence of the ancient belief in the existence of tainted 'syphilitic blood', and on the other because of the great fear of syphilis and its consequence, by the priority given by the public authorities to research on this disease. The conjunction of these two factors stimulated the collective effort to search for a blood test for the detection of syphilis, overcame the obstacle of scientific uncertainty and allowed the elaboration of a highly efficient test for the detection of this disease. Fleck believed also that lack of understanding of theoretical principles of the Wassermann reaction had led to the development of tests based solely on complex technical considerations, and, in consequence, to the confinement of syphilis testing to a narrow, esoteric circle of specialists: the serologists. The community of serologists developed unusually dense internal links, but at the same time isolated itself from other scientific disciplines and from the exoteric circles of biologists, general practitioners and the lay public.[4]

In his pioneering work Fleck made explicit the mechanism and the consequences of social construction of what he believed to be an uncontestable 'medical fact'. In all probability even such an unorthodox critic of science as Fleck did not suspect that the Wassermann test, the basis of compulsory premarital screening, was far from being well established as a 'medical fact' as it was believed in the 1920s and 30s. In this paper I will deal with the metamorphoses of the 'medical fact' studied by Fleck, and use this example to illustrate the difficulties of application of 'scientific facts' to medical practice. In the first part, I will describe the 'genesis and development' of the Wassermann test and of other tests based on similar principles in the years 1906–40, then, in the second part, I will follow the radical modifications in the interpretation of 'non-treponemal' tests for syphilis after the Second World War and their practical consequences. Finally, in the conclusion, I will consider the relevance of the history of syphilis testing for a contemporary problem: AIDS testing.

The Wassermann test: the 'genesis and development' phase

The puzzle of the Wassermann reaction

The discovery of the etiological agent of syphilis, Treponema pallidum, by Schaudinn (1905)[5] allowed in some cases (e.g. primary syphilitic lesions) for a direct diagnosis of syphilis. It also confirmed the possibility of developing a blood test for this disease. Wassermann and his collaborators, Neisser and Bruck, assumed that a syphilitic patient would carry in his/her blood specific anti-treponema antibodies. It was difficult, however, to demonstrate directly the presence of such antibodies because it was impossible to grow Treponema pallidum in a test tube. They attempted therefore to use the indirect method of complement fixation, developed by Bordet and Gengau in 1901,[6] which reveals the presence of specific antibodies in the blood of an infected individual. The complement fixation test is based on the principle that when antibody-containing serum is allowed to react with a specific antigen (in the case of the Wassermann test, an extract of a syphilitic liver, rich in treponema antigens), in the presence of guinea-pig complement, the complement will be absorbed by the antigen–antibody complexes. This disappearance of the complement from the reaction mixture can then be demonstrated by a revealing system. In their first publication, Wassermann, Neisser and Bruck[7] affirmed that about 80% of syphilitic sera – but no normal sera – reacted with an extract of syphilic liver. The new test was rapidly used to strengthen the strongly suspected (but, in 1907, not yet proven) etiological links between the primary Treponema pallidum infection and late clinical manifestations such as tabes and dementia paralityca.

When Wassermann and his collaborators described their test, they assumed automatically that it was a specific reaction, closely related to other tests of complement fixation mediated by specific antibodies. Soon, however, it was found that the reaction was in all probability a non-specific one: sera from syphilitic patients reacted also with extracts of organs from normal individuals. At first attempts were made to minimalise the importance of reactions with normal tissues.[8] However, in the years 1907–8, several studies independently confirmed that the Wassermann test might be made with extracts (in particular alcoholic extracts) of normal tissues. Those results put an end to the discussion on the immunological specificity of the 'Wassermann antibody' (called 'reagin', in order to distinguish it from classical antibodies) and opened a debate on the chemical nature of the substances which react in this test and on their relationships to pathological phenomena induced by Treponema pallidum.[9] The theoretical and practical questions were rapidly dissociated. While the elucidation of the biochemical nature of the substance(s) reactive in the Wassermann test and the understanding of the pathological process underlying this reaction was slow to come, physicians and serologists rapidly consolidated the links between Wassermann reaction and treponemal infection, and perfected the technical aspects of this test.

In 1909, it was largely accepted that a positive Wassermann reaction is the result of the 'modification of the colloid properties of the serum'. Such modification, usually viewed as a quantitative and not a qualitative one, was somehow related to the presence of an active pathological process. It was found that, unlike the 'classical' antibodies which usually persist in the serum long after the disappearance of an infection, the presence of 'reagins' is often correlated with the presence of an active disease, and they tend to disappear from the serum after a successful anti-syphilitic treatment. Some authors explained that the

'Wassermann reagins' were decomposition products of tissular origin which appear in the serum as a result of the destructive action of the treponema upon the host tissue.[10] Other investigators believed that the treponemal infection somehow modified the equilibrium between the colloids of the serum and/or alternated their physico-chemical properties.[11] Finally, it was postulated that the reagins are auto-immune antibodies ('auto-cytotoxins') directed against the host's tissues.[12]

Early chemical studies of 'Wassermann reagins' and the lipoid 'antigens' with which they react failed to elucidate the link between the 'colloidal modification of the serum' and the pathological processes in primary, secondary and tertiary syphilis.[13] This was not surprising. In the 1910s and 20s the chemical nature of 'classical' specific antibodies was not much better understood than those of 'Wassermann reagins', allowing for the claim that 'classical' immunological reactions are, like the Wassermann reaction, based on unspecified 'colloidal modifications' of the serum.[14] These studies allowed, however, the perfection of the Wassermann test through optimisation of the 'antigen' source (usually, alcoholic extract of beef heart mixed with lecithin) and detailed codification of the technical aspects of the reaction.[15]

In the late 1930s the development of a new technology – ultracentrifugation – led to a demonstration that antibodies are not, as Fleck believed, names given to symbolic properties of the serum, but are well-defined chemical molecules, the immunoglobulins. At the same time, a growing body of evidence pointed to a structural similarity between 'Wassermann reagins' and 'classical' antibodies.[16] The elucidation of the chemical nature of Wassermann reagins put an end to the speculations that 'reagins' were unspecified 'colloidal modifications' of the serum, or that they were decomposition products of tissues. Two non-mutually exclusive hypotheses remained: the 'reagin' is an antibody directed against a cross-reactive, non-species-specific lipoid component of the treponema, and/or it is an auto-antibody directed against a lipoid component of the host's cells.[17] The finding that reagins were *in fine* true antibodies, perhaps related to an auto-immune process, did not explain, however, why a high concentration of these antibodies appear in syphilitic serum, and what precisely their link with the pathological phenomena induced by an infection with Treponema pallidum is.

The specificity of the Wassermann test: 1906–40

The question of the relationship between the appearance of atypical 'Wassermann antibody' in the blood and the pathology of syphilis, although undoubtedly of interest to scientists, may have been viewed as relatively unimportant by clinicians. The Wassermann test and its derivative, the flocculation test,[18] had above all a practical aim: the specific diagnosis of syphilis. Before the Second World War, this goal was viewed as fully achieved. The Wassermann test, Fleck explained in 1935, demonstrated how the collective effort of the community of serologists transformed the initial doubtful results and false assumptions into an uncontestable scientific truth. Thanks to an impressive collective labour, summed up in more than 10,000 scientific papers, the specific links between Wassermann reaction and syphilis became one of the best established medical facts.[19]

But what was precisely the nature of this 'medical fact'? A serological reaction is evaluated according to its sensitivity – its ability to react in the presence of a given disease, and its specificity – its ability not to react in the absence of this disease. Ideally, a test should be both highly sensitive (i.e. yield few, if any, false negative results) and highly specific (i.e. yield few, if any, false positive results), but in real-life conditions tests usually have either higher specificity or higher sensitivity. In the years 1906–40 the Wassermann reaction was viewed as a test with limited sensitivity and high specificity. The 'scientific fact' discussed by Fleck was in all probability not only the observation that confirmed syphilitic patients have a positive Wassermann test, but that in doubtful cases a positive result of a Wassermann test indicated the presence of syphilis, and of syphilis only. This affirmation was made from the earliest period of the introduction of this test. In 1907, one of the first articles on the Wasser-mann reaction in the US medical press explained that 'a sure conclusion from a positive reaction seems certain. This is especially valuable in diseases in which the determination of etiologic reaction to syphilis is in question and, which, if certain, so much depends on prompt antiluetic treatment.'[20] While a negative response to the Wassermann test was considered of doubtful diagnostic value, a positive response was seen as a solid proof of active syphilis. If, in a properly executed test, 'a suspicious serum is found positive, it can be said without hesitancy that the patient has syphilis'.[21]

One of the problems with the Wassermann reaction was its technical com-plexity. The test was very delicate, and it was necessary to constantly verify each of the components of the reaction. The belief in the high specificity of the Wassermann reaction was always based on the assumption that the test was properly executed. On the other hand, the fact that the original Wassermann test was technically complicated made possible maintaining the faith in the specificity of the method by attributing all the inexplicable results to laboratory errors. A doubtful result of the Wassermann reaction, claimed one specialist, 'in practically every instance is traceable to a failure of controls and to improper use of materials',[22] while another affirmed that 'it is true that in certain diseases other than syphilis positive reactions have been reported, but before these can be accepted it is necessary that every possible technical error be definitively excluded'.[23] The Rockefeller Institute bacteriologist Hideyo Noguchi affirmed that studies in which a high percentage of positive results of the Wassermann test was found in patients suffering from a variety of acute and chronic diseases should not be believed: 'it should be suspected that when one obtains a high percentage of positive reactions in non-syphilitic cases one is not doing the test properly'.[24]

Aware of the technical difficulties of Wassermann reaction, Noguchi attempted to develop a simplified form of the test and the introduction of standardised reagents, dried and distributed on filter paper. Such reagents, Noguchi explained, might be prepared on a large scale by commercial biological laboratories under the supervision of a competent serologist, and might be placed on the market within the ready reach of physicians. This method (a precursor of the present 'kit' methods for antibody testing) should allow the test to be performed by any clinician who is used to making clinical laboratory tests.[25] Noguchi's colleagues strongly disagreed. The Wassermann reaction, they affirmed, is too delicate to permit its use by non-specialists. While the reaction is highly specific in the hands of expert laboratory men who know all about the principles of hemolysis, its diffusion among non-specialists would lead to a considerable increase in the occurrence of 'false positive results', the more so because the Noguchi reaction was of somewhat lower specificity than the original Wassermann test. Such 'false positive' results have potentially disastrous consequences for the patient and his family.[26] Following this debate, Noguchi accepted the principle that specific training is indispensable in order to obtain reliable results in syphilis testing. As to the lower specificity of his test, he admitted that his method might indeed produce some 'false positive results'. On the other hand this limitation of his test is compensated by its higher sensitivity, and thus its higher efficiency in cases in which the goal is not diagnosis but elimination of the possibility of infection: 'for selecting wet-nurses, recruiting for the military or naval services, choosing a donor of blood for transfusion etc., a system which will not miss the reaction whenever there is one should be recommended'.[27]

The modified Noguchi method was finally adopted by some laboratories. It is advantageous, affirmed a laboratory manual in 1914, to use simultaneously two methods, one with lower specificity (Noguchi) and another with lower sensitivity (Wassermann): 'The Noguchi method gives a positive reaction with non-syphilitic sera in about 7% of the cases. The Wassermann gives a negative result in about 9% of syphilitic sera. These figures show the advantage of checking one against the other.'[28] This statement illustrates the general agreement on the high specificity of the original Wassermann method, at least in non-tropical countries. It was found that the Wassermann reaction was positive in some tropical diseases: other treponemal infections (framboesia, yaws) leprosy and trypanosomiasis. But 'so far as the inhabitants of the temperate zones are concerned, a positive reaction practically excludes every disease but syphilis'.[29]

A consensus on syphilis testing was established around 1910. Although several technical modifications and simplifications of the test were proposed, the original (and the most complex) Wassermann method was viewed as the most trustworthy one. As a consequence, it was strongly recommended that in order to avoid false positive and false negative results, syphilis testing would be confined to specialised laboratories only. This conclusion later played an important role in the development of serology as a distinct sub-speciality of clinical bacteriology. On the other hand, if performed by competent specialists the Wassermann reaction was considered highly trustworthy, and a positive result was seen as a nearly absolute proof of syphilis, able to reveal hidden cases of this disease.[30] For example, an American physician, Dr Litterer, affirmed that the Wassermann test disclosed the high incidence of syphilis among city blacks:

> it is evident from the above that a good percentage of the city negroes have syphilis, either acquired or congenital, and do not know it, or else their statements could not be depended on concerning this affection . . . I am of the opinion that a good percentage of the city negroes of the south giving negative syphilis histories will show a positive Wassermann reaction as modified by Noguchi, since many have hereditary syphilis.[31]

Several factors contributed to the uncritical acceptance of the positive results of the Wassermann test as a proof of hidden treponema infection. One was the chronic character and proteiform manifestations of the late stages of infection by Treponema pallidum. In cases of doubtful or poorly defined pathological manifestations, syphilis was always suspected. The second factor was the widespread conviction, fuelled by the popular fear of this disease, that syphilis was highly prevalent, in particular among persons of low socio-economic status. During the Budapest Congress of Medicine of 1909, a German physician, Dr Blashko claimed that 20% of the mortality in Berlin's hospitals was due to syphilis.[32] A high percentage of positive results in the Wassermann test were viewed as a confirmation of this shared conviction. 'The specialists of syphilis have often been accused of "seeing syphilis everywhere"', explained a French specialist, Dr Leredde: 'But, it is proven today that the syphilis specialists themselves were unable to see syphilis in all the places where it really exists, and, on the other hand, that they have not sufficiently recognised its gravity . . . It is difficult to conceive the number of mistakes of which the syphilitic patients are victims.' Thus, Leredde added, the Wassermann test revealed the presence of syphilis in young women with a lupus diagnosis, and in numerous elderly patients suffering from cardiovascular or neurological disorders.[33]

The diagnosis of the syphilitic origin of a given illness was often made on the basis of a positive Wassermann reaction alone. The first rule was: if in doubt, test. The physician should never give credence to the patient's affirmations that he had never had syphilis, and 'in each case of an individual presenting doubtful symptoms, even if syphilis seems highly improbable, one should apply the sero-reaction'.[34] The second rule was: if the Wassermann test is positive, start immediately an anti-syphilitic treatment. The positive Wassermann reaction, viewed as a highly trustworthy indication of active syphilis, became a central diagnostic element in affections of unknown etiology, and 'energetic treatment should be commenced at once after a positive reaction has been obtained in every case, without waiting for the development of further symptoms'.[35] And, one should remember, this was not an innocuous proposition. Before the discovery of penicillin syphilis was treated for prolonged periods (often several years) with drugs such as mercury and arsphenamine which were considerably toxic and which in some cases induced severe secondary effects.

In the 1920s and 30s, the conviction that the Wassermann reaction was highly specific was maintained. A few reports of unusually high percentages of false positive cases were published, but such results were usually attributed to technical errors and inadequate performance of the tests.[36] A better co-ordination among specialists should, it was believed, limit the number of such errors. The Hygiene Committee of the League of Nations organised three international conferences on the serodiagnostics of syphilis (Copenhagen, 1923; Copenhagen, 1928; Montevideo, 1930). There were also two North American conferences organised by the American Society of Clinical Pathologists and the US Public Health Services (1934, 1935–6). In these conferences, samples of both positive and negative sera were distributed to well-known serologists and to serology laboratories in order to estimate the variability between several variants of the Wassermann test, and later to compare data obtained in complement fixation tests to those of flocculation tests (tests based on the principle of directly detecting the presence of 'reagins' in a suspected serum). The comparative tests revealed the existence of differences between individual investigators and between laboratories. These findings reinforced the organisers' conviction that syphilis testing should be performed only in specialised laboratories. They also recommended, whenever possible, checking one kind of test against another (e.g. confirming flocculation results by a complement fixation test). Under optimal conditions, and in the hands of experienced serologists, the tests were, however, found to be trustworthy, and the syphilis testing highly specific.[37]

A similar study, sponsored by the United States Public Health Service in 1935, aimed more specifically at comparing different laboratories. It revealed marked differences between tests performed by expert serologists and those made by standard analysis laboratories. As expected, the state, municipal and private laboratories obtained less trustworthy results, and some of the tests performed in such laboratories showed less than 50% sensitivity, as compared with the 65–88% sensitivity of tests performed by specialists: 'an excellent proof that the methods of these laboratories sadly need correction'. As to the specificity of the tests, the study confirmed the existence of a high (60%) percentage of false positive tests in leprosy, and revealed the – previously unknown – existence of false positive tests (15%) in malaria. The low (and inconsistent) percentage of false positive results found in several other acute diseases (tuberculosis, jaundice, febrile conditions) and in pregnancy was viewed as devoid of practical importance. When sera from patients suffering from acute diseases conducive to false positive results were removed, tests performed in routine laboratories had a low of 91% (and a high of 100%) specificity, while in the hands of specialists

> in general the tests showed a rather high specificity, although four of the participating serologists had a rating of less than 99%, and only five had a rating of 100%. The committee feels very strongly that any test which fails to show a rating of over 99% specificity should be corrected, as it is believed that a false diagnosis of syphilis is, in the words of Moore, 'a major calamity'.[38]

It was felt, however, that at least in expert hands a satisfactory specificity might be achieved.

The faith in the high specificity of the Wassermann reaction was shared by leading microbiologists and immunologists. Jules Bordet affirmed in 1920 that 'the extreme rarity in our countries of leprosy and trypanosomiasis, makes in practice the serodiagnosis of syphilis highly specific'. This affirmation was reiterated by him in the second edition of his book in 1939. And the bacteriologist and historian of medicine William Bulloch explained in 1938 that 'the Wassermann reaction has been practiced to an enormous extent in the diagnosis of syphilis, and is regarded as a test of deadly accuracy'.[39]

While the specificity of the Wassermann reaction and related tests was not questioned before the Second World War, from the mid-1930s on – perhaps as a result of accumulation of clinical experience on this subject – several authors started to question the wisdom of using this reaction as the sole proof of syphilis. In the 1936 edition of *The Principles of Bacteriology and Immunity*, Topley and Wilson discussed the evidence for a low percentage of false positive tests in acute diseases other than syphilis, and affirmed that 'in any case the onus of interpreting the test must rest with the clinician, when he has made due allowance for the stage of the disease, if the case is one of syphilis, and for the possible or probable existence of one of the infections that may sometimes induce similar changes in the serum'. Describing the control of venereal disease in Denmark, the Danish immunologist Thorvald Madson explained in 1937 that 'in no case where the serological result does not agree with clinical symptoms is the doctor to base his diagnosis on serological examination alone'. Finally, a textbook on bacteriology affirmed in 1942 that the Wassermann test 'is a valuable aid in diagnosis, but it must be remembered that it is only an aid and not the diagnosis itself'.[40] A modification attributed to the meaning of a positive Wassermann reaction started thus to be perceptible in the late 1930s and early 1940s. A true revision of the meaning of the positive result of this reaction was made, however, only after the Second World War, as a result of two independent events: the first results of massive routine syphilis testing and the elaboration of specific 'treponemal tests'.

The Wassermann test: the reassessment phase

The belief in the specificity of syphilis testing in all probability played an important role in two decisions: to introduce obligatory pre-marital syphilis tests in several US states, and to start mass syphilis testing of US soldiers during the Second World War. These screening campaigns – the first attempts at large-scale screening for the presence of a given disease – supplied data on Wassermann tests in large sectors of the US population.[41] The results often markedly conflicted with epidemiological observations on the frequency of syphilis in these populations. This finding led some physicians to a strong suspicion that the faith in the high specificity of syphilis tests was mistaken: at least in some sectors of the society the results of these tests might be grossly misleading.

In 1949 a direct test for anti-treponemal antibodies, the 'Nelson test' (later modified and renamed the treponema immobilisation test (TPI)), was developed. In this test living treponemas were immobilised by specific antibodies in the serum.[42] Later another, less expensive 'treponemal test' was developed – the FTA-fluorescein treponemal antibody test. This test revealed the presence of specific anti-treponema antibodies in the serum by the inhibition of the binding of specific, fluorescent anti-treponema antiserum.[43] Unlike the Wassermann test, both 'treponemal tests' detected the presence of specific antibodies in serum of an infected individual; they were therefore based on conventional immuno-logical and bacteriological knowledge. The development of the 'treponemal tests' ended the unique status of syphilis testing and its consequence – the professional isolation of serologists. The switch to treponema-specific tests enabled serologists to replace the esoteric terminology of their speciality[44] by the shared language of biological specificity and facilitated therefore the integration of serology in the mainstream of biological research.

The development of new methods of testing for syphilis made possible the comparison between the 'non-treponemal' (or 'reagin-based') syphilis tests and the 'treponemal tests' based on the presence of specific antibody and viewed as trustworthy indicators of infection with Treponema pallidum. This comparison had confirmed the suspicions of epidemiologists: the specificity of the non-treponemal tests was found to be strongly dependent on the prevalence of infec-tion with Treponema pallidum in the tested population. The 'non-treponemal' tests were found to have a surprisingly low specificity in populations with low incidence of clinical syphilis. In 1952 two American specialists, Drs Moore and Mohr explained that analysis of the results of screenings in large sectors of the US population and verification of the results through the treponema immobilis-ation test 'has led us to express the epidemiological opinion that in certain population groups in the United States (especially in white persons of relatively high socioeconomic status in the Northeastern, Northern and Northwestern states) at least half of the seropositive reactors discovered in mass blood testing do not have syphilis at all, but do instead have biologically false positive reactions'.[45] Thus the introduction of a new family of syphilis tests had resulted in redefinition of the meaning of a positive result in a 'non-treponemal' test for syphilis and in the creation of a new nosologic entity of 'biological false positives' (BFP), that is individuals who have a high level of 'Wassermann reagins' in their serum and tested negative in 'treponemal tests.'

Moore's and Mohr's findings were confirmed by other studies which demonstrated the inverse relation between the percentage of 'biologically false positive' results and the incidence of syphilis in the tested population.[46] For example, in an analysis of the frequency of false positive results in hospitalised patients in Massachusetts during the years 1954–61 a clear-cut correlation between socio-economic status, race and the frequency of BFP was found. Thus while among the black patients of a public hospital 97% of the sera positive in a 'non-treponemal' flocculation test (Hinton test) were found positive in a specific 'treponemal test' (TPI), among the white patients of private clinics only 59% of the Hinton positive sera were found positive in the TPI test.[47] Tests of populations with no known health problems (in contrast to patients in a hospital) showed even higher rates of 'biological false positives'. For example, among the 3,123 persons tested in California in 1962 and found to have a positive 'non-treponema test', 70% were described as 'BFPs'.[48]

Moore and Mohr divided the 'biologically false positive' reactions into two categories: the 'acute BFPs' and the 'chronic BFPs'.[49] 'Acute BFPs' (that is transitory positive Wassermann reactions that may appear in patients suffering from acute febrile diseases) are viewed today as relatively unimportant laboratory artifacts. This is not the case with 'chronic BFPs' – a persisting positive response in 'non-treponemal' syphilis tests. When 'Wassermann reagins' ceased to be exclusively associated with a treponemal infection, physicians were able to observe that the persistence of these 'reagins' in the serum may be an early indication of a severe chronic disorder such as auto-immune disease, collagen or vascular disease, rheumatoid arthritis, heart or liver disease. In the 1950s and 60s the centre of interest in reagin-based tests shifted from the diagnosis of syphilis to the 'diagnosis of BFP'. The description of the 'chronic BFP' state allowed therefore a redefinition of the failures of specificity of the 'non-treponemal' tests as a 'search for a BFP diagnosis'.

A positive Wassermann test, once viewed as a manifestation of a specific disease, acquired in the 1950s and 60s the status non-specific diagnostic indication, not unlike, e.g., abnormal blood sedimentation rate.[50] Physicians stressed the importance of 'BFP diagnosis' in young women, because in about 20% of such cases 'chronic BFP' was the earliest sign of a severe auto-immune disorder – lupus erythrematosus. Non-treponemal tests were found to be positive in other auto-immune diseases too, and in such cases the diagnosis was further complicated by the fact that in these diseases the specific treponemal tests were also often positive.[51] It was shown that in 20 to 25% of the cases 'chronic BFP' was linked with a vast array of chronic systemic disorders. Other conditions conducive to a chronic BFP state were determined to be heroin addiction, the use of certain anti-hypertension drugs and aging: about 10% of persons aged seventy to eighty were found to be BFP. Finally in numerous cases of 'chronic BFP' the reason for chronic persistence and, in some cases, family occurrence, of high levels of 'Wassermann reagins' in the serum remains unknown. The observation that high levels of 'Wassermann reagins' in the serum may be associated with a vast array of chronic diseases, together with the discovery of a highly efficient syphilis treatment – penicillin – radically modified the meaning of a positive Wassermann reaction for a patient. Before the discovery of antibiotics a physician was in some cases happy to be able to announce to a patient that in all probability he/she did not have syphilis and his/her positive Wassermann reaction was a laboratory mistake. Later the opposite was often true: a physician might be happy to explain to a patient that finally the reason for his/her persisting positive tests was nothing worse than syphilis.[52]

Conclusions

The history of the Wassermann reaction is far from being a story of a failure. In the early twentieth century the Wassermann test contributed to medical knowledge by reinforcing the long-suspected link between the primary syphilitic infection and later complications such as tabes or aortal aneurysm. It had important practical effects too: often this test had allowed the confirmation of a diagnosis of syphilis, and led to a treatment which had a real anti-treponemal efficiency. Moreover, the belief in the efficiency of the test and the treatment of syphilis strengthened the pragmatic view of this disease, and contributed to the development of a network of venereal disease clinics, which, even before the penicillin era, helped to curb the infection rate.

The 'non-treponemal tests' have maintained their usefulness up to the present: although new, more specific tests for syphilis have been developed, reactions based on the presence of 'Wassermann reagin' in the serum (e.g. Venereal Disease Research Laboratory test (VDRL)) are still widely applied today. 'Reagin-based' reactions, which are perceived as tests which possess an adequate sensitivity but very low specificity, have become the first step in a laboratory diagnosis of syphilis. During mass screening campaigns for syphilis, the main goal of these tests has been to eliminate the bulk of non-syphilitic sera, and thus artificially transform a population with a very low incidence of syphilis into one with a high incidence. In such a population, the accuracy of the more specific (but not absolutely specific) treponemal tests is viewed as very high. The 'reagin-based' tests which reveal the presence of active treponemal infection are also very useful in monitoring the treatment of confirmed cases of syphilis.[53] However, before the discovery of antibiotics, the Wassermann reaction was a mixed blessing. A positive test was viewed – in particular in the first period of enthusiasm for the new method – not as a diagnostic aid, but as an infallible proof of treponemal infection. As a consequence, thousands of persons who today would be defined as BFP were diagnosed with syphilis. They suffered not only from the psychological and social consequences of syphilis diagnosis – fear, guilt, shame and social opprobrium – but also from the severe toxic effects of the standard anti-syphilitic treatments.[54]

In the 1910s the Wassermann test represented the peak of contemporary medical science, and was viewed as an exemplary case of successful transfer of knowledge from the laboratory to the clinics. Before the Second World War the specialists believed that the continuation of the previous efforts of better standardisation of the reaction by serologists and a better understanding of the chemical nature of the Wassermann test by the fundamental scientists (or, as the unorthodox immunologist Fleck believed, a better understanding of the nature of serological reactions in general) will unfailingly lead to further improvements in syphilis testing.[55] From a more recent point of view the collective efforts of specialists in the 1920s and 30s may, however, appear singularly ineffective. Studies of the mechanism of the 'reagin' reaction, improvements of the technical aspects of the tests, comparative tests made on samples containing high percentages of positive sera, or the accumulation of thousands of papers dealing with small-scale syphilis testing, could not lead to the identification of an important discrepancy between the results of 'non-treponemal' tests for syphilis and the prevalence of treponemal infection in a given population.[56] Only the ulterior conjunction of two events – the development of specific 'treponemal tests' and the analysis of results of mass screening for syphilis – made possible the observation that (a) as a rule, the percentage of 'false positive' responses in a diagnostic test was dependent on the prevalence of a given pathology in the tested population and (b) regarding syphilis, numerous chronic diseases, the symptoms of which may be confused with those of tertiary syphilis, induce 'modifications of the serum' similar to those induced by a treponemal infection.

With the advent of penicillin syphilis has lost its threatening character, and anti-syphilitic treatment most of its dangers. But new epidemic diseases continue to appear,[57] and the obvious present parallel to syphilis is the AIDS epidemic. The similarity between these two diseases is not limited to the fact that both are sexually transmitted. AIDS, like syphilis, is a chronic, slowly developing illness, in which a long latent stage separates the initial – sometimes asymptomatic – infection from a possible late onset of severe, multiform complications. With syphilis, as with AIDS, 'the long term significance of a person being seropositive is unclear until many years of observation of the disease's natural history have elapsed. The choice of therapy remains controversial, particularly for persons with long-standing, asymptomatic infection. Persistent sero-positivity – even after the patient has received an appropriate therapy – frequently results in apprehension and stigmatization.'[58] Finally with AIDS, as with syphilis, the development and the rapid diffusion of tests for the detection of the infection have been fuelled by the powerful prevailing social attitude toward the problems of this disease, and 'the existence of a social tension seeking relief in research'.[59]

It is important to note that the lessons of syphilis testing have not been lost and they were remembered during the development of tests for AIDS. Unlike the Wassermann test and other 'non-treponemal' tests for syphilis, the HIV tests are based on the detection of either specific viral components, or of specific antibodies directed against viral antigens. Moreover, statisticians and epidemi-ologists have been from the very beginning associated with the development and application of HIV tests. The problem of the high ratio of 'false positives' in low risk populations, and the social cost of such 'false positives' have been important arguments in debates on mandatory or large-scale AIDS testing.[60] But although the scientific basis of HIV tests is in better agreement with the present scientific knowledge than was the case for the Wassermann test, the clinical and epidemiological meaning of the results of these tests is far from being entirely elucidated. Routine AIDS testing, based on tests which detect the presence of anti-HIV antibodies, is still facing two important problems. One is the existence of false-positive results, e.g. in parenteral drug users, or in individuals suffering from a variety of tropical diseases.[61] The other is the existence of the 'silent' phase of the disease during which the level of anti-HIV antibodies in the serum is too low to allow their detection by routine methods.[62] Moreover, the clinical and epidemiological interpretation of tests based on the measurement of anti-HIV antibodies is further complicated by the fact that HIV directly attacks its host's immune system, altering, among other things, his/her capacity to produce antibodies.[63]

The uncertainty about AIDS testing (and about other aspects of HIV-induced pathology as well) is acknowledged by the scientists.[64] It is, however, often viewed merely as a temporary obstacle. There is a widely shared conviction that the important facts about HIV infection are already known and AIDS studies are firmly engaged on the right road. The continuation of the present investigations should therefore lead to a much better understanding of the pathology, epidemi-ology and the natural history of HIV infection.[65] The history of the Wassermann reaction reminds us, however, of the possible fragility even of seemingly solid and uncontestable 'medical facts'. One cannot avoid the transformation of some of today's 'facts' into tomorrow's 'errors'. What perhaps may be avoided – and probably might have been at least partly avoided in syphilis testing – is an

88   Ilana Löwy

excessive enthusiasm for the latest scientific innovations and an undue haste in their application to the clinics. '*Primum non nocere.*'

Acknowledgements

I am indebted to Virginia Berridge, Gad Freudenthal, Giora Hon, Nancy Rockafellar, Philip Strong and Robert Westman for their comments on an earlier version of this paper.

1 Ludwik Fleck, *Genesis and Development of a Scientific Fact*, trans. Fred Bradley and Thaddeus Trenn (Chicago, 1979 (1st edn, 1935)), xxviii.

2 *Ibid.*, 15; Boris Zalc, 'Some comments on Fleck's interpretation of the Bordet–Wassermann reaction in view of present biochemical knowledge', in Robert S. Cohen and Thomas Schnelle (eds.), *Cognition and Fact: Materials on Ludwik Fleck* (Dordrecht, 1986), 399–406.

3 Julius Citron, *The Methods of Immunodiagnostic and Immunotherapy* (Leipzig, 1910), quoted in Fleck, *Genesis and Development*, 58.

4 Ludwik Fleck, 'O swoistych cechach myslenia serologicznego' ('Some specific features of the serological way of thinking') in W. Nowicki and D. Szymkiewicz (eds.), *Papers of the XVth Meeting of Polish Physicians and Biologists, Lwow, July 4–7, 1939* (n.p., n.d.), 287–99; English translation in *Science in Context*, 2 (1988), 343–4.

5 F. R. Schaudinn and E. Hoffmann, 'Vorlaüfiger über das Vorkommen von Spirochaeten in syphilischen Krankheitproducten und bei Papillomen', *Arbeiten aus dem Kaiserlichen Gesundheitsamte*, 22 (1905), 527–34.

6 Jules Bordet and Octave Gengou, 'Sur l'existence des substances sensibilitrices dans la plupart des sérums antimicrobiens', *Annales de L'Institut Pasteur*, 15 (1901), 289–302.

7 August Wassermann, Albert Neisser and Carl Bruck, 'Eine serodiagnostische Reaktion bei Syphilis', *Deutsche medizinische Wochenschrift*, 48 (1906), 745.

8 A. Marie and Constantin Levaditi, 'Les "anticorps syphilitiques" dans le liquide cephalo-rachidien des paralytiques généraux', *Annales de L'Institut Pasteur*, 21 (1907), 138–55; P. Fleishmann and W. J. Butler, 'Serum diagnosis of syphilis', *Journal of the American Medical Association*, 49 (1907), 934–8.

9 Constantin Levaditi and J. Roché, *La Syphilis: expérimentation, microbiologie, diagnostique* (Paris, 1909), 138–40; Fleck, *Genesis and Development*, 70–5. The historical name 'reagin' may be misleading, because later a very different category of antibodies – the IgE antibodies, active in allergic reactions – were also called 'reagins'.

10 Levaditi and Roché, *La Syphilis*, 133–4.

11 William Litterer, 'Serodiagnosis of syphilis', *Journal of the American Medical Association*, 53 (1909), 1537–41; James M'Intosh, 'The sero-diagnosis of syphilis', *The Lancet*, 1 (1909), 1515–21.

12 Stephan Mutermilch, 'Sur la nature des substances qui provoquent la réaction de

Wassermann dans le sérum des syphilitiques et des lapins trypanosomies', *Comptes Rendus de la Société de Biologie* (Paris), 67 (1909), 125–7. This hypothesis was first evoked by Weil. E. Weil, 'Uber den Leusantikörper nach weis im Blute von Luetischen', *Wiener klinische Wochenschrift*, 18 (1907), 527.

13 Jules Bordet, *Traité de l'immunité dans les maladies infectieuses* (Paris, 1920), 433–47; Jules Bordet, *Bacteriologie, parasitologie, infection et immunité* (Brussels, 1927), 162–9.

14 Marc Rubinstein, *Traité pratique de sérologie et de diagnostic* (Paris, 1921), 240; Fleck, *Genesis and Development*, 65; Arthur M. Silverstein, *A History of Immunology* (New York, 1989), 125–9.

15 Ivy McKenzie, 'The serum diagnostic of syphilis', *Journal of Pathology and Bacteriology*, 13 (1909), 311–24; Carl H. Browning, John Cruikshank and Ivy McKenzie, 'Constituent concerned in the Wassermann syphilis reaction, with special reference to leicithin and cholesterin', *Journal of Pathology and Bacteriology*, 14 (1910), 484–502; Paul Gastou and A. Girault, *Guide pratique du diagnostic de la syphilis* (Paris, 1910); Armand Deliele, *Techniques de diagnostic par la methode de deviation de complement* (Paris, 1911).

16 Karl Landsteiner, *The Specificity of Serological Reactions* (Cambridge, Mass., 1947), 102–4.

17 Henry Eagle, *The Laboratory Diagnosis of Syphilis* (London, 1937); Jules Bordet, *Traité de l'immunité* (2nd edn, Paris, 1939), 492–515.

18 Flocculation tests directly reveal the presence of the 'reagin' in the serum. The first flocculation tests were developed in the 1920s. Reuben Kahn, *The Kahn Test: A Practical Guide* (Baltimore, 1928).

19 Fleck, *Genesis and Development*, 78–81, xxviii.

20 Fleishmann and Butler, 'Serum diagnosis of syphilis', 938.

21 Levaditi and Roché, *La Syphilis*, 129; William J. Butler, 'Serum diagnosis of syphilis', *Journal of the American Medical Association*, 51 (1908), 824–30, on 830.

22 Litterer, 'Serodiagnosis of syphilis', 1538.

23 M'Intosh, 'The sero-diagnosis of syphilis', 1515.

24 Hideyo Noguchi, *Serum Diagnosis of Syphilis* (Philadelphia and London, 1910), 109.

25 Hideyo Noguchi, 'A new and simple method for the serum diagnosis of syphilis', *Journal of Experimental Medicine*, 11 (1909), 392–401; Hideyo Noguchi, 'The serodiagnostic of syphilis', *Journal of the American Medical Association*, 53 (1909), 934–6.

26 'Serodiagnosis of syphilis: abstract of discussion', *Journal of the American Medical Association*, 53 (1909), 1540–1.

27 Noguchi, in 'Serodiagnosis of syphilis: abstract of discussion', 1540.

28 E. R. Stitt, *Practical Bacteriology, Blood Work and Animal Parasitology* (Philadelphia, 1914), 154.

29 Carl H. Browning and Ivy McKenzie, 'The biological syphilis reaction: its significance and method of application', *The Lancet*, 1 (1909), 1521–3, on 1523.

30 P. Mauriac, 'Conclusions fournies par trois cent cas de séro-réaction de Wassermann', *Comptes Rendus de Séances de la Société de Biologie*, 66 (1909), 668–70.

31 Litterer, 'Serodiagnosis of syphilis', 1539.

32 Data reproduced by Gastou and Girault, *Guide pratique du diagnostic de la syphilis*, 85–9.

33 D. Leredde, *La Réaction de Wassermann* (Paris, 1912), 28, 29–30.

34 Mauriac, 'Conclusions fournies par trois cent cas', 669; Leredde, *La Réaction de Wassermann*, 30.

35 M'Intosh, 'The sero-diagnosis of syphilis', 1520; Leredde, *La Réaction de Wassermann*, 30, 42.

36 Rubinstein, *Traité pratique de sérologie*, 219–22.

37 Theodor Vogelsang, *Séro-diagnostic de la syphilis* (Bergen, 1940), 24–30.

38 H. H. Hazzen, 'The serodiagnosis of syphilis', *Journal of the American Medical Association*, 108 (1937), 785–8.

39 Bordet, *Traité de l'immunité* (1st edn, 1920), 444; Bordet, *Traité de l'immunité* (2nd edn, 1939), 506; William Bulloch, *The History of Bacteriology* (London and New York, 1938), 283.

40 W. W. C. Topley and G. S. Wilson, *The Principles of Bacteriology and Immunity* (London, 1936), 1441; Thorvald Madsen, *Lectures on Epidemiology and Control of Syphilis, Tuberculosis and Whooping Cough* (Baltimore, 1937), 11; T. B. Rice, *A Textbook of Bacteriology* (Philadelphia and London, 1942), 487.

41 Allan M. Brandt, *No Magic Bullet: A Social History of Venereal Disease in the United States since 1880* (2nd edn, New York and Oxford, 1987), 147–52.

42 Robert A. Nelson and Manfred M. Mayer, 'Immobilisation of Treponema pallidum in vitro by antibody produced in syphilitic infection', *Journal of Experimental Medicine*, 89 (1949), 369–93.

43 Wolfgang R. Joklik and David T. Smith, *Zinser's Microbiology* (15th edn, New York, 1972), 644–50.

44 Fleck, 'Some specific features of the serological way of thinking'.

45 J. E. Moore and C. F. Mohr, 'Biologically false positive serological tests for syphilis', *Journal of the American Medical Association*, 150 (1952), 467–73, on 471.

46 Frederick Sparling, 'Diagnosis and treatment of syphilis', *New England Journal of Medicine*, 284 (1971), 642–53. Syphilis testing was the first case of mass screening for the presence of a pathological condition. It allowed therefore the establishment of the epidemiological principle that in such screenings specificity is inversely linked to prevalence.

47 Nicholas J. Fiumara, 'Biologically false positive reactions for syphilis', *New England Journal of Medicine*, 268 (1963), 402–5.

48 C. Carpenter, R. A. Clair and R. A. Broak, 'Tests for syphilis: increasing incidence of false positive reactions as measured by Treponema pallidum immobilization', *California Medical Journal*, 103 (1965), 13–15.

49 Moore and Mohr, 'Biologically false positive serologic tests'.

50 D. L. Tufanelli, K. D. Wuepper, L. L. Bradford and R. M. Wood, 'Fluorescent treponemal antibody absorption tests: studies of false positive reactions to tests for syphilis', *New England Journal of Medicine*, 276 (1967), 258–62; D. L. Tufanelli, 'Aging and false positive reactions for syphilis', *British Journal of Venereal Diseases*, 42 (1966), 40–1; G. S. Wilson and A. Miles, *Topley's and Wilson's Principles of Bacteriology, Virology and Immunity* (6th edn, London, 1975), 2315–19; P. Balows and W. J. Hausler, *Diagnostic Procedures for Bacterial,*

Mycotic and Parasitic Infections (Washington, DC, 1981), 631–74; E. H. Lenuette, A. Ballows, W. J. Hauser and H. J. Shadomy, *Manual of Clinical Microbiology* (Washington, DC, 1985), 910–21.

51 J. L. Miller, M. Brodey and J. H. Hill, 'Studies on the significance of biologically false positive reactions', *Journal of the American Medical Association*, 164 (1957), 1461–6; M. A. Harvey, 'Auto-immune disease and the chronic biologic false positive tests for syphilis', *Journal of the American Medical Association*, 182 (1962), 513–18; Sidney Olansky, 'Current serodiagnostic and treatment of syphilis', *Journal of the American Medical Association*, 198 (1966), 165–8; S. J. Kraus, J. R. Haserick and N. A. Lonz, 'Atypical FIA-ADS fluorescent tests in lupus erythrematosus patients', *Journal of the American Medical Association*, 211 (1970), 2140–4; F. S. Aschar and R. Miller, 'Serological test for syphilis in diseases of the thyroid', *Journal of the American Medical Association*, 213 (1970), 872.

52 Fiumara, 'Biologically false positive reactions for syphilis'.

53 L. L. Bradford, *et al.*, 'FTA-200, FTA-ABS and TPI tests in serodiagnosis of syphilis', *Public Health Reports*, 80 (1965), 797–804; US Department of Health, Education and Welfare, *Manual of Test for Syphilis* (Atlanta, 1969); Russel C. Johnson (ed.), *The Biology of Parasitic Spirochetes* (New York, 1976); US Department of Health, *Manual of Tests for Syphilis*; L. L. Bradford and S. A. Larsen, 'Serological tests for syphilis', in Lenuette *et al.* (eds.), *Manual of Clinical Microbiology*, 910–21.

54 Walsh McDermott, 'Evaluating the physician and his technology', *Dedalus*, 106 (Winter 1977), 135–57, on 144.

55 The origins and physiological role of the 'Wassermann reagin' are not much better understood today than they were eighty years ago. Wilson and Miles, *Topley's and Wilson's Principles of Bacteriology*, 2318–19; Silverstein, *A History of Immunology*, 169. Recently, cases of syphilis in AIDS patients have pointed to a greater than suspected role of the patient's immune response in the prevention of neurosyphilis and called the attention of physicians to the insufficiency of the understanding of immune mechanism in syphilis. Edmund C. Tramont, 'Syphilis in the AIDS era', *The New England Journal of Medicine*, 316 (1987), 1600–1; Donald R. Johns, Maureen Tierney, and Donna Felenstein, 'Alternation in the natural history of neurosyphilis by concurrent infection with the human immunodeficiency virus', *Journal of the American Medical Association*, 316 (1987), 1569–72.

56 For discussion on 'unexpected errors', see Giora Hon, 'Experimental errors: an epistemological view', in Paul Weingartner and Gerhard Schurtz (eds.), *Philosophy of the Natural Sciences: Borderline Questions* (Vienna, 1989), 368–76; Giora Hon, 'Franck and Hertz versus Townsend: a study of two types of experimental error', *Historical Studies in the Physical and Biological Sciences*, 20 (1989), 79–106.

57 Charles Nicolle, *Destin des maladies infectieuses* (Paris, 1933).

58 Dale N. Lawrence, 'The acquired immunodeficiency syndrome: what it can teach us', Banquet address delivered by the author on 24 April 1984, at the Bay Harbor Inn, Tampa, Florida. Reproduced in A. Szentiavang and H. Friedman, *Viruses, Immunity and Immunodeficiency* (New York and London, 1986), 189–94, on 189–90.

59 Fleck, *Genesis and Development*, 77.

60 Klemens B. Meyer and Stephen G. Pauker, 'Screening for HIV: can we afford the
    false-positive rate?', *The New England Journal of Medicine*, 317 (1987), 238–41;
    Robin Weiss and Samuel O. Thier, 'HIV testing is the answer – what is the
    question?', *The New England Journal of Medicine*, 319 (1988), 1010–12.
61 James D. Moore, Edward J. Cone and Steve S. Alexander, 'HTLV-III seropositivity
    in 1971–1972 parenteral drug abusers – a case of false positives or evidence of viral
    exposure', *The New England Journal of Medicine*, 314 (1986), 1387–8; Robert J.
    Biggar, Paul L. Gigase, Mads Melbye *et al.*, 'Elisa HTLV retrovirus antibody
    reactivity associated with malaria and immune complexes in healthy Africans', *The
    Lancet*, 2 (1985), 520–3; Ulla Bredberg Raden, John Kiango, Fred Mhalu and
    Gunnel Biberfield, 'Evaluation of commercial enzyme immunoassays for anti-
    HIV-1 using East African sera', *AIDS*, 2 (1988), 281–5; Neil T. Constantine, Emile
    Fox, E. A. Abbate and James N. Woody, 'Diagnostic usefulness of five screening
    assays for HIV in an east African city where prevalence of infection is low', *AIDS*,
    3 (1989), 313–17.
62 Richard G. Marlink, Jonathan S. Alan, Mary McLane *et al.*, 'Low sensitivity of Elisa
    testing in early HIV infection', *The New England Journal of Medicine*, 315 (1986),
    1549; Sheldon H. Landesman, Harold M. Ginzburg and Stanley H. Weiss, 'Special
    report: the AIDS epidemic', *The New England Journal of Medicine*, 312 (1985),
    521–5; Annamari Ranki, Sirkka-Lisa Valle, Minerva Krohn *et al.*, 'Long latency
    preceded overt seroconversion in sexually-transmitted immunodeficiency virus
    infection', *The Lancet*, 2 (1987), 589–93; Michael Loche and Bernard Machi,
    'Identification of HIV infected seronegative individuals by a direct diagnostic test
    based on hybridization to amplified viral DNA', *The Lancet*, 2 (1988), 418–21; John
    W. Ward, Scott D. Holmberg, James R. Allen *et al.*, 'Transmission of human
    immunodeficiency virus (HIV) by blood transfusions screened negative for HIV
    antibody', *The New England Journal of Medicine*, 318 (1988), 473–8; David T.
    Imagawa, Moon H. Lee, Steven M. Wolinsky *et al.*, 'Human deficiency virus type I
    in homosexual men who remain seronegative for prolonged periods', *The New
    England Journal of Medicine*, 320 (1989), 1458–62; William A. Haseltine, 'Silent
    HIV infections', *The New England Journal of Medicine*, 320 (1989), 1487–9.
63 Maxime Seligmann, Leonard Chess, John L. Fahey *et al.*, 'AIDS – an immuno-
    logical evaluation', *The New England Journal of Medicine*, 311 (1984), 1286–92;
    P. Volberding, 'AIDS – variations on a theme of cellular immune deficiency',
    Bulletin de l'Institut Pasteur, 85 (1987), 87–94; Anthony Fauci, 'The human
    immunodeficiency virus: infectivity and mechanisms of pathogenesis', *Science*, 239
    (1988), 617–22.
64 Jay A. Levy, 'Mysteries of HIV: challenges for therapy and prevention', *Nature*, 333
    (1988), 519–22; Robert S. Root-Bernstein, 'Do we know the cause(s) of AIDS?',
    Perspectives in Biology and Medicine, 33 (1990), 480–500.
65 Margaret A. Hamburg and Anthony Fauci, 'AIDS the challenge to biomedical
    research', *Dedalus*, 118, 2 (Spring 1989), 19–40; David Baltimore and Mark B.
    Feinberg, 'HIV revealed: towards a natural history of the infection', *The New
    England Journal of Medicine*, 321 (1989), 1673–5.

5

The politics of international co-ordination to combat sexually transmitted diseases, 1900–1980s

PAUL WEINDLING

Organisations for the prevention and cure of sexually transmitted diseases (STDs) have been battlegrounds for social conflicts and international tensions. Debates on control of STDs expose tensions between officially condoned pro-natalism and social purity movements, and dissident internationally minded feminists, socialist sympathisers and pacifists, demanding removal of police controls on public morality, sex education, freely available contraceptives and the socialisation of health services. Medical scientists were themselves divided between these contrasting viewpoints. The emergence of any unitary international consensus on STDs let alone any single authority has been undermined by governmental hostility to a supranational agency, controversies over medical power and the efficacy and distribution of new drugs like salvarsan and penicillin, and by birth control propagandists challenging traditional notions of the family.

Imperialist conferences and conflicts

Imperialist concerns with promoting national efficiency by combating physical degeneration and declining birth rates arose at the same time that campaigners for the abolition of police controls on prostitution were seeking comprehensive strategies to prevent and treat STDs throughout the totality of populations. Voluntaristic models of self-help clashed with state and policing regulatory measures. Whether there should be targeting of specific groups like prostitutes or education of total populations (recognising that STDs were not a monopoly of prostitutes) were issues. The extent that STDs were precipitated by poverty, the lack of basic sex education or immorality was keenly debated. Imperial powers regarded STDs as a threat to the family, to military and economic power and to the nation's future generations; syphilis was a major cause of blindness and other disabilities, and concern increased over gonorrhea as a cause of sterility and miscarriage.

The first initiatives in international co-ordination of efforts to control STDs

93

were the *Conférence internationale pour la prophylaxie de la syphilis et des maladies vénériennes* held in Brussels during 1899 and a second conference in 1902.[1] Here the powers of police and medical authorities were criticised by feminists and socialists. A more moralistic tone was struck at the International Congress for Combating the Traffic in Women held by voluntary organisations in 1899. The foundation of the International Bureau for the Suppression of the Trade in Women and Children in 1904 led to a French government-sponsored conference. There resulted distinct strategies with different historical lines of development: medical controls on sexually transmitted diseases, and moral and policing efforts to control prostitution as an international vice.

These differences remained unresolved when societies to combat 'venereal diseases' were established first in France in 1901, in Germany in 1902, in the United States in 1905 and (significantly later) in Great Britain in 1914.[2] These societies had both lay and medical membership with greater lay involvement in the United States and Britain, and domination by the medical profession in continental Europe, where dermatology and venereology were more highly developed as medical specialisms. The pace-setting French and German societies placed greater stress on public understanding of medical means of prevention and treatment than the Americans emphasising moral education.[3] The Germans took an interest in prevention by recommending Alexander Metchnikov's antiseptic ointment for self-disinfection, condoms and highly controversial preventive health checks on prostitutes.[4] The Prussian state supported diagnosis with Wassermann testing, as well as developing curative chemotherapy with salvarsan.[5] The German sickness insurances and state authorities were also interested in compiling statistics on the incidence of STDs.

During the First World War there was a fiercely debated shift of priorities from moralistic notions of self-control to improving medical facilities. Military and civilian authorities established networks of primary health care for STDs. Improved facilities for diagnosis and treatment for soldiers and civilians became available in new outpatient clinics and dispensaries. To the indignation of campaigners for moral purity there was a greater readiness on the part of the authorities to accept condoms as a barrier to infection.[6] This coincided with the extension of welfare facilities to cater for the needs of single mothers and working women. Whereas imperialist ideologies prior to war had initially reinforced pro-natalism, during the war there was a new acceptance that improved medical and welfare provision as well as greater availability of condoms would help to diminish STDs.

Inter-war health and welfare bodies

Control of STDs was crucial in the transition from war to peace with the fear that infected soldiers might spread STDs among the civilian population. Groups targeted as reservoirs of STDs were – besides prostitutes – the armed services, demobilised soldiers and sailors, and merchant navies. The risks from STDs to seamen and to other migrant workers was a stimulus for free and universal provision of treatment and diagnosis irrespective of nationality. Radicals, critical of targeting specially infective groups, pointed out that socialisation of medicine with free and universal medical treatment for all health problems could cover STDs so rendering redundant various forms of special care.

The problems of establishing an international health organisation were compounded by disagreements between the allies, which resulted in competing international agencies. These included: the Health Organisation of the League of Nations (LNHO), the International Labour Office (ILO) which had a small medical division, the International Office of Public Health/Organisation internationale d'hygiène publique (OIHP) and the League of Red Cross Societies (LRCS). These bodies had very different constitutions which influenced their policies: the LHNO and OIHP were controlled by constituent states with Britain and France having dominant (but rival) roles. The ILO was a tripartite organisation of states, employers and trade unions, and was much influenced by its first Secretary-General, the French socialist Albert Thomas who challenged the hegemony of national ruling elites on the basis of univer-salist ideals and conventions. The LRCS had a philanthropic ethos derived from voluntary war work. The problem arose whether these organisations were to be staffed only by a small number of professional experts whose activities were restricted to comparisons of legislation, statistical and technical problems, or whether these international organisations should be able to take autonomous initiatives, and involve a broad range of lay and professional advisers. The LRCS promoted a framework based on US developments in 'social hygiene', which emphasised the need for constituent national societies to undertake preventive educative programmes on a voluntary basis, encouraging personal hygiene, and a sense of individual responsibility for future generations.[7] Certain national Red Cross societies – notably the Norwegian Red Cross – wished to take over the running of seamen's clinics, prompting debates on voluntaryism or state responsibility for STDs.[8]

First World War and post-war fears that soldiers might spread venereal infections to civilian populations enhanced the importance of the LRCS. In April 1919 the Committee (subsequently the League) of Red Cross Societies favoured an international council and central bureau of health with a section for venereal diseases.[9] The LRCS was in an expansionist phase of post-war optimism, which was boosted by the substantial funds from the American Red Cross, when it organised a series of conferences: a Pan-American Conference on Venereal Diseases in December 1920, a Burmese conference, and three regional conferences in western Europe (in Paris under the patronage of the French Ministry of Hygiene in December 1921), in northern Europe (in Copenhagen in

May 1921) and eastern Europe (in Prague in December 1921).[10] Yet the LRCS was at loggerheads with the International Committee of the Red Cross, and misgivings arose at the League of Nations' recognition of the LRCS as a voluntary body, particularly once the LN's own health organisation was formed. When the LRCS moved its headquarters to Paris in 1922, its expansionism was on the wane.

From the time of the Genoa maritime conference of 1920 the issue of venereal diseases among seamen was used by the ILO to assert its right to take initiatives in health matters against the LRCS, the emergent LNHO, OIHP and the National Council for Combating Venereal Disease (NCCVD).[11] In 1924 the ILO conducted a survey of treatment facilities in ports and harbours.[12] Thereafter the ILO gave occasional advice but maintained a 'politique d'abstention' on issues associated with STDs except for the issue of port welfare on which employers' organisations also held strong opinions.[13] The provision of treatment for seamen was taken up by the governmentally oriented OIHP. It secured the Brussels agreement of 1924 that governments should establish services for the treatment of STDs for seamen of all nationalities with medical facilities and drugs available free of charge.[14] The League of Nations felt compelled 'to nominate one or more public health men' to act as technical experts.[15] The initiative passed to governments, and the Belgian government negotiated an agreement of December 1924 for treatment facilities for merchant seamen (using a British-style *carnet* for treatment records). The agreement was endorsed by France and Great Britain but not the USA or USSR.[16] The monitoring of port facilities under the Brussels Agreement was a responsibility of the OIHP.[17] The issue of merchant seamen's welfare continued to preoccupy single-country organisations like the British Red Cross and NCCVD, and prompted efforts to maintain the separation of sailors from indigenous populations by enforcing systems of passes, the fencing in of dock areas and the exclusion of visitors to ships.[18]

The NCCVD was given official blessing by the British government keen to devolve a controversial area of policy to private initiatives.[19] The NCCVD undertook a global role with commissions to the Far East, Mediterranean and West Indies during 1920, and to Constantinople in 1921. In response to the Genoa conference of 1920 and the activities of the LN and ILO, the NCCVD set about improving facilities in ports in Britain and the Empire. In 1921 it distributed leaflets in French, Dutch and Danish on treatment facilities in North Sea ports.[20] Although by January 1922 the LRCS had decided to discontinue its division for combating venereal diseases, Sybil Neville-Rolfe (the formidable Secretary-General of the NCCVD and eugenicist) spurred it into taking further international initiatives, and liaised with Sir George Buchanan, the British representative of the LNHO.[21] Relations with the ILO revolved around the provision of medical and social facilities for sailors.[22]

The ILO and LNHO were suspicious when the Union Internationale contre le

Péril Vénérien (UIPV) was established in Paris in January 1923. But they were forced to support the UIPV by British Ministry of Health Officials arguing in favour of 'voluntary effort' at a national and international level.[23] The recognition of the UIPV meant that the moralistic NCCVD and LRCS (under Sir Claude Hill) could have a major say at an international level. The Director of the Venereal Diseases Section of the LRCS, Emile Weisweiller, became Secretary-General of the UIPV. The UIPV was composed of specialist societies, national Red Cross Societies, state representatives, and technical representatives from the ILO, the LNHO and the International Council of Women.[24] The UIPV was subject to conflicts between member organisations, as it moved from a moralistic Anglo-American position to a stance based on social medicine. British delegates were disappointed at the French dominance over the first congress in May 1923, and overcame French hostility to German participation.[25] Initially the organisation had a Secretariat financed by the LRCS, but by 1925 the UIPV had broken away from the dominance of the LRCS.[26] This can be seen as a reaction to the American-sponsored International Social Hygiene Congress of 1925. While freeing itself from the Anglo-American-dominated LRCS, it remained much influenced by its French location. In 1927 there was a change of Secretary-General from Weisweiller to J.-A. Cavaillon, a French ministerial public health official.[27] Cavaillon's appointment as technical adviser to the LRCS on 'all matters relating to VD' signalled a defeat of the LRCS's moralistic voluntaryism.[28] The UIPV was doggedly Euro-centric, encouraging European states like Sweden (where the state assumed a central role in comprehensive legislation for diagnosis and treatment of STDs since 1918) and Finland to form constituent organisations. Although having members from North and South America, with the exception of a single congress in Tunis, UIPV meetings were in Europe. Colonies and mandated territories were deemed to be represented by the colonial powers.[29] The Germans continued to be members after the Nazi takeover in 1933 – and consequent withdrawal from the LNHO and ILO – and a UIPV conference was held in Cologne in 1937, but the USSR was a conspicuous absentee despite negotiations in 1928.

The British NCCVD attempted to give the UIPV a moralistic tenor. In 1925 the NCCVD became the British Social Hygiene Council (BSHC), responding to the American point of view that attention should be shifted from the infected to the preventive education of the uninfected. It represented a move from the pre-war Franco-German medical models of improved access to treatment and preventive health education to the American stress on morals and personal hygiene with mass propaganda, deploying new media like the radio and cinema and advertising techniques in Health Weeks.[30] The BSHC jealously defended its colonial realm as its legitimate sphere of activity: colonies were discouraged from joining the UIPV in their own right. Given that the UIPV broke away from the American-influenced LRCS, a profound rift between Anglo-American and

European viewpoints can be discerned in 1925. Cavaillon later managed to heal the wounds through co-operation with Mrs Neville-Rolfe (an admiral's daughter and widow of a naval commander) who for her part came out in favour of abolitionism. In 1927 the LRCS resurrected its committee on venereal diseases, but ceded control to the UIPV.[31] The Ports Commission of the UIPV was funded by £1,000 respectively from the British Shipping Federation and the American Social Hygiene Association.[32] Mrs Neville-Rolfe continued to act as a global inspector of treatment facilities. Her vigilance exposed how countries tried to evade their obligations under the Brussels agreement, and she persuaded many port authorities, for example in Hamburg, to provide free diagnosis and treatment for seamen of all nations.[33] In 1928 she was invited to chair and direct the UIPV's Ports Committee, and thereafter took a prominent international role on behalf of the UIPV.[34]

The UIPV's moderately progressive stance meant that despite limited resources, it could claim constructive achievements in facilitating international comparisons and checking excessive policing or under-provision of state resources for diagnosis and therapy. The UIPV did not establish a major journal or other organ of publicity, leaving activities to constituent organisations; but Cavaillon published under UIPV aegis an important study of legislation throughout the world.[35] The UIPV served as a forum for the representatives of various organisations to meet and inspect each other's work in the course of conferences and study tours. Such visits facilitated comparison of different systems of regulation of prostitution and notification of STDs, for example Mrs Neville-Rolfe and the NCCVD studied Scandinavian procedures comparing statistics of the incidence and treatment of STDs with those in Britain.[36] The UIPV encouraged the foundation of national organisations where none existed, co-ordinated propaganda on the risks of infection, sought to remove social and moral stigma as well as any discriminatory measures in medical insurance and social security legislation and insisted on equal moral codes for both sexes.

The UIPV endorsed abolitionist demands for an end to the regimentation of prostitutes, and proposed measures embracing the totality of the population while respecting 'the principle of individual liberty'.[37] Its moralism was reflected in support for the censorship of books and films, and concern over the corruption of youth. It demanded disinfection facilities for merchant seamen and colonial troops, and screening of emigrants and frontier controls for carriers of STDs.[38] It was initially cautious as regards publicity for condoms as a barrier to infection, and – to the chagrin of the Pasteur Institute – condemned Metchnikov's self-disinfection ointment.[39] But by 1930 it was advocating a fully medical programme with self-disinfection as the starting point.[40] Symptomatic of the dominance of a professional lobby was opposition to native practitioners as 'quacks' and it did not seek to establish patients' rights in legislative schemes for compulsory detention and treatment, or in criminal sentences for infecting another with syphilis. The UIPV can be seen as moving away from moralistic concerns or US-dominated social hygiene of the early 1920s to medical and secular viewpoints by the 1930s.

Avoiding birth control

The UIPV like most other international medical organisations had male doctors in leading positions. Sybil Neville-Rolfe of the NCCVD/British Social Hygiene Council (BSHC) was the only woman representative and the only person without medical qualifications. The ILO, LRCS and LNHO also employed very few women, except in spheres concerned with the family and women's welfare. International efforts to protect women and children involved greater numbers of women welfare workers. The League of Nations took up the pre-war standards concerning the minimum age of prostitutes and penalties for procuration in a Convention of 1921. The issue of prostitution was dealt with by a separate social committee which tackled the question of 'white slavery' and 'the suppression of traffic in women and children'.[41] Although the USA was not a member of the League, it was represented on the Committees for Traffic in Women and Children, and on the Child Welfare Committee. The Rockefeller's Bureau of Social Hygiene provided $75,000 funding for an enquiry on the extent of the traffic in Europe, the Mediterranean region and the USA, and in 1930 contributed $125,000 for a Far Eastern survey. The committee supported the development of women police, and co-operation between the International Criminal Police Commission and the Traffic in Women and Children Committee.[42] In 1923 an international convention for the suppression of obscene publications was drawn up, and this was ratified by thirty-five member states by 1929. Some delegates wished to include 'birth control propaganda', although opinions differed over whether this was a special class of obscene literature.[43] The debate revealed the highly moralistic and pro-natalist tenor of the 'social and humanitarian activities' of the LN. The situation exposed the rift between moral and policing solutions to the problem of prostitution, and more strictly medical approaches.

The LNHO concentrated on a restricted range of scientific issues such as the standardisation of the Wassermann and flocculation tests, and of salvarsan therapy. Issues associated with the diagnosis of gonorrhea, soft chancre and other sexually transmitted infections were not tackled. Expert conferences on serodiagnosis were held in London in 1921 and in Paris in 1922. In 1923 a working laboratory conference was held in Copenhagen when 500 specimens from eight countries were tested using different techniques. Further working laboratory conferences were held in Frankfurt am Main, in Geneva in 1928 and in Montevideo in 1930.[44] Laboratories at Copenhagen and London were designated for establishing international standards for pharmaceutical products and vaccines, and the Copenhagen laboratory acted as a centre for studies of salvarsan. The LNHO paid scant regard to the practicalities of financing and gaining public acceptance for serodiagnosis and salvarsan therapies. In 1935 it proposed a protracted forty to sixty week standard treatment for syphilis, which required extensive systems of scientific medicine. Governments' suspicion of international agencies developing autonomously optimum but costly policies encouraged a minimalist reaction; this meant that contraception and the circumstances of non-European populations – particularly regarding non-venereal trypanosomes associated with poor hygiene and poverty – were virtually ignored. The colonial powers became obstructive: thus in 1930 the Secretary of the LNHO argued for its responsibility for the health of 'native populations', but this was strongly objected to by the British representative.[45] International health organisations could not operate on a global scale, and the LNHO was limited to the technical areas. Thus 'education' for the LNHO was not public education or health education in schools but professional postgraduate education, seen as part of the building up of viable professional specialisms of venereology as related to urology or dermatology.

There was broad international consensus over family allowances and over the need to have a system of medical insurance which supported treatment for STDs as for any other disease.[46] Within each member country there were tensions between more moralistic and more secular approaches, which condoned contraception. The League of Nations found itself unable to give frank consideration to – let alone endorse – birth control. Eric Drummond, Secretary-General of the LN was a convert to Catholicism; he opposed discussion of birth control. Dame Rachel Crowdy of the Social Questions Section and members of the Health Secretariat were more sympathetic when invited to attend the World Population Conference, but recognised that they could not act as official representatives of the LN as long as member states had not endorsed birth control. The ILO's constitutional basis provided for greater autonomy. The Director of the ILO, Albert Thomas took a prominent role at the World Population Congress encouraging the American birth control campaigner, Margaret Sanger, and suggesting the need for international research on the solution to population problems.[47] The congress was held in Geneva in 1927, and it inaugurated the International Union on Population. The conference tackled the population expansion as economically and medically damaging from a eugenic point of view, arguing the need for selective welfare benefits and immigration policies.[48] The conference could not advocate birth control as this was too controversial. The medical implications of degenerationism and abortion were discussed, but not the question of STDs. In 1932 the LNHO's committee on maternal and child welfare (chaired by Janet Campbell of the British Ministry of Health) cautiously raised the issues of medical indications for birth control and abortion. There were strong attacks from Catholic medical organisations, and from representatives from Catholic countries during 1932-3.[49] This situation meant that there was reluctance to tackle the complex moral and social issues concerning sex education, contraception and sexually transmitted diseases.

The birth control question was marginalised and consigned to various eugenics organisations and the left-liberal and socialist-inclined Malthusian leagues. Disagreements in Britain between the NCCVD's moralistic stance and the secularists who had in 1919 broken away to establish the Society for the Prevention of Venereal Diseases (SPVD) were projected onto the world stage of the neo-Malthusian and sexual reform movement.[50] Self-disinfection became part of a progressive package which included birth control, abortion, voluntary sterilisation, psycho-analysis, and campaigns for the removal of legal penalties against homosexuality, as well as broader links with feminism, socialism and secularism.[51] The Secretary of the SPVD, Hugh Wansy Bayly, addressed the World League for Sexual Reform Congress, held in London in 1929, arguing that preventive campaigns had been excessively moralistic resulting in 'the suppression of the sexual instinct outside marriage'. The SPVD stressed immediate self-disinfection after risk.[52] Although certain speakers supported the criminalisation of infecting another person with an STD, this was very much a minority attitude for the thrust of the sex reform movement since the abolitionist era was to replace the authority of the police by medical science. It was above all the Soviet Union which was hailed as an international model for radical approaches to STDs. In contrast to moralistic American views, Soviet social hygiene diagnosed prostitution as a result of poverty.[53] The raising of overall standards of prosperity and abolishing unemployment and class inequalities would – it was hoped – result in the disappearance of prostitution. Radical sex reformers like the German physician, Max Hodann, argued that the socialisation of medicine was the best way to tackle STDs. In this way every citizen would have free and equal access to all medical services, and so special measures for control of STDs would be rendered unnecessary. Hodann argued that 'sexphobia' – hostility to all extra-marital sexual relationships – underlay most health education literature on STDs. Thus treating STDs as any other disease and removing all social and moral stigmas was in the view of radical sex reformers a solution to wider problems of poverty and disease.[54]

The post-Second World War era: old conflicts among new bodies

The inter-war coyness over contraception was in marked contrast to the post-1945 attack on the 'population explosion' as a global issue. Whereas the inter-war period was characterised by a plurality of international agencies, the founding of the World Health Organisation (WHO) in September 1948 brought about new possibilities for global strategies. The prior Interim Commission and the WHO continued inter-war trends in social medicine but unified the disparate organisations. It sought support for a revised version of the 1924 Brussels agreement; among echoes of the past was Cavaillon of the UIPV attending as an observer.[55] The technical emphasis on standards was readily adapted to the new potential of penicillin. The WHO took initiatives concerning standardisation of serological tests and in drawing up treatment schedules for penicillin, and called on the facilities of United Nations Relief and Rehabilitation Administration (UNRRA) regarding penicillin manufacture and United Nations International Children's Emergency Fund (UNICEF) for financing penicillin programmes to combat syphilis in pregnant women.[56]

Lay and political pressures meant that inter-war health organisations were fragmented and enfeebled; by way of contrast, the WHO operated on more purely medical foundations. The resulting narrowness was restrictive. Although certain WHO officials and delegates were convinced from the start that birth control was a medical problem, pressure from member governments kept the WHO as a purely 'technical organisation' thereby excluding family planning from its responsibilities.[57] That the Second World War saw the introduction of antibiotics for military and then civilian populations also strengthened the view that sexually transmitted diseases were primarily a medical problem. Lay participation diminished, as the previously active anti-STD public associations became either defunct (as in Germany) or changed their focus (as in Britain where attention shifted to school biology and sex education). This can be seen in WHO's expert Committee on Venereal Infections. Initially the problem of STDs in post-war Europe was a major preoccupation, and can be seen with special concern for Rhine River Boatmen and conditions in Poland. Horizons broadened to endemic trepanosomes in poor countries, and mass penicillin campaigns were launched. Yet WHO initiatives for the eradication of syphilis were unsuccessful. Antibiotics made only a limited impact on gonorrheal infections, and other infections like chancroid were ignored.[58]

A dichotomy continued between population and health problems. Anglo-American influence secured a UN Population Commission in 1946 but its status was downgraded in 1955. In 1969 a UN population programme was initiated with a UN Fund for Population Activities. Although improvements in maternal and child health were recognised as incentives for family limitation, health matters were less of a priority than environmental and economic considerations, and the fundamental concern that world peace could be threatened by imbalance in birth rates.[59] The favouring of the birth control pill and sterilisation in the arising policies has restricted the availability of condoms in developing countries, as their importance in preventing infections was insufficiently appreciated.

The WHO's ideology of public health campaigns remained militaristic resonating with ideological echoes of *fin de siècle* imperialism. The transition from an 'attack phase' (with mass penicillin campaigns) to 'consolidation' (with the establishment of integrated systems of clinics) proved difficult. The hoped for eradication of endemic syphilis and yaws, using an ideal drug or 'magic bullet', was over-optimistic.[60] The WHO found that antibiotics had made little impact on gonorrheal infections, and underlying social problems were not being tackled. It is only recently that the emphasis has changed to primary health care, taking account of local variations in lifestyle, socio-economic structures and cultural values. The WHO recognised the need to deploy only 'socially acceptable technologies' and to encourage lay participation.[61]

Scientism, militarism and state controls have dominated international initiatives.[62] The powers and responsibilities of international organisations remain unresolved. The LNHO was subject to the conflicts between the minimalist tendency for international organisations to act as agencies of epidemiological intelligence for member governments, and the universalist drive to formulate optimum standards so transcending the interests of ruling elites in member states. Action remains a discretionary matter for national health authorities. All too often ruling national elites pose obstacles to humane measures, and there is an inherent narrowness to policies directed by medical elites. The military model of public health campaigns created an authoritarian and coercive ethos. This authoritarian model can be contrasted to alternatives already present in the liberalising movement to abolish state controls on prostitution in the late nineteenth century, and continued by feminists, sex educators and birth control campaigners in the inter-war period.

The primary focus of this account has been the politics of the plurality of inter-war health organisations. Ironically consensus over the UIPV's abolitionist and egalitarian programme over medical and social strategies was only emerging by the early 1930s when the international diplomatic situation was deteriorating. Today's discussions over AIDS resonate with the echoes of early lay criticisms of over-elaborate schemes for medical controls, and suggest the need for respect of cultural diversity and individual needs and feelings, the blending of medical priorities with humanitarian values, democratic accountability and popular participation.

NOTES

1 *Conférence internationale pour la prophylaxie de la syphilis et des maladies vénériennes* (Brussels, 1899). *IIe conférence internationale pour la prophylaxie de la syphilis et des maladies vénériennes* (Brussels, 1902).

2 C. Quétel, *History of Syphilis* (Oxford, 1990), 135. A. M. Brandt, *No Magic Bullet. A Social History of Venereal Disease in the United States since 1880* (expanded edn, New York and Oxford, 1987), 24–6. F. Tennstedt, 'Alfred Blaschko – das wissenschaftliche und sozialpolitische Wirken eines menschenfreundlichen Sozial-hygienikers im Deutschen Reich', *Zeitschrift für Sozialreform*, 25 (1979), 513–23, 600–14, 646–67. P. J. Weindling with U. B. S. L. Slevogt, *Alfred Blaschko*

(1858–1922) and the Problem of Sexually Transmitted Diseases in Imperial and Weimar Germany (Oxford, in press).

3 *Royal Commission on Venereal Diseases in the United Kingdom. Minutes of Evidence* (London, 1916), 104–7, evidence of A. Blaschko concerning the German Society, 5 June 1914.

4 S. Leibfried and F. Tennstedt (eds.), *Kommunale Gesundheitsfürsorge zwischen Kaiserreich und Nationalsozialismus – autobiographische, biographische und gesundheitspolitische Anmerkungen von Dr Georg Loewenstein* (Bremen, 1980). U. Linse, 'Alfred Blaschko: Der Menschenfreund als Überwacher. Von der Rationalisierung der Syphilis-Prophylaxe zur sozialen Kontrolle', *Zeitschrift für Sexualforschung* (1989), 301–16.

5 L. Fleck, *Genesis and Development of a Scientific Fact* (Chicago and London, 1979), 68–70.

6 E. H. Beardsley, 'Allied against sin: American and British responses to venereal disease in World War I', *Medical History*, 20 (1976), 189–202. B. A. Towers, 'Health education policy 1916–1926: venereal disease and the prophylaxis dilemma', *Medical History*, 24 (1980), 70–87.

7 League of Nations archives, Geneva (hereafter LN), 12B/27351/5923, 'Memorandum. Co-operation between the League of Red Cross Societies and other International Health Organisations' (c. August 1925).

8 National Council for Combating Venereal Diseases/British Social Hygiene Council papers, Wellcome Unit for the History of Medicine Oxford (hereafter NCCVD/ BSHC papers), Imperial and International Committee, 1 Oct. 1926, 31 May 1933.

9 *Proceedings of the Medical Conference Held at the Invitation of the Committee of Red Cross Societies, Cannes, France April 1 to 11, 1919* (Geneva, 1919), 82–96.

10 S. Neville-Rolfe, 'North European opinion on the venereal disease problem', *Health and Empire*, 1 (1921–2), 7. I. F. Ritchie, 'Western European conference on venereal diseases', *Health and Empire*, 1 (1921–2), 38–9.

11 International Labour Office archives, Geneva (hereafter ILO), HY 1100/1/0, L 6/1, concerning the opposition of Crowdy.

12 ILO HY 1000/4/3, 7 March 1924, Weisweiller to Thomas. ILO to Union Internationale, 2 April 1924.

13 ILO HY 1000/4/5, Memorandum by A. Thomas that the ILO should liaise with the UIPV, without Carozzi attending its meetings; HY 1000/4/6, Memorandum by Carozzi, 26 March 1926.

14 N. M. Goodman, *International Health Organizations and their Work* (London, 1952), 10–13.

15 LN Health R 880/28491, ILO letter of 4 Aug. 1920 and resolution concerning venereal diseases of 9 July 1920. R 815/5923, Rachel Crowdy to Secretary General, 19 Aug. 1920.

16 C. W. Hutt, *International Hygiene* (London, 1927), 134–8.

17 NCCVD/BSHC papers, Imperial and International Committee, 11 Oct. 1932, 3 Oct. 1933.

18 *BSHC Twentieth Annual Report (1932–1935)*, concerning 1936 recommendations by the ILO Sub-committee on Seamen's Welfare in Ports.

19 F. Mort, *Dangerous Sexualities. Medico-Moral Politics in England since 1830* (London, 1987), 199–200.

20 NCCVD, Minutes of the Services Committee, 26 Sept. 1921, 24 Oct. 1921.

21 NCCVD, Minutes of the Services Committee, 24 Oct 1921, 23 Jan 1922.

22 NCCVD/BSHC papers, Imperial and International Questions Committee, 20 Nov. 1923, 106–7, 15 Jan. 1924, 117, 19 Feb. 1924, 124, 30 Sept. 1924, 167, concerning leisure and social hygiene; 1 Oct. 1926 disagreeing that transmission of STDs should be a criminal offence; 13 Dec. 1926 concerning the International Labour Conference in 1927; 7 June 1934 concerning the 1935 International Labour Conference.

23 LN Health 12B, Doc. 27351 doss. 5923, G. S. Buchanan to Rajchman, 29 March 1923.

24 'Union Internationale contre le Péril Vénérien', *Health and Empire*, 2 (1923–4), 34–6.

25 H. C. King, 'The Paris Congress', *Health and Empire*, 2 (1923), 19–21; NCCVD/BSHC papers, Executive Committee, 3 Dec. 1923, 34–6. Imperial and International Questions Committee, 20 Nov. 1923, 107, 16 Jan. 1924, 114, 19 Feb. 1924, 123, 18 March 1924, 131.

26 ILO HY 1000/4/7–13 UIPV, Resolutions adoptées par le conseil de Direction, 9 Oct. 1925 (typescript). LN Health 12B/27351/5923, W. Snow to C. Hill, letter of 4 Aug. 1925, C. Hill to W. Snow, letter of 27 Aug. 1925. NCCVD/BSHC papers, Imperial and International Questions Committee, 20 Feb. 1925, 190, 17 March 1925, 197–8, 10 Sept. 1925, 224–5, 14 Dec. 1927, concerning Snow's report on the UIPV; 11 Jan. 1928, concerning BSHC and SPVD representation.

27 For French policies on STDs, see W. H. Schneider, *Quality and Quantity. The Quest for Biological Regeneration in Twentieth-Century France* (Cambridge, 1990), 146–69, 270–1.

28 NCCVD/BSHC papers, Imperial and International Committee, 3 April 1928.

29 ILO HY 1000/4/7–13 UIPV, Comité executatif, 9 Dec. 1928.

30 Quétel, *Syphilis*, p. 181. *BSHC Tenth Annual Report June 1924–June 1925*, 16–17.

31 NCCVD/BSHC papers, Imperial and International Committee, 22 June 1927, 10 Dec. 1928, concerning joint UIPV and LRCS representation to the ILO.

32 NCCVD/BSHC papers, Imperial and International Questions Committee, 30 Sept. 1924, 166.

33 NCCVD/BSHC papers, Imperial and International Questions Committee, 30 Sept. 1924, 162, 1 Oct. 1926, concerning an interview with Dr Knack on the non-regulation of prostitution; 31 Oct. 1928, concerning a meeting with the Hamburg MOH.

34 S. Neville-Rolfe, *Social Hygiene in the Mercantile Marine – the Brussels Agreement, a Survey of Action Taken from 1920 to 1934* (London, 1934). NCCVD/BSHC papers, Imperial and International Committee, 3 Apr. 1928, 18 Apr. 1928, 13 June 1928, 11 Oct. 1932, 16 July 1936, concerning the International Conference on the Welfare of the Mercantile Marine.

35 L. Cavaillon, *Les Législations antivénériennes dans le monde* (Paris, 1931). A second edition was issued in 1948.

36 S. Neville-Rolfe, *Social Biology and Welfare* (London, 1949), 261–4.

37 M. Hodann, *History of Modern Morals* (London, 1937), 99–100.

38 'Programme adopted at the first meeting of the UIPV. 27–28 January 1923', in NCCVD, Minutes of the Executive Committee (20 July 1922–7 Jan. 1923), 70, meeting on 7 Feb. 1923.

39 UIPV, resolution of 28 May 1928.

40 Hodann, *History of Modern Morals*, 103.

41 Hutt, *International Hygiene*, 138–46.

42 *League of Nations. Ten Years of World Co-operation* (Geneva, 1930), 289–96.

43 *Ibid.*, 296–7.

44 *International Conference on the Standardisation of Sera and Serological Tests* (London, 1921). *Second International Conference on the Standardisation of Sera and Serological Tests* (Geneva, 1922). *Investigations of the Serodiagnosis of Syphilis; Report of the Technical Laboratory Conference (Held at Copenhagen 1923)* (Geneva, 1924). *Report of the 2nd Laboratory Conference on the Sero-diagnosis of Syphilis held at Copenhagen* (Geneva, 1928). *Report of the 3rd Laboratory Conference on the Sero-diagnosis of Syphilis Convened at Montevideo* (Geneva, 1931). *Report on the Meeting of Experts on Syphilis and Cognate Subjects* (Geneva, 1928). *Progress of the Enquiry into Treatment of Syphilis* (Geneva, 1930).

45 *Sixteenth Session* (December 1930).

46 ILO N 102/4/2/0, Enquiry into the Effects of Family Allowances on the Physical and Moral Wellbeing of Children and their Birthrate and Mortality.

47 R. Symonds and M. Carder, *The United Nations and the Population Question 1945–1970* (London, 1973), 12–15.

48 M. Sanger (ed.), *Proceedings of the World Population Conference Held at the Salle Centrale, Geneva, August 29th to September 3rd, 1927* (London, 1927).

49 Symonds and Carder, *The United Nations*, 25–9.

50 For the SPVD, see Towers, 'Venereal disease', 80–7 and R. Davenport-Hines, *Sex, Death and Punishment. Attitudes to Sexuality in Britain since the Renaissance* (London, 1990).

51 Bayly, however, was a right-wing campaigner for Nordic racial purity, see Davenport-Hines, *Sex, Death and Punishment*, 239.

52 H. Wansy Bayly, 'Sexual reform and the prevention of venereal disease', in N. Haire (ed.), *The Sexual Reform Congress. London. 8.–14.:IX:1929* (London, 1930), 242–8. On the impact of Bayly's speech, see Hodann, *History of Modern Morals*, 88, 91, 93.

53 H. E. Sigerist, *Socialised Medicine in the Soviet Union* (London, 1937), 241–51.

54 Hodann, *History of Modern Morals*, 109–13.

55 The UIPV was a precursor of the IUVDT (the International Union against VD and Trepanatides).

56 'International Control of Venereal Disease. Excerpts from the Report on the Second Session of the Expert Committee on Venereal Diseases', *Bulletin of the World Health Organisation*, 2 (1949), 139–54.

57 Symonds and Carder, *The United Nations*, 58–66.

58 *The Second Ten Years of the World Health Organisation 1958–1967* (Geneva, 1968), 120.

59 S. P. Johnson, *World Population and the United Nations. Challenge and Response* (Cambridge, 1987).

60 *The First Ten Years of the World Health Organisation* (Geneva, 1958). *The Second Ten Years of the World Health Organisation*, 120.
61 WHO, *AIDS: Prevention and Control: Invited Presentations and Papers for the World Summit of Ministers of Health on Programmes for AIDS Prevention* (Oxford, 1988).
62 For these themes in a British context, see Mort, *Dangerous Sexualities*, 167, 175.

6

Hepatitis B as a model (and anti-model) for AIDS

WILLIAM MURASKIN

In the 1970s, a decade before AIDS became epidemic, it was discovered that a hepatitis B (HB) pandemic existed. Hepatitis B, often referred to as serum, or transfusion hepatitis, had been thought to be an iatrogenic disease, caused by western medical technology, and of limited spread outside the developed world. Due to the work of the geneticist Baruch Blumberg, an antigen associated with hepatitis B (the so-called Australian antigen) was accidentally discovered, and from that discovery a blood test for the virus developed. With the aid of the test, it was found that hepatitis B was the most widespread viral disease in the world, infecting billions of people, especially in Asia and sub-Sahara Africa. It was also discovered that between 200,000,000 and 300,000,000 people were chronic carriers of the disease and constituted an infectious reservoir for the virus. In some Asian countries, such as Vietnam, fully 15–20% of the population were carriers of the disease.[1]

In addition, researchers discovered that chronic hepatitis B infection was highly associated with the development of liver cancer; hepatitis B being a necessary (though not sufficient) cause of most of the world's liver cancer; and, in turn, liver cancer was the most frequent cancer in developing countries. Chronic carriership was also correlated with cirrhosis of the liver; most cirrhosis being caused by HB infection, not alcohol consumption. While hepatitis B infection in the developing world takes place at birth or during childhood, the fatal effects of the disease usually appear only in later decades, after the carrier has become a productive member of society; thus its economic effects on the developing world are more extreme than if it directly increased childhood mortality. It was estimated that approximately 25% of the carriers would ultimately die of HB-related illness (i.e. 15% of the females, but fully 40% of the males). This translates into 1–2 million deaths a year.[2]

The United States, along with western Europe, became designated as an area of low endemicity for hepatitis B. However, that status was not incompatible with 200,000 cases per year, an estimated 1,000,000 chronic carriers and 5,000 deaths.

Epidemiological studies revealed that hepatitis B in America was a disease contracted in adulthood rather than childhood, and that it was usually spread through sex, blood exposure and drug use. It could, however, be spread, as it was in Asia and Africa, from mother to child, or from child to child.

Dozens of identifiable groups were found to be at heightened risk of hepatitis exposure: health care workers, especially those intimately involved with blood such as heart and oral surgeons, dialysis workers, dentists, laboratory researchers, pathologists, emergency room nurses; morticians; institutionalised children with Down's Syndrome; multi-partner heterosexuals; gays and bisexuals; intravenous (IV) drug users; immigrants from Asia and sub-Sahara Africa; poor blacks; soldiers stationed in endemic areas (e.g. Vietnam and the Mediterranean); overseas travellers; Eskimos; American Indians; immigrants from Latin America; recipients of blood transfusions, etc. In addition, 40% of the cases fell outside any known risk group.

The hepatitis studies done in the 1970s made it possible for perceptive medical observers in the early 1980s to hypothesise the existence of a viral agent behind the appearance of immune deficiency related disorders spreading through the nation, since the cases were following the hepatitis B transmission routes: sex (gays), drugs (IV drug users), blood (haemophiliacs and transfusion recipients), and perinatal exposure (infants). With hepatitis B as a guide it was possible to devise, very early in the epidemic, effective guidelines for prevention of HIV infection. The recommendation to avoid sharing 'bodily fluids' came directly out of hepatitis B research. Indeed, some of the recommendations may have been overly restrictive (i.e. those dealing with oral sex) because of the power of the hepatitis B model.

While the two diseases are very similar in their manner of spread there are, nevertheless, vital differences. Hepatitis B virus is far more contagious than HIV. The amount of active virus concentrated in even tiny amounts of HB-contaminated blood is astronomical. It is a uniquely hearty virus that resists all but the most determined attempts at disinfection. It can survive for extended periods outside the body on environmental surfaces. Most importantly, hepatitis B, unlike HIV, can be spread 'casually', through rough non-sexual bodily contact (children's sports), by inanimate objects (e.g. towels, haircut scissors, ear-piercing stakes, tattooing needles, shared food that injures the gums – hard candy, or fruit) and insects (e.g. bedbugs). While the chances of infection from a single needle prick exposure to HIV is 1 in 100, for HB it is closer to 1 in 4.

One of the most important similarities between the two viruses is that they can be carried silently for years without the development of overt symptoms or warnings of potential infectiousness. The existence of this carrier state has created for both 'diseases' a whole series of major political, social, economic and moral problems. Both conditions raise the question of how to protect simultaneously the public's health and the rights of the infected. All the social problems faced by people with HIV in the 1980s were relevant for HB carriers during the previous decade. However, while HB served as a useful, indeed life-saving, model for understanding HIV transmission, it did not serve a similar role in raising and settling the social and moral problems surrounding chronic carriership. While useful scientific lessons were learned from the HB experience, humane and responsible social lessons were not. A major opportunity to create a model designed to balance equitably both the rights and obligations of the individual and the community was lost. Hepatitis B, more than AIDS, offered such an opportunity because the disease was usually not fatal, and it struck a far larger, more diversified and less stigmatised population – ranging from the family dentist to the troops stationed overseas.

Thus, in a crucial way, hepatitis B did not function as a model for AIDS. The failure to confront adequately the issues of disease carriership in the 1970s made it harder and more costly to deal with it in the 1980s. In addition, not facing and resolving the social and moral problems surrounding asymptomatic carriership was an important factor in frustrating efforts to curb the hepatitis B epidemic, despite the rapid development of a safe and effective vaccine. Indeed, in the years after the licensing of the vaccine (1982) the number of cases in the United States, instead of declining, soared from 200,000 to 300,000 cases a year.

In this paper we will look at why the hepatitis B carriers and the problems they raised were not adequately dealt with, and why no usable model for dealing with HIV carriers was in place when the second epidemic struck. Of especial importance will be the fact that HB was kept a low profile disease during the 1970s and 80s, and attempts to curb it were conducted outside public awareness. This lack of publicity and public debate did provide a limited number of benefits, but only at the cost of reduced disease prevention and the failure to generate solutions that would desperately be needed during the AIDS epidemic.

The early results of the hepatitis B epidemiological investigations painted an increasingly frightening picture of transmission. The disease seemed spreadable by countless everyday routes. The medical detective work tracking this was inspiring, but the implications were horrendous. In one case, cross-country runners passed through sticker bushes; a lead runner cut himself and left a small amount of blood on the sharp point of the sticker. The runners who came after him were cut on the same point and were infected because the lead runner was an asymptomatic HB carrier. In another case, poor children shared the same chewing gum. When one child was finished with it he stuck it to a bed post where the other children could pick it up and re-chew it. Hepatitis B virus was passed from child to child via the gum. In a third study, clerical workers were found to be infected with HB as a result of paper cuts they received while working with computer cards contaminated with minute amounts of blood. Numerous studies showed HB virus hidden on environmental surfaces in many hospital settings, and in dental offices as well. It looked like transmission might be uncontrollable.[3]

The research also started to identify groups at heightened risk of infection and carriership. One of those groups was health care workers.[4] Indeed, one piece of evidence that convinced Blumberg that the 'Australian antigen' he discovered was related to hepatitis B was that after one of his laboratory assistants was accidentally infected by hepatitis B blood, her serum converted from 'Australian antigen' negative to positive. In many medical fields the chances of infection with HB were overwhelming. Dentists over time had better than a 30% chance of being infected. Cardiovascular surgeons had rates of 50%, and pathologists even higher.[5] It was estimated that health care workers as a group had a 1% chance of becoming chronic carriers – and even higher in a number of specialities. The question arose, could, and would, health care workers infect their patients. To the dismay of many, a number of spectacular cases were discovered in which dentists or oral surgeons infected scores of clients; in one case more than fifty.

What should be done? At this time there was no vaccine, and special hepatitis B immune globulin (HBIG) was in very short supply, prohibitively expensive and only provided temporary protection. Stories of nurses and doctors being forced to leave hospitals when they were accidentally discovered to be carriers were becoming frequent.

A spectre haunted medicine, or at least the most aware members of the professions: the health care worker carrier as 'leper'. Indeed, the *New England Journal of Medicine* editorialised against the creation of a whole new leper class; as did Nobel Laureate Blumberg in a series of emotionally moving speeches and articles. The initial danger came from within the health care sector itself, especially from hospital administrators and clinical laboratory directors. The situation as it existed in the early 1970s was put very clearly by James Mosley:

> As soon as a relationship was recognized between the then recently described Australia antigen and viral hepatitis, it was found that health-care personnel, as a result of their occupation, had not only a greater risk of disease than most segments of the general population, but also a higher relative frequency of the carrier state . . . In view of the emphasis at the time upon what was called 'non-parenteral' transmission, concern was caused by [a] . . . report that a nurse . . . was associated with 11 cases for whom she provided care on a surgical ward . . . other reports of nonpercutaneous transmission . . . were being mentioned anecdotally. This circumstance . . . created an emotional climate in which there was serious discussion of HBsAG [HB antigen] testing of all health-care personnel, and prohibiting those who were positive from having further association with patients. There was even a proposal that persons contemplating a career in health care be tested before they enter professional training.[6]

But an even greater future danger existed: public panic and witch-hunting of the problem of hepatitis B carriers became a high profile issue. If the public became anxious about the health status of its doctors, nurses and dentists, carriers might be driven out of their professions in substantial numbers. And even the uninfected would live under the shadow of future HB exposure, potential carriership and occupational catastrophe. The fear of public panic and negative action continued throughout the 1970s, and into the 80s. In 1981, Mosley put it this way:

> Public concern about viral hepatitis as a menace to its health has continued to increase, and legal action, even if unjustified, would probably be pursued by any patient who did develop symptoms [from a health care worker carrier]. At present, our system of detecting persons with easily communicated hepatitis B infection is surveillance of all cases of viral hepatitis uncovered by routine morbidity reporting. Most states utilize follow-up [that] . . . inquires about antecedent medical, surgical, and dental procedures . . . How long this system of *post facto* identification of [medical personnel] communicable carriers will be accepted by the public is difficult to say . . . we may expect increasing pressure to do something.[7]

The position ultimately taken by the medical research establishment, and supporting public health agencies, was presented as early as 1971 by two eminent medical scientists, Harvey Alter and Thomas Chalmers: 'The implications of removing trained professionals from patient contact is too broad, the number too great, and the psychosocial cost too devastating to base decisions on anything but conclusive data.'[8] As a result it became common to play down the danger until that 'conclusive' evidence was produced and in the interim assume the most favourable scenario, that health care worker carriers were not a major source of infection. Not a very conservative policy where the public's health and safety was concerned.

When Alter and Chalmers published an interesting but limited study that showed a low risk of health care worker infection, it was heralded by health professionals as 'proof' that the fears were groundless. It was cited in article after article as the justification for the developing official policy of 'benign neglect'. Medical people also took comfort in Baruch Blumberg's study of hepatitis in haemodialysis units, which showed that good hygienic technique alone could change a catastrophic area of infectiousness into a safe environment. Governmental statements insisted that good hygiene offered adequate protection for patients regardless of the status of the health care worker. They also advised that carrier education should focus as much on hygiene in private life as on hygiene in the workplace.

Unfortunately, the actual situation did not live up to the claims. Good hygiene, rubber gloves, masks and extra care in handling blood might indeed protect patient and worker alike, but no mechanism to assure good hygiene and technique or the wearing of protective gear was instituted. Dental association journals well into the 1980s were full of the laments that dentists would not wear gloves or protective clothing. In 1981 Mosely could report that hospital staff often flagrantly disregarded simple hygienic requirements to wash their hands after seeing each patient. And 'As far as laboratory workers are concerned, it is apparent from several of the reports about nosocomial HBV that casual handling of specimens, failure to comply with safety measures such as the wearing of gloves, poor work habits, and sloppiness have contributed heavily to the frequent acquisition of HBV infection.'[9] Good technique is not protective if it is not applied, though claims as to its (theoretical) efficacy could and did justify failures to devise other policies.

In theory, a determined research effort was supposed to be undertaken to produce the hard evidence necessary to demonstrate the existence (or non-existence) of a health care worker carrier danger. This effort, however, was severely handicapped. Powerful forces in the health field were opposed to any prospective studies that might uncover carrier infection of patients. Almost no hospital wanted studies that might lay it open to law suits. The major physician organisations forbade large-scale research testing of their members for signs of chronic carriership. Individual doctors would not co-operate with studies that might threaten their careers. Governmental policy (as reiterated by the National Research Council (NRC) and the Advisory Committee on Immunization Policy (ACIP) of the Public Health Service) promoted only voluntary testing, and then suggested nothing be done to carriers unless clear evidence of patient infection was uncovered; and, even then, only suggested that restrictive action 'might' be considered, rather than required.

During the 1970s and 80s a great deal of impressive research on hepatitis B and its spread were carried out. The Centers for Disease Control (CDC) scrupulously investigated every report of possible patient infection by health care workers. But in the absence of large-scale controlled prospective studies, evidence remained anecdotal, and the policy of assuming the best remained in place. Mosely's comment in 1981 retains much of its force today: 'Unfortunately, 10 years of discussion have not produced data that are likely to be considered conclusive.'[10]

In sum, key figures and groups in the medical community, first came up against the problem of the hepatitis B carrier in relationship to health care providers. They thus faced a severe conflict of interest. They were dedicated to protecting the public's health but they were also committed to protecting their colleagues and associates from occupational catastrophe. They chose, in a situation of doubt and uncertainty, to err, if necessary, on the side of protecting the health care workers rather than the public. As a result they claimed that good hygiene, careful technique and worker education, by themselves, were capable of solving the problem. That position, however, was not combined with an effective system to ensure that adequate levels of hygiene were in fact maintained or an effort to prove that careful technique actually delivered the infection protection claimed for it. While the medical authorities insisted that future research would provide conclusive proof that this policy was correct, they were unable, or unwilling, adequately to carry out that research, at least in part because of the fear that the policy would be proven inadequate.

Influential members of the medical community also decided to maintain the hepatitis B carrier problem as a low profile issue. They felt that public debate of such a sensitive matter would be unfortunate, and lead to needless social and economic stigma and discrimination. The problem could be best solved by health professionals and researchers working outside the glare of public scrutiny. As a result, for most of the 1970s and 80s hepatitis B remained a 'silent epidemic' as far as the American people were concerned. During the period, most educated people could not tell the difference between hepatitis B and A, nor were they aware of the existence of a hepatitis B epidemic raging in the United States.

The strategy originally formulated for health care worker carriers became the model for treating all hepatitis B carriers. The policy included: (1) no active search for carriers, (2) voluntary, not mandatory, testing, (3) support for education of carriers in good personal hygiene, (4) education of household contacts of carriers in ways to reduce their risk of infection, (5) concentration by public health authorities on high risk groups and (6) avoidance of general public education about hepatitis B.

The general position toward carriers taken by the NRC and the ACIP assumed that all carriers, just like the health care workers, could protect their social contacts if they learnt and practised good personal hygiene. The type of care required is well summarised in the following passage:

> A general list of do's and don'ts can be formulated for the carrier . . . The carrier should not share articles that could penetrate his/her skin or be contaminated with blood, such as razor blades, nail files and clippers, scissors, toothbrushes, and douche and enema equipment. A carrier should take care of his/her own abrasions and lacerations or seek medical attention. Blood contamination should be promptly cleaned, and soiled items disposed of or laundered. Skin breaks should be covered. The carrier must inform medical personnel of his/her status, and he/she must not donate blood . . . the carrier . . . [has] the responsibility of informing sexual partners of the risk of transmission of hepatitis B. Partners may agree on the use of a condom.[11]

This is rather important information for carriers and their contacts to possess. However, in the absence of programmes actively to locate and test possible carriers no such hygienic education could be given. Most carriers did not know they were infected; and their household contacts and sex partners had no way of knowing that they were at risk. Neither carriers nor contacts could learn or practise protective hygiene in such a situation. The policy sounded reasonable and potentially effective on paper, but was meaningless without some plan to find carriers. In fact, it could be only offered to the small fraction of carriers who were accidentally discovered through donations to blood banks or as a side effect of other medical testing. (Even in these cases, the blood banks and Red Cross did minimal carrier education – often only contacting them through the mails, and informing them of their status in language difficult for the lay person to comprehend.)[12]

While dozens of known high risk groups existed, medical and governmental agencies had links with almost none of them except for health care workers. Even small, easily notifiable groups like morticians were never contacted and warned of their high risk status. Many of the named groups, such as gays, bisexuals and IV drug users, were primarily secret groups whose actual memberships were unknown, and whose spouses and sexual contacts were unknowable.

Surprisingly, hospitals neglected to test in-coming patients for their hepatitis antigen status. On the face of it, hospital admissions offered an easy way to locate large numbers of carriers. Testing patients on entry would have offered both increased protection to hospital personnel and would have permitted extensive education of carriers and their household contacts about ways to prevent transmission. However, routine testing was not instituted. In the eyes of at least some medical participants, there was a tacit, 'social contract' involved: we (health care workers) will not test the public for carriers (and thus continue to accept a higher risk of hepatitis infection from patients) and the public in turn will not demand testing of medical personnel for carriership.

The failure to institute routine testing provided a clear answer to the three ethical dilemmas Baruch Blumberg saw raised by hepatitis B screening: 'How much biological knowledge about an individual should be divulged and subsequently permitted to impinge on their daily lives . . . [; s]hould routine screening of health personnel be mandatory . . . [; and s]hould we regulate the risks inherent in people living together?'[13] The lack of hospital testing was also in harmony with the general American way of handling such problems. As Blumberg put it: 'most infectious diseases are communicated from person-to-person; therefore, the most obvious way to avoid infection is isolate the carrier. Since the disadvantages to this are numerous, our society generally opts to risk exposure to a particular disease'.[14] The answer to almost all the problems created by carriership seemed to be to minimise knowledge and accept risks.

Such 'philosophical' views were reinforced by questions of cost and effectiveness:

It has been suggested by some that patients newly admitted to hospital or newly accepted in dental practice might be pre-screened for HBsAg. Identified carriers of HBsAg would presumably be subject to the establishment of 'special' precautions for the handling of their clinical specimens. It is not yet clear, however, whether such identification of HBsAg carrier patients would result in any greater reduction of risk of HBV exposure than the scrupulous enforcement of procedures for the safe handling of *all* clinical specimens might provide. Given the extremely high cost of mass HBsAg screening of patients without concurrent knowledge of the benefits to be gained by such screening, introduction of this procedure presently cannot be recommended.[15]

The problem with the Blumberg approach was that since no one had informed the American people about the problems of hepatitis B carriership, the society had no opportunity to 'opt' for the risk of exposure to this particular disease. The cost and effectiveness argument, even if meritorious (and that is far from clear), totally ignored the stated public health goal of informing carriers of their status in order to educate them (and their household contacts) in ways to minimise transmission.

For many in the medical and public health communities, their real belief was that in the absence of a vaccine or effective treatment nothing could or should be done about carriers. They saw carrier hygienic education as of little value, and notification of hepatitis B surface antigen (HBsAG) positive status as psychologically traumatic and socially dangerous. But if one accepted that perception it radically undermined the standard justification for the low profile, minimal interventionist, high risk group oriented, hygiene and education strategy: that it could control the epidemic without more restrictive or intrusive measures.

The official policy was in fact, no-policy. As far as the carrier reservoir of infection went, nothing was being done. And instead of looking for legal and administrative solutions to the danger of unnecessary social and economic discrimination against carriers, the problem was avoided by simply not trying to find them.

The licensing of a safe and effective vaccine in 1982 promised to change the situation dramatically. While the vaccine had no direct therapeutic effect on carriers, it provided the means to stop the spread of the epidemic. It also made the necessity of finding carriers more urgent: now household and sexual contacts could be protected by vaccination, not just education in hygienic procedures.

Unfortunately, the hoped for benefits from the vaccine were not realised. The epidemic was not only not stopped, but in the years after the vaccine's development it spread with increased vigour. By the mid-1980s the number of cases had escalated from 200,000 to 300,000 a year. This spectacular increase occurred despite the increasingly successful control of the epidemic among homosexuals, the largest risk group. The adoption of 'safe sex' practices by gay and bisexual men brought about by the AIDS epidemic offered protection not only against HIV, but also against HB infection. Before 'safe sex', 80% of gay men were exposed to hepatitis B infection within the first few years of initiating sexual activity; and the chronic carrier rate among gays was between 6% and 10%. Death from hepatitis B related illness was a significant cause of mortality in the gay community. After the safe sex campaign, gay exposure and illness dropped dramatically.[16] However, multi-partner, unprotected heterosexual transmission more than compensated for the drop among gays, and sexually active heterosexuals became the engine of the epidemic's intensification.[17]

The failure of the new vaccine to curb the epidemic was the result of a number of factors. The chief problem was its price. The vaccine required three separate shots, at a cost of $100 for adults, around half that for children. The administrative costs for the vaccine raised the consumer price considerably higher. The price came as a shock to the hepatitis research community. The fact that Saul Krugman had developed a proto-vaccine by simply boiling infected serum, and that Baruch Blumberg had patented his early vaccine work, made the astronomical price that much harder to understand. Unfortunately, Blumberg had discovered that the actual development of a practical vaccine required the aid of a major pharmaceutical company. And no one would co-operate without exclusive rights in various markets. Merck Sharpe & Dohme finally developed the vaccine but then possessed a monopoly in the United States. It was widely believed in public health circles that the price bore no relationship to developmental cost, but the drug companies guard their costs, as they do their lives. Recently, an independent study of hepatitis B production has shown that when the vaccine is produced in large quantities the unit price falls to as low as $0.10 a dose![18] For many years, public health officials hoped that when a DNA form of the vaccine was developed, and a second pharmaceutical firm entered the competition, the price would finally fall. However, when SmithKline entered the American market in the late 1980s, the consumer price rose to $170 for the adult series.

It could be argued that the price structure alone, especially in an era of governmental cut backs under both Carter and Reagan, doomed any successful use of the vaccine to end the epidemic. Many medical people believe that. But the situation was much more complex. First, the mind-set that dominated the pre-vaccine period continued to operate after the vaccine was developed. Fears concerning the problem of health care worker carriers continued. The vaccine did not solve the problem of patient infection from health care workers. Patients were unvaccinated and vulnerable. Thus, the danger of public hostility to health care worker carriers was still a real one even after 1982.

In the discussions surrounding the ACIP's recommendations for hepatitis vaccine usage, the question of the health care worker carriers and the occupational and social problems they faced were still of great importance. The ACIP recommendations continued to discourage any attempt aggressively to find hepatitis B carriers – in health care or in the general population. Where official recommendations had previously asserted that carrier education and good hygiene alone would solve the problem of transmission, the new guidelines said that vaccination of carrier household contacts would accomplish the same goal even more efficiently. However, in the absence of the ability to locate carriers and inform them of their status, there was no way to vaccinate those at risk around them. Again, on paper it sounded like everything was under control, but in reality, very little was being done. In addition, powerful but parochial financial concerns of the hospitals had an exceptional effect on the shape of the recommendation. If we look closely at the debates around the issuance of the ACIP's recommendations on the new hepatitis B vaccine, the nature of the concerns felt by powerful groups in the medical community becomes clearer.

Recommendations by the Immunization Practices Advisory Committee (still called the ACIP) carried immense weight in both the public and private health care sectors. In order to protect the group from partisan political manipulation the committee was primarily composed of experts who were independent of the government. Thus, the ACIP was the voice of the Public Health Service (and the Centers for Disease Control), but at the same time independent and superior to it. Despite its nominal freedom, the group was composed of men who often represented important outside interests (e.g. the hospitals, professional associations, the universities). Politics with a capital 'P' was avoided, but not professional politics.

The ACIP in order to issue guidelines asked that a number of position papers be prepared, by both CDC people and outside experts, on important issues surrounding the new vaccine. Some of that material concerned the problem of carriers and was incorporated into early drafts of the recommendations. They, however, did not make it into the final draft. That material, coming from the hepatitis experts in the CDC, tried explicitly to lay out the problems surrounding the issue of chronic carriership and the limitations of current programmes. In the part called 'Identification of and Implications for Hepatitis B Virus (BHV) Carriers in the U.S.' the author was quite straightforward about how little was being done:

> The advent of a licensed hepatitis B virus vaccine (HBV) . . . calls for an examination of the implications of identifying HBV carriers in the U.S. . . . Since 1971, routine HBsAg screening of blood donors has been carried out in the U.S. An estimated 56,000 HBV carriers have been identified via this national program. These carriers are listed in blood bank registries which are utilized for the sole purpose of excluding . . . carriers from donating blood . . . Most medical workups of hepatitis cases . . . involve . . . testing to identify the type of hepatitis. The extent to which followup studies of hepatitis B cases are carried out to determine . . .

carrier[ship] is not known . . . no routine system exists in most States for reporting an HBV carrier identified as part of such medical studies . . . Only a small proportion of the estimated 12,000 new HBV carriers which result from infections each year in the U.S. are identified, and an even smaller proportion of those identified are reported to public health units . . . [A]nnual births in the U.S. include a minimum 10,000 babies born to HBV carrier mothers. Very few of these carrier mothers are currently being identified . . . Some refugee clinics in the U.S. have tested for HBV carriers, but this has not been a uniform practice in most clinics. No Statewide or national registry of these identified HBV carriers exists.[19]

The author went on to say that because of the high cost of the vaccine 'consideration must be given' to only administering it to individuals in high risk groups; however, he explicitly pointed out that 'Screening only the known high-risk groups will not identify the vast majority of HBV carriers.'

The draft went on to spell out succinctly the basic problem for dealing with carriership:

> Aside from those programs whose specific objective is to identify HBV carriers, such as the blood donor and prenatal screening programs, there is no agreement that other programs which potentially could identify HBV carriers should or will do so. HBV carriers should be identified in order to assess an individual's medical prognosis and risk of transmission of infection to others. However, from the standpoint of ethical and legal issues regarding patient confidentiality, and the potential need to restrict carriers from entering some types of employment, many facilities and individuals would prefer that HBV carriers not be identified.[20]

The document recommends carrier education for those (few) carriers who are identified.

This draft of the recommendation proposed no solution to the carrier problem. It certainly did not call for new aggressive programmes to find carriers, to educate them and to vaccinate their contacts. In that respect it was not a break with the past consensus. But, by its candour, and openness, it clearly revealed how extensive the problem was, and how insufficient current policies were. It simultaneously accepted the status quo as it laid the groundwork for undermining it.

These comments were not included in the final document. Rather, like previous reports, the recommendations gave the impression that education, and now vaccination, would be available to carriers (in general) and their contacts, and thus could achieve control of the epidemic.

The CDC's hepatitis people were also in the minority on the problem of vaccination of health care workers in the hospitals.[21] Their position of protection of health care workers with blood contact was quite aggressive: all of them should be offered vaccine. The hospitals were vehemently opposed to such a recommendation. Cost, not control of the epidemic, was their primary concern. The ACIP received many letters that made the hospitals' position quite clear: 'As you probably know, the proposed recommendations of the [ACIP] . . . appear to be quite broad, and would include most (if not all) hospital workers. Many of our hospitals have limited financial resources . . . Indeed, for many hospitals the financial resources may never permit the immunization of all hospital employees.'[22] Another one said: 'members of the Society of Hospital Epidemiologists of America who are fearful that CDC Phoenix [the hepatitis research centre] will promulgate vaccination recommendations which might not be appropriate for their situation and might be extremely burdensome financially.'[23] Robert Haley, Director of Hospital Infections Program, CDC, reassured those anxious about the forthcoming recommendations that their views were well represented by people sitting on the ACIP, which they certainly were.[24]

The position taken by the ACIP was very responsive to the hospitals. So responsive, that it drew a fierce letter of outrage from the distinguished hepatitis expert Jules Dienstag:

> one of the sentences [in the latest draft] . . . is quite ill-conceived: 'Since the risk of hospital personnel acquiring hepatitis B varies . . . among hospitals . . . , each individual hospital should formulate its own specific immunization strategy' . . . It appears that at least certain Committee members were more concerned with 'protecting' hospitals from the costs of vaccination than with protecting health care personnel . . . The role of the APIC should be, instead, to foster the prevention of hepatitis B infection; anything short of a strong statement will provide hospitals with an excuse to avoid involvement in vaccination programs for their employees at risk.

He went on to say,

> In bending over backwards not to commit hospitals with ostensibly lower risk of hepatitis, the APIC will have done an immeasurable disservice to hospitals with substantial . . . risks. Moreover, it is rather debatable that *any* hospital has a low hepatitis risk . . . I cannot stress enough how detrimental the impact of the current version of the recommendations would be; its most unfortunate effect would be to interfere with vaccination of the one group for whom the vaccine was originally intended and upon whom its impact would be the most profound.[25]

(It is interesting to note that Dienstag, who had been requested by the ACIP to write up an outline dealing with 'the vexing legal and ethical dilemmas physicians, hospital administrators, and public health officials will' confront because of the vaccine, focused exclusively on health care workers – even going so far as to assume that the vaccine was designed primarily for them. This narrowness of vision, in a very thoughtful observer, was typical of the pre- and post-vaccine period.)

The hospitals were not only afraid of the cost of vaccinating their employees, but they were afraid of other financial dangers as well:

How does vaccine availability affect the liability of a hospital or health care provider when . . . a health provider transmits hepatitis B to a patient. Presumably, availability of the vaccine and its administration to health care personnel will increase the visibility of the problem of hepatitis B health care workers to the general public. This in turn might lead to an increase in the number of lawsuits by patients who have acquired or who suspect they acquired hepatitis B from their physician or other health provider . . . theoretically liability could be increased by the availability of vaccine; the hospital [can] . . . prevent hepatitis B with vaccine. Not having done so, would their liability be even higher?[26]

Fear of public awareness of the carrier issue continued to remain a potent influence on policy.

The final ACIP document adopted a 'high risk strategy' for curbing the hepatitis B epidemic. The strategy was aimed exclusively at 'Persons at substantial risk of HBV infection who are demonstrated or judged likely to be susceptible.'[27] The recommendations did not recognise obstacles in carrying out that policy except in so far as it allowed the hospitals to decide their own needs. The adoption of such a policy was strongly affected by the cost of the vaccine. With a limited supply, and a prohibitively high price, one had to choose targets carefully. Nevertheless, here as elsewhere, the pressures for this strategy were not purely economic. The high risk group emphasis kept the epidemic out of public consciousness and supported the low profile approach. It treated the epidemic as if it could be controlled by closely focused public health work without the larger society's involvement.

On the face of it, the high risk emphasis was from its inception fatally flawed. First, 40% of all cases of HB were among people in no assignable risk group. Second, the largest risk groups (IV drug users, married bisexuals, gays not out of the closet) were hidden and largely unreachable through low visibility channels. (Public health authorities often lacked broad or deep links even to the highly visible, organised gay community.)[28] Third, since carriers generally were not actively searched for, there was no way to find, let alone vaccinate, household and sexual contacts of hepatitis B virus (HBV) carriers. Even in theory, the epidemic could not be controlled when people at risk could not be adequately identified, educated and vaccinated.

On a visit to the Hepatitis Branch of the CDC in 1990 I asked why such a no-win policy was adopted. I was told that it was generally believed in the Branch that it was an unworkable approach from the start. The Branch had to prove to its numerous constituencies (e.g. ACIP, State Epidemiologists, Medical Professional Associations) 'the Null Hypothesis'.[29] It had to amass facts and figures that demonstrated that a narrowly focused high risk strategy was not practical. This is exactly what was done as the epidemic inexorably spread in the years after the licensing of the vaccine.

The hepatitis people said that in 1982 there was no support for the obvious alternative to a high risk strategy: universal child and adolescent vaccination. The reasons for the lack of support were many. First, the cost would be astronomical; and who would pay for it? The manufacturer had a stranglehold on the vaccine in the United States and severely limited the possibilities. Hepatitis Branch researchers continually raised the question of lowering the price with representatives of the company, but found they were hitting their heads against a stone wall. In addition, their best contacts at Merck were primarily with fellow scientists who were 'outside the loop' of price determination. Second, in the eyes of many public health officials outside of CDC, Atlanta, hepatitis B was not perceived as a national problem at all. It was seen as a problem of the east and west coasts, and of limited groups in those areas. Also, for many such observers, HB was pigeonholed as a sexually transmitted disease (STD), primarily striking stigmatised and unpopular populations. Such a label was the kiss of death in much of the country. Those people were 'not found in our states'. No political leaders on the local level would provide money for protecting such people; and state public health authorities would not ask them to.[30] Third, most medical personnel were generally ignorant about the full extent of the epidemic, or who in the larger population was at risk, or even the many ways the virus was transmitted.[31] What the Branch had to do was collect its data and then slowly win over the key groups that were seen as forming its natural audience – medical and public health organisations.[32]

For years, the scientists and public health officials at the Centers for Disease Control worked tirelessly to overcome the many external hindrances to an effective hepatitis B programme in the United States.[33] However, the Hepatitis Branch members tended to be unaware of their own involvement in creating or supporting some of the problems that frustrated them. There was less inevitability about many of the obstacles they faced than they realised.

Most of the problems that prevented the Branch from recommending to the ACIP a more adequate approach to curbing the epidemic stemmed directly from the long-established tradition of avoiding publicity about hepatitis B. As a result, there was no public agitation, or even knowledge, about the epidemic. Thus, there was no mass support for raising money or creating mechanisms to do anything about it. Since there was no public concern, there was no public outrage at the high cost of the vaccine or the quasi-monopoly that Merck had obtained for itself. People did not know, and therefore did not care. While most hepatitis B was indeed sexually transmitted, and stigmatised groups were indeed numerically the likeliest victims, it was not inevitable that the disease would be socially constructed as an STD. It was a disease that almost anyone could come into contact with: in the hospital through transfusion (even after the blood test was developed), in the armed forces, as a traveller overseas to endemic areas, from one's dentist, or surgeon; from an ear-piercing, a tattoo, a haircut. The groups affected included one's local mortician, the neighbour's retarded child, the Latin immigrant down the block, the waiter at the local Chinese restaurant, the Korean or Vietnamese orphan adopted by a prominent church member, the business man at his yearly convention, the college student on a Saturday night. There was nothing that required the disease to be perceived by local public health authorities or anyone else as simply an STD suffered by 'Them'. Of course, it would have required a major public educational effort to provide an alternative image of the disease's victims.

The hepatitis people at CDC did not think of themselves as having such a public educational role. They were not trained for such a function. They also did not think to search out non-medical organisations that might share their goal of a more sweeping strategy.[34] Quite revealing is an incident that occurred in 1990. In that year, the Occupational, Safety and Health Administration (OSHA) made known that it planned to issue guidelines that required all employers of workers who came into contact with blood to offer hepatitis B vaccination free of charge to its workers. That would have included millions of health care workers, as well as policemen, firemen, sanitation and urban park workers. It was a great victory in the eyes of the Hepatitis Branch people for a more comprehensive and effective policy; they had never been about allowing the hospitals to determine their own vaccination needs. What they did not realise was the role played by the Service Employees International Union (SEIU) in the announcement. The union had been relentlessly pressuring OSHA for years to issue guidelines to protect workers, going so far as to threaten OSHA with a court law suit if they were not issued.[35] Significantly, the union had discovered that fears about hepatitis B infection were a top concern of its large health care worker membership. The union had for years fruitlessly tried to make contact with people at the Centers for Disease Control, asking to be included in 'the information loop' in connection with hepatitis B (and AIDS). They received no positive response. The CDC as a whole, not just the Hepatitis Branch, was not oriented to deal with the non-medical public. They did not think of such people as a major resource. More commonly, when the public was thought about, it was perceived as a threat to rational public health policy.

The Hepatitis Branch people had, like everyone else who was knowledgeable about hepatitis B, been opposed to public debate for fear of the negative social/occupation effects it would create for chronic carriers. This orientation becomes exceptionally clear in their handling of the problem of Asian immigrant and refugee hepatitis carriers.

While most of the discussion of the dangers of discrimination and stigma against carriers in the medical and public health literature focused overwhelmingly on health care workers, there had always been concern about foreign carriers entering the United States, especially from Asia.

The issue surfaced very early in the 1970s:

A particular difficult issue arose in respect to adoption of children from Vietnam. Many orphans had been brought to the United States and placed for adoption. What if these children had been screened and some of them found to be carriers? Would this affect their chance of adoption? Would a single blood test determine the fate of a young child? The Public Health Service decided not to test these orphans for HBV as a condition of entry.[36]

The problem was also acute for non-Vietnamese orphans. Most foreign adopted children in the United States come from Korea, another country with high carrier rates. If screening children as a condition of entry was undesirable on humanitarian grounds, so was informing would-be adoptive parents: 'Should such identification deter adoption? . . . consider the plight of potentially adoptive parents who see 10 or 15 children available for adoption and then are told that one or two of them may carry hepatitis. That finding alone could deter prospective parents.'[37] Ultimately, a system was set up in the United States that made notification of would-be adoptive parents of the HBsAg status of their child very unlikely. Except in the case of South-East Asian refugees, the government never got involved in testing orphans outside the United States. For example, there was no programme to test orphans from the major donor nation, Korea. When the American government decided to test 'unaccompanied minors' in the South-East Asian refugee camps, there was no procedure to pass that information on directly to prospective parents. The decision to notify was left up to the private philanthropic organisations that sponsored adoption – groups that were reluctant to undermine the adoption process. While CDC policy recommended the vaccination of adoptive family household members, it was emphatic that carrier adoption should not be dependent on or delayed until the household was vaccinated; but since many (probably most) families were never informed of the hepatitis carrier problem, family vaccination often never occurred.

The Hepatitis Branch itself became deeply involved in the question of discrimination against Asian carrier children. As the number of Asians radically increased in the United States, so did the number of carriers. Indeed, at one point two-thirds of all new carriers added to the American population came from immigrants – primarily from Asia.[38] A significant public health question arose around the question of carriers in day care facilities. There was much evidence that horizontal transmission, especially among toddlers, was a major form of transmission, especially in unsanitary situations. Horizontal transmission was the overwhelming type of spread in Africa, and accounted for most infection even in Asia where perinatal transmission was common. The possibility existed that in home-like conditions, such as day care or nursery school, similar infection could occur.

The Hepatitis Branch received many inquiries from day care centre directors about the question of infection-risk.[39] The Branch emphatically informed the directors that there was no problem, that with good hygiene, and a little extra care, there was little or no danger of contagion. The rules for good hygiene were easily spelled out:

> Specific hygienic standards should be maintained in all settings involving close contact between an HBV carrier child and other persons for an extended period of time. The implementation of such standards by supervising adults is most important in settings in which contacts are unvaccinated and carriers are too young to adhere reliably to personal hygienic standards . . . In general the carrier child should be discouraged from placing others' fingers in his/her mouth or his/her own fingers in others' mouth, sharing food and mouthing objects that other might use. Attempts should be made to curtail aggressive behavior such as biting and scratching . . . Open skin lesions of carriers and contacts should be covered. Items soiled by the carrier's blood or saliva should be either thoroughly cleaned by detergent and water before reuse or discarded . . . Blood-contaminated objects and surfaces should be disinfected . . . Persons who clean up blood spills or dress wounds of carrier children should wear gloves.[40]

This was not an easy (or likely) regimen to be carried out in a day care centre. Not surprisingly the directors were not reassured, and rejected the carriers.

While the CDC recommended maintaining good hygiene for all carrier situations, they had extra recommendations for aggressive carriers. However, the CDC opposed testing children for carriership before acceptance or after admittance. The only way they would know about the presence of a carrier, especially an aggressive one, was to be voluntarily informed by the parent. However, parents usually did not know their child was a carrier. There was no immigrant testing programme. While there was a superb pregnant-refugee testing programme, it was concerned almost exclusively with identifying carrier mothers in order to vaccinate their newborns. It did have an interest in vaccinating susceptible household members – especially children, but it was not concerned with existing non-pregnant carriers. While there was no official policy concerning what to do after a child carrier was stumbled upon, refugee programme workers were unofficially told by the CDC not to pass carrier information on to schools and day care centres, for fear of stigmatising the child. The danger of discrimination against the children, and the larger groups from which they came, seemed much greater than any risk to uninfected children.

Unfortunately, the reassurances that the CDC gave day care centre directors was not based upon persuasive scientific studies. The data was not available to be sure how great the risk of toddler transmission actually was. There were excellent reasons why the proof was lacking – especially the problem of informed consent, which, by alerting the parents of susceptible children to the presence of a carrier, led to flight rather than co-operation. But the fact was that the proof was missing, the studies not done. Exaggerated CDC claims for the safety of integrating carriers into day care were based more on humanitarianism than scientific research.

In the late 1980s, a Hepatitis Branch study of Asian refugees living in Georgia documented significant horizontal transmission to children in households where a carrier was not present. This study showed that conditions similar to South-East Asia could be duplicated in the United States. On the basis of this finding ACIP recommended that all Asian children, below the age of five, immigrant as well as refugee, be vaccinated. However, neither the study nor the CDC raised the question of the implication of these unsettling finds to day care centres.

For the CDC the danger of discrimination against carrier children was a pressing moral problem. They saw the public (in this case, day care centre directors, and parents of susceptible children) as irrational about hepatitis B when they became aware of it. They responded (1) by claiming a greater level of safety for integrated settings than they could document; (2) by championing unrealistic levels of 'good hygiene' rather than expensive vaccination, as protection for the uninfected; (3) by rejecting the need for antigen testing; (4) by recommending that mothers of rejected carriers stop informing the directors and (5) by insisting that health workers who knew of refugee carrier children not pass that information on to the schools and centres.

Their motivation was humane and understandable. But they put the protection of carriers above the rights of the uninfected population, just as the medical community had always done with health care worker carriers. They also continued to support the traditional policy of shunning public discussion about the issue. What they did not realise was that the problem of hepatitis B among Asians presented opportunities not just dangers.

If the goal of the Hepatitis Branch was to build a constituency supportive of universal childhood vaccination against hepatitis B, and by the late 1980s that was their explicit goal, then the problem of Asian immigrants was more a potential asset than a liability. There exists a lot of goodwill in the United States for the Asian newcomers, and a significant amount of guilt for the South-East Asian refugees and orphans. The enlarged Asian presence in the United States has increased the drive to reconceptualise the country as a unique type of multiracial society. The existence of large-scale HB carriership, while threatening temporarily to increase racial prejudice and discrimination, provides a powerful rationale and impetus for universal childhood vaccination as a necessary (and affordable) investment in allowing America to live up to that evolving ideal. Open democratic controversy is not neat, or painless, and certainly has its risks, but it is the best hope for resolving issues of conflicting rights. Candidly dealing with the problem of Asian carriers, like health care worker carriers, has always presented the danger of stigma and discrimination but also the possibility of a creative debate leading to protective laws guaranteeing confidentiality, protection against job, housing and social harassment, and safeguards for preserving medical and insurance coverage.[41] Today, it also has the potential to provide moral support for large-scale vaccination. The immediate effect of publicity would probably be painful, the racists would come out of the woodwork, but the democratic process should not be jettisoned or undermined because of it, as it too often has been in the case of hepatitis B.

The negative results of not directly and publicly facing the moral and social problems surrounding the hepatitis carriers have been many. First, it has made it much harder successfully to fight the hepatitis epidemic. Without public concern and outrage, resources for the battle have been meagre and inadequate. People at risk were left in ignorance, hygienic safety procedures have been left uncommunicated and unenacted by those who needed to learn them. Second, the scientific miracle of a safe and effective vaccine has been subverted by a monopoly-dictated price, that the public did not know about and thus could not protest. Third, the medical and public health literature has been distorted by self-serving or humanitarian claims about carrier safety, that were premature or unwarranted as the medical community tried to protect health care workers, immigrants and others from the dangers of an uninformed and ignorant populace. Fourth, the public has been purposefully kept ignorant, and then placed at risk in vulnerable situations (from their dentist's office to their toddler's day care centre) without their consent or agreement; they could not 'opt for the risk', since they were not consulted.

In addition, it left the public unprepared for the social and ethical dilemmas surrounding HIV carriers during the AIDS epidemic. All of the AIDS social/ ethical issues were relevant to HB carriers. Hepatitis B should have been the model for a humane, fair and responsible balancing of carrier rights and the public welfare. All of the problems that had to be dealt with from scratch in a climate of mortal fear and homophobia could have been already settled. The fact that hepatitis B was a less fatal disease than AIDS and potentially affected a much broader spectrum of the population made it a better disease over which to fight the issues of individual rights versus the public health. Thus, hepatitis B should have been both the transmission model and the social/ethical model for dealing with the issues surrounding asymptomatic disease carriers. Unfortunately much of that opportunity was lost – to the detriment of adequately dealing with both the hepatitis B and AIDS epidemics.[42]

Perhaps even more tragic, the hepatitis B epidemic demonstrated the existence of a series of infectious super 'highways'; transmission routes paved by major social, technological and cultural changes: increased medical innovations requiring significant exposure to blood, sexual revolution (straight and gay), large-scale recreational and addictive IV drug use and massive international travel. Looking at that new thoroughfare one could predict that other diseases would ultimately come rolling down it. What was needed was a series of road blocks. Widespread use of condoms was an obvious start. If hepatitis B had become the public issue it should have in the 1970s, anti-hepatitis B 'safe sex' could have conceivably been one result, and the AIDS blitzkrieg immobilised before it began. But it did not become a public issue, no one wanted to risk panic and hysteria, stigma and discrimination. Were the gains worth the losses? I do not believe they were.

1 Documentation for most of the material in this chapter can be found in William Muraskin, 'The silent epidemic: the social, ethical, and medical problems surrounding the fight against hepatitis B', *Journal of Social History*, 22 (1988), 277–98; William Muraskin, 'Individual rights versus the public health: the controversy over the integration of retarded hepatitis B carriers into the New York City public school system', *Journal of the History of Medicine and Allied Sciences*, 24 (1990), 64–98; and William Muraskin, 'Individual rights vs. the public health: the problem of the Asian hepatitis carriers in America' (manuscript sent out to scholarly journals, April 1991). Additional references will be provided for material not found in those articles.

2 Ian Gust, 'Public health control of HBV: worldwide HBV vaccination programme', in John L. Gerin, Robert H. Purcell and Mario Rizzetto, *The Hepatitis Delta Virus* (New York, 1991), 333. When hepatitis B infection occurs at or near birth (a common situation in Asia) the chances of becoming a chronic carrier are exceptionally great. The risk of developing carriership from infection is very high throughout childhood, in adolescence and adulthood. In the west most infection occurs in the late teens and early 20s, with carrier rates varying from 1 to 10%, depending upon the risk group.

3 These studies discovered transmission routes, but could not quantify the risks involved; thus, they made transmission seem more likely than they turned out to be.

4 In the late 1980s, despite the fact that a large minority of health care workers had been vaccinated against HB, between 10,000–15,000 continued to be infected each year, with 300 dying as a result of the infection. See Baruch Blumberg, 'Feasibility of controlling or eradicating the hepatitis B virus', *American Journal of Medicine*, 87 (suppl. 3A) (1989), 3A–2S–4S.

5 Comments of James Maynard, in Wolf Szmuness, Harvey J. Alter and James Maynard, *Viral Hepatitis: 1981 Symposium* (Philadelphia, 1982), 309.

6 *Ibid.*, 555–6

7 *Ibid.*, 560.

8 *Ibid.*, 556.

9 *Ibid.*, 552.

10 *Ibid.*, 556.

11 Richard E. Sampliner, 'Follow-up and management of hepatitis B carriers', in Robert Gerety (ed.), *Hepatitis B* (New York, 1985), 167.

12 For example, when I was interviewing at the CDC in 1990 I saw such a Red Cross letter notifying a donor of his/her carrier status – the letter's message bordered on the unintelligible even to someone studying hepatitis. The receiver would have little reason to assume there was a major problem worth worrying about.

13 Baruch Blumberg, 'The bioethical dilemma of the hepatitis carrier', *P&S Journal*, 25–9 (Winter 1977), 27–8.

14 *Ibid.*, 28.

15 James Maynard, 'Viral hepatitis as an occupational hazard', in T. Oda (ed.), *Hepatitis Viruses* (Baltimore, 1978), 303.

16 See Mark Kane, Miriam J. Alter, Stephen C. Hadler and Harold S. Margolis, 'Hepatitis B infection in the United States', *American Journal of Medicine*, 87 (suppl. 3A) (1989), 3A–11S–20S, 3A–12S.

17 *Ibid.*, 3A–12S.

18 See Richard Mahoney, 'Cost of plasma-derived hepatitis B vaccine production', *Vaccine*, 8 (1990), 397–401.

19 Preliminary draft of ACIP recommendations, dated 14 May 1982, 16–19. Draft from J. Michael Lane to members of the committee. Found in ACIP files, CDC, Atlanta.

20 *Ibid.*, 20.

21 See *Hospital Employee Health*, 1, 7 (July 1982), in the files of the ACIP, which discusses the final document as a compromise between the ACIP and the CDC consultants to the committee.

22 Letter to Robert Haley, CDC, from John McGowan, Jr, President, Nonsocomial Infections Division, American Society for Microbiology, 31 March 1982, ACIP files.

23 Letter from Donald Goldman to Robert Haley, CDC, 30 March 1982. ACIP files.

24 Letter from Haley to George Counts, President-Elect of the Association for Practitioners of Infection Control, 4 May 1982, ACIP files.

25 Letter from Jules Dienstag to Michael Lane, 28 May 1982. ACIP files. Dienstag in other letters made clear that he, and Massachusetts General Hospital, recommended that health care workers at highest risk should be offered vaccine at the hospital's expense. He also said that 'in the best of all possible worlds, health care personnel would be vaccinated as they begin clinical training . . . but these educational institutions are even less likely to be able to afford the vaccine' than hospitals. See letter from Jules Dienstag to Michael Lane, 5 May 1982, ACIP files.

26 Letter from Jules Dienstag to Michael Lane, 7 May 1982, ACIP files.

27 *Morbidity and Mortality Weekly Report*, 31, 24 (25 June 1982), 317–22, 327–8.

28 There were attempts to communicate with the gay community. David Ostrow, founder of the Howard Brown Memorial Clinic in Chicago and a leading gay medical leader, helped organise a 'Task Force on Vaccination Strategies for Sexually Transmitted hepatitis B Virus Infection' that included Bruce Dull of the CDC, Saul Krugman of New York University, Cladd Stevens of the New York Blood Center, and a number of CDC Resource Personnel. There was a bridge between gay medical activists and the CDC. That group also prepared a paper for inclusion in the ACIP recommendations that called for important outreach programmes aimed at the gay community: 'Specifically, all school health education programs should communicate to their students the high risks of HBV infection that will be experienced by homosexually active males. In addition, college and community organizations of homosexually active persons and public health departments and clinics should make special efforts to identify high risk individuals

and encourage them to seek serologic testing. Publicity and educational programs should include a full variety of approaches such as special publications, leaflets, posters, and the gay media, and may be developed cooperatively with plasma collection centers and the vaccine manufacturer' (*Homosexual Health Report*, 1, 2 (1982), 25, found in ACIP documents). It sounded like a good approach, but the public health authorities were not all that comfortable about outreach and publicity and the gay medical activists did not well represent the organised gay community. Little came of those recommendations. In addition, they were not incorporated into the ACIP publication. Mark Kane says, 'Efforts to control HBV infection in [gays] ... with hepatitis B vaccine have been unsuccessful ... [in part because of] minimal efforts to reach this group through health education and advertising' (Kane *et al.*, 'Hepatitis', 3A–12S).

29 Interview with Harold Margolis, Chief, Hepatitis Branch, CDC, January 1990. A similar statement was made to me by James Maynard, who until his retirement from the CDC was for two decades the key public health official concerned with hepatitis (interview, June 1991). This policy has just recently borne fruit. For years, the ultimate, though unexpressed, goal of the Branch was universal childhood immunisation. If all children could be routinely vaccinated, then when they experimented with sex or drugs as late adolescents and adults they would be protected without the difficulties inherent in searching out individuals engaged in private (and secret) activities. This in-house goal existed for key people probably as early as 1982 when the vaccine was licensed, certainly by the mid-1980s. By the end of the decade the data was strong enough to start publicly calling for universal vaccination. Universal vaccination for hepatitis B is now on the agenda at the CDC and is being aggressively championed on the federal level. It is hoped that the programme will be in place by 1995. (However, childhood vaccination will have little effect in actively curbing the epidemic until those children reach their early adulthood, fifteen to twenty years later.)

30 Interview with Harold Margolis, January 1990.

31 Draft, Gary Schatz, Harold Margolis and James Popham, 'Hepatitis B vaccination in the U.S.: an assessment of physicians' attitude, knowledge and behaviors' (files of Hepatitis Branch, CDC).

32 The worsening hepatitis B epidemic in the United States was fed by a number of social and cultural changes that occurred in the period 1950–90: (1) the sexual revolution, both among homosexuals and heterosexuals, which linked large numbers of people in multi-partner sex chains without the protection of barrier contraceptives such as condoms; (2) the increasing use of intravenous drugs; (3) large-scale immigration from high and moderate areas of hepatitis endemicity (Asia, Central and South America, the Caribbean); (4) the increased use of transfusions and blood exposure as the result of advances in medical technology and techniques.

33 The weaknesses of the Branch's approach to hepatitis control discussed here should not obscure their generally untiring efforts in combating the epidemic for the last two decades. That work will be discussed in greater, and more admiring, detail in a future article.

34 This view was common throughout the CDC. In 1990 when William Roper became the head of the CDC, the *New York Times* highlighted the problem, and a new desire to deal with it: 'Dr. Roper is taking over the helm at C.D.C. at a time when he and

many others believe the field of public health itself is ailing . . . One reason for the decline, . . . [a] study [by the Institute of Medicine of the National Academy of Sciences] said, is that the public health field has had difficulty adjusting to the dynamics of American politics . . . The report said it had found "much evidence of isolation and little evidence of constituency building, citizen participation" or communications with elected officials or the public by public health workers.' Dr Roper agreed with that assessment, though with the reservation that he did not want to place politics ahead of scientific fact (*New York Times*, 27 February 1990, C3).

35 Interview with Bill Borwegen, Director, Occupational Health and Safety Department, Service Employees International Union (SEIU), AFL–CIO.

36 Baruch Blumberg, 'Hepatitis B virus and the carrier problem', *Social Research*, 55, 3 (1988), 401–12, at 405.

37 Blumberg, 'Bioethical', 27.

38 14 May 1982, draft of the ACIP recommendations, 16: 'about 12,000 new carriers are added each year' as a result of new HBV infections. Others are added by migration into the US especially from South-East Asia (up to 20,000 to 25,000 per year).

39 Interview with Stephan Hadler, CDC, January 1990.

40 See Ronald Hershow, Stephen C. Hadler and Mark A. Kane, 'Adoption of children from countries with endemic hepatitis', *Pediatric Infectious Disease Journal*, 6 (1987), 431–7, at 433–4.

41 In recent years under the guidance of Harold Margolis, the Hepatitis Branch has made major headway in building a medical community constituency for universal childhood vaccination. He has been significantly helped by the creation of the National Foundation for Infectious Diseases (NFID) which has adopted hepatitis B as its special interest. The unrelenting and sophisticated 'lobbying' of the NFID was a significant factor in leading Congress to 'demand' that the CDC come up with a more effective strategy for combating the hepatitis B epidemic. The CDC hierarchy has come to endorse universal vaccination, and the ACIP has put out preliminary 'hints' to the same effect. However, these achievements may be more apparent than real. The combination of budget deficits, economic crisis and lack of extensive public knowledge and discussion of the epidemic makes the chances of actually implementing universal vaccination in the near future far from certain. There is also a real question whether the momentum for change at the CDC, in key medical professional organisations and in some congressional committees may not outstrip support in the country at large, even among state and local public health officials. Mark Kane, head of the World Health Organisation's hepatitis programme (on loan from the CDC) has clearly stated this danger (interview, July 1990). In interviews with public health officials in California and New Mexico (June and July 1990) I have found reason to believe this to be the case.

42 In one instance, in the late 1970s, there was a semi-public fight over hepatitis B carriers which eventually had a positive impact on the AIDS epidemic. It involved two court hearings concerning the integration of retarded HB carriers into the New York Public School system. The rulings ultimately offered some civil protection to people infected with AIDS. The use of those rulings for HIV people was more appropriate, unfortunately, than their applicability to hepatitis B carriers, for which

they were originally made. The decisions were legally reasonable given the presentations offered the Court, but they equalled poor public health policy for hepatitis. It is interesting that the decisions made about one disease, incorrectly I believe, were nevertheless more justifiable when applied to a later one.

II

AIDS as history

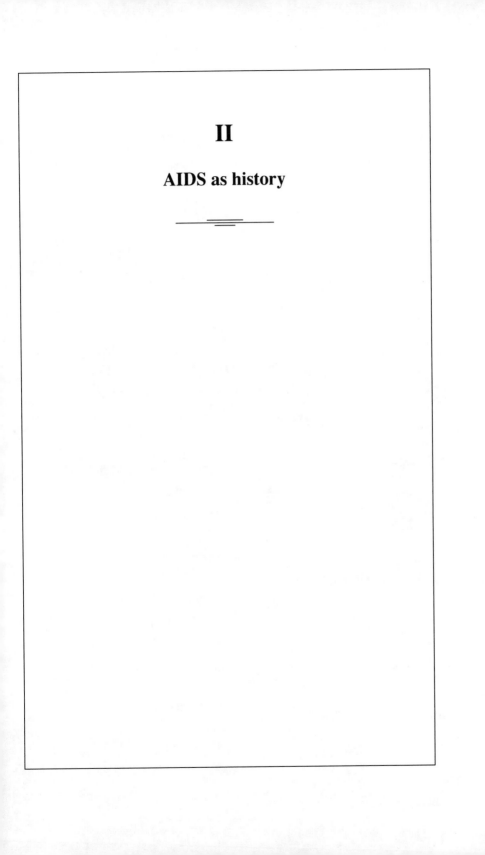

7

AIDS and British drug policy: continuity or change?

VIRGINIA BERRIDGE

There appear to have been some radical changes in British drug policy since the advent of AIDS. Since the discovery of the HIV virus among British drug users at the end of 1985, the pace of policy change has been rapid. Two major reports on AIDS and Drug Misuse have followed, together with £17 million for the development of drug services. At least a hundred needle exchanges offering new for used syringes are the most tangible public expression of new developments, underlining the view that the danger of the spread of AIDS from drug users into the general population is a greater threat to the nation's health than the dangers of drug misuse itself. British drug policy and in particular the visible manifestation of a harm-minimisation approach in the form of needle exchanges, has attracted world-wide attention. Some commentators have as a result argued that AIDS has changed the direction of British drug policy. 'The only instance of AIDS overriding established policy objectives has been in the field of drugs . . . The Government had abandoned its previous stance of augmenting its restrictive and punitive policies on drugs now that AIDS had come to be seen as the greater danger.'[1] Others have been more cautious. Gerry Stimson comments: 'these new ideas appear as a distinct break with earlier ones, but as with many conceptual and practical changes, the possibilities are inherent in earlier ideas and work. It is perhaps a matter of emphasis and direction, rather than abrupt rupture with the recent past.'[2] Susanne MacGregor is also more sceptical: 'Are we now entering a new fourth phase in British policy and practice regarding drugs, or are we seeing merely a modification to the third phase?'[3]

This paper aims to look at the question of the 'newness' of British drug policy post-AIDS. How far has drug policy been changed under the impact of AIDS? How far has AIDS been simply a vehicle whereby developments inherent in existing policy have been achieved more quickly than might otherwise have been possible? From a longer term perspective, how much is really new at all; how far do recent changes merely exemplify some very long-standing themes and tensions in British drug policy? One historical analogy is with the debates around the impact of war on social policy. Historians have in

135

recent years begun to look more closely at the impact of the First and Second World Wars on social and health policy in particular. They have questioned the view that war was the only catalyst for radical change. In the Second World War, for example, the 'national consensus for social change' appears to have been less than unanimous; and the particular alliance of labour activism and senior civil servants of significance.[4] The roots of the National Health Service, established in 1948, can also be found not just in war-time change, but in pre-war debates and blueprints for health care. What war did was to enable this to happen more quickly and in rather a different fashion (the nationalisation of the hospitals, for example, rather than local authority control) than might otherwise have been the case. War served, too, to lay bare the deficiencies of the existing system. The chaotic overlap of hospital services and structures pre-war was quickly rationalised in the Emergency Medical Service in the war; war served to overcome vested interests and opposition to change, but essential continuities with the pre-war service remained.[5] AIDS, too, fits into this paradigm. Like war, it evoked a period of political emergency reaction which was at its peak from 1986 to 1987, but which, in the case of drugs, spilled over into 1988 with the government reaction to the Advisory Council on the Misuse of Drugs Part I Report on *AIDS and Drug Misuse*. Many of the actions of central government in this period had a war-time flavour – the creation of an interdepartmental Cabinet committee chaired by William Whitelaw, Deputy Prime Minister, the 'AIDS week' on television in February 1987, when both television companies joined together on a war-time model; the Commons emergency debate in November 1986.[6]

Drug policy in the 1980s: before AIDS

But how far did this emergency reaction stimulate genuine new departures? To analyse this question in relation to drug policy, it is first necessary briefly to sketch in developments in the preceding years. Drug policy in Britain has been characterised historically in terms of four distinct phases. The first, in the nineteenth century, saw gradually increasing professional controls inserted into a system of open availability of opiate drugs.[7] A more stringent reaction established during the cocaine 'epidemic' of the First World War heralded a new phase of policy.[8] The 1920 Dangerous Drugs Act marked a penal reaction to drug use; but the Rolleston Report of 1926 reasserted what became known as the 'British System' of medical prescribing of opiates, a system of medical control operating within a more penal framework of national and international controls.[9] It was not until the late 1960s that a new and third phase began. The development of a drugs subculture, over-prescribing by a number of London doctors, were among the factors leading to a change in policy. The second Brain Committee Report in 1965 led to changes in drug policy, in particular the limitation of the prescribing of heroin and cocaine to doctors licensed to do so by the Home Office; treatment of addiction was re-located in the 'clinics', hospital-based drug dependency units. These initially operated as prescribing centres, in the belief that 'competitive prescribing' would undercut and curtail the development of a black market in drugs. Changes in clinic policies in the 1970s, however, brought a decline in opiate prescribing and a rise in more active treatment methods, based on short-term methadone prescribing or on no prescribing at all.[10]

The 'new drug problem'

In the early 1980s, drug policy again entered a new phase. What were the main changes which characterised it? First, a 'new' drug problem began to emerge. At the beginning of the 1980s, the numbers of addicts notified to the Home Office underwent a sharp increase although the numbers had in fact been rising more slowly since the mid-1970s. The 3,425 addicts notified in 1975 had risen to over 12,000 by 1984. At the same time the amount of heroin seized by customs rocketed – from under 50 kg in 1980 to over 350 kg in 1984. The real price of heroin in London is estimated to have fallen by 20% between 1980 and 1983. The number of people involved in drug-related offences also rose steeply – from under 500 in 1975 to 2,500 in 1984. Beneath this worrying surface rise in drug-related indicators there was also a realisation that the numbers of addicts or drug users was in reality far higher than the number notified to the Home Office – a multiplier of between five and ten was suggested. Customs and police between them probably at best seized only a tenth of the drugs coming into the country; a significant black market in drugs had developed. After some years of calm, Britain was clearly in the throes of a 'new drug problem'.[11] That problem was dealt with, as this section of the paper will indicate, by changes in policy which nevertheless continued the twin track focus established in the 1920s. British drug policy remained, for all its surface change, a system of medical control operating within a framework of penal national and international policy.

Drugs and political consensus

This coincided with the emergence of drugs as a concern for politicians. Crucially, however, they became not a political issue, but one of political consensus. From about 1984, the Conservative government took a direct interest in the formation of drug policy. In 1984 an interdepartmental working group of ministers and officials, the Ministerial Group on the Misuse of Drugs, was established, for the first time bringing together the thirteen departments, from the Home Office and Department of Health to the Welsh Office and Overseas Development Administration, with an interest in the subject.[12] The Group was chaired by a Home Office Minister. This chairmanship was undertaken initially by David Mellor, who, during his tenureship of the office, adopted a high political profile as the public exponent of the 'war on drugs'. This reawakened political interest in drugs was reflected in the Commons Select Committee System also with reports from the Social Services Committee (1984–5) and the Home Affairs Committee.[13] The latter, reporting in 1986, commented that 'drug misuse, especially of hard drugs like heroin and cocaine, is still one of the UK's most distressing and difficult problems. Drug dealers still make princely profits and threaten us all, including our children, with a nightmare of drug addiction which has now become a reality for America.'[14] There were some signs that drugs might even emerge as an issue for political division between the parties. In 1985, David Owen, leader of the Social Democratic Party, gave a lecture in which he cited research evidence linking drug use with youth unemployment, and deprivation.[15] But the incipient debate did not develop. In the 1987 general election the SDP/Liberal Alliance manifesto did not mention drugs and an election leaflet on health policy gave it no more than a mention. Labour's manifesto was likewise silent. Any argument was, as one commentator noted, 'about how *much* rather than *what* should be done'.[16] Some commentators have seen the 1980s as characterised by the politicisation of drug policy.[17] But drugs in fact never became a party political issue, an issue for division between the parties. Drug control became an issue particularly associated with the Conservative government. But policy was essentially consensual and the main opposition parties did not significantly differ in their approach. In this drug policy was a model for later AIDS policy making, where issues of political difference between the parties were equally blurred.

The 'war on drugs'

The public face of Conservative political interest was a policy focused on a strong penal response to drugs, on both domestic and international fronts. In 1985, the government published the first version of its strategy document for drugs, *Tackling Drug Misuse*.[18] The strategy had five main aspects, three of which were penal in orientation. Its aims were:

1. Reducing supplies from abroad
2. Making enforcement even more effective
3. Maintaining effective deterrents and tight domestic controls
4. Developing prevention
5. Improving treatment and rehabilitation

In the same year, the Commons Home Affairs Committee, in its interim report, called for continued enforcement of the law; the stationing overseas of additional customs and police intelligence liaison officers; harsher penalties for trafficking offences; help for crop eradication and substitution schemes; legislation to attack and seize the profits of traffickers; and changes in banking law to impede the disposal of money derived from drug trafficking.[19] Much of this was put into effect. The Drug Trafficking Offences Act 1986 (in force since 1987) provided (with all-party support) comprehensive powers for tracing, freezing and confiscating drug money, along with measures to stop the laundering of drug money. The Controlled Drugs (Penalties) Act 1985 increased the maximum penalty for drug trafficking from fourteen years to life. Drug policy assumed new visibility at the level of international control. Increasingly, too, it acquired a European dimension. Britain had chaired the Pompidou Group (the Council of Europe Co-operation Group to Combat Drug Abuse and Illicit Trafficking in Drugs) since 1984. The arrival of a single European market in 1992 brought questions of drug control to the fore. Clearly a penal reaction largely out of favour since the 1920s was back in fashion. What it meant in actual practice was rather more uncertain; but certainly the penal response remained a powerful political, if rhetorical, symbol.

Health policy on drugs: a time of change

One aspect of policy which it did symbolise was the decline of a primarily medical response to drugs. British drug policy, as established in the 1920s, had a twin-track approach of penal control, symbolised by the lead role in policy taken by the Home Office, but also of a medical reaction, underpinned by the departmental interest of the Ministry of Health. Since the 1926 Rolleston Report British drug policy had been based on a medical response to drug addiction, symbolised in that report by its reaffirmation of the disease model of addiction and by a doctor's clinical freedom to provide maintenance doses of opiate drugs as a form of treatment. The Rolleston Committee, although arising out of Home Office concern, was established as a Health Ministry Committee, and serviced by the Ministry, in particular by its doctor–civil servant Secretary, E. W. Adams. But the resultant 'British system' of medical control operated as part of a legal system based on penal sanctions and international controls as laid down in the 1912 Hague Convention and the 1919 Versailles settlement.[20] How the balance operated could vary over time.

In the 1980s, that balance did begin to shift towards a penal response. But the 'British System' had in fact been in decline well before the Conservative government introduced its package of penal measures in 1984–6. The shift in the health side of drug policy had begun in the mid-1970s. It was marked by a number of factors; a decline in medical prescribing of opiate drugs and of the clinics as centres for the treatment of drug addiction; a change in the character-isation of drug addiction; the rise of the voluntary sector and of drug treatment as part of primary health care. Perhaps most important of all, it had seen the consolidation of a new 'policy community' round drugs and the emergence (or re-emergence) of the concept of harm-minimisation as an objective of policy. It is worth looking briefly at all of these developments. The specialist model for the treatment of drug addiction within the National Health Service as exemplified by the clinic system did not long adhere to the original blueprint. Between 1971 and 1978, the amount of heroin prescribed fell by 40%.[21] Increasingly, injectable and oral methadone were used as substitutes for heroin, following the American example; short-term treatment contracts based on withdrawal replaced longer term prescribing. The clinics were effectively treating only addicts who were highly motivated to come off drugs. The reasons behind this change in treatment policy were complex and focused on clinic doctors' need to provide 'real treatment', rather than simply acting as glorified shopkeepers by handing out injectable heroin. The conflicts between the professional perceptions and needs of doctors working in the clinic system and the 'non-medical' paradigm of junkies who simply wanted an available source of heroin, recur in the medical literature of the time. This change in clinic policy was legitimated by research. A controlled trial of oral methadone prescribing versus injectable heroin conducted by researchers at University College Drug Dependence Unit (DDU) provided the rationale for seeing the change of approach as a scientific issue rather than as one driven by professional needs.[22] These developments, together with cuts in funding and resources, ensured that the clinics, by the early 1980s, had become what Mike Ashton called 'a backwater of our social response to drug abuse'.[23] Withdrawal from prescribing was a central feature of the medical response. This change of tactic was enshrined in the *Guidelines of Good Clinical Practice* distributed to all doctors in 1984, which emphasised the limited role prescribing had to play.[24] The weight of professional opinion against prescribing was demonstrated by the case of Dr Ann Dally, brought before the General Medical Council in 1987 for technical offences involved in prescribing in her private practice.

The 'medical model' of addiction as a disease requiring specialist treatment was disappearing in practice – and in theory as well. The older concept of addiction had given place, in official language at least, in the late 1960s, to the concept of dependence, enshrined in an official World Health Organisation definition.[25] But in the 1980s, this changed to the concept of the problem drug taker, paralleling similar developments in the alcohol field. The change in definitions received official sanction in the 1982 Advisory Council on the Misuse of Drugs Report on *Treatment and Rehabilitation*, which declared

> most authorities from a range of disciplines would agree that not all individuals with drug problems suffer from a disease of drug dependence. While many drug misusers do incur medical problems through their use of drugs some do not. The majority are relatively stable individuals who have more in common with the

general population than with any essentially pathological sub-group . . . There is no evidence of any uniform personality characteristic or type of person who becomes either an addict or an individual with drug problems.[26]

The 'normality' of the drug taker, an essential component of the sociology of deviance since the 1960s along with the sociological critique of disease and deviance, thereby received legitimation at an official policy level.

Accompanying this change in definitions was an emphasis on a multi-disciplinary approach, based on regional and district drug problem teams and local drug advisory committees. Although medical personnel would continue to take the lead, the involvement of other agencies, local authorities, police and voluntary agencies was actively sought. The voluntary agencies in particular had already been playing a more prominent role in the provision of services since the late 1970s. The *Treatment and Rehabilitation* Report encouraged a partnership between them and the statutory services. In 1983, the Department of Health mounted a Central Funding Initiative for the development of drug services on a national basis. Between 1983 and 1987, £17.5 million was made available for the development of new community-based services. The majority of grants, 56%, were administered through health authorities; 42% through the voluntary sector.[27] The aim was to displace the old hospital-based London-focused specialist treatment system. A senior Department of Health civil servant recalled,

Brain had bunged clinics into London . . . The most important thing was to try and get a few more services up and running . . . We had to get the voluntary and hospital services working together. We had to say to generalists and generic workers that the problems of drug users are the same as others – get on and deal with this homeless person and forget he's a drug user.[28]

This approach met resistance from a variety of quarters, from some of the London clinic establishment and from some voluntary agencies, suspicious of incorporation.

But the first half of the 1980s was marked also by the formation of a new 'policy community' around drugs. Richardson and Jordan have used this concept to delineate the way in which the central policy-making machinery is divided into sub-systems in departments (organised round areas such as alcohol or drugs).[29] Close relationships can develop between these sub-systems and outside pressure groups, involving shared policy objectives and priorities. For drugs, the 1980s saw a shift from a primarily medical policy community to one which was more broadly based, involving revisionist doctors, the voluntary agencies, researchers and, most crucially, like-minded civil servants within the Department of Health. The change can be characterised through the changed membership of the Advisory Council on the Misuse of Drugs (ACMD), the main expert advisory body on drug policy. In the 1980s, it recruited to an originally mainly medical membership representatives of the voluntary agencies, health education, social science research, the probation service and general practice.[30] The increase in drug use in Liverpool and Wirral attracted much attention; non-medical researchers and service workers there were of key importance in advocating the thesis of the 'normalisation' of drug use. But doctors also played a key role there; and it was in the Manchester area that revisionism received its clearest expression. The Regional Drug Dependence consultant introduced a 'new model service' based on satellite clinics, community drug teams and a regional drug training unit.[31] Developments such as these were actively encouraged by civil servants in the Department of Health. The aim was to encourage a more bottom-up approach, to try and bring the voluntary agencies, drug and ex-drug users into a more active relationship with services.

This new policy community took the conclusions of the *Treatment and Rehabilitation* Report as its bible. There were differences over questions of implementation and practice. The 1982 report's recommendations were, for example, criticised for establishing the regional drug problem team as basically the staff of a specialist service, headed by a consultant psychiatrist, rather than a genuine multi-disciplinary and agency partnership; and there were also differences over questions of prescribing. But another policy objective, that of the minimisation of harm from drug use, found general support. This was an aim which had long received support from within the voluntary sector of drug services and also from doctors critical of the clinics' non-prescribing policies and their consequent effect on the black market. But it also became an official policy objective in the 1980s. In 1984, the ACMD's Report on *Prevention* abandoned earlier divisions into primary, secondary and tertiary prevention in favour of two basic criteria: (a) reducing the risk of an individual engaging in drug misuse; (b) reducing the harm associated with drug misuse.[32] But such objectives remained difficult to enunciate publicly in relation to drug use. When, in 1981, the Institute for the Study of Drug Dependence published a pamphlet, *Teaching about a Volatile Situation*, advocating harm-minimisation techniques (safe sniffing) for glue sniffing, there was an outcry which nearly brought an end to the Institute.[33] There was still a yawning gap between the 'political' and 'policy community' view of drugs. This gap was epitomised in the furore surrounding the government's decision to mount a mass media anti-heroin campaign in 1985–6. This essentially political decision ran counter to received research and internal policy advice which concluded that such campaigns should not be attempted and were potentially counter-productive.[34] Here again, drug policy provided a model for later developments over AIDS. The model of a mass media campaign proved uncontroversial once the anti-heroin campaign had preceded it.

To sum up, 1980s drug policy pre-AIDS had a dual face – a 'political' penal policy with a high public and mass media profile; and an 'in-house' health policy based on a rhetoric of de-medicalisation and the development of community services and harm-minimisation. There were undoubtedly similarities and continuities between both wings of policy – the focus on community mobilisation, for example (although the parents' groups on Merseyside differed from the 'junkie union' model of drug user participation). The relationship between the rhetoric of policy and the nature of practice in both wings was also paradoxical. Changes in the health aspects of policy were still largely dependent on the power of medical expertise in policy formation. Medicine might, as Jerry Jaffe commented in his 1986 Okey lecture, no longer sit at the top of the table, but the new system could not have moved forward if doctors and doctor civil servants had not wanted it.[35]

The impact of AIDS: the crisis response

What was the impact of AIDS upon an area of policy already in a state of flux? The nature of the problem presented by drug use changed. Late in 1985 reports from Edinburgh revealed a prevalence of HIV antibody seropositivity among injecting drug misusers which was considerably higher than in the rest of the United Kingdom and also higher than in parts of Europe and the United States.[36] The issue of potential heterosexual spread was not new. The blood transfusion question and the spread of the virus among haemophiliacs had in 1983/4 raised the question of the spread of the virus into the general population.[37] This was already part of the emergent AIDS 'policy community's' position. But drugs made the issue of spread into the general population more urgent. A Scottish Committee chaired by Dr D. McClelland, Director of the South-East Scotland Regional Blood Transfusion Service, was set up to review the Scottish situation and to report on how to contain the spread of HIV infection and allay public concern. The report of this committee, published in September 1986, foreshadowed many of the more publicised statements of the later ACMD Reports.[38] It enunciated harm-minimisation as a primary objective. The threat of the spread of HIV into the general population justified a response based on the minimisation of harm from drug use and on attracting drug users into contact with services.

> There is . . . a serious risk that infected drug misusers will spread HIV beyond the presently recognised high risk groups and into the sexually active general population. Very extensive spread by heterosexual contacts has already occurred in a number of African countries . . . There is . . . an urgent need to contain the spread of HIV infection among drug misusers not only to limit the harm caused to drug misusers themselves but also to protect the health of the general public. The gravity of the problem is such that on balance the containment of the spread of the virus is a higher priority in management than the prevention of drug misuse.

Substitute prescribing and the provision of sterile injecting equipment to addicts were two major means by which these ends were to be achieved.

Members of the new policy community began to voice these objectives more openly. David Turner, co-ordinator of SCODA, the Standing Conference On Drug Abuse, the national co-ordinating body for the voluntary drug sector, commented at an AIDS conference in Newcastle in 1986, 'it is essential that no risk-reduction option is rejected out of hand because it appears to conflict with a service's stated goal of abstinence'.[39] Reports of Dutch harm-reduction strategies and needle exchange projects became more frequent.[40] Social science researchers joined in. These objectives were, as before AIDS, shared by civil servants in the Department of Health. 'We're going to get harm minimisation much more quickly' commented one senior non-medical civil servant (to the author) in the autumn of 1986.[41] Another saw it as the opportunity

to go out and push out a bit further. Almost fortuitously the fact we'd already shifted our policy . . . was . . . a fertile seed bed from which we've been able to develop . . . We'd be weeping in our tea now . . . The pre-existing development of community services enabled us to get harm-minimisation approaches off the ground more rapidly than if we'd been rooted in the old hospital based approach to drug misuse.[42]

The urgency of the situation enabled what had been a stumbling block to the unspoken objectives of drug policy pre-AIDS – political and media opposition to any suspicion of 'softness' on drugs – to be quietly overcome. Research was an important legitimating factor. In December 1986, Norman Fowler, Secretary of State for Social Services, announced the intention to set up a number of pilot needle exchange schemes (building on some already in operation, in Liverpool and Swindon, for example). Assessment of effectiveness in preventing the spread of the virus was an important consideration. There were doubts in the Cabinet Committee on AIDS (set up in October 1986) about the provision of syringes; and early in 1987 a project to monitor and evaluate the pilot schemes was established at Goldsmith's College. In May 1987, the ACMD set up its own working group on AIDS and drug misuse, chaired by Ruth Runciman, a non-medical member of the Council. Of the working group's thirteen members, six were non-medical. Part of the ACMD's Report, ready in the autumn of 1987, was not published by the government until March 1988, causing disquiet among some members of the working party.[43] The report, like the McClelland committee before it, declared the danger of the heterosexual spread of the virus to be a greater menace than the danger of drug use itself. It called for a range of harm-minimisation strategies, most notably needle exchange and over the counter sales of syringes by pharmacists. Prescribing, too, was seen as an option to attract drug users into services. But the initial political reaction was lukewarm.

Although the goal of harm-reduction was accepted by Tony Newton, Minister of Health, in his statement to the Commons on 29 March 1988, only £1 million was provided for the development of services and the further results of evaluation were awaited. The response from Michael Forsyth, Scottish Health Minister, saw central funding of the two pilot schemes still in operation at an end – and a generally negative response to the particular criticisms of the Scottish situation in the ACMD Report. It seemed as though policy would founder on the rocks of political opposition. The summer of 1988 saw intense pressure from civil servants for a more positive response from ministers which brought a turn-around in the autumn, aided by research results from the Goldsmiths' group which showed that users did change to lower risk behaviours (although a disappointingly small proportion of attenders stayed on to achieve them).[44] David Mellor, the new Health Minister, announced an extra £3 million for the provision of services in England. The money was specifically to enable services to expand and develop in such a way as to make contact with more drug misusers in order to offer help and advice on reducing the risk of HIV infection. Only £300,000 was allocated to Scottish services, despite the disparity in numbers of HIV positive drug users there by comparison with England. Further money followed for 1989/90 with an extra £5 million available for the development of drug services. Coming on top of pre-existing AIDS allocations, the extra funding since 1986 gave health authorities at least £17 million to spend on drug services; money was being provided, too, on a recurrent basis. In Scotland the 1989/90 figure of £2.1 million for drug services was less significant than the doubling of the general AIDS allocation to £12 million. For some English projects funded by the Central Funding Initiative (CFI), the money came just in time.

The 'normalisation' of drug policy through AIDS

What, then, had AIDS really meant for drug policy? At the level of policy formulation it had clearly, on the war-time model, meant the public establishment of the previous largely unspoken aims of policy. Drug policy in general and services in particular had ostensibly come out of the ghetto and the process, instigated pre-AIDS, of integration into the normal range of services had been intensified. The message of government advertising on drugs changed, initially away from the mass shock approach to targeted harm-minimisation. A senior medical officer commented, 'AIDS may be the trigger that brings care for drug users into the mainstream for the first time ever . . . The drug world can come "in from the cold" through AIDS . . . it's a golden opportunity to get it right for the first time.'[45] Drugs, so it was argued, became a problem of public health rather than a question of individual pathology. Gerry Stimson argued,

> HIV has simplified the debate and we now see the emergence of what I will call the public health paradigm. Rather than seeing drug use as a metaphorical disease, there is now a real medical problem associated with injecting drugs. All can agree that this is a major public health problem for people who inject drugs, their sexual partners, and their children.[46]

AIDS, so it seems, went some way to achieving the normalisation of drug use. In declaring prescribing to be a legitimate option, it appeared to deal with the prescribing question which had bedeviled drug policy in the 1970s and 80s. The new 1980s policy community around drugs was strengthened by the support of some key politicians. References to normalisation and attracting drug users to services began to appear in Hansard as well as the pages of the in-house drug journals.[47] The media were diverted away from heroin into the cocaine issue. For some members of the policy community AIDS opened up the wider agenda of the liberalisation of drug policy.[48] British policy had historically differed from the American approach to drug control although some commentators had argued that the two systems were drawing closer in the 1970s. But AIDS served to underline some radical differences in approach; harm-minimisation was not adopted as official policy in the United States. Why that was so is a complex story which cannot be fully addressed here and to which Warwick Anderson refers in the succeeding chapter. Among the salient factors were a less signifi- cant and shorter history of medical involvement in policy making in the US; the decentralisation of aspects of health policy by comparison with the Federal and political nature of the 'war on drugs'; and the ethnic dimension to the harm- minimisation issue in the US (official black leaders condemned the approach as 'genocide') which was completely absent in the UK.

A new departure for drug policy?

Policy in the UK is clearly in a state of flux and any historian would be unwise to attempt to lay down definitive statements about either present or future directions. The rest of this paper will simply raise a number of questions about the 'new drug policy' in the light of an historical perspective. It will argue that in general the changes, although real enough, exemplify and expand on long- standing themes and tensions within British drug policy. It will look specifically at five areas; at questions of the implementation of policy and whether this represents demedicalisation or remedicalisation; at the 'newness' of the 'new public health approach' to drugs; at the issue of syringe exchange in the light of the past history of technological change and of scientific research on drug policy; at tensions between penal and medical approaches; and finally, at the long-term history of harm-minimisation as a policy objective.

The implementation of policy: demedicalisation or remedicalisation?

The nature of the implementation of policy is important, for the rhetoric of policy and its practice can differ significantly.[49] Undoubtedly, local 'policy traditions' have been important, as, for example, in Scotland, where psychiatrists traditionally had little to do with drug users and where infectious disease specialists and GPs initially took on the increased medical involvement in drug use which resulted from the spread of HIV. AIDS while nominally 'normalising' drug use, in some respects appears to have brought a revival of medical involvement both in practical terms and in conceptualisation of the issue. Doctors have become more central through the emphasis on prescribing as an option and the focus on the role of the general practitioner. There is also a new emphasis on the general health of drug users. Clinic doctors have begun to become interested in issues such as hepatitis B and the general health of drug users, whereas previously these had hardly figured as part of clinic work. A consultant commented,

> What's disturbing is that I have had to change positions. I hadn't seen doctors as being that important in services . . . There were nineteen CDTs in X, each one autonomous and funded by the NHS, but only one headed by a doctor and the others would be headed by a community nurse, a social worker, a voluntary worker . . . Now I've started arguing strongly that all drug services need a lot of doctor input . . . The impact of AIDS means an urgent need for medical care . . . Drug services will have to do routine health checks and be proactive in selling it.[50]

Such views were echoed at an official level. The need, underlined by the McClelland and the two ACMD Reports of contacting drug users not normally in contact with services served to elevate the notion of treatment which resumed its place as an unchallengeable good. Part of the critique of drug policy in the 1970s aimed to move away from drug abuse/addiction as a medical condition requiring treatment. But AIDS served to bring treatment back to the centre of attention and the earlier arguments fell from favour. In another respect, too, AIDS served to revive earlier 'medical' arguments and themes in drug policy. The arguments for prescribing methadone as a 'bait' to attract people into services and hence away from syringe sharing practices reproduced arguments in favour of the medical approach originally advanced in the 1960s and 70s. Then, too, prescribing was an option which, so it was considered, would attract addicts to services and undercut the black market. The 'competitive prescribing' argument, criticised at the time, revived via AIDS.

The role of the voluntary sector in drug services and its relationship to medical practice has also been affected. Ben Pimlott's comment that the Thatcher government, with its rhetoric of voluntarism, had seen the virtual abolition of the voluntary sector may have been exaggeration, but it did contain an element of truth.[51] The voluntary sector, in drug services as in AIDS more generally, was drawing closer to the statutory sector, and was often funded by it. The 'contract culture' brought about by National Health Service (NHS) funding changes made this tendency clearer. Even within the voluntary sector, drug use, because of HIV, had become associated with illness. 'They champion the drug users' rights to treatment and to use drugs if they want because they have an illness and need a script . . . The voluntary sector ends up holding a disease model.'[52] Increasingly, voluntary (non-medical) and statutory (medical) services were being brought into a closer relationship and the differences between them blurred. This was a process which pre-dated AIDS and owed much to more general trends in health policy.

Whether this can be seen as demedicalisation or remedicalisation largely depends on individual perspective. But so far as the power relationships in policy making went the situation exemplified the long-standing policy influence of the medical profession. Without the support of influential and centrally placed doctors, the 'new departures' in policy could not have been sustained. Drug policy making after, as before, AIDS has exemplified the influence of doctor civil servants as important in policy making, a tradition going back to Dr E. W. Adams, a Ministry of Health civil servant and Secretary of the Rolleston Committee in 1924–6.[53] The role of Dr Dorothy Black, senior medical civil servant in the Department of Health was an important one. Social science expertise was brought into a policy advisory role; but medical expertise in defining policy as for example through the role of the medical expert adviser to the Department of Health remained central. To sum up, then, the 'non-medical' rhetoric of policy post-AIDS disguised some clear tendencies towards sustained or even increased medical input in terms of treatment and services and revived some old medical-focused arguments of the 1960s. The nature of the symbiosis between medical and non-medical at the practical level is unclear and varied locally. Quite who was incorporating whom depends on perspective. At a national policy level, however, the centrality of medical influence remained.

The 'new public health' approach?

One aspect of this symbiotic inter-relationship between medical and non-medical has been the incorporation of drug use into a public health model of response. Two issues are central here. First that a 'public health' response to drug use is nothing new. Historically such responses have often been triggered in times of perceived crisis. Secondly, definitions of public health are themselves historically specific; the image of nineteenth-century environmentalist public health which this language conveys is far from the individual focused public health of the 1980s and 90s. To take crisis and the public health response first – one observer commented in 1988 on the parallels between the Advisory Council's Part I Report on *AIDS and Drug Misuse* and the second Brain Committee's Report on drug addiction in 1965.[54] Like the ACMD, Brain also justified change in drug policy on public health grounds – addiction was a 'socially infectious condition', a disease which 'if allowed to spread unchecked, will become a menace to the community'. The remedies suggested by Brain – including notification and compulsory treatment – were classic public health responses. The balance required in drug policy in the 1980s between minimising the harm from drug use but not thereby promoting drug use is paralleled by Brain's attempt to graft the public health objective of preventing infection on to a system geared to individual treatment; drug workers had to prescribe opiates to undercut the black market, but not so much that the market was supplied and new addicts created. There have always been tensions in drug policy, not simply between penal and medical forms of control, but between different forms of medical input either focused on the community or on the individual. In the nineteenth century, a 'public health' focus on opium adulteration, on child doping or working-class industrial opiate use was stimulated by the urban crisis of industrialisation. This gave place to individually focused medical theories of addiction and disease.[55] Roy MacLeod has pointed to the focus on individual pathology rather than an environmentalist approach in late nineteenth-century discussions of inebriety.[56] Likewise, Brain's public health focus in 1965 was modified in practice to a focus on active medical treatment. There has always been an implicit tension between preventive and curative approaches, in this as in other areas of health policy.

The 'public health' paradigm itself, too, is worth closer examination – for 'public health' has not been an unchanging absolute. Its definition and remit has changed in the twentieth century, as the nature of state intervention in social issues has itself shifted.[57] The environmentalist public health of the mid-nineteenth century narrowed under the impact of the bacteriological revolution. Social hygiene with its emphasis on individual responsibility for health was the reformulated public health of the 1900s; the 1970s and 1980s public health has, in its emphasis on individual lifestyle and on prevention, revived these earlier social hygienist concerns. Drug policy, both pre- and post-AIDS, with its emphasis on health education, on the role of the voluntary sector, on the drug user as a 'normal' individual responsible for his or her own actions and health, has epitomised some key elements of the redefinition. Certainly the 'public health paradigm' of post-AIDS policy is nothing new.[58] As with past 'public health' responses the potential for a shift to an individualistic medical response is present. The conceptual distance is, on current definitions, not a large one.

Syringe exchange: the history of technological change, research and policy

Changes in British drug policy have been particularly associated with the role of syringe exchange. The acceptance of this institutional practice has been seen by many commentators as epitomising the radical change in British drug policy brought by AIDS. There is no doubt that British policy is, in this respect, significantly different from that of some other countries, most notably the United States. But the conceptualisation of syringe exchange as a radical new non-medical departure in policy is not wholly convincing, given the past history of policy change. Two issues come into focus here: the relationship between changing medical technology and the impetus for policy change; and the legitimation of controversial policy change through its redefinition as a technical medical and scientific issue. Both of these issues have a history in the drug policy arena; and both are illustrated in the case of the adoption and policy use of syringe exchange. Carol Smart, in her analysis of twentieth-century British drug policy, noted the connection between developments in scientific knowledge and consequent new technologies capable of regulating and processing addicts and the impetus for policy change. Methadone, urine screening and rational systems of collecting information via notification were, in her argument, particular examples of technological regulation of relevance to the policy changes of the 1960s.[59] Moving back into the nineteenth century, the introduction of another technical medical procedure – the hypodermic syringe – also helped dramatically to shift the response to drug use in the 1870s and 80s.[60] The change of focus from a public health to an individualist medical response to drug use via disease theories of addiction was linked to perceptions of the dangers brought by this form of technological change. In the 1980s, too, policy change was again symbolised in syringe exchange by a technical medical procedure. Yet the association between harm-minimisation approaches and the hypodermic syringe was not automatic. Some of the pre-AIDS discussion of this overall objective had envisaged the evaluation of a range of different non-technical, non-medical 'safe use' procedures. Smoking heroin was among them. The danger of encouraging injecting use where the local culture was not an injecting one was also discussed.[61] But policy change post-AIDS was closely entwined with the syringe exchange approach, a focus which had its antecedents in the 1880s and 1960s.

The association of policy change with syringe exchange was also legitimated at a political level by its redefinition as a technical issue. Responsibility for controversial decision making was deflected on to the 'objective' process of research. The epidemiologically focused research of the Monitoring Research Group at Goldsmiths' College was of central importance in winning political acceptability for a potentially controversial policy change. The involvement in the research of a leading social scientist, Gerry Stimson, symbolised one aspect of the alliance between medical and non-medical expertise which has been a continuing theme of recent policy. Reginald Smart, of the Canadian Addiction Research Foundation, noted, in a commentary on the Goldsmiths' group's results, that the support given in the findings for the efficacy of syringe exchange as a means of achieving the objective of harm-minimisation was hardly convincing.[62] But in policy terms, this type of comment mattered less than the legitimation the research provided for politicians nervous about a policy change urged by the drug 'policy community'. The relationship between research and policy in this instance again recalls policy change in the 60s and 70s. The Hartnoll-Mitcheson controlled trial of heroin versus methadone had legitimated policy change in the clinics via a 'scientific' procedure. As in the 1980s, some critics had then argued that the substantive data did not fully support the policy change laid upon it. Oral methadone was in fact found to lead to decreased clinic attendance and a greater degree of involvement in the black market. Again the important issue was less the detailed results of the research and more the policy change it appeared to support. In both cases the redefinition and refocusing of controversial policy change into a scientific and technical issue (epidemiology in both instances) secured the relatively painless passage of a policy objective into practice.

Tensions between penal and medical approaches in policy

It is a commonplace to analyse drug policy in terms of competing penal and medical forms of control. Here AIDS has brought change – but the continuities with historical themes are also strong. Most obviously the twin-track nature of British drug policy remains in existence post-AIDS. Penal policy still remains, albeit modified at the local level. Britain still adheres to a system of international control of drugs and there has been little modification of this at the international or European levels. In 1989, one senior Conservative politician succinctly summed up his view of drug control as 'increased controlled availability at home and stronger prohibition round the edges'.[63] How far the 'normalisation' of the drug user has penetrated beyond specialist drug and political circles is also debatable. Some of the exchanges in the House of Commons Social Services Committee hearings on AIDS in 1987 were notable by a distinctly harsher attitude on the part of politicians to drug users than to gays.[64] At the local level in Britain there have been changes in the balance between penal and medical with police co-operation in the establishment of needle exchanges, police participation in local drug advisory committees and links between police and services. The prisons issue has in particular symbolised the shifting balance between penal and medical. At one level, British prison policy has not changed to accommodate the demands for syringe and condom provision to prison populations enshrined in a 1986 World Health Organisation (WHO) document. But the balance between penal and medical is changing. The potential impact of HIV among over-crowded prison populations has been one impetus among many behind the government's *Crime, Justice and Protecting the Public White Paper* (1990) which introduces the option of the diversion of drug users into treatment rather than imprisonment.[65] An historically minded observer could point to a long tradition of compulsory treatment in the drug and alcohol area with its roots in the inebriates legislation of the late nineteenth century. As Timothy Harding has commented, HIV 'has emphasised the health aspects of the penal response'.[66] As with the medical/non-medical alliance, the balance of power within the relationship is currently unclear.

The history of harm-minimisation

This article has suggested that, despite the apparent revolution in the public rhetoric of drug policy achieved by AIDS, many aspects of post AIDS policy were already inherent in drug policy in the 1980s. Harm-minimisation is one obvious example which has already been discussed. But harm-minimisation itself also has its history before the 1980s. It is only a restatement in different circumstances of the principles enumerated in the Rolleston Report of 1926.

> When, therefore, every effort possible in the circumstances has been made, and made unsuccessfully, to bring the patient to a condition in which he is independent of the drug, it may . . . become justifiable in certain cases to order regularly the minimum dose which has been found necessary, either in order to avoid serious withdrawal symptoms, or to keep the patient in a condition in which he can lead a useful life.[67]

Harm-minimisation, although not categorised in those terms received a clear expression in the 1920s; and it has been the basis of the British approach to drug control for much of the twentieth century. If one looks back even further, into the nineteenth century, one focus of the professional self-regulation approach (apart from the establishment of professional status) was also the minimisation of harm to the customer.[68]

Conclusion: the long-term impact of policy change

The question of the long-term impact of policy change should also be considered. How long will the revived 'public health paradigm' persist? It would be an unwise historian or policy scientist who attempted to predict what the long-term balance of policy might be. The analogy of war and policy change with which this paper began does offer some suggestive indications. The 'public health' response to alcohol in the First World War with state control of the alcohol industry and limited pub opening hours only partially survived the war.[69] The 'hard-line' emergency response to drugs at the same period was moderated in the 1920s.[70] War does lead to change – but long-standing themes and tendencies also express and reassert themselves. As this paper has argued, the overall balance of power within policy is too complex and historically specific to be adequately subsumed under rhetorical barriers such as the 'public health' approach or the 'normalisation' of drug policy. Indeed, the overall impression is of some long-standing tendencies – the role of medicine, the penal approach, even the revival of the nineteenth-century role of the pharmacist – which have not been undermined and may even have been enhanced by the impact of AIDS.[71] Whatever the future of drug policy in its post-AIDS years, it will not escape from its history.

Acknowledgements

I am grateful to Philip Strong for comments on an earlier draft and to the Nuffield Provincial Hospitals Trust for financial support for the research on which this paper is based. My thanks are due to Ingrid James for secretarial assistance.

NOTES

1 D. M. Fox, P. Day and R. Klein, 'The power of professionalism: AIDS in Britain, Sweden and the United States', *Daedalus*, 118 (1989), 93-112.

2 G. Stimson, 'AIDS and HIV: the challenge for British drug services', *British Journal of Addiction*, 85 (1990), 329–39.

3 S. MacGregor, 'Choices for policy and practice', in S. MacGregor (ed.), *Drugs and British Society. Responses to a Social Problem in the 1980s* (London, 1989), 171–200.

4 C. Webster, 'Conflict and consensus: explaining the British health service', *Twentieth Century British History*, 1, 2 (1990), 115–51.

5 For discussion of these issues, see C. Webster, *The Health Services since the War*, vol. I: *Problems of Health Care. The National Health Service before 1957* (London, 1988); also Daniel M. Fox, 'The National Health Service and the Second World War: the elaboration of consensus', in H. L. Smith (ed.), *War and Social Change. British Society in the Second World War* (Manchester, 1986), 32–57.

6 V. Berridge and P. Strong, 'AIDS policies in the UK: a preliminary analysis', in E. Fee and D. Fox (eds.), *AIDS: The Making of a Chronic Disease* (Berkeley, 1992).

7 V. Berridge and G. Edwards, *Opium and the People: Opiate Use in Nineteenth Century England* (London, 1987).

8 V. Berridge, 'War conditions and narcotics control: the passing of Defence of the Realm Act 40B', *Journal of Social Policy*, 1 (1978), 285–304.

9 V. Berridge, 'Drugs and social policy: the establishment of drug control in Britain, 1900–1930', *British Journal of Addiction*, 79 (1984), 17–29.

10 MacGregor, 'Choices for policy and practice'; P. Bean, *The Social Control of Drugs* (London, 1974); G. Edwards, 'Some years on: evolutions in the "British System"', in D. H. West (ed.), *Problems of Drug Abuse in Britain* (Cambridge, 1978); H. B. Spear, 'The growth of heroin addiction in the United Kingdom', *British Journal of Addiction*, 64 (1969), 245–55.

11 G. Stimson, 'British drug policies in the 1980's: a preliminary analysis and suggestions for research', *British Journal of Addiction*, 82 (1987), 477–88.

12 Home Office, *Tackling Drug Misuse: A Summary of the Government's Strategy* (London, 1986).

13 Social Services Committee, *Fourth Report of the Social Services Committee: Misuse of Drugs with Special Reference to the Treatment and Rehabilitation of Misusers of Hard Drugs* (London, 1985).

14 Home Affairs Committee, *First Report from the Home Affairs Committee, Session 1985–86: Misuse of Hard Drugs* (London, 1986).

15 D. Owen, 'Need for a scientific strategy to curb the epidemic of drug abuse in the United Kingdom', *Lancet*, 26 (October 1985), 958.

16 'Election 87, What the parties said about drugs', *Druglink*, 2, 5 (1987), 7.

17 For example, G. Stimson, 'The war on heroin: British policy and the international trade in illicit drugs', in N. Dorn and N. South (eds.), *A Land Fit for Heroin? Drug Policies, Prevention and Practice* (London, 1978), 35–61.

18 Home Office, *Tackling Drug Misuse.*

19 Home Affairs Committee, *Interim Report. Misuse of Hard Drugs* (London, 1985).

20 V. Berridge, 'Drugs and social policy'.

21 R. Lewis, R. Hartnoll, S. Bryer, E. Daviaud and M. Mitcheson, 'Scoring smack: the illicit heroin market in London, 1980–83', *British Journal of Addiction*, 80 (1985), 281–90.

22 R. L. Hartnoll, M. C. Mitcheson, A. Battersby, G. Brown, M. Ellis, P. Fleming and N. Hedley, 'Evaluation of heroin maintenance in controlled trial', *Archives of General Psychiatry*, 37 (1980), 877.

23 M. Ashton, 'Controlling addiction: the role of the clinics', *Druglink*, 13 (1980), 1–6.

24 Department of Health and Social Security (DHSS), *Guidelines of Good Clinical Practice in the Treatment of Drug Misuse. Report of the Medical Working Group on Drug Dependence* (London, 1984).

25 G. Edwards, A. Arif and R. Hodgson, 'Nomenclature and classification of drug and alcohol related problems', *Bulletin of World Health Organisation*, 59 (1981), 225–42.

26 DHSS, *Treatment and Rehabilitation. Report of the Advisory Council on the Misuse of Drugs* (London, 1982).

27 S. MacGregor, B. Ettorre, R. Coomber and A. Crosier, *The Impact on Drug Services in England of the Central Funding Initiative* (London, 1991).

28 Dr Dorothy Black speaking at Hatfield Polytechnic conference, June 1989.

29 A. G. Jordan and J. J. Richardson, *British Politics and the Policy Process* (London, 1987).

30 The membership of the ACMD is listed at the front of DHSS, *Treatment and Rehabilitation*, and Home Office, *Prevention. Report of the Advisory Council on the Misuse of Drugs* (London, 1984). Membership of the Working Group on AIDS and Drug Misuse is listed in the two ACMD AIDS reports, *AIDS and Drug Misuse, Parts 1 and 2* (London, 1988 and 1989).

31 J. Strang, 'A model service: turning the generalist on to drugs', MacGregor (ed.), *Drugs and British Society*, 143–69.

32 Home Office, *Prevention.*

33 H. Shapiro, 'Press review July 1980–May 1981', *Druglink*, 16 (1981), 6–8.

34 N. Dorn, 'Media campaigns', *Druglink*, 1, 2 (1986), 8–9.

35 J. Jaffe, 'Drug addiction: the American experience', Okey memorial lecture, Institute of Psychiatry, 1986. Key figures were Dr John Strang, regional consultant in Manchester, Dr Dorothy Black, senior medical officer at the Department of Health and Dr Philip Connell, chairman of the Advisory Council on the Misuse of Drugs.

36 J. F. Peutherer, E. Edmonds, P. Simmonds, J. D. Dickson *et al.*, 'HTLV-III antibody in Edinburgh drug addicts', *Lancet*, 2 (1985), 1129; J. R. Robertson, A. B. V. Bucknall, P. D. Welsby *et al.*, 'Epidemic of AIDS related virus (HTLV-III/LAV)

infection among intravenous drug abusers', *British Medical Journal*, 292 (1986), 527.
37 Berridge and Strong, 'AIDS policies in the UK'.
38 Scottish Home and Health Department, *HIV Infection in Scotland. Report of the Scottish Committee on HIV Infection and Intravenous Drug Misuse* (Edinburgh, 1986).
39 D. Turner, 'AIDS and injecting', *Druglink*, 1, 3 (1986), 8–9.
40 R. Newcombe, 'High time for harm reduction', *Druglink*, 2, 1 (1987), 10-11.
41 Department of Health civil servant, observation to author, 1986.
42 Dr Dorothy Black speaking at Hatfield Polytechnic conference, June 1989.
43 DHSS, *AIDS and Drug Misuse Part 1* (London, 1988).
44 G. Stimson, L. Alldritt, K. Dolan, M. Donoghoe and R. Lart, *Injecting Equipment Exchange Schemes – Final Report* (Goldsmiths' College, Monitoring Research Group, 1988).
45 Dr Dorothy Black, conference paper, June 1989.
46 Stimson, 'AIDS and HIV'.
47 See speech by Chris Butler in House of Commons Debate on Drug Abuse, *Hansard*, 9 June 1989, cols. 470–4.
48 M. Wolf, 'Thinking about drug legalisation', *Financial Times*, 4 September 1989.
49 For example, an evaluation of Liverpool's 'prescribing' clinic found its actual practice little different from 'non-prescribing' clinics. See C. Fazey, *An Evaluation of Liverpool Drug Dependency Clinic. The First Two Years 1985 to 1987* (Liverpool, 1988).
50 Interview, drug consultant, January 1989.
51 B. Pimlott, paper on 'Thatcher: the first ten years' (Conference, London School of Economics, 1989).
52 Interview, drug consultant, January 1989.
53 Berridge, 'Drugs and social policy'. Alcohol and drug policy has long been an interesting example of the relationship between medicine and the state. See R. M. MacLeod, 'The edge of hope: social policy and chronic alcoholism, 1870–1900', *Journal of the History of Medicine and Allied Sciences*, 22 (1967), 215–45.
54 'HIV top priority, says official report', *Druglink*, 3, 3 (1988), 6.
55 Berridge and Edwards, *Opium and the People*.
56 MacLeod, 'The edge of hope'.
57 J. Lewis, *What Price Community Medicine? The Philosophy, Practice and Politics of Public Health Since 1919* (Brighton, 1986).
58 For similar comments from a sociological perspective, see G. Stimson and R. Lart, 'HIV, drugs and public health in England: new words, old tunes' (unpublished paper).
59 C. Smart, 'Social policy and drug addiction: a critical study of policy development', *British Journal of Addiction*, 79 (1984), 31–9.
60 Berridge and Edwards, *Opium and the People*.
61 See the Report of the Drug Addiction Research Initiative and N. Dorn, 'The agenda for prevention', in V. Berridge (ed.), *Drugs Research and Policy in Britain: A Review of the 1980s* (Aldershot, 1990).
62 R. Smart, 'A comment on the "Syringe Exchange Schemes Final Report"', *British Journal of Addiction*, 84 (1989), 1289–90.

63 Senior Conservative politician. Comment at private meeting, 1989.

64 House of Commons, Third Report from the Social Services Committee. Problems Associated with AIDS. Volumes I–III. *Report, Proceedings of Committee and Minutes of Evidence* (London, 1987).

65 U. Padel, 'Fair trial for justice proposals', *Druglink*, 5 (1991), 6–7.

66 T. Harding, 'HIV infection and AIDS in the prison environment: a test case for the respect of human rights', in J. Strang and G. Stimson (eds.), *AIDS and Drug Misuse. The Challenge for Policy and Practice in the 1990's* (London, 1990), 197–207.

67 Rolleston Report, *Report of the Departmental Committee on Morphine and Heroin Addiction* (London, 1926).

68 Berridge and Edwards, *Opium and the People.*

69 M. Rose, 'The success of social reform? The Central Control Board (Liquor Traffic) 1915–21', in M. R. D. Foot (ed.), *War and Society* (London, 1973).

70 Berridge, 'Drugs and social policy'.

71 In Scotland, the role of the pharmacist in the prevention of HIV spread has been important. There are parallels with the nineteenth-century role of the pharmacist in dispensing opiates and providing medical care to poor clients. See Berridge and Edwards, *Opium and the People.*

8

The New York needle trial: the politics of public health in the age of AIDS

WARWICK ANDERSON

In January 1988 Dr Stephen C. Joseph, the New York City Health Commissioner, gained approval from the state health administration for a medical experiment, a controlled clinical trial. Usually the conduct of a clinical trial is respectfully left to experts; rarely will its origins be announced on the front page of the *New York Times*, with its fortunes chronicled in subsequent editions. But this was no ordinary scientific trial. Law enforcement officials immediately called the experiment 'unthinkable', and many of the city's minority leaders denounced it as 'genocide'. The trial was designed to recruit a limited number of drug addicts to a treatment group permitted to trade-in used needles and syringes for sterile equipment, and to compare their progress with a control group not given the same access to clean paraphernalia. From the beginning, New York's experimental needle exchange scheme, like so many other public health initiatives aimed at controlling HIV infection, was controversial, a focus for fear, frustration and political manoeuvre in the city. The troubled history of the needle exchange scheme illustrates the constraints on health promotion in a liberal American city overwhelmed by AIDS, drug addiction and racial tension.

Although it has recently been argued that the development of AIDS policy offers 'many examples of the triumph of the ethic of professionalism over the confused and conflicting claims of morality and ideology', the attempt to establish a needle exchange scheme in New York is not such an instance. Here there was no broad agreement about policy, or who was in charge of it; no 'reassertion of the authority of conventional medical and public health leaders' occurred in this case.[1] Instead, the attempt to explain and to legitimate a needle exchange scheme revealed the limits of the health professionals' power in the city. Neither their institutional authority nor their access to the expertise and rhetoric of medical science ever allowed them to control the course of the debate.

This is only one incident in the response to AIDS in New York City, but it is a telling one. For the historian and for the social critic, AIDS serves, in Rosenberg's words, as 'an extraordinarily useful sampling device' that illuminates 'fundamental patterns of social value and institutional practice'.[2]

Weeks, too, has pointed out that conflicting social possibilities shape the ways in which we interpret illness and therefore organise the ways in which we respond. 'What gives AIDS a particular power', he suggests, 'is its ability to represent a host of fears, anxieties and problems in our current post-permissive society.'[3] The methodological point has become commonplace, but rarely have its adherents provided us with the detailed and provocative social history one might expect. Indeed, for many of the more contemplative social analysts of AIDS, the epidemic has seemed principally an opportunity for historical analogy and sociological apriorism, an event apparently detached from the conditions of contemporary human suffering.[4]

My account of the social challenges of intravenous drug use and HIV infection in New York City focuses on the strategies that public health officials employed in order to legitimate a needle exchange. In Europe and Australia, the organised exchange of drug paraphernalia from the start met with considerably less opposition – with less ethnic hostility in particular.[5] Public health officials were able to 'sell' such exchanges as unpleasant but probably effective mechanisms for harm-reduction, and then conduct further research on the relatively 'user-friendly' programmes. But in New York City a pilot needle exchange scheme, in order to have even a remote chance of acceptance, was packaged from the start as a controlled clinical trial, as a scientific experiment.

Health professionals – arguing that a rigorous scientific assessment of needle exchanges was still necessary – attempted to overcome contention and deflect responsibility for a controversial decision by invoking the 'objective' process of the clinical trial, and so represent their actions as a 'scientific' response to the crisis. Advocates of needle exchanges had reached a stalemate with the promoters of law enforcement, and the use of clinical science to structure public policy – a policy which in another political context would have been more pragmatic – seemed to offer a solution. That health professionals should seek a recourse both scientific and polemical to the clinical trial is not surprising. In this century, the controlled clinical trial has replaced anecdotal evidence as the irreproachable standard for evaluating and representing new medical intervention.[6] But the use of such a restrictive research process in part to secure a broad political consensus on public policy, as in this case, raises some difficult ethical questions – or, rather, it should have.

The conduct of a clinical trial requires constant vigilance to ensure that an effective treatment is not withheld from any untreated group during the course of the test. In order to establish and continue a clinical trial, the physician must be able to make an 'intellectually honest admission that the best therapy is not known'.[7] Fried has called this state of genuine uncertainty about effective therapy investigator 'equipoise'.[8] It is, of course, a condition often aimed at, but rarely attained. The clinical investigator's failure to achieve equipoise has frequently appeared to present an obstacle to the ethical commencement or completion of a clinical trial. To overcome the ethical objection, Freedman has recently suggested the concept of 'clinical equipoise'.[9] According to this theory the ethical requirements for a clinical trial are met so long as there is genuine uncertainty within the expert medical community about the preferred intervention. But by late 1988, that part of the medical community whose expertise lay in the study of disease prevention and public health – the experts who would design and analyse any trial – could be reasonably sure that providing clean needles to intravenous drug users was one of the few interventions that might slow the transmission of the human immunodeficiency virus and improve outreach education, without encouraging addiction. By then, European and Australian studies (although no North American ones) offering evidence of these outcomes could be cited – as indeed they frequently were.

On the face of it, the rapidly improving scientific understanding of the subject that occurred during 1988 would make the maintenance of equipoise among the investigators, or in the relevant medical community, quite challenging. Yet, at the same time, the only politically acceptable, and practically efficacious, way to distribute clean needles in New York City was by representing the intervention as a controlled clinical trial, and setting aside consideration of any potential ethical infractions. The efforts to establish the New York needle exchange trial thus illustrate some general problems for AIDS prevention: this commentary on recent events in New York examines the practical limitations on health promotion, the use (under constraint) of a restrictive research process to organise public policy, and the ethical hazards of health professionals seeking a polemical recourse to the clinical trial.

Public health or law enforcement?

Dr David Sencer, then New York City's Health Commissioner, had first proposed the pragmatic distribution of clean needles to drug users in September 1985. By refusing them access to clean needles, he said, 'we are condemning large numbers of addicts to death from AIDS'.[10] But the recommendation provoked vehement opposition. Law enforcement officials argued that addicts were not responsible enough to use clean needles to safeguard their own health: making needles freely available would appear to condone addiction and only encourage young people to try drugs. One of the plan's principal opponents, Sterling Johnson Jr, the special narcotics prosecutor in the Manhattan District Attorney's office, wrote an impassioned letter to the Mayor. 'Drug addicts,' he advised, ' in the frenzied and desperate minutes before injecting a needle into their veins, could not care less about contamination.' Experience had taught him that 'slaves of addiction do not change their daily habits'.[11] Within a few days, Mayor Koch had rejected Sencer's recommendation, observing wryly that the idea was obviously one 'whose time has not come and, based upon the response, will never come'.[12]

By late 1985, over a million Americans had been exposed to the human immunodeficiency virus (HIV). The number of cases of AIDS was doubling each year. Almost 30% of the 4,387 cases reported in New York since 1981 were IV drug users, and increasingly the experts feared that this group would transmit the virus to their spouses and children, passing the disease into the general community. Yet the prevention of HIV infection among drug users, who were mostly African-American and Hispanic, had scarcely begun. All through the summer of 1985, city officials had been working to persuade homosexuals to avoid the bathhouses.[13] They were also engaged in a debate with angry parents in Queens who were trying to exclude children with AIDS from the schools. The Schools Chancellor and health officials attempted to reassure parents, promising them that all classrooms would have supplies of alcohol swabs and rubber gloves.[14] But no specific measures were taken to reduce the spread of the virus among drug users: there was, instead, a vague hope that an expansion of drug treatment programmes might take care of the problem.[15] Of the approximately 250,000 IV drug users in New York City, only 30,000 received treatment, and 1,500 were on the waiting lists.

At the time there was only one model of a successful needle exchange project. A year earlier, the Amsterdam municipal health service, at the prompting of an association of drug users (the Junkies' Union), had set up a needle and syringe exchange scheme in order to combat the spread of the hepatitis B virus. The clients of the exchange received one needle and syringe for each set they returned; the procedure was anonymous; and it was popular among the user community. Indeed, during 1985 over 100,000 needles and syringes were handed out. It provided opportunities for educational outreach, counselling and the distribution of condoms. Although clients were encouraged to stop injecting or to stabilise their habits with methadone maintenance, the approach generally was pragmatic rather than moralistic. 'If it is impossible to cure an addict,' wrote a promoter of the project, then 'one should at least try to create a situation that greatly reduces the risk that the addict harms himself or his environment.'[16]

During 1986, news of the Amsterdam scheme began to spread. A growing awareness of the dangers of HIV infection among drug users prompted an international conference sponsored by the World Health Organisation to conclude that 'initiatives of this kind could have an important role to play in stopping the spread of HIV'.[17] The Institute of Medicine of the National Academy of Sciences, in its report *Confronting AIDS*, discussed the Amsterdam project and suggested that it was time 'to begin experimenting with public policies to encourage the use of sterile needles and syringes by removing legal and administrative barriers to their possession and use'.[18]

In May 1986, the New York State Health Department and the Milbank Memorial Fund sponsored an international conference in Manhattan to assess the impact of AIDS on public policy. Many of the delegates discussed the need for needle exchanges. Dr Frederick Robins, the former president of the Institute of Medicine, admitted it was a difficult issue 'but it seems to me that the time has come to seriously consider providing needles and syringes to drug users to avoid the necessity of using common instruments'. His opinion was confirmed by Dr James Curran, the director of the AIDS programme at the National Center for Disease Control, who offered his support for a test programme. 'I would not discount anything in trying to combat this disease', he continued. 'The problem we face is bigger than politics.'[19] But Mayor Koch again declared himself against the idea. 'How can I support something that the police and law-enforcement leaders are totally against?'[20] Dr David Axelrod, the State Commissioner of Health, also expressed his opposition to making needles and syringes more widely available, for he feared that this could lead to an increase in drug addiction. Yet Dr Julian Gold, a member of Australia's national AIDS task force, reported that needles and syringes were now freely available to drug addicts in Sydney, and drug addiction had not increased.[21] Andrew Moss, from the Department of Epidemiology at University College of San Francisco, reflected on the opposition to needle exchanges:

> You cannot legalize use here. It's politically impossible. It's been brought up in many jurisdictions, and uniformly gets squelched by mayors or attorney-generals or police chiefs. But you can do it in Europe, it's being done in Holland . . . We could go and look at them and find out how it works. If it's found to be successful, then we can come back and fill a huge gap in our own public policy discussions about this issue here.[22]

Needle exchange or scientific experiment?

During 1987, the city's new Health Commissioner, Dr Stephen C. Joseph, announced that the number of AIDS-related deaths among IV drug users was probably 1,000 more than reported. He also estimated that, over the next year, nearly 800 babies infected with HIV would be born in the city, virtually all of them born to mothers who were IV drug users. The Health Department predicted that by the end of 1991 there would be at least 40,000 AIDS cases in New York City and close to 30,000 deaths. Each year IV drug users would make a larger contribution to these figures.[23]

The *New York Times* had recently published a number of articles describing European needle exchange schemes. One of these reported that the Scottish Committee on HIV Infection had recommended that free clean needles and syringes should be provided to IV drug users. After a crackdown on drug paraphernalia had forced Edinburgh's addicts to share dirty needles, the city recorded the highest infection rate in Britain, mostly among drug users. In contrast, Glasgow, with no similar needle restrictions, had nearly twice as many drug users but far fewer AIDS cases. 'The gravity of the problem', the Scottish Committee declared, 'is such that on balance the containment of the spread of the virus is a higher priority in management than the prevention of drug misuse.'[24]

The same concern was expressed elsewhere in Europe, fuelled by grim statistics. In Italy, it was estimated that more than half the 100,000 addicts were HIV positive; in France, the incidence of infection was probably 30%. Several countries were now prepared to try the Dutch model. Britain had decided to allow the exchange of needles and syringes in more than ten cities. The Swiss government permitted pharmacies to sell syringes to anyone who wanted them. In France, drug users could exchange needles and syringes in pharmacies.[25]

Yet, as the *New York Times* pointed out in an editorial, little had been done in the US to control HIV infection among drug users. In 1987, some 50% to 60% of New York's 200,000 heroin users were believed to be infected. And still there were long waits for methadone maintenance clinics and drug-free rehabilitation programmes. In the 'shooting galleries', meanwhile, addicts continued to rent and share dirty needles. Although dispensing clean needles might retard the transmission of HIV, law enforcement officers would resist on principle even 'experiments' to test the possibility.[26]

But when Dr Stephen Joseph, the city's Health Commissioner, proposed such an experiment, his chief critics initially were state health officials, who faulted the trial on technical grounds.[27] Dr Joseph had suggested that the city should dispense clean needles and syringes to several hundred addicts who were not HIV positive and who were waiting the many months it took to join a methadone maintenance programme. An identical control group, addicts not given clean needles and syringes, would also be monitored to assess behavioural change and to measure relative rates of infection. This would be the nation's first trial of a needle exchange. But the proposed experiment did not satisfy the state's scientific requirements. State health officials doubted that the applicants for methadone programmes were a truly representative sample of drug addicts; and the demonstration would, in any case, have to enrol several thousand addicts to provide scientifically valid results. Dr Joseph, contending that AIDS infection among drug users was a major threat to the city's health, promised he would come up with a revised, more rigorous, trial.

The least controversial policy, though, remained a 'war on drugs'. Citing a 'state of emergency', city and state officials in June announced a new programme that would provide treatment for another 3,000 of New York's estimated 225,000 IV drug users.[28] The new clients would join the 30,000 people already enrolled at the city's 100 methadone clinics. But city officials, fearing neighbourhood opposition, declined to give the proposed addresses of the new clinics, except to say that most would be located in parts of Harlem and Brooklyn that have high rates of addiction. Evidently, there was no policy that would not incite some opposition.

Saying no to pragmatism

In the midst of a crackdown on illicit drug use, there seemed no acceptable camouflage for any pragmatic schemes that made it safer to inject drugs. But, in January 1988, the issue was forced. A community action group, the Association for Drug Abuse Prevention and Treatment (ADAPT), decided to defy state law and distribute free needles and syringes in the city. ADAPT was a private, non-profit group, formed in 1980 to counsel addicts to stop using drugs and enter treatment. It was based in Brooklyn, and relied on donations and grants to support its ten full-time staff members, most of whom were ex-users or sympathetic outreach workers. Unlike similar organisations in Amsterdam and Australia, current users were not active in its leadership.[29] The president of ADAPT, Yolanda Serrano, told the press that her agency was prepared to face prosecution in order to 'protect the public and save lives'.[30]

Dr Joseph praised the group's commitment and responsibility, but felt that he could not condone this illegal action. 'It's regrettable', he said, 'that the issue has come to a head in this way, when it's scientifically uncontrolled.'[31] Sterling Johnson condemned the plan more vehemently. He speculated on whether it might be a prosecutable offence; perhaps there were even grounds for a criminal charge of homicide if an addict overdosed using one of the clean needles. But Ms Serrano thought the risks of the project were overstated. New York was one of eleven states restricting needles, yet it had the highest rate of drug abuse in the country. In any case, ADAPT intended to give clean needles only to those who already had dirty ones. It was too late, Ms Serrano declared, to engage in the research process. 'Something has to be done now. Someone has to take the initiative to challenge the state in the name of public health.'[32]

Dr Axelrod refused to comment on ADAPT's plans, but pointed out that the state was still considering a revised experimental needle exchange. Mayor Koch said that the law must be obeyed, though he would favour a limited experiment at some stage. 'I have an open mind', Governor Cuomo was reported as saying, adding that the issue has been 'tormenting me – it's very, very difficult'.[33] But not everyone encountered the same difficulties. The Surgeon-General, C. Everett Koop, mentioned at the launching of an information brochure on AIDS that needle exchange schemes would be worth considering, even though they faced public resistance. 'With a fatal epidemic, that's spreading as this one is, you do anything in the world that you can do to stop it', he said. 'And if providing free needles will stop it, that's fine.'[34]

The clinical trial

Three days later, the Cuomo administration announced that it would let New York City conduct a revised clinical trial of needle and syringe distribution. State and city health officials stressed that the plan, the first time in the US that a government would provide drug paraphernalia to addicts, was a scientific experiment, and it would be discontinued if it failed to retard the spread of AIDS. Dr Axelrod had previously opposed the idea of a needle exchange, arguing that addicts' behaviour was so unpredictable that it would be impossible to monitor the programme. But now he was confident that the trial in its revised form could produce scientifically valid results.[35]

The New York study initially would involve 400 IV drug users awaiting rehabilitation. At this stage, Joseph proposed to draw addicts from targeted neighbourhoods, rather than from the whole city, in order to make the experiment easier to manage. The participant would be issued with an identification card, with a photograph and fingerprint on it, then enter the treatment group or the control group depending on the site attended. All subjects were to receive counselling and general medical assistance. The proposal called for the randomisation of the sites where the programme was offered, rather than the randomisation of individual subjects. Anyone who had enrolled in a control site would be free to withdraw and then re-enrol at a treatment site, though this may mean travelling across town. No one had yet worked out how to entice the control group back for regular monitoring; and no one could discern any obvious endpoint for the study. But since the average waiting time to enter a methadone maintenance programme was one to three months, and six months to get into a drug-free programme, the problem of finding an endpoint seemed unlikely to arise.

Law enforcement officers and drug rehabilitation experts soon found fault with the plan. To representatives of the law, and conservative politicians, the very idea was inimical, even in the guise of medical science. 'It sends out the message that it is right to shoot drugs', declared Sterling Johnson. 'It may be well meaning, but I think it is a very bad mistake.'[36] The State Assembly's Republican minority went on record unanimously to oppose any needle exchange scheme. The minority leader, Clarence Rappleyea, stated that: 'The notion of state-subsidized drug abuse is abhorrent.'[37] The Catholic church also opposed the scheme: Cardinal O'Connor accused the city of 'dragging down the standards of all society'.[38]

Managers of drug treatment programmes criticised both the design of the trial and its principles. Many such as Dr Beny J. Primm, the director of the Addiction Research and Treatment Corporation, feared that distributing needles would become a cheap substitute for rehabilitation. Dr Robert Newman, the president of Beth Israel Medical Center, the largest provider of methadone maintenance programmes in the city, said he supported the idea of a needle exchange scheme, but wondered how communities that resisted drug treatment centres would react to practising addicts appearing regularly to pick up their needles and syringes. Few of these experts could see how the experiment could come up with any meaningful scientific conclusion. According to Dr Mitchell Rosenthal, the president of Phoenix House, the chief provider of drug-free rehabilitation in New York, addicts were 'the most disordered people in society', hardly likely to travel across Manhattan to register for an identification card.[39] This debate focused on the scientific legitimacy and the feasibility of the experiment: no one questioned the ethical aspects of not providing clean needles to a control group, or asked if a clinical trial was the best way to deal with a public health crisis.

'They don't want to give out free needles . . . '

But the idea of distributing clean needles and syringes, one way or another, did have its non-medical supporters – only they were often difficult to find. Thomas Morgan, a reporter with the *New York Times*, ventured into a 'shooting gallery' to talk to some of them.[40] There, in an abandoned building near the Williamsburg Bridge in Brooklyn, he met a man who called himself Cano, 'the man with the needles'. A packet of ten syringes, illegally acquired, cost him $4, he said, and he sold them to others for $2 each to support his heroin and cocaine habit. 'People are buying them a lot because they don't want to share', he said. 'People are afraid of AIDS.' In the dim glow of the candles, Morgan also talked to a thirty-two-year-old man called Willenski who was fidgeting as he awaited his turn. 'This talk about addicts liking to share needles is a lie', he said. 'They don't want to give out free needles because they want us to die, and they see it as a good way to get rid of us.'

Since 1984, ethnographic studies in New York City had suggested that addicts knew about AIDS and had taken steps to protect themselves. Drug users have an addiction and a culture that make risk reduction difficult: there is a deep mistrust of the outside world, a refusal to share needles can endanger personal relationships and an addict keeping clean injection equipment runs the risk of arrest. Yet, when fifty-nine patients were interviewed at a Manhattan methadone maintenance clinic, 93% knew that sharing needles could spread the disease, 59% reported having made behavioural changes to avoid AIDS, 31% used clean needles more often and 29% had reduced needle sharing.[41] Further studies indicated that blacks were significantly more likely than other groups to report that they had decreased the sharing of works with other IV drug users: 48% compared to 26% of whites and 23% of Hispanics.[42] Des Jarlais and his colleagues observed, though, that 'the extent of increased use of new needles would depend not only on the person's general intention to avoid sharing needles but also on market supply mechanisms for providing new needles at the appropriate times'.[43] Outreach workers reported that the illicit market in New York for sterile needles had in fact expanded greatly, though perhaps not enough, since AIDS began. The threat of disease had even helped advertising. 'Get the good needles, don't get the bad AIDS', one seller chanted.[44]

Through the summer of 1988, the debate continued. The increasing severity of the AIDS problem led more health professionals to push for a needle exchange scheme. Dr Mervyn Silverman, president of the American Foundation for AIDS Research, was reported in the *New York Times* in June as saying: 'I never heard of anybody starting drugs because needles were available or stopping because they couldn't find a clean one.'[45] With needle sharing now the leading means of HIV transmission in New York, Kathleen Oliver, the head of Outside-In, a private social service agency, thought that distributing clean needles was the sensible thing to do. By refusing to provide needles and syringes, 'what you're really saying is these people are expendable, that you'd rather have them die of AIDS than give them needles'.[46]

Don Des Jarlais pointed out that in foreign cities where pragmatic needle exchanges had operated for many years now, no one could detect any rise in drug addiction. Recent evidence from Amsterdam, where 700,000 needles were given out over the previous year, implied that some addicts injected less frequently, or decided to enter treatment programmes after counselling.[47] These findings were supported by preliminary studies in Sweden, England, Scotland, France and Australia, countries where pragmatic distribution of drug injection equipment was permitted.[48] Yet it would probably take more years of observation to confirm that needle exchanges actually slowed the rate of sero-conversion.

But was it advisable to wait for further gains in scientific assurance?[49] Recent studies indicated that each year about 6% of IV drug users in New York City who were not formerly infected became HIV positive.[50] Before long, the prevalence of HIV infection might rival the 80–95% figures for hepatitis B infection found among drug users in New York and San Francisco. Even in late 1987, a survey had shown that one of every sixty-one babies born in New York City carried antibodies to HIV, with most of the affected babies born in poorer neighbourhoods.[51] With a public health disaster looming, needle exchange programmes were now proposed in Boston, the District of Columbia, New Jersey and San Francisco, as well as New York. San Francisco had been distributing bleach and telling addicts how to sterilise needles for over a year.[52] The Vancouver health authorities, convinced of 'the success of needle exchange programs and, in particular, that such programs clearly did not encourage new drug users', had recently 'sold' the idea of a pragmatic scheme in their city.[53] In New York, though, the search for more 'conclusive' scientific evidence was just about to begin.

A pilot programme

In February, Dr Joseph had told Peter Kerr, a reporter from the *Times*: 'We shouldn't delude ourselves. It is not a static situation. We don't have that much time.'[54] But ten months later, Joseph's proposed experiment was still not operating. As the months passed, even the tentative plans had been scaled down.

Predictably, no neighbourhood wanted a needle exchange anywhere near it. Dr John V. Natoli, the principal of Public School 33 in Chelsea, was incensed when he heard that a needle exchange would soon open next door. 'I have no objection to the program as an experiment', he said, 'but as an educator, I don't see how you can place such a facility right next to a school.'[55] He was worried that the area would become littered with used needles. Dr Joseph, though, pointed out that the Chelsea centre already did HIV testing, so 'hundreds if not thousands' of addicts passed the school every day. He believed the pilot programme was under siege from critics 'not because of any actual harm it could cause, but because it symbolizes the worst fears of its detractors'.[56] But Mayor Koch stepped in and cancelled the plans for neighbourhood exchanges. Since Koch's decision suddenly meant that only one site was available, the proposal for a randomisation of sites had to be abandoned just a few days before the start of the trial.[57] Now all subjects would have to travel across town to the Health Department's headquarters in lower Manhattan.

The 'clinical trial' began on 7 December 1988, three years after David Sencer had first suggested the distribution of clean needles, and after two years of planning and redesign. The New York State Health Department's institutional review board had approved the new proposal, and the state Health Commissioner had finally promulgated the necessary regulations identifying the persons authorised to obtain or furnish hypodermic syringes (10 NYCRR section 80.134). But the trial was now called a 'pilot study' and seemed less consequential than ever. Most likely, it would simply determine whether drug addicts could comply with the conditions of a clinical trial, though it might still provide some information on how effectively a needle exchange scheme slowed the spread of HIV infection. According to Don Des Jarlais, for a large-scale trial to be feasible, the pilot study would have to attract enough volunteers, who would have to exchange regularly their used needles for clean ones, and be prepared to enter drug treatment programmes when vacancies occurred. Another important criterion of success was community support for the experiment.[58]

The number of IV drug users that could be enrolled was still limited to 400. To participate, addicts eighteen years and older had to register at the Health Department's headquarters in lower Manhattan, where they would be interviewed and examined by doctors, sign consent forms and be tested for tuberculosis, sexually transmitted diseases and HIV infection. These tests were to be repeated regularly throughout the trial. Only drug users who had applied to a drug rehabilitation programme and had been turned away because it was full were eligible for the study. When they came in to register they had to show a letter of referral from the programme.[59]

Participants could exchange injection equipment between 10 a.m. and 3 p.m., Monday through Friday at the lone distribution site in downtown Manhattan, where they also received counselling and education. Each participant had an identification card with a photograph attached, to prevent others from getting access to the clean needles. Furthermore, the researchers planned to check the returned needles and syringes to make sure the blood in them was the same type as the participant's. If it was not, the participant would be warned, but no one had decided yet how many warnings were allowed before the refractory needle sharer had to be dropped from the study.

The initial proposal had included non-exchanging sites where members of a 'comparison group' would also receive counselling, bleach kits and basic medical assessment, but not injection equipment. This was to allow researchers to make statistical comparisons of behavioural changes and HIV infection rates between the 'treated' and 'untreated' groups.[60] But Koch's sudden decision to restrict the trial had thrown plans for a control group into confusion. Des Jarlais suggested using an historical control, consisting of drug users that his group had been following for some years.[61] Eventually, though, a 'comparison group' was found in the South Bronx. The needle exchange's staff gained access to a clinic where they counselled the patients who injected drugs. Sixty-one patients decided to 'pre-enrol' in the programme, that is they 'completed all aspects of the enrolment procedure although they were unwilling to travel from the South Bronx to 125 Worth St to receive an ID card and hypodermic equipment'.[62] This became the 'comparison group' which was followed for relative rates of needle sharing, and seroconversion.

'Encouragement of drug abuse'

Only two people had enrolled by the end of the first day of the experiment. They first had to pass the barricades that police had erected in anticipation of protests against the scheme. In fact, by 10 a.m. only twenty demonstrators had gathered outside the Health Department, most of them from ADAPT, chanting slogans like: 'Free needles save lives.' The poor response from IV drug users did not surprise the demonstrators. Several of them pointed out that the single distribution centre was inconvenient, with limited hours. Others observed that the study required addicts to identify themselves to a government agency.[63] Only eight applicants had shown up by the end of the week.

Meanwhile, criticism of the study became more vehement. Rarely, though, did critics bother any longer to challenge the scientific validity of the small, constrained trial, which even its promoters now seemed to assume was negligible. Instead, its opponents – including prosecutors, the police, black and Hispanic politicians and operators of drug treatment programmes – expressed their concern that the government appeared to sanction IV drug use. The distribution of clean needles and syringes seemed to them a cynical, cheap solution to a drug problem that had brought not only AIDS but also crime, social breakdown and other illnesses – such as tuberculosis – to the city's black and Hispanic neighbourhoods. A new sign was posted on lampposts in Harlem: 'When will all the junkies die so the rest of us can go on living?'[64] The Police Commissioner, Benjamin Ward, told the *New York Times*: 'As a black person, I have a particular sensitivity to doctors conducting experiments, and they too frequently seem to be conducted against blacks.'[65] The New York City Council voted overwhelmingly to approve a non-binding resolution calling on the Koch administration to abandon the pilot needle exchange project. Enoch Williams, the chairman of the Council's black and Hispanic caucus, argued that 'The city is sending the wrong message when it distributes free needles to drug addicts while we are trying to convince our children to say no to drugs.'[66] According to City Councilman Hilton B. Clark of Harlem, needle distribution was 'genocide' and the programme's architect, Dr Stephen C. Joseph, 'should be arrested for murder and drug distribution'.[67]

In response, Yolanda Serrano from ADAPT exclaimed: 'They talk about genocide – this is the real genocide. People can survive addiction, but they can't survive AIDS.'[68] Dr Joseph tried to calm things down and distance himself from the dispute: 'People are taking positions based on opinions and assumptions without any data, and that's what we want to get.'[69] But this appeal to the 'objectivity' of medical research seemed no longer convincing enough to dissolve the controversy.

During January, in another interview with the *Times*, Joseph agreed that 'It obviously has been a very tough row to hoe because of constraints placed on the program and the intensity of opposition to it.'[70] After two months, only fifty-six addicts had enrolled, and only seventy-six needles had been dispensed. Health officials decided to alter the experiment so they could concentrate more on getting drug users into rehabilitation programmes. Joseph conceded that the number of addicts so far enrolled would be too few to draw any valid 'scientific' conclusions.

For the last five months on a street corner in Tacoma, Washington, just a few steps from a 'shooting gallery', David Purchase had successfully handed out clean syringes in exchange for used ones. His volunteer efforts proved more popular than the New York 'experiment' – 13,000 needles had already been exchanged – even though fewer than 3,000 IV drug users lived in Tacoma. Purchase, a forty-nine-year-old drug counsellor disabled from a motorbike accident, told reporters that needle exchanges elsewhere had been hampered by 'ignorance, politics and moral fascism'. He believed that if dispensing clean needles and syringes turned out not to slow the spread of HIV infection, then he would just look foolish, but if those who blocked needle exchanges were wrong, 'their children will be dead'.[71] In Tacoma, Purchase had the support of the local Police Chief, who suspended enforcement of the law on possession of drug paraphernalia. But at the same time in Boston, a similar volunteer effort met a different fate, and the distributor was arrested. Another proposal to distribute clean needles, from a private social service agency in Portland, Oregon, was being delayed by insurance problems.[72]

Uncertain policies

In early 1989 the government response to AIDS in New York City was fragmented, contentious and inadequately funded. Koch and other city officials blamed state agencies for cutting reimbursements to AIDS patients, failing to expand hospitals and stalling on clinics to treat drug addiction. State officials, in turn, attacked the city for neglecting public hospitals and shirking on drug treatment. Axelrod, the State Health Commissioner, was confronted with extraordinary overcrowding in the hospitals and nursing homes he was responsible for. His city counterpart, Joseph, had antagonised minority politicians with his promotion of a needle exchange programme and recently upset AIDS advocacy groups when he reduced the estimate of the number of New Yorkers infected with HIV.[73]

During that spring, a number of federal officials commented on the needle exchange experiment, initially in support of it. The National Research Council, the research division of the National Academy of Sciences, produced a report on the national response to AIDS. To reduce the spread of HIV infection among IV drug users, the committee recommended an expansion of needle exchange programmes.[74] Dr Louis W. Sullivan, President Bush's new Secretary of Health and Human Services, also endorsed needle exchange schemes. 'I don't subscribe to the view that it condones drug abuse', he said. 'It is an idea that certainly deserves some investigation to see if it does work.'[75] But Representative Charles B. Rangel, a Manhattan Democrat who headed the Select Committee on Narcotics Abuse and Control, immediately condemned Sullivan's comments, calling them 'tragic, ill-advised and illegal'. Needle exchange programmes, he declared, 'would keep addicts out of sight, out of mind, and sweep them under the rug instead of restoring their dignity and giving them drug-free lives'.[76] Don Hamilton, a spokesman for William J. Bennett, the head of the Bush administration's anti-drug efforts, told the *New York Times* that needle exchange schemes were ineffective and, since they were likely to encourage drug abuse, also 'pernicious'.[77] Marlin Fitzwater, the President's spokesman, assured the press that 'The President is opposed to the exchange of needles under any condition.'[78] When asked about the apparent conflict, Campbell Gardett, a spokesman for Dr Sullivan, said 'We're in an in-between period when an awful lot has to be worked out.'[79]

So the confusion over US needle exchange policy continued. In Europe and Australia the distribution of needles and syringes had been less contentious. In April 1989, directors of AIDS prevention programmes in Britain and the Netherlands told the House Energy and Commerce subcommittee on health and the environment that providing clean needles and syringes to addicts had reduced needle sharing, without increasing drug abuse. Allan Parry, who was in charge of thirteen needle exchange programmes in the Liverpool area, told the committee that since 1986 he had not found one case of HIV infection among the 1,050 addicts that had received clean needles.[80] In Amsterdam, HIV infection among IV drug users had stabilised for two years, and new cases of hepatitis B had dropped 75%. Evidence from the only successful US exchange also suggested the project's effectiveness. According to Dr Alfred Allen, the Pierce County, WA, health director, since David Purchase began distributing clean needles in Tacoma admissions to drug treatment programmes had increased by one third. Local surveys indicated that 90% of addicts no longer shared needles. Purchase himself told the committee that he was convinced that protecting IV drug users from a fatal disease was more important than moral concerns about drug abuse. 'You can get over being stupid', he said 'but you can't get over being dead.'[81]

But after seven months, the carefully regulated New York needle exchange experiment had attracted only 160 participants. Axelrod had recently permitted the programme to accept addicts off the street, without letters of referral, but the other barriers to participation remained. Eventually, over 250 IV drug users enrolled in the programme during its first ten months, but there was still no sign that the 'data' on these subjects and on the comparison group 'will begin a new less confrontational era of AIDS prevention policy'.[82] Councilman Hilton Clark continued to argue that the programme was a failure as an experiment, and the 'data' showed nothing of any value. 'People are not participating', he said. 'We are going to call for a cessation of the program because it is still sending out the wrong message: using drugs is O.K.'[83]

A public health agenda?

The message that city health officials had hoped to send out was that the exchange scheme was a valuable scientific experiment in the prevention of HIV infection. Instead, the project was read as an endorsement of drug use. Never a popular suggestion, any hint of tolerance of addiction was, in the summer of 1989, politically unthinkable.

In September, George Bush warned that drugs were 'sapping our strength as a nation', and announced a national drug control strategy that stressed law enforcement.[84] His televised address from the Oval Office paid little attention to prevention efforts, or to the rehabilitation of addicts. Drug experts complained that neither Bush's programme nor any existing state approach provided nearly enough clinics for addicts who wanted to break the habit. According to Salvatore di Menza, special assistant to the director of the National Institute on Drug Abuse, perhaps a million addicts wanted treatment that was simply not available.[85] Many of them languished on waiting lists for eight months or more.[86] Many did not bother even signing up.

When David Dinkins became Mayor of New York, he confirmed the emphasis on the policing of drug use, appointing Nicholas DeB. Katzenbach, a former US Attorney-General, to head a study group to recommend a strategy for fighting addiction.[87] Dinkins had always opposed the needle exchange experiment, arguing that to provide addicts with needles was to give in to drug abuse. 'I think we need to go at fighting drug addiction in the first instance', he told the *Times*, 'and I don't want to give people the paraphernalia to keep using drugs.'[88] So when he announced the abandonment of the trial, in February 1990, it came as no surprise. Joseph, though, who had been replaced as Health Commissioner by Dr Woodrow A. Myers, expressed his disappointment with the decision. 'Black leadership has consistently opposed it and I think they made a big mistake', he said, 'because some people who might have survived are going to die.'[89]

At his first news conference, in April 1990, Dr Myers explained that he intended to concentrate on expanding drug treatment. He was 'ideologically opposed' to the government distribution of needles and syringes, and could not, he said, imagine any evidence that would convince him that such schemes were worthwhile.[90] Myers also felt it was not the city's responsibility to teach addicts safer injection techniques, or to give them bleach to disinfect needles and syringes. In response, Des Jarlais told the *Times* that he had reviewed needle exchange programmes in Tacoma; Portland, Oregon; Seattle; San Francisco; Britain; the Netherlands; Sweden; Australia; and Canada. He would be happy to discuss these studies with Myers. 'They are really quite clear', he said. 'Safe injection practices have not led to increased drug use, and have led to large reductions in AIDS risk behavior.'[91] Yolanda Serrano, one of the few minority officials to have supported the idea of a needle exchange, was even more blunt. She pointed out that drug treatment was not readily available, and some addicts were unwilling or unable to enter rehabilitation programmes. 'What do we do, just let them die and take their families with them?'[92]

In May, a coalition of major AIDS organisations, including the Gay Men's Health Crisis and the American Foundation for AIDS Research (AmFAR), appealed to Myers to change his opinion on the promotion of safe injection techniques. Dr David Rogers, head of the New York State AIDS Advisory Council and the Mayor's AIDS Task Force, claimed that eliminating prevention programmes was 'indefensible'. Myers's actions had left him 'absolutely bewildered'.[93] Dr Mathilde Krim, co-founder of AmFAR, said she was in favour of 'all these life-saving measures' – to be otherwise would doom many drug users and their spouses and babies as 'dispensable'.[94]

Myers also advocated withdrawing city funds from ADAPT's rather perfunctory bleach distribution efforts. The Black Leadership Commission on AIDS, a group of sixty-five doctors, lawyers, politicians and business executives, supported his stand. They accused white public health officials of being too quick to endorse cheap ways of stopping AIDS, while failing to spend enough on drug treatment. Bleach distribution contained 'a grave element of risk' to the African-American community, the Commission said.[95] But according to Mathilde Krim, their statement was 'contemptible, absurd and irrational'. The debate was polarising blacks against whites. 'The majority of whites are in favor of preventing HIV transmission by any means', she said, but blacks 'are obsessed with the demand for treatment.'[96]

Yet, in May 1990, it was John C. Daniels, the first black Mayor of New Haven, who gained his Council's authorisation of a local needle exchange scheme. He had argued that with 75% of the AIDS cases in New Haven linked to IV drug use, and over 4,000 addicts in the city, making clean needles available would keep people alive until they could be helped. Officials hoped to dispense 500 needle kits each week, and planned to expand the programme to Hartford and Bridgeport by 1992. They had decided that the needle and syringe distribution would be more pragmatic than it had been in New York. For a start, kits would be dispensed from a van travelling around the neighbourhoods where addicts lived. The programme had received enthusiastic support from New Haven's Police Chief, Nicholas Pastore. 'The 1990's is calling for some new thinking in dealing with these issues', he said. 'I like to see the Police Department's moving toward a social engineering role.'[97] Alvin Novick, a professor of biology at Yale and chairman of the Mayor's Task Force on AIDS, told reporters: 'This is not a political agenda: it's a public health agenda.'[98]

Conclusion

I have described here the history of one effort to curtail the spread of HIV among drug users. My intention, however, is not to point out the 'rational' course of action, or the 'correct' public policy. There are lessons to be learnt from this case, certainly, but they are not easily expressed in terms of right and wrong. I have tried, rather, to illustrate the contested meanings of health promotion and clinical research during the late 1980s in New York City – a diverse community facing an array of health crises and moral uncertainties. A number of groups – including public health officials, drug treatment experts, law enforcement officers, local community leaders, drug users and federal, state and city politicians – all had an interest in controlling the meaning of both the problem of HIV transmission among IV drug users and any intervention to curtail it. On a practical level, the various interpretations of the nature and severity of AIDS and illicit drug use determined each interested party's response to the needle exchange trial. The experimental programme was promoted by health professionals as the most rational and scientific approach possible in the circumstances, but undoubtedly it was seen by other groups – ultimately more influential ones – as a symbolic endorsement of illegal drug use, the major perceived threat to the integrity of the community.

The failure of the New York needle exchange illustrates a social resistance to defining HIV infection as a technical problem, and reveals local limitations on the role of expert groups in the formation of controversial policy. Invoking the prestige of medical science is not always sufficient to compel acceptance of contested policies. Indeed, the opinions of city health officials were treated with suspicion, making it difficult for them to avoid creating the impression that they were hiding political decisions in technical assessments. While evidence from abroad by early 1989 suggested that the distribution of clean needles and syringes could reduce the sharing of drug paraphernalia without increasing addiction, this evidence clearly, in the end, was outweighed by the magnitude of the policy's symbolic affront to social order. Thus the control over the definition of the relevant issues had been wrested from the health professionals and, in the end, the explicit moral and political aspects of the problem proved paramount in defining society's response.

In New York, the ineffectiveness of expert opinion that Fox detected in the initial response to AIDS was never rectified.[99] The epidemic challenged a health system increasingly preoccupied with cost containment and the decentralisation of authority. It was a fractured system poorly prepared to devise and enforce a co-ordinated and convincing programme to curtail the spread of the virus.[100] The intensity of disagreement over access to sterile injection equipment thus continues to illustrate how 'the public rhetorical dramas of symbolic politics are a mechanism for coping with the fragmentation of political authority'.[101] And at least in part, it confirms Porter's speculation that 'the appalling slowness and ineptitude of the United States response to AIDS arose out of the mixed blessings of the decentralised state and of City Hall caucus politics'.[102]

It is not surprising that Dinkins's political decision should finally have ruled out a needle exchange in any guise in New York City. Intravenous drug users in New York were too unorganised and socially stigmatised to force government action, or to enter into negotiations over the appropriate policy response. They were the city's poor, mostly African-American and Hispanic, an embarrassment to their families and communities – no one's constituency. In the past, drug treatment professionals had often claimed to speak for many addicts, but it was not necessarily in their interests to promote needle exchanges.

African-American communities had been slow to mobilise against AIDS, and when they did, the leadership usually opposed the distribution of sterile injection equipment out of a concern that it would endorse drug use and substitute for rehabilitation. The churches that traditionally had taken the major role in mobilising black communities remained strongly opposed on moral grounds to any action that appeared to condone drug use. Only ADAPT, a small group of outreach workers and past users, campaigned for access to sterile needles and syringes, but their contribution to policy negotiations remained marginal.[103]

The attempt to formulate public policy in terms of the research process – even though it failed – deserves careful study, for there is a danger that political restrictions on access to care are simply replaced by research restrictions constructed on insecure scientific grounds. As soon as the provision of needle exchanges was structured as a scientific trial in New York, a recurrent anxiety emerged among the investigators: how to identify a control group that would give the experiment legitimacy. Political constraints on needle distribution were reiterated in scientific protocols that attempted to find an untreated 'comparison group' to monitor, or simply limited the trial to the few prepared to negotiate a bureaucratic maze. The experiment, or the pilot study, was predicated on exclusion. This exclusion on scientific grounds, for research purposes, itself can be read as throwing doubt on the perceived rationality of needle exchange policy, as challenging an emerging international clinical consensus. In New York City – as in few other cities abroad – public health officials maintained an agnosticism (or equipoise) on needle exchanges, and maintained it in practice long after they were able to quote studies indicating that the distribution of clean needles and syringes in a pragmatic fashion, with counselling, would be of superior therapeutic merit to the alternative of counselling alone, or perhaps counselling with bleach distribution too. This equipoise permitted them a polemical and scientific recourse to the clinical trial, and the local credibility needed to exert an influence over events.

The tension between acceptance of pragmatic exchanges on the basis of existing knowledge, and the need to construct an acceptably limited experiment is readily apparent. Even the city Health Department's report on the trial and the comparison group referred to needle exchange as 'a promising – and necessary – intervention' in a 'health crisis', and pointed out that 'no empirical data' supported the principal arguments against such programmes.[104] In a letter to Axelrod in December 1989, Stephen Joseph described needle exchanges as an 'anti-HIV intervention already researched and adopted in many parts of the world' – though not yet 'field tested' in the US.[105] Generally, the scientists involved argued that needle exchanges needed much more local controlled field testing (just as a vaccine might need more than one field trial) and that exchanges should not yet be accepted as a standard of care[106] – yet in Europe and Australia they increasingly, in response to a crisis, were becoming so accepted. In the circumstances one might have expected at least more debate on the ethics of limiting 'treatment' to a few, or making access to it difficult for a 'comparison group', for purposes of further US research of doubtful statistical power.[107] But then again, the interests of the population from which the trial drew its participants were not well represented.

But what if the configuring of policy as a restricted trial *had* been challenged on ethical grounds? Considering the balance of forces, such an attempt to bring AIDS prevention back into the middle of the political arena would most likely have resulted not in an expansion of access to clean needles, but in the abandonment of even the limited scheme – as eventually happened, although not from a squeamishness about restricting access for research purposes. But even if the choice was therefore between rigid political control over access to clean needles and a more flexible 'scientific' control, one should bear in mind that our society has chosen to hold scientists to higher ethical standards in these matters than it demands of politicians. The issue, though, became so enmeshed in politics that no one can now say with certainty who was talking as a scientist and who as a politician: there was no room left for a relatively autonomous science. Nevertheless, when clinical science is used in an effort to attain a broader community consensus or political legitimacy for public policy – as much as to resolve a genuine clinical uncertainty – then one hopes scientists will be even more vigilant than usual in guarding against a refusal of effective treatment to an untreated population either in the trial, or outside it altogether.

Since the rejection of the formulation of needle exchange policy as a research process, even fewer IV drug users in the United States now have authorised access to clean needles and syringes.[108] Yet in Europe and Australia, needle exchange schemes continue to expand in pragmatic ways. Thus a persisting irony of this story is that when the New York experiment ended, and the few local IV drug users ever permitted access to clean needles dispersed, the real international 'experiment' on the effectiveness of needle exchange schemes had just begun: only now the majority of drug injectors in the United States will serve as the control group for the rest of the world.

Acknowledgements

I am grateful to the editors of the *American Journal of Public Health* for permission to reprint this essay in its revised form. Rosemary Stevens, Charles Rosenberg, Virginia Berridge and Elizabeth Fee made helpful comments on earlier versions of the paper.

NOTES

1 D. M. Fox, P. Day and R. Klein, 'The power of professionalism: policies for AIDS in Britain, Sweden and the United States', *Daedalus*, 112 (1989), 110–11 and 107. Until the last two decades the medical profession's role in the formulation of US drug policy had been particularly limited: considering the historical context, then, it is not surprising that the aspects of AIDS prevention strategy most closely related to drug policy are the policies least amenable to expert medical control. For an account of US drug policy, see D. F. Musto, *The American Disease: Origins of Narcotic Control* (New Haven, 1973).

2 C. E. Rosenberg, 'What is an epidemic: AIDS in historical perspective', *Daedalus*, 112 (1989), 2.

3 Jeffrey Weeks, 'AIDS: the intellectual agenda', in P. Aggleton, G. Hart and P. Davies (eds.), *AIDS: Social Representation, Social Practices* (London, 1989).

4 E. Fee and D. M. Fox, 'The contemporary historiography of AIDS', *Journal of Social History*, 23 (1989), 303–14. AIDS Social History Groups in both the UK and the US have recently attempted to remedy this problem.

5 See Berridge's paper in this volume for an analysis of the way in which scientific authority in the UK provided an acceptable and apparently rational justification for pragmatic policy change. Also, more generally, see P. Strong and V. Berridge, 'No one knew anything: some issues in British AIDS policy', in P. Aggleton, P. Davies and G. Hart (eds.), *AIDS: Individual, Cultural and Policy Dimensions* (London, 1990).

6 L. Friedman, C. D. Furburg and D. L. DeMers, *et al.*, *Fundamentals of Clinical Trials* (Boston, Mass., 1981). US Congress, Office of Technology Assessment, *Impact of Randomized Clinical Trials on Health Policy and Medicine* (Washington, DC, 1983).

7 D. P. Byar, R. M. Simon and W. T. Friedewald, *et al.*, 'Randomized clinical trials: perspectives in some recent ideas', *New England Journal of Medicine*, 295 (1976), 74–80, at 74.

8 C. Fried, *Medical Experimentation: Personal Integrity and Social Policy* (Amsterdam, 1974).

9 B. Freedman, 'Equipoise and the ethics of clinical research', *New England Journal of Medicine*, 317 (1987), 141–5. See also A. R. Feinstein, 'An additional basic science for clinical medicine. II. The limitations of randomized trials', *Annals of Internal Medicine*, 99 (1983), 544–50.

10 D. Sencer, 'Choosing between two killers', *New York Times* (hereafter *NYT*), 15 Sept. 1985.

11 J. Purnick, 'Koch bars easing of syringe sales in AIDS fight', *NYT*, 4 Oct. 1985.

12 *Ibid.*

13 R. D. McFadden, 'Cuomo and Koch reconsidering their opposition to closing of bathhouses', *NYT*, 5 Oct. 1985. See R. Bayer, *Private Acts, Social Consequences: AIDS and the Politics of Public Health* (New York, 1989).

14 D. Nelkin and S. Hilgartner, 'Disputed dimensions of risk: a public school controversy over AIDS', *Milbank Quarterly*, 64 (suppl. 1) (1986), 118–42.

15 J. Barbanel, 'To combat AIDS, Koch urges anti-drug effort', *NYT*, 17 Dec. 1985.

16 E. C. Bunning, R. Coutinho and G. H. van Brussel, *et al.*, 'Preventing AIDS in drug addicts in Amsterdam', *Lancet*, 1 (1986), 1435.

17 World Health Organisation, *AIDS among Drug Abusers* (Copenhagen, 1987), 190.

18 National Academy of Sciences, Institute of Medicine, *Confronting AIDS: Directions for Public Health, Health Care and Research* (Washington, DC, 1986).

19 R. Sullivan, 'Official favors a test program to curb AIDS', *NYT*, 30 May 1986.

20 *Ibid.*

21 *Ibid.*

22 A. Moss, quoted in R. F. Hummel, W. R. Leavy and M. Rampolla, *et al.* (eds.), *AIDS: Impact on Public Policy* (New York, 1986), 56–7.

23 R. Sullivan, 'Addicts' AIDS deaths may be higher than reported, official says', *NYT*, 26 Mar. 1987.

24 F. X. Clines, 'Via addicts' needles, AIDS spreads in Edinburgh', *NYT*, 4 Jan. 1987. See also G. V. Stimson, L. Alldritt and K. Dolan, *et al.*, 'Syringe-exchange schemes in England and Scotland: evaluating a new service for drug users', in Aggleton, Hart and Davies (eds.), *AIDS: Social Representations.*

25 'Some nations giving addicts clean needles', *NYT*, 9 Mar. 1987.

26 'AIDS, sex and needles' (edit.), *NYT*, 29 Mar. 1987.

27 R. Sullivan, 'New York State rejects plan to give drug users needles', *NYT*, 17 May 1987.

28 R. Sullivan, 'Citing "state of emergency", New York starts drug-clinic program to fight AIDS', *NYT*, 12 June 1987.

29 S. R. Friedman, W. M. de Jong, D. C. Des Jarlais, 'Problems and dynamics of organizing intravenous drug users for AIDS prevention', *Health Education Research*, 3 (1986), 49–59.

30 B. Lambert, 'Drug group to offer free needles to combat AIDS in New York City', *NYT*, 8 Jan. 1988.

31 *Ibid.*

32 *Ibid.*

33 B. Lambert, 'Reaction to needles-for-addicts plan', *NYT*, 9 Jan. 1988.

34 'U.S. homes to get a booklet on AIDS', *NYT*, 28 Jan. 1988.

35 J. Schmalz, 'Addicts to get needles in plan to curb AIDS', *NYT*, 30 Jan. 1988. Plans are also described in 'AIDS and drug abuse: no quick fix', *Science*, 239 (12 Feb. 1988), 717–19.

36 P. Kerr, 'Weighing of two perils leads to needles-for-addicts plan', *NYT*, 1 Feb. 1988.

37 'Fighting AIDS and addiction: a start' (edit.), *NYT*, 18 Feb. 1988.

38 H. Evans and M. Santangelo, 'O'C blasts addict plan', *NY Daily News*, 1 Feb. 1988.

39 P. Kerr, 'Experts find fault in new AIDS plan', *NYT*, 7 Feb. 1988. See L. S. Brown and B. J. Primm, 'Intravenous drug abuse and AIDS in minorities', *AIDS and Public Policy Journal*, 3 (1988), 5–15.

40 T. Morgan, 'Inside a "shooting gallery": new front in the AIDS war', *NYT*, 4 Feb. 1988.

41 S. R. Friedman, D. C. Des Jarlais and J. L. Southeran, 'AIDS health education for intravenous drug users', *Health Education Quarterly*, 13 (1986), 383–93. On the cultural significance of needle sharing, see D. C. Des Jarlais, S. R. Friedman and D. Strug, 'AIDS and needle-sharing within the intravenous drug use subculture', in

D. A. Feldman and T. M. Johnson (eds.), *The Social Dimensions of AIDS: Method and Theory* (New York, 1986).

42 S. R. Friedman, D. C. Des Jarlais, J. L. Southeran, *et al.*, 'The AIDS epidemic among blacks and Hispanics', *Milbank Quarterly*, 65 (suppl. 2) (1986), 455–99.

43 D. C. Des Jarlais, S. R. Friedman and W. Hopkins, 'Risk reduction for the acquired immunodeficiency syndrome among intravenous drug users', *Annals of Internal Medicine*, 103 (1985), 755–9, at 758.

44 *Ibid.*

45 B. Lambert, 'Needles for addicts: test phase begins', *NYT*, 26 June 1988.

46 *Ibid.*

47 B. Lambert, 'Study supports New York's needle plan', *NYT*, 6 June 1988. Also E. C. Buning, G. H. A. van Brussel and V. van Santen, *et al.*, 'Amsterdam's drug policy and its implications for controlling needle sharing', in R. J. Battjes and R. W. Pickens (eds.), *Needle Sharing among Intravenous Drug Users: National and International Perspectives*, NIDA Research Monograph No. 80 (Washington, DC, 1989). Battjes and Pickens concluded that 'Preliminary evaluation of the Amsterdam program suggests that the program has been successful in reducing needle sharing among IV drug abusers, and it has not resulted in increased drug use among program participants', p. 181.

48 P. W. Brickner, R. A. Torres, M. Barnes, *et al.*, 'Recommendations for control and prevention of human immunodeficiency virus (HIV) infection in intravenous drug users', *Annals of Internal Medicine*, 110 (1989), 833–7; G. Mulleady, P. Roderick, S. Burnyeat, *et al.*, 'HIV and drug abuse: essential factors in providing a syringe exchange scheme', *Proceedings of the IV International Conference on AIDS* (Stockholm, 1988) (Abstract 8519); D. Flanagan, S. Burnyeat, B. Wade, H. Clarice, and R. Marten, 'Evaluation of a syringe exchange scheme', *Proceedings of the IV International Conference on AIDS* (Stockholm, 1988) (Abstract 8519); P. Espinoza, I. Bouchard, P. Ballian and J. Polo Devoto, 'Has the open sale of syringes modified the syringe exchange habits of drug addicts?', *Proceedings of the IV International Conference on AIDS* (Stockholm, 1988) (Abstract 8522); G. J. Hart, A. Carvell, A. M. Johnson, C. Feinmann, N. Woodward and A. W. Adler, 'Needle exchange in central London', *Proceedings of the IV International Conference on AIDS* (Stockholm, 1988) (Abstract 8512); D. Goldberg, H. Watson, F. Stuart, M. Miller, L. Gruer and E. Follett, 'Pharmacy supply of needles and syringes – the effect on HIV in intravenous drug users', *Proceedings of the IV International Conference on AIDS* (Stockholm, 1988) (Abstract 8521); and J. S. Wolk, A. Wodak, J. J. Guinan, *et al.*, 'HIV prevalence in syringes of intravenous drug users using syringe exchanges in Sydney, Australia', *Proceedings of the IV International Conference on AIDS* (Stockholm, 1988) (Abstract 8504).

49 H. W. Feldman and P. Biernacki, 'The ethnography of needle sharing among IV drug users and implications for public policies and intervention strategies', in Battjes and Pickens (eds.), *Needle Sharing*. They commented: 'Nor do we have the luxury of awaiting controlled experiments before developing public policies and intervention strategies' (38).

50 L. K. Altman, 'Spread of AIDS virus found slowing among drug users in 3 cities', *NYT*, 16 June 1988.

51 Kerr, 'Weighing of two perils'.

52 J. A. Newmeyer, 'Why bleach? Development of a strategy to combat HIV contagion among San Francisco IV drug users', in Battjes and Pickens (eds.), *Needle Sharing*.

53 J. Blatherwick, 'How to "sell" a needle exchange program', *Canadian Journal of Public Health*, 80 (suppl. 1) (1989), S26–S27.

54 Kerr, 'Weighing of two perils'.

55 N. A. Lewis, 'P.S. 33 fights needle test next door', *NYT*, 2 Nov. 1988.

56 *Ibid.*

57 D. C. Des Jarlais (interview), 2 Aug. 1991.

58 L. K. Altman, 'Needle program is a small one to test concept', *NYT*, 8 Nov. 1988.

59 New York City Department of Health, *The Pilot Needle Exchange Study in New York City: A Bridge to Treatment. A Report on the First Ten Months of Operation* (New York, Dec. 1989).

60 *Ibid.*

61 D. C. Des Jarlais (interview), 2 Aug. 1991.

62 New York City Department of Health, *The Pilot Needle Exchange Study*.

63 Altman, 'Needle program is a small one'.

64 E. Quimby and S. R. Friedman, 'Dynamics of black mobilization against AIDS in New York City', *Social Problems*, 36 (1989), 403–13.

65 B. Lambert, 'The free needle program is under way and under fire', *NYT*, 13 Nov. 1988.

66 E. Williams, quoted in 'Council calls for end to free needles plan', *NYT*, 7 Dec. 1988.

67 B. Lambert, 'New York alters needle plan for addicts to combat AIDS', *NYT*, 13 Nov. 1988.

68 *Ibid.*

69 *Ibid.*

70 M. Marriott, 'Needle plan fails to attract addicts, so it's revised', *NYT*, 30 Jan. 1989.

71 J. Gross, 'Needle exchange for addicts wins foothold against AIDS in Tacoma', *NYT*, 23 Jan. 1989.

72 'Deadly reach of needle proves difficult to block', *NYT*, 8 Feb. 1989.

73 B. Lambert, 'New York's confusing war on AIDS', *NYT*, 19 Feb. 1989.

74 W. E. Leary, 'U.S. needs data on drug and sex habits to halt AIDS, study says', *NYT*, 9 Feb. 1989. See C. F. Turner, H. G. Miller and L. E. Moses (eds.), *AIDS: Sexual Behavior and Intravenous Drug Use* (Washington, DC, 1989).

75 L. W. Sullivan, quoted in 'Sullivan backs needle trading to fight AIDS', *NYT*, 9 Mar. 1989.

76 M. Tolchin, 'Health chief seeks better care for poor', *NYT*, 10 Mar. 1989.

77 M. Tolchin, '2 Bush aides at odds on giving needles to addicts', *NYT*, 11 Mar. 1989.

78 *Ibid.*

79 C. Gardett, quoted in 'U.S. sending mixed signals on trade-ins of dirty needles', *NYT*, 15 Mar. 1989.

80 K. J. Cooper, 'Officials laud free needle programs', *Philadelphia Inquirer*, 25 Apr. 1989.

81 *Ibid.*

82 New York City Department of Health, *The Pilot Needle Exchange Study*.

83 M. Marriott, 'Drug needle exchange is gaining but still under fire', *NYT*, 7 June 1989.

84 B. Weinraub, 'President offers strategy for U.S. on drug control', *NYT*, 6 Sept. 1989;
    M. Marriott, 'Doubts greet drug plan in New York', *NYT*, 7 Sept. 1989.
85 A. H. Malcolm, 'In making drug strategy, no accord on treatment', *NYT*, 19 Nov.
    1989.
86 M. Marriott, 'Addicts awaiting treatment often face delays and panic', *NYT*, 10 Jan.
    1990.
87 T. S. Purdom, 'Dinkins appoints advisors on drugs and top positions', *NYT*, 24 Jan.
    1990.
88 T. S. Purdom, 'Dinkins to end needle plan for drug users', *NYT*, 14 Feb. 1990.
89 *Ibid.*
90 B. Lambert, 'Myers opposes needle project to curb AIDS', *NYT*, 10 Apr. 1990.
91 *Ibid.*
92 *Ibid.*
93 B. Lambert, 'Health chief is criticized on AIDS shift', *NYT*, 10 May 1990.
94 *Ibid.*
95 G. Kolata, 'Black group attacks using bleach to slow spread of AIDS', *NYT*, 17 June
    1990.
96 *Ibid.*
97 K. Johnson, 'New Haven plans to give drug addicts new needles', *NYT*, 24 May
    1990.
98 *Ibid.* Also, 'New Haven needle project gets 20 addicts on first day', *NYT*, 15 Nov.
    1990.
99 D. M. Fox, 'AIDS and the American health polity: the history and prospects of a
    crisis of authority', in E. Fee and D. M. Fox (eds.), *AIDS: The Burdens of History*
    (Berkeley, 1988).
100 J. C. Rossman and S. D. Pomrinse, 'New York City', in L. H. W. Paine (ed.), *Health
    Care in Big Cities* (New York, 1978); and P. S. Arno and R. G. Hughes, 'Local
    policy responses to the AIDS epidemic: New York and San Francisco', *New York
    State Journal of Medicine*, 87 (1987), 264–72.
101 Fox, Day and Klein, 'Power of professionalism', 104.
102 R. Porter, 'Epidemic of fear', *New Society*, 4 Mar. 1988, 24–5.
103 Quimby and Friedman, 'Dynamics and black mobilization'.
104 New York City Department of Health, *The Needle Exchange Pilot Study*.
105 S. C. Joseph to D. Axelrod (letter), 27 Dec. 1989.
106 D. C. Des Jarlais (interview), 5 Aug. 1991.
107 C. Levine, 'Has AIDS changed human subjects research?', *Law, Medicine and
    Health Care*, 16 (1988), 167–73.
108 At the time of writing there are officially sanctioned needle exchanges in New
    Haven, Conn.; Hawaii; Portland, Oreg.; Seattle, Wash.; and Boulder, Colo.
    Unauthorised exchanges operate in many other US cities, including New York. See
    Gay Wachman, 'Our druggies' (letter), *The Nation*, 15 Apr. 1991.

9

Context for a new disease: aspects of biomedical research policy in the United States before AIDS

VICTORIA A. HARDEN and DENNIS RODRIGUES

In the decade since AIDS was recognised in the United States, extraordinary public debate has surrounded the response of the medical establishment, especially the biomedical research enterprise, to the disease. Particular facets of this response have been considered by a number of authors. Gerald M. Oppenheimer, for example, has analysed factors involved in the epidemiological identification of AIDS at the Centers for Disease Control (CDC), and Daniel M. Fox has included biomedical research policy in his identification of a wider 'crisis of authority' in the United States health polity.[1] Lacking, however, has been an interpretation of the capacities, policies, opportunities and restraints that governed how and to what extent federal research organisations could respond to AIDS.[2]

Although such a full-scale evaluation is far too large for a single paper, we will examine two major policy issues and present two case studies that illuminate the context in which the emerging problem of AIDS was integrated into the existing framework of biomedical research sponsored by the National Institutes of Health (NIH).[3] The two policy issues are the structure of the NIH system for distributing grants and the emergence of targeted disease programmes and planning. The NIH grants system had been constructed carefully over three decades and, when confronted with the AIDS challenge, we will argue, functioned with adequate flexibility within its historic edifice. The agency's implementation of targeted research programmes and planning efforts provided an administrative context in which knowledge used to understand AIDS had been created and through which an AIDS research strategy was initially formulated.

The two case studies concern the formulation of guidelines for research on recombinant DNA and the 1976 epidemic of Legionnaires' disease. The former illuminates political concerns during the 1970s about the direction and control of science and, we believe, undergirded the agency's mandate to seek public advice in structuring AIDS advisory boards. The latter, which examines the roles of the

NIH and the CDC in response to another new disease, provides data for comparison with AIDS.

Research funding and NIH grants system

Although precedents for government patronage of medical research extend back to the late nineteenth century, the present system of federal support emerged after the Second World War, fuelled by wartime medical achievements, especially the development of antibiotics.[4] It was necessarily predicated on the assumption that practical results would soon follow the investment of public money, because creation of such a programme required that Americans suspend a deeply ingrained suspicion of government patronage for special groups.[5] Historically, Congress had preferred to support practical scientific endeavours over open-ended basic research, even when a lack of basic knowledge regarding the ventures undertaken resulted in wasted time, effort and money.[6]

The NIH grants system was modelled on the process for allocating scientific funds during the Second World War. Known as the 'peer review' system, its goal was to fund research on the basis of merit and of priorities determined by the granting agency. University-based investigators submitted research proposals, which were separated by the NIH according to subject area and referred to groups of non-federal scientists who were experts in each area – i.e. the peers of the proposers. After receiving ratings on their scientific merit from the review panels, the applications were reviewed a second time by the advisory councils for each institute. These bodies were comprised of physicians, scientists and laypersons, who considered the proposals from the perspective of each institute's mission, placing them in the context of nation-wide policy concerns about diseases and of the need for further research in selected areas. From the time an investigator submitted a proposal until the time funds were received, about eight or nine months elapsed, under normal circumstances. Grant monies were channelled to the principal investigators through the institutions with which they were affiliated.[7]

Studies of the peer review system began almost immediately after it was established. By 1976, some twenty-two studies had been conducted by congressional committees, by both Republican and Democratic administrations, by the scientific community and by NIH itself. Major issues discussed in these deliberations included conflict of interest, inability to provide adequate review in highly specialised areas, concern that the review groups were not representative of the current trends in science, fear of missing the unrecognised genius by funding only 'safe science', the volume of grants assigned to study section members and the burden for both applicants and reviewers imposed by new laws and regulations.[8] In the years just before AIDS was identified, the studies continued. Concerns about fairness, for example, surfaced in a 1977 appropriation hearing. A congressman queried NIH director Donald S. Fredrickson about allegations that the system was 'really an old boys' club' and that there was no 'provision for appeals'. Fredrickson noted that another committee had conducted yet another intensive review of the system and produced recommendations for establishing an appeals system and for reducing even further the possibility of cronyism or conflict of interest in awarding grants.[9]

Also of major concern in the late 1970s was the impact of economic forces on research funds awarded under the system. One measure of this was the increase in 'indirect costs' to support research. Indirect costs were defined as compensation to institutions for overhead expenses incurred in housing federally sponsored research. Heating and cooling, additional laboratory space and added maintenance costs fell into this category. The total cost of any grant represented the sum of direct and indirect costs. In 1947, when the first funds were awarded, indirect costs had been set at 8% of the direct costs of research. In 1955 Congress raised the indirect cost rate to 15% and by 1963, the rate had risen only to 16%.[10] Beginning with the oil crisis in 1974, however, indirect costs began to spiral upward, and by 1979 they had risen to 26.7%. The sharp increase in energy costs was the factor cited most frequently by recipient institutions as responsible for the increase. By the end of the 1970s, inflation had so increased the total cost of funding research that fewer grants could be supported. If the percentage of indirect costs for 1979 had been the same as the 1966 rate, for example, an additional $228 million would have been available in 1979 for research projects.[11]

During the years before AIDS was identified, the NIH grants system had become an elaborate, much-studied process designed to identify and support meritorious research through the judicious expenditure of taxpayer dollars. NIH and university administrators, Congress and biomedical scientists were most concerned with the impact of inflation on grants and with questions of accountability, fairness and scientific merit. Within this larger framework, as will be discussed below, the agency projected lines of research in annual plans and attempted to guide the course of research toward those health problems with which large segments of the public were concerned.

Managing the research enterprise: planning initiatives and targeted research

A second policy objective during the decade before AIDS was the refinement of existing policies to ensure progress in biomedicine toward specifically defined goals. In part, it was expressed through initiatives for planning programmes and for targeted research efforts. Both emerged after the grants programme had already functioned for more than a decade, and they represented a slight philosophical shift in management of the enterprise, which had been based on two major premises: (1) that biomedical science would advance best by allowing individual scientists to propose lines of research and to follow up serendipitous observations, and (2) that a substantial investment in basic laboratory research was the method most efficient in the long term for producing practical clinical applications.[12] By the 1970s, however, these concepts had been modified after extensive study by Congress and outside groups.

Reliance on individual initiative to guide research came into question in 1965 when a blue ribbon panel appointed by President Lyndon B. Johnson stipulated that one of the most important organisational needs of NIH was 'strengthening of its capacity for long-term planning'. The next year a congressional committee investigation of the Department of Health, Education and Welfare (DHEW) pointedly noted 'the lack of effective planning procedures' as the 'most glaring deficiency' observed.[13] These studies did not negate the importance of the individual initiative concept but rather reflected the growing size and complexity of the research enterprise. Furthermore, they coincided with the introduction by the Johnson administration of a new budgeting system, called Planning–Programming–Budgeting (PPB), which sought to integrate agency planning and budgeting for greater administrative control and efficiency.[14] In response, the NIH elevated the Office of Program Planning within the administration and instructed it to place emphasis on working with individual institutes in developing long-range plans.[15]

A decade later the Assistant Secretary for Health launched another planning initiative, articulated in the 1974 publication, *Forward Plan for Health*. In this document the DHEW detailed activities to be supported by all of its agencies, including the NIH, for the fiscal years 1976–80. By 1977 individual agencies published their own annual planning documents separately. At the NIH, two major goals of the process were to identify research that spanned categorical institute lines and thereby promote co-ordination of effort and to integrate the planning process with both the budget and the legislative processes during each year. This integrated approach produced plans that included as many different scientific opportunities as possible.[16]

Closely allied with the concept of planning for research was an increasing emphasis on targeting specific diseases for intensified research. This initiative challenged the premise that free-ranging scientific inquiry into fundamental biological questions was the most direct route to clinical applications. By the waning years of the Johnson administration, the President and research lobbyists were calling for results from the investment in a quarter-century of basic research. Noting in 1966, for example, that 'a great deal of basic research has been done', Johnson stated that 'the time has come to zero in on the targets by trying to get our knowledge fully applied'.[17] This trend was continued and escalated during the administration of Richard Nixon with enactment of the

National Cancer Act that launched a 'War on Cancer' and with subsequent initiatives against heart disease and stroke.[18] Between 1971 and 1975, in fact, Congress passed seventeen public laws directing NIH to emphasise research on particular areas, including sickle-cell anaemia, Cooley's anaemia, multiple sclerosis, sudden infant death syndrome, diabetes, arthritis, Huntington's disease and epilepsy.[19]

Although research on specific diseases was to be emphasised in these programmes, considerable leeway existed in deciding how best to attack each malady. Much targeted money was utilised in projects that had broad implications, such as studies of a possible link between cancer and viruses, research on the immune system and improved techniques in molecular biology. In the decade before AIDS was identified, NIH research plans noted the high priority given to studies in these basic fields.[20] Funds designated for cancer research, for example, were utilised in support of immunology and virology, fields that had proved fruitful in the 1970s and had implications for many different diseases. In 1977 the National Cancer Institute (NCI) provided 48% of the total NIH investment in immunology and 69% of NIH support in virology.[21]

The planning and targeted research efforts reflected Congress's concern with assuring steady progress toward defined goals. Both of these initiatives arose outside the NIH, and implementation strategies reflect the agency's efforts to comply with congressional mandates. Neither introduced radical restructuring within the NIH; indeed, both had the effect of refining policies and procedures toward what Congress perceived as a more effective implementation of the agency's mission. The plans sought to identify and foster promising areas of research that might otherwise be missed and to minimise duplication of effort. Targeted research programmes raised the visibility of particular diseases with which substantial segments of the public were concerned. In concert with the modifications in the grants process, these management imperatives reveal the NIH in the pre-AIDS era as a mature institution, whose policies and procedures were directed at fine-tuning a broadly accepted and widely supported mission.

Policy making on the frontiers of science: recombinant DNA

In addition to responding to broad areas of policy concern in the 1970s, NIH addressed a number of issues concerning the ethics of science. These included investigation of fraud and misconduct in research, the ethics of research on human subjects and regulation of recombinant DNA research. The last provides an excellent case study for examining the emergence of new scientific techniques and the politics of biomedicine in the years preceding AIDS.

In 1974, a group of eminent scientists called attention to the potential hazards of newly discovered recombinant DNA techniques.[22] Their announcement sparked debates over control of this powerful new biological tool. These occurred within a social climate sceptical of science. Discoveries in the 1960s about toxic side effects of antibiotics, the environmental dangers of chemical pesticides, carcinogens in food and the ethical dilemmas posed by manipulation of individuals in behavioural research had produced misgivings about the value and humanity of modern science and technology.[23]

In response to both scientific and lay concerns, the Secretary of the Department of Health, Education and Welfare chartered a Recombinant DNA Advisory Committee (RAC), headed by the director of intramural research at NIH and comprised of scientists and laypersons.[24] In February 1975 an international conference of molecular biologists convened at the Asilomar conference centre in California. Participants reached consensus about the appropriate levels of laboratory safeguards for experiments of differing potential risks and about the types of experiments that would be prohibited voluntarily until knowledge increased about the hazards or safety of the technology. Working from these findings, the RAC drafted guidelines that were promulgated in 1976.[25]

Some environmental activists complained that, in formulating the guidelines, the RAC had been dominated by 'technocratic' interests focused on safety alone to the exclusion of democratic debate on the ethics of recombinant experiments. A number of bills were introduced into Congress to legislate regulations for the research, but none was enacted. As the 1970s drew to a close, the highly vocal debate subsided, experience having demonstrated that biological disaster was unlikely. During the early 1980s, the controls were loosened, but the RAC was retained as a standing committee to evaluate research that broke new ground in recombinant DNA research.[26]

This case study illustrates several characteristics of federal biomedical research policy during the later 1970s. First, NIH leadership was expected by the larger biomedical community in dealing with such issues. Since recombinant DNA technology cut across disciplinary and geographic lines, no single professional scientific society could claim leadership, nor could any single institution. Second, the agency was implicitly charged by the scientific community with making the case for voluntary guidelines to Congress and thereby heading off legislative regulations that most scientists believed would be detrimental to research. Finally, in assuming leadership of the recombinant DNA discussions, the NIH had to respond to lay concerns about the potential social consequences of scientific decisions. The political benefits gleaned from lay participation in the RAC reinforced the wisdom of existing NIH practice to include lay members on major advisory committees.

Research and public health crises: Legionnaires' disease

The formulation of recombinant DNA guidelines raised broad questions about leadership and regulation in science. A second case study, focusing on the 1976

Victoria A. Harden and Dennis Rodrigues

Table 1. *NIH and CDC initial expenditures on AIDS and Legionnaires' disease (dollars in thousands)*

				AIDS			
				Fiscal year			
	82	83	84	85	86	87	88
CDC	2,050	6,202	13,750	33,298	62,152	136,007	304,942
NIH	3,355	21,668	44,121	63,737	134,667	260,907	430,570
				Legionnaires' disease			
				Fiscal year			
	76	77	78	79	80	81	82
CDC	162	1,533	1,931	2,047	1,521	1,647	1,115
NIH	—	—	—	622	1,266	1,635	1,027

Sources: Office of Financial Management, CDC; NIH Data Book 1990, US Dept. of Health and Human Services, Public Health Service, NIH.

outbreak of Legionnaires' disease, provides insight into the functioning of well-established federal protocols. It also provides perspective on the respective roles of the CDC and the NIH in addressing an extraordinary public health problem in the pre-AIDS period.[27]

As many authors have detailed, in 1976 at an American Legion convention in Philadelphia, Pennsylvania, a mysterious respiratory malady struck 182 Legionnaires or members of their families. Twenty-nine of them died. The microbial cause of this epidemic eluded identification for some months, during which questions were raised about the ability of biomedicine to respond to unknown pathogens. Eventually, however, CDC microbiologists identified a gram-negative bacterium as the etiological agent. This organism, *Legionella pneumophilia*, had long been known to microbiologists. What had been unknown was its affinity for growing in modern air handling systems, which distributed the pathogen through the air to unwary victims. Subsequent studies of stored sera revealed that this organism also had been the cause of previous unsolved respiratory epidemics.[28]

Research on Legionnaires' disease was initially conducted by the CDC and, after October 1979, also by the NIH. As the first line of defence against epidemic outbreaks, the CDC launched an epidemiological investigation and utilised standard laboratory methodology in searching for the etiological agent. Once *Legionella pneumophilia* had been identified, the agency researched the biology, immunology and pathogenic microbiology of the organism. It also instituted serologic and pneumonic surveillance and investigated rapid diagnostic techniques. Research sponsored by the NIH fell into four categories:

clarification of the etiologic niche, elucidation of the mode of transmission, delineation of the pathology through the development of animal models and characterisation of different stains and surface antigens in order to develop diagnostic tests and possible vaccines.[29]

Legionnaires' disease was reminiscent of classic epidemics in that it struck rapidly, with considerable mortality, then waned just as rapidly. As the figures in Table 1 show, research expenditures by the CDC rose rapidly, peaked and then levelled off as the disease was understood. Those by NIH started later, and rose to a level comparable with those of CDC. Within a year, Legionnaires' disease had reaffirmed the belief that infectious disease problems were understood and controllable within the existing medical and scientific paradigm. The very success, moreover, of the CDC in identifying the cause of Legionnaires' disease and in developing diagnostic and preventive methods against it may have strengthened the expectation that other new diseases, including AIDS, would be quickly resolved through existing techniques.

Placing the NIH response to AIDS in context

This brief examination of the two issues and two case studies offers some insight to the historical context in which the NIH responded to AIDS. Broadly speaking, the NIH mission in the post-Second World War era had been defined by Congress as research, especially on chronic diseases, for which few or no medical interventions were effective. Steady progress toward specific goals, accountability and fairness in awarding grants were issues of primary concern. The advent of AIDS brought stress to the carefully built biomedical research system when political advocates suggested that it should have been structured to permit a more rapid response to the deadly new disease.

AIDS came as a surprise to the medical community. It was not just an outbreak of a well-known pathogen or even a new organism within a well-understood family of pathogens. Since no previous transmissible agent had been known that killed by undermining the immune system, research aimed at understanding such an agent had not previously been conducted, nor had it been contemplated in structuring plans for future research. In this sense, the research planning process was useless. By proposing support for lines of research in fruitful areas, however, such as molecular immunology and retrovirology, the planning process had fostered the new production of knowledge that proved useful in understanding the new disease. The 1981 NIH research plan, for example, which was prepared during the spring of 1981, before publications about AIDS had appeared, highlighted as promising areas new immunologic techniques, such as recombinant DNA technology and hybridoma cell fusion, and studies on interferon and other biological response modifiers – all fields that were utilised in research on AIDS.[30]

Once AIDS was identified, moreover, it was rapidly incorporated in the planning process as a promising area for research support. The plan written in 1982 contained two items of note with regard to AIDS. In the National Institute of Allergy and Infectious Diseases section, the institute proposed to redirect some funds during fiscal year 1983 (which began in October 1982) for new initiatives 'in response to unusual or emerging new opportunities, including acquired and inherited immunologic disorders'. Since AIDS was the only known 'acquired' immunologic disorder, this notation reflects the institute's interest in the new disease. Similarly, in the NCI section, 'Kaposi's sarcoma in homosexual men and concurrent viral infections' was specified as one area to be emphasised. These comments not only reveal institute awareness of AIDS as a research problem but also underscore the difficulty of formulating focused research programmes in the absence of knowledge about the etiological agent.[31]

Perhaps the single issue most assailed by critics of the NIH response to AIDS was the length of time between identification of a new disease threat and the receipt of the first grant dollars by university researchers who wished to investigate it. In *AIDS in the Mind of America*, for example, Dennis Altman asserted: 'There were two major problems in funding AIDS research, the first being the question of how much money would be available, the second involving the very cumbersome process whereby that money was made available to researchers.'[32] As we have seen, however, the question of whether the grants system could or should be a vehicle for rapid distribution of funds in response to public health emergencies had not been considered in studies of the process.[33] Given the history of the system and its many modifications, it could be compared to a vast ship laboriously constructed over many years. Critics who complained that the system did not distribute funds rapidly were denouncing the ship because it could not fly.[34]

Further, the impact of indirect costs had taken a severe toll on the number of new grants that could be awarded and on the percentage of approved grants, both new and continuing, that could be funded. During the time that AIDS emerged, the NIH leadership struggled to maintain a minimum number of new awards that would be funded each year in order to prevent further erosion in the number of investigators pursuing federally sponsored research.[35] The constrained situation, which was exacerbated by the budget-cutting policies of Ronald Reagan's administration, compromised the agency's flexibility to initiate new activities, including research on AIDS. Operating in a 'zero sum game' meant that, in the absence of new appropriations, substantial amounts of research support for new initiatives could be generated only by reducing or eliminating existing programmes or by transferring funds from one agency to another.[36]

In August 1982, just over one year after the first paper identifying AIDS had appeared, the NCI issued its first request for investigators to submit grant applications relating specifically to AIDS.[37] This formal request was designed to bring into AIDS work those institutions that did not already participate in an NCI co-operative agreement, a funding mechanism similar to a grant, but one in which the awarding institute retained substantial programmatic involvement. Institutions already involved in co-operative agreements were eligible to apply for supplemental funds to inaugurate research on AIDS.[38] In addition, individual scientists could submit proposals relating to AIDS through the normal grants process, and recipients of grants whose work could be redirected towards AIDS were permitted to alter their projects if their home institutions agreed.[39] In April 1982 Bruce Chabner, director of NCI's Division of Cancer Treatment noted this flexibility in his testimony before California Representative Henry Waxman's Subcommittee on Health and the Environment during the first congressional hearing on AIDS: 'It is hard to account for the amount of money that they [NIH grantees] have invested through redirection of their grant support, but we feel it is considerable in view of the number of publications that have appeared.'[40]

Within the NIH intramural programme, flexibility to redirect research was considerably greater.[41] The first AIDS patient was treated in the NIH Clinical Center in June 1981, the same month that the initial publication about AIDS appeared.[42] During the ensuing year, a group of physicians and scientists redirected some or all of their research to explore the unusual disease and treat additional patients. One of them described the process: 'When we first started studying AIDS, just by word of mouth, there were a lot of people who wanted to look at various aspects [of the disease] . . . Very quickly we got a group of people . . . who didn't need an organized program because they all had a common interest.'[43] Another recalled that no one initially dropped existing projects to work on AIDS, 'they simply worked longer', into the evenings and on weekends.[44] In 1982 Robert C. Gallo, chief of the Laboratory of Tumor Cell Biology in the NCI, redirected his laboratory's research toward searching for the etiological agent after hearing evidence presented by James Curran, chief of the CDC's venereal disease branch, that AIDS was transmitted via blood and compromised the function of T-lymphocytes, white blood cells that were key components of the immune system. Curran's presentation suggested to Gallo that AIDS might be caused by an agent closely related to the retroviruses on which his laboratory was already working.[45]

These experiences of researchers in the intramural NIH programme reveals the existence of an informal network of investigators – inside and outside of government – in which information about AIDS was shared actively. In addition, internal correspondence files attest to official co-ordination and liaison efforts between agencies of the Public Health Service (PHS) within the Department of Health and Human Services (DHHS). In a memorandum dated 31 July 1981, for example, William H. Foege, director of the CDC, requested NCI co-operation in studying the 'outbreak' of Kaposi's sarcoma. Specifically, Foege asked that NCI augment the CDC's epidemiologic studies with therapy trials and with 'studies designed to define possible microbiologic, immunologic, and/or toxic roles in oncogenesis'. Vincent T. DeVita, Jr, director of NCI, referred the memo to Bruce Chabner, then acting director of NCI's Division of Cancer Treatment, asking Chabner to arrange for 'someone to join in'. Chabner responded by organising a national conference in September 1981 aimed at developing a 'coordinated strategy regarding the etiology and treatment of Kaposi's sarcoma'. In January 1982 Edward N. Brandt, Jr, the Assistant Secretary for Health in DHHS, officially requested 'greater participation' in AIDS investigation by NCI, the National Institute of Allergy and Infectious Diseases and the National Institute on Drug Abuse to supplement epidemiologic work by the CDC. The directors of each institute reported on activities underway, and on 3 March the CDC hosted a conference on AIDS for PHS scientists. Further liaison activities continued, including the formation in July 1982 of an NIH 'working group' that co-ordinated efforts among institutes and provided agency representation on AIDS matters.[46]

The 1970s emphasis on targeted research made AIDS a candidate for earmarked funds as soon as it was established that the disease was no ordinary epidemic outbreak that would be quickly controlled. Expenditures on AIDS rose dramatically during the first three years after the disease was identified, and continued their exponential climb for years thereafter. The only parallel to this striking growth in funds for a single disease was the sharp rise in cancer funds after enactment of the 1971 National Cancer Act. Comparing funding patterns for AIDS and Legionnaires' disease underscores the magnitude of the difference. Figure 1 compares the overall pattern of research funding for Legionnaires' and AIDS during the years after each was first identified. Although some authors have suggested that public and political sentiment compelled a larger research effort for Legionnaires' disease, our analysis shows that spending on AIDS outstripped Legionnaires' research in overall magnitude and in acceleration of spending over time. Furthermore, NIH funding for Legionnaires' began only after the etiologic agent was identified. In the case of AIDS, however, NIH provided more funds for research than did the CDC within the first full fiscal year after the disease was recognised – two years before a retrovirus was accepted as the etiological agent. The differences in funding patterns for these diseases reflect early recognition of the differences between the diseases themselves. Legionnaires' disease proved to be a transient and limited disease event in sharp contrast to AIDS' relentless exponential growth.

The experience of developing guidelines for recombinant DNA research also had an impact on NIH's AIDS policy. Although there were important differences between recombinant DNA and AIDS – the former, though worrying, posed a hypothetical problem while the latter involved actual death and suffering – both confronted the biomedical community with critical issues relating to the

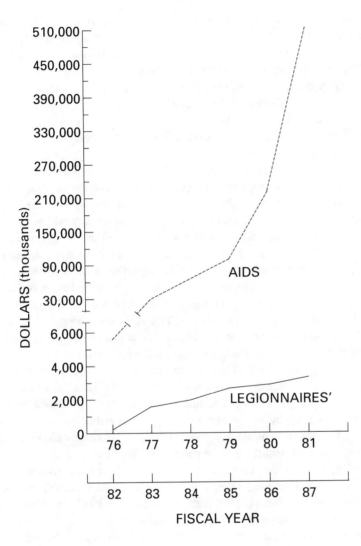

Figure 1   Initial PHS funding for AIDS and Legionnaires' disease

Sources: Office of Financial Management, CDC; NIH Data Book 1990, US Dept. of Health and Human Services, Public Health Service, NIH.

public health and welfare. The emergence of guidelines governing recombinant DNA research followed recognition of a theoretical but discernible risk. Response to AIDS was similar, once the magnitude of the risk had been ascertained. In 1980 and 1981, however, as unusual cases of what came to be known as AIDS were discussed between medical experts, the magnitude of the risk was not apparent. When epidemiological evidence mounted that it was a communicable disease with identifiable risk factors and that it was recognised in other countries as well as in the United States, both medical and lay communities mobilised to combat it.

Although it is impossible to pinpoint an exact moment when the enormity of this new disease became apparent, the evolution of phrases describing AIDS provides some clues. During the summer and autumn of 1981, the terms 'epidemic' – usually placed within quotation marks – and 'outbreak' were often used, sometimes in association with phrases such as 'dramatic increase'. By early 1982, the phrases 'accident of nature' or 'experiment of nature' appeared, indicating recognition of a problem that was larger than a limited 'outbreak'. During the next few months, however, the terminology escalated as appreciation increased about the scope of the disease and its lethal nature. In April 1982, Bruce Chabner of the NCI testified that AIDS was a 'new, complex, and very serious illness', which had become 'a public health problem of great magnitude'. At the same hearing, James Curran of the CDC suggested that known cases might be 'merely the tip of the iceberg', and that although the entire range of manifestations of the disease remained unclear, they were 'quite disturbing'. By mid-1982, epidemiological evidence had convinced many investigators that AIDS was caused not by an environmental agent but rather by an infectious pathogen, probably transmitted by blood as well as by sexual activity. This finding may well represent the turning point in medical understanding of AIDS because of its ominous implications. An environmentally caused disease might be limited geographically and/or controlled with existing public health methods, while an unknown, communicable pathogen would be much more difficult to identify, prevent and cure. Reflecting this realisation in his rhetoric, one investigator returning from a scientific meeting on AIDS in July 1982 strongly stressed the need for 'a most urgent response'.[47]

Internal NIH administrative structures for addressing AIDS also emerged parallel with funding increases as the scope of the disease became better understood. The NCI, concerned with the incidence of Kaposi's sarcoma, organised an informal 'working group' relating to AIDS in March 1982, four months before the agency-level group was established.[48] By 1985 all the NIH working groups had been consolidated and elevated into the NIH AIDS executive committee, and in 1987, the Secretary of the Department of Health and Human Services, chartered the AIDS Program Advisory Committee (APAC), with four of the thirteen appointed members designated as 'members of the general public'.[49] To strengthen internal co-ordination further, an NIH Office of AIDS Research was created the following year.[50] The careful attention by NIH to lay involvement in the APAC was doubtless reinforced by the recent experience of constituting the RAC, as well as by earlier precedents of lay representation on advisory councils. Conversely, the demands of AIDS activists to participate in such official bodies reflected their assumption that power should be shared in making some medical decisions, an attitude that was in part an outgrowth of the experience with recombinant DNA.

In a 1989 article, historian Charles Rosenberg described social reaction to an epidemic as occurring in a predictable pattern like the acts in a drama.[51] In act three pressure is generated for decisive and visible community response. In the past, such ritualist actions have included quarantines and religious fasting or prayer. Large congressional allocations for research and the establishment of visible bureaucratic structures may be seen as a similar response in our secular, scientifically oriented society. Viewed in this light, much of the stridency directed against the federal biomedical research enterprise had its origin in the need to propel such an appropriate community response. The few issues addressed in this paper, however, suggest that considerable flexibility existed in the federal biomedical research response to AIDS even before external criticism appeared. They also indicate that careful attention to historic medical, scientific and organisational forces is indeed necessary to understand how the biomedical research community formulated and implemented its response to the deadly disease.

NOTES

1 Gerald M. Oppenheimer, 'In the eye of the storm: the epidemiological construction of AIDS', in Elizabeth Fee and Daniel M. Fox (eds.), *AIDS: The Burdens of History* (Berkeley, 1988), 267–300; Daniel M. Fox, 'AIDS and the American health polity: the history and prospects of a crisis of authority', in Ronald Bayer, Daniel M. Fox and David P. Willis (eds.), 'AIDS: the public context of an epidemic', special issue, *Milbank Quarterly*, 64 (suppl. 1) (1986), 7–33; reprinted in Fee and Fox (eds.), *AIDS: The Burdens of History*, 316–43. See also Stephen P. Strickland, *Research and the Health of Americans: Improving the Policy Process* (Lexington, Mass., 1978).

2 'Introduction', in Bayer, Fox and Willis (eds.), 'AIDS: the public context of an epidemic', 3.

3 The NIH is the research arm of the Public Health Service in the US Department of Health and Human Services. This department was created in 1980 out of the health and welfare programmes of the former Department of Health, Education and Welfare.

4 The two precedents for federal support of medical research by non-federal scientists were the grants given for research on yellow fever by the National Board of Health between 1879 and 1883 and those given for research on venereal diseases by the

Interdepartmental Social Hygiene Board between 1918 and 1921. See Peter Bruton, 'The National Board of Health', PhD dissertation, University of Maryland, 1974; Wyndham D. Miles, 'A history of the National Board of Health, 1879–1893', 2 vols., manuscript, National Library of Medicine, 1970. Within its own laboratories, first called the Hygienic Laboratory and later renamed the National Institute of Health, the US Public Health Service and its predecessor agencies had sponsored research since 1887. See Victoria A. Harden, *Inventing the NIH: Federal Biomedical Research Policy, 1887–1937* (Baltimore, 1986). Standard references on the emergence of the post-Second World War NIH include James A. Shannon, 'The advancement of medical research: a twenty-year view of the role of the National Institutes of Health', *Journal of Medical Education*, 42 (1967), 97–108; Elizabeth Brenner Drew, 'The health syndicate: Washington's noble conspirators', *Atlantic Monthly*, 220 (December 1967), 75–82; Stephen P. Strickland, *Politics, Science, and Dread Disease: A Short History of U.S. Medical Research Policy* (Cambridge, Mass., 1972); G. Burroughs Mider, 'The federal impact on biomedical research', in John Z. Bowers and Elizabeth F. Purcell (eds.), *Advances in American Medicine: Essays at the Bicentennial*, 2 vols. (New York, 1976), II, 806–71; Donald S. Fredrickson, 'The National Institutes of Health yesterday, today, and tomorrow', *Public Health Reports*, 93 (1978), 642–7; Daniel M. Fox, 'The politics of the NIH extramural program, 1937–1950', *Journal of the History of Medicine and Allied Sciences*, 42 (1987), 447–66; Stephen P. Strickland, *The Story of the NIH Grants Program* (Lanham, Md., 1989).

5 Alvin M. Weinberg, 'In defense of science', *Studium Generale*, 23 (1970), 797–807; reprinted in *Science*, 169 (1970), 141–5. On republicanism and suspicion of patronage for any special group, see Daniel T. Rodgers,'Republicanism: the career of a concept', *Journal of American History* 79 (1992), 11–38.

6 One of the earliest examples of this is found in efforts to survey and map the US coast. See A. Hunter Dupree, *Science in the Federal Government: A History of Policies and Activities* (Cambridge, Mass., 1957; reprint Baltimore, 1986), 29–33. Dupree also noted that in the nineteenth century, Congress created most scientific agencies through the appropriations process in order that they could be controlled – and, if necessary, terminated – by the simple act of withholding funding. Indeed, the organic legislation authorising the existence of the federal laboratory that became the National Institutes of Health was buried in a 1901 sundry civil appropriations act. See *ibid.*, 214–15; Harden, *Inventing the NIH*, 17.

7 Catherine Henley, 'Peer review of research grant applications at the National Institutes of Health 1: the assignment and referral processes', *Federation Proceedings*, 36 (1977), 2066–8; *idem*, 'Peer review of research grant applications at the National Institutes of Health 2: review by an initial review group', *ibid.*, 2186–90; *idem*, 'Peer review of research grant applications at the National Institutes of Health 3: review by an advisory board council', *ibid.*, 2335–8. On political questions relating to the peer review system, see Don K. Price, 'Endless frontier or bureaucratic morass?', *Daedalus*, 107 (Spring 1978), 75–92.

8 Major studies of the NIH peer review system are summarised in 'Selected studies, investigations, and recommendations related to the National Institutes of Health: an annotated bibliography', in Appendix D, 'Selected staff papers', of US President's Biomedical Research Panel, *Report of the President's Biomedical Research Panel,*

30 April 1976, 4 appendices, 4 suppl. (Washington, DC, DHEW Publication Nos. (OS) 76–500 through 76–509, 1976), 1–32.

9 US Congress, House Committee on Appropriations, *Departments of Labor and Health, Education and Welfare Appropriations for 1978: Hearings before a Subcommittee of the Committee on Appropriations*, part 3, 'National Institutes of Health' (Washington, DC, 1977), 56–7.

10 The rate set in 1963 was 20% of 'allowable' direct costs, which, because of the accounting methods used, resulted in a net rate of about 16% of total direct costs. See Kenneth T. Brown, 'Indirect costs of federally supported research', *Science*, 212 (1981), 411–18.

11 Brown, 'Indirect costs of federally supported research'; *Report by the Comptroller General of the U.S.: Indirect Costs of Health Research. How They are Computed, What Actions are Needed* (Washington, DC, General Accounting Office Publication No. HRD–79–67, 1979), esp. 9–10; Saunders MacLane, 'Total reporting for scientific work', *Science*, 210 (1980), 158–63. Because indirect cost rates were negotiated with individual institutions and because accounting practices in calculating direct and indirect costs varied among institutions, these figures represent overall trends.

12 These concepts have been discussed in most historical studies of the NIH grants programme. See, for example, *The Nation's Medical Research*, vol. 5 of US President's Scientific Research Board, *Science and Public Policy: A Report to the President*, by John R. Steelman, 5 vols. (Washington, DC, 1947), esp. 9, 27; Strickland, *Politics, Science, and Dread Disease*, 174; Shannon, 'The advancement of medical research', 105.

13 US President's NIH Study Committee, *Biomedical Science and its Administration. A Study of the National Institutes of Health*, Report to the President (Washington, DC, 1965), 1; US Congress, House Committee on Interstate and Foreign Commerce, *Investigation of HEW*, Report of the Special Subcommittee on Investigation of the Department of Health, Education and Welfare, 89th Cong., 2nd sess., 13 October 1966, House Rept. No. 2266 (Washington, DC, 1966), 110.

14 There is a large literature on this programme. Two review papers with useful citations are W. Ken Fisher, Jr, 'PPBS in proper perspective', *Federal Accountant*, 21 (1972), 22–32; B. H. DeWoolfson, 'Federal PPB: A ten year perspective', *ibid.*, 24 (1975), 52–61. In 1971 strict adherence to PPB format was abandoned as a requirement for submission of agency budgets, although many agencies continued to utilise its planning and programme analysis features.

15 The NIH did not implement the recommendation of the President's NIH Study Committee (known as the Wooldridge Committee after its chairman, physicist Dean E. Wooldridge) that a policy and planning council be formed to assist the NIH director in formulating programmes. The NIH position was explained in 'The initial NIH commentary, biomedical science and its administration, the Wooldridge Committee Report', staff paper, April 1965, Office of the Director central files, NIH (hereafter cited as OD central files, NIH).

16 US Congress, House Committee on Appropriations, *Departments of Labor and Health, Education, and Welfare Appropriations for 1975: Hearings before a Subcommittee of the Committee on Appropriations*, part 3, 'Department of Health, Education, and Welfare' (Washington, DC, 1974), 2–3; *Forward Plan for Health,*

198   Victoria A. Harden and Dennis Rodrigues

FY 1976–80 (Washington, DC, 1974); US National Institutes of Health, *Forward Plan, FY 1979–83*, administrative document (Bethesda, 1977), copy in NIH Historical Office.

17 Johnson's remarks to medical and hospital leaders, 15 June 1966, quoted in *Research in the Service of Man: Biomedical Knowledge, Development, and Use*, proceedings of a conference sponsored by the subcommittee on government research (pursuant to S. Res. 218, 89th Cong.) and the Frontiers of Science Foundation of Oklahoma for the Committee on Government Operations, United States Senate, 24–7 October 1966 (Washington, DC, 1967), 5. See also Strickland, *Politics, Science, and Dread Disease*, chapters 9–10.

18 R. A. Rettig, *Cancer Crusade: The Story of the National Cancer Act of 1971* (Princeton, 1977); Natalie Davis Spingarn, *Heartbeat: The Politics of Health Research* (Washington, DC, 1976).

19 The specific initiatives with citations and appropriation amounts are listed in 'Congressional initiatives in biomedical and behavioral research', in Appendix D of *Report of the President's Biomedical Research Panel*, 36–8, 40.

20 See, for example, US National Institutes of Health, *Draft Research Plan, FY 1981–1983*, administrative document (Bethesda, 1979), copy in NIH Historical Office, 35–6.

21 *Ibid.*, 65. NCI also supported Robert C. Gallo's research in retrovirology during the 1970s. In 1979 Gallo announced his discovery of the first human retrovirus. See Robert Gallo, *Virus Hunting: AIDS, Cancer and the Human Retrovirus: A Story of Scientific Discovery* (New York, 1991), 99–115.

22 Stanley N. Cohen, Annie C. Y. Chang, Herbert W. Boyer and Robert B. Helling, 'Construction of biologically functional bacterial plasmids *in vitro*', *Proceedings of the National Academy of Sciences, U.S.A.*, 70 (1973), 3240–4. Paul Berg, David Baltimore, H. W. Boyer, Stanley N. Cohen, R. W. Davis, D. S. Hogness, D. Nathans, R. Roblin, J. D. Watson, S. Weissman and N. D. Zinder, 'Potential biohazards of recombinant DNA molecules', *ibid.*, 71 (1974), 2593–4. On the recombinant DNA controversy, see John Richards, *Recombinant DNA: Science, Ethics, and Politics* (New York, 1978); Nicholas Wade, *The Ultimate Experiment: Man-Made Evolution* (New York, 1977; rev. edn, 1979); David Archer and Stephen P. Stich, *The Recombinant DNA Debate* (Englewood Cliffs, NJ, 1979); Joan Morgan and W. J. Whelan (eds.), *Recombinant DNA and Genetic Experimentation* (New York, 1979); Sheldon Krimsky, *Genetic Alchemy: The Social History of the Recombinant DNA Controversy* (Cambridge, Mass., 1982). Initial research on recombinant DNA was supported by grants from the National Institute of Child Health and Human Development and the National Institute of General Medical Sciences.

23 On the anti-science movement, see Herbert Marcuse, 'The individual in the great society', in B. M. Gross (ed.), *A Great Society* (New York, 1968); Jacques Ellul, *The Technological Society* (New York, 1964); Theodor Roszak, *The Making of a Counter Culture* (New York, 1969); *idem*, *Where the Wasteland Ends* (Berkeley, 1972); Don K. Price, 'Purists and politicians', *Science*, 163 (1969), 25–31; Philip M. Boffey, 'AAAS convention: radicals harass the establishment', *Science*, 171 (1971), 47–9; Philip Handler, 'The federal government and the scientific community', *Science*, 171 (1971), 144–51; Harvey Brooks, 'Can science survive in the modern age?', *Science*, 174 (1971), 21–30.

24 Initially the committee was comprised primarily of experts on recombinant DNA technology, with few lay members, but, over the ensuing years, its composition changed to include a greater proportion of non-scientists.

25 Donald W. Fredrickson, 'Values and the advance of medical science', in *Integrity in Institutions: Humane Environments for Teaching, Inquiry, and Healing*, proceedings of a conference sponsored by the Association of Academic Health Centers, at the University of Texas Health Science Center, Houston, Texas, 25 May 1989 (in press), 18–23; quotation from 20. See also *idem, Decision of the Director, National Institutes of Health, to Release Guidelines for Research on Recombinant DNA Molecules* (Bethesda, Md., 1976); *idem*, 'A history of the recombinant DNA guidelines in the United States', in Morgan and Wheelan (eds.), *Recombinant DNA and Genetic Experimentation*, 151–60.

26 The guidelines were published in the *Federal Register*, 41, 131 (7 July 1976), part 2, 27902–943, and as National Institutes of Health, *Guidelines for Research Involving Recombinant DNA Molecules* (Bethesda, Md., 1976). For views of scientists on the guidelines, see, for example, Stanley N. Cohen, 'Recombinant DNA: fact and fiction', *Science*, 195 (1977), 654–7; for criticism, see David Dickson, *The New Politics of Science* (Chicago, 1984; 2nd edn, 1988), pp. 243–60; Wade, *Ultimate Experiment*, chapter 11. Principal regulatory bills were sponsored by Senator Edward M. Kennedy and Representative Paul G. Rogers. See Barbara J. Culliton, 'Recombinant DNA bills derailed: Congress still trying to pass a law', *Science*, 199 (1978), 274–7.

27 Before the Second World War, the NIH mission had included responding to epidemics of infectious diseases and monitoring incidence of mortality and morbidity. In the post-war era, as the federal health bureaucracy expanded, these responsibilities were assumed by the newly created Centers for Disease Control, whose initials, CDC, originally stood for Communicable Disease Center. See Elizabeth Etheridge, *Sentinel for Health: A History of the Centers for Disease Control* (Berkeley, 1992); Fitzhugh Mullan, *Plagues and Politics: The Story of the United States Public Health Service* (New York, 1989), 128–65.

28 Gary L. Lattimer and Richard A. Ormsbee, *Legionnaires' Disease* (New York, 1981), 1–8, quotation from 1. On the history of this epidemic, see also Gordon Thomas and Max Morgan-Witts, *Trauma: The Search for the Cause of Legionnaires' Disease* (London, 1981); *idem, Anatomy of an Epidemic* (Garden City, NY, 1982); Paul Clinton, comp., *Legionnaires' Disease: A Bibliography* (London, 1989). For an evaluation of the biomedical response to the epidemic, see also Barbara J. Culliton, 'Legion fever: postmortem on an investigation that failed', *Science*, 194 (1976), 1025–7; *idem*, 'Legion fever: "failed" investigation may be successful after all', *Science*, 195 (1977), 469–70.

29 Information on funding was supplied by the Financial Management Offices, CDC and NIH. Information on areas of NIH research, which included both intramural and extramural projects, was supplied by the Research Documentation Section, Information Systems Branch, Division of Research Grants, NIH.

30 US National Institutes of Health, *Draft Research Plan, FY 1984*, administrative document (Bethesda, 1982), copy in NIH Historical Office.

31 *Ibid.*, 66, 116.

32 Dennis Altman, *AIDS in the Mind of America* (Garden City, NY, 1986), 48.

33 The only report in which we have found concern about the speed of the process was a General Accounting Office study of grants made by the National Cancer Institute, which complained about 'significant delays' in the funding process. See US General Accounting Office, Comptroller General of the United States, *Administration of Contracts and Grants for Cancer Research, National Institutes of Health, Department of Health, Education, and Welfare B–164031(2)* (Washington, DC, 1971), 2–3. The National Cancer Act of 1971 (and later the National Heart, Blood Vessel, Lung, and Blood Act) authorised those institutes to award grants up to $35,000 without review by the institute advisory councils. These small grants, however, were not exempted, as the General Accounting Office report had recommended, from peer review by scientific panels.

34 In 1983 Representative Theodore S. Weiss of New York utilised the ship metaphor in a slightly different argument. He stated that 'persuading NIH to pay greater attention to the AIDS epidemic is like rerouting a luxury liner that takes ten miles to turn'. See US *Congressional Record*, House, 3 May 1983, 2587.

35 Donald S. Fredrickson, 'Communal resources, community responsibilities', *Clinical Research*, 29 (1981), 239–47.

36 Donald S. Fredrickson, 'Biomedical research in the 1980s', *New England Journal of Medicine*, 304 (1981), 509–17.

37 National Cancer Institute, 'Request for cooperative agreement applications: RFA NIH–NCI–DCT–CTRP–82–13. Studies of AIDS (Kaposi's sarcoma and opportunistic infections)', *NIH Guide for Grants and Contracts*, 11, 9 (13 August 1982), 3–7.

38 William D. DeWys to Michael A. Friedman, 18 November 1981, file 'Kaposi's sarcoma', Division of Cancer Treatment, National Cancer Institute, Bethesda, Maryland (hereafter cited as DCT, NCI).

39 US Public Health Service, *Grants Policy Statement* (Washington, DC, DHEW Publication No. (OS) 77–50,000 (Rev.), 1 October 1976), 36. Grantees must discuss changes in the scope of their research with their home institution, which receives and distributes NIH grant funds. This provision in grants policy provides one of the essential differences between the grant and the contract instruments for funding research.

40 US Congress, House Committee on Energy and Commerce, Subcommittee on Health and Environment, *Kaposi's Sarcoma and Related Opportunistic Infections: Hearing before the Subcommittee on Health and the Environment of the Committee on Energy and Commerce*, 97th Cong., 2nd sess., 13 April 1982 (Washington, DC: Government Printing Office (Serial No. 97–125), 1982), 32. In preparing for the testimony, Chabner's office had identified twenty-seven existing grants and contracts 'with some applicability to the subject' of Kaposi's sarcoma and estimated that $433,000 of the 1981 funding for these projects might be utilised in studying the new disease. See 'National Cancer Institute, Kaposi's sarcoma', table with attachments, 6 Apr. 1982, file 'Kaposi's sarcoma', DCT, NCI.

41 Intramural investigators do not have to apply for grant funds to support their research. Their work is reviewed by their administrative superiors and, periodically, by each institute's board of scientific counsellors, comprised of non-federal scientists who are experts in fields supported by the institute. Within this structure

and within the limitations of budgets, intramural scientists can redirect their research at any time if they believe a new direction is more promising.

42 Victoria A. Harden and Dennis Rodrigues, interview with Thomas Waldmann, 14 March 1990, Bethesda, Maryland, copy in NIH Historical Office. Dr Waldmann was the admitting physician for this patient.

43 Victoria A. Harden and Dennis Rodrigues, interview with Henry Masur, 22 November 1989, Bethesda, Maryland, copy in NIH Historical Office.

44 Victoria A. Harden and Dennis Rodrigues, interview with Robert B. Nussenblatt, 25 April 1990, Bethesda, Maryland, copy in NIH Historical Office.

45 Gallo, *Virus Hunting*, 134–5. Gallo's account of his decision to investigate AIDS is representative of the approach taken by many scientists. Most investigators, whether on the staff of the intramural programme on the Bethesda campus or supported by grants at universities, were committed to particular research projects on a long-term basis. Seeing the research through to its conclusion and publishing experimental findings were prerequisites for continued funding and for status among scientific peers. A serendipitous finding could lead research projects in new directions, but most investigators were wary of jumping from topic to topic. A decision to redirect research towards AIDS was usually made only after it became clear that a laboratory's existing expertise could be utilised to illuminate some aspect of the disease. See comments on this in Alan N. Schechter, 'Basic research related to AIDS', in Victoria A. Harden and Guenter B. Risse (eds.), *AIDS and the Historian: Proceedings of a Conference at the National Institutes of Health 20–21 March 1989* (Washington, DC, NIH Publication No. 91–1584, 1991), 45–50.

46 William H. Foege to Vincent T. DeVita, Jr, memorandum re 'Kaposi's sarcoma and opportunistic infections', 30 July 1981; DeVita to Bruce Chabner, n.d., handwritten note on same memorandum; Chabner to Foege, memorandum re 'Kaposi's sarcoma conference', 6 August 1981; Vincent T. DeVita, Jr, to Edward N. Brandt, Jr, memorandum re 'Current work on Kaposi's sarcoma', 18 February 1982; William H. Foege to Bruce A. Chabner, 23 February 1982, all in file 'Kaposi's sarcoma', DCT, NCI; Edward N. Brandt, Jr, to Vincent DeVita, Richard Krause and William Pollin, memorandum re 'Kaposi's sarcoma', 7 January 1982; Richard M. Krause to Edward N. Brandt, Jr, 15 January 1982; James B. Wyngaarden to BID Directors, memorandum re 'Working group on epidemic of acquired immunosuppression, opportunistic infections, and Kaposi's sarcoma', 13 July 1982, all in file 'Kaposi's sarcoma, January 1982', Intramural Research 5–15, OD central files, NIH.

47 The words 'epidemic' and 'outbreak' are found in numerous early documents; Chabner and Curran testimony from the April 1982 hearing on *Kaposi's Sarcoma and Related Opportunistic Infections* (see n. 40), 34, 10; Arthur S. Levine to Vincent T. DeVita, Jr, memorandum re 'Update on the epidemic of acquired immuno-deficiency sarcoma-opportunistic infection', 2 July 1982, file 'Kaposi's sarcoma, July 1982', Intramural Research 5–15, OD central files, NIH.

48 Associate Director for Field Studies and Statistics, DCCP, NCI to William Blattner, Mark Greene, James Goedert, Robert Biggar, Dean Mann, Robert Hoover and Deborah Winn, memorandum re 'Epidemiology working group on Kaposi [*sic*] sarcoma', 8 March 1982, file 'Intramural research 5–15, March 1982', OD central files, NIH.

49 Documentation of the creation of the NIH AIDS executive committee is in Director, NIH to Acting Assistant Secretary for Health, memorandum re 'NIH coordination of AIDS research', 15 October 1985, file 'Intramural research 5–15, October 1985', OD central files, NIH. On creation of the APAC, see Otis R. Bowen, 'Formal determination', 21 August 1987; 'Charter, acquired immunodeficiency syndrome program advisory committee', 21 August 1987; and 'Amendment to the charter of the acquired immunodeficiency syndrome program advisory committee', 23 November 1987, copies in files of the NIH Office of AIDS Research.

50 Statutory authorisation for the NIH Office of AIDS Research is in the Omnibus Health Bill, PL 100–607, 4 November 1988, US *Statutes at Large*, vol. 102, 3076.

51 Charles E. Rosenberg, 'What is an epidemic? AIDS in historical perspective', in 'Living with AIDS', special issue, *Daedalus*, 118 (Spring 1989), 1–17.

10

The NHS responds to HIV/AIDS

EWAN FERLIE

Introduction[1]

The unexpected and sudden emergence of the HIV/AIDS epidemic in Britain in the 1980s – as in other countries – posed difficult issues for individuals, pressure groups and social movements, health care organisations, and the national political and policy process alike. This experience has to be captured quickly if memories are not to erode and while accounts are beginning to emerge of the governmental and ministerial process,[2] of the formation of policy 'communities' and lobbies acting on formal policy making;[3] and the role of professional experts[4] in influencing the formation of national policy, there is still work to be done on the response by District Health Authorities which represent the operational tier of the National Health Service (NHS) although we can build on an earlier analysis of a single case in a high prevalence locality.[5] Some American work has examined the organisational response in particular localities[6] suggesting interesting local sources of variation. But we need to know more about how British health care organisations responded to an unanticipated epidemic – and new epidemics have been rare in First World health care systems – which has had such important societal consequences.

HIV can be seen as a single health care issue but one which was processed within a particular organisational form (District Health Authorities (DHAs)) which span a multiplicity of issues, involve a wide variety of interest groups, contain a strong political component and also a range of powerful professional groups. Some political theorists have questioned the ability of any single issue to retain profile within such political settings,[7] so the politics of neglect may characterise the handling of the HIV issue – particularly in its later stages – as much as the politics of attention. The two hundred or so District Health Authorities were created as fully independent authorities only in 1982, but all have their own personalities, and (as we shall see) central guidance often exerts only a limited influence on what is decided in particular localities. Decision making is often diffuse in as much as a variety of internal interest groups lobby and form coalitions, but often external influence is weaker, especially in teaching Districts where clinicians and clinical academics exert most power. The power structure is best described as one of 'bounded pluralism'. From April 1991 the role of the DHA began to undergo major changes as White Paper reforms providing for a 'managed market' were progressively introduced and the split between the new purchaser and provider roles started to intensify.

Between 1982 and 1991, therefore, the District Health Authority (and its affiliated Units) represented the key operational tier of the NHS responding to the HIV issue, yet we know little about the nature of this response. DHAs were of course themselves changing and restructuring in the 1980s as the pull of the new Thatcherite political economy became evident, most notably with the introduction of general management in 1984/5. By the end of the decade, the general managerial cadre was – at least in some localities and some issues – able to act as a countervailing force against the professional blocs. The HIV/AIDS issue can also be used as a tracer to explore more general theories of innovation in health care organisations. HIV/AIDS may force the question of change: effective organisational and managerial responses to such a complex and uncertain issue might be thought to be very different from the incrementalist or steady state responses which have previously characterised health care management.[8]

The methodology used is one of longitudinal, comparative, case studies, stretching back now for almost a decade but often with more distant pre-histories (such as the prior response to hepatitis B in the locality) to consider as well. The knowledge base for such longitudinal case study work draws both on contemporary history and the sociology of organisations, and thus both has to develop a history which is interpretive as well as chronological, and which can present a plurality of accounts from different viewpoints, and a sociology which is empirically grounded, inductive and sensitive to the impact of time, rather than concerned to build high level theory. Initial analysis has concentrated on individual case studies,[9] but there is now the opportunity to move on to comparative case study work, where patterns may begin to emerge in the data.

The first section of the paper therefore reviews some of the broader literature which will be considered. The second section describes in more detail the methodology and the data base, while in the third section some patterns across the case studies are considered. The fourth section explores questions of role creation and organisational design, and the paper concludes by summarising the analytic themes identified and speculating about possible developments in the 1990s.

Some organisational and managerial aspects to the HIV/AIDS epidemic

In this section some organisational and managerial literature is reviewed in order to identify a perspective with which to interrogate the case study material.

The problem of strategic service change in the NHS

The problem of ensuring rapid change in complex health care systems is of course a general one, but one which applies with particular force to the conditions of urgency created by the emergence of a new epidemic. The wider literature on organisational change in the NHS highlights the obstacles of effecting strategic change and the frequency of implementation failure so that policies which are agreed in principle are often not put into practice.[10] Often health care systems have been seen as exhibiting 'institutional paralysis', so that any coalition for change is likely to be insufficiently powerful to reconfigure services and will be unable to switch resources away from dominant groupings.[11] 'Implementation deficits' within the NHS increasingly emerged as a research and policy problem for the centre in the 1980s, as national policies for change (for example in mental illness services) were not reflected in change at local level. Nowhere were the pressures towards institutional inertia more acute than in dense metropolitan settings such as Inner London (which is precisely where HIV/AIDS first emerged as an issue) and where managerial agendas were retrenchment led rather than centred on service development.

A further question relates to the leadership of change in such a fragmented system. It is not obvious who are the champions of change, and four potential and alternative bases should be considered. The first scenario is that the push for service development could come from social movements such as gay organisations, either by lobbying and influencing the response of the public statutory sector, or by constructing a lively and vigorous non-statutory sector to which workload might be contracted out.[12]

A second potential basis could be the appointed members on DHAs. While there is a controversy about the extent to which such members who are formally expected to perform a policy making role in the localities in effect act as no more than 'rubber stamps', some writers argue that they can exert an influence either through setting boundaries and local rules of the game[13] or more proactively, especially through proposals coming from a small but influential subgroup of member 'strategists'.[14]

A third potential basis of leadership could be general management. Indeed part of the Thatcherite political economy of health care has consisted of the attempt to create a clearer managerial focus for driving through change. However, the agendas of the new cadre of general managers appointed in 1984/5 in practice seem to have revolved around financial control, rather than managing strategic service change or organisational development, both of which represent possible alternative constructions of their early brief.[15]

Fourthly, clinicians might emerge as 'product champions' of service innovation, which is a concept which has been used both in studies of industrial innovation[16] and health care innovation.[17] Some of the personal characteristics of the effective product champion have been outlined as follows: a risk taker; a willingness to use all informal as well as formal channels to promote the cause; drive and energy (perhaps to the point of obsessionality).[18] But the social role and the power position of the product champion was also found to be of importance. There may be an interesting further distinction between a 'product champion' whose enthusiasm may be needed to get an idea off the ground and an 'organisational champion' who will be able to work the wider organisation diplomatically.[19] The whole product championing literature draws attention to the importance of people within organisations, and the need for an internal push from particular individuals if rapid service development is to take place.

The role of crisis: its construction, management and aftermath

The naive view that 'necessity is the mother of invention' and that high caseload would force the HIV/AIDS issue up agendas is not confirmed by a comparison of the response in New York and San Francisco, where HIV/AIDS attracted less governmental attention in New York despite (at least initially) a higher caseload.[20] The balance of local political and organisational forces and the way in which issues are received into pre-existing networks may then be important mediating factors, but the degree to which the new issue is accorded 'crisis' status may also play a crucial role.

The theme of crisis management has traditionally provided a rich seam for organisation theorists to mine and the managerial processing of strategic issues may be different in crisis and non-crisis situations.[21] Certainly between 1983 and late 1986–7, HIV/AIDS quickly emerged nationally in the UK as a high profile health issue to a point where it was often labelled as a 'crisis': the early epidemiology was taken as indicating that the UK was only four or so years behind America; an unparalleled national health education programme was launched; and there was high media interest. The HIV/AIDS issue acquired many of the characteristics of a crisis as used by Dutton (importance, immediacy and uncertainty): indeed, it was often said that there had been nothing like it in health care since the Second World War.

Here was a crisis which contained both real and constructed elements but, as predicted, maintenance of the HIV issue on a national policy agenda was to prove more problematic than creation.[22] Issue succession took place and by 1989 the focus of attention had moved on to the health care White Paper. Some have even suggested that the natural history of public policy issues is from crisis to complacency.[23]

How might the perception of HIV as a potential crisis affect the response from health care organisations? Much of the existing literature on organisational crisis[24] stresses the pathological consequences for organisations of the emergence of crisis-as-threat: increased centralisation and formalisation, with a breakdown in integrating structures; the erosion of information channels; the exiting of key human resources; a loss of trust and loyalty as a low commitment organisation emerges; the emergence of groupthink and scapegoating at a small group level. Crisis is here seen as making the creativity and flexibility needed even less likely to occur.

There is, however, a less considered counter scenario of crisis-as-opportunity.[25] Major change can only take place when the perception of a crisis forces an awkward issue up crowded agendas. The construction of crisis-as-opportunity by a band of early learners may lead to very different patterns of behaviour from that envisaged in the earlier model: continuing pressure from pioneers; the formation of special groups who reach out to the rest of the organisation; high energy and commitment levels; strong integration and cohesion within the newly emergent group. Even in this more optimistic scenario, however, there remains the problem of how to manage the post-crisis aftermath perhaps as disillusion or burn out sets in. Tracing through the response by DHAs to the HIV/AIDS issue provides an opportunity to develop some of the literature on the management of crisis within a health care setting.

HIV/AIDS – a naturally occurring opportunity for organisational design and development

The perception that the NHS has remained in many ways a frustratingly under-developed organisation created in some localities an alternative general managerial agenda throughout the service: the creation of greater autonomy and flexibility in organisational design.[26] Certainly this had resonance in the localities: in one of the case study districts, the District General Manager wrote: 'it was recognised from an early stage that one of the key management challenges was not just to implement change, but to develop the organisation's capacity to cope with change. The aim, in a sense, was to create a different kind of organisation, capable of learning, responding to and even generating change, rather than simply reacting to it.'[27] We see here a more global attempt in the 1980s to create a new form of 'learning' NHS which would have a much better developed capacity to change. Such an organisation might look very different from the old highly rule-bound decision making structures and emphasise more fluid forms of decision making, such as task forces or *ad hoc* groups. HIV/AIDS can be used as a tracer issue to assess the extent to which this broader agenda was actually operationalised.

This is because these general arguments for organisational design and development were highly applicable in the rapidly emerging HIV/AIDS issue where there was a requirement for speedy action; strategic planning was taking place under conditions of gross uncertainty; and there was a premium on much better

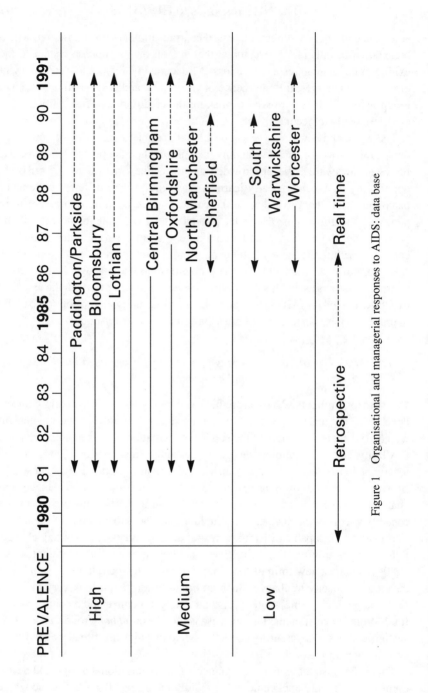

Figure 1   Organisational and managerial responses to AIDS: data base

forms of lateral communication as a host of very different specialties which had historically never had contact found themselves unexpectedly going to the same meetings (for example, sexually transmitted diseases (STDs) and dentistry). Moreover, the emergence of earmarked resources provided a windfall which could be used to accelerate such processes of service development. But while windfall growth can promote the politics of extraordinary change, new interest groups may quickly emerge into a dominant coalition to capture the new resources, excluding constituencies which emerged just that little bit later.[28] This points to the critical importance of very early choices in designing machinery to process the new HIV/AIDS issue and the retaining of control over the new resources.

Case studies and approach

The basic methodology adopted is that of the comparative, longitudinal, case study. Figure 1 describes the nine case studies which are being considered in this analysis.

As the key questions were essentially historical, processual and related to the meanings which actors attributed to their actions, qualitative methodology was indicated. Methods included: interviews with a wide range of stakeholders in each of the systems (forty to fifty per case); attendance at meetings; and examination of archival material (both formal minutes, informal memos and ephemera). Typically an intensive period of analysis (say five months) would be followed up by more limited monitoring over time. By use of these methods the aim is to produce research on organisations which move beyond the ahistorical, aprocessual and acontextual limitations of previous work, but which can engage with micro organisational processes through time.[29]

An interesting methodological question concerns the relationship between the perspectives of history and of organisation theory. While some branches of organisational theory (such as the contingency theoretic approach popular in the 1960s and 1970s) are indeed ahistorical, other methodologies are far more sensitive to the importance of history in shaping organisational power structures, attitudes and assumptions. Sometimes the skills of an historian have not always been apparent within these analyses but there are now some important and interesting exceptions. For example, Chandler's[30] analysis is essentially a business history of the rise of the modern corporation as an institutional form and of management as a social grouping. For contemporary historians the understanding of institutions which so dominate decision making processes in modern societies might also be thought to be important. In the 1980s there has been if anything a growing move within organisation theory towards more processual and historical perspectives (for example Pettigrew's study of strategic change processes in ICI).[31] The life cycle and organisational transitions approaches to the study of organisations indeed explicitly organise themselves around the passage of time.[32]

At the same time sociology continues to influence even those branches of organisation theory which are sympathetic to historically informed analysis. As a result there is a greater emphasis on the building and testing of formal theoretical models than in many purely historical accounts. However, as in many historical accounts (narrative history excluded), the pluralist nature of reality is acknowledged and competing interpretations of the past presented. There are thus areas of overlap and continuity of interest between the disciplines. The potential for a fruitful dialogue between history and organisation theory is now apparent.

The pattern of service development in the 1980s

What observations can be made from reviewing these nine case studies?

Local variation in service development

The first relates to the substantial variation apparent at local level in the development of service strategies: the localities did not mechanistically replicate national guidelines. Although health services are formally organised within a National Health Service designed to promote territorial equity, the higher tiers played an indirect and facilitative role – especially through the provision of financial incentives – and the periphery (especially the big inner city DHAs) retained much of the initiative. Thus neighbouring authorities or even particular hospitals within the same authority exhibited quite different responses.

Most obviously this is because the local epidemiology (and perception of it) varies: the bulk of the caseload has fallen upon perhaps twenty mainly inner city DHAs, while most districts still report very low caseloads. One analysis of different case studies suggests that this metropolitan/regional divide may be crucial, distinguishing between two types of response.[33] The first pattern is metropolitan hospital-based, perhaps professionally dominated with an emphasis on disease prevention through control of infection and laboratory measures such as blood screening. The treatment model was based on open access genito-urinary medicine (GUM) clinics with in patient care in specialist units. The second community-based model was characterised by multi-sectoral networks, involving or even led by the voluntary sector. There was an emphasis on health education. Care was provided where possible in community settings with the emphasis on support groups.

But the present case studies indicate that differences in the pattern of development are even more finely grained than this two-category model. While clinical 'product champions' emerged in all three of the high prevalence districts, they were drawn from very different backgrounds (immunology, infectious diseases, public health) and included clinical academics as well as service clinicians. In addition the nature of the developing service system has clearly been affected by the local environment and by local antecedent conditions. Responses are thus not only issue-based, but are shaped by the wider histories of the host systems into which this new issue is received. Local political cultures were also important: the context was perhaps more receptive in Inner London (where the gay social movement was best developed), while some of the councils in the regional centres showed greater nervousness about dealing with issues related to sexuality, and the Scottish political culture complicated efforts to develop services for drug injectors.

There were some other sources of local variation. Hospitals under long-term threat of closure have sometimes diversified into HIV/AIDS more readily than those whose future was secure. Teaching hospitals offer an important 'supply side' motor of service development, with clinical academics able and anxious to develop research into new diseases. The recent experience of other epidemics (hepatitis B, tuberculosis), or a local infection control tradition represented other examples of how the past could affect patterns of development.[34]

A good example of how antecedent conditions affected responses can be drawn from St Mary's, Paddington, London, which was one of the very first hospitals to respond clinically: not only was there a need in the local population, but the existence of an infection control tradition and facility, the formation of a prior research group around hepatitis B, and the international networks of clinical academics which could be used to access the earlier American experience all helped to provide local clues in advance of the issue being constructed nationally.

Finally, in the face of loose top down guidance localities quickly built up service systems around early product champions and centres of activity. There is organisational process as well as structure. Who emerged in the earliest days to raise consciousness around the issue was found to vary widely across the Districts, and some product champions were much more powerful than others. Under these circumstances, organisational histories soon diverged as virtuous and vicious circles built up. An issue quickly attracts a history, a label and an image, and becomes seen as either a good or a bad service to be associated with.

The dominant role of health care agencies

We can, however, advance some tentative generalisations on the basis of the early case study evidence. The first is that the prime focus at operational level has generally been the District Health Authority (or its Units) – given its control over key resource flows – and that therefore it is here that we should look if we want to understand how the key service development decisions in the localities have been made.

Certainly lobbying from social movements (rapidly organising from 1984/5 within voluntary groups such as the Terrence Higgins Trust) managed to achieve influence at departmental level and at field level, at least in London (especially over non-resource issues such as ward regime and counselling). But their influence wilted in the middle of the hierarchy, and there was little evidence that voluntary groups were integrated into district planning and policy machinery nor was there large-scale contracting out to the voluntary sector. Outside Inner London, the nervousness of some local authority councils on gay issues given restrictive national guidance could force DHAs to choose priorities for the development of links. There were some examples of statutory facilities (such as phonelines) being set up in competition with voluntary provision. Links between HIV/AIDS projects and education departments were also made more difficult by local authority loss of nerve over sex education following new legislation which increased the power of Boards of Governors. This sometimes made it more difficult for special HIV projects to gain access to schools.

Another potential lead at local level were local authority social services departments, but these agencies generally came on stream later than DHAs, reflecting the lag in special national funding mechanisms, and lacked the powerful product champions found in DHAs. In the absence of a specific budget, joint care planning around HIV/AIDS between health and social care agencies often remained at the useful but limited information exchange level, rather than moving on to the formation of joint strategy.

The stance of the higher tiers (Regions and the Department) during the early years of the epidemic can be broadly seen as facilitative, supplying resources which could enable bottom up developments from the Districts to happen given fairly broad policy guidelines. As the HIV issue matured, however, and as flows of resources escalated, this picture began to change. There was also increasing pressure from the centre to monitor the spend by Districts. While the pace of regional development varied (North West Thames was often seen as the 'lead region' on HIV/AIDS), regional 'offices', procedures and strategies were also emerging elsewhere by 1988/9, beginning to place constraints around Districts' freedom of manoeuvre. Regions often adopted policies to 'spread the workload', although implementation was patchy.

Crisis, crisis management and its aftermath

The notion of 'crisis' provides a useful construct which must itself be deconstructed. While every DHA experienced the national 'crisis' constructed around HIV/AIDS in 1986/7, local 'crises' varied in length and intensity, according to perceptions of local caseload and skill in crisis construction. Once the national stimulus had been removed, it could be difficult to keep the HIV/AIDS issue going in low prevalence districts, but in 1986/7 mobilisation of the national crisis could generate funding even in areas of low prevalence. Local perceptions of crisis did not always emerge: in one low prevalence district studied, the early response did not emerge from a 'crisis' at all (cases had not yet emerged), but a gradual process of people becoming aware of HIV/AIDS as an issue, and thereafter reflecting on how it might impact on their professional roles.

Despite this variation in most Districts there was a perception that HIV/AIDS posed urgent, immediate and uncertain issues that amounted to a label of 'crisis'. It is useful to distinguish between the initial, medium-term and long-term effects of organisational crisis. In many Districts, there was evidence of an initial short-term crisis driven by the arrival of patients which was associated with pathological reactions from the organisation. There is a link here to Goffman's (1963) work on stigma, where it is suggested that interactions with stigmatised patients may be characterised by withdrawal and irrational beliefs about the dangers posed by the stigmatised person. Crisis construction and a focus on 'infection' may of course have negative implications for quality of the treatment and care of those already infected.

Local control of infection crises blew up in the early days, often characterised by rumour, staff anxiety and even panic. These were routed to clinical control of infection fora which were largely independent of management. In Paddington, for example, the AIDS/HIV issue was received into the organisation as a control of infection issue.[35]

In the Scottish Board studied, an epidemiological crisis arose when a virologist who was practising using the new HTLV-3 test examined stored bloods from drug users: quite unexpectedly 38% tested positive.[36]

In the medium term experience of local crisis seemed on the whole to have had energising and creative effects in the Districts. An extraordinary outburst of energy, enthusiasm and activity took place as high commitment groups began to emerge. In one medium prevalence regional centre an energetic special team arose as the centrepiece of the DHA's response, linking into a wide variety of DHA and external agencies as 'change agents'.

By 1989, however, it was possible to take a longer term and less rosy view on the aftermath of crisis. Crisis-based structures were clearly vulnerable when early projections had to be revised downwards: had the HIV/AIDS lobby been crying wolf all along? Even services which had developed rapidly now faced a less benign climate.[37] Staff burn out was another problem in these centres of high activity, as exceptionally high activity levels could not always be sustained.[38]

Thus by 1989 it was clear that a number of early innovators were withdrawing from the field as a result of burn out, and that a new generation might be needed for the 1990s. The HIV/AIDS issue still poses questions of how to manage continuing rather than episodic change. While the first wave of the epidemic around gay men in the mid-1980s aroused a high level of energy, this may prove difficult to sustain in the 1990s when there may be a further requirement to develop service systems for drug users and women and children.

From innovation to institutionalisation

A transition from birth and early development on the one hand to maturity and institutionalisation on the other may be particularly difficult for innovative organisations, as the institutionalisation stage involves removing the freedom of manoeuvre, space for entrepreneurial activity and creativity which were welcomed in the organisation's infancy, and which became part of the organisation's self-image and ideology.[39]

Initially innovation had often taken place by delegation down to self-starters who had been selected on the basis of their potential. These innovations were thus developed and managed in a highly unusual fashion.[40]

Yet in a number of districts 1988/9 was seen as a difficult period of transition from these crisis-based early years to a period of 'normalisation', in which the projects which had emerged were to be more closely tied to mainstream machinery. A number of first stage 'innovators' got out of HIV/AIDS and into still newer growth points; staff became increasingly aware of their inability constantly to expand their brief and even started to be labelled as 'veterans'; more managerial capacity arose to complement much of the clinically based early response; and formal 'offices' and structures emerged to place boundaries around action. The transition is essentially a Weberian one from the personal to the impersonal, and from the charismatic to the bureaucratic.[41]

Yet given the need for continuous rather than episodic change, such normalisation and institutionalisation may be premature. HIV services may instead need the ability to cope with continuing change over a much longer timescale. It will be interesting to see how many of the original service developers are driven out by the new more rule bound order.

Strategy formulation and implementation

The development of strategies for HIV/AIDS has severely tested the planning and management capacity of DHAs as responding to such a complex and uncertain issue requires the development of methodologies very different from formal long-range corporate planning. At the very least, uncertainty has to be scripted in rather than scripted out; different scenarios considered; and as much flexibility as possible retained.[42]

Strategy was an important issue for many Districts in their attempt to structure the gross uncertainty which they faced, but there was much variation: some had produced formal documents (which were not always embedded in organisational behaviour); in others the uncodified but purposeful behaviour of small groups represented the real strategy. While there were attempts to create special machinery, the construction of a capacity to think strategically and retain strategic flexibility was more elusive. An unfortunate consequence of the special allocation was a tendency to plan for the annual round, with little 'visioning' of what the future might look like.

Using Mintzberg's[43] framework, strategy can be seen as containing both emergent and purposeful elements and we should not assume that strategy always proceeds in a rational-analytic manner but can also be seen as consistency in a stream of decisions through time. In many cases 'strategy' can bless actions which have already emerged as a retrospective labelling of activity. But there were also decision points (such as the construction of the first bid for resources) where the quality of the forward look could have important long-term consequences for the emergent service system. A good example of purposeful strategy would be the first (Community Medicine-based) bid to come out of Bloomsbury DHA (1985) which could be seen as: well founded in local epidemiological evidence (highlighting the importance of the rational component of strategy); shrewd in its assessment of the need to use the windfall to put a coalition together (the political component); and taking care to be broadly based in its assessment of needs outside the acute sector.

Clearly the development of HIV/AIDS services was clearly influenced by covert as well as overt strategies, as HIV/AIDS represented a well-resourced peg on which other issues could fit. In one District HIV/AIDS was a stalking horse in a much wider debate about how health education projects were to be managed; in another it was a way of developing women's services through a prostitutes' outreach project; in others the unspoken objective – especially for finance – was to tear down the ringfence around the special monies and transfer them to pressured base budgets. Formal documentation alone would give a very partial view of some of these covert processes.

There is some evidence that the most effective strategy making combined top down and bottom up planning. The first attempt by one District to develop a strategy led by Community Medicine initially ran into implementation difficulties, due in part to the lack of ownership of the issue in the operating divisions. The response by the centre was to support the creation of Unit level groups which could supply such ownership, and develop strategy through a dialogue between the centre and the units.

Role creation and organisational design

In the first section, it was suggested that leadership around HIV/AIDS could have been supplied from a number of sources and this section considers how such roles have been constructed. Of course the case studies are disproportionately likely to be drawn from high and medium prevalence teaching districts, which may operate distinctive labour markets.

DHA members played a generally reactive role although a friend on the DHA could prove useful in safeguarding funds. In some cases, 'managing up' to the chairman to ensure political cover for sensitive work emerged as an issue for service developers, but members were unlikely to come along with proactive proposals. Nor was HIV/AIDS generally constructed as a major political issue at DHA level (unlike hospital closure proposals), but retained bipartisan support, so even major bids could go through with little discussion.

Their agenda dominated by questions of financial control, the new general managers were on the whole dull in their response to HIV/AIDS. As one respondent remarked: 'general managers are not turned on by AIDS, but by the tag that attaches to AIDS.' Indeed another respondent was developing a financial model of general managerial behaviour: what was the point beyond which the special financial allocation would have to rise before general managers would start to attend HIV/AIDS meetings? Giving the HIV/AIDS issue to a general manager who lacked a sense of personal ownership was counterproductive, and could lead to a damping down of the whole management process. Nor – on the whole – was there much evidence of conscious utilisation of the HIV/AIDS issue as a containable test bed for a more general organisational development and design brief, perhaps reflecting the lack of interest among action oriented managers in developing theories of managerial action.

There were some important redeeming features and interesting exceptions. Those managers who developed the greatest interest in HIV/AIDS tended either to be drawn from clinical backgrounds (and thus retain an interest in strategic service development) or to have had a prior background in service development processes (for instance in drugs services) or to be strong conceptualisers and lateral thinkers (perhaps these managers are also more likely to be found in teaching Districts), and hence interested in the organisational design implications of HIV/AIDS. Nor should the learning curve along which managers had to move be forgotten, given their lack of international clinical networks which could have fed early knowledge in.[44]

Certainly the case studies illustrated the critical importance of clinical product champions in driving change. In all the case studies enthusiasts emerged who pushed for service development, often in the face of scepticism from elsewhere in the organisation. These champions could be some way down the formal hierarchy (such as health education officers in low prevalence areas), but in each of the three high prevalence districts and in some of the medium prevalence districts, an elite consultant (drawn from different specialties) emerged as an important early focus.

These champions were self-confident in their academic backgrounds, skilled in the black arts of running rings around systems (such as using soft research monies as a way around manpower controls), were able to gain access to national policy making and media channels over the heads of the District, and showed drive and energy over a long period of time in building up services. The achievement of a position of power was crucial, and there were also examples of clinical product champions coming up with ideas for service development (for example in drugs services) which faced severe difficulties in their adoption in part because of the peripheral power base of the champions in the organisation. There were also some interesting differences in the balance placed between interfirm diplomacy on the one hand and zeal on the other, and the degree to which HIV/AIDS confirmed a long-standing interest in the world of policy or whether it represented a transforming experience in which champions left the relative shelter of the laboratory for the world of policy and politics. The emergence of active product champions can then have dysfunctional as well as functional consequences for the organisation, as their highly individualistic approaches can pose wider integrating problems. Initially these product champions emerged organically but there have been attempts to create a new cadre in the appointment of a new generation of GUM consultants to develop services in their Districts. It will be interesting to see whether they will in the future emerge as powerful and effective champions of change.

Some of the most effective clinical product champions did not operate in isolation, but were embedded in a wider institutional setting, able to call on the support of Young Turks (such as Senior Registrars) who could undertake much of the planning or service development work, in effect helping to write the first rules for that District. Highly motivated and energetic, they were already senior enough to have won some autonomy, and were making fundamental long-run career choices, but in the end fitted into the world of formal health care organisations.

A little remarked upon consequence of the escalating financial allocations has been the creation of a specialist and largely unregulated HIV labour market, with a growing number of workers employed on very different conditions of service by different authorities, but often on junior grades and on short-term contracts. These posts pulled in younger, mission driven and countercultural workers from social movements who sometimes faced a difficult period of acculturation to the NHS.[45]

Where the acute sector had developed an interest in HIV/AIDS, such workers had only a peripheral impact. Where, however, prevention was more of a priority and such workers were organised into cohesive and energetic teams (perhaps utilising empowerment ideology), then their influence was stronger. It will be interesting to see how many of these workers remain in the NHS, or whether many move back into less formal organisations.

Public health medicine of course represents the crossover point between medicine and policy, and as such could potentially play a major role in the development of services in the early stages of an epidemic. Yet there is also evidence that community medicine was sometimes unable to secure a firm foothold in the local policy process as a whole after the 1974 reorganisation, and was potentially marginalised as a result of the introduction of general management: 'In some parts of the country community physicians seized the opportunity which was presented to them in 1974 and created vigorous departments which continue to make important contributions to the planning and development of health services for the populations they serve. In other places, some simply failed to make the transition.'[46]

HIV/AIDS should be seen as perhaps the first issue to come along after the introduction of general management which clearly related to the health of populations. How did public health respond to the challenge? The case studies indicate that public health was always important in the early response to HIV/AIDS, but in very different ways. In some cases public health departments represented an empty shell from which front line service developers could operate. Some public health physicians concentrated on the epidemiology rather than the policy. But others became intensely involved in the policy process around HIV/AIDS, writing strategies, bids for funds and distributing resources (although probing for value for money and the reduction of implementation deficits were managerial tasks which were more foreign to them). In some localities public health was itself adapting through its response to HIV/AIDS to the new world of general management, for example, giving the task of planning for service development to a Specialist in Community Medicine (SCM) who would take advice from a group.[47]

Leadership could be supplied from small groups as well as from individuals, and in one locality an effective and cohesive team emerged and was kept together which networked well with local authorities and the voluntary sector. Leadership from such a core group offered a broader base for service development, especially where the group was characterised by a range of complementary skills.

We now briefly consider the question of organisational development and design. While there seems to have been little self-conscious intervention by Organisational Development or Human Resource Departments, nevertheless in a number of the case studies opportunity was taken following the introduction of general management to introduce more flexible forms of decision making better able to process a high change issue. Most obviously the appointment of AIDS co-ordinators could help build lateral networks between specialties and vertical links between District and Units (the most fruitful planning could emerge as a dialogue between the top down and the bottom up) but in some instances more radical organisational change was evident, particularly where more conceptual managers or public health physicians had been drawn into the process.

Sometimes a small mixed advisory group would form around a general manager offering readily accessible advice on epidemiology, service development and finance (as in Bloomsbury's 'kitchen cabinet') which was a small, highly informal group which advised the lead general manager. In one regional centre, the opportunity was taken to construct around HIV/AIDS a new type of project-based Health Promotion Team which (on the basis of careful selection of staff, confidence about team performance and frequent reporting up) was given a buffer space within which to develop in its first phase.[48]

Here the shared and energising values of the team were of key importance. In another regional centre, similar themes of the winning of space within which service development could take place on the basis of securing political support at Chair level emerged. A small core group formed around the product champion as an initial bridgehead into the DHA. Perhaps the principal long-term danger associated with the creation of such small in groups is 'groupthink', so that deviant or heretical opinions are squeezed out, and external groups which do not share such values are labelled as 'bigots', thus narrowing the basis of potential organisational support.

Discussion and implications

A number of general and concluding points should now be made. The substantial local variation found to exist and the major role played by liberal professional elites do not confirm the crude theories of state repression sometimes advanced as a way of understanding the government response to HIV/AIDS. The picture is rather one of 'bounded pluralism'. At DHA level the debate was rather dominated by internal clinical and managerial elites which decomposed into liberal and conservative wings, but little space was accorded either to social movements or elected members. The outcome of these debates was highly unpredictable, depending on the local balance of forces, and just who established the early roles, but there was little evidence of an effective top down political drive to 'put the lid' on AIDS. Indeed, the provision of earmarked funds nationally was a crucial motor of change as significant earmarked sums were won from the Treasury. This potentially could finance significant growth even in inner city districts where services generally were under pressure to contract, although this also depended on the relative ability of the AIDS lobby to retain control of these resources locally, in competition with the finance function. The micropolitics of the District were crucial in the struggle for control over the money.

Secondly, the HIV/AIDS issue also highlights some well-established organisational theoretic themes, albeit in new contexts. The following themes were identified which all relate to various problems caused by the management of growth: processes of service innovation and in particular the nature and role of product champions and product championing; strategy making and the retention of strategic flexibility; crisis construction, management and its aftermath; the organisational politics of budgetary windfalls; and aspects of organisational design and development.

Thirdly, the comparative case study analysis allowed us to test and develop organisational literature. A three-phase model was advanced to explain patterns of crisis management which incorporated a first 'crisis as threat' phase, a second 'crisis as opportunity' phase and a third 'aftermath and burn out phase'. The concept of the clinical product champion was also utilised, and some clinical product champions observed in process. The importance of core groups as well as individuals in supplying leadership was also apparent. On the other hand, the general managerial role was often found to have been dull, albeit with some important exceptions. Only modest attempts had been made to unravel the consequences of HIV/AIDS for organisational development and design and while the introduction of general machinery had facilitated the creation of more flexible decision making machinery, the building up of a strategic flexibility was not on the whole evident.

Finally, there is a question of what happens after this period of rapid change. There were indications that by 1989–90 conditions were beginning to change and that a point of discontinuity was approaching: the period of rapid increase in earmarked funding was coming to an end; 'normalisation' and integration with the host organisation was replacing reliance on specialist services; political and managerial attention had switched to White Paper issues; and some of the early innovators had undergone burn out. The new agenda related both to the stabilisation of the rapid growth which had been experienced since 1985 (middle management capacity underwent strengthening in many of the case study localities) and an awareness that ways had to be found for keeping the momentum going. Second generation districts outside metropolitan centres where caseloads were beginning to approach significant levels were beginning to come on stream (for example some of the regional centres or Outer London DHAs), and even within the first generation sites there was sometimes a search for second generation leadership, either because of burn out or because the focus of development had switched to drugs services or services for women and children. Local histories of the organisational and managerial response to HIV/AIDS will therefore continue to develop in the 1990s, although in a different form from the 1980s.

NOTES

1 The Parkside and Bloomsbury cases were undertaken by Ewan Ferlie and Andrew Pettigrew; the Lothian, Central Birmingham, Oxfordshire and Worcester cases by Chris Bennett and Andrew Pettigrew. The Sheffield case was undertaken by Ewan

Ferlie and Pippa Stilwell, while the South Warwickshire case was undertaken by Caroline Watts.

2 J. Street, 'British government policy on AIDS', *Parliamentary Affairs*, 41 (1988), 490–508; P. Day and R. Klein, *Two Way Signals: The Case of AIDS Policy Making in Britain*, Centre for the Analysis of Social Policy, University of Bath (Bath, 1989). Prepared for the WZB Symposium, 'Signals for Steering Government', Berlin, May 1989.

3 V. Berridge and P. Strong, 'AIDS policies in the UK: a preliminary analysis', in E. Fee and D. Fox (eds.), *AIDS: The Making of a Chronic Disease* (Berkeley, 1992).

4 D. M. Fox, P. Day and R. Klein, 'The power of professionalism: policies for AIDS in Britain, Sweden and the United States', *Daedalus*, 118, 2 (1989), 93–112.

5 E. B. Ferlie and A. M. Pettigrew, 'Coping with change in the NHS: a frontline district's response to AIDS', *Journal of Social Policy*, 19, 2 (1990), 191–200.

6 E. H. Thomas and D. M. Fox, 'AIDS on Long Island: the regional history of an epidemic, 1981–1986', *Long Island Historical Journal*, 1, 2 (1989), 93–111; D. M. Fox, 'Financing health care for persons with HIV infection: guidelines for state action', *American Journal of Law and Medicine*, 16, 1 and 2 (1990), 223–47.

7 A. Downs, 'Up and down with ecology – the issue attention cycle', *The Public Interest*, 28 (1972), 38–50.

8 D. Hunter, *Coping with Uncertainty* (Chichester, 1980).

9 Ferlie and Pettigrew, 'Coping with change'.

10 A. M. Pettigrew, L. McKee and E. B. Ferlie, 'Understanding change in the NHS', *Public Administration*, 66, 3 (1988), 297–317.

11 R. Alford, *Health Care Politics* (London, 1975); Hunter, 'Coping with uncertainty'.

12 P. Arno, 'The non profit sector's response to the AIDS epidemic: community based services in San Francisco', *American Journal of Public Health*, 76, 11 (1986), 1325–30.

13 R. Stewart, J. Gabbay, S. Dopson and P. Smith, *District General Managers and the District Health Authority*, Templeton Series Number 3 (Bristol, 1987).

14 W. Ranade, 'Motives and behaviours in district health authorities', *Public Administration*, 63 (Summer 1985), 183–200.

15 See R. Griffiths, *NHS Management Enquiry* (London, 1983), for the seminal document which first proposed the introduction of a general management function in the NHS.

16 R. Rothwell, 'Intracorporate entrepreneurs', *Management Decision*, 13, 3 (1976), 142–54.

17 B. Stocking, *Initiative and Inertia: Case Studies in the NHS* (London, 1985).

18 Rothwell, 'Intracorporate entrepreneurs'.

19 R. A. Burgleman and L. R. Sayles, *Inside Corporate Innovation: Strategy, Structure and Managerial Skills* (London, 1986).

20 R. Shilts, *And the Band Played On* (London, 1987).

21 J. Dutton, 'The processing of crisis and non crisis strategic issues', *Journal of Management Studies*, 23, 5 (1987), 501–17.

22 Downs, 'Up and down with ecology'.

23 B. Hogwood, *From Crisis to Complacency* (Oxford, 1987).

24 C. F. Hermann, 'Some consequences of crisis which limit the viability of organisations', *Administrative Science Quarterly*, 8, 1 (1963), 61–82; T. D. Jick and

V. V. Murray, 'The management of hard times: budget cutbacks in public sector organisations', *Organisation Studies*, 3, 2 (1982), 141–69.

25 W. H. Starbuck, A. Greve and B. L. T. Hedberg, 'Responding to crisis', *Journal of Business Administration*, 9 (1978), 111–37.

26 Griffiths, *NHS Management Enquiry*.

27 A. Liddell, 'General management in a DHA', in B. Stocking (ed.), *In Dreams Begins Responsibility: A Tribute to Tom Evans* (London, 1987).

28 C. H. Levine, I. S. Levine and G. Wolohojian, *The Politics of Retrenchment: How Local Governments Manage Fiscal Stress* (London, 1981).

29 A. M. Pettigrew, 'Contextualist research: a natural way to link theory and practice', in Ed Lawler (ed.), *Doing Research that is Useful in Theory and in Practice* (San Francisco, 1985).

30 A. Chandler, *The Visible Hand* (London, 1977).

31 A. M. Pettigrew, *The Awakening Giant* (Oxford, 1985).

32 J. R. Kimberly, R. H. Miles and associates, *The Organisational Life Cycle* (London, 1980).

33 M. Pye, 'The challenge of AIDS – towards a model for public health response', in M. Pye, M. Kapila, G. Buckley and D. Cunningham (eds.), *Responding to the AIDS Challenge* (Harlow, 1989).

34 In one District, there was a vivid folk memory around hepatitis B which transferred across to HIV. As one respondent put it: 'Hepatitis B hit us and we had about 29 patients and a lot of them died, we lost two members of the medical staff, not actually our own staff, we lost a nurse, we lost a lab technician, people were very worried about it . . . People were really very anxious, it was like a medieval plague city.'

35 In Paddington, realisation over the 1983 August Bank holiday weekend that the number of patients was beginning to escalate, and that media interest was apparent, led the Control of Infection Officer to call an emergency meeting with two clinical academic colleagues to draw up control of infection guidelines to combat rising staff hysteria:

> This caused a lot of tension and pressure because we could not get other people to take it seriously. We knew that we were going to have real patients and real problems, and people seemed to flip between not being bothered and not caring, and it was something minor and peripheral, to being something that was so serious that it was untouchable.

36 A key article is J. F. Peutherer, E. Edmond, P. Simmonds, J. D. Dickson and G. E. Bath, 'HTLV-iii antibody in Edinburgh drug addicts', *Lancet*, 2 (1985), 1129–30.

37 For example, in one regional centre, one respondent said:

> Here we are with a well resourced, properly thought out project, perhaps at just the time when people think 'well, it never really happened did it, the AIDS epidemic in Britain? . . . ' now more than ever we are in a position to provide quite detailed programmes for AIDS education at a time probably when not many people want it.

38 Staff sometimes took on extremely high workloads which proved unsustainable. As one Paddington respondent put it: 'By mid-1985, we were a publishing house, a health education house, as well as a treatment house, and we were very rapidly becoming exhausted.'

39 Kimberly, Miles and associates, *The Organisational Life Cycle*.

40 For example, a number of special teams sprang up in one regional centre. As one member of staff there put it:

> I've never been able to work with so little answerability to any management structure and so little documentation of decisions . . . this is partly because of the sort of person that [the Director] is, he just keeps saying 'Go ahead and do it and we will sort out the mess afterwards', which I find I can cope with . . . I see the whole thing having worked very much on personalities and philosophies, and not on meetings and seminal documents at all.

41 A good example is the change in the nature of the District HIV/AIDS Action Group in late 1988 in our analysis of a low prevalence District:

> The arrival of new people is also likely to influence the nature of the Action Group. Two of the people who were most committed to it have left, and the feeling of being an informal ad hoc group with a shared goal is likely to be replaced by pressure for it to become a more formal, structured, group.

42 E. B. Ferlie and L. McKee, 'Planning for alternative futures in the NHS', *Health Services Management Research*, 1, 1 (1988), 4–18.

43 H. Mintzberg, 'Patterns in strategy formation', *Management Science*, 24, 9 (1978), 934–48.

44 For example, one manager moved some eight miles in 1985 from an Outer London Borough DHA to become the first District General Manager (DGM) in Paddington and was propelled into a new world:

> The funny thing was that AIDS had not impinged on my consciousness at all until I got the job here . . . I became aware that (a) there was such a thing as AIDS and (b) that Paddington and North Kensington was in the thick of it. And then I got here, it went WROOM!, from that moment on, more and more time was taken up. I sat on the AIDS subgroup just to get the hang of it, and it was clear that it was getting bigger and very soon a district ethic that AIDS is important takes over.

45 One worker in a health education team in a regional centre described how personal platforms changed between 1987 and 1989:

> So I think that it was important that the homophobia, racism, and sexism were confronted . . . it was not actually until I had been in the work for a few months that I began to think about people as a group of real people who were depressed and stigmatised and needed support, which would be my platform now.

46 *Public Health in England: The Report of the Committee of Enquiry into the Future Development of the Public Health Function* (London, 1988).

47 As another respondent managing an innovatory team put it in describing the new form of management arrangement adopted: 'That is another implication, we went for the Griffiths 1 idea that jobs were given to people, not groups, those people then discharged that task. If they wanted to call together a group to help them do it, that was fine.'

48 As another respondent in the same District described the new team: 'Never before has there been a project like this, never before has a Health Promotion Project regularly kept the Health Authority updated on its every move in the way that this did.'

11

A fall in interest? British AIDS policy, 1986–1990

JOHN STREET

Introduction

Many of the problems which face a society never disappear completely, but political interest in them often does. Political attention spans rarely do justice to the issue at hand. In 1972, the political scientist Anthony Downs described the 'issue attention cycle' that then applied to environmental issues. The cycle was characteristic of most public problems. 'Each of these problems suddenly leaps into prominence, remains there but a short time, and then – though still largely unresolved – gradually fades from the centre of public attention'.[1] This thought has become so common that it is now enshrined in the title of a textbook on British policy making: *From Crisis to Complacency.*[2] There is a strong temptation to fit this conventional wisdom on to British AIDS policy.

The story would run something like this. From 1982 to late 1986, a sense of panic gradually developed within government. The spread of AIDS came to be seen as a 'threat' for which crisis action was needed. This impression was fostered in the pages of tabloid papers, and in a wave of television documentaries. The government had to be seen to act. A special Cabinet Committee was created, the budget for public education was vastly increased, as was research and treatment funding; television adverts were broadcast and every home received a leaflet explaining how AIDS was spread and how it could be avoided. And then, just as suddenly, AIDS disappeared from the front pages of the papers. Politicians no longer rushed to talk about it. Or when they did, it was to wonder aloud whether the threat had not been exaggerated. In 1989 the special Cabinet Committee was wound up. It seemed that political interest in AIDS had indeed run the familiar course from crisis to complacency.

Part of the purpose of this chapter is to assess this version of the later history of AIDS policy, to ask whether in fact it has been dropped from the political agenda. I want to set this examination against a more general backdrop: the way in which party political values and interests have played their part in the form and content of AIDS policy in Britain. The story of the passage from crisis to complacency is, after all, a story about politicians and the way they behave to protect their personal and party interests. It suggests that the attention span devoted to an issue is determined by the electoral cycle and by cynical political calculation.

Though the crisis-complacency model is tempting, it needs to be treated with caution. A clear distinction has to be made between party politics and policy making. The fact that political interest may wane does not mean that policy interest will follow the same course. It might flourish precisely because political interest has faded. Equally, we need to avoid conflating the public, media-generated profile of an issue with the actual development of the policy process. The attention span of the media and the public is much shorter than that of policy makers, and is determined by quite different interests and criteria. Nonetheless, the thought that AIDS may have lost political support and commitment cannot be discounted *a priori*; we need to look closely at the trajectory it has followed since the 1986 watershed.

This paper, therefore, has two tasks. The first is to look critically at the history of AIDS policy after 1986. The second is to explore the ways in which political interests have shaped that history. To make these tasks more manageable, I have narrowed the focus. The account of AIDS policy begins with the work of the House of Commons Select Committee on the Social Services. Its 1987 report was, at the time, the most comprehensive statement on AIDS policy in Britain. In the context of this paper, it not only provides a critical perspective on AIDS policy, it also acts as a guide to political opinion on AIDS. Using the Select Committee Report enables me to examine government performance in the political climate of the time. After all, the Select Committee is itself part of the policy process and an expression of the political values and interests at play in the response to AIDS. Although the Select Committee system encourages the development of cross-party consensus, it does not produce objective analysis. Political compromises and trade-offs are built into the committee's work. It establishes a common ground for MPs concerned about their role as representatives, parliamentarians, careerists, party loyalists and ideologists. The Select Committee Report, therefore, represents a political benchmark against which to measure changes in government policy. It does not set an absolute standard, rather it provides a way of assessing the development of AIDS policy in the period after 1986.

The focus of this paper's second task – the examination of political influence – is narrowed by concentrating on the elite policy process, on the way in which political values in the core executive influenced the outcome. Rather than looking at the policy process as a whole, therefore, my concern is with the way in which political judgements were included or excluded from the decisions being made about the response to AIDS. Were decisions about AIDS policy inspired by party political calculation?

The government's response to AIDS 1986–90

The dramatic announcement in November 1986 that the government was to commit itself to tackling AIDS did little to change the basic components of existing policy. These remained the four elements of: (a) public education; (b) treatment of those with AIDS; (c) prevention of the spread of HIV; (d) research into the causes and cures for AIDS. While the basic policy strategy was unaffected by the 1986 political intervention, there were major shifts as a result of it. Most obviously each benefited from a substantial increase in resources – the public education campaign gained by £20 million, for example. It also altered the political profile of, and responsibility for, the policy. Before then AIDS policy was largely the business of the health authorities, the Department of Health and a number of other interested parties (from the Terrence Higgins Trust to the Medical Research Council). The creation of a special Cabinet Committee was a way of expressing the new commitment, giving public attention to the policy and adding another layer of control. It also added to the political capital invested in AIDS. Cabinet Committees have long been regarded as the main centres of power in the executive, but they have also been kept as official secrets. The AIDS committee, by contrast, was launched in full public view. The combination of power and publicity provided the means for introducing major changes. And there was certainly, as the Select Committee on the Social Services heard, a need for change.

Criticisms of AIDS policy 1986–7

The Select Committee heard evidence from many different sources when it scrutinised British AIDS policy in February–March 1987. Witnesses testified about every aspect of the policy, from the way it was made to the way it was implemented. The Committee's conclusions were published in May 1987. Although it was generally complimentary about the government's response, the Select Committee voiced a number of criticisms. These criticisms fell into two categories. One set of comments was directed at the way the problem of AIDS was being assessed, in particular how it was spread and the extent of its spread. The other set of criticisms focused on the content of the policy itself.

The Committee's first line of criticism, therefore, was directed at policy formulation. It argued that too little had been done to discover what sexual practices were engaged in by men and women, and how that behaviour, where risky, might be changed. Too much attention, it was said, was given to medical and clinical research, and too little to sociological research.[3] At the same time, the Committee was critical both of the funding of basic research and clinical research.[4] These gaps in knowledge were compounded by the government's reluctance to use the voluntary sector, especially the Terrence Higgins Trust.

The other main line of criticism focused on policy implementation. Doubts were raised about whether the public health campaigns were sufficiently explicit and whether they were reaching their targets.[5] These comments were fuelled by a general scepticism about whether sexual behaviour was being changed by the posters, television advertisements and school packs. If government, the Committee said, was unhappy about spreading a more explicit message, then the task should be handed to the voluntary sector.[6]

The Committee also argued that the government should expand the range and funding of treatment services – from genito-urinary medicine (GUM) clinics, to counselling, to community care.[7] This advice was combined with a demand for more prevention work. The government ought to promote the use of condoms, albeit 'only in the most general sense', and to encourage the development of needle exchange schemes, beyond the few existing experimental local schemes, and develop schemes in the prison system.[8] Finally, the Committee wanted the government to do more to protect the rights of those people who were HIV positive or who had AIDS.[9] The insurance industry was the main target. The Committee complained that not only did insurance companies insist that people reveal whether they had been tested for HIV, they also retained the right to refuse cover to those they deemed to constitute an unacceptable risk.[10]

Although each of these criticisms called for particular actions to correct them, the Select Committee argued that there was a general weakness underlying the government's response to AIDS: the lack of central co-ordination. Despite the creation of the AIDS Cabinet Committee, it was argued that policy making was made in a pragmatic, *ad hoc* fashion.[11]

In summarising the Select Committee's critique, I do not want to pretend that these were the only criticisms to be made of government policy in 1986–7. What they constitute, however, are the criticisms to which the political leadership was most susceptible. They were ones to which there was a direct, if vague, responsibility to respond. The same was not true, for instance, of the criticisms coming from gay activists or the moral right. Neither of these groups had established connections with the political elite, although, as we shall see, the moral right had an important ally in Mrs Thatcher. The Select Committee's criticisms expressed a highly mediated version of public opinion and a more direct expression of electoral political interests. It helped to set the political climate which enveloped AIDS policy making and which established an agenda which the government could either respond to or ignore. Hence, it establishes a basis from which to ask whether the Thatcher Cabinet's crisis response faded into complacency.

Appeasing the critics?

Before looking at the specific criticisms, we need first to look at the general problem with which the government was dealing: the spread of HIV and the incidence of AIDS.

The figures in Table 1 tell a complicated story, from which few conclusions can be drawn. It is difficult to make sensible comparisons between the period before and after 1986. The data are more accurate in the latter period, thereby creating an impression of increase in the spread. Similarly, the incubation period between infection and the development of AIDS also distorts the later picture. It seems that the rate of increase from homosexual contact is much lower than that for drug users, albeit with much smaller absolute figures. While increase in homosexual spread fell from 91% in 1986–7 to 40% in 1988–9, the number of infected drug users has increased by 100% each year since 1986. There is no sign of a downturn in the heterosexual spread, although importantly the main contributor to the increase is exposure to HIV abroad. The figures in themselves, though, only reveal the general conditions under which the policy process is analysed. They tell us little about what contribution, whether positive or negative, the policy itself makes. This is a general problem of the study of AIDS policy. In a recent review of AIDS policy throughout the world, Mildred Blaxter comments: 'given the variety of . . . background variables, together with differences in the magnitude and nature of each country's epidemic, overall "success" or "failure" of policy can barely be judged, much less accounted for'.[12] Here, all we can do is compare one political response to another, the Select Committee's to the government's.

Policy formulation since 1986

There has undoubtedly been a marked increase in research into and knowledge of sexual behaviour. This research, begun in the mid-1980s and financed mainly by the Medical Research Council, is being published and disseminated.[13] The store of knowledge is likely to expand, at least in the short term, because of work underwritten by the Economic and Social Research Council (ESRC). The responsibility of the government in promoting this change is, at best, ambiguous.

While the Economic and Social Research Council's involvement in AIDS research can itself be seen as a consequence of the issue's change in political salience in 1986, its contribution has been hedged in by political constraints. Throughout the decade of Mrs Thatcher's rule, the ESRC felt vulnerable. The knowledge in which it traded was not highly valued by Conservative ideologues, who tended to see social science as socialism under an academic guise. The ESRC, which depended on the government for its funds, was therefore circum-spect about the research it funded. Thus, when in 1985 it was asked to support

Table 1. *People with AIDS*

Category	1983	1984	1985	1986	1987	1988	1989	1990
Homosexual/bisexual	25	93	245	538	1,032	1,634	2,288	3,234
Intravenous drug abusers			2	9	19	39	80	161
Homosexual/bisexual + IVDA				6	19	31	38	61
Haemophiliac		3	9	25	70	127	169	228
Blood recipient								
Abroad			5	6	16	20	26	37
UK			5	4	8	15	21	30
Heterosexual contact								
Partner with above risk factor						15	22	34
Others abroad		6	11	14	35	54	100	208
No evidence of exposure abroad				4	9	19	13	26
Child of at risk/infected parent				3	13	19	23	36
Other	6	5	1	1	6	21	50	43
Total	31	108	280	610	1,227	1,994	2,830	4,098

Source: Department of Health.

research into gay sexual behaviour and the spread of HIV, it rejected the project on the grounds that it did not accord with the Council's research priorities. (The work was subsequently financed by the Medical Research Council (MRC)). The ESRC made no further effort to solicit or direct AIDS research until the 1986 political watershed. Subsequently, in the summer of 1988, the ESRC announced that it was making £1.9 million available for three years of AIDS research, particularly in the area of sexual behaviour.

The value of this new commitment has, however, to be qualified. Despite encouraging the thought that more money would be available in subsequent years, the ESRC has in fact added nothing to its original commitment. And the government has done nothing to cause a change of heart. Quite the opposite. A planned National Survey on Sexual Behaviour, to be financed jointly by the ESRC and the Department of Health, was cancelled. Two sets of decisions were involved, one in Downing Street the other in the ESRC.

It was widely reported that Mrs Thatcher was personally responsible for vetoing the survey. The proposal for the survey had been held in Whitehall for several months. It needed formal approval because it involved the commitment of resources. While such a decision would normally fall to the relevant department, the style of Mrs Thatcher's leadership entailed her frequent involvement in relatively small matters of particular concern. The survey was one such matter. Her biographer, Hugo Young, records his impression of the event: 'The Prime Minister's veto on public money appeared to derive from an instinctive distaste for invasion of heterosexual privacy – although homosexuals were fair game. Her decision was never explicitly defended. It simply happened, without a public rationale and without the relevant minister, in possession of the scientific facts, feeling able to challenge it'.[14]

The Department of Health backed out, leaving the ESRC on its own. Formally, the ESRC could have continued with the survey. It, after all, was responsible for its design and conduct. But it lacked the necessary resources, and without political support, it too withdrew from the enterprise. If the fortunes of the ESRC were taken as a test of the government's determination to increase knowledge about sexual behaviour, then we might conclude that its will was weak. But the reason for the lack of determination seems to owe less to complacency or indifference, and rather more to an excess of concern.

The government has, however, made some attempt to improve the monitoring of the spread of AIDS, if not the behaviour that causes it. After much prevarication, the government conceded the need for a more systematic mapping of the spread of HIV. From January 1990, it introduced a limited system of anonymous screening. In doing so, it acceded to demands that had been voiced for some time. It seems to have occurred through the collapse of counter arguments, rather than the emergence of any positive initiative. One of the obstacles to be surmounted was the Select Committee's Report which opposed screening, largely on the strength of the ethical arguments of Ian Kennedy, a Professor of Law at King's College, London.[15] It was significant that when the government introduced screening, it spoke of the absence of legal or ethical constraints.[16] These words were uttered at a time when Kennedy himself had become part of the government's own Expert Advisory Group on AIDS, although he had not changed his position on screening. It seems, though, that this advice did not carry the Committee. Perhaps this is not surprising, the advisory system continued to be dominated by medical expertise, albeit mediated by the departmental secretariat.

The exclusivity of the advisory system is further demonstrated by the treatment of the voluntary sector. The Terrence Higgins Trust, Body Positive and other such groups have remained on the outside, although the grants they receive from central government have increased.[17]

Importantly, though, these grants contribute only a portion of the organisation's operating costs, and are only awarded on an annual basis. The groups' position, therefore, remains precarious, and may become more so with the 1991 reforms of the NHS which makes it necessary for agencies to compete for contracts and funds.

Although the 1986 watershed signalled an increase in funds for voluntary groups, it has done little for the access granted them. If anything, the political attention actually led to a decrease in outside advice. The demise of the Health Education Advisory Group exemplified this trend.

The Health Education Advisory Group (HEAG) was set up in the mid-80s by the Chief Medical Officer to advise on prevention policy, about which he had little direct knowledge. The HEAG was in some respects a normal advisory group, and in others an exception to the rule. It was an exception in that it contained a social scientist, Professor Tony Coxon, a sociologist who specialised in research methodology and a member of the Gay Research Group. HEAG also contained representatives of Body Positive and the Terrence Higgins Trust, as well as a member of the Gay Medical Association.

The HEAG undoubtedly made an impact in the early days of AIDS public education. The Department of Health was uncertain about how to proceed. One official thought that the two key public health messages should be: 'avoid London' and 'avoid male prostitutes', neither of which addressed the real problem. The HEAG persuaded Acheson to focus on condoms. The secretariat obliged by furnishing the Group with extensive documentation on condom promotion campaigns throughout the world (including Australia's 'rubber dubber' campaign). HEAG managed to force the Department to make its campaigns more explicit and to give greater prominence to the use of condoms.

The HEAG, however, eventually fell into disuse. There were a variety of reasons for this. The HEAG's influence was, it seems, inversely proportional to the political interest taken in their work. As political responsibility for public education increased, so expertise became more selectively chosen, and groups like the Terrence Higgins Trust (THT) pushed to one side.

It was not just politics, though, that limited the effect of HEAG's advice. The character of that advice also mattered. The HEAG was not offering hard science, instead its advice was grounded in psychology and the study of social behaviour. This type of knowledge tended to be viewed as 'common sense', despite the evidence to the contrary. Reflecting upon his experience on the HEAG, Professor Coxon remarked: 'The feeling I have, particularly, was that there was a very strong mix of concern and expertise which, in the event, was not actually used and that whilst in particular medical skills were being called upon and used and respected, other sorts of non-medical skills were being ignored'.[18] The HEAG was replaced by advice from a more selectively drawn body, Coordination of AIDS – Public Education (CAPE). CAPE was made up of the Health Department, health education agencies, the Health Education Authority (HEA) and interested government departments. In short, CAPE represented the dominant consensus.

Policy implementation since 1986

The government has continued to increase the funding for education campaigns (£44 million was allocated in 1986–9). Equally important, responsibility for public education shifted from the Department of Health and the Health Education Council, to the Health Education Authority. The HEA was granted considerably more power and more resources than its predecessor. But, like the ESRC, the gain in the HEA's profile was paid for in increased policy scrutiny.

The content of its campaigns have had to pay heed to the character of the political climate. Dr Mukesh Kapila, Deputy Director of the HEA's AIDS programme, summed up the effect of political involvement:

> it is clear that UK government leadership has been an important driving force to get things going and, in general, our politicians have made wise decisions. But it is also true that in countries in which political expediency dictates social policy, the personalities and personal beliefs of key individual politicians and civil servants have profound influence on how programmes evolve, including their tone, credibility, public and professional acceptability and ultimately their impact.[19]

When the HEA's special AIDS unit was wound up in 1989, it was surmised that this signalled further evidence of political interference and a wariness about the tone of public education campaigns. This charge is denied by both the HEA and the government. What cannot be overlooked, however, is that the HEA's education campaigns are shaped by more than simple disinterested concern for getting its message across. In education policy, political factors played their part in constraining policy, but in other policy areas, politics had a different effect.

Like spending on education, the money made available for AIDS treatment (and related services) rose markedly in the period from 1986, especially when set against the provision for other parts of the health service. The government's formal (ideological) position was that problems could not be solved by throwing money at them. With AIDS, though, this was precisely what they seem to have done. Operating against the formulas normally applied to the allocation of funds within the National Health Service (NHS), the government underwrote 70% of the costs centrally. As a result of this beneficence, the genito-urinary services have been immeasurably improved both physically and in terms of the service they offer. The inequities in the allocation have not, however, changed (see Table 2). AIDS patients are costed differently in different parts of the country. The explanation for this distribution was not discrimination between regions, but, it was claimed, the *ad hoc* and inefficient character of the allocation system.

Whatever the gaps in the response on the treatment front, it is in marked contrast to the way the government has moved on prevention. The bulk (more than 90%) of the funding has been concentrated on the health authorities. For critics, this has been an inefficient use of resources because health authorities are ill-equipped to work with other agencies and at reaching key groups, a problem made all the greater by the health authorities' general reluctance to give prevention a high priority.[20]

Change in prevention policy has been slow and selective. A considerable battle had to be fought, mostly by the government's own Advisory Council on

Table 2. *Allocation of funds per people with*
AIDS (PWA) for different regions (1989)

Region	Allocation per PWA (£s)
Yorkshire	52,500
Trent	58,000
East Anglia	75,000
Oxford	72,500
Mersey	49,500
Lothian (Scotland)	20,000

the Misuse of Drugs, before there was any increase in commitment to needle exchange schemes. A change of minister was also necessary to expedite the process. The system of needle exchanges continued to depend upon regional initiatives, and, as a result, reflected local practices and policies. Little or nothing was done about increasing the availability of condoms. If anything, things got worse, following cutbacks in the Family Planning Association. Meanwhile the Home Office steadfastly refused to allow needle exchanges or condoms to be introduced within the prison service.

Finally, despite the protests of groups like the Terrence Higgins Trust and the criticisms of the Select Committee, the government has been unwilling to intervene in the activities of the insurance industry. The government's only concession has been to agree to meet the industry representatives to discuss the policy. This was, it seems, a mere gesture, because the government was already convinced of 'the need of the insurance industry to find out relevant information before providing life insurance'.[21]

Summary

AIDS policy since the 1986 watershed has clearly changed, but the question is how these developments should be assessed. Do they demonstrate a decline in the interest-attention cycle and a rise in complacency? Certainly, they have not formed part of a clear political strategy. The lack of co-ordination that concerned the Select Committee in 1987 has not been corrected. The only gesture towards central planning, the special Cabinet Committee, ceased to operate after September 1989. Since then political control of AIDS policy has largely reverted to the various agencies responsible for its implementation. This does not mean, however, that politics has ceased to influence AIDS policy and to determine its fortunes. The absence of central co-ordination or of deliberate strategic planning is not proof of political indifference. It merely indicates that there is no single route through which that interference is organised. The rest of this chapter, therefore, explores the way in which political judgements and interests have shaped AIDS policy and determined whether complacency has ruled.

Politics and AIDS policy

The impact of politics on AIDS policy has taken many forms and emerged from many different sources. It has sometimes been direct, sometimes indirect; it has been the result of individual initiative, or the playing out of structural processes. What follows is by no means a comprehensive picture. Instead it aims to explore the different general ways in which policy and politics have intersected. We begin with the most politically obvious form of influence, that exercised by Mrs Thatcher.

The impact of Mrs Thatcher

The decade since AIDS first appeared in Britain has coincided with the era of Thatcherism, in which the British political agenda and British political practices were significantly altered. The temptation is, therefore, to see AIDS policy as the child of Thatcherism and of the person from whom the era took its name. Such a response is too easy.

One of the most distinctive features of Mrs Thatcher's influence on AIDS policy is her apparent *lack* of interest. When the special Cabinet Committee was established, the job of chairing it was given to her deputy, Lord Whitelaw. And on his resignation it went to the even more junior John Moore. Students of Mrs Thatcher's style of government have observed that when she wanted to impose her will, she chaired the relevant Cabinet Committee. With AIDS policy, she remained at one remove from the political centre and she made very few public statements on the subject. When she did comment, it seemed that she thought that countering AIDS was really the responsibility of the individual citizen, not the government.

Of course in taking such a view and remaining distanced from policy making, she was having a political impact; she was refusing AIDS the kind of support that other policies enjoyed. And when she did intervene directly, it was to dull the policy. Not only did she undermine the national survey of sexual behaviour, she also caused health education campaigns to remain cautiously inexplicit. It was also possible to detect her influence on the ministers directly responsible for AIDS policy. The reluctance of the Department of Health to expand the needle exchange scheme seemed to owe something to John Moore's unwillingness to take the political risks involved. There is, though, another dimension to Mrs Thatcher's mixture of indifference and interference. Where she chose not to get involved, she allowed, albeit by default, the emergence of policies which accorded with liberal thinking on AIDS and which allowed for more funding than might otherwise have been available. In so far as decisions on AIDS were being made away from Mrs Thatcher's gaze and the political limelight, it was possible for them to reflect the consensual approach that the Department of Health officials and their ministers were disposed to follow. In short, Mrs Thatcher's indirect impact had two dimensions. Her values and presence created a climate which ministers felt inclined to acknowledge. This restricted the development of some aspects of AIDS policy. At the same time, her decision to remain aloof allowed for progress in other areas.

The extent of her direct influence was eloquently demonstrated by the impact of her departure. Her successor, almost immediately, reversed her policy on compensation for haemophiliacs. In doing so, John Major showed that political intervention need not work negatively. It does, though, suggest that the calculations upon which intervention is based do not derive directly from rational assessment of the policy problems. The attention and resources devoted to public education campaigns have been much greater than those devoted to research (approximately £62 million has been spent on publicity; £50 million on research). While this imbalance may owe something to the nature of the problem, it also owes much to the fact that the education campaign provided an easier demonstration of political action. For the ambitious minister, it provided a route to popular attention. A similar rationale might be ascribed to the decision to make payments to the haemophiliacs with HIV. Not only had the Haemophiliac Society lobbied MPs very effectively, it also offered a group of people who could be portrayed as 'innocent victims' demanding public sympathy and political action. Haemophiliacs, in this sense, were turned into a good party political issue.

The politics of the policy process

Political influence, though, can be exercised without the deliberate intention or intervention of individuals. It can simply be the consequence of particular political relationships, such as existed between the government and the Health Education Authority. In early 1990, a series of advertisements was run on prime-time TV. They had the same black and white format: a single talking head. The budget was £2.3 million and the campaign ran for six weeks. The talking heads were all experts in the AIDS field: Sir Donald Acheson, Professor Michael Adler, Dr Anthony Pinching, Dr Anne Johnson, Dr Raymond Maw and others. Each uttered a simple statement about HIV and AIDS. The Chief Medical Officer, for example, said: 'We know for certain that HIV, the virus that causes AIDS, can be spread by sexual intercourse from man to man, man to woman and from woman to man. It is also spread by sharing infected needles and syringes during drug abuse.' It was, said the HEA, a very successful campaign.

But why was this low key approach adopted? Partly it reflected a changing perception of the problem of AIDS, from that of an immediate crisis to that of a long-term policy. But there were more direct, political causes for the change of tone. There had been renewed media interest in AIDS. This time it took the form of scepticism about the heterosexual spread. The *Sunday Times* serialised the book by Michael Fumento[22] which cast doubt on the idea of 'heterosexual AIDS'; the same theme was taken up by various people in the letter columns of the 'serious' press; and a television documentary gave publicity to the Californian scientist, Professor Duesberg, who claimed that HIV was not the cause of AIDS. This new interest in the disease coincided with reports of the scrapping of the HEA's AIDS unit.[23] It also coincided with a decline in the political fortunes of the Conservative government, as it trailed behind Labour in the opinion polls. This made the government politically sensitive to anything that might detract further from its popularity, a popularity that it had chosen to build around the family and morality.

It was in this political climate that the HEA advised the 'experts' campaign. It was designed both to maintain the credibility of the HEA and its message, conveying the necessary information in an unsensational fashion. The campaign, in short, was informed as much by the politics of the day as by the spread of the disease.

A parallel form of political influence could be detected in the advisory system which played such a vital part in determining how the 'problem' of AIDS was defined. This was evident in the experience of the HEAG, but it also seems to be true of the way in which the Expert Advisory Group on AIDS was used. The Department of Health's secretariat played an important role in determining what issues were considered and what solutions were advanced. It was through the secretariat that political boundaries were set. Equally significant, however, was the way in which the personnel of such organisations were dominated by certain types of knowledge and interests. Primarily, it was clinical medicine that established the general concerns of the advisory bodies.[24]

Finally, it is worth observing how parliament responded to AIDS. Although Parliament plays a relatively small direct part in the political process, it does contribute to the political capital invested in outcomes. Where some issues – like *in vitro* fertilisation – have become a source of intense political concern, causing problems within the policy process, AIDS has remained remarkably free of blatant political axe-grinding. If anything, it has been characterised by parliamentary indifference. The main debates on AIDS have been sparsely attended. Parliamentary questions have come from a very limited number of MPs, and almost always from people with a genuine concern for the adequacy of the government's response. One explanation for this political quiescence lies with the role taken by the All-Party Committee on AIDS. The All-Party group has helped to build a consensus around AIDS which has been reinforced by the consensual practices of the Select Committee. It has created a barrier against the emergence of maverick self-publicists who might have been tempted to make political capital out of the disease. Attempts within Parliament to raise doubt about the heterosexual spread of AIDS have met with little sympathy or support. This is not to deny that political interests and values have played a part in the parliamentary consensus on AIDS. There has been a clear attempt to manage opinion and to forge agreement around a containment strategy. In doing this, party politics have been of relatively little importance, and it is a more general corporatist politics that has counted. The attempt has been to fit AIDS into existing political and administrative operating procedures, and to avoid the kind of radical politicisation favoured by the political fringes, whether represented by gay groups like Outrage or the Conservative Family Group.

The impact of other policy issues

The role of politics in AIDS policy cannot be confined to the specific policy arena. The emergence of AIDS policy coincided with a number of other important political changes which had an impact upon its course and its effect. The two most obvious of these were the reforms to local government legislation and to the health service.

While the formal position of the Department of Health was that of equal concern and care for all who had AIDS, there were other messages also emanating from central government. A general disposition in favour of the 'traditional family', together with a particular animosity to homosexuality, was apparent in Conservative rhetoric. Within AIDS policy, this found expression in the idea that haemophiliacs with HIV were 'innocent victims', the implication being, of course, that other people were responsible for their plight. Outside AIDS, such attitudes were confirmed in Section 28 of the Local Government Act which sought to outlaw the 'promotion of homosexuality'. By sanctioning homophobia in this way, the government threatened an important element of AIDS policy: to encourage openness and equality in the response to the disease.

The delivery of AIDS policy has also been threatened by another feature of government policy: the reform of the National Health Service. Although the full implications of these reforms are only slowly emerging, those who worked with AIDS saw the devolution of responsibility for health care and the system of contract provision as undermining some of the principles which previously shaped AIDS health care. They warn that GPs may be reluctant to take on HIV positive patients because of the costs thereby imposed on drug budgets; that the co-ordination of other services will become increasingly difficult because of the complex contracting arrangements to be established; and that voluntary groups like the THT will have to compete for scarce funds with statutory services.[25] Whether or not these expectations are borne out, it is clear that AIDS policy is not immune to political decisions taken elsewhere, and that those decisions have sometimes worked against AIDS policy.

Conclusion

This chapter began with the question as to whether AIDS policy has suffered the same fate as is typically attributed to other policies born of crisis. Has that crisis led swiftly to complacency as Downs's 'issue-attention cycle' is played out? In trying to give an answer, two riders were introduced. The first involved clarifying the different aspects of policy that might be involved in the passage from crisis to complacency – ebbs and flows in public and party opinion do not translate neatly into similar movements in the policy process. The second rider was to suggest that the measure of shifts in interest was to be found in the politics of the policy process, the way in which values were imposed and interests organised.

The evidence discussed here indicates that no simple generalisation, whether it refers to attention cycles or to crisis-complacency continuums, can be applied. Public opinion, as measured by media coverage, has fluctuated and taken a variety of forms. AIDS, though, remains a public issue. Equally, party political opinion has followed no straightforward pattern, and has in any case to be explained more by the activities of groups like the All-Party Committee on AIDS than by some 'natural law' of politics and policy making. The same is true of the government. While it has not met the demands made by its critics, in particular in the Select Committee on the Social Services, it has amended and developed its AIDS policies over the period since the 1986 watershed. Moreover, these changes cannot be attributed to a decline in political interest or in response to fluctuations in public opinion. Explicit political intervention, and less direct forms of political influence, have been a constant feature of the way the AIDS 'problem' has been defined and responded to.

Superficial impressions of a decline in AIDS' political salience have to be heavily qualified by the realisation that AIDS policy continues to be subject to changes of political leadership and political circumstances. Its fortune owes less to any 'law' of political behaviour and much more to the playing out of complex political processes, in which party political interests, ideology, 'expertise' and many other factors intersect. Any impression of a 'cycle' is undercut by the realisation that shifts in interest and changes in policy are to be accounted for by detailed analysis of particular circumstances, in which the electoral process is but one element. The fluctuating passions of politicians are a poor guide to the operation of the policy process; at the same time, political values and interests can never be eliminated from the creation and implementation of policy.

Acknowledgements

This chapter draws on research financed by the University of California and carried out with Professor Albert Weale at the University of East Anglia; he also helped with this paper, as did the editors of this volume. They are absolved of blame, but are due much thanks.

NOTES

1 A. Downs, 'Up and down with ecology – the "issue attention cycle"', *Public Interest*, 28 (1972), 38.

2 B. W. Hogwood, *From Crisis to Complacency? Shaping Public Policy in Britain* (Oxford, 1987).

3 Social Services Committee, *Problems Associated with AIDS*, vol. 1, HC 182–1 (London, 1987), para. 51.

4 *Ibid.*, paras. 23 and 26.

5 *Ibid.*, paras. 61–2.

6 *Ibid.*, para. 65.

7 *Ibid.*, paras. 111–12, 113–14 and 133–6.

8 *Ibid.*, paras. 78, 86 and 95.

9 *Ibid.*, paras. 167–70.

10 *Ibid.*, paras. 178–80.

11 *Ibid.*, paras. 181–5.

12 M. Blaxter, *AIDS: worldwide policies and problems* (London, 1991), 32.

13 See, for example, P. Aggleton, P. Davies and G. Hart (eds.), *AIDS: Individual, Cultural and Policy Dimensions* (London, 1990).

14 H. Young, *One of Us* (London, 1990), 548.

15 Social Services Committee, *AIDS*, HC 202 (London, 1989).

16 Department of Health, *AIDS*, Cm. 925 (London, 1989), para. 14.

17 Grants to the Terrence Higgins Trust: 1985–6, £35,000; 1986–7, £100,000; 1987–8, £300,000; 1988–9, £400,000.

18 Social Services Committee, *Problems with AIDS*, vol. 2, 35.

19 M. Kapila, 'AIDS prevention through public education: the work of the Health Education Authority', *Royal Society of Medicine: The AIDS Letter*, 15 (1989), 3–4.

20 V. Beardshaw, 'Blunted weapons', *New Statesman and Society*, 2, 78 (1989), 24–5.

21 Social Services Committee, *AIDS*, para. 19. Meanwhile, evidence emerged that an increasing number of people were refusing to be tested for HIV for fear of the consequences of their insurance status.

22 M. Fumento, *The Myth of Heterosexual AIDS* (New York, 1990).

23 Health Education Authority, *AIDS and Sexual Health Programme: Summary of Second Annual Report* (London, 1990), 7.

24 This argument is more fully discussed in J. Street and A. Weale, 'British AIDS policy', in R. Bayer and D. Kirp (eds.), *AIDS in the Industrialized Democracies* (Rutgers Press, 1992).

25 C. Bentley and M. Adler, 'Choice cuts for patients with AIDS?', *British Medical Journal*, 301 (1990), 501–2.

12

AIDS policies in France

MONIKA STEFFEN

AIDS is a difficult health issue which mainly concerns medicine, hospitals and public health policies. But the epidemic also concerns the political system. The definition of the nature of risk and of the rank it should occupy amongst the different risks society may be facing is a political task. A new problem and its possible consequences can be evaluated in many different ways. Different social groups will develop various conceptions of the problem according to their position in society and of the danger it may present for them and for society as a whole. Therefore, negotiation is needed between different possible perceptions of the problem and a large consensus is necessary to make the choice legitimate. Priorities as defined will automatically legitimate certain actors and certain means to deal with the problem and exclude others which are considered as irrelevant. The AIDS epidemic offers an excellent case for studying these strategic moments of problem definition and consensus building which shape public policies from their very beginning.

International comparison is of particular interest here, because every country faces a similar problem. But as no legitimate knowledge pre-existed to interpret the new epidemic when it occurred and the threat it might represent to society, problem definition and policy construction largely depended on the character-istics of national policy systems, institutional networks and decision making processes in health policies.[1] France has a higher number of AIDS cases than any other European country (except Switzerland which shows a higher level of cases per inhabitants) but France took longer than Britain to formulate public policy. Figures for 1987 (the turning period for public policies in most countries) as well as recent data, illustrate the discrepancy between the policy process and the concrete reality of the epidemic (see table). As in most countries, the geo-graphical spread of the epidemic in France was unequal. As in Britain (although to a lesser extent) it is concentrated in two regions. From the 13,145 cases

This article publishes first results of an ongoing research project, funded by the Agence Nationale de Recherches sur le Sida (ANRS), France.

	31 December 1987		31 December 1990	
	Total number of declared cases	Per one million inhabitants	Total number of declared cases	Per one million inhabitants
France	3,073	55	13,145	234
West Germany	1,669	27	5,612	71
Italy	1,411	25	8,227	143
UK	1,227	22	4,098	71

Source: World Health Organisation, European AIDS Centre, Paris.

declared at the end of 1990, 52% were located in the Parisian area (Ile de France) and 14% in the Marseille area (Provence-Alpes-Côte d'Azur).

Important national differences exist on all major levels that determine public health policies. They have to be taken into account when analysing national policies against the AIDS epidemic:

the organisation of health care and the social security system;

the type of relationships between public and private institutions in sectors of medical and social care, and of scientific research;

the social status, degree of organisation and capacity for collective action of the groups concerned: homosexuals, haemophiliacs, doctors, researchers, moral authorities, health and social administrations;

the relationship between medical research, the pharmaceutical industry and clinicians;

the national issues raised by AIDS in terms of economic, ethical and symbolic issues.

French AIDS policies were marked by special characteristics which can be summarised under five provisional points:

1. Defining a public policy on such a new and unexpected issue as AIDS was disturbed, occasionally delayed, by electoral uncertainty which weakened the capacity for consensus of French society and the legitimacy of public intervention. The strong criticisms of the 'political class' during the 80s illustrate this weakness.

2. The characteristics of the French policy system, especially of decision making in health and social sectors, made the AIDS issue dependent on political decisions. As this level was weakened, policy decisions depended entirely on scientific legitimacy but here, too, consensus was lacking during the first years of AIDS because of internal differences within the scientific community. Since health policies in France depend to a great extent on professional and scientific expertise, the twofold lack was crucial and explains certain hesitations and delays in public action.

3.　New actors and 'owners' of possible policies had first to emerge. It was a long process because they could only emerge on the periphery of established groups. Internal debates had to be overcome and alliances across different fields built up between researchers, homosexuals and public officials, in order to establish and reinforce authority.

4.　The new set of norms the first AIDS experts proposed proved acceptable because they fitted into the previous norms of health and social policies more easily than other alternatives. Neither the traditional message of the Catholic church nor the demands for social segregation put forward by the National Front had any influence on central policy adoption. On the contrary, the homosexuals' message of social solidarity, individual responsibility and the right to sexual liberty was consistent with the norms of social policies over the last thirty years (abortion and divorce were legitimised on the grounds of individual choice).

5.　The government's role was to invent new administrative and technical modalities to integrate the new issues into existing legislation, medical systems and social negotiation. When the legitimacy of the political system was reinforced, the new policy was implemented with surprising speed, according to the well-proven model of a big 'national project'.

It is an open question, too early to be assessed, to what extent the innovations introduced through the AIDS issue will contribute to a modification of traditional patterns of health policies in France. Will the new model of public action strengthen the position of public health? Will it favour new relationships between hospital and ambulatory care? Between social action and medical care? Between private and public institutions? Will it contribute to enlarged social negotiation and interest representation in the health sector? To promote patients' representation and new ways of arbitration between professional, economic and social interests?

The context of French AIDS policy

Four general contextual issues have influenced the French case. Each represents a major level of policy formation and has to be regarded as an independent variable.

The general political situation

France experienced major political changes during the 80s. The 'decade of AIDS' coincided with unusually frequent elections, several changes of government and major electoral reforms. In the 1981 presidential and general elections, the socialists came into power for the first time for nearly fifty years. The following local (1983) and general elections (1986) gave the majority to the opposition and thus created an entirely new situation for the Fifth Republic, the so-called *cohabitation* between a liberal Prime Minister, from the Rassemblement pour la République (RPR) Party, and a socialist President (1986–8). Traditional alliances also changed during the 80s. The Communist Party lost its influence, the conservative parties split whilst an extreme right movement, the Front National, gained considerable electoral influence, up to 30% in some regions, with slogans of insecurity, anti-immigration and national decline. As all other social issues during the last decade, AIDS became a battlefield for general political competition. Growing politicisation of national life led to criticism of what the press called the 'political class' and weakened its legitimacy.

Health administration and medicine

Health and social administrations occupy a rather weak position within the hierarchy of public administration. The different departments inside the Ministry of Health and Social Affairs are subject to divergent pressures. On the one hand, there is growing control by the Ministry of Finance, on the other hand, direct intervention from professional groups, especially an influential medical lobby. Reforms that would threaten either established frontiers between administrative and professional territories or the internal hierarchy of the medical profession are difficult to carry through.[2] They lead to absence of decision making, especially when the borders between what is regarded as being 'medical' and as being 'social' or the relationship between hospital care and ambulatory care are to be reconsidered.[3] Fighting the AIDS epidemic obviously interferes with these traditional boundaries.

The position of public health within the decision making process, and more generally within the health system, is particularly weak. The information system is mainly orientated towards statistics concerning the range and the cost of medical services. These priorities result from the cost coverage system which is organised for reimbursement on a fee per item basis. Epidemiology developed rather late in France and then merely for research purposes and not necessarily according to public health goals. With the historical decline of infectious disease, the position of infectious illness and of virology within medical research also became less important. Some indicators may illustrate this weakness. The discovery of the AIDS virus by a research team from the Pasteur Institute did not result from institutional mobilisation, but direct personal relationships with clinicians caring for the first French AIDS patients.[4] If press articles of well-informed daily newspapers like *Le Monde* may be considered as an indicator, the discovery of the virus early in 1983 was hardly noticed in France. It became of public interest only after the same discovery was announced by the Americans and when the vital interests of the French medical research and pharmaceutical industry were at stake.

The first medical term used in France was 'AIDS', the French equivalent 'SIDA' coming into use only several months later, at the end of 1983.[5] This indicates the degree of dependence of European science and public concern on American standards. This external dependence might be linked with the weak internal position of particular fields of medical research and public health. But at the same time, the French discovery and the existence of a well-established institution, the Pasteur Institute, has made AIDS an issue of national interest for France, in terms of the international prestige of French research and the potential economic benefits. Such vital issues, however, are far beyond the competence of the French health policy sector.

The public policy process

Health and more generally social policies in France are traditionally conducted by an alliance of certain segments of the politico-administrative system and certain segments of professional groups. These rather closed systems tend to reproduce existing conditions and to oppose reforms. Innovations emerge either in exceptional circumstances, like the 1958 hospital reform and the 1960 medical agreement,[6] or as a result of initiatives from high public officials acting in connection with private associations they promote as external pressure groups. National policies in favour of the elderly and of the handicapped during the 60s and 70s are examples of this model of change.[7] In industry and technology, innovation often proceeds in the form of 'big national projects' promoted by the state. The electrification of France, the nuclear power programme, ambitious projects like Concorde and the TGV high speed train are examples of changes promoted as national priorities.[8] When the AIDS problem arrived, there was no professional or administrative constituency to take it up and provide sufficient legitimacy for a big national project. Opinion polls, however, showed that the fear of contamination was a growing preoccupation among the public during the early years of AIDS.

Social negotiation and interest representation in the health sector

As a result of the situation described above, or as one of its reasons, there is little public mobilisation for health issues in France. They occupy very little space in the programmes of political parties or of trade unions and there are few debates on health issues in Parliament. Several movements of 'health service users' emerged during the 70s but they were closely linked with militant doctors who opposed the dominating structures of public hospitals and private medicine. These movements disappeared along with the militancy of the professionals.

Unlike in Great Britain where the National Health Service is under direct state authority and therefore a 'political ' issue, the French social security system is managed by social partners, i.e. the trade unions and employers' unions, but without competence over the organisation of services and structural evolution which remain in the hands of the government. Unlike in Germany where health policies have always been considered as part of general economic and social policies, health policies in France are considered as medical issues, concerning doctors. Health insurance merely operates as a payment office, a function which does not give rise to major public mobilisation.

The French homosexual community was initially not prepared to take up the AIDS problem which caused great uncertainty about the future of the community, fear of renewed marginalisation and internal conflict about the basis on which to organise the struggle against the epidemic and its consequences. The national organisation of haemophiliacs was not able to break its traditional dependence on the blood transfusion centres through which patients were contaminated. These centres provide daily medical care and emergency services to haemophiliac patients. The latter prefer the traditional service structures they have always known to other hospital services with changing staff and priorities. In fact, the blood transfusion centres acted as representatives of the haemophiliac patients and as their mediator in all public relations. Feeling deeply betrayed and isolated, the National Association of Haemophiliacs has started only now to integrate into its self-perception a dimension of political mobilisation and autonomy from medical guardianship. The AIDS epidemic struck France in a sort of social and administrative vacuum and at a period where general political issues made decision making a particularly difficult exercise.

The policy process

Three phases in the policy construction process can be distinguished. Until 1984–5, established elites ignored the emerging problem whilst newcomers mobilised problem perception and provided technical tools. In spite of the conflicts that then arose over the use of blood tests, major public policy lines were established between 1985 and 1988, but implementation of the AIDS programme suffered from the difficult political context of the 'cohabitation' period. After the re-election of President Mitterrand in 1988, the reinforced social consensus favoured rapid implementation of the policy which was then conducted as a national priority.

1981–3: problem emergence and definition

The first news about AIDS reached France in June 1981 when the Morbidity and Mortality Weekly Report published details of the first cases. At the same time, a

Parisian hospital doctor met a case showing similar symptoms. As other cases soon followed, he set up an informal group to observe the new illness and discuss scientific literature. The group was soon joined by a psychiatrist, an immunologist, two officials from the Ministry of Health and an epidemiologist. The group obtained some formal status, attached to the Ministry's General Department of Health who agreed, in early 1982, to study leave for the epidemiologist. It was through the initiative of this first working group on AIDS, convinced of the gravity of the problem, that infected cells from a Parisian patient were provided to researchers from the Pasteur Institute who succeeded in isolating the HI-virus early in 1983. After the discovery, with the arrival of the virologists, the first expert group evolved in two distinct directions: on the one hand, an epidemiological surveillance system was set up as part of the General Department of Health; and, on the other hand, an association ('ARSIDA') aiming to develop research on AIDS and to obtain funding was set up under the leadership of the Pasteur group.

The first press articles on what they still called 'a mysterious epidemic in the United States' were published in January 1982, reporting on medical questions without mentioning the first French expert group. There was little mention in the general press about the isolation of the virus and the first blood test for which a patent demand was submitted in September in Europe and for the United States in December 1983. These events were reported only later, from 1984 onwards, when the 'scientific war' brought French and American institutions into open opposition.

The 'Association of gay doctors', which had been founded just before AIDS was recognised in France[9] in order to meet growing concern about specific health problems in the community, especially syphilis and hepatitis B, was already confronted with the first patients presenting the symptoms of AIDS. The association was also asked by the first expert group to collect and spread information within the gay community and the medical profession. It preferred, however, a discreet attitude in order to preserve the gay community from a public backlash. This reluctant attitude of gay doctors began to change during 1984 and the first specifically AIDS-orientated associations started operating within the gay community.

The first public intervention began in the summer of 1983. In June and August, the General Department of Health issued three 'recommendations'. These reminded health workers of hygiene and security measures; suggested to the blood transfusion centres (which organise all blood donation in France) that they 'avoid risk groups' (homosexuals, intravenous drug users, persons of African and Caribbean origin and their partners); established a surveillance system, in order to know whether the first French cases presaged epidemiological developments such as those in the States and eventually to prepare an adequate intervention structure. At the same time, the first funds were made available for research, from the National Institute for Health and Medical Research, the Ministry of Research and Technology and the Foundation for Medical Research. Allocation of these funds led to conflict between leading medical professors, especially from the fields of cancer and immunology, and the existing expert group from the General Department of Health (this 'French working group on AIDS' was chosen as the World Health Organisation (WHO) group for Europe in October 1983 and the European WHO centre for AIDS was set up in Paris in November 1984). The French scientific community developed at that time two hypotheses concerning the nature of AIDS:

the majority of cancer, immunology and virology specialists considered that AIDS was some normal infection that would only strike persons already weakened from other infections or disease and therefore, it would not be easily transmitted;

a minority of less known specialists, among them a number of virologists and the Pasteur research team led by Professor Montagnier, declared that AIDS was an infectious disease caused by an active viral agent.

During the autumn and winter of 1983–4, each of these different scientific disciplines organised its own working sessions on AIDS, with international participation in Paris. Commenting on these debates to the press a year later, Professor J. P. Levy, now the President of the National Research Agency for AIDS (ANRS), recalled the history of medical science and the relationship between cancer, retro-viruses and the immune system which had been known since the beginning of the century.[10] This was a call for interdisciplinary collaboration.

By the end of 1983, more than 100 cases of AIDS were already diagnosed in France, most of them in the Parisian area with an overwhelming majority of homosexual men, half of whom had travelled to the States, Haïti or central Africa. One haemophiliac case was already known but no intravenous drug users at that stage. The first year of AIDS policies in France was characterised by a lack of consensus within the scientific community. Health authorities were thus unable to take any further action.

1984–5: policy emergence

The Pasteur blood test was developed experimentally during 1984 and large-scale production started in the spring of 1985. The provision of a technical tool helped to define scientific consensus over the nature of the disease and indicated specific policies to be followed. Implementation, however, depended on national priorities, international legitimacy and initiatives from civil society. These issues and important controversies between policy deciders marked the period of 1984–5.

The most important private association in the AIDS field, called 'AIDES',[11] emerged at the end of 1984 and started operating in early 1985. It aimed to promote solidarity with patients, to spread information and to establish preventive measures both against the epidemic and against the risk of group stigmatisation. This mobilisation coincided with growing media interest. Well-known French intellectuals and artists were among the first AIDS victims. Famous patients from abroad began to arrive in French hospitals to seek the best available treatment (Rock Hudson died in Paris in 1985). The World Health Organisation chose the French epidemiological survey group to set up the WHO Centre for Europe. However, the major event which mobilised French authorities and the press was the announcement by the American Secretary of State for Health of the discovery of the virus in the US. A patent was rapidly granted to the American team; the earlier French application remained unanswered. Tension with the American authorities grew into an open legal battle during 1985. This focused on free access for the French test to the American market and to other continents (mainly to Africa where branches of the Pasteur Institute are traditionally well established). It was in this climate of intense international competition that the first compulsory measures were decided upon in the summer of 1985. At the same time the Minister of Social Affairs announced to the press an 'important AIDS treatment success', with cyclosporine after experimentation on a very limited number of patients for only one week, a declaration immediately criticised by the entire scientific community and by the Secretary of State for Health. This rather unusual incident illustrated the central preoccupation of the French government. It was concerned to preserve national interests, an economic priority which caused latent conflicts between government departments, the first AIDS experts and other health policy constituencies, mainly the blood transfusion establishment.

The first tests, available in limited quantities since early 1984, were used to study HIV prevalence in the population of haemophiliacs and in blood donation. Nearly half of the haemophiliacs tested were found HIV positive. As early as March 1984 numbers were concentrated in the Paris region – these corresponded to the high local prevalence of blood donation. They were also particularly high in the group of patients regularly using concentrated blood products. Since no immediate alternative seemed to exist, these alarming results were not communicated to the public, nor to the patients and their associations. The AIDS experts insisted on a series of measures which had to be taken immediately. There had to be systematic testing of all blood donations with information and medical advice to be given to all donors who proved positive; provision of voluntary and free of charge test facilities for everyone; limitation of the prescription of blood products and the provision of heat-treated blood products. All these measures marked a profound change in the traditional ethical basis of the blood institutions. They brought radical change to an organisation which had previously been based on concepts of voluntary donation and of a system of provision which was considered safe because it was national, voluntary and non-commercial in origin. The heating process also necessitated an important technical transformation of all blood donation centres. The safety of the blood supply was based on systematic screening of all donated blood for various viruses, especially hepatitis B. This was thought to make heat treatment unnecessary. The blood transfusion and related industries were publicly funded, so all centres had to be equipped at the same time, in order to provide all patients with equally safe products. This meant that increased imports, withdrawal from the market of all untreated French products and the destruction of stocks would be necessary if the recommendations put forward by the AIDS experts were to be put into practice. These public health measures were in opposition to other important policy goals the government was pursuing. If the Pasteur test was to get a good share of the market, then it had to be competitive before the establishment of systematic screening of blood donation and the development of voluntary test facilities. All these measures also meant increases in health expenditure, already subject to severe restriction. Last but not least, differences of opinion existed among the blood and haemophilia specialists on risk appreciation and the means to reduce the risk. In order not to discourage blood donation, the blood centres had been reluctant to select and refuse risk groups on the lines recommended by the Ministry of Health in June 1983. Haemophilia patients and their doctors also resisted any moves which might limit access to the new coagulation treatments which had been hailed as major medical progress, increasing the patient's autonomy and security.

In this context, a lack of expert consensus, an absence of patient protest, decision making proved difficult and was delayed for a few months. The government followed AIDS experts in areas where consensus existed with the haemophiliac community, for example compulsory blood screening and voluntary test facilities. It followed the haemophiliac and blood transfusion establishment in not limiting the distribution of unheated blood products, although these were already known as unsafe, until the stocks were used and provision of heat-treated products had been guaranteed both by imported heat-treated material and by the production of such material in France. The question of responsibility for these 'unacceptable delays' has now become the subject of intense public scandal, with important legal consequences. Decisions were taken by the Prime Minister in June 1985. The Order (*arrêté*) of 23 July 1985 introduced compulsory testing of all blood donations, applicable from 1 August 1985. This measure was extended to organ donors in 1987. The question of whether donors should be informed or not of positive results remained open until the National Committee on Ethics decided that they should be. The circular of 20 October 1985 confirmed this duty to inform and issued guidelines on how people should be informed of their seropositivity. This was always to be during a personal consultation with a doctor. A second Order of 23 July fixed prices for heat-treated blood products and cancelled health insurance reimbursements for non-heat-treated products, but only from 1 October. This specific delay, between the decision and its application, was the starting point for mobilisation around the French 'blood scandal'.

There were important developments in society during this period of difficult public choice. Unlike the United States of America, the homosexual community was not organised as such in France. Special group identities are not recognised and sexual behaviour is not considered as a matter of public concern. The gay community existed through its specialist press and meeting places. Some gay militancy had emerged in the early 80s when an obsolete discrimination law was abolished, but the impact of AIDS put the movement back to its infancy. AIDS militancy grew from the personal initiative taken by Daniel Defert, the intimate friend of Michel Foucault. He founded the 'AIDES' association with the aim of representing the interests of all AIDS victims, irrespective of whether they were homosexuals or not, acute patients or sero-positive people, and to build alliances with laymen and specialists from all fields of relevant knowledge against the risk of excessive medical or state power over the AIDS issue.[12] His strategy relied on Foucault's philosophy of 'micro-powers' and a previous experience as an extreme left militant. The leader of the association, although gay himself, considered the homosexual community as too marginal to cope with the AIDS problem and its social identity, only based on sexual liberty, as too fragile. His strategy encountered opposition in the gay community, an opposition which lost support, however, as blood tests and the first medical treatment became available. AIDES started operating in early 1985 and focused initially on improving the conditions around acute medical care in hospitals. The association rapidly became a pressure group urging voluntary, free test facilities and preventive measures, such as publicity for condoms and free sale of syringes. It became evident to the AIDES activists that despite Foucault's aim to keep the state out of sexual regulation, large-scale AIDS prevention and social solidarity needed state support. But the government was struggling through a difficult decision making process, as new general elections approached. This was the origin of the argument that France was 'late' in developing policies on AIDS.

In the autumn of 1985, two months after the introduction of compulsory testing of blood donations, the number of contaminated donors was known. This was the equivalent of one per thousand donors, with important regional differences. In several regions not a single positive person was detected. There was a strong concentration in urban areas, especially in Paris and Marseille. Statistical extrapolation for the whole population suggested a total of 50,000 infected people in France. This figure became subject to passionate debate. Was this a minimum hypothesis because the risk groups had already been filtered out by the preliminary questionnaires filled in before giving blood? Or, on the contrary, was the figure an overestimation? AIDS experts argued that risk groups continued to use the blood collection centres, in particular to obtain AIDS tests which were not yet easily available outside hospitals. The idea of creating special centres for AIDS information and anonymous HIV testing took shape during these debates.

1986–mid-1988: public intervention

Major AIDS legislation was passed in a most difficult period of general politicisation and in a situation which the French political system had not experienced before. The Fifth Republic had previously always had a President and a government coming from the same political party. Between the 1986 general election and the 1988 presidential election, the socialist President had to deal with a conservative government, whilst the entire political system was under growing electoral pressure from the extreme right-wing Front National.

The new Chirac government was initially set up without any particular person in charge of health, an omission that illustrates the low position of public health in the hierarchy of French administration. After protests from the medical profession, Michelle Barzach (unknown till then) was appointed as Minister of Health. It was her task to legislate the prevention policy formulated by the first AIDS expert group. As she took office, the AIDS group attached to the General Department of Health passed her an internal report outlining the way they saw the problem and the measures which should be taken.[13] The French position on the scientific front was strengthened by the isolation of the second AIDS virus in the Pasteur Institute in February 1986 and by growing consensus in the international scientific community. An international commission proposed to call the virus 'HIV', as a compromise between the American and the French research teams and the Second International Conference on AIDS was held in Paris in June 1986. It provided an excellent platform for the new Minister of Health to publicise her policy.

Two significant measures were put into practice almost immediately. AIDS was added to the list of compulsorily notifiable diseases (decree of 10 June 1986); a circular on 3 September 1986 opposed restrictions on patients with AIDS travelling by air. This was the first step towards preserving freedom of international travel and cutting down demands for segregationist policies. In November, Madame Barzach announced her programme. It had three major strands: the creation of a research centre on AIDS; the promotion of international collaboration; and the declaration of AIDS as a 'national cause' for 1987. The Health Minister appointed a medical professor[14] as 'Mr. AIDS', a general co-ordinator for research and medical options; and a special research council was set up to supervise the distribution of funds. The effectiveness of these structures, however, remained uncertain. They did not gain sufficient support either from the medical elite or from the public research institutions. International collaboration aimed essentially at resolving the French/American conflict. A high level meeting between Reagan and Chirac, followed by meetings at the Health Minister level, aimed at a compromise, one much criticised by members of the French research teams. They considered the financial compromise as 'capitulation'; and also expressed concerns about the equitable distribution of the French section of benefits between the different French institutions covered by the agreement. For the first time large-scale public funding was allocated to AIDS in 1987. There was 110 million francs for research projects on treatment and vaccine (for a two-year period, 1987 and 1988); 40 million francs of extra funding to Parisian hospitals; and a subsidy of half a million to the 'AIDES' association to promote information and prevention campaigns. The 1988 budget made a special allowance of 760 million francs to the national health insurance fund which henceforth had to reimburse the cost of all voluntary blood tests, according to the ordinary procedures for medical services.

Public prevention policies were based on three premises. First, public information was disseminated through television campaigns and through school-based education. The first French television campaigns were rather careful and indirect, far less explicit than in northern European countries. In schools, the campaigns remained under the supervision of the Ministry of Education. Here, AIDS was not to be treated as a specific issue but integrated within more general subjects such as the prevention of drug use or sexually transmitted diseases, as part of general sexual education. Promotion of safer individual behaviour was the second strand of the prevention policy. The emphasis on condom use made it necessary to abolish a 1967 law prohibiting the advertising of contraceptives, including condoms (law of 21 January 1987). The open sale of syringes was allowed by Order of 13 May 1987, despite some initial protest from the chemists. These two measures naturally raised conservative criticism, in particular from the National Front, the only political organisation to mount an anti-AIDS crusade. Thirdly, new service structures were provided to offer easy access to information, care and HIV blood testing. By February 1987, eleven centres for ambulatory care and information were in service and two centres for anonymous and free of charge HIV testing. The latter were rapidly developed to form a network covering the country, according to the law of 30 July 1987 which required at least one centre in each administrative district (*département*). By June 1988, 109 testing centres were in operation and 118 exist currently.

The controversial issues of compulsory screening for foreigners entering the country, pregnant women and pre-marital medical examination arose at this time. These issues appeared under various guises, for example the compatibility of seropositivity with certain professional occupations and the general screening of the population or of certain groups considered as particularly at risk. Demands came up for the systematic screening of pilots, train and road transport conductors, supported by some medical professors arguing on the grounds of 'nervous risks'. The state set the example in the field of occupational rights. Although entry into public service jobs is normally subject to precise health conditions (excluding for instance persons with tuberculosis), HIV screening or questions about lifestyle were banned from selection procedures. The first concrete case concerned a young teacher with pre-AIDS symptoms. He was supported by his trade union, colleagues and the parents' association, probably with some guidance from official levels,[15] as his case constituted a precedent. The case was dealt with through the normal procedures of examining the teacher's aptitude for the particular job as well as by the usual medical commission. Henceforth it was established that AIDS specialists have a role on these commissions when an HIV positive case is under examination. A leading organisation for cancer research urged general population screening but the Health Minister and leaders of her party (RPR) refused any debate on this subject. Demands for compulsory screening or for segregation were localised. They arose from defined professional groups defending specific corporatist interests and from a single extremist party. Official policy focused on voluntary testing, public information and personal responsibility.

The law of 30 July 1987 constituted an indirect but quite definite answer to these controversies. The first article ordered that 'the definition of policy against AIDS is the responsibility of the state', to avoid divergent local policies linked with electoral issues. Consequently, and for the same reason, AIDS was not added to the list of 'sexually transmitted diseases' which are the responsibility of local government, although information campaigns often treat AIDS within the chapter of sexually transmitted diseases (STDs) in order to prevent particularisation and dramatisation of the subject and treat it as part of more general issues. The second article established the network of centres for voluntary, anonymous and free blood testing. Madame Barzach's efforts to implement an active prevention policy gave rise to social debates with political and ethical issues. Four discussion centres can be distinguished.

1. The main debate was of a partisan nature. The conservative parties in government had to clarify their position against the extreme right-wing National Front, a potential political ally, which was demanding compulsory screening of the population and isolation of the seropositive and ill persons in 'sidatoriums'. The National Front linked its AIDS strategy with its general ideology in favour of traditional morality and nationalism, based on opposition to abortion and immigration and a rhetoric of national decline. In May 1987, the RPR ministers officially rejected all arguments by the Front National on AIDS and on immigration. Henceforth, a firm consensus

existed within the political elite, from the right as well as the left, against restrictive and segregationist AIDS policies.

2. Activist organisations in the AIDS area based their militancy on a respect for human rights. They aimed to preserve AIDS victims from social and medical discrimination and to protect their access to work, housing, insurance cover and normal human contact. In October 1987, the AIDES association and a well-established humanitarian organisation, Médecins du monde, published together a 'Bill of rights for AIDS victims', which aimed to provide guidelines for the ethical and social dimensions of AIDS policies.

3. The French Catholic church was confronted with the very traditional position of the Vatican and growing internal criticism. The French bishops supported the Vatican position on solidarity with the sick but remained distant from the Pope's demand for a new sexual morality. They declared officially that 'AIDS was not a divine punishment', a statement aimed to establish a clear distinction between the official church and a wing of religious traditionalists that had split from the official Roman Catholic church and maintained links with the National Front. The internal debate progressively shrunk to focus finally on condoms which it was argued could not be considered as 'the only solution to the AIDS problem'.

4. The last area of debate, confidential at that time, confined to expert circles and ministerial departments, concerned haemophiliacs and blood transfusion. Some blood centres admitted that unsafe products might have been distributed and suggested autologous transfusion for non-urgent operations. When demands for compensation for victims were discreetly put forward by the president of the National Association of Haemophiliacs (a top diplomat), the official response was firmly to refuse any negotiation. When the president died of AIDS, in July 1988, there was a split in the association. A splinter group engaged in open protest, burning the car of the Director of the National Centre of Blood Transfusion.

The period from 1986 to mid-1988 was marked by social debates over the question of how to use the technical tools now available (blood tests) and by conflict over the influence groups promoting different policies should have in the decision process. Although consensus existed within the political elite over the principles underlying AIDS policies, this period was characterised by a need for legitimacy from outside, by reference to international norms. Policy discussion on the question of screening foreigners entering the country was based on European EC and WHO recommendations, Madame Barzach used international platforms and frequent press conferences to publicise her policy. President Mitterrand, much in favour of ethical councils acting as independent expert advisory bodies for government action in new medical and scientific issues, put forward his proposal for an international ethical council on AIDS at the meeting of the seven industrialised countries in Venice in June 1987.

From mid-1988 onwards: a national priority

Although major regulation was achieved and essential principles clearly established during her period in office, Madame Barzach did not have the means fully to implement the policy. The Chirac government was committed to reduction of public expenditure; the next Presidential election was due in May 1988. The re-election of President Mitterrand strengthened consensus within French society and the legitimacy of public intervention. AIDS policies were implemented in these more favourable circumstances. One surprising incident, however, marked the change. The newly appointed Minister of Health, a popular medical professor known for his outstanding opinions, had to resign after just one week in office. He had announced without consultation a number of innovations, including compulsory HIV screening for all pregnant women and candidates for operations. Two months later, after having taken advice from all ethical institutions in the medical field, the government recommended that HIV tests should be 'systematically offered' to all pregnant women. They remained free to refuse the test.

The newly appointed Minister of Health (Claude Evin) asked a well-known public health specialist to report on the AIDS situation and propose policies to deal with it. In November 1988, the 'Got Report',[16] named after the author, confirmed the previous policy principles of public information: strict prohibition of compulsory screening, the emphasis on voluntary testing and condom use. He insisted on the previous choice of treating AIDS and related problems with reference to existing rules and avoiding specific AIDS regulations or structures. He castigated the ineffective French official infrastructure dealing with AIDS (three people with part-time responsibility and a single small office were the total ministerial input, and this for a problem officially termed a 'national cause'). He criticised the low research investment in a case where the country could lose a predominant place in the international market. He proposed a strategy based on the model of big national projects: the AIDS issue should move from the level of the Health Ministry to an interministerial approach. The major recommendations of the report may be summarised as follows:

The creation of a national research agency to promote and co-ordinate all AIDS linked research. Research budgets should be tripled immediately from 50 million francs in 1988 to 150 million in 1989. This national structure would define and orient research policies, and replace the modest research council previously established by the Minister of Health and whose function was in fact limited to arbitration in fund allocation between the competing medical constituencies.

The creation of a national council on ethical questions related to AIDS, consisting of independent scientists, academics and intellectuals from all fields of social and philosophical knowledge. The ethical council should report directly to the Prime Minister. Its members should be appointed by high state authority to advise the government 'which should not be left alone to deal with the AIDS situation' (Got, p. 125).

Important financial support for information and prevention campaigns which should be directly targeted towards condom use. Budgets should quadruple immediately from 31 million francs in 1988 to 120 million francs in 1989. The task should be carried out by the existing Committee of Health Education, a public body reporting to the Ministry of Health; its standing and authority should be reinforced; it should therefore have a scientific council of unquestionable authority.

Special funding for the public hospitals in Paris which dealt with most French AIDS patients. Additional funding for hospitalisation of AIDS patients should be extended from 1,000 million francs in 1987–8 to 2,750 million francs in 1990 with an additional 36 million francs for community care facilities.

Promotion of social solidarity with AIDS victims, in every field from medical care to human rights.

Creation of an 'interministerial governmental action committee on AIDS'. This committee should be attached to the Health Ministry but report directly to the Prime Minister and be directed by a high state official, trained at the famous ENA School[17] in order to exert a credible authority over AIDS issues in all ministries. The committee should be responsible for international relationships and for providing society and public administration with exact information on AIDS, to prevent the diffusion of misunderstood scientific debates and the political abuse of ignorance. The previous solution of a 'Mister AIDS' nominated only by the Health Minister was obviously less than the type of the mission at which Got was aiming.

The Got Report recommended that future AIDS problems should always form part of general frameworks for similar problems. Controversial issues were discussed in the light of this guideline. The report argued that it was difficult for insurance companies not to demand medical tests when the applicants were free to take them, because the entire insurance business was based on the logic of 'probability'. The insurance problem for AIDS victims should be considered with reference to insuring other chronic diseases. The problem of penalising deliberate transmission of the virus should not be dealt with through the existing legal categories (injury, poisoning, attempt to hurt or to kill) but required a new more general category, centred on the idea of 'risky behaviour dangerous to the health of others' which would include dangerous driving, pollution and adding dangerous ingredients to food. The haemophiliacs' demand for compensation, he argued, was difficult to meet as a specific issue since no such compensation exists for other illnesses contracted through medical treatment. To limit the transmission of the virus in prisons, the report suggested the improvement of general living conditions and medical care in prisons and the provision of facilities for conjugal visits. For drug addicts, the report proposed an official investigation of the 'Patriarch' organisation, a private international organisation treating drug users and confronted with a high concentration of HIV positive patients. Its services should be evaluated in order to assess how far they conformed to French legislation and the possibility that they could collaborate with public services for drug users.

The government followed most of the recommendations of the Got Report and implemented them with surprising rapidity, as far as research, funding and promotion of condom use were concerned. The Minister of Health announced his 'National Plan against AIDS' to the press in early November 1988, stating that 'AIDS is no more a group specific illness but concerns everyone.' The first television campaign promoting condom use started the same month. In December, the first working group on AIDS was set up in Parliament. The National Agency for Research on AIDS was fully operational in February 1989. It is linked to the Ministry of Research and INSERM, the national institute for medical research. An ethical advisory body was set up by Order of 8 February 1989, as the 'National Council on AIDS', and its president – an anthropologist – was appointed directly by the President of the Republic. Its major work so far has been on the ethics of information and on insurance.

On two major points, the government did not follow the Got Report. First, a specialised 'French Agency for AIDS Prevention' was set up in January 1989, to elaborate and pilot mass campaigns and specific prevention action, in collaboration with the newly created AIDS Division in the Ministry's General Department of Health and the private AIDES association acting as a service provider. Unlike the research agency, it took a full year to install and staff the prevention agency, which has private status despite its direct attachment to the Health Minister. This unusual compromise may allow the government not to appear directly involved. Secondly, the 'Governmental Action Committee on AIDS', a key element of the infrastructure proposed by Got, was not set up. This leaves decisions in the hands of the Prime Minister and the President of the Republic.

This national AIDS policy was based on a broad consensus in French society, from researchers as well as from political actors. The National Front lost much of its support over AIDS. The condom campaigns only mobilised consumer associations who found that a third of condoms tested were not safe (France does not produce condoms but has to import them). The government reacted immediately by imposing strict French technical standards and withdrew five brands from the market. The Protestant church officially approved publicity for condoms in November 1988 and the Catholic church finally declared that there was no official line on these subjects. Bishops were free to adopt the position they judged reasonable according to their own conscience and the needs of those they had to care for.

Policy content and implementation

Two contradictory characteristics mark French public policy. On the one hand, it is a guiding principle that special structures for AIDS patients should not be created, the epidemic should be treated within the existing channels of social administration and health services, in order to avoid the risk of social stigmatisation through technical specialisation. On the other hand, specialised agencies were created and AIDS experts on the national level conduct the policy outside the ordinary decision making processes. Two specialised AIDS divisions function within the Ministry, one in the General Department of Health and the second, less important, within the Department of Hospital Management. Each is established separately from normal bureaucratic structures and directly attached to the Director of the Departments. There is a national expert community, composed of executives of the National Agency for Research on AIDS, the executives of the two special AIDS divisions of the Ministry of Health, the president of the Ethical Council on AIDS and the director of the National Agency of Campaigns against AIDS. These structures (which now have a permanent staff of more than fifty persons) represent an important innovation in French administration. The AIDS issue was not only taken out of the ordinary hierarchy of health and research administration, but for the first time in the history of the Health Ministry, organisation proceeds *according to illness*, with special horizontal units treating the whole range of problems connected with that one illness. On the contrary, medical care for patients with AIDS and most prevention activities are integrated into the normal system of services and the social security coverage. The compulsory notification of AIDS diagnoses, like all other AIDS relevant information, are collected and analysed by the AIDS division operating in the General Department of Health which deals with declarations of all other infectious diseases.

AIDS was simply added to the list of some thirty illnesses which, under the health insurance, are reimbursed up to 100% of expenses (Order, 31 December 1986). Patients with AIDS related complex (ARC) have approximately 70–80% of expenses reimbursed. Hospitals are advised to treat AIDS patients in their normal infectious diseases and other services. Special funding was provided to extend the capacity of home care units, but the home care associations have not always been able to define their special needs as quickly as the government expected. All doctors can prescribe HIV tests. Since 1986, they are paid for and reimbursed like any other medical examinations. Free and anonymous HIV tests are provided within local prevention centres, in vaccine centres or in the new units set up as part of local public health services. According to the AIDES association, which should be the most critical observer, 'there is no problem for medical care in France . . . and the line of social integration and solidarity was perfectly maintained by public authority' (interview). All medical and dental services are expected to accept seropositive patients. Respect for the normal rules of hygiene is considered an ordinary professional responsibility which should offer sufficient security.

The necessity of treating growing numbers of AIDS patients has led to the development of community care and to limitations on the traditional liberty of doctors to prescribe the medicine they see fit. By far the major part of AIDS treatment (80%) occurs in public hospitals, leaving only 20% to the private sector. The day-hospital has become the central point in the organisation of AIDS care and 'hospitalisation at home' an important part of the care structures. The most prescribed medicine is AZT, which is prescribed twice as often as any other form of Retrovir. According to a recent study,[18] at the stage of acute AIDS there is little difference in access to medical care between social groups, for example the homosexuals and intravenous drug (IVD) addicts. By comparison, social inequality still continues in the field of pre-AIDS care for seropositive persons: drug addicts have far less access to care than homosexuals. Only hospital doctors can prescribe AZT, independent practitioners can only renew the prescription.[19] National training programmes on AIDS for health and social workers are conducted by the AIDS unit of the General Department for Health, with the aim of providing professional advice and psychological support to clients everywhere when AIDS related problems arise.

The Ministry now wants to limit the number of HIV tests prescribed by general practitioners and to favour the role of the anonymous testing centres where the percentage of positive results is higher. A more focused strategy for HIV testing and prevention seems about to emerge. Up till now and against all epidemiological evidence, AIDS has been presented as concerning 'everyone' in the same way. Prevention policy was the same for the whole country. But France is clearly confronted with three different epidemics: AIDS is concentrated in the Parisian area dominated by homosexual transmission; in the south-eastern area (Marseille–Nice) dominated by IVD transmission; and the Caribbean overseas territories with heterosexual transmission patterns. The dilemma of how to warn the public of contamination risks without stigmatising the groups known as risk carriers, was solved in France by disassociating AIDS from homosexuality. This choice was in line with the state's tradition of not intervening in matters of private lifestyle and of not recognising special group identities. It may be the explanation (rather than any sense of discretion about homosexuality or sexual matters) why French public campaigns did not use moral arguments in any way. The second feature of public policy was a determination to avoid spreading information not yet the subject of scientific and political consensus. Haemophiliacs, drug addicts and prisoners paid a heavy price in this consensus orientated policy. Decisions on prevention of contamination through blood products were left to the closed community of specialists on transfusion and haemophilia.[20] The state is now confronted with severe criticisms for not having faced up to its specific responsibilities. Apart from the free sale of syringes, AIDS strategies in the field of drug abuse and in prisons remained largely limited to prohibition of testing without consent.

In areas where norms of behaviour are part of a particular group identity, special action has to be taken in alliance with insiders. The National Agency for Campaigns against AIDS covers these types of areas, together with the special AIDS division of the Ministry and the private AIDES association. There are frequent problems with respect to their respective areas of competence and functions. The AIDES movement spread geographically throughout the country. Local associations, affiliated to the national federation, now exist in every large town. They offer a variety of services, according to local needs, ranging from the collection and diffusion of information inside and outside the risk groups and professions concerned with AIDS, telephone hotlines, legal advice, discussion groups, individual psychological and social support from volunteers in hospitals and at home, accompanying the dying[21] and initiatives to promote home care in order to preserve social links. AIDES perceives its role as that of a pilot movement proposing new public policies and representing the interests of AIDS concerned people. It played this role with remarkable success, shaping public opinion and developing social visibility around the epidemic. On the service level, however, AIDES depends entirely on project bound funding from public authorities which might limit its independence as a social actor.

During 1991 three important measures have further marked implementation. Article 187 of the penal code which outlaws discrimination on the basis of nationality, race, sex and religion was extended to cover health handicaps. It is now illegal to exclude people from employment, public places, public transport, housing, shops or restaurants, etc. The organisations representing patients or handicapped people can take offenders to court. France thus implemented the WHO recommendations on social rights for the sick. The second decision, taken jointly by the Health Minister and the Minister of Finance, concerns access to insurance for HIV positive people. Any questions related to lifestyle are henceforth prohibited in insurance questionnaires; demands for HIV tests are only allowed in conjunction with other medical examination and for policies paying over one million francs (the sum is subject to revision according to price indexes and the evolution of the epidemic). Seropositive applicants are entitled to insurance, via the category of 'aggravated health risks' with a higher subscription fee according to the rules already in use for people with other chronic disease. Penal sanctions can be applied to insurers who do not respect this law.

A third series of decisions since the autumn of 1991 concerns compensation for AIDS victims through blood transfusion or products. Unlike a first scheme set up in 1989–90, which provided only a fixed sum to help a defined group of haemophiliacs and excluded the idea of public responsibility, the new scheme explicitly recognises the public responsibility for solidarity with the victims. It includes all haemophiliacs and patients who were contaminated through transfusion. Compensation will be decided according to each individual case and with reference to common law principles. A special fund has been made available, funded jointly by the government and the national federation of insurance companies, managed by the latter who have been charged with negotiating compensation with individual victims, their families or lawyers. Acceptance of compensation does not exclude further legal action for specific medical negligence or mistakes. Reform of the entire blood transfusion system is under way to prevent similar accidents in the future.

Conclusions

The case of AIDS has often been presented as a major innovation in public policy. But was it really so new? French policy was initiated by scientific and professional experts linked with sections of the public administration, by a minority against established hierarchies. It followed one of the typical models of innovation in French public policy. The liberal approach, centred on voluntary testing and on medical confidentiality, was congruent with key principles of social policy established over the past few decades. Personal liberty and choice were continuously extended in fields of health care, abortion, contraception, divorce, age of retirement. It would have been difficult for the state to draw on authoritarian methods in the case of AIDS. All governments from the right and the left continued the same policy. This consistency might cause surprise in the case of France, better known for her passionate ideological debates than for her traditions of individual liberty and social solidarity. The National Front's attempt to oppose individual and public interests was not shared by society and ruled out by the political elite.

Was France late in promoting public policies against AIDS, as was often stated by activist groups? Precise international comparisons would be needed to answer this question. In certain fields, 'la grande Nation' was well ahead. France discovered the virus and was the first European country to set up a specific epidemiological surveillance system. French legislation was among the first to include systematic screening of blood donation and even the controversial distribution of untreated blood products was banned relatively early compared to other countries. Last but not least, France developed an extensive system of free and voluntary testing facilities. Delays occurred in two defined circumstances. On the one hand, each time political power changed hands on the national level, decision making or implementation was delayed. On the other hand, in fields traditionally dominated by closed professional groups (blood transfusion) or where a coherent anti-AIDS strategy would require joint action across existing professional and administrative borders (drug addicts, prisoners, extended home care), policies were not developed or were only partially implemented. Situated on the margins of medical and social action, these fields are traditionally difficult to co-ordinate. In its content as well as in its delays, AIDS policy seems to have followed the general logic of the French policy system.

However, the AIDS issue did introduce changes into the health system. The doctor's freedom to prescribe was limited. Home care facilities were developed and professional hierarchies and elite positions were challenged, under the pressure of newcomers and a social movement representing the patients' interests. The policy of social integration and solidarity with AIDS victims met the demands of the early AIDS militants, especially from the gay community, but these social demands had to be legitimated by science and by international references before a political consensus could emerge and enable the political system to establish them as policies. The AIDES movement filled a social vacuum. For the first time in France, social interests in the health sector were represented outside medical leadership. The haemophiliacs, reluctant to join a movement dominated by homosexuals, took several more years to break their traditional dependence on their doctors and caring institutions. Their isolation and silence were finally overcome with press support. Gay representatives obtained their place in the policy process at a certain price. They left behind group specific demands. The recognition of homosexual marriage or inheritance, promoted by gay groups linked with the Socialist Party did not reach the official discussion agenda. The AIDES leaders, on the contrary, built up their movement on a general philosophy of human rights and considered their campaigns for safer sexual behaviour and free access to syringes 'not only as a medical necessity but also as a way of integrating minority choices into socially accepted norms and values' (interview).

The French state reacted to the unexpected and quite special issue of AIDS by reinforcing the protection of private life and individual liberties. The administration was used to provide society with prevention facilities and useful statistical data to enable doctors, public health experts, trade unions and insurance to exercise their social function. New intellectual and administrative tools had to be elaborated and prove their efficiency in the special AIDS context; this meant delay. The 'normalising' process of the AIDS issue and these newly invented modalities illustrate the capacity of the welfare state to deal with unexpected social danger and new types of social risks.

NOTES

1 R. Klein and P. Day, 'Interpreting the unexpected: the case of AIDS policy making in Britain', *Journal of Public Policies*, 9, 3 (1989), 337–53.

2 B. Jobert and M. Steffen, 'Décisions et non-décisions en matière de politique de santé', *Contribution to the Congress of the Société Française de la Santé Publique*, Lyons, 16–17 May 1988 (Grenoble, 1988).

3 M. Steffen, 'Les politiques alternatives dans le domaine de la santé', Research report, 2 vols. (Grenoble, 1987).

4 M. Pollak, *Les Homosexuels et le sida; sociologie d'une épidémie* (Paris, 1988), 131.

5 C. Herzlich and J. Pierret, 'Le sida dans l'espace public', *Annales; Economie, société, civilisation*, 5 (1988), 1109–33.

6 H. Jamous, 'Professions ou systèmes auto-perpetués? Changements dans le système hospitalo-universitaire français', in *Rationalisation, mobilisation sociale et pouvoir*, Centre de Sociologie de l'Innovation (Paris, 1973), 5–55; H. Hatzfeld, *Le Grand Tournant de la médecine libérale* (Paris, 1963).

7 M. Steffen, 'Les politiques de la santé devant les alternatives', *Cahiers de Sociologie, de Démographie et d'Economie Médicales*, 28, 2 (1988), 163–78.

8 J. J. Salomon, *Le Gaullois, le cowboy et le samouraï; la politique française de la technologie* (Paris, 1986); J. Zysman, *L'Industrie française entre l'Etat et le marché* (Paris, 1982) (first English edition: *Political Strategies for Industrial Order* (Berkeley, 1977)).

9 The association had 240 members in 1988, according to Pollak, *Les Homosexuals et le sida*, 132.

10 *Le Monde*, 25 April 1985.

11 'Aides' means 'help' and 'support' in French (plural form).

12 Daniel Defert, 'Un nouveau reformateur social: le malade', *Communication Presented at the Vth International Conference on AIDS* (plenary session), Montreal, Canada, 6 June 1989.

13 'Rapport du groupe de travail sur le Sida' (Rappin Report), Direction Générale de la Santé, Ministère de la Santé, May 1986.

14 Alain Pompidou, the son of the famous ex-President.

15 'It was quite clear for us, that for public administration, there should not be any employment of screening, but we could not always speak up and say so. Generally, we arranged that some organisation, the trade unions of the public service or some other organisation would speak up for this. We also had contacts about it with the employers' unions' (interview, a member of the first AIDS expert group, Ministry of Health).

16 C. Got, *Rapport sur le sida* (Paris, 1989).

17 ENA (Ecole Nationale de l'Administration), the famous elite school which prepares candidates for high positions in the public administration and provides the state elite with a common culture.

18 Y. A. Flori, Y. Souteyrand and A. Triomphe, 'Les fillières de soins des patients VIH; les interrelations de médecine de ville et de médecine hospitalière', *Communication at the first French Seminar on Health Economics* (Dijon, 1990).

19 It was only in 1991 that doctors outside public hospitals were allowed to *renew* prescriptions for AZT. Young people who are not yet employed and therefore still covered by their parents' health insurance, but who do not wish their family to be

informed of their serological state can receive AZT treatment, free of charge, in Family Planning Centres, even if they are under the age of majority (eighteen years). This solution follows the model tried during the 70s for contraception.

20 M. Lucas, 'Transfusion sanguine et Sida en 1985, chronologie des faits et des décisions pour ce qui concerne les hémophiles', *Report Presented to the Minister of Social Affairs and Integration and to the Minister Delegated to Health, Inspection Générales des Affaires Sociales* (Paris, 1991).

21 Based on the French concept of *accompagner les mourants*; it means giving 'tender loving care', based on being present, listening, counselling and comforting.

Appendix

AIDS: the archive potential

JANET FOSTER

Archival holdings available for research of all kinds in the UK are among the most rich and extensive in the world. The wealth of these collections is shown in *British Archives* which contains details of the material held by more than 1,000 archive repositories, libraries, institutions and societies.[1] However, this is not exhaustive. There is more material to be discovered and records are being created continually.

The AIDS Social History Programme, based at the London School of Hygiene and Tropical Medicine and financed by Nuffield Provincial Hospitals Trust, has been engaged, since 1988, upon researching and writing the social history of AIDS in the UK. The work is concentrating on official policy making in the context of the various influences upon it from the statutory and voluntary sectors, the medical establishment and medical research.[2] An initial aim of the Programme was to establish an AIDS archive. However, before any decisions could be made about taking in material it was desirable to investigate the records being generated by those individuals and organisations involved in the AIDS arena. As an initial phase, a pilot survey was established, in January 1990, as a four-month project to identify the extent and scope of primary documentation for the history of AIDS in the UK.

Surveys of primary source material are not new. The Royal Commission on Historical Manuscripts was established in 1869 to locate and register archives throughout the country and its National Register of Archives now holds in excess of 31,000 lists and reports of papers available for the study of British history. In recent years surveys of primary documentation available for the historical study of specific subjects have become quite common. *Surveys of Historical Manuscripts in the United Kingdom* details almost 200 such surveys completed or in progress.[3] However, these have concentrated on historical material which is generally already to be found in archive repositories. The AIDS archive survey was completely different in being concerned with identifying potential archives, as they were being created.

Archivists have always been professionally interested in the full life-cycle of records – from creation through working life to destruction or selection for permanent preservation. But this has been a function of management within the record-producing body, concerned with regulating record-keeping whilst ensuring that the documents essential to recording the history of the organisation are identified and permanently kept as archives. However the AIDS archive survey took a subject approach to records management, locating and surveying records created by a variety of agencies, which would provide the source material for writing the history of an epidemic in progress. It is believed this is the first time an archivist has been directly involved in identifying primary source material for a specific topic of British contemporary history.

The aim of the pilot survey was to report on potential AIDS archive material in the UK by:

1. Locating collections of relevant personal papers
2. Locating archive material in organisations which are or were active in the AIDS arena
3. Identifying existing collections of material with relevance to the history of AIDS in the UK, for example press-cuttings, films, oral histories

A further aim was to encourage an awareness of the importance of record-keeping in the AIDS arena, where, for the first time, there was an opportunity to document an epidemic, and the responses to it, as it happened.

A start was made with a checklist of about twenty-five individuals and organisations which previous research for the Programme suggested should be contacted. Further details for most of them were gleaned from the *National AIDS Manual*,[4] an invaluable, and regularly updated, compendium of information on organisations nation-wide concerned in full or in part with AIDS. Further names were added to the original list by recommendation and eventually contact was made with more than forty organisations and individuals in the statutory and voluntary sectors, principally in London and Edinburgh. However, not all of these participated in the survey either because shortage of time prevented it or because they claimed not to keep records. Finally a small sample of existing collections of AIDS-related archive material or information was added to the survey. A full list appears at the end of this article.

Because of the time restriction on the project, the number of contacts was limited to provide a core sample and contact was to be personal, by phone and follow-up visit, rather than by letter or questionnaire. This decision was reinforced by the fact that the people to be contacted would be unfamiliar with the concept of archives. Previous experience had shown that even archivists found difficulty in completing questionnaires about archives and information-gathering was much more likely to be effective through personal interviews. However, a leaflet was written, explaining the aims and objectives of the survey, and copies of this were sent to contacts between phone call and visit to give them some preparation. The utility of the leaflet for its intended purpose proved debatable (often it was not read until the time of my visit), nonetheless, it was something tangible to send to enquirers and saved repetition of the same information.

Details of the initial telephone contacts, reactions and arrangements were kept on conventional index cards. The subsequent visits generated computerised reports of the information gained from the interviews. These reports typically summarised the work/involvement of the organisation/individual, comments or perceptions from the interviewee, details of the documentation produced and conditions for access to it, with my general comments including the long-term prospects for preservation of the material where appropriate.

An interesting and unexpected aspect of the visit was that many of the interviewees, in addition to providing a straightforward account of their work and that of the organisation, took the opportunity of my presence as an objective listener to rehearse the history of their involvement in the AIDS story. These oral histories both informed my subsequent questioning about the archives produced and provided research material from a different perspective for the main Programme.

As anticipated, the interviewees' perceptions of archives could be hazy. In general, the day-to-day work of an archivist is not well known and the archive profession does not have a high profile, so this was not surprising. Archives tend to be thought of in terms of dusty, old parchments and archivists are similarly regarded. It is difficult for people to equate archives with modern papers and much less with letters and documents that they have produced themselves. More authority is given to printed material and on several occasions I was assured that archives were certainly kept only to be shown collections of press-cuttings or leaflets. This is not to denigrate the value of such material as an historical resource but I was interested in the records produced by the organisations themselves, documenting their decisions, plans and activities.

When this has been explained it was usually possible systematically to review the work of the organisation and establish what documentation was produced by its various activities. Often this was done by question and answer based on the information gleaned from the interview, allowing details of the existence, quantity and quality of records to be gathered and noted. Thus there might be committee minutes and supporting papers such as reports; correspondence files; staff records; client files; training programmes and evaluations; annual reports and publications. Obviously the type and quantity of records varied from comprehensive to minimal – one organisation had meticulously documented its activities, keeping a separate bookcase for its archive files, whilst another interviewee when pressed about the records of the outreach sessions he had been describing produced a file containing one sheet of paper with a few scribbled notes. However, in the majority of cases, despite the compelling nature of the work being undertaken, time had been found to maintain records.

Interviewees were then asked to consider the possibility of research use of the material. In general this was welcomed except for confidential files, usually those relating to clients, with the proviso that researchers should be bona fide and/or submit details of their research before access to the documents was agreed. The only exceptions were documents which were covered by legislation, notably records which are designated as public records under the Public Records Acts, 1957 and 1968. These include records of government, for example the Department of Health, and the health service, including the records of the Health Education Authority and its predecessor the Health Education Council. In these cases administrative records are closed for thirty years. This gap in the availability of records central to the study of AIDS in the UK has been compounded by the insistence that all members of government committees are bound by the Official Secrets Act and cannot, therefore, release their personal copies of minutes and papers.

The final consideration was the possibility of long-term preservation of the records which had been surveyed. Public records more than thirty years old, which have been selected for preservation, should be transferred to the Public Record Office, or a place of deposit approved by the Lord Chancellor. Tower Hamlets Health Authority for example, which was included in the survey, has established an Archive Centre which has been so approved and the records of the Authority and its constituent hospitals will be maintained there. The Centre may also take in non-National Health Service health care records from the surrounding area such as those of the Mildmay Mission Hospital, the first AIDS hospice.

In many other cases an existing agency which will assume archival responsibility can be identified. For example the records of the All-Party Parliamentary Group on AIDS might be placed in the House of Lords Record Office, whilst those of the Association of London Authorities, including their HIV Co-ordinator's files, will go to Greater London Record Office. The records of organisations having a purely local remit will usually be of interest to the local authority record office for the area. Examples in the survey are the Aled Richards Trust in Bristol and Druglink in Swindon where the appropriate repositories would be Bristol City Record Office and Wiltshire Record Office respectively. For personal papers also the local record office might be appropriate or there may be a specialist repository such as the Contemporary Medical Archives Centre at the Wellcome Institute in London which would consider taking records relating to the medical aspects of AIDS, either research or treatment.

However, these instances served to confirm an initial feeling that the records most at risk are those of the voluntary sector organisations with a national role, for which there is no existing archival safety net. One of the initial aims of the Programme was to establish an AIDS archive which found general support among the people interviewed. The survey has certainly shown that a repository is needed to safeguard the records of the national voluntary response to AIDS. It has also highlighted the necessity for existing repositories to include AIDS material in their collecting policies. Additionally, there is a perceived need for archival education to prevent the loss of material. Whilst people involved with HIV and AIDS mostly have a realisation of being in the middle of history-in-the-making and welcomed the survey as a first step towards documenting their contribution to the story of HIV and AIDS, they also realise that they need advice and guidance in record-keeping, selection and preservation.

A selection of the survey reports has now been published as *AIDS Archives in the UK* (London, 1990). This also includes an introduction describing the survey methodology and results with an educational section giving guidance on what constitutes an archive and what material should be kept. The survey identified a core sample of AIDS-related archive material with the possibilities for its long-term preservation and demonstrated very positively the archive potential for documenting all aspects of HIV infection and AIDS.

Survey contacts

Statutory sector

Central government
All-Party Parliamentary Group on AIDS

Local government
Association of London Authorities (ALA), HIV Co-ordinator
Local Authority Associations' Officer Working Group on AIDS
Oxford City Council AIDS Liaison Working Party

Health education
Health Education Authority
Lothian Health Board, Take Care Campaign
Scottish Health Education Group

Health service
North West Thames Regional HA, HIV Project
Tower Hamlets HA

Non-statutory sector

Charities
AIDS Policy Unit
AVERT (AIDS Education & Research)
Haemophilia Society
National AIDS Trust

Drug agencies
Druglink, Swindon
Standing Conference on Drug Abuse (SCODA)

Gay organisations
London Lesbian & Gay Switchboard

Health education
Bristol Polytechnic, Faculty of Education
Family Planning Association

Health workers support groups
Forum of HIV Information Workers
Network Association of HIV/AIDS Workers (NOVOAH)

Helplines
National AIDS Helpline
Sussex AIDS Helpline

Hospices
London Lighthouse
Mildmay Mission Hospital

Self-help agencies
Immunity: legal issues and welfare rights
Landmark: drop-in centre
National AIDS Manual
Scottish AIDS Monitor
Terrence Higgins Trust

Business

London International (LRC Products)
Wellcome Foundation

Medical Research

Dr Ray Brettle, Edinburgh City Hospital: HIV/AIDS and pregnancy
Dr Tony Pinching, St Mary's Hospital, London
Dr Roy Robertson, GP Edinburgh: IV Drug Users and HIV/AIDS
Prof. Robin Weiss, Institute of Cancer Research: retrovirologist

Individuals

Ewan Armstrong, Community Health Dept, South Bank Polytechnic
Jonathan Grimshaw, Body Positive and Landmark
Simon Watney, gay historian and activist
Tony Whitehead, Terrence Higgins Trust

Existing collections

British Universities Film & Video Council
London School of Economics Library
Mass-Observation Archive, University of Sussex
National Sound Archive, Hall Carpenter Oral Histories

NOTES

1 J. Foster and J. Sheppard, *British Archives: A Guide to Archive Resources in the United Kingdom* (2nd edn, London, 1989).
2 V. Berridge and P. Strong, 'AIDS policies in the UK: a preliminary analysis', in E. Fee and D. M. Fox (eds.), *AIDS: The Making of a Chronic Disease* (Berkeley, 1992).
3 Royal Commission on Historical Manuscripts, *Surveys of Historical Manuscripts in the United Kingdom: A Select Bibliography* (HMSO, 1989).
4 P. Scott, *National AIDS Manual* (3rd rev. edn, London, 1991).

Index

Numbers in italics refer to Tables and Figures.

272

Cambridge history of medicine

Health, medicine and morality in the sixteenth century   EDITED BY CHARLES WEBSTER

The Renaissance notion of woman: A study in the fortunes of scholasticism and medical science in European intellectual life   IAN MACLEAN

Mystical Bedlam: madness, anxiety and healing in sixteenth century England
MICHAEL MACDONALD

From medical chemistry to biochemistry: The making of a biomedical discipline
ROBERT E. KOHLER

Joan Baptista Van Helmont: Reformer of science and medicine   WALTER PAGEL

A generous confidence: Thomas Story Kirkbride and the art of asylum-keeping, 1840–1883
NANCY TOMES

The cultural meaning of popular science: Phrenology and the organization of consent in nineteenth-century Britain   ROGER COOTER

Madness, morality and medicine: A study of the York Retreat, 1796–1914   ANNE DIGBY

Patients and practitioners: Lay perceptions of medicine in pre-industrial society
EDITED BY ROY PORTER

Hospital life in enlightenment Scotland: Care and teaching at the Royal Infirmary of Edinburgh
GUENTER B. RISSE

Plague and the poor in Renaissance Florence   ANNE G. CARMICHAEL

Victorian lunacy: Richard M. Bucke and the practice of late-nineteenth-century psychiatry
S. E. D. SHORTT

Medicine and society in Wakefield and Huddersfield 1780–1870   HILARY MARLAND

Ordered to care: The dilemma of American nursing, 1850–1945   SUSAN M. REVERBY

Morbid appearances: The anatomy of pathology in the early nineteenth century
RUSSELL C. MAULITZ

Professional and popular medicine in France, 1770–1830: The social world of medical practice
MATTHEW RAMSEY

Abortion, doctors and the law: Some aspects of the legal regulation of abortion in England 1803–1982   JOHN KEOWN

Public health in Papua New Guinea: Medical possibility and social constraints, 1884–1984
DONALD DENOON

Health, race and German politics between national unification and Nazism, 1870–1945
PAUL WEINDLING

The physician-legislators of France: Medicine and politics in the early Third Republic, 1870–1914
JACK D. ELLIS

The science of woman: Gynaecology and gender in England, 1800–1929   ORNELLA MOSCUCCI

Science and empire: East Coast fever in Rhodesia and the Transvaal   PAUL F. CRANEFIELD

The colonial disease: A social history of sleeping sickness in northern Zaire, 1900–1940
MARYINEZ LYONS

Quality and quantity: The quest for biological regeneration in twentieth-century France
WILLIAM H. SCHNEIDER